The Irish R.M.

SOMERVILLE & ROSS

SPHERE BOOKS LIMITED

First published in Great Britain in 1928 by
Faber & Faber under the title
The Irish R.M. Complete
© First Sphere Books edition, 1970. All rights reserved
27 Wrights Lane, London W8 5TZ
Reprinted 1982, 1983 (twice), 1984 (twice), 1985, 1986
Trade paperback edition 1987

*Any similarity or apparent connection between
the characters in this story and actual persons,
whether alive or dead is purely coincidental.*

Also by Somerville and Ross in Sphere Books:
AN ENTHUSIAST

TRADE
MARK

Printed and bound in Great Britain by
Cox & Wyman Ltd, Reading

CONTENTS

Ireland and Fox-hunting are the twin subjects of these immortal stories. First published at the turn of the century, the EXPERIENCES OF AN IRISH R.M. were quickly recognised as a classic of sporting literature and as some of the funniest stories in the English language.

Although the post of R.M. (Resident Magistrate) is no more, the antics of Major Yeates will keep his readers in fits of laughter for as long as the sun rises and sets on the West of Ireland.

This edition contains all three of the books of stories told by the R.M.—thirty-four stories in all.

"Their achievement remains, solitary, immortal, like *Hamlet* or *The Diary of a Nobody*."

THE OBSERVER

PREFACE

The arduous post of Resident Magistrate in Ireland exists no more. It has been extinguished, like many other features of an earlier régime, and its incumbents no longer vie with the snipe and the dispensary doctor in endurance of conditions which test even those exponents of the art of being jolly in creditable circumstances.

Yet, in some ways, an Irish R.M. had his compensations. A southern or western Irish Petty Sessions Court can teach many things, often useful, still more often entertaining.

Major Sinclair Yeates left his Regiment and England "equipped" (as we have elsewhere said) "with a feeling heart, and the belief that two and two inevitably make four, whereas in Ireland two and two are just as likely to make five, or three, and are still more likely to make nothing at all."

The duty—which I cannot but think was also something of a privilege—of the Irish Resident Magistrate was to flit from Courthouse to Courthouse in order to impart, as it were, a dispassionate, even an exotic flavour to the local administration of justice. For anyone whose powers of endurance were fortified by the sense of humour, the long hours on "The Bench" of an Irish country-town were not without their enjoyable moments. There, with Flurry Knox at his right hand, and Mr. Jeremiah Flynn on his left, and with that able solicitor, Mr. John Mooney ("widely known and respected as Roaring Jack") pleading a case before him, Major Yeates learned the finer shades of definition of various offences.

That—for example—although in the considered opinion of the prosecuting Sergeant of Royal Irish Constabulary, a man might have "drink taken" and be "a contrary little man and never duly sober", and one also who was in the habit of "swearing unearthly oaths", yet the extenuating fact would be offered that "it was all that was the matter with him he had no sense". Again, in the matter of a case of Assault and Battery, even though one of the combatants might have admitted to "having a howlt" of the other "by the beard, for about a minute or two", nevertheless the outcome of the contest might be no more than what an impartial witness defined as "a few swings".

Cases such as these might give pause to Solomon, but from an unjudicial point of view they can prove a solace.

Not only in the sphere of his recognized duties did Major Yeates experience a widening of his horizon. To know Flurry Knox (who, it may be remembered, "looked like a gentleman among stableboys, and a stableboy among gentlemen") was in itself a liberal education in the high science of Horse-dealing (if in nothing else).

Flurry's grandmother, old Mrs. Knox of Aussolas, taught the R.M. that "cold age cannot quench or allay the noble fires within", and that although she might look like "a rag-bag held together by diamond brooches" her personality was the only thing that counted, and reduced all externals, even old age itself, to a proper insignificance.

It may be admitted that from Slipper, the egregious Slipper, with his eye "like a profligate pug", Major Yeates learned little, save indeed, the chastening knowledge that never in this world (or, probably, in any other) would he succeed in plumbing the depths of what might be assumed to be his soul.

More than one Irish county has believed itself to have been the scene of these experiences of Major Yeates, that are now, for the first time, assembled between two covers, and the originals of most of his friends have been confidently identified, and claimed as members of many Hunts that might have been, but were not, Mr. Knox's.

I should like, once more, to declare that of them all, Slipper and Maria alone had prototypes in the world as Martin Ross and I knew it.

E. Œ. SOMERVILLE

January 1928

GREAT-UNCLE McCARTHY

A resident Magistracy in Ireland is not an easy thing to come by nowadays; neither is it a very attractive job; yet on the evening when I first propounded the idea to the young lady who had recently consented to become Mrs. Sinclair Yeates, it seemed glittering with possibilities. There was, on that occasion, a sunset, and a string band playing "The Gondoliers", and there was also an ingenuous belief in the omnipotence of a godfather of Philippa's—(Philippa was the young lady) who had once been a member of the Government.

I was then climbing the steep ascent of the Captains towards my Majority. I have no fault to find with Philippa's godfather; he did all and more than even Philippa had expected; nevertheless, I had attained to the dignity of mud major, and had spent a good deal on postage stamps, and on railway fares to interview people of influence, before I found myself in the hotel at Skebawn, opening long envelopes addressed to "Major Yeates, R.M."

My most immediate concern, as anyone who has spent nine weeks at Mrs. Raverty's hotel will readily believe, was to leave it at the earliest opportunity; but in those nine weeks I had learned, amongst other painful things, a little, a very little, of the methods of the artisan in the west of Ireland. Finding a house had been easy enough. I had had my choice of several, each with some hundreds of acres of shooting, thoroughly poached, and a considerable portion of the roof intact. I had selected one; the one that had the largest extent of roof in proportion to the shooting, and had been assured by my landlord that in a fortnight or so it would be fit for occupation.

"There's a few little odd things to be done," he said

easily; "a lick of paint here and there, and a slap of plaster——"

I am short-sighted; I am also of Irish extraction; both facts that make for toleration—but even I thought he was understating the case. So did the contractor.

At the end of three weeks the latter reported progress, which mainly consisted of the facts that the plumber had accused the carpenter of stealing sixteen feet of his inch-pipe to run a bell wire through, and that the carpenter had replied that he wished the devil might run the plumber through a wran's quill. The plumber having reflected upon the carpenter's parentage, the work of renovation had merged in battle, and at the next Petty Sessions I was reluctantly compelled to allot to each combatant seven days, without the option of a fine.

These and kindred difficulties extended in an unbroken chain through the summer months, until a certain wet and windy day in October, when, with my baggage, I drove over to establish myself at Shreelane. It was a tall, ugly house of three stories high, its walls faced with weather-beaten slates, its windows staring, narrow, and vacant. Round the house ran an area, in which grew some laurustinus and holly bushes among ash heaps, and nettles, and broken bottles. I stood on the steps, waiting for the door to be opened, while the rain sluiced upon me from a broken eaveshoot that had, amongst many other things, escaped the notice of my landlord. I thought of Philippa, and of her plan, broached in to-day's letter, of having the hall done up as a sitting-room.

The door opened, and revealed the hall. It struck me that I had perhaps overestimated its possibilities. Among them I had certainly not included a flagged floor, sweating with damp, and a reek of cabbage from the adjacent kitchen stairs. A large elderly woman, with a red face, and a cap worn helmet-wise on her forehead, swept me a magnificent curtsy as I crossed the threshold.

"Your honour's welcome——" she began, and then every door in the house slammed in obedience to the gust that drove through it. With something that sounded

8

like "Mend ye for a back door!" Mrs. Cadogan abandoned her opening speech and made for the kitchen stairs. (Improbable as it may appear, my housekeeper was called Cadogan, a name made locally possible by being pronounced Caydogawn.)

Only those who have been through a similar experience can know what manner of afternoon I spent. I am a martyr to colds in the head, and I felt one coming on. I made a laager in front of the dining-room fire, with a tattered leather screen and the dinner table, and gradually, with cigarettes and strong tea, baffled the smell of must and cats, and fervently trusted that the rain might avert a threatened visit from my landlord. I was then but superficially acquainted with Mr. Florence McCarthy Knox and his habits.

At about 4.30, when the room had warmed up, and my cold was yielding to treatment, Mrs. Cadogan entered and informed me that "Mr. Flurry" was in the yard, and would be thankful if I'd go out to him, for he couldn't come in. Many are the privileges of the female sex; had I been a woman I should unhesitatingly have said that I had a cold in my head.

My landlord was there on horseback, and with him there was a man standing at the head of a stout grey animal. I recognized with despair that I was about to be compelled to buy a horse.

"Good afternoon, Major," said Mr. Knox in his slow, sing-song brogue; "it's rather soon to be paying you a visit, but I thought you might be in a hurry to see the horse I was telling you of."

I could have laughed. As if I were ever in a hurry to see a horse! I thanked him, and suggested that it was rather wet for horse-dealing.

"Oh, it's nothing when you're used to it," replied Mr. Knox. His gloveless hands were red and wet, the rain ran down his nose, and his covert coat was soaked to a sodden brown. I thought that I did not want to become used to it. My relations with horses have been of a purely military character. I have endured the Sandhurst

9

riding-school, I have galloped for an impetuous general, I have been steward at regimental races, but none of these feats has altered my opinion that the horse, as a means of locomotion, is obsolete. Nevertheless, the man who accepts a resident magistracy in the south-west of Ireland voluntarily retires into the prehistoric age; to institute a stable became inevitable.

"You ought to throw a leg over him," said Mr. Knox, "and you're welcome to take him over a fence or two if you like. He's a nice flippant jumper."

Even to my unexacting eye the grey horse did not seem to promise flippancy, nor did I at all desire to find that quality in him. I explained that I wanted something to drive, and not to ride.

"Well, that a fine raking horse in harness," said Mr. Knox, looking at me with his serious grey eyes, "and you'd drive him with a sop of hay in his mouth. Bring him up here, Michael."

Michael abandoned his efforts to kick the grey horse's forelegs into becoming position, and led him up to me.

I regarded him from under my umbrella with a quite unreasonable disfavour. He had the dreadful beauty of a horse in a toy-shop, as chubby, as wooden, and as conscientiously dappled, but it was unreasonable to urge this as an objection, and I was incapable of finding any more technical drawbacks. Yielding to circumstance, I "threw my leg" over the brute, and after pacing gravely round the quadrangle that formed the yard, and jolting to my entrance gate and back, I decided that as he had neither fallen down nor kicked me off, it was worth paying twenty-five pounds for him, if only to get in out of the rain.

Mr. Knox accompanied me into the house and had a drink. He was a fair, spare young man, who looked like a stableboy among gentlemen, and a gentleman among stableboys. He belonged to a clan that cropped up in every grade of society in the county, from Sir Valentine Knox of Castle Knox down to the auctioneer Knox, who bore the attractive title of Larry the Liar. So far as I could judge, Florence McCarthy of that ilk occupied a shifting position about midway in the tribe. I had met him at dinner at Sir Valentine's, I had heard of him at an illicit auction, held by Larry the Liar, of brandy stolen from a wreck. They were "Black Protestants", all of them, in virtue of their descent from a godly soldier of Cromwell, and all were prepared at any moment of the day or night to sell a horse.

"You'll be apt to find this place a bit lonesome after the hotel," remarked Mr. Flurry, sympathetically, as he placed his foot in its steaming boot on the hob, "but it's a fine sound house anyway, and lots of rooms in it, though indeed, to tell you the truth, I never was through the whole of them since the time my great-uncle, Denis McCarthy, died here. The dear knows I had enough of it that time." He paused, and lit a cigarette—one of my best, and quite thrown away upon him. "Those top floors, now," he resumed, "I wouldn't make too free with them. There's some of them would jump under you like a spring bed. Many's the night I was in and out of those attics, following my poor uncle when he had a bad turn on him—the horrors, y'know—there were nights he never stopped walking through the house. Good Lord! will I ever forget the morning he said he saw the devil coming up the avenue! 'Look at the two horns on him', says he, and he out with his gun and shot him, and, begad, it was his own donkey!"

Mr. Knox gave a couple of short laughs. He seldom laughed, having in unusual perfection the gravity of manners that is bred by horse-dealing, probably from the habitual repression of all emotion save disparagement.

The autumn evening, grey with rain, was darkening in the tall windows, and the wind was beginning to make bullying rushes among the shrubs in the area; a shower of soot rattled down the chimney and fell on the hearth-rug.

"More rain coming," said Mr. Knox, rising composedly; "you'll have to put a goose down these chimneys some day soon, it's the only way in the world to

11

clean them. Well, I'm for the road. You'll come out on the grey next week, I hope; the hounds'll be meeting here. Give a roar at him coming in at his jumps." He threw his cigarette into the fire and extended a hand to me. "Good-bye, Major, you'll see plenty of me and my hounds before you're done. There's a power of foxes in the plantations here."

This was scarcely reassuring for a man who hoped to shoot woodcock, and I hinted as much.

"Oh, is it the cock?" said Mr. Flurry; "b'leeve me, there never was a woodcock yet that minded hounds, now, no more than they'd mind rabbits! The best shoots ever I had here, the hounds were in it the day before."

When Mr. Knox had gone, I began to picture myself going across country roaring, like a man on a fire-engine, while Philippa put the goose down the chimney; but when I sat down to write to her I did not feel equal to being humorous about it. I dilated ponderously on my cold, my hard work, and my loneliness, and eventually went to bed at ten o'clock full of cold shivers and hot whisky-and-water.

After a couple of hours of feverish dozing, I began to understand what had driven Great-Uncle McCarthy to perambulate the house by night. Mrs. Cadogan had assured me that the Pope of Rome hadn't a better bed undher him than myself; wasn't I down on the new flog mattherass the old masther bought in Father Scanlan's auction? By the smell I recognized that "flog" meant flock, otherwise I should have said my couch was stuffed with old boots. I have seldom spent a more wretched night. The rain drummed with soft fingers on my window panes; the house was full of noises. I seemed to see Great-Uncle McCarthy ranging the passages with Flurry at his heels; several times I thought I heard him. Whisperings seemed borne on the wind through my keyhole, boards creaked in the room overhead, and once I could have sworn that a hand passed, groping, over the panels of my door. I am, I may admit, a believer in ghosts; I even take in a paper that deals with their culture, but I cannot pretend that on that night I looked forward to a manifestation of Great-Uncle McCarthy with any enthusiasm.

The morning broke stormily, and I woke to find Mrs. Cadogan's understudy, a grimy nephew of about eighteen, standing by my bedside, with a black bottle in his hand.

"There's no bath in the house, sir," was his reply to my command; "but me a'nt said, would you like a taggeen?"

This alternative proved to be a glass of raw whisky. I declined it.

I look back to that first week of housekeeping at Shreelane as to a comedy excessively badly staged, and striped with lurid melodrama. Towards its close I was positively home-sick for Mrs. Raverty's, and I had not a single clean pair of boots. I am not one of those who hold the convention that in Ireland the rain never ceases, day or night, but I must say that my first November at Shreelane was composed of weather of which my friend Flurry Knox remarked that you wouldn't meet a Christian out of doors, unless it was a snipe or a dispensary doctor. To this lamentable category might be added a resident magistrate. Daily, shrouded in mackintosh, I set forth for the Petty Sessions Courts of my wide district; daily, in the inevitable atmosphere of wet frieze and perjury, I listened to indictments of old women who plucked geese alive, of publicans whose hospitality to their friends broke forth uncontrollably on Sunday afternoons, of "parties" who, in the language of the police sergeant, were subtly defined as "not to say dhrunk, but in good fighting thrim".

I got used to it all in time—I suppose one can get used to anything—I even became callous to the surprises of Mrs. Cadogan's cooking. As the weather hardened and the woodcock came in, and one by one I discovered and nailed up the rat holes, I began to find life endurable, and even to feel some remote sensation of home-coming when the grey horse turned in at the gate of Shreelane.

The one feature of my establishment to which I could not become inured was the pervading subpresence of some thing or things which, for my own convenience, I summarized as Great-Uncle McCarthy. There were nights on which I was certain that I heard the inebriate shuffle of his foot overhead, the touch of his fumbling hand against the walls. There were dark times before the dawn when sounds went to and fro, the moving of weights, the creaking of doors, a far-away rapping in which was a workmanlike suggestion of the undertaker, a rumble of wheels on the avenue. Once I was impelled to the perhaps imprudent measure of cross-examining Mrs. Cadogan. Mrs. Cadogan, taking the preliminary precaution of crossing herself, asked me fatefully what day of the week it was.

"Friday!" she repeated after me. "Friday! The Lord save us! 'Twas a Friday the old masther was buried!"

At this point a saucepan opportunely boiled over, and Mrs. Cadogan fled with it to the scullery, and was seen no more.

In the process of time I brought Great-Uncle McCarthy down to a fine point. On Friday nights he made coffins and drove hearses; during the rest of the week he rarely did more than patter and shuffle in the attics over my head.

One night, about the middle of December, I awoke, suddenly aware that some noise had fallen like a heavy stone into my dreams. As I felt for the matches it came again, the long, grudging groan and the uncompromising bang of the cross door at the head of the kitchen stairs. I told myself that it was a draught that had done it, but it was a perfectly still night. Even as I listened, a sound of wheels on the avenue shook the stillness. The thing was getting past a joke. In a few minutes I was stealthily groping my way down my own staircase, with a box of matches in my hand, enforced by scientific curiosity, but none the less armed with a stick. I stood in the dark at

14

the top of the back stairs and listened; the snores of Mrs. Cadogan and her nephew Peter rose tranquilly from their respective lairs. I descended to the kitchen and lit a candle; there was nothing unusual there, except a great portion of the Cadogan wearing apparel, which was arranged at the fire, and was being serenaded by two crickets. Whatever had opened the door, my household was blameless.

The kitchen was not attractive, yet I felt indisposed to leave it. None the less, it appeared to be my duty to inspect the yard. I put the candle on the table and went forth out into the outer darkness. Not a sound was to be heard. The night was very cold, and so dark that I could scarcely distinguish the roofs of the stables against the sky; the house loomed tall and oppressive above me; I was conscious of how lonely it stood in the dumb and barren country. Spirits were certainly futile creatures, childish in their manifestations, stupidly content with the old machinery of raps and rumbles. I thought how fine a scene might be played on a stage like this; if I were a ghost, how bluely I would glimmer at the windows, how whimperingly chatter in the wind. Something whirled out of the darkness above me, and fell with a flop on the ground, just at my feet. I jumped backwards, in point of fact I made for the kitchen door, and, with my hand on the latch, stood still and waited. Nothing further happened; the thing that lay there did not stir. I struck a match. The moment of tension turned to pathos as the light flickered on nothing more fateful than a dead crow.

Dead it certainly was. I could have told that without looking at it; but why should it, at some considerable period after its death, fall from the clouds at my feet? But did it fall from the clouds? I struck another match, and stared up at the impenetrable face of the house. There was no hint of solution in the dark windows, but I determined to go up and search the rooms that gave upon the yard.

How cold it was! I can feel now the frozen musty air of those attics, with their rat-eaten floors and wallpapers

15

furred with damp. I went softly from one to another, feeling like a burglar in my own house, and found nothing in elucidation of the mystery. The windows were hermetically shut, and sealed with cobwebs. There was no furniture, except in the end room, where a wardrobe without doors stood in a corner, empty save for the solemn presence of a monstrous tall hat. I went back to bed, cursing those powers of darkness that had got me out of it, and heard no more.

My landlord had not failed of his promise to visit my coverts with his hounds; in fact, he fulfilled it rather more conscientiously than seemed to me quite wholesome for the cock-shooting. I maintained a silence which I felt to be magnanimous on the part of a man who cared nothing for hunting and a great deal for shooting, and wished the hounds more success in the slaughter of my foxes than seemed to be granted to them. I met them all, one red frosty evening, as I drove down the long hill to my demesne gates, Flurry at their head, in his shabby pink coat and dingy breeches, the hounds trailing dejectedly behind him and his half-dozen companions.

"What luck?" I called out, drawing rein as I met them.

"None," said Mr. Flurry briefly. He did not stop, neither did he remove his pipe from the down-twisted corner of his mouth; his eye at me was cold and sour. The other members of the hunt passed me with equal hauteur; I thought they took their ill luck very badly.

On foot, among the last of the straggling hounds, cracking a carman's whip, and swearing comprehensively at them all, slouched my friend Slipper. Our friendship had begun in Court, the relative positions of the dock and the judgement-seat forming no obstacle to its progress, and had been cemented during several days' tramping after snipe. He was, as usual, a little drunk, and he hailed me as though I were a ship.

"Ahoy, Major Yeates!" he shouted, bringing himself

up with a lurch against my cart; "it's hunting you should be, in place of sending poor divils to gaol!"

"But I hear you had no hunting," I said.

"Ye heard that, did ye?" Slipper rolled upon me an eye like that of a profligate pug. "Well, begor, ye heard no more than the thruth."

"But where are all the foxes?" said I.

"Begor, I don't know no more than your honour. And Shreelane—that there used to be as many foxes in it as there's crosses in a yard of check! Well, well, I'll say nothin' for it, only that it's quare! Here, Vaynus! Naygress!" Slipper uttered a yell, hoarse with whisky, in adjuration of two elderly ladies of the pack who had profited by our conversation to stray away into an adjacent cottage. "Well, good-night, Major. Mr. Flurry's as cross as briars, and he'll have me ate!"

He set off at a surprisingly steady run, cracking his whip, and whooping like a madman. I hope that when I also am fifty I shall be able to run like Slipper.

That frosty evening was followed by three others like unto it, and a flight of woodcock came in. I calculated that I could do with five guns, and I dispatched invitations to shoot and dine on the following day to four of the local sportsmen, among whom was, of course, my landlord. I remember that in my letter to the latter I expressed a facetious hope that my bag of cock would be more successful than his of foxes had been.

The answers to my invitations were not what I expected. All, without so much as a conventional regret, declined my invitation; Mr. Knox added that he hoped the bag of cock would be to my liking, and that I need not be "affraid" that the hounds would trouble my coverts any more. Here was war! I gazed in stupefaction at the crooked scrawl in which my landlord had declared it. It was wholly and entirely inexplicable, and instead of going to sleep comfortably over the fire and my newspaper as a gentleman should, I spent the evening in irritated ponderings over this bewildering and exasperating change of front on the part of my friendly squireens.

17

My shoot the next day was scarcely a success. I shot the woods in company with my gamekeeper, Tim Connor, a gentleman whose duties mainly consisted in limiting the poaching privileges to his personal friends, and whatever my offence might have been, Mr. Knox could have wished me no bitterer punishment than hearing the unavailing shouts of "Mark cock!" and seeing my birds winging their way from the coverts, far out of shot. Tim Connor and I got ten couple between us; it might have been thirty if my neighbours had not boycotted me, for what I could only suppose was the slackness of their hounds.

I was dog-tired that night, having walked enough for three men, and I slept the deep, insatiable sleep that I had earned. It was somewhere about 3 a.m. that I was gradually awakened by a continuous knocking, interspersed with muffled calls. Great-Uncle McCarthy had never before given tongue, and I freed one ear from blankets to listen. Then I remembered that Peter had told me the sweep had promised to arrive that morning, and to arrive early. Blind with sleep and fury I went to the passage window, and thence desired the sweep to go to the devil. It availed me little. For the remainder of the night I could hear him pacing round the house, trying the windows, banging at the doors, and calling upon Peter Cadogan as the priests of Baal called upon their god. At six o'clock I had fallen into a troubled doze, when Mrs. Cadogan knocked at my door and imparted the information that the sweep had arrived. My answer need not be recorded, but in spite of it the door opened, and my housekeeper, in a weird *déshabille*, effectively lighted by the orange beams of her candle, entered my room.

"God forgive me, I never seen one I'd hate as much as that sweep!" she began; "he's these three hours—arrah, what three hours!—no, but all night, raising tallywack and tandem round the house to get at the chimbleys."

"Well, for Heaven's sake let him get at the chimneys

18

and let me go to sleep," I answered, goaded to desperation, "and you may tell him from me that if I hear his voice again I'll shoot him!"

Mrs. Cadogan silently left my bedside, and as she closed the door she said to herself, "The Lord save us!"

Subsequent events may be briefly summarized. At seven-thirty I was awakened anew by a thunderous sound in the chimney, and a brick crashed into the fireplace, followed at a short interval by two dead jackdaws and their nests. At eight, I was informed by Peter that there was no hot water, and that he wished the divil would roast the same sweep. At nine-thirty, when I came down to breakfast, there was no fire anywhere, and my coffee, made in the coach-house, tasted of soot. I put on an overcoat and opened my letters. About fourth or fifth in the uninteresting heap came one in an egregiously disguised hand.

"Sir," it began, "this is to inform you your unsportsmanlike conduct has been discovered. You have been suspected this good while of shooting the Shreelane foxes, it is known now that you do worse. Parties have seen your gamekeeper going regular to meet the Saturday early train at Salters Hill Station, with your grey horse under a cart, and your labels on the boxes, and we know as well as *your agent in Cork* what it is you have in those boxes. Be warned in time.—Your Wellwisher."

I read this through twice before its drift became apparent, and I realized that I was accused of improving my shooting and my finances by the simple expedient of selling my foxes. That is to say, I was in a worse position than if I'd stolen a horse, or murdered Mrs. Cadogan, or got drunk three times a week in Skebawn.

For a few moments I fell into wild laughter, and then, aware that it was rather a bad business to let a lie of this kind get a start, I sat down to demolish the preposterous charge in a letter to Flurry Knox. Somehow, as I selected my sentences, it was borne in upon me that, if the letter spoke the truth, circumstantial evidence was rather against me. Mere lofty repudiation would be unavailing, and by my infernal facetiousness about the woodcock had effectively filled in the case against myself. At all events, the first thing to do was to establish a basis and have it out with Tim Connor. I rang the bell.

"Peter, is Tim Connor about the place?"

"He is not, sir. I heard him say he was going west the hill to mend the bounds fence." Peter's face was covered with soot, his eyes were red, and he coughed ostentatiously. "The sweep's after breaking one of his brushes within in yer bedroom chimney, sir," he went on, with all the satisfaction of his class in announcing domestic calamity; "he's above on the roof now, and he'd be thankful to you to go up to him."

I followed him upstairs in that state of simmering patience that any employer of Irish labour must know and sympathize with. I climbed the rickety ladder and squeezed through the dirty trapdoor involved in the ascent to the roof, and was confronted by the hideous face of the sweep, black against the frosty blue sky. He had encamped with all his paraphernalia on the flat top of the roof, and was good enough to rise and put his pipe in his pocket on my arrival.

"Good morning, Major. That's a grand view you have up here," said the sweep. He was evidently far too well bred to talk shop. "I travelled every roof in this counthry and there isn't one where you'd get as handsome a prospect!"

Theoretically he was right, but I had not come up to the roof to discuss scenery, and demanded brutally why he had sent for me. The explanation involved a recital of the special genius required to sweep the Shreelane chimneys; of the fact that the sweep had in infancy been sent up and down every one of them by Great-Uncle McCarthy; of the three ass-loads of soot that by his peculiar skill he had this morning taken from the kitchen chimney; of its present purity, the draught being such that it would "dhraw up a young cat with it". Finally—realizing that I could endure no more—he explained that my bedroom chimney had got what he called "a wynd" in it, and he proposed to climb down a little way in the stack to try "would he get to come at the brush". The sweep was very small, the chimney very large. I stipulated that he should have a rope round his waist, and despite the illegality, I let him go. He went down like a monkey, digging his toes and fingers into the niches made for the purpose in the old chimney; Peter held the rope. I lit a cigarette and waited.

Certainly the view from the roof was worth coming up to look at. It was rough, heathery country on one side, with a string of little blue lakes running like a turquoise necklet round the base of a firry hill, and patches of pale green pasture were set amidst the rocks and heather. A silvery flash behind the undulations of the hills told where the Atlantic lay in immense plains of sunlight. I turned to survey with an owner's eye my own grey woods and straggling plantations of larch, and espied a man coming out of the western wood. He had something on his back, and he was walking very fast; a rabbit poacher no doubt. As he passed out of sight into the back avenue he was beginning to run. At the same instant I saw on the hill beyond my western boundaries half a dozen horsemen scrambling by zigzag ways down towards the wood. There was one red coat among them; it came first at the gap in the fence that Tim Connor had gone out to mend, and with the others was lost to sight in the covert, from which, in another instant, came clearly through the frosty air a shout of "Gone to ground!" Tremendous horn blowings followed, then, all in the same moment, I saw the hounds break in full cry from the wood, and come stringing over the grass and up the back avenue towards the yard gate. Were they running a fresh fox into the stables?

I do not profess to be a hunting-man, but I am an Irishman, and so, it is perhaps superfluous to state, is Peter. We forgot the sweep as if he had never existed, and precipitated ourselves down the ladder, down the stairs, and out into the yard. One side of the yard is

21

formed by the coach-house and a long stable, with a range of lofts above them, planned on the heroic scale in such matters that obtained in Ireland formerly. These join the house at the corner by the back door. A long flight of stone steps leads to the lofts, and up these, as Peter and I emerged from the back door, the hounds were struggling helter-skelter. Almost simultaneously there was a confused clatter of hoofs in the back avenue, and Flurry Knox came stooping at a gallop under the archway followed by three or four other riders. They flung themselves from their horses and made for the steps of the loft; more hounds pressed, yelling, on their heels, the din was indescribable, and justified Mrs. Cadogan's subsequent remark that "when she heard the noise she thought 'twas the end of the world and the divil collecting his own!"

I jostled in the wake of the party, and found myself in the loft, wading in hay, and nearly deafened by the clamour that was bandied about the high roof and walls. At the farther end of the loft the hounds were raging in the hay, encouraged thereto by the whoops and screeches of Flurry and his friends. High up in the gable of the loft, where it joined the main wall of the house, there was a small door, and I noted with a transient surprise that there was a long ladder leading up to it. Even as it caught my eye a hound fought his way out of a drift of hay and began to jump at the ladder, throwing his tongue vociferously, and even clambered up a few rungs in his excitement.

'There's the way he's gone!' roared Flurry, striving through hounds and hay towards the ladder. 'Trumpeter has him! What's up there, back of the door, Major? I don't remember it at all."

My crimes had evidently been forgotten in the supremacy of the moment. While I was futilely asserting that had the fox gone up the ladder he could not possibly have opened the door and shut it after him, even if the door led anywhere which, to the best of my belief, it did not, the door in question opened, and to my amazement the sweep appeared at it. He gesticulated violently, and over the tumult was heard to asserverate that there was nothing above there, only a way into the flue, and anyone would be destroyed with the soot——

"Ah, go to blazes with your soot!" interrupted Flurry, already half-way up the ladder.

I followed him, the other men pressing up behind me. That Trumpeter had made no mistake was instantly brought home to our noses by the reek of fox that met us at the door. Instead of a chimney, we found ourselves in a dilapidated bedroom, full of people. Tim Connor was there, the sweep was there, and a squalid elderly man and woman on whom I had never set eyes before. There was a large open fireplace, black with the soot the sweep had brought down with him, and on the table stood a bottle of my own special Scotch whisky. In one corner of the room was a pile of broken packing-cases, and beside these on the floor lay a bag in which something kicked.

Flurry, looking more uncomfortable and nonplussed than I could have believed possible, listened in silence to the ceaseless harangue of the elderly woman. The hounds were yelling like lost spirits in the loft below, but her voice pierced the uproar like a bagpipe. It was an unspeakable vulgar voice, yet it was not the voice of a countrywoman, and there were frowsy remnants of respectability about her general aspect.

"And is it you, Flurry Knox, that's calling me a disgrace! Disgrace, indeed, am I? Me that was your poor mother's own uncle's daughter and as good a McCarthy as ever stood in Shreelane!"

What followed I could not comprehend, owing to the fact that the sweep kept up a perpetual undercurrent of explanation to me as to how he had got down the wrong chimney. I noticed that his breath stank of whisky—Scotch, not the native variety.

Never, as long as Flurry Knox lives to blow a horn, will he hear the last of the day that he ran his mother's first cousin to ground in the attic. Never, while Mrs. Cadogan can hold a basting spoon, will she cease to recount how, on the same occasion, she plucked and roasted ten couple of woodcock in one torrid hour to provide luncheon for the hunt. In the glory of this achievement her confederacy with the stowaways in the attic is wholly slurred over, in much the same manner as the startling outburst of summons for trespass, brought by Tim Connor during the remainder of the shooting season, obscured the unfortunate episode of the bagged fox. It was, of course, zeal for my shooting that induced him to assist Mr. Knox's disreputable, relations in the deportation of my foxes; and I have allowed it to remain at that.

In fact, the only things not allowed to remain were Mr. and Mrs. McCarthy Gannon. They, as my landlord informed me, in the midst of vast apologies, had been permitted to squat at Shreelane until my tenancy began, and having then ostentatiously and abusively left the house, they had, with the connivance of the Cadogans, secretly returned to roost in the corner attic, to sell foxes under the ægis of my name, and to make inroads on my belongings. They retained connection with the outer world by means of the ladder and the loft, and with the house in general, and my whisky in particular, by a door into the other attics—a door concealed by the wardrobe in which reposed Great-Uncle McCarthy's tall hat.

It is with the greatest regret that I relinquish the prospect of writing a monograph on Great-Uncle McCarthy for a Spiritualistic Journal, but with the deparure of his relations he ceased to manifest himself, and neither the nailing up of packing-cases, nor the rumble of the cart that took them to the station, disturbed my sleep for the future.

I understand that the task of clearing out the McCarthy Gannons' effects was of a nature that necessitated two glasses of whisky per man; and if the remnants of rabbit and jackdaw disinterred in the process were anything like the crow that was thrown out of the

24

window at my feet, I do not grudge the restorative.

As Mrs. Cadogan remarked to the sweep, "A Turk couldn't stand it."

WHEN I FIRST MET DR. HICKEY

There was a wonderful chandelier in the hotel dining-room. Fine bronze it was made of, with mermaids, and Tritons, and dolphins flourishing their tails up towards the dingy ceiling-paper, and beaked galleys, on whose prows sat six small lamps, with white china receptacles for paraffin, and smoky brown chimneys. Gone were the brave days when each prow had borne a galaxy of tall wax candles; the chandelier might consider itself lucky in that it had even the paraffin lamps to justify its existence, and that it still hung from a ceiling, instead of sharing the last resting-place of its twin brother, in the bed of the tidal river under the hotel windows.

James, the hotel waiter, knew the family history of the chandelier, as he knew that of most people and things in the county. I commented upon it to a young gentleman with a pointed beard, who sat next to me at dinner, and said that it looked to me like Renaissance. The young gentleman suggested, alternatively, that it looked more like bronze. I did not dispute the point, but I think he found the subject precarious, as he turned to the young lady on his left, and I heard him embark upon a new theme.

"I was half dead with the toothache all day," he observed.

The young lady replied sympathetically that toothache was a fright.

"Well, indeed, that's true,' 'said James, smoothly entering the conversation from behind my chair. "I got my own share of it. Sure there was one time I used to be roaring like a banshee all night with it."

"Wer you so?" said the gentleman, with a wink at me. "That must have been a long time ago, James."

26

"Well, indeed, it is too, Doctor," replied James meditatively, "going on forty years, I dare say. I went to Dublin, and I went to a great dentist that was in it that time, and he pulled all the teeth I had, andhe gave me a new set entirely."

"Oh, my!" said the young lady, "that must have been very expensive."

"It was so," said James, not without pride. "Twenty pounds I gave him."

"That was awful," said the young lady, feelingly; "it was well to be you that had it to spend."

"Well, it wasn't all out so bad," said James; "sure I only wore them a few times—I wouldn't be bothered with them, and a doctor that was a friend of mine gave me ten pounds for them."

"I suppose they were a fit for a patient of his?" said the Doctor.

"They were a bad fit for me, anyway," returned James, glancing over his shoulder at the clattering operations of his two female subordinates, with the eye of the sergeant-major—the eye that always contains a grievance. "I was a footman with the old Lord Garretmore that time. Sure that was where the chandelier came from. A grand house it was, too—big slabs of marble on the tables, and gold legs under them, and ye'd bog to the knees in the carpets. Well, it was the first night after me getting the teeth, there was a gentleman stayed for dinner, and he was to go away by the night train. Forty horses were in the stables, and there wasn't one but was out at grass, and I had to go out beating the bushes for an old mare that was round the house always, herself and her foal, to put her under the side car. 'Prua! Prua!' says I, calling the mare in the dark, and with that the teeth leeped out of my mouth, with respects to you!"

"Oh, fie!" said the mother of the young lady.

"What did you do then, James?" inquired the Doctor.

"I took the white tie off me, and I tied it to the bush that was next me, for a token, and 'twas that way I got them again the next morning, thanks be to God."

Having concluded his story, James started on a perfunctory tour of the table with the wine card. He stopped
to pull the turf fire together, and, with a furtive eye at
the glass over the chimney-piece, he rearranged the long
lock of hair that draped his bald pate. It was dyed of
that peculiar shade of chestnut that disdains subterfuge,
and the fact and its suggestions were distressing where an
old servant was concerned; so also was the manner in
which he hobbled on his heels.

"His walk's full of corns," said the young Doctor, eyeing him not without sympathy. "He's a great old
character. I believe they keep him here to talk to the
tourists."

It is a melancholy fact that in Ireland, in these later
days, "characters" have become aware of their position,
and palpably live up to their reputation. But James was
in a class of his own.

I said didactically, even combatively, that "characters"
wer free and easy, but that James was easy without being
free.

"I'll bet he's not easy in his feet, anyhow!" said the
Doctor brutally. "Have you any more soup there,
James?"

The mother of the young lady, who had hitherto preserved a silence, broken only by the audible assimilation
of her soup, here laid down her spoon and said in
cryptic disparagement:

"Tin!"

"Well, I'd say it was the best we had yet," said the
Doctor. "I'd undertake to pull a puppy through dis-
temper with it."

"That's the soup she has always for th' assizes," said
James. "Grand soup it is, and I declare to ye, she makes
it out of egg shells and every old rubbish!"

The young lady's mother emitted a short laugh, but
her empty soupplate told heavily against her.

The meal wore slowly on. A sea fish, of a genus unknown to me, and amazingly endowed with bones, was
consumed in distracted silence.

"I hear you have a fish shop opened in Ballinagar, Mrs. M'Evoy," remarked the Doctor, taking his last fish bone out of action with professional adroitness, and addressing the mother of the young lady. "That's very up-to-date. There wasn't one I met from Ballinagar but was bragging of it."

"It was the Hoolahanes that had it," said Mrs. M'Evoy. "It's closed."

"Oh dear, why so?" said the Doctor. "Why did they do that, I wonder?"

"They said that morning, noon, and night people were bothering them for fish," returned Mrs. M'Evoy, to whom this triumph of the artistic temperament presented no exceptional feature.

"Unless it might be on a fast day, I'd never ask to taste a bit of fish," remarked James, giving a helping hand to the conversation. "There was a man I knew from this place got his death in Liverpool from a bit of fish. It stuck to the upper gum. 'Bill,' says he to the one that was with him, 'so help me God,' says he, 'I'm dyin',' says he; and sure that's how he met his death! It was in some grand hotel he was, and he was too shy to give the puff to send out the bit."

"I'd like to send that to the 'B.M.J.'," said the Doctor gravely. "Maybe you could give me the man's name, James?"

"There was them that could swear to it," said James, depositing a syphon on the table in a determined manner, "but they were before your day, Doctor Hickey."

"How young he is!" said Miss M'Evoy archly. "Don't be flattering him, James."

"Indeed I'll not flatter him," returned James, "there's plenty doing that."

It was at about this point that a dish containing three roast ducks was placed in front of me. Circumstances had decreed that I sat at the end of the table; it was my task to deal with the ducks, and during the breathless and steamy struggle that ensued, I passed out of the conversation, which, indeed, had resolved itself into a more personal affair between Dr. Hickey and Miss M'Evoy.

It was somewhere in the reposeful period that came with the cheese that Dr. Hickey ordered a bottle of port, of which he very handsomely invited the ladies and me to partake. He leaned back in his chair.

"Was this in the cellar the time of the flood?" he said, putting down his glass. "I don't mean Noah's flood, James; you mightn't remember that; but the time the river came up in the town here."

"If it was Noah's flood itself," said James, instantly accepting combat, "it couldn't get into *our* cellars. But, faith, it was up in this room you're sitting in, and I had to get up on the table from it, and it ruz to the table, and I had to hang out of the chandelier, and a boat came into the room then and took me out. Sure that was the time that the porpoise came up the river, with the dint of the flood, and she was in it for a week, in front of the hotel."

"In compliment to the visitors, I suppose?" said the Doctor. "And what happened her, James?"

"She was in it till a whale came up the river," replied James, with the simplicity of Holy Writ, "and b'Jove he banished her!"

"It's a wonder you'd let him treat a lady that way, James," said Dr. Hickey.

It was still twilight when we left the dining-room, and strayed to the open hall door, and out into the September evening. In the east a rose-pink moon was rising in lavender haze, and a faint wind blew from it; the subtle east wind of September, warmed by its journey across the cornfields, turf-scented by the bogs. There was a narrow garden between the hotel and the river, a place where were new and already-neglected flower-beds, and paths heavy with coarse gravel, and grass that had been cut, not too recently, with a scythe. A thatched summer-house completed the spasmodic effort of the hotel to rise to smartness. The west of Ireland cannot be smart, nor should any right-minded person desire that it should be so.

Dr. Hickey and I sat and smoked on the parapet wall above the river, while the slated and whitewashed town darkened into mystery. Little lights came slowly out, and behind the town the grey shape of Dreelish mountain lowered in uncompromising abruptness, a brooding presence, felt rather than seen. In the summer-house James was lighting a Chinese lantern, of a somewhat crumpled and rheumatic outline.

"Well, now, that's a great notion!" said Dr. Hickey, with the lethargic and pessimistic humour of his type. "That'll be in the prospectus—'Hotel grounds illuminated every night'. I wonder did they buy that at the Jumble Sale after the Fancy Fair in the Town Hall?"

We sat there, and the moon and the round red Chinese lantern looked at each other across the evening, and had a certain resemblance, and I reflected on the fact that an Irishman is always the critic in the stalls, and is also, in spirit, behind the scenes.

"Look at James now," said the Doctor. "He's inviting the ladies out to have coffee in the summer-house. That's very fashionable. I suppose we should go there too."

We sat with Mrs. and Miss M'Evoy in the summer-house, and drank something that was unearthly black in the red light, and was singularly unsuggestive of coffee. The seats were what is known as "rustic", and had aggressive knobs in unexpected places; the floor held the invincible dampness of the West, yet the situation was not disagreeable. At the other side of the river men were sitting on a wall, and talking, quietly, inexhaustibly; now and then a shout of laughter broke from one of them, like a flame from a smouldering fire.

"These lads are waiting to go back on the night mail," said the Doctor; "you wouldn't think they're up since maybe three this morning to come in to the fair."

Here a railway whistle made a thin bar of sound somewhere out under the low moon, that had now lifted

31

herself clear of the haze. A voice called from the hill-side:

"Hora-thu! Tommeen! Let yee be coming on!"

The men tumbled on to the road, and hurried, heavy-footed, in the direction of the station.

"Sure, they've half an hour yet, the creatures," said Mrs. M'Evoy.

"They have, and maybe an hour before they have the pigs shunted," said James, re-entering with a plate of biscuits, adorned with pink and white sugar.

"Ah! what signifies half an hour here or there on this line!" said Dr. Hickey. "I'm told there was a lady travelling on it last week, and she had a canary in a cage, and the canary got loose and flew out of the window, and by George, the lady pulled the communication cord and stopped the train!"

"Well, now, she showed her sense," said Mrs. M'Evoy, with an utterance slightly muffled in pink biscuit.

"She and the guard went then trying to catch the canary," continued Dr. Hickey, "and he'd sit till they'd get near him, and then he'd fly on another piece. Everyone that was in the train was hanging out of it, and betting on it, from one carriage to another, and some would back the lady and some would back the bird, and everyone telling them what to do."

"It's a pity *you* weren't in it," said Miss M'Evoy, "they'd have been all right then."

"It was that bare bit of bog near Bohirmeen," pursued Dr. Hickey, without a stagger, "not a tree in it, 'If he have a fly left in him at all', says a chap out of a Third Smoker, 'ye'll get him in Mike Doogan's bush.' That was the only bush in the country."

"'Twas true for him," said James.

"Well, they got him in the bush," proceeded Dr. Hickey, "singing away for himself; but they had some trouble crossing the drains. I'm told the guard said the lady lepped like a horse!"

"You had it right, all to the singing," commented

Mrs. M'Evoy, advancing as it were to the footlights. "I have the little bird upstairs this minute, and she never sang a note yet!"

Mrs. M'Evoy here permitted herself to subside into fat and deep-seated chuckles, and Miss M'Evoy, James, and I gave way suitably to our feelings.

"Well, now, I thought it was a nice idea, the canary to be singing," said Dr. Hickey, emerging from the situation as from a football scrimmage in which he had retained possession of the ball. "The next time I tell the story I'll leave that out, and I can say that the lady that lepped like a horse was Mrs. M'Evoy. They'll believe me then."

"Why wouldn't you say the canary was an eagle?" said Miss M'Evoy. "There used to be plenty eagles in these mountains back here."

"Well, indeed, I might too," said Dr. Hickey. "I remember it was somewhere in these parts that an uncle of mine was staying one time, and a man came to the hotel with an eagle to sell to the tourists. My uncle was like Mrs. M'Evoy here, he was very fond of birds; and the man said the eagle'd be a lovely pet. Whatever way it was, he bought it." He paused to light a cigarette, and James pretended to collect the coffee cups.

"He gave the eagle to the Boots to mind for him," resumed the Doctor, "and the Boots puts it into an empty bedroom. It wasn't more than seven o'clock next morning when my uncle was wakened up, and the waiter came in. 'There's a man in the kitchen, your honour,' says he, 'and he has a great fighting aigle, and he says he'll fight your honour's aigle in the passage.' They had a grand fight between the two o' them in the spare room, and in the end my uncle's eagle went up the chimney, and the man's eagle went out through the glass in the window. My uncle had a nice bill to pay for all that was broken in the room, and in the end he gave the eagle to the Zoo."

"Faith, he did not!" shouted James suddenly. "He left him stuck in the chimbley! And sure it was I that got him out, and meself that sold him to a gentleman that was going to Ameriky. Sure, I was the waiter!"

Dr. Hickey threw himself back in his rustic chair.

"Holy smoke! This is no place for me," he said; "every story I have is true in spite of me."

Soon afterwards the ladies went to bed, and Dr. Hickey and I smoked on for a time. He explained to me that he was here as "locum" for a friend of his; it wasn't much of a catch, but he was only just after passing for his Medical, and you'd nearly go as locum for a tinker's dog after you had three years' grinding in Dublin put in. This was a God-forsaken sort of a hole, not a hound within fifty miles, nor anyone that would know a hound if they saw one, but the fishing was middling good. From this point the conversation flowed smoothly into channels of sport, and the dual goals of Dr. Hickey's ambition were divulged to me.

"There was a chap I was at school with—Knox his name was—that has a little pack of foxhounds down in the South, and he's as good as promised me I'm to whip-in to him if I can get the Skebawn Dispensary that's vacant now, and I might have as good a chance of it as another."

My own ambitions were also, at the moment, dual, being matrimonial, with a Resident Magistracy attached, but I did not feel it necessary to reveal them. I mentioned that I was having a day's fishing here on my way to Donegal to shoot grouse, but did not add that Philippa, to whom I was newly engaged, was implicated in the grouse party, still less that it was my intention to meet her the next afternoon at Carrow Cross Junction, an hour away, and proceed with her to the home of her uncle, an hour or so further on.

"You might have three hours, or maybe four, to wait at Carrow Cross," said Dr. Hickey, as if tracking my thought; "why wouldn't you drive out to the Sports at Carrow Bay? It's only four miles, and there's a regatta there to-morrow, and when the tide goes out they have

34

races on the sands. I believe there's a trotting-match too, and an exhibition of crochet."

It did not seem to me that I wanted to go to Carrow Bay, but it was not necessary to say so.

Trucks at the station were banging into their neighbours, with much comment from the engine; I thought of Tommeen and his comrades, up since 3 a.m., and still waiting to get home, and it suggested the privileges of those who could go to bed.

It was over a whisky and soda in the heavily reminiscent atmosphere of the smoking-room that Dr. Hickey told me he was going to take the ladies to the Sports, and mentioned that there would be a train at eleven, and a spare seat on the car from Carrow Cross. It required no special effort to see the position that I was to occupy in relation to Mrs. M'Evoy; I followed the diplomatic method of my country; I looked sympathetic, and knew certainly that I should not be there.

I leaned out of my window that night, to look at the river, with the moon on it, hustling over the shallows, and thought of the porpoise, who had been so unchivalrously banished by the whale. I also wondered when the English post got in. I was presently aware of a head projecting from a window just below, and a female voice said, as if in continuance of a conversation:

"We should coax James for the cold duck to take with us."

"That's a good idea," replied the rotund voice of Mrs. M'Evoy; "we'll get nothing out there that a Christian could eat, and there might be that gentleman too." (That gentleman closed one eye.) "Come in now, Ally! There's an east wind coming in that would perish the crows."

The guillotine slam of the sash followed. The river warbled and washed through the stillness; its current was not colder, more clear, than "that gentleman's" resolve that he would not grace the luncheon party at Carrow Bay Sports.

I breakfasted late and in solitude, ministered to by one of the female underlings of James; the voice of James himself, I heard distinclty, in war and slaughtering, somewhere behind the scenes. The letter that I wanted had not failed me, and I smoked a very honeyed cigarette over it in the garden afterwards. A glimpse of Dr. Hickey at the hotel door in a palpably new tie, and of Mrs. and Miss M'Evoy in splendour in the hall, broke into my peace. I quietly but unhesitatingly got over the wall of the garden, and withdrew by way of the river bank.

When the eleven o'clock train had left I returned to the halcyon stillness of the hotel; my own train left at one-thirty; it was a time favourable, and almost attractive, for letter writing. As I wrote, I heard the voice of James demanding in thunder where was Festus O'Flaherty, and why hadn't he the chickens plucked. A small female voice replied that the Doctor and the ladies had left their lunch after them, and that Festus had run up to the station to try would he overtake them with it, and the thrain was gone.

"And if it was themselves they left after them," retorted James, still in thunder, "what was that to him?"

To this conclusion no answer was attempted; I bestowed upon Mrs. M'Evoy some transient compassion, and she and her company departed, hull down, below the horizon of my thoughts.

A few hours afterwards, I trod the solitudes of Carrow Cross Junction, and saw the train that had brought me there bend like a caterpillar round a spur of hill, and disappear. When I looked round again the little bookstall was shuttered up, and the bookstall lady was vanishing down a flight of steps; the porter had entrenched himself in the goods store; the stationmaster was withdrawn from human ken with the completeness only achieved by his kind. I was suspended in space for three hours, and the indifference of my fellow-creatures was unconcealed. A long walk to nowhere and back again was the obvious resource of the destitute.

The town of Carrow Cross lay in a hollow below the station, with the blue turf smoke stagnant above its muddle of slate and thatched roofs; I skirted it, and struck out into the country. I did not find it attractive. Potato fields in September are not looking their best; there were no trees, and loose, crooked walls overran the landscape. The peak of Dreelish mountain was visible, but the dingy green country rose high between me and it, like the cope on the neck of a priest. I walked for an hour; I sat on a wall and read Philippa's letter again, and found, with a shock, that I had only one cigarette left. A fatuous fear of missing the train turned me back in the direction of the station, slightly hungry, and profoundly bored. I came into the town by a convent, and saw the nuns walking flowingly in twos, under chestnut trees; asceticism in its most pictorial aspect, with the orange leaves and the blue September haze, and the black robes and white headgear. I wondered how they managed to go on walking neatly to nowhere and back again with such purpose, and if they felt as jaded as I, and as little enlivened by the environs of Carrow Cross.

The town was an unprepossessing affair of two or three streets, whitewash and thatch squeezed between green and gold pubs, like old country-women among fashionable daughters. Everything was closed; as I looked along the empty street an outside car drawn by a dun pony turned into it at high speed, the pony forging with a double click-clack. As the car swung towards me someone flourished a stick, someone else a red parasol.

"We got a bit tired waiting for the sports," Dr. Hickey said, as he assisted Mrs. M'Evoy to alight at a house labelled Lynch's Railway Hotel, in royal blue; "it seemed that the tide wasn't going out as fast as the Committee expected. It might be another hour or more before the racecourse would be above water, and we thought we might as well come on here and get something to eat at the hotel."

"It has the appearance of being closed," said Mrs. M'Evoy, in a voice thinned by famine.

"That might be a fashion it has in the afternoon, when themselves does be at their dinner," said the car-driver.

The front door was certainly closed, and there was neither knocker nor bell, nothing but a large well-thumbed keyhole. Dr. Hickey hammered with his stick; nothing happened.

"They're gone to the races so," said the car-driver.

In the silence that followed it seemed that I could hear the flagging beat of Mrs. M'Evoy's heart.

"Wait awhile," said Dr. Hickey, "the window isn't bolted!"

The sill was no more than two feet from the ground, the sash yielded to pressure and went up; Dr. Hickey dived in, and we presently heard him assail the front door from inside.

It was locked, and its key had apparently gone to the races. I followed Dr. Hickey by way of the window, so did Miss M'Evoy; we pooled our forces, and drew her mamma after us through the opening of two foot by three, steadily, as the great god Pan drew the pitch from the reed.

We found ourselves in a small sitting-room, almost filled by a table; there was a mature smell of cabbage, but there was nothing else to suggest the presence of food. We proceeded to the nether regions, which were like a chapter in a modern realistic novel, and found a sickly kitchen fire, the horrid remains of the Lynch family breakfast, an empty larder, and some of the home attire of the race-goers, lying, as the tree lies, where it fell.

"There's a sort of a butcher in the town," said Dr. Hickey, when the search-parties had converged on each other, empty-handed, "maybe we could cook something——"

"If it was even a bit of salt pork——" said Mrs. M'Evoy, seizing the poker and attacking the sleepy fire.

"Let you get some water, and I'll wash the plates," said Miss M'Evoy to Dr. Hickey.

I looked at my watch, saw that I had still an hour and a half to play with, and departed to look for the butcher.

Neither by sign-board nor by shop front did the Carrow Cross butcher reveal himself. I was finally investigating a side street, where the houses were one-storied, and thatched, and wholly unpromising, when a heavy running step, that might have been a horses's, thundered behind me, and a cumbrous pale woman, with the face of a fugitive, plunged past me, and burst in at a cottage door like a mighty blast of wind. A little girl, in tears, thudded bare-footed after her. The big woman turned in the doorway, and shrieked at me:

"Thim's madmen, from th'Asylum! Come inside from them, for God's sake!"

I looked behind me up the street, and saw a small, decorous party of men, flanked by a couple of stalwart keepers in uniform. One of the men, a white-faced being in seedy black, headed them, playing an imaginary fiddle on his left arm, and smiling secretly to himself. Whether the lady had invited me to her house as a protector, or as a refugee, I did not know: she herself had vanished, but through the still open door I saw, miraculously, a fragment or two of meat, hanging in the interior. I had apparently chanced upon the home of the Carrow Cross butcher.

A greasy counter and a chopping-block put the matter beyond doubt; I beat upon an inner door; a wail of terror responded, and then a muffled voice:

"Come in under the bed to me, Chrissie, before they ketch ye!"

There was nothing for it but to take from a hook a grey and white fragment that looked like bacon, place half a crown on the counter, and depart swiftly.

"I gave a few of the Asylum patients leave to go to the Sports," said Dr. Hickey, a little later, when we were seated between the large bare table and the wall of the little sitting-room, with slices of fried pork weltering on our plates. "I saw the fellow waltzing down the street. Ah! he's fairly harmless, and they've a couple o' keepers with them anyway."

"The only pity was that you left the half-crown," said Mrs. M'Evoy; "a shilling was too much for it."

Mrs. M'Evoy was considerably flushed, and had an effective black smear on her forehead, but her voice had recovered its timbre. There was a tin of biscuits on the table, there was a war-worn brown teapot, and some bottles of porter; it was now four hours since I had eaten anything; in spite of the cold and clear resolve of the night before. I was feeding, grossly yet enjoyable, with Dr. Hickey and his friends.

"This is a Temperance Hotel for the past year," remarked Dr. Hickey, delicately knocking off the head of a porter bottle with the sitting-room poker. "That's why it was upstairs I found the porter. I suppose they took the corkscrew to the Sports with them."

"How did they lose the license at all?" said Mrs. M'Evoy; "I thought there wasn't a house in Carrow Cross but had one."

"It was taken from them over some little mistake about selling potheen," replied Dr. Hickey, courteously applying the broken neck of the bottle to Mrs. M'Evoy's tumbler. "The police came to search the house, and old Lynch, that was in bed upstairs, heard them, and threw a two-gallon jar of potheen out of the top back window, to break it. The unlucky thing was that there was a goose in the yard, and it was on the goose it fell."

"The creature!" said Miss M'Evoy, "was she killed?"

"Killed to the bone, as they say," replied the Doctor; "but the trouble was, that on account of falling on the goose the jar wasn't broken, so the bobbies got the potheen."

"Supposing they summons you now for the porter!" said Mrs. M'Evoy, facetiously, casting her eye through the open window into the bare sunshiny street.

"They'll have summonses enough at Carrow Bay to keep them out of mischief," returned Dr. Hickey. "It's a pity now, Major, you didn't patronize the Sports. They might have put you on judging the cakes with Mrs. M'Evoy."

"Why then, the one they put on with me was the man they had judging the vegetables," said Mrs. M'Evoy, after a comfortable pull at the contraband porter. "That's a fine weighty cake,' says me lad, weighing a sponge-cake on his hand. 'We'll give that one the prize.' "

"I wish you brought it here with you," said her daughter, "as weighty as it was."

"They put *me* judging the row-boats," said Dr. Hickey, "but after the third race I had to give up, and put five stitches in one of the men that was in the mark-boat."

I said that the mark-boat ought to have been a fairly safe place.

"Safe!" said Dr. Hickey. "It was the hottest corner in the course. I thought they were sunk twice, but they might have been all right if they hadn't out-oars and joined in the race on the second round. They got in first, as it happened, and it was in the course of the protest that I had to put in the stitches. It was a good day's sport, as far as it went."

"Ah ,there's no life in a regatta without a band," said Miss M'Evoy languidly, with her elbows on the table and her cup in her hand. "Now Ringsend Regatta's sweet!"

"I'm afraid Miss M'Evoy didn't enjoy herself to-day," said Dr. Hickey. "Of course she's used to so much attention in Dublin——"

"It's kind of you to say that," said Miss M'Evoy; "I'm sure you're quite an authority on Dublin young ladies."

"Is it me?" said Dr. Hickey; "I'd be afraid to say Boo to a goose. But I've a brother that could tell you all about them. He's not as shy as I am."

"He must be a great help and comfort to you," returned Miss M'Evoy.

"He's very romantic," said Dr. Hickey, "and poetical. He was greatly struck with two young ladies he met at the Ringsend Regatta last month. He mistook their

41

address, someway, and when he couldn't find them, what did he do but put a poem in the papers—the Agony Column, y'know——"

"We'd like to hear that," said Mrs. M'Evoy, putting her knife into the salt with unhurried dexterity.

"I forget it all, only the last verse," said Dr. Hickey, "it went this way:

> You are indeed a charming creature,
> Perfect alike in form and feature,
> I love you and none other.
> Oh, Letitia—Here's your Mother!"

As Dr. Hickey, his eyes modestly on his plate, concluded the ode, I certainly intercepted a peculiar glance between the ladies.

"I call that very impident," said Mrs. M'Evoy, winking at me.

"It was worth paying a good deal to put that in print!" commented Miss M'Evoy unkindly. "But that was a lovely regatta,' 'she continued, "and the music and the fireworks were grand, but the society's very mixed. Do you remember, M'ma, what happened to Mary and me that evening, the time we missed you in the dark?"

"Indeed'n I do," said Mrs. M'Evoy, her eyes still communing with her daughter's, "and I remember telling you it was the last evening I'd let you out of my sight."

"It was a gentleman that picked up my umbrella," began Miss M'Evoy artlessly.

Dr. Hickey dropped his knife on the floor, and took some time to pick it up.

"And he passed the remark to me that it was a nice evening," went on Miss E'Evoy. " 'It is,' said I. Now, M'ma, why wouldn't I give him a civil answer?"

"That's according to taste," said Mrs. M'Evoy.

"Well indeed I didn't fancy his looks at all. It was pitch dark only for the fireworks, but I thought he had a nasty kind of a foreign look, and a little pointed beard on him too. If you saw the roll of his eye when the green

fire fell out of the rockets you'd think of Mephistopheles——"

"There's no doubt Mephistopheles was one of
Shakespeare's grandest creations," said Dr. Hickey
hurriedly. His eyes besought my aid. It struck me that
this literary digression was an attempt to change the
conversation.

Miss M'Evoy resumed her narrative.

" 'That's a pretty flower you have in your button-
hole,' said he. 'It is,' said I."

"You didn't tell him a great deal he didn't know,"
said her mother.

" 'Maybe you might give it to me?' said he. 'Maybe I
might not!' said I. 'And where do you live?' said he.
'Percy Place,' says Mary, before you could wink. Anyone would have to believe her. 'Upon my soul,' said he,
'I'll have the pleasure of calling upon you. Might I ask
what your name is?' 'O'Rooney,' says Mary, 'and this is
my cousin, Miss Letitia Gollagher.' Well, when Mary
said 'Gollagher', I *burst*!"

Miss M'Evoy here put down her cup, and to some
slight extent repeated the operation.

"I suppose the foreign gentleman told you his own
name then?" said Dr. Hickey, whose complexion had
warmed up remarkably.

"He did not," said Miss M'Evoy; "but perhaps that
was because he wasn't asked, and it was then M'ma
came up. I can tell you he didn't wait to be introduced!"

"I have a sister-in-law living in Percy Place," said
Mrs. M'Evoy, passing her handkerchief over her brow,
and addressing no one in particular, "and it was some
day last month she was telling me of a young man that
was knocking at all the doors down the street, and she
thought he was a collector of some sort. He came to her
house too, and he told the girl he was looking for some
ladies of the name of Gollagher or O'Rooney."

She paused, and regarded Dr. Hickey.

"I wonder did he find them?" asked Dr. Hickey, who
was obviously being forced on to the ropes.

"I thought *you* might be able to tell us that!" said Mrs. M'Evoy, delivering her knock-out blow with the suddenness that belongs to the highest walks of the art.

Miss M'Evoy, with equal suddenness, uttered a long and strident yell, and lay back in her place, grasping my arm as she did so, in what I am convinced was wholly unconscious sympathy. She and I were side by side, facing the window, and through the window, which, as I have mentioned, was wide open, I was aware of a new element in the situation.

It was a figure in blue in the street outside; a soft and familiar blue, and it bore a parasol of the same colour. The figure was at a standstill; and very blue, the burning blue of tropical heavens, were the eyes that met mine beneath the canopy of the parasol. Even before my own had time to blink I foreknew that never, in time or in eternity, should I be able to make Philippa accept thoroughly my explanation.

Philippa's explanation was extremely brief, and was addressed rather to the empty street of Carrow Cross than to me, as I crawled by her side. There had been, she said, half an hour to wait, and as I was not at the station—the blue eyes met mine for a steely moment— she had gone for a little walk. She had met some horrid drunken men, and turned into another street to avoid them, and then——

A brimming silence followed. We turned up the road that led to the station.

"There are those men again!" exclaimed Philippa, coming a little nearer to me.

In front of us, deviously ascending the long slope, was the Asylum party; the keepers, exceedingly drunk, being assisted to the station by the lunatics.

IN THE CURRANHILTY COUNTRY

It is hardly credible that I should have been induced to depart from my usual walk of life by a creature so uninspiring as the grey horse that I bought from Flurry Knox for £25.

Perhaps it was the monotony of being questioned by every other person with whom I had five minutes' conversation, as to when I was coming out with the hounds, and being further informed that in the days when Captain Browne, the late Coastguard officer, had owned the grey, there was not a fence between this and Mallow big enough to please them. At all events, there came an epoch-making day when I mounted the Quaker and presented myself at a meet of Mr. Knox's hounds. It is my belief that six out of every dozen people who go out hunting are disagreeably conscious of a nervous system, and two out of the six are in what is brutally called "a blue funk". I was not in a blue funk, but I was conscious not only of a nervous system, but of the anatomical fact that I possessed large, round legs, handsome in their way, even admirable in their proper sphere, but singularly ill adapted for adhering to the slippery surfaces of a saddle. By a fatal intervention of Providence, the sport, on this my first day in the hunting-field, was such as I could have enjoyed from a bathchair. The hunting-field was, on this occasion, a relative term, implying long stretches of unfenced moorland and bog, anything, in fact, save a field; the hunt itself might also have been termed a relative one, being mainly composed of Mr. Knox's relations in all degrees of cousinhood. It was a day when frost and sunshine combined went to one's head like iced champagne; the distant sea looked like the Mediterranean, and for four sunny hours the Knox

45

relatives and I followed nine couple of hounds at a tranquil footpace along the hills, our progress mildly enlivened by one or two scrambles in the shape of jumps. At three o'clock I jogged home, and felt within me the new-born desire to brag to Peter Cadogan of the Quaker's doings, as I dismounted rather stiffly in my own yard.

I little thought that the result would be that three weeks later I should find myself in a railway carriage at an early hour of a December morning, in company with Flurry Knox and four or five of his clan, journeying towards an unknown town, named Drumcurran, with an appropriate number of horses in boxes behind us and a van full of hounds in front. Mr. Knox's hounds were on their way, by invitation, to have a day in the country of their neighbours, the Curranhilty Harriers, and with amazing fatuity I had allowed myself to be cajoled into joining the party. A northerly shower was striking in long spikes on the glass of the window, the atmosphere of the carriage was blue with tobacco smoke, and my feet, in a pair of new blucher boots, had sunk into a species of Arctic sleep.

"Well, you got my letter about the dance at the hotel to-night?" said Flurry Knox, breaking off a whispered conversation with his amateur whip, Dr. Jerome Hickey, and sitting down beside me. "And we're to go out with the Harriers to-day, and they've a sure fox for our hounds to-morrow. I tell you you'll have the best fun ever you had. It's a great country to ride. Fine honest banks, that you can come racing at anywhere you like."

Dr. Hickey, a saturnine young man, with a long nose and a black torpedo beard, whose acquaintance I had, some months before, been privileged to make, returned to his pocket the lancet with which he had been trimming his nails.

"They're like the Tipperary banks," he said; "you climb down nine feet and you fall the rest."

It occurred to me that the Quaker and I would most probably fall all the way, but I said nothing.

46

"I hear Tomsy Flood has a good horse this season," resumed Flurry.

"Then it's not the one you sold him," said the Doctor.

"I'll take my oath it's not," said Flurry with a grin. "I believe he has it in for me still over that one."

Dr. Jerome's moustache went up under his nose and showed his white teeth.

"Small blame to him! when you sold him a mare that was wrong of both her hind-legs. Do you know what he did, Major Yeates? The mare was lame going into the fair, and he took the two hind-shoes off her and told poor Flood she kicked them off in the box, and that was why she was going tender, and he was so drunk he believed him."

The conversation here deepened into trackless obscurities of horse-dealing. I took out my stylograph pen, and finished a letter to Philippa, with a feeling that it would probably be my last.

The next step in the day's enjoyment consisted in trotting in cavalcade through the streets of Drumcurran, with another northerly shower descending upon us, the mud splashing in my face, and my feet coming torturingly to life. Every man and boy in the town ran with us; the Harriers were somewhere in the tumult ahead, and the Quaker began to pull and hump his back ominously. I arrived at the meet considerably heated, and found myself one of some thirty or forty riders, who, with traps and bicycles and foot-people, were jammed in a narrow, muddy road. We were late, and a move was immediately made across a series of grass fields, all considerately furnished with gates. There was a glacial gleam of sunshine, and people began to turn down the collars of their coats. As they spread over the field I observed that Mr. Knox was no longer riding with old Captain Handcock, the Master of the Harriers, but had attached himself to a square-shouldered young lady with effective coils of dark hair and a grey habit. She was riding a fidgety black mare with great decision and a not disagreeable swagger.

47

It was at about this moment that the hounds began to run, fast and silently, and everyone began to canter.

"This is nothing at all," said Dr. Hickey, thundering alongside of me on a huge young chestnut; "there might have been a hare here last week, or a red herring this morning. I wouldn't care if we only got what'd warm us. For the matter of that, I'd as soon hunt a cat as a hare."

I was already getting quite enough to warm me. The Quaker's respectable grey head had twice disappeared between his forelegs in a brace of most unsettling bucks, and all my experiences at the riding-school at Sandhurst did not prepare me for the sensation of jumping a briary wall with a heavy drop into a lane so narrow that each horse had to turn at right angles as he landed. I did not so turn, but saved myself from entire disgrace by a timely clutch at the mane. We scrambled out of the lane over a pile of stones and furze bushes, and at the end of the next field were confronted by a tall, stone-faced bank. Every one, always excepting myself, was riding with that furious valour which is so conspicuous when neighbouring hunts meet, and the leading half-dozen charged the obstacle at steeplechase speed. I caught a glimpse of the young lady in the grey habit, sitting square and strong as her mare topped the bank, with Flurry and the redoubtable Mr. Tomsy Flood riding on either hand; I followed in their wake, with a blind confidence in the Quaker, and none at all in myself. He refused it. I suppose it was in token of affection and gratitude that I fell upon his neck; at all events, I had reason to respect his judgment, as, before I had recovered myself, the hounds were straggling back into the field by a gap lower down.

It finally appeared that the hounds could do no more with the line they had been hunting, and we proceeded to jog interminably, I knew not whither. During this unpleasant process Flurry Knox bestowed on me many items of information, chiefly as to the pangs of jealousy he was inflicting on Mr. Flood by his attentions to the lady in the grey habit, Miss "Bobbie" Bennett.

48

"She'll have all old Handcock's money one of these days—she's his niece, y' know—and she's a good girl to ride, but she's not as young as she was ten years ago. You'd be looking at a chicken a long time before you thought of her! She might take Tomsy some day if she can't do any better." He stopped and looked at me with a gleam in his eye. "Come on, and I'll introduce you to her!"

Before, however, this privilege could be mine, the whole cavalcade was stopped by a series of distant yells, which apparently conveyed information to the hunt, though to me they only suggested a Red Indian scalping his enemy. The yells travelled rapidly nearer, and a young man with a scarlet face and a long stick sprang upon the fence, and explained that he and Patsy Lorry were after chasing a hare two miles down out of the hill above, and ne'er a dog nor a one with them but themselves, and she was lying beat out, under a bush, and Patsy Lorry was minding her until the hounds would come. I had a vision of the humane Patsy Lorry fanning the hare with his hat, but apparently nobody else found the fact unusual. The hounds were hurried into the fields, the hare was again spurred into action, and I was again confronted with the responsibilities of the chase. After the first five minutes I had discovered several facts about the Quaker. If the bank was above a certain height he refused it irrevocably, if it accorded with his ideas he got his forelegs over and ploughed through the rest of it on his stifle-joints, or, if a gripe made this inexpedient, he remained poised on top till the fabric crumbled under his weight. In the case of walls he butted them down with his knees, or squandered them with his hind-legs. These operations took time, and the leaders of the hunt streamed farther and farther away over the crest of a hill, while the Quaker pursued at the equable gallop of a horse in the Bayeux Tapestry.

I began to perceive that I had been adopted as a pioneer by a small band of followers, who, as one of their number candidly explained, "liked to have someone

49

ahead of them to soften the banks", and accordingly waited respectfully till the Quaker had made the rough places smooth, and taken the raw edges off the walls. They, in their turn, showed me alternative routes when the obstacle proved above the Quaker's limit; thus, in ignoble confederacy, I and the offscourings of the Curranhilty Hunt pursued our way across some four miles of country. When at length we parted it was with extreme regret on both sides. A river crossed our course, with boggy banks pitted deep with the hoof-marks of our forerunners; I suggested it to the Quaker, and discovered that Nature had not in vain endued him with the hindquarters of the hippopotamus. I presume the others had jumped it; the Quaker, with abysmal flounderings, walked through and heaved himself to safety on the farther bank. It was the dividing of the ways. My friendly company turned aside as one man, and I was left with the world before me, and no guide save the hoof-marks in the grass. These presently led me to a road, on the other side of which was a bank, that was at once added to the Quaker's black list. The rain had again begun to fall heavily, and was soaking in about my elbows; I suddenly asked myself why, in Heaven's name, I should go any farther. No adequate reason occurred to me, and I turned in what I believed to be the direction of Drum-curran.

I rode on for possibly two or three miles without seeing a human being, until, from the top of a hill I descried a solitary lady rider. I started in pursuit. The rain kept blurring my eye-glass, but it seemed to me that the rider was a schoolgirl with hair hanging down her back, and that her horse was a trifle lame. I pressed on to ask my way, and discovered that I had been privileged to overtake no less a person than Miss Bobbie Bennett.

My question as to the route led to information of a varied character. Miss Bennett was going that way herself; her mare had given her what she called "a toss and a half", whereby she had strained her arm and the mare her shoulder, her habit had been torn, and she had lost all her hairpins.

"I'm an awful object," she concluded; "my hair's the plague of my life out hunting! I declare I wish to goodness I was bald!"

I struggled to the level of the occasion with an appropriate protest. She had really very brilliant grey eyes, and her complexion was undeniable. Philippa has since explained to me that it is a mere male fallacy that any woman can look well with her hair down her back, but I have always maintained that Miss Bobbie Bennett, with the rain glistening on her dark tresses, looked uncommonly well.

"I shall never get it dry for the dance to-night," she complained.

"I wish I could help you," said I.

"Perhaps you've got a hairpin or two about you!" said she, with a glance that had certainly done great execution before now.

I disclaimed the possession of any such tokens, but volunteered to go and look for some at a neighbouring cottage.

The cottage door was shut, and my knockings were answered by a stupefied-looking elderly man. Conscious of my own absurdity, I asked him if he had any hairpins.

"I didn't see a hare this week!" he responded in a slow bellow.

"Hairpins!" I roared; "has your wife any hairpins?"

"She has not." Then, as an after-thought, "She's dead these ten years."

At this point a young woman emerged from the cottage, and, with many coy grins, plucked from her own head some half-dozen hairpins, crooked, and grey with age, but still hairpins, and as such well worth my shilling. I returned with my spoil to Miss Bennett, only to be confronted with a fresh difficulty. The arm that she had strained was too stiff to raise to her head.

Miss Bobbie turned her handsome eyes upon me. "It's no use," she said plaintively, "I can't do it!"

51

I looked up and down the road; there was no one in sight. I offered to do it for her.

Miss Bennett's hair was long, thick, and soft; it was also slippery with rain. I twisted it conscientiously, as if it were a hay rope, until Miss Bennett, with an irrepressible shriek, told me it would break off. I coiled the rope with some success, and proceeded to nail it to her head with the hairpins. At all the most critical points one, if not both, of the horses moved; hairpins were driven home into Miss Bennett's skull, and were with difficulty plucked forth again; in fact, a more harrowing performance can hardly be imagined, but Miss Bennett bore it with the heroism of a pin-cushion.

I was putting the finishing touches to the coiffure when some sound made me look round, and I beheld at a distance of some fifty yards the entire hunt approaching us at a foot-pace. I lost my head, and instead of continuing my task, I dropped the last hairpin as if it were red-hot, and kicked the Quaker away to the far side of the road, thus, if it were possible, giving the position away a shade more generously.

There were fifteen riders in the group that overtook us, and fourteen of them, including the Whip, were grinning from ear to ear; the fifteenth was Mr. Tomsy Flood, and he showed no sign of appreciation. He shoved his horse past me and up to Miss Bennett, his red moustache bristling, truculence in every outline of his heavy shoulders. His green coat was muddy, and his hat had a cave in it. Things had apparently gone ill with him.

Flurry's witticisms held out for about two miles and a half; I do not give them, because they were not amusing, but they all dealt ultimately with the animosity that I, in common with himself, should henceforth have to fear from Mr. Flood.

"Oh, he's a holy terror!" he said conclusively; "he was riding the rails off the hounds to-day to best me. He was near killing me twice. We had some words about it, I can tell you. I very near took my whip to him. Such a bull-rider of a fellow I never saw! He wouldn't so much as stop to catch Bobbie Bennett's horse when I picked her up, he was riding so jealous. His own girl, mind you! And such a crumpler as she got too! I declare she knocked a groan out of the road when she struck it!"

"She doesn't seem so much hurt!" I said.

"Hurt!" said Flurry, flicking casually at a hound. "You couldn't hurt that one unless you took a hatchet to her!"

The rain had reached a pitch that put further hunting out of the question, and we bumped home at that intolerable pace known as a "hound's jog". I spent the remainder of the afternoon over a fire in my bedroom in the Royal Hotel, Drumcurran, official letters to write having mercifully provided me with an excuse for seclusion, while the bar and the billiard-room hummed below, and the Quaker's three-cornered gallop wreaked its inevitable revenge upon my person. As this process continued and I became proportionately embittered, I asked myself, not for the first time, what Philippa would say when introduced to my present circle of acquaintances.

I have already mentioned that a dance was to take place at the hotel, given, as far as I could gather, by the leading lights of the Curranhilty Hunt. A less jocund guest than the wreck who at the pastoral hour of nine crept stiffly down to "chase the glowing hours with flying feet" could hardly have been encountered. The dance was held in the coffee-room, and a conspicuous object outside the door was a saucer bath full of something that looked like flour.

"Rub your feet in that," said Flurry; "that's French chalk! They hadn't time to do the floor, so they hit on this dodge."

I complied with this encouraging direction, and followed him into the room. Dancing had already begun, and the first sight that met my eyes was Miss Bennett, in a yellow dress, waltzing with Mr. Tomsy Flood. She

53

looked very handsome, and, in spite of her accident, she was getting round the sticky floor and her still more sticky partner with the swing of a racing cutter. Her eye caught mine immediately, and with confidence. Clearly our acquaintance that, in the space of twenty minutes, had blossomed tropically into hair-dressing, was not to be allowed to wither. Nor was I myself allowed to wither. Men, known and unknown, plied me with partners, till my shirt cuff was black with names, and the number of dances stretched away into the blue distance of to-morrow morning. The music was supplied by the organist of the church, who played with religious unction and at the pace of a processional hymn. I put forth into the mêlée with a junior Bennett, inferior in calibre to Miss Bobbie, but a strong goer, and, I fear, made but a sorry début in the eyes of Drumcurran. At every other moment I bumped into the unforeseen orbits of those who reversed, and of those who walked their partners backwards down the room with faces of ineffable supremacy. Being unskilled in these intricacies of an elder civilization, the younger Miss Bennett fared but ingloriously at my hands; the music pounded interminably on, until the heel of Mr. Flood put a period to our sufferings.

"The nasty dirty filthy brute!" shrieked the younger Miss Bennett in a single breath; "he's torn the gown off my back!"

She whirled me to the cloak-room; we parted, mutually unregretted, at its door, and by, I fear, common consent, evaded our second dance together.

Many, many times during the evening I asked myself why I did not go to bed. Perhaps it was the remembrance that my bed was situated some ten feet above the piano in a direct line; but, whatever the reason, the night wore on and found me still working my way down my shirt cuff. I sat out as much as possible, and found my partners to be, as a body, pretty, talkative, and ill dressed, and during the evening I had many and varied opportunities of observing the rapid progress of Mr.

Knox's flirtation with Miss Bobbie Bennett. From No. 4 to No. 8 they were invisible; that they were behind a screen in the commercial-room might be inferred from Mr. Flood's thunder-cloud presence in the passage outside.

At No. 9 the young lady emerged for one of her dances with me; it was a barn dance, and particularly trying to my momently stiffening muscles; but Miss Bobbie, whether in dancing or sitting out, went in for "the rigour of the game". She was in as hard condition as one of her uncle's hounds, and for a full fifteen minutes I capered and swooped beside her, larding the lean earth as I went, and replying but spasmodically to her even flow of conversation.

"That'll take the stiffness out of you!" she exclaimed, as the organist slowed down reverentially to a conclusion. "I had a bet with Flurry Knox over that dance. He said you weren't up to my weight at the pace!"

I led her forth to the refreshment table, and was watching with awe her fearless consumption of a claret cup that I would not have touched for a sovereign, when Flurry, with a partner on his arm, strolled past us.

"Well, you won the gloves, Miss Bobbie!" he said. "Don't you wish you may get them!"

"Gloves without the g, Mr. Knox!" replied Miss Bennett, in a voice loud enough to reach the end of the passage, where Mr. Thomas Flood was burying his nose in a very brown whisky-and-soda.

"Your hair's coming down!" retorted Flurry. "Ask Major Yeates if he can spare you a few hairpins!"

Swifter than lightning, Miss Bennett hurled a macaroon at her retreating foe, missed him, and subsided laughing on to a sofa. I mopped my brow and took my seat beside her, wondering how much longer I could live up to the social exigencies of Drumcurran.

Miss Bennett, however, proved excellent company. She told me artfully, and inch by inch, all that Mr. Flood had said to her on the subject of my hair-dressing; she admitted that she had, as a punishment, cut him out

55

of three dances and given them to Flurry Knox. When I remarked that in fairness they should have been given to me, she darted a very attractive glance at me, and pertinently observed that I had not asked for them.

As steals the dawn into a fevered room,
And says, "Be of good cheer, the day is born!"
so did the rumour of supper pass among the chaperons, male and female. It was obviously due to a sense of the fitness of things that Mrs. Bennett was apportioned to me, and I found myself in the gratifying position of heading with her the procession to supper. My impressions of Mrs. Bennett are few but salient. She wore an apple-green satin dress and filled it tightly; wisely mistrusting the hotel supper, she had imported sandwiches and cake in a pocket-handkerchief, and, warmed by two glasses of sherry, she made me the recipient of the remarkable confidence that she had but two back teeth in her head, but, thank God, they met. When, with the other starving men, I fell upon the remains of the feast, I regretted that I had declined her offer of a sandwich.

Of the remainder of the evening I am unable to give a detailed account. Let it not for one instant be imagined that I had looked upon the wine of the Royal Hotel when it was red, or, indeed, any other colour; as a matter of fact, I had espied an inconspicuous corner in the entrance hall, and there I first smoked a cigarette, and subsequently sank into uneasy sleep. Through my dreams I was aware of the measured pounding of the piano, of the clatter of glasses at the bar, of wheels in the street, and then, more clearly, of Flurry's voice assuring Miss Bennett that if she'd only wait for another dance he'd get the R.M. out of bed to do her hair for her—then again oblivion.

At some later period I was dropping down a chasm on the Quaker's back, and landing with a shock; I was twisting his mane into a chignon, when he turned round his head and caught my arm in his teeth. I awoke with the dew of terror on my forehead, to find Miss Bennett leaning over me in a scarlet cloak with a hood over her head. and shaking me by the coat sleeve.

"Major Yeates," she began at once in a hurried whisper, "I want you to find Flurry Knox and tell him there's a plan to feed his hounds at six o'clock this morning so as to spoil their hunting!"

"How do you know?" I asked, jumping up.

"My little brother told me. He came in with us to-night to see the dance, and he was hanging round in the stables, and he heard one of the men telling another there was a dead mule in an outhouse in Bride's Alley, all cut up ready to give to Mr. Knox's hounds."

"But why shouldn't they get it?" I asked in sleepy stupidity.

"Is it fill them up with an old mule just before they're going out hunting?" flashed Miss Bennett. "Hurry and tell Mr. Knox; don't let Tomsy Flood see you telling him—or anyone else."

"Oh, then it's Mr. Flood's game?" I said, grasping the situation at length.

"It is," said Miss Bennett, suddenly turning scarlet; "he's a disgrace! I'm ashamed of him! I'm done with him!"

I resisted a strong temptation to shake Miss Bennett by the hand.

"I can't wait," she continued. "I made my mother drive back a mile—she doesn't know a thing about it— I said I'd left my purse in the cloak-room. Good night! Don't tell a soul but Flurry!"

She was off, and upon my incapable shoulders rested the responsibility of the enterprise.

It was past four o'clock, and the last bars of the last waltz were being played. At the bar a knot of men, with Flurry in their midst, were tossing "Odd man out" for a bottle of champagne. Flurry was not in the least drunk, a circumstance worthy of remark in his present company, and I got him out into the hall and unfolded my tidings. The light of battle lit in his eye as he listened.

"I knew by Tomsy he was shaping for mischief," he

said coolly; "he's taken as much liquor as'd stiffen a tinker, and he's only half-drunk this minute. Hold on till I get Jerome Hickey and Charlie Knox—they're sober; I'll be back in a minute."

I was not present at the council of war thus hurriedly convened; I was merely informed when they returned that we were all to "hurry on". My best evening pumps have never recovered the subsequent proceedings. They, with my swelled and aching feet inside them, were raced down one filthy lane after another, until, somewhere on the outskirts of Drumcurran, Flurry pushed open the gate of a yard and went in. It was nearly five o'clock on that raw December morning; low down in the sky a hazy moon shed a diffused light; all the surrounding houses were still and dark. At our footsteps an angry bark or two came from inside the stable.

"Whisht!" said Flurry. "I'll say a word to them before I open the door."

At his voice a chorus of hysterical welcome arose; without more delay he flung open the stable door, and immediately we were all knee-deep in a rush of hounds. There was not a moment lost. Flurry started at a quick run out of the yard with the whole pack pattering at his heels. Charlie Knox vanished; Dr. Hickey and I followed the hounds, splashing into puddles and hobbling over patches of broken stones, till we left the town behind and hedges arose on either hand.

"Here's the house!" said Flurry, stopping short at a low entrance gate; "many's the time I've been here when his father had it; it'll be a queer thing if I can't find a window I can manage, and the old cook he has is as deaf as the dead."

He and Doctor Hickey went in at the gate with the hounds; I hesitated ignobly in the mud.

"This isn't an R.M.'s job," said Flurry in a whisper, closing the gate in my face; "you'd best keep clear of housebreaking."

I accepted his advice, but I may admit that before I turned for home a sash was gently raised, a light had sprung up in one of the lower windows, and I heard Flurry's voice saying, "Over, over, over!" to his hounds.

There seemed to me to be no interval at all between these events and the moment when I woke in bright sunlight to find Dr. Hickey standing by my bedside in a red coat with a tall glass in his hand.

"It's nine o'clock," he said. "I'm just after waking Flurry Knox. There wasn't one stirring in the hotel till I went down and pulled the Boots from under the kitchen table! It's well for us the meet's in the town; and, by-the-bye, your grey horse has four legs on him the size of bolsters this morning; he won't be fit to go out, I'm afraid. Drink this anyway, you're in the want of it."

Dr. Hickey's eyelids were rather pink, but his hand was as steady as a rock. The whisky-and-soda was singularly untempting.

"What happened last night?" I asked eagerly as I gulped it.

"Oh, it all went off very nicely, thank you," said Hickey, twisting his black beard to a point. "We benched as many of the hounds in Flood's bed as'd fit, and we shut the lot into the room. We had them just comfortable when we heard his latchkey below at the door." He broke off and began to snigger.

"Well?" I said, sitting bolt upright.

"Well, he got in at last, and he lit a candle then. That took him five minutes. He was pretty tight. We were looking at him over the banisters until he started to come up, and according as he came up, we went on up the top flight. He stood admiring his candle for a while on the landing, and we wondered he didn't hear the hounds snuffing under the door. He opened it then, and, on the minute, three of them bolted out between his legs." Dr. Hickey again paused to indulge in Mephistophelian laughter. "Well, you know," he went on, "when a man in poor Tomsy's condition sees six dogs jumping out of his bed he's apt to make a wrong diagnosis. He gave a roar, and pitched the candlestick at them, and ran for his life downstairs, and all the hounds after him.

'Gone away!' screeches that devil Flurry, pelting down-stairs on top of them in the dark. I believe I screeched too.'

"Good heavens!" I gasped. "I was well out of that!"

"Well, you were," admitted the Doctor. "However, Tomsy bested them in the dark, and he got to ground in the pantry. I heard the cups and saucers go as he slammed the door on the hounds' noses, and the minute he was in Flurry turned the key on him. 'They're real dogs, Tomsy, my buck!' says Flurry, just to quiet him; and there we left him."

"Was he hurt?" I asked, conscious of the triviality of the question.

"Well, he lost his brush," replied Dr. Hickey. "Old Merrylegs tore the coat-tails off him; we got them on the floor when we struck a light; Flurry has them to nail on his kennel door. Charlie Knox had a pleasant time too", he went on, "with the man that brought the barrow-load of meat to the stable. We picked out the tastiest bits and arranged them round Flood's breakfast table for him. They smelt very nice. Well, I'm delaying you with my talking——"

Flurry's hounds had the run of the season that day. I saw it admirably throughout—from Miss Bennett's pony cart. She drove extremely well, in spite of her strained arm.

TRINKET'S COLT

It was Petty Sessions day in Skebawn, a cold, grey day of February. A case of trespass had dragged its burden of cross summonses and cross swearing far into the afternoon, and when I left the bench my head was singing from the bellowings of the attorneys, and the smell of their clients was heavy upon my palate.

The streets still testified to the fact that it was market day, and I evaded with difficulty the sinuous course of carts full of soddenly screwed people, and steered an equally devious one for myself among the groups anchored round the doors of the public-houses. Skebawn possesses, among its legion of public-houses, one establishment which timorously, and almost imperceptibly, proffers tea to the thirsty. I turned in there, as was my custom on court days, and found the little dingy den, known as the Ladies' Coffee-Room, in the occupancy of my friend Mr. Florence McCarthy Knox, who was drinking strong tea and eating buns with serious simplicity. It was a first and quite unexpected glimpse of that domesticity that has now become a marked feature in his character.

"You're the very man I wanted to see," I said as I sat down beside him at the oilcloth-covered table; "a man I know in England who is not much of a judge of character has asked me to buy him a four-year-old down here, and as I should rather be stuck by a friend than a dealer, I'd wish you'd take over the job."

Flurry poured himself out another cup of tea, and dropped three lumps of sugar into it in silence.

Finally he said, "There isn't a four-year-old in this country that I'd be seen dead with at a pig fair."

61

This was discouraging, from the premier authority of horse-flesh in the district.

"But it isn't six weeks since you told me you had the finest filly in your stables that was ever foaled in the County Cork," I protested; "what's wrong with her?"

"Oh, is it that filly?" said Mr. Knox with a lenient smile; "she's gone these three weeks from me. I swapped her and £6 for a three-year-old Ironmonger colt, and after that I swapped the colt and £19 for that Bandon horse I rode last week at your place, and after that again I sold the Bandon horse for £75 to Welply, and I had to give him back a couple of sovereigns luck-money. You see I did pretty well with the filly after all."

"Yes, yes—oh rather," I assented, as one dizzily accepts the propositions of a bimetallist; "and you don't know of anything else——?"

The room in which we were seated was closely screened from the shop by a door with a muslin-curtained window in it; several of the panes were broken, and at this juncture two voices that had for some time carried on a discussion forced themselves upon our attention.

"Begging your pardon for contradicting you, ma'am," said the voice of Mrs. McDonald, proprietress of the tea-shop, and a leading light in Skebawn Dissenting circles, shrilly tremulous with indignation, "if the servants I recommend you won't stop with you, it's no fault of mine. If respectable young girls are set picking grass out of your gravel, in place of their proper work, certainly they will give warning!"

The voice that replied struck me as being a notable one, well bred and imperious.

"When I take a barefooted slut out of a cabin, I don't expect her to dictate to me what her duties are!"

Flurry jerked up his chin in a noiseless laugh. "It's my grandmother!" he whispered. "I bet you Mrs. McDonald don't get much change out of her!"

"If I set her to clean the pig-sty I expect her to obey me," continued the voice in accents that would have made me clean forty pig-sties had she desired me to do so.

"Very well, ma'am," retorted Mrs. McDonald, "if that's the way you treat your servants, you needn't come here again looking for them. I consider your conduct is neither that of a lady nor a Christian!"

"Don't you, indeed?" replied Flurry's grandmother. "Well, your opinion doesn't greatly distress me, for, to tell you the truth, I don't think you're much of a judge."

"Didn't I tell you she'd score?" murmured Flurry, who was by this time applying his eye to a hole in the muslin curtain. "She's off," he went on, returning to his tea. "She's a great character! She's eighty-three if she's a day, and she's as sound on her legs as a three-year-old! Did you see that old shandrydan of hers in the street a while ago, and a fellow on the box with a red beard on him like Robinson Crusoe? That old mare that was on the near side—Trinket her name is—is mighty near clean bred. I can tell you her foals are worth a bit of money."

I had heard of old Mrs. Knox of Aussolas; indeed, I had seldom dined out in the neighbourhood without hearing some new story of her and her remarkable ménage, but it had not yet been my privilege to meet her.

"Well, now," went on Flurry in his slow voice, "I'll tell you a thing that's just come into my head. My grandmother promised me a foal of Trinket's the day I was one-and-twenty, and that's five years ago, and deuce a one I've got from her yet. You never were at Aussolas? No, you were not. Well, I tell you the place there is like a circus with horses. She has a couple of score of them running wild in the woods, like deer."

"Oh, come," I said, "I'm a bit of a liar myself——"

"Well, she has a dozen of them anyhow, rattling good colts, too, some of them, but they might as well be donkeys for all the good they are to me or anyone. It's not once in three years she sells one, and there she has them walking after her for bits of sugar, like a lot of dirty lapdogs," ended Flurry with disgust.

"Well, what's your plan? Do you want me to make a bid for one of the lapdogs?"

"I was thinking," replied Flurry, with great deliberation, "that my birthday's this week, and maybe I could work a four-year-old colt of Trinket's she has out of her in honour of the occasion."

"And sell your grandmother's birthday present to me?"

"Just that, I suppose," answered Flurry with a slow wink.

A few days afterwards a letter from Mr. Knox informed me that he had "squared the old lady, and it would be all right about the colt". He further told me that Mrs. Knox had been good enough to offer me, with him, a day's snipe shooting on the celebrated Aussolas bogs, and he proposed to drive me there the following Monday, if convenient. Most people found it convenient to shoot the Aussolas snipe bog when they got the chance. Eight o'clock on the following Monday morning saw Flurry, myself, and a groom packed into a dogcart, with portmanteaus, gun-cases, and two rampant red setters.

It was a long drive, twelve miles at least, and a very cold one. We passed through long tracts of pasture country, fraught, for Flurry, with memories of runs, which were recorded for me, fence by fence, in every one of which the biggest dog-fox in the country had gone to ground, with not two feet—measured accurately on the handle of the whip—between him and the leading hound; through bogs that imperceptibly melted into lakes, and finally down and down into a valley, where the fir-trees of Aussolas clustered darkly round a glittering lake, and all but hid the grey roofs and pointed gables of Aussolas Castle.

"There's a nice stretch of a demesne for you," remarked Flurry, pointing downwards with the whip, "and one little old woman holding it all in the heel of her fist. Well able to hold it she is, too, and always was, and she'll live twenty years yet, if only to spite the whole lot of us, and when all's said and done goodness knows how she'll leave it!"

Flurry administered a composing kick to the ceaseless strivings of the red setters under the seat.

"I used to be rather a pet with her," he said, after a pause; "but mind you, I haven't got him yet, and if she gets any notion I want to sell him I'll never get him, so say nothing about the business to her."

The tall gates of Aussolas shrieked on their hinges as they admitted us, and shut with a clang behind us, in the faces of an old mare and a couple of young horses, who, foiled in their break for the excitements of the outer world, turned and galloped defiantly on either side of us. Flurry's admirable cob hammered on, regardless of all things save his duty.

"He's the only one I have that I'd trust myself here with," said his master, flicking him approvingly with the whip; "there are plenty of people afraid to come here at all, and when my grandmother goes out driving she has a boy on the box and a basketful of stones to peg at them. Talk of the dickens, here she is herself!"

A short, upright old woman was approaching, preceded by a white woolly dog with sore eyes and a bark like a tin trumpet; we both got out of the trap and advanced to meet the lady of the manor.

I may summarize her attire by saying that she looked as if she had robbed a scarecrow; her face was small and incongruously refined, the skinny hand that she extended to me had the grubby tan that bespoke the professional gardener, and was decorated with a magnificent diamond ring. On her head was a massive purple velvet bonnet.

"I am very glad to meet you, Major Yeates," she said with an old-fashioned precision of utterance; "your grandfather was a dancing partner of mine in old days at the Castle, when he was a handsome young aide-de-camp there, and I was—— You may judge for yourself what I was."

She ended with a startling little hoot of laughter, and

65

I was aware that she quite realized the world's opinion of her, and was indifferent to it.

Our way to the bogs took us across Mrs. Knox's home farm, and through a large field in which several young horses were grazing.

"There now, that's my fellow," said Flurry, pointing to a fine-looking colt, "the chestnut with the white diamond on his forehead. He'll run into three figures before he's done, but we'll not tell that to the old lady!"

The famous Aussolas bogs were as full of snipe as usual, and a good deal fuller of water than any bogs I had ever shot before. I was on my day, and Flurry was not, and as he is ordinarily an infinitely better snipe shot than I, I felt at peace with the world and all men as we walked back, wet through, at five o'clock.

The sunset had waned, and a big white moon was making the eastern tower of Aussolas look like a thing in a fairy tale or a play when we arrived at the hall door. An individual whom I recognized as the Robinson Crusoe coachman, admitted us to a hall, the like of which one does not often see. The walls were panelled with dark oak up to the gallery that ran round three sides of it, the balusters of the wide staircase were heavily carved, and blackened portraits of Flurry's ancestors on the spindle side stared sourly down on their descendant as he tramped upstairs with the bog mould on his hobnailed boots.

We had just changed into dry clothes when Robinson Crusoe showed his red beard round the corner of the door, with the information that the mistress said we were to stay for dinner. My heart sank. It was then barely half-past-five. I said something about having no evening clothes and having to get home early.

"Sure the dinner'll be in another half-hour," said Robinson Crusoe, joining hospitably in the conversation; "and as for evening clothes——God bless ye!"

The door closed behind him.

"Never mind," said Flurry, "I dare say you'll be glad enough to eat another dinner by the time you get home."

He laughed. "Poor Slipper!" he added inconsequently, and only laughed again when I asked for an explanation.

Old Mrs. Knox received us in the library, where she was seated by a roaring turf fire, which lit the room a good deal more effectively than the pair of candles that stood beside her in tall silver candlesticks. Ceaseless and implacable growls from under her chair indicated the presence of the woolly dog. She talked with confounding culture of the books that rose all round her to the ceiling; her evening dress was accomplished by means of an additional white shawl, rather dirtier than its congeners; as I took her into dinner she quoted Virgil to me, and in the same breath screeched an objurgation at a being whose matted head rose suddenly into view behind an ancient Chinese screen, as I have seen the head of a Zulu woman peer over a bush.

Dinner was as incongruous as everything else. Detestable soup in a splendid old silver tureen that was nearly as dark in hue as Robinson Crusoe's thumb; a perfect salmon, perfectly cooked, on a chipped kitchen dish; such cut glass as is not easy to find nowadays; sherry that, as Flurry subsequently remarked, would burn the shell off an egg; and a bottle of port, draped in immemorial cobwebs, wan with age, and probably priceless. Throughout the vicissitudes of the meal Mrs. Knox's conversation flowed on undismayed, directed sometimes at me—she had installed me in the position of friend of her youth, and talked to me as if I were my own grandfather—sometimes at Crusoe, with whom she had several heated arguments, and sometimes she would make a statement of remarkable frankness on the subject of her horse-farming affairs to Flurry, who, very much on his best behaviour, agreed with all she said, and risked no original remark. As I listened to them both, I remembered with infinite amusement how he had told me once that "a pet name she had for him was 'Tony Lumpkin', and no one but herself knew what she meant by it". It seemed strange that she made no allusion to Trinket's colt or to Flurry's birthday, but, mindful of my instructions, I held my peace.

As, at about half-past-eight, we drove away in the moonlight, Flurry congratulated me solemnly on my success with his grandmother. He was good enough to tell me that she would marry me to-morrow if I asked her, and he wished I would, even if it was only to see what a nice grandson he'd be for me. A sympathetic giggle behind me told me that Michael, on the back seat, had heard and relished the jest.

We had left the gates of Aussolas about half a mile behind when, at the corner of a by-road, Flurry pulled up. A short squat figure arose from the black shadow of a furze bush and came out into the moonlight, swinging its arms like a cabman and cursing audibly.

"Oh murdher, oh murdher, Misther Flurry! What kept ye at all? 'Twould perish the crows to be waiting here the way I am these two hours——"

"Ah, shut your mouth, Slipper!" said Flurry, who, to my surprise, had turned back the rug and was taking off his driving coat, "I couldn't help it. Come on, Yeates, we've got to get out here."

"What for?" I asked, in not unnatural bewilderment.

"It's all right. I'll tell you as we go along," replied my companion, who was already turning to follow Slipper up the by-road. "Take the trap on, Michael, and wait at the River's Cross." He waited for me to come up with him, and then put his hand on my arm. "You see, Major, this is the way it is. My grandmother's given me that colt right enough, but if I waited for her to send him over to me I'd never see a hair of his tail. So I just thought that as we were over here we might as well take him back with us, and maybe you'll give us a help with him; he'll not be altogether too handy for a first go-off."

I was staggered. An infant in arms could scarcely have failed to discern the fishiness of the transaction, and I begged Mr. Knox not to put himself to this trouble on my account, as I had no doubt I could find a horse for my friend elsewhere. Mr. Knox assured me that it was no trouble at all, quite the contrary, and that, since his grandmother had given him the colt, he saw no reason why he should not take him when he wanted him; also, that if I didn't want him he'd be glad enough to keep him himself; and finally, that I wasn't the chap to go back on a friend, but I was welcome to drive back to Shreelane with Michael this minute if I liked.

Of course I yielded in the end. I told Flurry I should lose my job over the business, and he said I could then marry his grandmother, and the discussion was abruptly closed by the necessity of following Slipper over a locked five-barred gate.

Our pioneer took us over about half a mile of country, knocking down stone gaps where practicable and scrambling over tall banks in the deceptive moonlight. We found ourselves at length in a field with a shed in one corner of it; in a dim group of farm buildings a little way off a light was shining.

"Wait here," said Flurry to me in a whisper; "the less noise the better. It's an open shed, and we'll just slip in and coax him out."

Slipper unwound from his waist a halter, and my colleagues glided like spectres into the shadow of the shed, leaving me to meditate on my duties as Resident Magistrate, and on the questions that would be asked in the House by our local member when Slipper had given away the adventure in his cups.

In less than a minute three shadows emerged from the shed, where two had gone in. They had got the colt.

"He came out as quiet as a calf when he winded the sugar." said Flurry; "it was well for me I filled my pockets from grandmamma's sugar-basin."

He and Slipper had a rope from each side of the colt's head; they took him quickly across a field towards a gate. The colt stepped daintily between them over the moonlit grass; he snorted occasionally, but appeared on the whole amenable.

The trouble began later, and was due, as trouble often

is, to the beguilements of a short cut. Against the maturer judgement of Slipper, Flurry insisted on following a route that he assured us he knew as well as his own pocket, and the consequence was that in about five minutes I found myself standing on top of a bank hanging on to a rope, on the other end of which the colt dangled and danced, while Flurry, with the other rope, lay prone in the ditch, and Slipper administered to the bewildered colt's hindquarters such chastisement as could be ventured on.

I have no space to narrate in detail the atrocious difficulties and disasters of the short cut. How the colt set to work to buck, and went away across a field, dragging the faithful Slipper literally *ventre-à-terre*, after him, while I picked myself in ignominy out of a briar patch, and Flurry cursed himself black in the face. How we were attacked by ferocious cur dogs, and I lost my eyeglass; and how, as we neared the River's Cross, Flurry espied the police patrol on the road, and we all hid behind a rick of turf, while I realized what an exceptional ass I was, to have been beguiled into an enterprise that involved hiding with Slipper from the Royal Irish Constabulary.

Let it suffice to say that Trinket's infernal offspring was finally handed over on the high-road to Michael and Slipper, and Flurry drove me home in a state of mental and physical overthrow.

I saw nothing of my friend Mr. Knox for the next couple of days, by the end of which time I had worked up a high polish on my misgivings, and had determined to tell him that under no circumstances would I have anything to say to his grandmother's birthday present. It was like my usual luck that, instead of writing a note to this effect, I thought it would be good for my liver to walk across the hills to Tory Cottage and tell Flurry so in person.

It was a bright, blustery morning, after a muggy day. The feeling of spring was in the air, the daffodils were already in bud, and crocuses showed purple in the grass on either side of the avenue. It was only a couple of miles to Tory Cottage by the way across the hills; I walked fast, and it was barely twelve o'clock when I saw its pink walls and clumps of evergreens below me. As I looked down at it the chiming of Flurry's hounds in the kennels came to me on the wind; I stood still to listen, and could almost have sworn that I was hearing again the clash of Magdalen bells, hard at work on May morning.

The path that I was following led downwards through a larch plantation to Flurry's back gate. Hot wafts from some hideous caldron at the other side of a wall apprised me of the vicinity of the kennels and their cuisine, and the fir-trees round were hung with gruesome and unknown joints. I thanked Heaven that I was not a master of hounds, and passed on as quickly as might be to the hall door.

I rang two or three times without response; then the door opened a couple of inches and was instantly slammed in my face. I heard the hurried paddling of bare feet on oilcloth, and a voice, "Hurry, Bridgie, hurry! There's quality at the door!"

Bridgie, holding a dirty cap on with one hand, presently arrived and informed me that she believed Mr. Knox was out about the place. She seemed perturbed, and she cast scared glances down the drive while speaking to me.

I knew enough of Flurry's habits to shape a tolerably direct course for his whereabouts. He was, as I had expected, in the training paddock, a field behind the stable-yard, in which he had put up practice jumps for his horses. It was a good-sized field with clumps of furze in it, and Flurry was standing near one of these with his hands in his pockets, singularly unoccupied. I supposed that he was prospecting for a place to put up another jump. He did not see me coming, and turned with a start as I spoke to him. There was a queer expression of mingled guilt and what I can only describe as divilment in his grey eyes as he greeted me. In my dealings with

71

Flurry Knox, I have since formed the habit of sitting tight, in a general way, when I see that expression.

"Well, who's coming next, I wonder!" he said, as he shook hands with me; "it's not ten minutes since I had two of your d——d peelers here searching the whole place for my grandmother's colt!"

"What!" I exclaimed, feeling cold all down my back; "do you mean the police have got hold of it?"

"They haven't got hold of the colt anyway," said Flurry, looking sideways at me from under the peak of his cap, with the glint of the sun in his eye. "I got word in time before they came."

"What do you mean?" I demanded; "where is he? For Heaven's sake don't tell me you've sent the brute over to my place!"

"It's a good job for you I didn't," replied Flurry, "as the police are on their way to Shreelane this minute to consult you about it. *You!*" He gave utterance to one of his short diabolical fits of laughter. "He's where they'll not find him, anyhow. Ho! ho! It's the funniest hand I ever played!"

"Oh yes, it's devilish funny, I've no doubt," I retorted, beginning to lose my temper, as is the manner of many people when they are frightened; "but I give you fair warning that if Mrs. Knox asks me any questions about it, I shall tell her the whole story."

"All right," responded Flurry; "and when you do, don't forget to tell her how you flogged the colt out on to the road over her own bounds ditch."

"Very well," I said hotly, "I may as well go home and send in my papers. They'll break me over this——"

"Ah, hold on, Major," said Flurry soothingly, "it'll be all right. No one knows anything. It's only on spec the old lady sent the bobbies here. If you'll keep quiet it'll all blow over."

"I don't care", I said, struggling hopelessly in the toils; "if I meet your grandmother, and she asks me about it, I shall tell her all I know."

"Please God you'll not meet her! After all, it's not once

72

in a blue moon that she——" began Flurry. Even as he said the words his face changed. "Holy fly!" he ejaculated, "isn't that her dog coming into the field? Look at her bonnet over the wall! Hide, hide for your life!" He caught me by the shoulder and shoved me down among the furze bushes before I realized what had happened.

"Get in there! I'll talk to her."

I may as well confess that at the mere sight of Mrs. Knox's purple bonnet my heart had turned to water. In that moment I knew what it would be like to tell her how I, having eaten her salmon, and capped her quotations, and drunk her best port, had gone forth and helped to steal her horse. I abandoned my dignity, my sense of honour; I took the furze prickles to my breast and wallowed in them.

Mrs. Knox had advanced with vengeful speed; already she was in high altercation with Flurry at no great distance from where I lay; varying sounds of battle reached me, and I gathered that Flurry was not—to put it mildly—shrinking from that economy of truth that the situation required.

"Is it that curby, long-backed brute? You promised him to me long ago, but I wouldn't be bothered with him!"

The old lady uttered a laugh of shrill derision. "Is it likely I'd promise you my best colt? And still more, is it likely that you'd refuse him if I did?"

"Very well, ma'am." Flurry's voice was admirably indignant. "Then I suppose I'm a liar and a thief."

"I'd be more obliged to you for the information if I hadn't known it before," responded his grandmother with lightning speed: "if you swore to me on a stack of Bibles you knew nothing about my colt I wouldn't believe you! I shall go straight to Major Yeates and ask his advice. I believe *him* to be a gentleman, in spite of the company he keeps!"

I writhed deeper into the furze bushes, and thereby discovered a sandy rabbit run, along which I crawled,

with my cap well over my eyes, and the furze needles
stabbing me through my stockings. The ground shelved
a little, promising profounder concealment, but the
bushes were very thick, and I laid hold of the bare stem
of one to help my progress. It lifted out of the ground in
my hand, revealing a freshly cut stump. Something
snorted, not a yard away; I glared through the opening,
and was confronted by the long, horrified face of Mrs.
Knox's colt, mysteriously on a level with my own.

Even without the white diamond on his forehead I
should have divined the truth; but how in the name of
wonder had Flurry persuaded him to couch like a woodcock in the heart of a furze brake? For a full minute I
lay as still as death for fear of frightening him, while the
voices of Flurry and his grandmother raged on alarmingly close to me. The colt snorted, and blew long
breaths through his wide nostrils, but he did not move. I
crawled an inch or two nearer, and after a few seconds
of cautious peering I grasped the position. They had
buried him.

A small sandpit among the furze had been utilized as
a grave; they had filled him in up to his withers with
sand, and a few furze bushes, artistically disposed round
the pit, had done the rest. As the depth of Flurry's guile
was revealed, laughter came upon me like a flood; I
gurgled and shook apoplectically, and the colt gazed at
me with serious surprise, until a sudden outburst of barking close to my elbow administered a fresh shock to my
tottering nerves.

Mrs. Knox's woolly dog had tracked me into the
furze, and was now baying the colt and me with mingled
terror and indignation. I addressed him in a whisper,
with perfidious endearments, advancing a crafty hand
towards him the while, made a snatch for the back of
his neck, missed it badly, and got him by the ragged
fleece of his hindquarters as he tried to flee. If I had
flayed him alive he could hardly have uttered a more
deafening series of yells, but, like a fool, instead of
letting him go, I dragged him towards me, and tried to

stifle the noise by holding his muzzle. The tussle lasted engrossingly for a few seconds, and then the climax of the nightmare arrived.

Mrs. Knox's voice, close behind me, said, "Let go my dog this instant, sir! Who are you——"

Her voice faded away, and I knew that she also had seen the colt's head.

I positively felt sorry for her. At her age there was no knowing what effect the shock might have on her. I scrambled to my feet and confronted her.

"Major Yeates!" she said. There was a deathly pause. "Will you kindly tell me," said Mrs. Knox slowly, "am I in Bedlam, or are you? And *what is that*?"

She pointed to the colt, and that unfortunate animal, recognizing the voice of his mistress, uttered a hoarse and lamentable whinny. Mrs. Knox felt around her for support, found only furze prickles, gazed speechlessly at me, and then, to her eternal honour, fell into wild cackles of laughter.

So, I may say, did Flurry and I. I embarked on my explanation and broke down; Flurry followed suit and broke down too. Overwhelming laughter held us all three, disintegrating our very souls. Mrs. Knox pulled herself together first.

"I acquit you, Major Yeates, I acquit you, though appearances are against you. It's clear enough to me you've fallen among thieves." She stopped and glowered at Flurry. Her purple bonnet was over one eye. "I'll thank you, sir," she said, "to dig out that horse before I leave this place. And when you've dug him out you may keep him. I'll be no receiver of stolen goods!"

She broke off and shook her fist at him. "Upon my conscience, Tony, I'd give a guinea to have thought of it myself!"

THE WATERS OF STRIFE

I knew Bat Callaghan's face long before I was able to put a name to it. There was seldom a court day in Skebawn that I was not aware of his level brows and superfluously intense expression somewhere among the knot of corner-boys who patronized the weekly sittings of the bench of magistrates. His social position appeared to fluctuate: I have seen him driving a car; he sometimes held my horse for me—that is to say, he sat on the counter of a public-house while the Quaker slumbered in the gutter; and, on one occasion, he retired, at my bidding, to Cork gaol, there to meditate upon the inadvisability of defending a friend from the attentions of the police with the tailboard of a cart.

He next obtained prominence in my regard at a regatta held under the auspices of "The Sons of Liberty", a local football club that justified its title by the patriot green of its jerseys and its free interpretation of the rules of the game. The announcement of my name on the posters as a patron—a privilege acquired at the cost of a reluctant half-sovereign—made it incumbent on me to put in an appearance, even though the festival coincided with my Petty Sessions day at Skebawn; and at some five of the clock on a brilliant September afternoon I found myself driving down the stony road that dropped in zigzags to the borders of the lake on which the races were to come off.

I believe that the selection of Lough Lonen as the scene of the regatta was not unconnected with the fact that the secretary of the club owned a public-house at the cross-roads at one end of it; none the less, the president of the Royal Academy could scarcely have chosen more picturesque surroundings. A mountain towered steeply up from the lake's edge, dark with the sad green of beech-trees in September; fir woods followed the curve of the shore, and leaned far over the answering darkness of the water; and above the trees rose the toppling steepnesses of the hill, painted with a purple glow of heather. The lake was about a mile long, and, tumbling from its farther end, a fierce and narrow river fled away west to the sea, some four or five miles off.

I had not seen a boat race since I was at Oxford, and the words still called up before my eyes a vision of smart parasols, of gorgeous barges, of snowy-clad youths, and of low slim outriggers, winged with the level flight of oars, slitting the water to the sway of the line of flat backs. Certainly undreamed-of possibilities in aquatics were revealed to me as I reined in the Quaker on the outskirts of the crowd, and saw below me the festival of the Sons of Liberty in full swing. Boats of all shapes and sizes, outrageously overladen, moved about the lake, with oars flourishing to the strains of concertinas. Black swarms of people seethed along the water's edge, congesting here and there round the dingy tents and stalls of green apples; and the club's celebrated brass band, enthroned in a wagonette, and stimulated by the presence of a barrel of porter on the box-seat, was belching forth "The Boys of Wexford", under the guidance of a disreputable ex-militia drummer, in a series of crashing discords.

Almost as I arrived a pistol-shot set the echoes clattering round the lake, and three boats burst out abreast from the throng into the open water. Two of the crews were in shirt-sleeves, the third wore the green jerseys of the football club; the boats were of the heavy sea-going build, and pulled six oars apiece, oars of which the looms were scarcely narrower than the blades, and were, of the two, but a shade heavier. None the less the rowers started dauntlessly at thirty-five strokes a minute, quickening up, incredible as it may seem, as they rounded the mark-boat in the first lap of the two-mile course. The rowing was, in general style, more akin to

77

the action of beating up eggs with a fork than to any other form of athletic exercise: but in its unorthodox way it kicked the heavy boats along at a surprising pace. The oars squeaked and grunted against the thole-pins, the coxswains kept up an unceasing flow of oratory, and superfluous little boys in punts contrived to intervene at all the more critical turning-points of the race, only evading the flail of the oncoming oars by performing prodigies of "waggling" with a single oar at the stern. I took out my watch and counted the strokes when they were passing the mark-boat for the second time; they were pulling a fraction over forty; one of the shirt-sleeved crews was obviously in trouble, the other, with humped backs and jerking oars, was holding its own against the green jerseys amid the blended yells of friends and foes. When for the last time they rounded the green flag there were but two boats in the race, and the foul that had been imminent throughout was at length achieved with a rattle of oars and a storm of curses. They were clear again in a moment, the shirt-sleeved crew getting away with a distinct lead, and it was at about this juncture that I became aware that the cox-swains had abandoned their long-handled tillers, and were standing over their respective "strokes", shoving frantically at their oars, and maintaining the while a ceaseless bawl of encouragement and defiance. It looked like a foregone conclusion for the leaders, and the war of cheers rose to frenzy. The word "cheering", indeed, is but a euphuism, and in no way expresses the serrated yell, composed of epithets, advice, and imprecations, that was flung like a live thing at the oncoming boats. The green jerseys answered to this stimulant with a wild spurt that drove the bow of their boat within a measurable distance of their opponents' stroke oar. In another second a thoroughly successful foul would have been effected, but the cox of the leading boat proved himself equal to the emergency by unshipping his tiller, and with it dealing "bow" of the green jerseys such a blow over the head as effectually dismissed him from the sphere of practical politics.

A great roar of laughter greeted this feat of arms, and a voice at my dogcart's wheel pierced the clamour—

"More power to ye, Larry, me owld darlin'!"

I looked down and saw Bat Callaghan, with shining eyes, and face white with excitement, poising himself on one foot on the box of my wheel in order to get a better view of the race. Almost before I had time to recognise him, a man in a green jersey caught him round the legs and jerked him down. Callaghan fell into the throng, recovered himself in an instant, and rushed, white and dangerous, at his assailant. The Son of Liberty was no less ready for the fray, and what is known in Ireland as "the father and mother of a row" was imminent. Already, however, one of those unequalled judges of the moral temperature of a crowd, a sergeant of the R.I.C., had quietly interposed his bulky person between the combatants, and the coming trouble was averted.

Elsewhere battle was raging. The race was over, and the committee boat was hemmed in by the rival crews, supplemented by craft of all kinds. The "objection" was being lodged, and in its turn objected to, and I can only liken the process to the screaming warfare of seagulls round a piece of carrion. The tumult was still at its height when out of its very heart two four-oared boats broke forth, and a pistol shot proclaimed that another race had begun, the public interest in which was specially keen, owing to the fact that the rowers were stalwart country girls, who made up in energy what they lacked in skill. It was a short race, once round the mark-boat only, and, like a successful farce, it "went with a roar" from start to finish. Foul after foul, each followed by a healing interval of calm, during which the crews, who had all caught crabs, were recovering themselves and their oars, marked its progress; and when the two boats, locked in an inextricable embrace, at length passed the winning flag, and the crews, oblivious of judges and public, fell to untrammelled personal abuse and to doing

79

up their hair, I decided that I had seen the best of the fun, and prepared to go home.

It was, as it happened, the last race of the day, and nothing remained in the way of excitement save the greased pole with the pig slung in a bag at the end of it. My final impression of the Lough Lonen Regatta was of Callaghan's lithe figure, sleek and dripping, against the yellow sky, as he poised on the swaying pole with the broken gold of the water beneath him.

Limited as was my experience of the south-west of Ireland, I was in no way surprised to hear on the following afternoon from Peter Cadogan that there had been "sthrokes" the night before, when the boys were going home from the regatta, and that the police were searching for one Jimmy Foley.

"What do they want him for?" I asked.

"Sure it's according as a man that was bringing a car of bogwood was tellin' me, sir," answered Peter, pursuing his occupation of washing the dogcart with unabated industry: "they say Jimmy's wife went roaring to the police, saying she could get no account of her husband."

"I suppose he's beaten some fellow and is hiding," I suggested.

"Well, that might be, sir," asserted Peter respectfully. He plied the mop vigorously in intricate places about the springs, which would, I knew, have never been explored save for my presence.

"It's what John Hennessy was saying, that he was hard set to get his horse past Cluin Cross, the way the blood was sthrewn about the road," resumed Peter; "sure they were fighting like wasps in it half the night."

"Who were fighting?"

" I couldn't say indeed, sir. Some o' thim low rakish lads from the town, I suppose," replied Peter with virtuous respectability.

When Peter Cadogan was quietly and intelligently candid, to pursue an inquiry was seldom of much avail.

Next day in Skebawn I met little Murray, the district

inspector, very alert and smart in his rifle-green uniform, going forth to collect evidence about the fight. He told me that the police were pretty certain that one of the Sons of Liberty, named Foley, had been murdered, but, as usual, the difficulty was to get anyone to give information; all that was known was that he was gone, and that his wife had identified his cap, which had been found, drenched with blood, by the roadside. Murray gave it as his opinion that the whole business had arisen out of the row over the disputed race, and that there must have been a dozen people looking on when the murder was done; but so far no evidence was forthcoming, and after a day and a night of search the police had not been able to find the body.

"No," said Flurry Knox, who had joined us, "and if it was any of those mountainy men did away with him you might scrape Ireland with a small-tooth comb and you'll not get him!"

That evening I smoked an after-dinner cigarette out of doors in the mild starlight, strolling about the rudimentary paths of what would, I hoped, some day be Philippa's garden. The bats came stooping at the red end of my cigarette, and from the covert behind the house I heard once or twice the delicate bark of a fox. Civilization seemed a thousand miles off, as far away as the falling star that had just drawn a line of pale fire half-way down the northern sky. I had been nearly a year at Shreelane House by myself now, and the time seemed very long to me. It was slow work putting by money, even under the austerities of Mrs. Cadogan's regime, and though I had warned Philippa I meant to marry her after Christmas, there were moments, and this was one of them, when it seemed an idle threat.

"Peter!" the strident voice of Mrs. Cadogan intruded upon my meditations. "Go tell the Major his coffee is waitin' on him!"

I went gloomily into the house, and, with a resignation born of adversity, swallowed the mixture of chicory and liquorice which my housekeeper possessed the secret of

81

distilling from the best and most expensive coffee. My theory about it was that it added to the illusion that I had dined, and moreover, that it kept me awake, and I generally had a good deal of writing to do after dinner.

Having swallowed it I went downstairs and out past the kitchen regions to my office, a hideous whitewashed room, in which I interviewed policemen, and took affidavits, and did most of my official writing. It had a door that opened into the yard, and a window that looked out in the other direction, among lanky laurels and scrubby hollies, where lay the cats' main thorough-fare from the scullery window to the rabbit holes in the wood. I had a good deal of work to do, and the time passed quickly. It was Friday night, and from the kitchen at the end of the passage came the gabbling murmur in two alternate keys that I had learned to recognize as the recital of a litany by my housekeeper and her nephew Peter. This performance was followed by some of those dreary and heart-rending yawns that are, I think, peculiar to Irish kitchens, then such of the cats as had returned from the chase were loudly shepherded into the back scullery, the kitchen door shut with a slam, and my retainers retired to repose.

It was nearly half an hour afterwards when I finished the notes I had been making on an adjourned case of "stroke-hauling" salmon in the Lonen River. I leaned back in my chair and lighted a cigarette preparatory to turning in; my thoughts had again wandered on a senti-mental journey across the Irish Channel, when I heard a slight stir of some kind outside the open window. In the wilds of Ireland no one troubles themselves about burglars; "more cats", I thought, "I must shut the window before I go to bed".

Almost immediately there followed a faint tap on the window, and then a voice said in a hoarse and hurried whisper, "Them that wants Jim Foley, let them look in the river!"

If I had kept my head I should have sat still and encouraged a further confidence, but unfortunately I acted on the impulse of the natural man, and was at the window in a jump, knocking down my chair, and making noise enough to scare a far less shy bird than an Irish informer. Of course there was no-one there. I listened, with every nerve as taut as a violin string. It was quite dark; there was just breeze enough to make a rustling in the evergreens, so that a man might brush through them without being heard; and while I debated on a plan of action there came from beyond the shrubbery the jar and twang of a loose strand of wire in the paling by the wood. My informant, whoever he might be, had vanished into the darkness from which he had come as irrecoverably as had the falling star that had written its brief message across the sky, and gone out again into infinity.

I got up very early next morning and drove to Skebawn to see Murray, and offer him my mysterious information for what it was worth. Personally I did not think it worth much, and was disposed to regard it as a red herring drawn across the trail. Murray, however, was not in a mood to despise anything that had a suggestion to make, having been out till nine o'clock the night before without being able to find any clue to the hiding-place of James Foley.

"The river's a good mile from the place where the fight was," he said, straddling his compasses over the Ordnance Survey map, "and there's no sort of a road they could have taken him along, but a tip like this is always worth trying. I remember in the Land League time how a man came one Saturday night to my window and told me there were holes drilled in the chapel door to shoot a boycotted man through while he was at Mass. The holes were there right enough, and you may be quite sure that chap found excellent reasons for having family prayers at home next day!"

I had sessions to attend on the extreme outskirts of my district, and could not wait, as Murray suggested, to see the thing out. I did not get home till the following day, and when I arrived I found a letter from Murray awaiting me.

"Your pal was right. We found Foley's body in the river, knocking about against the posts of the weir. The head was wrapped in his own green jersey, and had been smashed in by a stone. We suspect a fellow named Bat Callaghan, who has bolted, but there were a lot of them in it. Possibly it was Callaghan himself who gave you the tip; you never can tell how superstition is going to take them next. The inquest will be held to-morrow."

The coroner's jury took a cautious view of the cause of the catastrophe, and brought in a verdict of "death by misadventure", and I presently found it to be my duty to call a magisterial inquiry to further investigate the matter. A few days before this was to take place, I was engaged in the delicate task of displaying to my landlord, Mr. Flurry Knox, the defects of the pantry sink, when Mrs. Cadogan advanced upon us with the information that the Widow Callaghan from Cluin would be thankful to speak to me, and had brought me a present of "a fine young goose".

"Is she come over here looking for Bat?" said Flurry, withdrawing his arm and the longest kitchen-ladle from the pipe that he had been probing; "she knows you're handy at hiding your friends, Mary; maybe it's he that's stopping the drain!"

Mrs. Cadogan turned her large red face upon her late employer.

"God knows I wish yerself was stuck in it, Master Flurry, the way ye'd hear Pether cursin' the full o' the house when he's striving to wash the things in that unnatural little trough."

"Are you sure it's Peter does all the cursing?" retorted Flurry. "I hear Father Scanlan has it in for you this long time for not going to confession."

"And how can I walk two miles to the chapel with God's burden on me feet?" demanded Mrs. Cadogan in purple indignation; "the Blessed Virgin and Docthor Hickey knows well the hardship I get from them. If it wasn't for a pair of the Major's boots he gave me, I'd he hard set to thravel the house itself!"

84

The contest might have been continued indefinitely, had I not struck up the swords with a request that Mrs. Callaghan might be sent round to the hall door. There we found a tall, grey-haired countrywoman waiting for us at the foot of the steps, in the hooded blue cloak that is peculiar to the south of Ireland; from the fact that she clutched a pocket-handkerchief in her right hand I augured a stormy interview, but nothing could have been more self-restrained and even imposing than the reverence with which she greeted Flurry and me.

"Good morning to your honours," she began, with a dignified and extremely imminent snuffle. "I ask your pardon for troubling you, Major Yeates, but I haven't a one in the country to give me an adwice, and I have no confidence only in your honour's experiments."

'Experience, she means," prompted Flurry. "Didn't you get advice enough out of Mr. Murray yesterday?" he went on aloud. " I heard he was at Cluin to see you."

"And if he was itself, it's little adwantage any one'd get out of that little whipper-shnapper of a shnap-dhragon!" responded Mrs. Callaghan tartly; "he was with me for a half-hour giving me every big rock of English till I had a reel in me head. I declare to ye, Mr. Flurry, after he had gone out o' the house, ye wouldn't throw threefarthings for me!"

The pocket-handkerchief was here utilized, after which, with a heavy groan, Mrs. Callaghan again took up her parable."

"I towld him first and last I'd lose me life if I had to go into the coort, and if I did itself sure th' attorneys could rip no more out o' me than what he did himself."

"Did you tell him where was Bat?" inquired Flurry casually.

At this Mrs. Callaghan immediately dissolved into tears.

"Is it Bat?" she howled. "If the twelve Apostles came down from heaven asking me where was Bat, I could give them no satisfaction. The divil a know I know what's happened him. He came home with me sober and good-natured from the rogatta, and the next morning he axed a fresh egg for his breakfast, and God forgive me, I wouldn't break the score I was taking to the hotel, and with that he slapped the cup o' tay into the fire and went out the door, and I never got a word of him since, good nor bad. God knows 'tis I got trouble with that poor boy, and he the only one I have to look to in the world!"

I cut the matter short by asking her what she wanted me to do for her, and sifted out from amongst much extraneous detail the fact that she relied upon my renowned wisdom and clemency to preserve her from being called as a witness at the coming inquiry. The gift of the goose served its intended purpose of embarrassing my position, but in spite of it I broke to the Widow Callaghan my inability to help her. She did not, of course, believe me, but she was too well bred to say so. In Ireland one becomes accustomed to this attitude.

As it turned out, however, Bat Callaghan's mother had nothing to fear from the inquiry. She was by turns deaf, imbecile, garrulously candid, and furiously abusive of Murray's principal witness, a frightened lad of seventen, who had sworn to having seen Bat Callaghan and Jimmy Foley "shaping at one another to fight", at an hour, when, according to Mrs. Callaghan, Bat was "lying stretched on the beddeen with a sick shtomach" in consequence of the malignant character of the porter supplied by the last witness's father. It all ended, as such cases so often do in Ireland, in complete moral certainty in the minds of all concerned as to the guilt of the accused, and entire impotence on the part of the law to prove it. A warrant was issued for the arrest of Bartholomew Callaghan; and the clans of Callaghan and Foley fought rather more bloodily than usual, as occasion served; and at intervals during the next few months Murray used to ask me if my friend the murderer had dropped in lately, to which I was wont to reply with condolences on the failure of the R.I.C. to find the Widow Callaghan's only son for her; and that was about all that came of it.

Events with which the present story has no concern took me to England towards the end of the following March. It so happened that my old regiment, the—th Fusiliers, was quartered at Whincastle, within a couple of hours by rail of Philippa's home, where I was staying, and, since my wedding was now within measurable distance, my former brothers-in-arms invited me over to dine and sleep, and to receive a valedictory silver claret jug that they were magnanimous enough to bestow upon a backslider. I enjoyed the dinner as much as any man can enjoy his dinner when he knows he has to make a speech at the end of it; through much and varied conversation I strove, like a nervous mother who cannot trust her offspring out of her sight, to keep before my mind's eye the opening sentences that I had composed in the train; I felt that if I could only "get away" satisfactorily I might trust the Ayala ('89) to do the rest, and of that fount of inspiration there was no lack. As it turned out, I got away all right, though the sight of the double line of expectant faces and red mess jackets nearly scattered those precious opening sentences, and I am afraid that so far as the various subsequent points went that I had intended to make, I stayed away; however, neither Demosthenes, nor a Nationalist member at a Cork election, could have been listened to with more gratifying attention, and I sat down, hot and happy, to be confronted with my own flushed visage, hideously reflected in the glittering paunch of the claret jug.

Once safely over the presentation, the evening mellowed into frivolity, and it was pretty late before I found myself settled down to whist, at sixpenny points, in the ancient familiar way, while most of the others fell to playing pool in the billiard-room next door. I have played whist from my youth up; with the preternatural seriousness of a subaltern, with the self-assurance of a senior captain, with the privileged irascibility of a major; and my eighteen months of abstinence at Shree-lane had only whetted my appetite for what I consider the best of games. After the long lonely evenings there, with rats for company, and, for relaxation, a "deck" of that specially demoniacal American variety of patience known as "Fooly Ann", it was wondrous agreeable to sit again among my fellows, and "lay the longs" on a severely scientific rubber of whist, as though Mrs. Cadogan and the Skebawn Bench of Magistrates had never existed.

We were in the first game of the second rubber, and I was holding a very nice playing hand; I had early in the games moved forth my trumps to battle, and I was now in the ineffable position of scoring with the small cards of my long suit. The cards fell and fell in silence, and Ballantyne, my partner, raked in the tricks like a machine. The concentrated quiet of the game was suddenly arrested by a sharp, unmistakable sound from the barrack yard outside, the snap of a Lee-Metford rifle.

"What was that?" exclaimed Moffat, the senior major.

Before he had finished speaking there was a second shot.

"By Jove, those were rifle-shots! Perhaps I'd better go and see what's up," said Ballantyne, who was captain of the week, throwing down his cards and making a bolt for the door.

He had hardly got out of the room when the first long high note of the "assembly" sang out, sudden and clear. We all sprang to our feet, and as the bugle-call went shrilly on, the other men came pouring in from the billiard-room, and stampeded to their quarters to get their swords. At the same moment the mess sergeant appeared at the outer door with a face as white as his shirt-front.

"The sentry on the magazine guard has been shot, sir!" he said excitedly to Moffat. "They say he's dead!"

We were all out in the barrack square in an instant; it was clear moonlight, and the square was already alive with hurrying figures cramming on clothes and caps as they ran to fall in. I was a free agent these times, and I followed the mess sergeant across the square towards the distant corner where the magazine stands. As we doubled round the end of the men's quarters, we nearly ran into a small party of men who were advancing slowly and heavily in our direction.

" 'Ere he is, sir!" said the mess sergeant, stopping himself abruptly.

They were carrying the sentry to the hospital. His busby had fallen off; the moon shone mildly on his pale, convulsed face, and foam and strange inhuman sounds came from his lips. His head was rolling from side to side on the arm of one of the men who were carrying him; as it turned towards me I was struck by something disturbingly familiar in the face, and I wondered if he had been in my old company.

"What's his name, sergeant?" I said to the mess sergeant.

"Private Harris, sir," replied the sergeant; "he's only lately come up from the depot, and this was his first time on sentry by himself."

I went back to the mess, and in process of time the others straggled in, thirsting for whiskies-and-sodas, and full of such information as there was to give. Private Harris was not wounded; both the shots had been fired by him, as was testified by the state of his rifle and the fact that two of the cartridges were missing from the pocket in his pouch.

"I hear he was a queer, sulky sort of chap always," said Tomkinson, the subaltern of the day, "but if he was having a try at suicide he made a bally bad fist of it."

"He made as good a fist of it as you did of putting on your sword, Tommy," remarked Ballantyne, indicating a dangling white strap of webbing, that hung down like a tail below Mr. Tomkinson's mess jacket. "Nerves, obviously in both cases!"

The exquisite satisfaction afforded by this discovery, to Mr. Tomkinson's brother officers found its natural outlet in a bear fight that threatened to become more or less general, and in the course of which I slid away unostentatiously to bed in Ballantyne's quarters, and took the precaution of barricading my door.

Next morning, when I got down to breakfast, I found Ballantyne and two or three others in the mess room, and my first inquiry was for Private Harris.

"Oh, the poor chap's dead," said Ballantyne; "it's a very queer business altogether. I think he must have been wrong in the top story. The doctor was with him when he came to out of the fit, or whatever it was, and O'Reilly—that's the doctor y' know, Irish of course, and, by the way, poor Harris was an Irishman too—says that he could only gibber at first, but then he got better, and he got out of him that when he had been on sentry-go for about half an hour, he happened to look up at the angle of the barrack wall near where it joins the magazine tower, and saw a face looking at him over it. He challenged and got no answer, but the face just stuck there staring at him; he challenged again, and then, as O'Reilly said, he 'just oop with his royfle and blazed at it'.'. Ballantyne was not above the common English delusion that he could imitate an Irish brogue.

"Well, what happened then?"

"Well, according to the poor devil's own story, the face just kept on looking at him and he had another shot at it, and 'My God Almighty', he said to O'Reilly, 'it was there always!' While he was saying that to O'Reilly he began to chuck another fit, and apparently went on chucking them till he died a couple of hours ago."

"One result of it is," said another man, "that they couldn't get a man to go on sentry there alone last night. I expect we shall have to double the sentries there every night as long as we're here."

"Silly asses!" remarked Tomkinson, but he said it without conviction.

After breakfast we went out to look at the wall by the magazine. It was about eleven feet high, with a coped top, and they told me there was a deep and wide dry ditch on the outside. A ladder was brought, and we examined the angle of the wall at which Harris said the face had appeared. He had made a beautiful shot, one of his bullets having flicked a piece off the ridge of the coping exactly at the corner.

"It's not the kind of shot a man would make if he had been drinking," said Moffat, regretfully abandoning his first simple hypothesis; "he must have been mad."

"I wish I could find out who his people are," said Brownlow, the adjutant, who had joined us; "they found in his box a letter to him, from his mother, but we can't make out the name of the place. By jove, Yeates, you're an Irishman, perhaps you can help us."

He handed me a letter in a dirty envelope. There was no address given, the contents were very short, and I may be forgiven if I transcribe them:

My dear Son,
    I hope you are well as this leaves me at present, thanks be to God for it. I am very much unaisy about the cow. She swelled up this morning, she ran in and was frauding and I did not do but to run up for tom sweeney in the minute. We are thinking it is too much lairels or an eirub she took. I do not know what I will do with her. God help one that's alone with himself I had not a days luck since ye went away. I am thinkin' them that wants ye is tired lookin' for ye. And so I remain,

YOUR FOND MOTHER.

"Well, you don't get much of a lead from the cow, do you? And what the deuce is an eirub?" said Brownlow.

"It's another way of spelling herb," I said, turning over the envelope abstractedly. The postmark was almost obliterated, but it struck me it might be construed into the word Skebawn.

"Look here," I said suddenly, "let me see Harris. It's just possible I may know something about him."

The sentry's body had been laid in the dead-house near the hospital, and Brownlow fetched the key. It was a grim little whitewashed building, without windows, save a small one of lancet shape, high up in one gable, through which a streak of April sunlight fell sharp and slender on the whitewashed wall. The long figure of the sentry lay sheeted on a stone slab, and Brownlow, with his cap in his hand, gently uncovered the face.

I leaned over and looked at it—at the heavy brows, the short nose, the small moustache lying black above the pale mouth, the deep-set eyes sealed in appalling peacefulness. There rose before me the wild dark face of the young man who had hung on my wheel and yelled encouragement to the winning coxswain at the Lough Lonen Regatta.

"I know him," I said, "his name is Callaghan."

LISHEEN RACES, SECOND-HAND

It may or may not be agreeable to have attained the age of thirty-eight, but, judging from old photographs, the privilege of being nineteen has also its drawbacks. I turned over page after page of an ancient book in which were enshrined portraits of the friends of my youth, singly, in David and Jonathan couples, and in groups in which I, as it seemed to my mature and possibly jaundiced perception, always contrived to look the most immeasurable young bounder of the lot. Our faces were fat, and yet I cannot remember ever having been considered fat in my life; we indulged in low-necked shirts, in "Jemima" ties with diagonal stripes; we wore coats that seemed three sizes too small, and trousers that were three sizes too big; we also wore small whiskers.

I stopped at last at one of the David and Jonathan memorial portraits. Yes, here was the object of my researches; this stout and earnestly romantic youth was Leigh Kelway, and that fatuous and chubby young person seated on the arm of his chair was myself. Leigh Kelway was a young man ardently believed in by a large circle of admirers, headed by himself and seconded by me, and for some time after I had left Magdalen for Sandhurst, I maintained a correspondence with him on large and abstract subjects. This phase of our friendship did not survive; I went soldiering to India, and Leigh Kelway took honours and moved suitably on into politics, as is the duty of an earnest young Radical with useful family connections and an independent income. Since then I had at intervals seen in the papers the name of the Honourable Basil Leigh Kelway mentioned as a speaker at elections, as a writer of thoughtful articles in the reviews, but we had never met, and nothing could have been less expected by me than the letter, written from Mrs. Raverty's Hotel, Skebawn, in which he told me he was making a tour in Ireland with Lord Waterbury, to whom he was private secretary. Lord Waterbury was at present having a few days' fishing near Killarney, and he himself, not being a fisherman, was collecting statistics for his chief on various points connected with the Liquor Question in Ireland. He had heard that I was in the neighbourhood, and was kind enough to add that it would give him much pleasure to meet me again.

With a stir of the old enthusiasm I wrote begging him to be my guest for as long as it suited him, and the following afternoon he arrived at Shreelane. The stout young friend of my youth had changed considerably. His important nose and slightly prominent teeth remained, but his wavy hair had withdrawn intellectually from his temples; his eyes had acquired a statesmanlike absence of expression, and his neck had grown long and bird-like. It was his first visit to Ireland, as he lost no time in telling me, and he and his chief had already collected much valuable information on the subject to which they had dedicated the Easter recess. He further informed me that he thought of popularizing the subject in a novel, and therefore intended to, as he put it, "master the brogue" before his return.

During the next few days I did my best for Leigh Kelway. I turned him loose on Father Scanlan; I showed him Mahona, our champion village, that boasts fifteen public-houses out of twenty buildings of sorts and a railway station; I took him to hear the prosecution of a publican for selling drink on a Sunday, which gave him an opportunity of studying perjury as a fine art, and of hearing a lady, on whom police suspicion justly rested, profoundly summed up by the sergeant as "a woman who had th' appairance of having knocked at a back door".

The net result of these experiences has not yet been given to the world by Leigh Kelway. For my own part,

I had at the end of three days arrived at the conclusion that his society, when combined with a notebook and a thirst for statistics, was not what I used to find it at Oxford. I therefore welcomed a suggestion from Mr. Flurry Knox that we should accompany him to some typical country races, got up by the farmers at a place called Lisheen, some twelve miles away. It was the worst road in the district, the races of the most grossly unorthodox character; in fact, it was the very place for Leigh Kelway to collect impressions of Irish life, and in any case it was a blessed opportunity of disposing of him for the day.

In my guest's attire next morning I discerned an unbending from the role of cabinet minister towards that of sportsman; the outlines of the notebook might be traced in his breast pocket, but traversing it was the strap of a pair of field-glasses, and his light grey suit was smart enough for Goodwood.

Flurry was to drive us to the races at one o'clock, and we walked to Tory Cottage by the short cut over the hill, in the sunny beauty of an April morning. Up to the present the weather had kept me in a more or less apologetic condition; anyone who has entertained a guest in the country knows the unjust weight of responsibility that rests on the shoulders of the host in the matter of climate, and Leigh Kelway, after two drenchings, had become sarcastically resigned to what I felt he regarded as my mismanagement.

Flurry took us into the house for a drink and a biscuit, to keep us going, as he said, till "we lifted some luncheon out of the Castle Knox people at the races", and it was while we were thus engaged that the first disaster of the day occurred. The dining-room door was open, so also was the window of the little staircase just outside it, and through the window travelled sounds that told of the close proximity of the stableyard; the clattering of hoofs on cobble stones, and voices uplifted in loud conversation. Suddenly from this region there arose a screech of the laughter peculiar to kitchen flirtation,

95

followed by the clank of a bucket, the plunging of a horse, and then an uproar of wheels and galloping hoofs. An instant afterwards Flurry's chestnut cob, in a dogcart, dashed at full gallop into view, with the reins streaming behind him, and two men in hot pursuit. Almost before I had time to realize what had happened, Flurry jumped through the half-opened window of the dining-room like a clown at a pantomime, and joined in the chase; but the cob was resolved to make the most of his chance, and went away down the drive and out of sight at a pace that distanced every one save the kennel terrier, who sped in shrieking ecstasy beside him.

"Oh merciful hour!" exclaimed a female voice behind me. Leigh Kelway and I were by this time watching the progress of events from the gravel, in company with the remainder of Flurry's household. "The horse is desthroyed! Wasn't that the quare start he took! And all in the world I done was to slap a bucket of wather at Michael out the windy, and 'twas himself got it in place of Michael!"

"Ye'll never ate another bit, Bridgie Dunnigan," replied the cook, with the exulting pessimism of her kind. "The Master'll have your life!"

Both speakers shouted at the top of their voices, probably because in spirit they still followed afar the flight of the cob.

Leigh Kelway looked serious as we walked on down the drive. I almost dared to hope that a note on the degrading oppression of Irish retainers was shaping itself. Before we reached the bend of the drive the rescue party was returning with the fugitive, all with the exception of the kennel terrier, looking extremely gloomy. The cob had been confronted by a wooden gate, which he had unhesitatingly taken in his stride, landing on his head of the farther side with the gate and the cart on top of him, and had arisen with a lame foreleg, a cut on his nose, and several other minor wounds.

"You'd think the brute had been fighting the cats, with all the scratches and scrapes he has on him!" said

Flurry, casting a vengeful eye at Michael, "and one shaft's broken and so is the dashboard. I haven't another horse in the place; they're all out at grass, and so there's an end of the races!"

We all three stood blankly on the hall-door steps and watched the wreck of the trap being trundled up the avenue.

"I'm very sorry you're done out of your sport," said Flurry to Leigh Kelway, in tones of deplorable sincerity; "perhaps, as there's nothing else to do, you'd like to see the hounds——?"

I felt for Flurry, but of the two I felt more for Leigh Kelway as he accepted this alleviation. He disliked dogs, and held the newest views on sanitation, and I knew what Flurry's kennels could smell like. I was lighting a precautionary cigarette, when we caught sight of an old man riding up the drive. Flurry stopped short.

"Hold on a minute," he said "here's an old chap that often brings me horses for the kennels; I must see what he wants."

The man dismounted and approached Mr. Knox, hat in hand, towing after him a gaunt and ancient mare with a big knee.

"Well, Bennett," began Flurry, surveying the mare with his hands in his pockets, "I'm not giving the hounds meat this month, or only very little."

"Ah, Master Flurry," answered Bennett, "it's you that's pleasant! Is it give the like o' this one for the dogs to ate! She a vallable strong young mare, no more than sixteen years of age, and ye'd sooner be lookin' at her going under a side-car than eatin' your dinner."

"There isn't as much meat on her a'd fatten a jackdaw," said Flurry, clinking the silver in his pockets as he searched for a matchbox. "What are you asking for her?"

The old man drew cautiously up to him.

"Master Flurry," he said solemnly, "I'll sell her to

97

your honour for five pounds, and she'll be worth ten after you give her a month's grass."

Flurry lit his cigarette; then he said imperturbably, "I'll give you seven shillings for her."

Old Barrett put on his hat in silence, and in silence buttoned his coat and took hold of the stirrup leather. Flurry remained immovable.

"Master Flurry," said old Bennett suddenly, with tears in his voice, "you must make it eight, sir!"

"Michael!" called out Flurry with apparent irrevevance, "run up to your father's and ask him would he lend me a loan of his side-car."

Half an hour later we were, improbable as it may seem, on our way to Lisheen races. We were seated upon an outside-car of immemorial age, whose joints seemed to open and close again as it swung in and out of the ruts, whose tattered cushions stank of rats and mildew, whose wheels staggered and rocked like the legs of a drunken man. Between the shafts jogged the latest addition to the kennel larder, the eight-shilling mare. Flurry sat on one side, and kept her going at a rate of not less than four miles an hour; Leigh Kelway and I held on to the other."

"She'll get us as far as Lynch's anyway," said Flurry, abandoning his first contention that she could do the whole distance, as he pulled her on to her legs after her fifteenth stumble, "and he'll lend us some sort of a horse, if it was only a mule."

"Do you notice that these cushions are very damp?" said Leigh Kelway to me, in a hollow undertone.

"Small blame to them if they are!" replied Flurry. "I've no doubt that they were out under the rain all day yesterday at Mrs. Hurly's funeral."

Leigh Kelway made no reply, but he took his note-book out of his pocket and sat on it.

We arrived at Lynch's at a little past three, and were there confronted by the next disappointment of this disastrous day. The door of Lynch's farmhouse was locked, and nothing replied to our knocking except a puppy, who barked hysterically from within.

"All gone to the races," said Flurry philosophically, picking his way round the manure heap. "No matter, here's the filly in the shed here. I know he's had her under a car."

An agitating ten minutes ensued, during which Leigh Kelway and I got the eight-shilling mare out of the shafts and the harness, and Flurry, with our inefficient help, crammed the young mare into them. As Flurry had stated that she had been driven before, I was bound to believe him, but the difficulty of getting the bit into her mouth was remarkable, and so also was the crab-like manner in which she sidled out of the yard, with Flurry and myself at her head, and Leigh Kelway hanging on to the back of the car to keep it from jamming in the gateway.

"Sit up on the car now," said Flurry when we got out on to the road; "I'll lead her on a bit. She's been ploughed anyway; one side of her mouth's as tough as a gad!"

Leigh Kelway threw away the wisp of grass with which he had been cleaning his hands, and mopped his intellectual forehead; he was very silent. We both mounted the car, and Flurry, with the reins in his hand, walked beside the filly, who, with her tail clasped in, moved onward in a succession of short jerks.

"Oh, she's all right!" said Flurry, beginning to run, and dragging the filly into a trot; "once she gets started——" Here the filly spied a pig in a neighbouring field, and despite the fact that she had probably eaten out of the same trough with it, she gave a violent side spring, and broke into a gallop.

"Now we're off!" shouted Flurry, making a jump at the car and clambering on; "if the traces hold we'll do!"

The English language is powerless to suggest the view-halloo with which Mr. Knox ended his speech, or to do more than indicate the rigid anxiety of Leigh

Kelway's face as he regained his balance after the preliminary jerk, and clutched the back rail. It must be
said for Lynch's filly that she did not kick; she merely
fled, like a dog with a kettle tied to its tail, from the
pursuing rattle and jingle behind her, with the shafts
buffeting her dusty sides as the car swung to and fro.
Whenever she showed any signs of slackening, Flurry
loosed another yell at her that renewed her panic, and
thus we precariously covered another two or three miles
of our journey.

Had it not been for a large stone lying on the road,
and had the filly not chosen to swerve so as to bring the
wheel on top of it, I dare say we might have got to the
races; but by an unfortunate coincidence both these
things occurred, and when we recovered from the consequent shock, the tyre of one of the wheels had come
off, and was trundling with cumbrous gaiety into the
ditch. Flurry stopped the filly and began to laugh; Leigh
Kelway said something startlingly unparliamentary under
his breath.

"Well, it might be worse," Flurry said consolingly as
he lifted the tyre on to the car, "we're not half a mile
from a forge."

We walked that half-mile in funereal procession
behind the car; the glory had departed from the weather,
and an ugly wall of cloud was rising up out of the west
to meet the sun; the hills had darkened and lost colour,
and the white bog cotton shivered in a cold wind that
smelt of rain.

By a miracle the smith was not at the races, owing, as
he explained, to his having "the toothaches", the two
facts combined producing in him a morosity only
equalled by that of Leigh Kelway. The smith's sole
comment on the situation was to unharness the filly, and
drag her into the forge, where he tied her up. He then
proceeded to whistle viciously on his fingers in the direction of a cottage, and to command, in tones of thunder,
some unseen creature to bring over a couple of baskets
of turf. The turf arrived in process of time, on a

100

woman's back, and was arranged in a circle in a yard at the back of the forge. The tyre was bedded in it, and the turf was with difficulty kindled at different points.

"Ye'll not get to the races this day," said the smith, yielding to a sardonic satisfaction; "the turf's wet, and I haven't one to do a hand's turn for me." He laid the wheel on the ground and lit his pipe.

Leigh Kelway looked pallidly about him over the spacious empty landscape of brown mountain slopes patched with golden furze and seamed with grey walls; I wondered if he were as hungry as I. We sat on stones opposite the smouldering ring of turf and smoked, and Flurry beguiled the smith into grim and calumnious confidences about every horse in the country. After about an hour, during which the turf went out three times, and the weather became more and more threatening, a girl with a red petticoat over her head appeared at the gate of the yard, and said to the smith:

"The horse is gone away from ye."

"Where?" exclaimed Flurry, springing to his feet.

"I met him walking wesht the road there below, and when I thought to turn him he commenced to gallop."

"Pulled her head out of the headstall," said Flurry, after a rapid survey of the forge. "She's near home by now."

It was at this moment that the rain began; the situation could scarcely have been better stage-managed. After reviewing the position, Flurry and I decided that the only thing to do was to walk to a public-house a couple of miles farther on, feed there if possible, hire a car, and go home.

It was an uphill walk, with mild generous raindrops striking thicker and thicker on our faces; no one talked, and the grey clouds crowded up from behind the hills like billows of steam. Leigh Kelway bore it all with egregious resignation. I cannot pretend that I was at heart sympathetic, but by virtue of being his host I felt responsible for the breakdown, for his light suit, for

101

everything, and divined his sentiment of horror at the first sight of the public-house.

It was a long, low cottage, with a line of dripping elm-trees overshadowing it; empty cars and carts round its door, and a babel from within made it evident that the racegoers were pursuing a gradual homeward route. The shop was crammed with steaming countrymen, whose loud brawling voices, all talking together, roused my English friend to his first remark since we had left the forge.

"Surely, Yeates, we are not going into that place," he said severely; "those men are all drunk."

"Ah, nothing to signify!" said Flurry, plunging in and driving his way through the throng like a plough. "Here, Mary Kate!" he called to the girl behind the counter, "tell your mother we want some tea and bread and butter in the room inside."

The smell of bad tobacco and spilt porter was choking; we worked our way through it after him towards the end of the shop, intersecting at every hand discussions about the races.

"Tom was very nice. He spared his horse all along, and then he put into him——" "Well, at Goggin's corner the third horse was before the second, but he was goin' wake in himself." "I tell ye the mare had the hind leg fasht in the fore." "Clancy was dipping in the saddle." " 'Twas a dam nice race whatever——"

We gained the inner room at last, a cheerless apartment, adorned with sacred pictures, a sewing-machine, and an array of supplementary tumblers and wineglasses; but, at all events, we had it so far to ourselves. At intervals during the next half-hour Mary Kate burst in with cups and plates, cast them on the table and disappeared, but of food there was no sign. After a further period of starvation and listening to the noise in the shop, Flurry made a sortie, and, after lengthy and unknown adventures, reappeared carrying a huge brown teapot, and driving before him Mary Kate with the remainder of the repast. The bread tasted of mice, the butter of turf-smoke, the tea of brown paper, but we had got past the critical stage. I had entered upon my third round of bread and butter when the door was flung open, and my valued acquaintance, Slipper, slightly advanced in liquor, presented himself to our gaze. His bandy legs sprawled consequentially, his nose was redder than a coal of fire, his prominent eyes rolled crookedly upon us, and his left hand swept behind him the attempt of Mary Kate to frustrate his entrance.

"Good evening to my vinerable friend, Mr. Flurry Knox!" he began, in the voice of a town crier, "and to the Honourable Major Yeates, and the English gintleman!"

This impressive opening immediately attracted an audience from the shop, and the doorway filled with grinning faces as Slipper advanced farther into the room.

"Why weren't ye at the races, Mr. Flurry?" he went on, his roving eye taking a grip of us all at the same time; "sure the Miss Bennetts and all the ladies was asking where were ye."

"It'd take some time to tell them that," said Flurry, with his mouth full; "but what about the races, Slipper? Had you good sport?"

"Sport is it? Divil so pleasant an afthernoon ever you seen," replied Slipper. He leaned against a side table, and all the glasses on it jingled. "Does your honour know O'Driscoll?" he went on irrelevantly. "Sure you do. He was in your honour's stable. It's what we were all sayin': it was a great pity your honour was not there, for the likin' you had to Driscoll."

"That's thrue," said a voice at the door.

"There wasn't one in the Barony but was gethered in it, through and fro," continued Slipper, with a quelling glance at the interrupter; "and there was tints for sellin' porther, and whisky as pliable as new milk, and boys goin' round the tints outside, feeling for heads with the big ends of their blackthorns, and all kinds of recreations, and the Sons of Liberty's piffler and dhrum band from Skebawn; though faith! there was more of

103

thim runnin' to look at the races than what was playin'
in it; not to mintion different occasions that the bandmasther was atin' his lunch within in the whisky tint."

"But what about Driscoll?" said Flurry.

"Sure it's about him I'm tellin' ye," replied Slipper,
with the practised orator's watchful eye on his growing
audience. " 'Twas within in the same whisky tint meself
was, with the bandmasther and a few of the lads, an'
we buyin' a ha'porth of crackers, when I seen me brave
Driscoll landin' into the tint, and a pair o' them long
boots on him; him that hadn't a shoe nor a stocking to
his foot when your honour had him picking grass out o'
the stones behind in your yard. 'Well,' says I to meself,
'we'll knock some sport out of Driscoll.'

" 'Come here to me, acushla!' says I to him; 'I suppose it's some way wake in the legs y'are,' says I, 'an'
the docthor put them on ye the way the people wouldn't
thrample ye!'

" 'May the divil choke ye!' says he, pleasant enough,
but I knew by the blush he had he was vexed.

" 'Then I suppose 'tis a left-tenant colonel y'are,' says
I; 'yer mother must be proud out o' ye!' says I, 'an'
maybe ye'll lend her a loan of thim waders when she's
rinsin' your bauneen in the river!' says I.

" 'There'll be work out o' this!' says he, lookin' at
me both sour and bitther.

" 'Well indeed, I was thinkin' you were blue-moulded
for want of a batin',' says I. He was for fightin' us then,
but afther we had him pacificated with about a quarther
of a naggin of sperrits, he told us he was goin' ridin' in
a race.

" 'An' what'll ye ride?' says I.

" 'Owld Bocock's mare,' says he.

" 'Knipes!' says I, sayin' a great curse; 'is it that little
staggeen from the mountains; sure she's somethin' about
the one age with meself,' says I. 'Many's the time Jamesy
Geoghegan and meself used to be dhrivin' her to
Macroom with pigs an' all soorts,' says I; ''an'is it
leppin' stone walls ye want her to go now?'

" 'Faith, there's walls and every vari'ty of obstackle in it,' says he.

" 'It'll be the best o' your play, so,' says I, 'to leg it away home out o' this.'

" 'An' who'll ride her, so?' says he.

" 'Let the divil ride her,' says I."

Leigh Kelway, who had been leaning back seemingly half asleep, obeyed the hypnotism of Slipper's gaze, and opened his eyes.

"That was now all the conversation that passed between himself and meself," resumed Slipper, "and there was no great delay afther that till they said there was a race startin' and the dickens a one at all was goin' to ride only two, Driscoll and one Clancy. With that then I seen Mr. Kinahane, the Petty Sessions Clerk, goin' round clearin' the coorse, an' I gethered a few o' the neighbours, an' we walked the fields hither and over till we seen the most of th' obstackles.

" 'Stand aisy now by the plantation,' says I; 'if they get to come as far as this, believe me ye'll see spoort,' says I, 'an' 'twill be a convenient spot to encourage the mare if she's anyway wake in herself,' says I, cuttin' somethin' about five foot of an ash sapling out o' the plantation.

" 'That's yer sort!' says Owld Bocock, that was thravellin' the race-coorse, peggin' a bit o' paper down with a thorn in front of every lep, the way Driscoll'd know the handiest place to face her at it.

"Well, I hadn't barely thrimmed the ash plant——"

"Have you any jam, Mary Kate?" interrupted Flurry, whose meal had been in no way interfered with by either the story or the highly scented crowd who had come to listen to it.

"We have no jam, only thraycle, sir," replied the invisible Mary Kate.

"I hadn't the switch barely thrimmed," repeated Slipper firmly, "when I heard the people screechin', and I seen Driscoll an' Clancy comin' on, leppin' all before them, an' Owld Bocock's mare bellusin' and powderin' along, an' bedad! whatever obstackle wouldn't throw *her* down, faith, she'd throw *it* down, an' there's the thraffic they had in it.

" 'I declare to me sowl,' says I, 'If they continue on this way there's a great chance some one o' thim'll win,' says I.

" 'Ye lie!' says the bandmasther, bein' a thrifle fulsome after his luncheon.

" 'I do not,' says I, 'in regard of seein' how soople them two boys is. Ye might observe,' says I, 'that if they have no convanient way to sit on the saddle, they'll ride the neck o' the horse till such time as they gets an occasion to lave it,' says I.

" 'Arrah, shut yer mouth!' says the bandmasther; 'they're puckin' out this way now, an' may the divil admire me!' says he, 'but Clancy has the other bet out, and the divil such leatherin' and beltin' of Owld Bocock's mare ever you seen as what's in it!' says he.

"Well, when I seen them comin' to me, and Driscoll about the length of the plantation behind Clancy, I let a couple of bawls.

" 'Skelp her, ye big brute!' says I. 'What good's in ye that ye aren't able to skelp her?' "

The yell and the histrionic flourish of his stick with which Slipper delivered this incident brought down the house. Leigh Kelway was sufficiently moved to ask me in an undertone if "skelp" was a local term.

"Well, Mr. Flurry, and gintlemen," recommenced Slipper, "I declare to ye when Owld Bocock's mare heard thim roars she sthretched out her neck like a gandher, and when she passed me she gave a couple of grunts, and looked at me as ugly as a Christian.

" 'Hah!' says I, givin' her a couple of dhraws o' th' ash plant across the butt o' the tail, the way I wouldn't blind her; 'I'll make ye grunt!' says I, 'I'll nourish ye!'

"I knew well she was very frightful o' th' ash plant since the winter Tommeen Sullivan had her under a sidecar. But now, in place of havin' any obligations to me, ye'd be surprised if ye heard the blaspheemious

106

expressions of that young boy that was ridin' her; and whether it was over-anxious he was, turnin' around the way I'd hear him cursin', or whether it was some slither or slide came to Owld Bocock's mare, I dunno, but she was bet up agin the last obstackle but two, and before ye could say 'Shnipes', she was standing on her two ears beyond in th' other field! I declare to ye, on the vartue of me oath, she stood that way till she reconnoithered what side would Driscoll fall, an' she turned about then and rolled on him as cosy as if he was meadow grass!"

Slipper stopped short; the people in the doorway groaned appreciatively; Mary Kate murmured "The Lord save us!"

"The blood was dhruv out through his nose and ears," continued Slipper, with a voice that indicated the cream of the narration, " and you'd hear his bones crackin' on the ground! You'd have pitied the poor boy."

"Good heavens!" said Leigh Kelway, sitting up very straight in his chair.

"Was he hurt, Slipper?" asked Flurry casually.

"Hurt is it?" echoed Slipper in high scorn; "killed on the spot!" He paused to relish the effect of the *dénouement* on Leigh Kelway. "Oh, divil so pleasant an afthernoon ever you seen; and indeed, Mr. Flurry, it's what we were all sayin', it was a great pity your honour was not there for the likin' you had for Driscoll."

As he spoke the last word there was an outburst of singing and cheering from a carload of people who had just pulled up at the door. Flurry listened, leaned back in his chair, and began to laugh.

"It scarcely strikes one as a comic incident," Said Leigh Kelway, very coldly to me; "in fact, it seems to me that the police ought——"

"Show me Slipper!" bawled a voice in the shop; "show me that dirty little undherlooper till I have his blood! Hadn't I the race won only for him souring the mare on me! What's that you say! I tell ye he did. He left seven slaps on her with a handle of a hay-rake——"

There was in the room in which we were sitting a second door, leading to the back yard, a door consecrated to the unobtrusive visits of so-called "Sunday travellers". Through it Slipper faded away like a dream, and, simultaneously, a tall young man, with a face like a red-hot potato tied up in a bandage, squeezed his way from the shop into the room.

"Well, Driscoll," said Flurry, "since it wasn't the teeth of the rake he left on the mare, you needn't be talking!"

Leigh Kelway looked from one to the other with a wilder expression in his eye than I had thought it capable of. I read in it a resolve to abandon Ireland to her fate.

At eight o'clock we were still waiting for the car that we had been assured should be ours directly it returned from the races. At half-past eight we had adopted the only possible course that remained, and had accepted the offers of lifts on the laden cars that were returning to Skebawn, and I presently was gratified by the spectacle of my friend Leigh Kelway wedged between a roulette table and its proprietor on one side of a car, with Driscoll and Slipper, mysteriously reconciled and excessively drunk, seated, locked in each other's arms, on the other. Flurry and I, somewhat similarly placed, followed on two other cars. I was scarcely surprised when I was informed that the melancholy white animal in the shafts of the leading car was Owld Bocock's much-enduring steeplechaser.

The night was very dark and stormy, and it is almost superfluous to say that no one carried lamps; the rain poured upon us, and through wind and wet Owld Bocock's mare set the pace that showed she knew from bitter experience what was expected from her by gentlemen who had spent the evening in a public-house; behind her the other two tired horses followed closely, incited to emulation by shouting, singing, and a liberal allowance of whip. We were a good ten miles from Skebawn, and never had the road seemed so long. For mile after mile the half-seen low walls slid past us, with occasional plunges into caverns of darkness under trees. Sometimes from a wayside cabin a dog would dash out to bark at us as we rattled by; sometimes our cavalcade swung aside to pass, with yells and counter-yells, crawling carts filled with other belated racegoers.

I was nearly wet through, even though I received considerable shelter from a Skebawn publican, who slept heavily and irrepressibly on my shoulder. Driscoll, on the leading car, had struck up an approximation of the "Wearing of the Green" when a wavering star appeared on the road ahead of us. It grew momently larger; it came towards us apace. Flurry, on the car behind me, shouted suddenly—

"That's the mail car, with one of the lamps out! Tell those fellows ahead to look out!"

But the warning fell on deaf ears.

"When laws can change the blades of grass
    From growing as they grow——"

howled five discordant voices, oblivious of the towering proximity of the star.

A Bianconi mail car is nearly three times the size of an ordinary side car, and when on a dark night it advances, Cyclops-like, with but one eye, it is difficult for even a sober driver to calculate its bulk. Above the sounds of melody there arose the thunder of heavy wheels, the splashing trample of three big horses, then a crash and turmoil of shouts. Our cars pulled up just in time, and I tore myself from the embrace of my publican to go to Leigh Kelway's assistance.

The wing of the Bianconi had caught the wing of the smaller car, flinging Owld Bocock's mare on her side and throwing her freight headlong on top of her, the heap being surmounted by the roulette table. The driver of the mailcar unshipped his solitary lamp and turned it on the disaster. I saw that Flurry had already got hold of Leigh Kelway by the heels, and was dragging him from under the others. He struggled up hatless, muddy

109

and gasping, with Driscoll hanging on by his neck, still singing the "Wearing of the Green".

A voice from the mail car said incredulously, *"Leigh Kelway!"* A spectacled face glared down upon him from under the dripping spikes of an umbrella.

It was the Right Honourable the Earl of Waterbury, Leigh Kelway's chief, returning from his fishing excursion.

Meanwhile Slipper, in the ditch, did not cease to announce that "Divil so pleasant an afthernoon ever ye seen as what was in it!"

PHILIPPA'S FOX-HUNT

No one can accuse Philippa and me of having married in haste. As a matter of fact, it was but little under five years from that autumn evening on the river when I had said what is called in Ireland "the hard word", to the day in August when I was led to the altar by my best man, and was subsequently led away from it by Mrs. Sinclair Yeates. About two years out of the five had been spent by me at Shreelane in ceaseless warfare with drains, eaveshoots, chimneys, pumps; all those fundamentals, in short, that the ingenuous and improving tenant expects to find established as a basis from which to rise to higher things. As far as rising to higher things went, frequent ascents to the roof to search for leaks summed up my achievements; in fact, I suffered so general a shrinkage of my ideals that the triumph of making the hall-door bell ring blinded me to the fact that the rat-holes in the hall floor were nailed up with pieces of tin biscuit boxes, and that the casual visitor could, instead of leaving a card, have easily written his name in the damp on the walls.

Philippa, however, proved adorably callous to these and similar shortcomings. She regarded Shreelane and its floundering, foundering *ménage* of incapables in the light of a gigantic picnic in a foreign land; she held long conversations daily with Mrs. Cadogan, in order, as she informed me, to acquire the language; without any ulterior domestic intention she engaged kitchen-maids because of the beauty of their eyes, and housemaids because they had such delightfully picturesque old mothers, and she declined to correct the phraseology of the parlour-maid, whose painful habit it was to whisper "Do ye choose cherry or clarry?" when proffering the wine. Fast-days, perhaps, afforded my wife her first insight into the sterner realities of Irish housekeeping. Philippa had what are known as High Church proclivities, and took the matter seriously.

I don't know how we are to manage for the servants' dinner to-morrow, Sinclair," she said, coming in to my office one Thursday morning; "Julia says she 'promised God this long time that she wouldn't eat an egg on a fast-day', and the kitchen-maid says she won't eat herrings 'without they're fried with onions', and Mrs. Cadogan says she will 'not go to them extremes for servants'."

"I should let Mrs. Cadogan settle the menu herself," I suggested.

"I asked her to do that," replied Philippa, "and she only said she thanked God *she* had no appetite!"

The lady of the house here fell away into unseasonable laughter.

I made the demoralizing suggestion that, as we were going away for a couple of nights, we might safely leave them to fight it out, and the problem was abandoned.

Philippa had been much called on by the neighbourhood in all its shades and grades, and daily she and her trousseau frocks presented themselves at hall-doors of varying dimensions in due acknowledgement of civilities. In Ireland, it may be noted, the process known in England as "summering and wintering" a new-comer does not obtain; sociability and curiosity alike forbid delay. The visit to which we owed our escape from the intricacies of the fast-day was to the Knoxes of Castle Knox, relations in some remote and tribal way of my landlord, Mr. Flurry of that ilk. It involved a short journey by train, and my wife's longest basket-trunk; it also, which was more serious, involved my being lent a horse to go out cubbing the following morning.

At Castle Knox we sank into an almost forgotten environment of draught-proof windows and doors, of deep carpets, of silent servants instead of clattering belligerents. Philippa told me afterwards that it had only been by an effort that she had restrained herself from snatching up the train of her wedding-gown as she paced across the wide hall on little Sir Valentine's arm. After three weeks at Shreelane she found it difficult to remember that the floor was neither damp nor dusty.

I had the good fortune to be of the limited number of those who got on with Lady Knox, chiefly, I imagine, because I was as a worm before her, and thankfully permitted her to do all the talking.

"Your wife is extremely pretty," she pronounced autocratically, surveying Philippa between the candle-shades; "does she ride?"

Lady Knox was a short square lady, with a weather-beaten face, and an eye decisive from long habit of taking her own line across country and elsewhere. She would have made a very imposing little coachman, and would have caused her stable helpers to rue the day they had the presumption to be born; it struck me that Sir Valentine sometimes did so.

"I'm glad you like her looks," I replied, "as I fear you will find her thoroughly despicable otherwise; for one thing, she not only can't ride, but she believes that I can!"

"Oh come, you're not as bad as all that!" my hostess was good enough to say; "I'm going to put you up on Sorcerer to-morrow, and we'll see you at the top of the hunt—if there is one. That young Knox hasn't a notion how to draw these woods."

"Well, the best run we had last year out of this place was with Flurry's hounds," struck in Miss Sally, sole daughter of Sir Valentine's house and home, from her place half-way down the table. It was not difficult to see that she and her mother held different views on the subject of Mr. Flurry Knox.

"I call it a criminal thing in anyone's great-great-grandfather to rear up a preposterous troop of sons and plant them all out in his own country," Lady Knox said to me with apparent irrelevance. "I detest collaterals. Blood may be thicker than water, but it is also a great deal nastier. In this country I find that fifteenth cousins consider themselves near relations if they live within twenty miles of one!"

Having before now taken in the position with regard to Flurry Knox, I took care to accept these remarks as generalities, and turned the conversation to other themes.

"I see Mrs. Yeates is doing wonders with Mr. Hamilton," said Lady Knox presently, following the direction of my eyes, which had strayed away to where Philippa was beaming upon her left-hand neighbour, a mildewed-looking old clergyman, who was delivering a long dissertation, the purport of which we were happily unable to catch.

"She has always had a gift for the Church," I said.

"Not curates?" said Lady Knox, in her deep voice.

I made haste to reply that it was the elders of the Church who were venerated by my wife.

"Well, she has her fancy in old Eustace Hamilton; he's elderly enough!" said Lady Knox. "I wonder if she'd venerate him as much if she knew that he had fought with his sister-in-law, and they haven't spoken for thirty years! though for the matter of that," she added, "I think it shows his good sense!"

"Mrs. Knox is rather a friend of mine," I ventured.

"Is she? H'm! Well, she's not one of mine!" replied my hostess, with her usual definiteness. "I'll say one thing for her, I believe she's always been a sportswoman. She's very rich, you know, and they say she only married old Badger Knox to save his hounds from being sold to pay his debts, and then she took the horn from him and hunted them herself. Has she been rude to your wife yet? No? Oh, well, she will. It's a mere question of time. She hates all English people. You know the story they tell of her? She was coming home from London, and when she was getting her ticket the man asked if she had a ticket for York. 'No, thank God, Cork!' says Mrs. Knox."

"Well, I rather agree with her!" said I; "but why did she fight with Mr. Hamilton?"

"Oh, nobody knows. I don't believe they know themselves! Whatever it was, the old lady drives five miles to Fortwilliam every Sunday, rather than go to his church, just outside her own back gates," Lady Knox said with a laugh like a terrier's bark. "I wish I'd fought with him myself," she said; "he gives us forty minutes every Sunday."

As I struggled into my boots the following morning, I felt that Sir Valentine's acid comments on cub-hunting, bestowed on me at mid-night, did credit to his judgement. "A very moderate amusement, my dear Major," he had said, in his dry little voice; "you should stick to shooting. No one expects you to shoot before daybreak."

It was six o'clock as I crept downstairs, and found Lady Knox and Miss Sally at breakfast, with two lamps on the table, and a foggy daylight oozing in from under the half-raised blinds. Philippa was already in the hall, pumping up her bicycle, in a state of excitement at the prospect of her first experience of hunting that would have been more comprehensible to me had she been going to ride a strange horse, as I was. As I bolted my food I saw the horses being led past the windows and a faint twang of a horn told that Flurry Knox and his hounds were not far off.

Miss Sally jumped up.

"If I'm not on the Cockatoo before the hounds come up, I shall never get there!" she said, hobbling out of the room in the toils of her safety habit. Her small, alert face looked very childish under her riding-hat; the lamp-light struck sparks out of her thick coil of golden-red hair; I wondered how I had even thought her like her prim little father.

She was already on her white cob when I got to the hall-door, and Flurry Knox was riding over the glistening wet grass with his hounds, while his whip, Dr. Jerome Hickey, was having a stirring time with the young entry and the rabbit-holes. They moved on without stopping, up a back avenue, under tall and dripping trees, to a thick laurel covert, at some little distance

115

from the house. Into this the hounds were thrown, and the usual period of fidgety inaction set in for the riders, of whom, all told, there were about half a dozen. Lady Knox, square and solid, on her big confidential iron-grey, was near me, and her eyes were on me and my mount; with her rubicund face and white collar she was more than ever like a coachman.

"Sorcerer looks as if he suited you well," she said, after a few minutes of silence, during which the hounds rustled and crackled through the laurels; "he's a little high on the leg, and so are you, you know, so you show each other off."

Sorcerer was standing like a rock, with his good-looking head in the air and his eyes fastened on the covert. His manners, so far, had been those of a perfect gentleman, and were in marked contrast to those of Miss Sally's cob, who was sidling, hopping, and snatching unappeasably at his bit. Philippa had disappeared from view down the avenue ahead. The fog was melting, and the sun threw long blades of light through the trees; everything was quiet, and in the distance the curtained windows of the house marked the warm repose of Sir Valentine, and those of the party who shared his opinion of cubbing.

"Hark! hark to cry there!"

It was Flurry's voice, away at the other side of the covert. The rustling and brushing through the laurels became more vehement, then passed out of hearing.

"He never will leave his hounds alone," said Lady Knox disapprovingly.

Miss Sally and the Cockatoo moved away in a series of heraldic capers towards the end of the laurel planta-tion, and at the same moment I saw Philippa on her bicycle shoot into view on the drive ahead of us.

"I've seen a fox," she screeched, white with what I believe to have been personal terror, though she says it was excitement; "it passed quite close to me!"

"Which way did he go?" bellowed a voice which I

recognized as Dr. Hickey's, somewhere in the deep of the laurels.

"Down the drive!" returned Philippa, with a pea-hen quality in her tones with which I was quite unacquainted.

An electrifying screech of "Gone away!" was projected from the laurels by Dr. Hickey.

"Gone away!" chanted Flurry's horn at the top of the covert.

"This is what he calls cubbing!" said Lady Knox, "a mere farce!" but none the less she loosed her sedate monster into a canter.

Sorcerer got his hind-legs under him, and hardened his crest against the bit, as we all hustled along the drive after the flying figure of my wife. I knew very little about horses, but I realized that even with the hounds tumbling hysterically out of the covert, and the Cockatoo kicking the gravel into his face, Sorcerer comported himself with the manners of the best society. Up a side road I saw Flurry Knox opening half of a gate and cramming through it; in a moment we also had crammed through, and the turf of a pasture field was under our feet. Dr. Hickey leaned forward and took hold of his horse; I did likewise, with the trifling difference that my horse took hold of me, and I steered for Flurry Knox with single-hearted purpose, the hounds, already a field ahead, being merely an exciting and noisy accompaniment of this endeavour. A heavy stone wall was the first occurrence of note. Flurry chose a place where the top was loose, and his clumsy-looking brown mare changed feet on the rattling stones like a fairy. Sorcerer came at it, tense and collected as a bow at full stretch, and sailed steeply into the air; I saw the wall far beneath me, with an unsuspected ditch on the far side, and I felt my hat following me at the full stretch of its guard as we swept over it, then, with a long slant, we descended to earth some sixteen feet from where we had left it, and I was possessor of the gratifying fact that I had achieved a good-sized "fly", and had not perceptibly moved in my saddle. Subsequent disillusioning

117

experience has taught me that but few horses jump like Sorcerer, so gallantly, so sympathetically, and with such supreme mastery of the subject; but none the less the enthusiasm that he imparted to me has never been extinguished, and that October morning ride revealed to me the unsuspected intoxication of fox-hunting.

Behind me I heard the scrabbling of the Cockatoo's little hoofs among the loose stones, and Lady Knox, galloping on my left, jerked a maternal chin over her shoulder to mark her daughter's progress. For my part, had there been an entire circus behind me, I was far too much occupied with ramming on my hat and trying to hold Sorcerer, to have looked round, and all my spare faculties were devoted to steering for Flurry, who had taken a right-handed turn, and was at that moment surmounting a bank of uncertain and briary aspect. I surmounted it also, with the swiftness and simplicity for which the Quaker's methods of bank jumping had not prepared me, and two or three fields, traversed at the same steeplechase pace, brought us to a road and to an abrupt check. There, suddenly, were the hounds, scrambling in baffled silence down into the road from the opposite bank, to look for the line they had overrun, and there, amazingly, was Philippa engaged in excited converse with several men with spades over their shoulders.

"Did ye see the fox, boys?" shouted Flurry, addressing the group.

"We did! we did!" cried my wife and her friends in chorus; "he ran up the road!"

"We'd be badly off without Mrs. Yeates!" said Flurry, as he whirled his mare round and clattered up the road with a hustle of hounds after him.

It occurred to me as forcibly as any mere earthly thing can occur to those who are wrapped in the sublimities of a run, that for a young woman who had never before seen a fox out of a cage at the Zoo, Philippa was taking to hunting very kindly. Her cheeks were a most brilliant pink, her blue eyes shone.

118

"Oh, Sinclair," she exclaimed, "they say he's going for Aussolas, and there's a road I can ride all the way!"

"Ye can, Miss! Sure we'll show you!" chorused her *cortège*.

Her foot was on the pedal ready to mount. Decidedly my wife was in no need of assistance from me.

Up the road a hound gave a yelp of discovery, and flung himself over a stile into the fields; the rest of the pack went squealing and jostling after him, and I followed Flurry over one of those infinitely varied erection pleasantly termed "gaps" in Ireland. On this occasion the gap was made of three razor-edged slabs of slate leaning against an iron bar, and Sorcerer conveyed to me his thorough knowledge of the matter by a lift of his hindquarters that made me feel as if I were being skilfully kicked downstairs. To what extent I looked it, I cannot say, nor providentially can Philippa as she had already started. I only know that undeserved good luck restored to me my stirrup before Sorcerer got away with me in my next field.

What followed was, I am told, a very fast fifteen minutes; for me time was not; the empty fields rushed past uncounted, fences came and went in a flash, while the wind sang in my ears, and the dazzle of the early sun was in my eyes. I saw the hounds occasionally, sometimes pouring over a green bank, as the charging breaker lifts and flings itself, sometimes driving across a field, as the white tongues of foam slide racing over the sand; and always ahead of me was Flurry Knox, going as a man goes who knows his country, who knows his horse, and whose heart is wholly and absolutely in the right place.

Do what I would, Sorcerer's implacable stride carried me closer and closer to the brown mare, till, as I thundered down the slope of a long field, I was not twenty yards behind Flurry. Sorcerer had stiffened his neck to iron, and to slow him down was beyond me; but I fought his head away to the right, and found myself coming hard and steady at a stone-faced bank with

119

broken ground in front of it. Flurry bore away to the left, shouting something that I did not understand. That Sorcerer shortened his stride at the right moment was entirely due to his own judgement; standing well away from the jump, he rose like a stag out of the tussocky ground, and as he swung my twelve stone six into the air the obstacle revealed itself to him and me as consisting not of one bank but of two, and between the two lay a deep grassy lane, half choked with furze. I have often been asked to state the width of the bohereen, and can only reply that in my opinion it was at least eighteen feet; Flurry Knox and Dr. Hickey, who did did not jump it, say that it is not more than five. What Sorcerer did with it I cannot say; the sensation was of a towering flight with a kick back in it, a biggish drop, and a landing on cee-springs, still on the downhill grade. That was how one of the best horses in Ireland took one of Ireland's most ignorant riders over a very nasty place.

A sombre line of fir-wood lay ahead, rimmed with a grey wall, and in another couple of minutes we had pulled up on the Aussolas road, and were watching the hounds struggling over the wall into Aussolas demesne.

"No hurry now," said Flurry, turning in his saddle to watch the Cockatoo jump into the road, "he's to ground in the big earth inside. Well, Major, it's well for you that's a big-jumped horse. I thought you were a dead man a while ago when you faced him at the bohereen!"

I was disclaiming intention in the matter when Lady Knox and the others joined us.

"I thought you told me your wife was no sportswoman," she said to me, critically scanning Sorcerer's legs for cuts the while, "but when I saw her a minute ago she had abandoned her bicycle and was running across country like——"

"Look at her now!" interrupted Miss Sally. "Oh!—oh!" In the interval between these exclamations my incredulous eyes beheld my wife in mid-air with a couple of stalwart country boys, with whom she was

120

leaping in unison from the top of a bank on to the road.

Every one, even the saturnine, Dr. Hickey, began to laugh; I rode back to Philippa, who was exchanging compliments and congratulations with her escort.

"Oh, Sinclair!" she cried, "wasn't it splendid? I saw you jumping, and everything. "Where are they going now?"

"My dear girl," I said, with marital disapproval, "you're killing yourself. Where's your bicycle?"

"Oh, it's punctured in a sort of lane, back there. It's all right; and then they"—she breathlessly waved her hand at her attendants—"they showed me the way."

"Begor! you proved very good, miss!" said a grinning cavalier.

"Faith she did!" said another, polishing his shining brow with his white flannel coat-sleeve, "she lepped like a haarse!"

"And may I ask how you propose to go home?" said I.

"I don't know and I don't care! I'm not going home!" She cast an entirely disobedient eye at me. "And your eyeglass is hanging down your back and your tie is bulging out over your waistcoat!"

The little group of riders had begun to move away.

"We're going on into Aussolas," called out Flurry; "come on, and make my grandmother give you some breakfast, Mrs. Yeates; she always has it at eight o'clock."

The front gates were close at hand, and we turned in under the tall beech-trees, with the unswept leaves rustling round the horses' feet, and the lovely blue of the October morning sky filling the spaces between smooth grey branches and golden leaves. The woods rang with the voices of the hounds, enjoying an untrammelled rabbit hunt, while the Master and the Whip, both on foot, strolled along unconcernedly with their bridles over their arms, making themselves agreeable to my wife, an occasional touch of Flurry's horn, or a crack of Dr.

Hickey's whip, just indicating to the pack that the authorities still took a friendly interest in their doings.

Down a grassy glade in the wood a part of old Mrs. Knox's young horses suddenly swept into view, headed by an old mare, who, with her tail over her back, stampeded ponderously past our cavalcade, shaking and swinging her handsome old head, while her youthful friends bucked and kicked and snapped at each other round her with the ferocious humour of their kind.

"Here, Jerome, take the horn," said Flurry to Dr. Hickey; "I'm going to see Mrs. Yeates up to the house, the way these tomfools won't gallop on top of her."

From this point it seems to me that Philippa's adventures are more worthy of record than mine, and as she has favoured me with a full account of them, I venture to think my version may be relied on.

Mrs. Knox was already at breakfast when Philippa was led, quaking, into her formidable presence. My wife's acquaintance with Mrs. Knox was, so far, limited to a state visit on either side, and she found but little comfort in Flurry's assurances that his grandmother wouldn't mind if he brought all the hounds in to breakfast, coupled with the statement that she would put her eyes on sticks for the Major.

Whatever the truth of this may have been, Mrs. Knox received her guest with an equanimity quite unshaken by the fact that her boots were in the fender instead of on her feet, and that a couple of shawls of varying dimensions and degrees of age did not conceal the inner presence of a magenta flannel dressing-jacket. She installed Phillippa at the table and plied her with food, oblivious as to whether the needful implements with which to eat it were forthcoming or no. She told Flurry where a vixen had reared her family, and she watched him ride away, with some biting comments on his mare's hocks screamed after him from the window.

The dining-room at Aussolas Castle is one of the many rooms in Ireland in which Cromwell is said to have stabled his horse (and probably no one would have objected less than Mrs. Knox had she been consulted in the matter). Philippa questions if the room had ever been tidied up since, and she endorses Flurry's observation that "there wasn't a day in the year you wouldn't get feeding for a hen and chickens on the floor". Opposite to Philippa, on a Louis Quinze chair, sat Mrs. Knox's woolly dog, its suspicious little eyes peering at her out of their setting of pink lids and dirty white wool. A couple of young horses outside the windows tore at the matted creepers on the walls, or thrust faces that were half-shy, half-impudent, into the room. Portly pigeons waddled to and fro on the broad window-sill, sometimes flying in to perch on the picture-frames, while they kept up incessantly a hoarse and pompous cooing.

Animals and children are, as a rule, alike destructive to conversation; but Mrs. Knox, when she chose, *bien entendu*, could have made herself agreeable in a Noah's ark, and Philippa has a gift of sympathetic attention that personal experience has taught me to regard with distrust as well as respect, while it has often made me realize the worldly wisdom of Kingsley's injunction:

Be good, sweet maid, and let who will be clever.

Family prayers, declaimed by Mrs. Knox with alarming austerity, followed close on breakfast, Philippa and a vinegar-faced henchwoman forming the family. The prayers were long, and through the open window as they progressed came distantly a whoop or two; the declamatory tones staggered a little, and then continued at a distinctly higher rate of speed.

"Ma'am! Ma'am!" whispered a small voice at the window.

Mrs. Knox made a repressive gesture and held on her way. A sudden outcry of hounds followed, and the owner of the whisper, a small boy with a face freckled like a turkey's egg, darted from the window and dragged a donkey and bath-chair into view. Philippa admits to having lost the thread of the discourse, but she thinks

that the "Amen" that immediately ensued can hardly
have come in its usual place. Mrs. Knox shut the book
abruptly, scrambled up from her knees, and said,
"They've found!"

In a surprisingly short space of time she had added to
her attire her boots, a fur cape, and a garden hat, and
was in the bath-chair, the small boy stimulating the
donkey with the success peculiar to his class, while
Philippa hung on behind.

The woods of Aussolas are hilly and extensive, and
on that particular morning it seemed that they held as
many foxes as hounds. In vain was the horn blown and
the whips cracked, small rejoicing parties of hounds,
each with a fox of its own, scoured to and fro: every
labourer in the vicinity had left his work, and was
sedulously heading every fox with yells that would have
befitted a tiger hunt, and sticks and stones when occasion
served.

"Will I pull out as far as the big rosydandhrum,
ma'am?" inquired the small boy. "I seen three of the
dogs go in it, and they yowling."

"You will," said Mrs. Knox, thumping the donkey on
the back with her umbrella; "here! Jeremiah Regan!
Come down out of that with that pitchfork! Do you
want to kill the fox, you fool?"

"I do not, your honour, ma'am," responded Jeremiah
Regan, a tall young countryman, emerging from a
bramble brake.

"Did you see him?" said Mrs. Knox eagerly.

"I seen himself and his ten pups drinking below at
the lake ere yesterday, your honour, ma'am, and he as
big as a chestnut horse!" said Jeremiah.

"Faugh! Yesterday!" snorted Mrs. Knox; "go on to
the rhododendrons, Johnny!"

The party, reinforced by Jeremiah and the pitchfork,
progressed at a high rate of speed along the shrubbery
path, encountering *en route* Lady Knox, stooping on to
her horse's neck under the sweeping branches of the
laurels.

"Your horse is too high for my coverts, Lady Knox," said the Lady of the Manor, with a malicious eye at Lady Knox's flushed face and dinged hat; "I'm afraid you will be left behind like Absalom when the hounds go away!"

"As they never do anything here but hunt rabbits," retorted her ladyship, "I don't think that's likely."

Mrs. Knox gave her donkey another whack, and passed on.

"Rabbits, my dear!" she said scornfully to Philippa. "That's all she knows about it. I declare it disgusts me to see a woman of that age making such a Judy of herself! Rabbits indeed!"

Down in the thicket of rhododendron everything was very quiet for a time. Philippa strained her eyes in vain to see any of the riders; the horn blowing and the whip cracking passed on almost out of hearing. Once or twice a hound worked through the rhododendrons, glanced at the party, and hurried on, immersed in business. All at once Johnny, the donkey-boy, whispered excitedly:

"Look at he! Look at he!" and pointed to a boulder of grey rock that stood out among the dark evergreens. A big yellow cub was crouching on it; he instantly slid into the shelter of the bushes, and the irrepressible Jeremiah, uttering a rending shriek, plunged into the thicket after him. Two or three hounds came rushing at the sound, and after this Philippa says she finds some difficulty in recalling the proper order of events; chiefly, she confesses, because of the wholly ridiculous tears of excitement that blurred her eyes.

"We ran," she said, "we simply tore, and the donkey galloped, and as for that old Mrs. Knox, she was giving cracked screams to the hounds all the time, and they were screaming too; and then somehow we were all out on the road!" What seems to have occurred was that three couple of hounds, Jeremiah Regan and Mrs. Knox's equipage amongst them, somehow hustled the cub out of Aussolas demesne and up on to a hill on the farther side of the road. Jeremiah was sent back by his

125

mistress to fetch Flurry, and the rest of the party pursued a thrilling course along the road, parallel with that of the hounds, who were hunting slowly through the gorse on the hillside.

"Upon my honour and word, Mrs. Yeates, my dear, we have the hunt to ourselves!" said Mrs. Knox to the panting Philippa, as they pounded along the road. "Johnny, d'ye see the fox?"

"I do, ma'am!" shrieked Johnny, who possessed the usual field-glass vision bestowed upon his kind. "Look at him over-right us on the hill above! Hi! The spotty dog have him! No, he's gone from him! *Gwan out o' that!*" This to the donkey, with blows that sounded like the beating of carpets, and produced rather more dust.

They had left Aussolas some half a mile behind, when, from a strip of wood on their right, the fox suddenly slipped over the bank on to the road just ahead of them, ran up it for a few yards and whisked in at a small entrance gate, with the three couple of hounds yelling on a red-hot scent, not thirty yards behind. The bath-chair party whirled in at their heels, Philippa and the donkey considerably blown, Johnny scarlet through his freckles, but as fresh as paint, the old lady blind and deaf to all things save the chase. The hounds went raging through the shrubs beside the drive, and away down a grassy slope towards a shallow glen, in the bottom of which ran a little stream, and after them over the grass bumped the bath-chair. At the stream they turned sharply and ran up the glen towards the avenue, which crossed it by means of a rough stone viaduct.

"'Pon my conscience, he's into the old culvert!" exclaimed Mrs. Knox; "there was one of my hounds choked there once, long ago! Beat on the donkey, Johnny!"

At this juncture Philippa's narrative again becomes incoherent, not to say breathless. She is, however, positive that it was somewhere about here that the upset of the bath-chair occurred, but she cannot be clear as to whether she picked up the donkey or Mrs. Knox, or whether she herself was picked up by Johnny while Mrs. Knox picked up the donkey. From my knowledge of Mrs. Knox I should say she picked up herself and no one else. At all events, the next salient point is the palpitating moment when Mrs. Knox, Johnny, and Philippa successively applying an eye to the opening of the culvert by which the stream trickled under the viaduct, while five dripping hounds bayed and leaped around them, discovered by more senses than that of sight that the fox was in it, and furthermore that one of the hounds was in it too.

"There's a sthrong grating before him at the far end," said Johnny, his head in at the mouth of the hole, his voice sounding as if he were talking into a jug, "the two of them's fighting in it; they'll be choked surely!"

"Then don't stand gabbling there, you little fool, but get in and pull the hound out!" exclaimed Mrs. Knox, who was balancing on a stone in the stream.

"I'd be in dread, ma'am," whined Johnny.

"Balderdash!" said the implacable Mrs. Knox. "In with you!"

I understand that Philippa assisted Johnny into the culvert, and presume that it was in so doing that she acquired the two Robinson Crusoe bare footprints which decorated her jacket when I next met her.

"Have you got hold of him yet, Johnny?" cried Mrs. Knox up the culvert.

"I have, ma'am, by the tail," responded Johnny's voice, sepulchral in the depths.

"Can you stir him, Johnny?"

"I cannot, ma'am, and the wather is rising in it."

"Well, please God, they'll not open the mill dam!" remarked Mrs. Knox philosophically to Philippa, as she caught hold of Johnny's dirty ankles. "Hold on to the tail, Johnny!"

She hauled, with, as might be expected, no appreciable result. "Run, my dear, and look for somebody, and we'll have that fox yet!"

Philippa ran, whither she knew not, pursued by fearful

127

visions of bursting mill-dams, and maddened foxes at bay. As she sped up the avenue she heard voices, robust male voices, in a shrubbery, and made for them. Advancing along an embowered walk towards her was what she took for one wild instant to be a funeral; a second glance showed her that it was a party of clergymen of all ages, walking by twos and threes in the dappled shade of the over-arching trees. Obviously she had intruded her sacrilegious presence into a Clerical Meeting. She acknowledges that at this awe-inspiring spectacle she faltered, but the thought of Johnny, the hound, and the fox, suffocating, possibly drowning together in the culvert, nerved her. She does not remember what she said or how she said it, but I fancy she must have conveyed to them the impression that old Mrs. Knox was being drowned, as she immediately found herself heading a charge of the Irish Church towards the scene of disaster.

Fate has not always used me well, but on this occasion it was mercifully decreed that I and the other members of the hunt should be privileged to arrive in time to see my wife and her rescue party precipitating themselves down the glen.

"Holy Biddy;" ejaculated Flurry, "is she running a paper-chase with all the parsons? But look! For pity's sake will you look at my grandmother and my Uncle Eustace?"

Mrs. Knox and her sworn enemy the old clergyman, whom I had met at dinner the night before, were standing, apparently in the stream, tugging at two bare legs that projected from a hole in the viaduct, and arguing at the top of their voices. The bath-chair lay on its side with the donkey grazing beside it, on the bank a stout Archdeacon was tendering advice, and the hounds danced and howled round the entire group.

"I tell you, Eliza, you had better let the Archdeacon try," thundered Mr. Hamilton.

"Then I tell you I will not!" vociferated Mrs. Knox,

with a tug at the end of the sentence that elicited a sub-
terranean lament from Johnny.

"Now who was right about the second grating? I told
you so twenty years ago!"

Exactly as Philippa and her rescue party arrived, the
efforts of Mrs. Knox and her brother-in-law triumphed.
The struggling, sopping form of Johnny was slowly
drawn from the hole, drenched, speechless, but clinging
to the stern of a hound, who, in its turn, had its jaws fast
in the hindquarters of a limp, yellow cub.

"Oh, it's dead!" wailed Philippa, "but I *did* think I
should have been in time to save it!"

"Well, if that doesn't beat all!" said Dr. Hickey.

A MISDEAL

The wagonette slewed and slackened mysteriously on the top of the long hill above Drumcurran. So many remarkable things had happened since we had entrusted ourselves to the guidance of Mr. Bernard Shute that I rose in my place and possessed myself of the brake, and in so doing saw the horses with their heads hard in against their chests, and their quarters jammed crookedly against the splashboard, being apparently tied into knots by some inexplicable power.

"Someone's pulling the reins out of my hand!" exclaimed Mr. Shute.

The horses and pole were by this time making an acute angle with the wagonette, and the groom plunged from the box to their heads. Miss Sally Knox, who was sitting beside me, looked over the edge.

"Put on the brake; the reins are twisted round the axle!" she cried, and fell into a fit of laughter.

We all—that is to say, Philippa, Miss Shute, Miss Knox, and I—got out as speedily as might be; but, I think, without panic; Mr. Shute alone stuck to the ship, with the horses struggling and rearing below him. The groom and I contrived to back them, and by so doing caused the reins to unwind themselves from the axle.

"It was my fault," said Mr. Shute, hauling them in as fast as we could give them to him; "I broke the reins yesterday, and these are the phaeton ones, and about six fathoms long at that, and I forgot and let the slack go overboard. It's all right, I won't do it again."

With this reassurance we confided ourselves once more to the wagonette.

As we neared the town of Drumcurran the fact that we were on our way to a horse fair became alarmingly

130

apparent. It is impossible to imagine how we pursued an uninjured course through the companies of horsemen, the crowded carts, the squealing colts, the irresponsible led horses, and, most immutable of all obstacles, the groups of country-women, with the hoods of their heavy blue cloaks over their heads. They looked like nuns of some obscure order; they were deaf and blind as ramparts of sandbags; nothing less callous to human life than a Parisian cabdriver could have burst a way through them. Many times during that drive I had cause to be thankful for the sterling qualities of Mr. Shute's brake; with its aid he dragged his overfed bays into a crawl that finally, and not without injury to the varnish, took the wagonette to the Royal Hotel. Every available stall in the yard was by that time filled, and it was only by virtue of the fact that the kitchenmaid was nearly related to my cook that the indignant groom was permitted to stable the bays in a den known as the calf-house.

That I should have lent myself to such an expedition was wholly due to my wife. Since Philippa had taken up her residence in Ireland she had discovered a taste for horses that was not to be extinguished, even by an occasional afternoon on the Quaker, whose paces had become harder than rock in his many journeys to Petty Sessions; she had also discovered the Shutes, new-comers on the outer edge of our vast visiting district, and between them this party to Drumcurran Horse Fair had been devised. Philippa proposed to buy herself a hunter. Bernard Shute wished to do the same, possibly two hunters, money being no difficulty with this fortunate young man. Miss Sally Knox was of the company, and I also had been kindly invited, as to a missionary meeting, to come, and bring my cheque-book. The only saving clause in the affair was the fact that Mr. Flurry Knox was to meet us at the scene of action.

The fair was held in a couple of large fields outside the town, and on the farther bank of the Curranhilty River. Across a wide and glittering ford, horses of all

131

sizes and sorts were splashing, and a long row of stepping-stones was hopped, and staggered, and scrambled over by a ceaseless variety of foot-passengers. A man with a cart plied as a ferry boat, doing a heavy trade among the applewomen and vendors of "crubeens", *alias* pigs' feet, a grisly delicacy peculiar to Irish open-air holiday-making, and the July sun blazed on a scene that even Miss Cecilia Shute found to be almost repayment enough for the alarms of the drive.

"As a rule, I am so bored by driving that I find it reviving to be frightened," she said to me, as we climbed to safety on a heathery ridge above the fields dedicated to galloping the horses; "but when my brother scraped all those people off one side of that car, and ran the pole into the cart of lemonade-bottles, I began to wish for courage to tell him I was going to get out and walk home."

"Well, if you only knew it," said Bernard, who was spreading rugs over the low furze bushes in the touching belief that the prickles would not come through, "the time you came nearest to walking home was when the lash of the whip got twisted round Nancy's tail. Miss Knox, you're an authority on these things—don't you think it would be a good scheme to have a light anchor in the trap, and when the horses began to play the fool, you'd heave the anchor over the fence and bring them up all standing?"

"They wouldn't stand very long," remarked Miss Sally.

"Oh, that's all right," returned the inventor; "I'd have a dodge to cast them loose, with the pole and the splinter-bar."

"You'd never see them again," responded Miss Knox demurely, "if you thought that mattered."

"It would be the brightest feature of the case," said Miss Shute.

She was surveying Miss Sally through her pince-nez as she spoke, and was, I have reason to believe, deciding

132

that by the end of the day her brother would be well on in the first stages of his fifteenth love affair.

It has possibly been suspected that Mr. Bernard Shute was a sailor, had been a sailor rather, until within the last year, when he had tumbled into a fortune and a property, and out of the navy, in the shortest time on record. His enthusiasm for horses had been nourished by the hirelings of Malta, and other resorts of her Majesty's ships, and his knowledge of them was, so far, bounded by the fact that it was more usual to come off over their heads than their tails. For the rest, he was a clean-shaved and personable youth, with a laugh which I may, without offensive intention, define as possessing a what-cheeriness special to his profession, and a habit, engendered no doubt by long sojourns at the Antipodes, of getting his clothes in large hideous consignments from a naval outfitter.

It was eleven o'clock, and the fair was in full swing. Its vortex was in the centre of the field below us, where a low bank of sods and earth had been erected as a trial jump, with a yelling crowd of men and boys at either end, acting instead of the usual wings to prevent a swerve. Strings of reluctant horses were scourged over the bank by dozens of willing hands, while exhortation, cheers, and criticism were freely showered upon each performance.

"Give the knees to the saddle, boy, and leave the heels slack." "That's a nice horse. He'd keep a jock on his back where another'd throw him!" "Well jumped, begor! She fled that fairly!" as an ungainly three-year-old flounced over the bank without putting a hoof on it. Then her owner, unloosing his pride in simile after the manner of his race:

"Ah ha! when she give a lep, man, she's that free, she's like a hare for it!"

A giggling group of country girls elbowed their way past us out of the crowd of spectators, one of the number inciting her fellows to hurry on to the other field "until they'd see the lads galloping the horses" to which

133

another responding that she'd "be skinned alive for the horses", the party sped on their way. We—i.e. my wife, Miss Knox, Bernard Shute, and myself—followed in their wake, a matter by no means as easy as it looked. Miss Shute had exhibited her wonted intelligence by remaining on the hilltop with the *Spectator*: she had not reached the happy point of possessing a mind ten years older than her age, and a face ten years younger, without also developing the gift of scenting boredom from afar. We squeezed past the noses and heels of fidgety horses, and circumnavigated their attendant groups of critics, while half-trained brutes in snaffles bolted to nowhere and back again, and whinnying foals ran to and fro in search of their mothers.

A moderate bank divided the upper from the lower fields, and as every feasible spot in it was commanded by a refusing horse, the choice of a place and moment for crossing it required judgement. I got Philippa across it in safety; Miss Knox, though as capable as any young woman in Ireland of getting over a bank, either on horseback or on her own legs, had to submit to the assistance of Mr. Shute, and the laws of dynamics decreed that a force sufficient to raise a bow anchor should hoist her seven stone odd to the top of the bank with such speed that she landed half on her knees and half in the arms of her pioneer. A group of portentously quiet men stood near, their eyes on the ground, their hands in their pockets; they were all dressed so much alike that I did not at first notice that Flurry Knox was among them; when I did, I perceived that his eyes, instead of being on the ground, were surveying Mr. Shute with that measure of disapproval that he habitually bestowed upon strange men.

"You're later than I thought you'd be," he said. "I have a horse half-bought for Mrs. Yeates. It's that old mare of Bobby Bennett's; she makes a little noise, but she's a good mare, and you couldn't throw her down if you tried. Bobby wants thirty pounds for her, but I think

134

you might get her for less. She's in the hotel stables, and you can see her when you go to lunch."

We moved on towards the rushy bank of the river, and Philippa and Sally Knox seated themselves on a low rock, looking, in their white frocks, as incongruous in that dingy preoccupied assemblage as the dreamy meadow-sweet and purple spires of loosestrife that thronged the river banks. Bernard Shute had been lost in the shifting maze of men and horses, who were, for the most part, galloping with the blind fury of charging bulls; but presently, among a party who seemed to be riding the finish of a race, we descried our friend, and a second or two later he hauled a brown mare to a standstill in front of us.

"The fellow's asking forty-five pounds for her," he said to Miss Sally; "she's a nailer to gallop. I don't think it's too much?"

"Her grandsire was the Mountain Hare," said the owner of the mare, hurrying up to continue her family history, "and he was the grandest horse in the four baronies. He was forty-two years of age when he died, and they waked him the same as ye'd wake a Christian. They had whisky and porther—and bread—and a piper in it."

"Thim Mountain Hare colts is no great things," interrupted Mr. Shute's groom contemptuously. "I seen a colt once that was one of his stock, and if there was forty men and their wives, and they after him with sticks, he wouldn't lep a sod of turf."

"Lep, is it!" ejaculated the owner in a voice shrill with outrage. "You may lead that mare out through the counthry, and there isn't a fence in it that she wouldn't go up to it as indepindent as if she was going to her bed, and your honour's ladyship knows that dam well, Miss Knox."

"You want too much money for her, McCarthy," returned Miss Sally, with her little air of preternatural wisdom.

"God pardon you, Miss Knox! Sure a lady like you

135

knows well that forty-five pounds is no money for that mare. Forty-five pounds!" He laughed. "It'd be as good for me to make her a present to the gentleman all out as take three farthings less for her! She's too grand entirely for a poor farmer like me, and if it wasn't for the long weak family I have, I wouldn't part with her under twice the money."

"Three fine lumps of daughters in America paying his rent for him," commented Flurry in the background. "That's the long weak family!"

Bernard dismounted and slapped the mare's ribs approvingly.

"I haven't had such a gallop since I was at Rio," he said. "What do you think of her, Miss Knox?" Then, without waiting for an answer, "I like her. I think I may as well give him the forty-five and have done with it!"

At these ingenuous words I saw a spasm of anguish cross the countenance of McCarthy, easily interpreted as the first pang of a life-long regret that he had not asked twice the money. Flurry Knox put up an eyebrow and winked at me; Mr. Shute's groom turned away for very shame. Sally Knox laughed with the deplorable levity of nineteen.

Thus, with a brevity absolutely scandalous in the eyes of all beholders, the bargain was concluded.

Flurry strolled up to Philippa, observing an elaborate remoteness from Miss Sally and Mr. Shute.

"I believe I'm selling a horse here myself to-day," he said; "would you like to have a look at him, Mrs. Yeates?"

"Oh, are you selling, Knox?" struck in Bernard, to whose brain the glory of buying a horse had obviously mounted like new wine; "I want another, and I know yours are the right sort."

"Well, as you seem so fond of galloping," said Flurry sardonically, "this one might suit you."

"You don't mean the Moonlighter?" said Miss Knox, looking fixedly at him.

"Supposing I did, have you anything to say against him?" replied Flurry.

Decidedly he was in a very bad temper. Miss Sally shrugged her shoulders, and gave a little shred of a laugh, but said no more.

In a comparatively secluded corner of the field we came upon Moonlighter, sidling and fussing, with flickering ears, his tail tightly tucked in and his strong back humped in a manner that boded little good. Even to my untutored eye, he appeared to be an uncommonly good-looking animal, a well-bred grey, with shoulders that raked back as far as the eye could wish, the true Irish jumping hindquarters, and a showy head and neck; it was obvious that nothing except Michael Hallahane's adroit chucks at his bridle kept him from displaying his jumping powers free of charge. Bernard stared at him in silence; not the pregnant and intimidating silence of the connoisseur, but the tongue-tied muteness of helpless ignorance. His eye for horses had most probably been formed on circus posters, and the advertisements of a well-known embrocation, and Moonlighter approximated in colour and conduct to these models.

"I can see he's a ripping fine horse," he said at length; "I think I should like to try him."

Miss Knox changed countenance perceptibly, and gave a perturbed glance at Flurry. Flurry remained impenetrably unamiable.

"I don't pretend to be a judge of horses," went on Mr. Shute. "I dare say I needn't tell *you* that!" with a very engaging smile at Miss Sally; "but I like this one awfully."

As even Philippa said afterwards, she would not have given herself away like that over buying a reel of cotton.

"Are you quite sure that he's really the sort of horse you want?" said Miss Knox, with rather more colour in her face than usual; "he's only four years old, and he's hardly a finished hunter."

The object of her philanthropy looked rather puzzled. "What! can't he jump?" he said.

137

"Is it jump?" exclaimed Michael Hallahane, unable any longer to contain himself; "is it the horse that jumped five foot of a clothes line in Heffernan's yard, and not a one on his back but himself, and didn't leave so much as the thrack of his hoof on the quilt that was hanging on it!"

"That's about good enough," said Mr. Shute, with his large friendly laugh; "what's your price, Knox? I must have the horse that jumped the quilt! I'd like to try him, if you don't mind. There are some jolly-looking banks over there."

"My price is a hundred sovereigns," said Flurry; "you can try him if you like."

"Oh don't!" cried Sally impulsively; but Bernard's foot was already in the stirrup. "I call it disgraceful!" I heard her say in a low voice to her kinsman—"you know he can't ride."

The kinsman permitted himself a malign smile. "That's his look-out," he said.

Perhaps the unexpected docility with which Moonlighter allowed himself to be manœuvred through the crowd was due to Bernard's thirteen stone; at all events, his progress through a gate into the next field was unexceptionable. Bernard, however, had no idea of encouraging this tranquillity. He had come out to gallop, and without further ceremony he drove his heels into Moonlighter's side, and took the consequences in the shape of a very fine and able buck. How he remained within even visiting distance of the saddle it is impossible to explain; perhaps his early experience in the rigging stood him in good stead in the matter of hanging on by his hands; but, however preserved, he did remain, and went away down the field at what he himself subsequently described as "the rate of knots".

Flurry flung away his cigarette and ran to a point of better observation. We all ran, including Michael Hallahane and various onlookers, and were in time to see Mr. Shute charging the least advantageous spot in a hollow-faced furzy bank. Nothing but the grey horse's extreme activity got the pair safely over; he jumped it on a slant, changed feet in the heart of a furze-bush and was lost to view. In what relative positions Bernard and his steed alighted was to us a matter of conjecture; when we caught sight of them again, Moonlighter was running away, with his rider still on his back, while the slope of the ground lent wings to his flight.

"That young gentleman will be apt to be killed," said Michael Hallahane with composure, not to say enjoyment.

"He'll be into the long bog with him pretty soon," said Flurry, his keen eye tracking the fugitive.

"Oh!—I thought he was off that time!" exclaimed Miss Sally, with a gasp in which consternation and amusement were blended. "There! He *is* into the bog!"

It did not take us long to arrive at the scene of disaster, to which, as to a dog-fight, other foot-runners were already hurrying, and on our arrival we found things looking remarkably unpleasant for Mr. Shute and Moonlighter. The latter was sunk to his withers in the sheet of black slime into which he had stampeded; the former, submerged to the waist three yards further away in the bog, was trying to drag himself towards firm ground by the aid of tussocks of wiry grass.

"Hit him!" shouted Flurry. "Hit him! he'll sink if he stops there!"

Mr. Shute turned on his adviser a face streaming with black mud, out of which his brown eyes and white teeth gleamed with undaunted cheerfulness.

"All jolly fine," he called back; "if I let go this grass I'll sink too!"

A shout of laughter from the male portion of the spectators sympathetically greeted this announcement, and a dozen equally futile methods of escape were suggested. Among those who had joined us was, fortunately, one of the many boys who pervaded the fair selling halters, and, by means of several of these knotted together, a line of communication was established. Moonlighter, who had fallen into the state of inane

139

stupor in which horses in his plight so often indulge, was roused to activity by showers of stones and imprecations but faintly chastened by the presence of ladies. Bernard, hanging on to his tail, belaboured him with a cane, and, finally, the reins proving good, the task of towing the victims ashore was achieved.

"He's mine, Knox, you know," were Mr. Shute's first words as he scrambled to his feet, "he's the best horse I ever got across—worth twice the money!"

"Faith, he's aisy plased!" remarked a bystander.

"Oh, do go and borrow some dry clothes," interposed Philippa practically; "surely there must be some-one——"

"There's a shop in the town where he can strip a peg for 13s. 9d.," said Flurry grimly; "I wouldn't care myself about the clothes you'd borrow here!"

The morning sun shone jovially upon Moonlighter and his rider, caking momently the black bog stuff with which both were coated, and as the group disintegrated, and we turned to go back, every man present was pleasurably aware that the buttons of Mr. Shute's riding breeches had burst at the knees, causing a large triangular hiatus above his gaiter.

"Well," said Flurry conclusively to me as we retraced our steps, "I always thought the fellow was a fool, but I never thought he was such a damned fool."

It seemed an interminable time since breakfast when our party, somewhat shattered by the stirring events of the morning, found itself gathered in an upstairs room at the Royal Hotel, waiting for a meal that had been ordained two hours before. The air was charged with the mingled odours of boiling cabbage and frying mutton; we affected to speak of them with disgust, but our souls yearned to them. Female ministrants, with rustling skirts and pounding feet, raced along the passages with trays that were never for us, and opening doors released roaring gusts of conversation, blended with the clatter of knives and forks, and still we starved. Even the ginger-coloured check suit, lately labelled "The Sandringham.

140

Wonderful value, 16s. 9d." in the window of Drum-curran's leading mart, and now displayed upon Mr. Shute's all too lengthy limbs, had lost its power to charm.

"Oh, don't tear that bell quite by the roots, Bernard," said his sister, from the heart of a lamentable yawn. "I dare say it only amuses them when we ring, but it may remind them that we are still alive. Major Yeates, do you or do you not regret the pigs' feet?"

"More than I can express", I said, turning from the window, where I had been looking down at the endless succession of horses' backs and men's hats, moving in two opposing currents in the street below. "I dare say if we talk about them for a little we shall feel ill, and that will be better than nothing."

At this juncture, however, a heavy-laden tray thumped against the door, and our repast was borne into the room by a hot young woman in creaking boots, who hoarsely explained that what kept her was waiting on the potatoes, and that the ould pan that was in it was playing Puck with the beefsteaks.

"Well," said Miss Shute, as she began to try con-clusions between a blunt knife and a bullet-proof mutton chop, "I never lived in the country before, but I have always been given to understand that the village inn was one of its chief attractions." She delicately moved the potato dish so as to cover the traces of a bygone egg, and her glance lingered on the flies that dragged their way across a melting mound of salt butter. "I like local colour, but I don't care about it on the tablecloth."

"Well, I'm feeling quite anxious about Irish country hotels now," said Bernard; "they're getting so civilized and respectable. After all, when you go back to England no one cares a pin to hear that you've been done up to the knocker. That don't amuse them a bit. But all my friends are as pleased as anything when I tell them of the pothouse where I slept in my clothes rather than face the sheets, or how, when I complained to the landlady next day, she said, 'Cock ye up! Wasn't it his Reverence the Dean of Kilcoe had them last!'"

We smiled wanly; what I chiefly felt was respect for any hungry man who could jest in presence of such a meal.

"All this time my hunter hasn't been bought," said Philippa presently, leaning back in her chair, and abandoning the unequal contest with her beefsteak. "Who is Bobby Bennett? Will his horse carry a lady?"

Sally Knox looked at me and began to laugh.

"You should ask Major Yeates about Bobby Bennett," she said.

Confound Miss Sally! It had never seemed worth while to tell Philippa all that story about my doing up Miss Bobby Bennett's hair, and I sank my face in my tumbler of stagnant whisky-and-soda to conceal the colour that suddenly adorned it. Any intelligent man will understand that it was a situation calculated to amuse the ungodly, but without any real fun in it. I explained Miss Bennett as briefly as possible, and at all the more critical points Miss Sally's hazel-green eyes roamed slowly and mercilessly towards me.

"You haven't told Mrs. Yeates that she's one of the greatest horsecopers in the country," she said, when I had got through somehow; "she can sell you a very good horse sometimes, and a very bad one too, if she gets the chance."

"No one will ever explain to me," said Miss Shute, scanning us all with her dark, half-amused, and wholly sophisticated eyes, "why horse coping is more respectable than cheating at cards. I rather respect people who cheat at cards; if everyone did, it would make whist so much more cheerful; but there is no forgiveness for dealing yourself the right card, and there is no condemnation for dealing your neighbour a very wrong horse!"

"Your neighbour is supposed to be able to take care of himself," said Bernard.

"Well, why doesn't that apply to card-players?"

returned his sister; "are they all in a state of helpless innocence?"

"I'm helplessly innocent," announced Philippa, "so I hope Miss Bennett won't deal me a wrong horse."

"Oh, her mare is one of the right ones," said Miss Sally: "she's a lovely jumper, and her manners are the very best."

The door opened and Flurry Knox put in his head. "Bobby Bennett's downstairs," he said to me mysteriously.

I got up, not without consciousness of Miss Sally's eye, and prepared to follow him. "You'd better come too, Mrs. Yeates, to keep an eye on him. Don't let him give her more than thirty, and if he gives that she should return him two sovereigns." This last injunction was bestowed in a whisper as we descended the stairs.

Miss Bennett was in the crowded yard of the hotel, looking handsome and overdressed, and she greeted me with just that touch of Auld Lang Syne in her manner that I could best have dispensed with. I turned to the business in hand without delay. The brown mare was led forth from the stable and paraded for our benefit; she was one of those inconspicuous, meritorious animals about whom there seems nothing particular to say, and I felt legs and looked hard at her hocks, and was not much the wiser.

"It's no use my saying she doesn't make a noise," said Miss Bobby, "because everyone in the country will tell you she does. You can have a vet. if you like, and that's the only fault he can find with her. But if Mrs. Yeates hasn't hunted before now, I'll guarantee Cruiskeen as just the thing for her. She's really safe and confidential. My little brother Georgie has hunted her—*you* remember Georgie, Major Yeates?—the night of the ball, you know—and he's only eleven. Mr. Knox can tell you what sort she is."

"Oh, she's a grand mare," said Mr. Knox, thus appealed to; "you'd hear her coming three fields off like a German band!"

143

"And well for you if you could keep within three fields of her!" retorted Miss Bennett. "At all events, she's not like the hunter you sold Uncle, that used to kick the stars as soon as I put my foot in the stirrup!"

" 'Twas the size of the foot frightened him," said Flurry.

"Do you know how Uncle cured him?" said Miss Bennett, turning her back on her adversary; "he had him tied head and tail across the yard gate, and every man that came in had to get over his back!"

"That's no bad one!" said Flurry.

Philippa looked from one to the other in bewilderment, while the badinage continued, swift and unsmiling, as became two hierarchs of horse-dealing; it went on at intervals for the next ten minutes, and at the end of that time I had bought the mare for thirty pounds. As Miss Bennett said nothing about giving me back two of them, I had not the nerve to suggest it.

After this Flurry and Miss Bennett went away, and were swallowed up in the fair; we returned to our friends upstairs, and began to arrange about getting home. This, among other difficulties, involved the tracking and capture of the Shutes' groom, and took so long that it necessitated tea. Bernard and I had settled to ride our new purchases home, and the groom was to drive the wagonette—an alteration ardently furthered by Miss Shute. The afternoon was well advanced when Bernard and I struggled through the turmoil of the hotel yard in search of our horses, and, the hotel hostler being nowhere to be found, the Shutes' man saddled our animals for us, and then withdrew, to grapple single-handed with the bays in the calf-house.

"Good business for me, that Knox is sending the grey horse home for me," remarked Bernard, as his new mare followed him tractably out of the stall. "He'd have been rather a handful in this hole of a place."

He shoved his way out of the yard in front of me, seemingly quite comfortable and at home upon the descendant of the Mountain Hare, and I followed as

144

closely as drunken carmen and shafts of erratic carts would permit. Cruiskeen evinced a decided tendency to turn to the right on leaving the yard, but she took my leftward tug in good part, and we moved on through the streets of Drumcurran with a dignity that was only impaired by the irrepressible determination of Mr. Shute's new trousers to run up his leg. It was a trifle disappointing that Cruiskeen should carry her nose in the air like a camel, but I set it down to my own bad hands, and to that cause I also imputed her frequent desire to stop, a desire that appeared to coincide with every fourth or fifth public-house on the line of march. Indeed, at the last corner before we left the town, Miss Bennett's mare and I had a serious difference of opinion, in the course of which she mounted the pavement and remained planted in front of a very disreputable public-house, whose owner had been before me several times for various infringements of the Licensing Acts. Bernard and the corner-boys were of course much pleased; I inwardly resolved to let Miss Bennett know how her groom occupied his time in Drumcurran.

We got out into the calm of the country roads without further incident, and I there discovered that Cruiskeen was possessed of a dromedary swiftness in trotting, that the action was about as comfortable as the dromedary's, and that it was extremely difficult to moderate the pace.

"I say! This is something like going!" said Bernard, cantering hard beside me with slack rein and every appearance of happiness. "Do you mean to keep it up all the way?"

"You'd better ask this devil," I replied, hauling on the futile ring snaffle. "Miss Bennett must have an arm like a prize-fighter. If this is what she calls confidential, I don't want her confidences."

After another half-mile, during which I cursed Flurry Knox, and registered a vow that Philippa should ride Cruiskeen in a cavalry bit, we reached the cross-roads at which Bernard's way parted from mine. Another difference of opinion between my wife's hunter and me here took place, this time on the subject of parting from our companion, and I experienced that peculiar inward sinking that accompanies the birth of the conviction one has been stuck. There were still some eight miles between me and home, but I had at least the consolation of knowing that the brown mare would easily cover it in forty minutes. But in this also disappointment awaited me. Dropping her head to about the level of her knees, the mare subsided into a walk as slow as that of the slowest cow, and very similar in general style. In this manner I progressed for a further mile, breathing forth, like Saint Paul, threatenings and slaughters against Bobby Bennett and all her confederates; and then the idea occurred to me that many really first-class hunters were very poor hacks. I consoled myself with this for a further period, and presently an opportunity for testing it presented itself. The road made a long loop round the flank of a hill, and it was possible to save half a mile or so by getting into the fields. It was a short cut I had often taken on the Quaker, and it involved nothing more serious than a couple of low stone "gaps" and an infantine bank. I turned Cruiskeen at the first of these. She was evidently surprised. Being in an excessively bad temper, I beat her in a way that surprised her even more, and she jumped the stones precipitately and with an ease that showed she knew quite well what she was about. I vented some further emotion upon her by the convenient medium of my cane, and galloped her across the field and over the bank, which, as they say in these parts, she "fled" without putting an iron on it. It was not the right way to jump it, but it was inspiriting, and when she had disposed of the next gap without hesitation my waning confidence in Miss Bennett began to revive. I cantered over the ridge of the hill, and down it towards the cottage near which I was accustomed to get out on to the road again. As I neared my wonted opening in the fence, I saw that it had been filled by a stout pole, well fixed into the bank at each end, but not more than three feet high. Cruiskeen pricked her ears at it with intelligence; I trotted her at it, and gave her a whack.

Ages afterwards there was someone speaking on the blurred edge of a dream that I was dreaming about nothing in particular. I went on dreaming, and was impressed by the shape of a fat jug, mottled white and blue, that intruded itself painfully, and I again heard voices, very urgent and full of effort, but quite outside any concern of mine.

I also made an effort of some kind; I was doing my very best to be good and polite, but I was dreaming in a place that whirred, and was engrossing, and daylight was cold and let in some unknown unpleasantness. For that time the dream got the better of the daylight, and then, *apropos* of nothing, I was standing up in a house with someone's arm round me; the mottled jug was there, so was the unpleasantness, and I was talking with most careful, old-world politeness.

"Sit down now, you're all right," said Miss Bobby Bennett, who was mopping my face with a handkerchief dipped in the jug.

I perceived that I was asking what had happened.

"She fell over the stick with you," said Miss Bennett; "the dirty brute!"

With another great effort I hooked myself on to the march of events, as a truck is dragged out of a siding and hooked to a train.

"Oh, the Lord save us!" said a grey-haired woman who held the jug, "ye're desthroyed entirely asthore! Oh, glory be to the merciful will of God, me heart lepped across me shesht when I seen him undher the horse!"

"Go out and see if the trap's coming," said Miss Bennett; "he should have found the doctor by this." She stared very closely at my face, and seemed to find it easier to talk in short sentences.

"We must get those cuts looking better before Mrs. Yeates comes."

After an interval, during which unexpected places in

my head ached from the cold water, the desire to be polite and coherent again came upon me.

"I am sure it was not your mare's fault," I said.

Miss Bennett laughed a very little. I was glad to see her laugh; it had struck me her face was strangely haggard and frightened.

"Well, of course it wasn't poor Cruiskeen's fault," she said. "She's nearly home with Mr. Shute by now. That's why I came after you!"

"Mr. Shute!" I said; "wasn't he at the fair that day?"

"He was," answered Miss Bobby, looking at me with very compassionate eyes; "you and he got on each other's horses by mistake at the hotel, and you got the worst of the exchange!"

"Oh!" I said, without even trying to understand.

"He's here within, your honour's ladyship, Mrs. Yeates, ma'am," shouted the grey-haired woman at the door; "don't be unaisy, achudth; he's doing fine. Sure, I'm telling Miss Binnitt if she was his wife itself, she couldn't give him better care!"

The grey-haired woman laughed.

HOLY ISLAND

For three days of November a white fog stood motionless over the country. All day and all night smothered booms and bangs away to the south-west told that the Fastnet gun was hard at work, and the sirens of the American liners uplifted their monstrous female voices as they felt their way along the coast of Cork. On the third afternoon the wind began to whine about the windows of Shreelane, and the barometer fell like a stone. At 11 p.m. the storm rushed upon us with the roar and the suddenness of a train; the chimneys bellowed, the tall old house quivered, and the yelling wind drove against it, as a man puts his shoulder against a door to burst it in.

We none of us got much sleep, and if Mrs. Cadogan is to be believed—which experience assures me she is not—she spent the night in devotional exercises, and in ministering to the panic-stricken kitchen-maid by the light of a blessed candle. All that day the storm screamed on, dry-eyed; at nightfall the rain began, and the next morning, which happened to be Sunday, every servant in the house was a messenger of Job, laden with tales of leakages, floods, and fallen trees, and inflated with the ill-concealed glory of their kind in evil tidings. To Peter Cadogan, who had been to early Mass, was reserved the crowning satisfaction of reporting that a big vessel had gone on the rocks at Yokahn Point the evening before, and was breaking up fast; it was rumoured that the crew had got ashore, but this feature, being favourable and uninteresting, was kept as much as possible in the background. Mrs. Cadogan, who had been to America in an ocean liner, became at once the latest authority on shipwrecks, and was of opinion that

149

"whoever would be dhrownded, it wouldn't be thim lads o' sailors. Sure wasn't there the greatest storm ever was in it the time meself was on the say, and what'd thim fellows do but to put us below entirely in the ship, and close down the doors on us, the way theirselves'd leg it when we'd be dhrownding!"

This view of the position was so startlingly novel that Philippa withdrew suddenly from the task of ordering dinner, and fell up the kitchen stairs in unsuitable laughter. Philippa has not the most rudimentary capacity for keeping her countenance.

That afternoon I was wrapped in the slumber, balmiest and most profound, that follows on a wet Sunday luncheon, when Murray, our D.I. of police, drove up in uniform, and came into the house on the top of a gust that set every door banging and every picture dancing on the walls. He looked as if his eyes had been blown out of his head, and he wanted something to eat very badly.

"I've been down at the wreck since ten o'clock this morning," he said, "waiting for her to break up, and once she does there'll be trouble. She's an American ship, and she's full up with rum, and bacon, and butter, and all sorts. Bosanquet is there with all his coastguards, and there are five hundred country people on the strand at this moment, waiting for the fun to begin. I've got ten of my fellows there, and I wish I had as many more. You'd better come back with me, Yeates, we may want the Riot Act before all's done!"

The heavy rain had ceased, but it seemed as if it had fed the wind instead of calming it, and when Murray and I drove out of Shreelane, the whole dirty sky was moving, full sailed, in from the south-west, and the telegraph wires were hanging in a loop from the post outside the gate. Nothing except a Skebawn car-horse would have faced the whooping charges of the wind that came at us across Corran Lake; stimulated mysteriously by whistles from the driver, Murray's yellow hireling pounded woodenly along against the blast, till the smell of the torn sea-weed was borne upon it, and we saw the Atlantic waves come towering into the bay of Tralagough.

The ship was, or had been, a three-masted barque; two of her masts were gone, and her bows stood high out of water on the reef that forms one of the shark-like jaws of the bay. The long strand was crowded with black groups of people, from the bank of heavy shingle that had been hurled over on to the road, down to the slope where the waves pitched themselves and climbed and fought and tore the gravel back with them, as though they had dug their fingers in. The people were nearly all men dressed solemnly and hideously in their Sunday clothes; most of them had come straight from Mass without any dinner, true to that Irish instinct that places its fun before its food. That the wreck was regarded as a spree of the largest kind was sufficiently obvious. Our car pulled up at a public-house that stood askew between the road and the shingle; it was humming with those whom Irish publicans are pleased to call "Bona feeds", and sundry of the same class were clustered round the door. Under the wall of the lee-side was seated a bagpiper, droning out "The Irish Washer-woman" with nodding head and tapping heel, and a very young man was cutting a few steps of a jig for the delectation of a group of girls.

So far Murray's constabulary had done nothing but exhibit their imposing chest measurement and spotless uniforms to the Atlantic, and Bosanquet's coastguards had only salvaged some spars, the débris of a boat, and a dead sheep, but their time was coming. As we stumbled down over the shingle, battered by the wind and pelted by clots of foam, someone beside me shouted, "She's gone!" A hill of water had smothered the wreck, and when it fell from her again nothing was left but the bows, with the bowsprit hanging from them in a tangle of rigging. The clouds, bronzed by an unseen sunset, hung low over her; in that greedy pack of waves, with

151

the remorseless rocks above and below her, she seemed the most lonely and tormented of creatures.

About half an hour afterwards the cargo began to come ashore on the top of the rising tide. Barrels were plunging and diving in the trough of the waves, like a school of porpoises; they were pitched up the beach in waist-deep rushes of foam; they rolled down again, and were swung up and shouldered by the next wave, playing a kind of Tom Tiddler's ground with the coastguards. Some of the barrels were big and dangerous, some were small and nimble like young pigs, and the bluejackets were up to their middles as their prey dodged and ducked, and the police lined out along the beach to keep back the people. Ten men of the R.I.C. can do a great deal, but they cannot be in more than twenty or thirty places at the same instant; therefore they could hardly cope with a scattered and extremely active mob of four or five hundred, many of whom had taken advantage of their privileges as "bona-fide travellers", and all of whom were determined on getting at the rum.

As the dusk fell the thing got more and more out of hand; the people had found out that the big puncheons held the rum, and had succeeded in capturing one. In the twinkling of an eye it was broached, and fifty backs were shoving round it like a football scrummage. I have heard many rows in my time: I have seen two Irish regiments—one of them Militia—at each other's throats in Fermoy barracks; I have heard Philippa's water spaniel and two fox-terriers hunting a strange cat around the dairy; but never have I known such untrammelled bedlam as that which yelled round the rum-casks on Tralagough strand. For it was soon not a question of one broached cask, or even of two. The barrels were coming in fast, so that it was impossible for the representatives of law and order to keep on any sort of terms with them. The people, shouting with laughter, stove in the casks, and drank rum at 34 degrees above proof, out of their hands, out of their hats, out of their boots. Women came fluttering over the hillsides through the

152

twilight, carrying jugs, milk-pails, anything that would hold the liquor; I saw one of them, roaring with laughter, tilt a filthy zinc bucket to an old man's lips.

With the darkness came anarchy. The rising tide brought more and yet more booty: great spars came lunging in on top of the waves, mixed up with cabin furniture, seamen's chests, and the black and slippery barrels, and the country people continued to flock in, and the drinking became more and more unbridled. Murray sent for more men and a doctor, and we slaved on hopelessly in the dark, collaring half-drunken men, shoving pig-headed casks up hills of shingle, hustling in among groups of roaring drinkers—we rescued perhaps one barrel in half a dozen. I began to know that there were men there who were not drunk and were not idle; I was also aware, as the strenuous hours of darkness passed, of an occasional rumble of cart wheels on the road. It was evident that the casks which were broached were the least part of the looting, but even they were beyond our control. The most that Bosanquet, Murray and I could do was to concentrate our forces on the casks that had been secured, and to organize charges upon the swilling crowds in order to upset the casks that they had broached. Already men and boys were lying about, limp as leeches, motionless as the dead.

"They'll kill themselves before morning, at this rate!" shouted Murray to me. "They're drinking it by the quart! Here's another barrel; come on!"

We rallied our small forces, and after a brief but furious struggle succeeded in capsizing it. It poured away in a flood over the stones, over the prostrate figures that sprawled on them, and a howl of reproach followed.

"If ye pour away any more o' that, Major," said an unctuous voice in my ear, "ye'll intoxicate the stones and they'll be getting up and knocking us down!"

I had been aware of a fat shoulder next to mine in the throng as we heaved the puncheon over, and I now recognized the ponderous wit and Falstaffian figure of

153

Mr. James Canty, a noted member of the Skebawn Board of Guardians, and the owner of a large farm near at hand.

"I never saw worse work on this strand," he went on. "I considher these debaucheries a disgrace to the counthry."

Mr. Canty was famous as an orator, and I presume that it was from long practice among his fellow P.L.G.'s that he was able, without aparent exertion, to out-shout the storm.

At this juncture the long-awaited reinforcements arrived, and along with them came Dr. Jerome Hickey, armed with a black bag. Having mentioned that the bag contained a pump—not one of the common or garden variety—and that no pump on board a foundering ship had more arduous labours to perform, I prefer to pass to other themes. The wreck, which had at first appeared to be as inexhaustible and as variously stocked as that in the *Swiss Family Robinson,* was beginning to fail in its supply. The crowd were by this time for the most part incapable from drink, and the fresh contingent of police tackled their work with some prospect of success by the light of a tar barrel, contributed by the owner of the public-house. At about the same time I began to be aware that I was aching with fatigue, that my clothes hung heavy and soaked upon me, that my face was stiff with the salt spray and the bitter wind, and that it was two hours past dinner-time. The possibility of fried salt herrings and hot whisky and water at the public-house rose dazzlingly before my mind, when Mr. Canty again crossed my path.

"In my opinion ye have the whole cargo under conthrol now, Major," he said, "and the police and the sailors should be able to account for it all now by the help of the light. Wasn't I the finished fool that I didn't think to send up to my house for a tar barrel before now! Well—we're all foolish sometimes! But indeed it's time for us to give over, and that's what I'm after saying to

154

the Captain and Mr. Murray. You're exhausted now the three of ye, and if I might make so bold, I'd suggest that ye'd come up to my little place and have what'd warm ye before ye'd go home. It's only a few perches up the road."

The tide had turned, the rain had begun again, and the tar barrel illumined the fact that Dr. Hickey's dreadful duties alone were pressing. We held a council and finally followed Mr. Canty, picking our way through wreckage of all kinds, including the human variety. Near the the public-house I stumbled over something that was soft and had a squeak in it; it was the piper, with his head and shoulders in an overturned rum-barrel, and the bagpipes still under his arm.

I knew the outward appearance of Mr. Canty's house very well. It was a typical southern farmhouse, with dirty whitewashed walls, a slated roof, and small, hermetically sealed windows staring at the morass of manure which constituted the yard. We followed Mr. Canty up the filthy lane that led to it, picked our way round vague and squelching spurts of the manure heap, and were finally led through the kitchen into a stifling best parlour. Mrs. Canty, a vast and slatternly matron, had evidently made preparations for us; there was a newly lighted fire pouring flame up the chimney from layers of bogwood, there were whisky and brandy on the table, and a plateful of biscuits sugared in white and pink. Upon our hostess was a black silk dress which indifferently concealed the fact that she was short of boot-laces, and that the boots themselves had made many excursions to the yard and none to the blacking-bottle. Her manners, however, were admirable, and while I live I shall not forget her potato cakes. They came in hot and hot from a pot-oven, they were speckled with caraway seeds, they swam in salt butter, and we ate them shamelessly and greasily, and washed them down with hot whisky and water; I knew to a nicety how ill I should be next day, and heeded not.

155

"Well, gentlemen," remarked Mr. Canty later on, in his best Board of Guardians' manner, "I've seen many wrecks between this and the Mizen Head, but I never witnessed a scene of more disgraceful ex-cess than what was in it to-night."

"Hear, hear!" murmured Bosanquet with unseemly levity.

"I should say," went on Mr. Canty, " there was at one time to-night upwards of one hundhred men dead dhrunk on the strand, or anyway so dhrunk that if they'd attempt to spake they'd foam at the mouth."

"The craytures!" interjected Mrs. Canty sympathetically.

"But if they're dhrunk to-day," continued our host, "it's nothing to what they'll be to-morrow and afther to-morrow, and it won't be on the strand they'll be dhrinkin' it."

"Why, where will it be?" said Bosanquet, with his disconcerting English way of asking a point-blank question.

Mr. Canty passed his hand over his red cheeks.

"There'll be plenty asking that before all's said and done, Captain," he said, with a compassionate smile, "and there'll be plenty that could give the answer if they'll like, but by dam I don't think ye'll be apt to get much out of the Yokahn boys!"

"The Lord save us, 'twould be better to keep out from the likes o' thim!" put in Mrs. Canty, sliding a fresh avalanche of potato cakes on to the dish; "didn't they pull the clothes off the gauger and pour potheen down his throath till he ran screeching through the streets o' Skebawn!"

James Canty chuckled.

"I remember there was a wreck here one time, and the undherwriters put me in charge of the cargo. Brandy it was—cases of the best Frinch brandy. The people had a song about it, what's this the first verse was—

156

One night to the rocks of Yokahn
Came the barque *Isabella* so dandy,
To pieces she went before dawn,
Herself and her cargo of brandy.
And all met a wathery grave
Excepting the vessel's car*pen*ther,
Poor fellow, so far from his home."

Mr. Canty chanted these touching lines in a tuneful if wheezy tenor. "Well, gentlemen, we're all friends here," he continued, "and it's no harm to mention that this man below at the public-house came askin' me would I let him have some of it for a consideration. 'Sullivan,' says I to him, 'if ye ran down gold in a cup in place of the brandy, I wouldn't give it to you. Of coorse,' says I, 'I'm not sayin' but that if a bottle was to get a crack of a stick, and it to be broken, and a man to drink a glass out of it, that would be no more than an accident.' 'That's no good to me,' says he, 'but if I had twelve gallons of that brandy in Cork,' says he, 'by the Holy German!' says he, saying an awful curse, 'I'd sell twenty-five out of it!' Well, indeed, it was true for him; it was grand stuff. As the saying is, it would make a horse out of a cow!"

"It appears to be a handy sort of place for keeping a pub," said Bosanquet.

"Shut to the door, Margaret," said Mr. Canty with elaborate caution. "It'd be a queer place that wouldn't be handy for Sullivan!"

A further tale of great length was in progress when Dr. Hickey's Mephistophelian nose was poked into the best parlour.

"Hullo, Hickey! Pumped out, eh?" said Murray.

"If I am, there's plenty more like me," replied the Doctor enigmatically, "and some of them three times over! James, did these gentlemen leave you a drop of anything that you'd offer me?"

"Maybe ye'd like a glass of rum, Doctor?", said Mr. Canty with a wink at his other guests.

157

Dr. Hickey shuddered.

I had next morning precisely the kind of mouth that I had anticipated, and it being my duty to spend the better part of the day administering justice in Skebawn, I received from Mr. Flurry Knox and other of my brother magistrates precisely the class of condolences on my "Monday head" that I found least amusing. It was unavailing to point out the resemblance between hot potato cakes and molten lead, or to dilate on their equal power of solidifying; the collective wisdom of the Bench decided that I was suffering from contraband rum, and rejoiced over me accordingly.

During the next three weeks Murray and Bosanquet put in a time only to be equalled by that of the heroes in detective romances. They began by acting on the hint offered by Mr. Canty, and were rewarded by finding eight barrels of bacon and three casks of rum in the heart of Mr. Sullivan's turf rick, placed there, so Mr. Sullivan explained with much detail, by enemies, with the object of getting his licence taken away. They stabbed potato gardens with crowbars to find the buried barrels, they explored the chimneys, they raided the cow-houses; and in every possible and impossible place they found some of the cargo of the late barque, *John D. Williams*, and, as the sympathetic Mr. Canty said, "For as much as they found, they left five times as much afther them!"

It was a wet, lingering autumn, but towards the end of November the rain dried up, the weather stiffened, and a week of light frosts and blue skies was offered as a tardy apology. Philippa possesses, in common with many of her sex, an inappeasable passion for picnics, and her ingenuity for devising occasions for them is only equalled by her gift for enduring their rigours. I have seen her tackle a moist chicken pie with a splinter of slate and my stylograph pen. I have known her to take the tea-basket to an auction, and make tea in a four-wheeled inside car, regardless of the fact that it was coming under the hammer in ten minutes, and that the kettle took twenty minutes to boil. It will therefore be readily understood that the rare occasions when I was free to go out with a gun were not allowed to pass uncelebrated by the tea-basket.

"You'd much better shoot Corran Lake to-morrow," my wife said to me one brilliant afternoon. "We could send the punt over, and I could meet you on Holy Island with——"

The rest of the sentence was concerned with ways, means, and the tea-basket, and need not be recorded.

I had taken the shooting of a long snipe bog that trailed from Corran Lake almost to the sea at Trala-gough, and it was my custom to begin to shoot from the seaward end of it, and finally to work round the lake after duck.

To-morrow proved a heavenly morning, touched with frost, gilt with sun. I started early, and the mists were still smoking up from the calm, all-reflecting lake, as the Quaker stepped out along the level road, smashing the thin ice on the puddles with his big feet. Behind the calves of my legs sat Maria, Philippa's brown Irish water-spaniel, assiduously licking the barrels of my gun, as was her custom when the ecstasy of going out shoot-ing was hers. Maria had been given to Philippa as a wedding-present, and since then it had been my wife's ambition that she should conform to the Beth Gelert standard of being "a lamb at home, a lion in the chase". Maria did pretty well as a lion: she hunted all dogs unmistakably smaller than herself, and whenever it was reasonably possible to do so she devoured the spoils of the chase, notably jack snipe. It was as a lamb that she failed; objectionable as I have no doubt a lamb would be as a domestic pet, it at least would not snatch the cold beef from the luncheon-table, not yet, if banished for its crimes, would it spend the night in scratching the paint off the hall door. Maria bit beggars (who valued their disgusting limbs at five shillings the square inch), she bullied the servants, she concealed ducks' claws and fishes' backbones behind the sofa cushions, and yet, when she laid her brown snout upon my knee, and rolled her blackguard amber eyes upon me, and smote me with her feathered paw, it was impossible to remember her iniquities against her. On shooting mornings Maria ceased to be a buccaneer, a glutton, and a hypocrite. From the moment when I put my gun together her breakfast stood untouched until it suffered the final degradation of being eaten by the cats, and now in the trap she was shivering with excitement, and agonizing in her soul lest she should even yet be left behind.

Slipper met me at the cross-roads from which I had sent back the trap; Slipper, redder in the nose than anything I had ever seen off the stage, very husky as to the voice, and going rather tender on both feet. He informed me that I should have a grand day's shooting, the head-poacher of the locality having, in a most gentle-man-like manner, refrained from exercising his sporting rights the day before, on hearing that I was coming. I understood that this was to be considered as a mark of high personal esteem, and I set to work at the bog with suitable gratitude.

In spite of Mr. O'Driscoll's magnanimity, I had not a very good morning. The snipe were there, but in the perfect stillness of the weather it was impossible to get near them, and five times out of six they were up, flickering and dodging, before I was within shot. Maria became possessed of seven devils and broke away from heel the first time I let off my gun, ranging far and wide in search of the bird I had missed, and putting up every live thing for half a mile round, as she went splashing and steeplechasing through the bog. Slipper expressed his opinion of her behaviour in language more appallingly picturesque and resourceful than any I have heard, even in the Skebawn Court-house; I admit that at the time I thought he spoke very suitably. Before she was recaptured every remaining snipe without earshot was lifted out of it by Slipper's steam-engine whistles and my own infuriated bellows; it was fortunate that the bog

160

was spacious and that there was still a long tract of it ahead, where beyond these voices there was peace.

I worked my way on, jumping treacle-dark drains, floundering through the rustling yellow rushes, circumnavigating the bog-holes, and taking every possible and impossible chance of a shot; by the time I had reached Corran Lake I had got two and a half brace, retrieved by Maria with a perfection that showed what her powers were when the sinuous adroitness of Slipper's woodbine stick were fresh in her mind. But with Maria it was always the unexpected that happened. My last snipe, a jack, fell in the lake, and Maria, bursting through the reeds with kangaroo bounds, and cleaving the water like a torpedo-boat, was a model of all the virtues of her kind. She picked up the bird with a snake-dart of her head, clambered with it on to a tussock, and there, well out of reach of the arm of the law, before our indignant eyes, crunched it twice and bolted it.

"Well," said Slipper complacently, some ten minutes afterwards, "divil such a bating ever I gave a dog since the day Prince killed owld Mrs. Knox's paycock! Prince was a lump of a brown tarrier I had one time, and faith I kicked the toes out o' me owld boots on him before I had the owld lady composed!"

However composing Slipper's methods may have been to Mrs. Knox, they had quite the contrary effect upon a family party of duck that had been lying in the reeds. With horrified outcries they broke into flight, and now were far away on the ethereal mirror of the lake, among strings of their fellows that were floating and quacking in preoccupied indifference to my presence.

A promenade along the lake-shore demonstrated the fact that without a boat there was no more shooting for me; I looked across to the island where, some time ago, I had seen Philippa and her punt arrive. The boat was tied to an overhanging tree, but my wife was nowhere to be seen. I was opening my mouth to give a hail, when I saw her emerge precipitately from among the trees and jump into the boat; Philippa had not in vain spent

161

many summers on the Thames, she was under way in a twinkling, sculled a score of strokes at the rate of a finish, then stopped and stared at the peaceful island. I called to her, and in a minute or two the punt had crackled through the reeds, and shoved its blunt nose ashore at the spot where I was standing.

"Sinclair," said Philippa in awestruck tones, "there's something on the island!"

"I hope there's something to eat there," said I.

"I tell you there *is* something there, alive," said my wife with her eyes as large as saucers; "it's making an awful sound like snoring."

"That's the fairies, ma'am," said Slipper with complete certainty; "sure I known them that seen fairies in that island as thick as the grass, and every one o' them with little caps on them."

Philippa's wide gaze wandered to Slipper's hideous pug face and back to me.

"It was not a human being, Sinclair!" she said combatively, though I had not uttered a word.

Maria had already, after the manner of dogs, leaped, dripping, into the boat: I prepared to follow her example.

"Major," said Slipper in a tragic whisper, "there was a man was a night on that island one time, watching duck, and Thim People cot him, and dhragged him through Hell and through Death, and threw him in the tide——"

"Shove off the boat," I said, too hungry for argument.

Slipper obeyed, throwing his knee over the gunwhale as he did so, and tumbling into the bow; we could have done without him very comfortably, but his devotion was touching.

Holy Island was perhaps a hundred yards long, and about half as many broad; it was covered with trees and a dense growth of rhododendrons; somewhere in the jungle was a ruined fragment of a chapel, smothered in ivy and briars, and in a little glade in the heart of the island there was a holy well. We landed, and it was

obviously a sore humiliation to Philippa that not a
sound was to be heard in the spell-bound silence of the
island, save the cough of a heron on a tree-top.

"It *was* there," she said, with an unconvinced glance
at the surrounding thickets.

"Sure, I'll give a thrawl through the island, ma'am,"
volunteered Slipper with unexpected gallantry, "an' if
it's the divil himself is in it, I'll rattle him into the
lake!"

He went swaggering on his search, shouting, "Hi,
cock!" and whacking the rhododendrons with his stick,
and after an interval returned and assured us that the
island was uninhabited. Being provided with refresh-
ments he again withdrew, and Philippa and Maria and
I fed variously and at great length, and washed the
plates with water from the holy well. I was smoking a
cigarette when we heard Slipper addressing the solitudes
at the farther end of the island, and ending with one
of his whisky-throated crows of laughter.

He presently came lurching towards us through the
bushes, and a glance sufficed to show even Philippa—
who was as incompetent a judge of such matters as many
of her sex—that he was undeniably screwed.

"Major Yeates!" he began, "and Mrs. Major Yeates,
with respex to ye, I'm bastely dhrunk! Me head is light
since the 'fluenzy, and the docthor told me I should
carry a little bottle-een o' sperrits——"

"Look here," I said to Philippa, "I'll take him across,
and bring the boat back for you."

"Sinclair," responded my wife with concentrated
emotion, "I would rather die than stay on this island
alone!"

Slipper was getting drunker every moment, but I
managed to stow him on his back in the bows of the
punt, in which position he at once began to uplift husky
and wandering strains of melody. To this accompaniment we, as Tennyson says,

> moved from the brink like some full-breasted swan,
> That, fluting a wild carol ere her death,
> Ruffles her pure cold plume, and takes the flood
> With swarthy web.

Slipper would certainly have been none the worse for taking the flood, and, as the burden of "Lannigan's Ball" strengthened and spread along the tranquil lake, and the duck once more fled in justifiable consternation, I felt much inclined to make him do so.

We made for the end of the lake that was nearest Shreelane, and, as we rounded the point of the island, another boat presented itself to our view. It contained my late entertainer, Mrs. Canty, seated bulkily in the stern, while a small boy bowed himself between the two heavy oars.

"It's a lovely evening, Major Yeates," she called out. "I'm just going to the island to get some water from the holy well for me daughter that has an impression on her chest. Indeed, I thought 'twas yourself was singing a song for Mrs. Yeates when I heard you coming, but sure Slipper is a great warrant himself for singing."

"May the divil crack the two legs undher ye!" bawled Slipper in acknowledgment of the compliment.

Mrs. Canty laughed genially, and her boat lumbered away.

I shoved Slipper ashore at the nearest point; Philippa and I paddled to the end of the lake, and abandoning the ducks as a bad business, walked home.

A few days afterwards it happened that it was incumbent upon me to attend the funeral of the Roman Catholic Bishop of the diocese. It was what is called in France *un bel enterrement*, with inky flocks of tall-hatted priests, and countless yards of white scarves, and a repast of monumental solidity at the Bishop's residence. The actual interment was to taks place in Cork, and we moved in long and imposing procession to the railway station, where a special train awaited the cortège. My friend Mr. James Canty was among the mourners: an important and active personage, exchanging condolences with the priests, giving directions to porters, and blowing his nose with a trumpeting mournfulness that penetrated all the other noises of the platform. He was condescending enough to notice my presence, and found time to tell me that he had given Mr. Murray "a sure word" with regard to some of *"the wreckage"*—this with deep significance, and a wink of an inflamed and tearful eye. I saw him depart in a first class carriage, and the odour of sanctity; seeing that he was accompanied by seven priests, and that both windows were shut, the latter must have been considerable.

Afterwards, in the town, I met Murray, looking more pleased with himself than I had seen him since he had taken up the unprofitable task of smuggler-hunting.

"Come along and have some lunch," he said, "I've got a real good thing on this time! That chap Canty came to me late last night, and told me that he knew for a fact that the island on Corran Lake was just stiff with barrels of bacon and rum, and that I'd better send out every man I could spare to-day to get them into the town. I sent the men out at eight o'clock this morning; I think I've gone one better than Bosanquet this time!"

I began to realize that Philippa was going to score heavily on the subject of the fairies that she had heard snoring on the island, and I imparted to Murray the leading features of our picnic there.

"Oh, Slipper's been up to his chin in that rum from the first," said Murray. "I'd like to know who his sleeping partner was!"

It was beginning to get dark before the loaded carts of the salvage party came lumbering past Murray's windows and into the yard of the police barrack. We followed them, and in doing so picked up Flurry Knox, who was sauntering in the same direction. It was a good haul, five big casks of rum, and at least a dozen smaller barrels of bacon and butter, and Murray and his Chief

165

Constable smiled seraphically on one another as the spoil was unloaded and stowed in a shed.

"Wouldn't it be as well to see how the butter is keeping?" remarked Flurry, who had been looking on silently, with, as I had noticed, a still and amused eye. "The rim of that small keg there looks as if it had been shifted lately."

The sergeant looked hard at Flurry; he knew as well as most people that a hint from Mr. Knox was usually worth taking. He turned to Murray.

"Will I open it, sir?"

"Oh! open it if Mr. Knox wishes," said Murray, who was not famous for appreciating other people's suggestions.

The keg was opened.

"Funny butter," said Flurry.

The sergeant said nothing. The keg was full of black bog-mould. Another was opened, and another, all with the same result.

"Damnation!" said Murray, suddenly losing his temper. "What's the use of going on with those? Try one of the rum casks."

A few minutes passed in total silence while a tap and a spigot were sent for and applied to the barrel. The sergeant drew off a mugful and put his nose to it with the deliberation of a connoisseur.

"Water, sir," he pronounced, "dirty water, with a small indication of sperrits."

A junior constable tittered explosively, met the light blue glare of Murray's eye, and withered away.

"Perhaps it's holy water!" said I, with a wavering voice.

Murray's glance pinned me like an assegai, and I also faded into the background.

"Well," said Flurry in dulcet tones, "if you want to know where the stuff is that was in those barrels, I can tell you, for I was told it myself half an hour ago. It's gone to Cork with the Bishop by special train!"

166

Mr. Canty was undoubtedly a man of resource. Mrs. Canty had mistakenly credited me with an intelligence equal to her own, and on receiving from Slipper a highly coloured account of how audibly Mr. Canty had slept off his potations, had regarded the secret of Holy Island as having been given away. That night and the two succeeding ones were spent in the transfer of the rum to bottles, and the bottles and the butter to fish boxes; these were, by means of a slight lubrication of the railway underlings, loaded into a truck as "Fresh Fish, Urgent", and attached to the Bishop's funeral train, while the police, decoyed far from the scene of action, were breaking their backs over barrels of bogwater. "I suppose," continued Flurry pleasantly, "you don't know the pub that Canty's brother has in Cork. Well, I do. I'm going to buy some rum there next week, cheap."

"I shall proceed against Canty," said Murray, with fateful calm.

"You won't proceed far," said Flurry; "you'll not get as much evidence out of the whole country as 'd hang a cat."

"Who was your informant?" demanded Murray.

Flurry laughed. "Well, by the time the train was in Cork, yourself and the Major were the only two men in the town that weren't talking about it."

THE POLICY OF THE CLOSED DOOR

The disasters and humiliations that befell me at Drum-curran Fair may yet be remembered. They certainly have not been forgotten in the regions about Skebawn, where the tale of how Bernard Shute and I stole each other's horses has passed into history. The grand-daughter of the Mountain Hare, bought by Mr. Shute with such light-hearted enthusiasm, was restored to that position between the shafts of a cart that she was so well fitted to grace; Moonlighter, his other purchase, spent the two months following on the fair in "favouring" a leg with a strained sinew, and in receiving visits from the local vet., who, however uncertain in his diagnosis of Moonlighter's leg, had accurately estimated the length of Bernard's foot.

Miss Bennett's mare Cruiskeen, alone of the trio, was immediately and thoroughly successful. She went in harness like a hero, she carried Philippa like an elder sister, she was never sick or sorry; as Peter Cadogan summed her up, "That one'd live where another'd die". In her safe keeping Philippa made her *début* with hounds at an uneventful morning's cubbing, with no particular result except that Philippa returned home so stiff that she had to go to bed for a day, and arose more determined than ever to be a fox-hunter.

The opening meet of Mr. Knox's foxhounds was on November the 1st, and on that morning Philippa on Cruiskeen, accompanied by me on the Quaker, set out for Ardmeen Cross, the time-honoured fixture for All Saints' Day. The weather was grey and quiet, and full of all the moist sweetness of an Irish autumn. There had been a great deal of rain during the past month; it had turned the bracken to a purple brown, and had filled the hollows with shining splashes of water. The dead leaves were slippery under foot, and the branches above were thinly decked with yellow where the pallid survivors of summer still clung to their posts. As Philippa and I sedately approached the meet the red coats of Flurry Knox and his whip, Dr. Jerome Hickey, were to be seen on the road at the top of the hill; Cruiskeen put her head in the air, and stared at them with eyes that understood all they portended.

"Sinclair," said my wife hurriedly, as a straggling hound, flogged in by Dr. Hickey, uttered a grievous and melodious howl, "remember, if they find, it's no use to talk to me, for I shan't be able to speak."

I was sufficiently acquainted with Philippa in moments of enthusiasm to exhibit silently the corner of a clean pocket-handkerchief; I have seen her cry when a police constable won a bicycle race in Skebawn; she has wept at hearing Sir Valentine Knox's health drunk with musical honours at a tenants' dinner. It is an amiable custom, but, as she herself admits, it is unbecoming.

An imposing throng, in point of numbers, was gathered at the crossroads, the riders being almost swamped in the crowd of traps, outside cars, bicyclists, and people on foot. The field was an eminently repre- sentative one. The Clan Knox was, as usual, there in force, its more aristocractic members dingily respectable in black coats and tall hats that went impartially to weddings, funerals, and hunts, and, like a horse that is past mark of mouth, were no longer to be identified with any special epoch; there was a humbler squireen element in tweeds and flat-brimmed pot-hats, and a good muster of farmers, men of the spare, black-muzzled, west of Ireland type, on horses that ranged from the cart mare, clipped trace high, to shaggy and leggy three-year-olds, none of them hunters, but all of them able to hunt. Philippa and I worked our way to the heart of things, where was Flurry, seated on his brown mare, in what appeared to be a somewhat moody silence. As we exchanged greetings I was aware that his eye was resting with extreme disfavour upon two approaching figures. I put up my eye-glass, and perceived that one of them was Miss Sally Knox, on a tall grey horse; the other was Mr. Bernard Shute, in all the flawless beauty of his first pink coat, mounted on Stockbroker, a well-known, hard-mouthed, big-jumping bay, recently purchased from Dr. Hickey.

During the languors of a damp autumn the neighbourhood had been much nourished and sustained by the privilege of observing and diagnosing the progress of Mr. Shute's flirtation with Miss Sally Knox. What made it all the more enjoyable for the lookers-on—or most of them—was that, although Bernard's courtship was of the nature of a proclamation from the housetops, Miss Knox's attitude left everything to the imagination. To Flurry Knox the romantic but despicable position of slighted rival was comfortably allotted; his sole sympathizers were Philippa and old Mrs. Knox of Aussolas, but no one knew if he needed sympathizers. Flurry was a man of mystery.

Mr. Shute and Miss Knox approached us rapidly, the latter's mount pulling hard.

"Flurry," I said, "isn't that grey the horse Shute bought from you last July at the fair?"

Flurry did not answer me. His face was as black as thunder. He turned his horse round, cursing two country boys who got in his way, with low and concentrated venom, and began to move forward, followed by the hounds. If his wish was to avoid speaking to Miss Sally it was not to be gratified.

"Good morning, Flurry," she began, sitting close down to Moonlighter's ramping jog as she rode up beside her cousin. "What a hurry you're in! We passed no end of people on the road who won't be here for another ten minutes."

"No more will I," was Mr. Knox's cryptic reply, as he spurred the brown mare into a trot.

Moonlighter made a vigorous but frustrated effort

to buck and indemnified himself by a successful kick at a hound.

"Bother you, Flurry! Can't you walk for a minute?" exclaimed Miss Sally, who looked about as large, in relation to her horse, as the conventional tomtit on a round of beef. "You might have more sense than to crack your whip under this horse's nose! I don't believe you know what horse it is even!"

I was not near enough to catch Flurry's reply.

"Well, if you didn't want him to be lent to me you shouldn't have sold him to Mr. Shute!" retorted Miss Knox, in her clear, provoking little voice.

"I suppose he's afraid to ride him himself," said Flurry, turning his horse in at a gate. "Get ahead there, Jerome, can't you? It's better to put them in at this end than to have everyone riding on top of them!"

Miss Sally's cheeks were still very pink when I came up and began to talk to her, and her grey-green eyes had a look in them like those of an angry kitten.

The riders moved slowly down a rough pasture-field, and took up their position along the brow of Ardmeen covert, into which the hounds had already hurled themselves with their customary contempt for the convenances. Flurry's hounds, true to their nationality, were in the habit of doing the right thing in the wrong way.

Untouched by autumn, the furze bushes of Ardmeen covert were darkly green, save for a golden fleck of blossom here and there, and the glistening grey cobwebs that stretched from spike to spike. The look of the ordinary gorse covert is familiar to most people as a tidy enclosure of an acre or so, filled with low plants of well-educated gorse; not so many will be found who have experience of it as a rocky, sedgy wilderness, half a mile square, garrisoned with brigades of furze bushes, some of them higher than a horse's head, lean, strong, and cunning, like the foxes that breed in them, impenetrable, with their bristling spikes, as a hedge of bayonets. By dint of infinite leisure and obstinate greed, the cattle had made paths for themselves through the

171

bushes to the patches of grass that they hemmed in; their hoof-prints were guides to the explorer, down muddy staircases of rock, and across black intervals of un-plumbed bog. The whole covert slanted gradually down to a small river that raced round three sides of it, and beyond the stream, in agreeable contrast, lay a clean and wholesome country of grass fields and banks.

The hounds drew slowly along and down the hill towards the river, and the riders hung about outside the covert, and tried—I can answer for at least one of them —to decide which was the least odious of the ways through it, in the event of the fox breaking at the far side. Miss Sally took up a position not very far from me, and it was easy to see that she had her hands full with her borrowed mount, on whose temper the delay and suspense were visibly telling. His iron-grey neck was white from the chafing of the reins; had the ground under his feet been red-hot he could hardly have sidled and hopped more uncontrollably; nothing but the most impassioned conjugation of the verb to condemn could have supplied any human equivalent for the manner in which he tore holes in the sedgy grass with a furious fore-foot. Those who were even superficial judges of character gave his heels a liberal allowance of sea-room, and Mr. Shute, who could not be numbered among such, and had, as usual, taken up a position as near Miss Sally as possible, was rewarded by a double knock on his horse's ribs that was a cause of heartless mirth to the lady of his affections.

Not a hound had as yet spoken, but they were forcing their way through the gorse forest and shoving each other jealously aside with growing excitement, and Flurry could be seen at intervals, moving forward in the direction they were indicating. It was at this juncture that the ubiquitous Slipper presented himself at my horse's shoulders.

" 'Tis for the river he's making, Major," he said, with an upward roll of his squinting eyes, that nearly made me seasick. "He's a Castle Knox fox that came in this morning, and ye should get ahead down to the ford!"

A tip from Slipper was not to be neglected, and Philippa and I began a cautious progress through the gorse, followed by Miss Knox as quietly as Moonlighter's nerves would permit.

"Wishful has it!" she exclaimed, as a hound came out into view, uttered a sharp yelp, and drove forward.

"Hark! hark!" roared Flurry with at least three *r*'s reverberating in each "hark"; at the same instant came a holloa from the farther side of the river, and Dr. Hickey's renowned and blood-curdling screech was uplifted at the bottom of the covert. Then babel broke forth, as the hounds, converging from every quarter, flung themselves shrieking on the line. Moonlighter went straight up on his hind-legs, and dropped again with a bound that sent him crushing past Philippa and Cruiskeen; he did it a second time, and was almost on to the tail of the Quaker, whose bulky person was not to be hurried in any emergency.

"Get on if you can, Major Yeates!" called out Sally, steadying the grey as well as she could in the narrow pathway between the great gorse bushes.

Other horses were thundering behind us, men were shouting to each other in similar passages right and left of us, the cry of the hounds filled the air with a kind of delirium. A low wall with a stick laid along it barred the passage in front of me, and the Quaker firmly and immediately decided not to have it until someone else had dislodged the pole.

"Go ahead!" I shouted, squeezing to one side with heroic disregard of the furze bushes and my new tops.

The words were hardly out of my mouth when Moonlighter, mad with thwarted excitement, shot by me, hurtled over the obstacle with extravagant fury, landed twelve feet beyond it on clattering slippery rock, saved himself from falling with an eel-like forward buck on to sedgy ground, and bolted at full speed down the muddy cattle track. There are corners—rocky, most of them—

in that cattle track, that Sally has told me she will remember to her dying day; boggy holes of any depth, ranging between two feet and half-way to Australia, that she says she does not fail to mention in the General Thanksgiving; but at the time they occupied mere fractions of the strenuous seconds in which it was hopeless for her to do anything but try to steer, trust to luck, sit hard down in the saddle and try to stay there. (For my part, I would as soon try to adhere to the horns of a charging bull as to the crutches of a side-saddle, but happily the necessity is not likely to arise.) I saw Flurry Knox a little ahead of her on the same track, jamming his mare into the furze bushes to get out of her way; he shouted something after her about the ford, and started to gallop for it himself by a breakneck short cut.

The hounds were already across the river, and it was obvious that, ford or no ford, Moonlighter's intentions might be simply expressed in the formula "Be with them I will". It was all downhill to the river, and among the furze bushes and rocks there was neither time nor place to turn him. He rushed at it with a shattering slip upon a streak of rock, with a heavy plunge in the deep ground by the brink; it was as bad a take-off for twenty feet of water as could well be found. The grey horse rose out of the boggy stuff with all the impetus that pace and temper could give, but it was not enough. For one instant the twisting, sliding current was under Sally, the next a veil of water sprang up all round her, and Moonlighter was rolling and lurching in the desperate effort to find foothold in the rocky bed of the stream.

I was following at the best pace I could kick out of the Quaker, and saw the water swirl into her lap as her horse rolled to the near-side. She caught the mane to save herself, but he struggled onto his legs again, and came floundering broadside on to the further bank. In three seconds she had got out of the saddle and flung herself at the bank, grasping the rushes, and trying, in spite of the sodden weight of her habit, to drag herself out of the water.

174

At the same instant I saw Flurry and the brown mare dashing through the ford, twenty yards higher up. He was off his horse and beside her with that uncanny quickness that Flurry reserved for moments of emergency, and, catching her by the arms, swung her on to the bank as easily as if she had been the kennel terrier.

"Catch the horse!" she called out, scrambling to her feet.

"Damn the horse!" returned Flurry, in the rage that is so often the reaction from a bad scare.

I turned along the bank and made for the ford; by this time it was full of hustling, splashing riders, through whom Bernard Shute, furiously picking up a bad start, drove a devastating way. He tried to turn his horse down the bank towards Miss Knox, but the hounds were running hard, and, to my intense amusement, Stockbroker refused to abandon the chase, and swept his rider away in the wake of his stable companion, Dr. Hickey's young chestnut. By this time two country boys had, as is usual in such cases, risen from the earth, and fished Moonlighter out of the stream. Miss Sally wound up an acrimonious argument with her cousin by observing that she didn't care what he said, and placing her water-logged boot in his obviously unwilling hand, in a second was again in the saddle, gathering up the wet reins with the trembling, clumsy fingers of a person who is thoroughly chilled and in a violent hurry. She set Moonlighter going, and was away in a moment, galloping him at the first fence at a pace that suited his steeple-chasing ideas.

"Mr. Knox!" panted Philippa, who had by this time joined us, "make her go home!"

"She can go where she likes as far as I'm concerned," responded Mr. Knox, pitching himself on his mare's back and digging in the spurs.

Moonlighter had already glided over the bank in front of us, with a perfunctory flick at it with his heels; Flurry's mare and Cruiskeen jumped it side by side with equal precision. It was a bank of some five feet high;

175

the Quaker charged it enthusiastically, refused it abruptly, and, according to his infuriating custom at such moments, proceeded to tear hurried mouthfuls of grass.

"Will I give him a couple o' belts, your honour?" shouted one of the running accompaniment of country boys. "You will!" said I, with some further remarks to the Quaker that I need not commit to paper.

Swish! Whack! The sound was music in my ears, as the good, remorseless ash sapling bent round the Quaker's dappled hindquarters. At the third stripe he launched both his heels in the operator's face; at the fourth he reared undecidely; at the fifth he bundled over the bank in a manner purged of hesitation.

"Ha!" yelled my assistants, "that'll put the fear o' God in him!" as the Quaker fled headlong after the hunt. "He'll be the betther o' that while he lives!"

Without going quite as far as this, I must admit that for the next half-hour he was astonishingly the better of it.

The Castle Knox fox was making a very pretty line of it over the seven miles that separated him from his home. He headed through a grassy country of Ireland's mild and brilliant green, fenced with sound and buxom banks, enlivened by stone walls, uncompromised by the presence of gates, and yet comfortably laced with lanes for the furtherance of those who had laid to heart Wolsey's valuable advice: "Fling away ambition; by that sin fell the angels." The flotsam and jetsam of the hunt pervaded the landscape: standing on one long bank, three dismounted farmers flogged away at the refusing steeds below them, like anglers trying to rise a sulky fish; half a dozen hats, bobbing in a string, showed where the road riders followed the delusive windings of a bohereen. It was obvious that in the matter of ambition they would not have caused Cardinal Wolsey a moment's uneasiness; whether angels or otherwise, they were not going to run any risk of falling.

Flurry's red coat was like a beacon two fields ahead of me, with Philippa following in his tracks; it was the first run worthy of the name that Philippa had ridden, and I blessed Miss Bobby Bennett as I saw Cruiskeen's undefeated fencing. An encouraging twang of the Doctor's horn notified that the hounds were giving us a chance; even the Quaker pricked his blunt ears and swerved in his stride to the sound. A stone wall, a rough patch of heather, a boggy field, dinted deep and black with hoof marks, and the stern chase was at an end. The hounds had checked on the outskirts of a small wood, and the field, thinned down to a panting dozen or so, viewed us with the disfavour shown by the first flight towards those who unexpectedly add to their select number. In the depths of the wood Dr. Hickey might be heard uttering those singular little yelps of encouragement that to the irreverent suggest a milkman in his dotage. Bernard Shute, who neither knew nor cared what the hounds were doing, was expatiating at great length to an uninterested squireen upon the virtues and perfections of his new mount.

"I did all I knew to come and help you at the river," he said, riding up to the splashed and still dripping Sally, "but Stockbroker wouldn't hear of it. I pulled his ugly head round till his nose was on my boot, but he galloped away just the same!"

"He was quite right," said Miss Sally; " I didn't want you in the least."

As Miss Sally's red-gold coil of hair was turned towards me during this speech, I could only infer the glance with which it was delivered from the fact that Mr. Shute's responded to it with one of those firm gazes of adoration in which the neighbourhood took such an interest, and crumbled away into incoherency.

A shout from the top of a hill interrupted the amenities of the check; Flurry was out of the wood in half a dozen seconds, blowing shattering blasts upon his horn, and the hounds rushed to him, knowing the "gone away" note that was never blown in vain. The brown mare came out through the trees and the undergrowth like a woodcock down the wind, and jumped across a

177

stream on to a more than questionable bank; the hounds splashed and struggled after him, and, as they landed, the first ecstatic whimpers broke forth. In a moment it was full cry, discordant, beautiful, and soul-stirring, as the pack spread and sped, and settled to the line. I saw the absurd dazzle of tears in Philippa's eyes, and found time for the insulting proffer of the clean pocket-handkerchief, as we all galloped hard to get away on good terms with the hounds.

It was one of those elect moments in fox-hunting when the fittest alone have survived; even the Quaker's sluggish blood was stirred by good company, and possibly by the remembrance of the singing ashplant, and he lumbered up tall stone-faced banks and down heavy drops, and across wide ditches, in astounding adherence to the line cut out by Flurry, Cruiskeen went like a book —a story for girls, very pleasant and safe, but rather slow. Moonlighter was pulling Miss Sally on to the sterns of the hounds, flying his banks, rocketing like a pheasant over three-foot walls—committing, in fact, all the crimes induced by youth and overfeeding; he would have done very comfortably with another six or seven stone on his back.

Why Bernard Shute did not come off at every fence and generally die a thousand deaths I cannot explain. Occasionally I rather wished he would, as, from my secure position in the rear, I saw him charging his fences at whatever pace and place seemed good to the thoroughly demoralized Stockbroker, and in so doing cannon heavily against Dr. Hickey on landing over a rotten ditch, jump a wall with his spur rowelling Charlie Knox's boot, and cut in at top speed in front of Flurry, who was scientifically cramming his mare up a very awkward scramble. In so far as I could think of anything beyond Philippa and myself and the next fence, I thought there would be trouble for Mr. Shute in consequence of this last feat. It was a half-hour long to be remembered, in spite of the Quaker's ponderous and unalterable gallop, in spite of the thump with which he came down off his banks, in spite of the confiding manner in which he hung upon my hand.

We were nearing Castle Knox, and the riders began to edge away from the hounds towards a gate that broke the long barrier of the demesne wall. Steaming horses and purple-faced riders clattered and crushed in at the gate; there was a moment of pulling up and listening, in which quivering tails and pumping sides told their own story. Cruiskeen's breathing suggested a cross between a grampus and a gramophone; Philippa's hair had come down, and she had a stitch in her side. Moonlighter, fresher than ever, stamped and dragged at his bit; I thought little Miss Sally looked very white. The bewildering clamour of the hounds was all through the wide laurel plantations. At a word from Flurry, Dr. Hickey shoved his horse ahead and turned down a ride, followed by most of the field.

"Philippa," I said severely, "you've had enough, and you know it."

"Do go up to the house and make them give you something to eat," struck in Miss Sally, twisting Moonlighter round to keep his mind occupied.

"And as for you, Miss Sally," I went on, in the manner of Mr. Fairchild, "the sooner you get off that horse and out of those wet things the better."

Flurry, who was just in front of us, said nothing, but gave a short and most disagreeable laugh. Philippa accepted my suggestion with the meekness of exhaustion, but under the circumstances it did not surprise me that Miss Sally did not follow her example.

Then ensued an hour of woodland hunting at its worst and most bewildering. I galloped after Flurry and Miss Sally up and down long glittering lanes of laurel, at every other moment burying my face in the Quaker's coarse white mane to avoid the slash of the branches, and receiving down the back of my neck showers or drops stored up from the rain of the day before; playing an endless game of hide-and-seek with the hounds, and never getting any nearer to them, as they turned and

179

doubled through the thickets of evergreens. Even to my limited understanding of the situation it became clear at length that two foxes were on foot; most of the hounds were hard at work a quarter of a mile away, but Flurry, with a grim face and a faithful three couple, stuck to the failing line of the hunted fox.

There came a moment when Miss Sally and I—who through many vicissitudes had clung to each other—found ourselves at a spot where two rides crossed. Flurry was waiting there, and a little way up one of the rides a couple of hounds were hustling to and fro, with the thwarted whimpers half breaking from them; he held up his hand to stop us, and at that identical moment Bernard Shute, like a bolt from the blue, burst upon our vision. It need scarcely be mentioned that he was going at full gallop—I have rarely seen him ride at any other pace—and as he bore down upon Flurry and the hounds, ducking and dodging to avoid the branches, he shouted something about a fox having gone away at the other side of the covert.

"Hold hard!" roared Flurry, "don't you see the hounds, you fool?"

Mr. Shute, to do him justice, held hard with all the strength of his body, but it was of no avail. The bay horse had got his head down and his tail up, there was a piercing yell from a hound as it was ridden over, and Flurry's brown mare will not soon forget the moment when Stockbroker's shoulder took her on the point of the hip and sent her staggering into the laurel branches. As she swung round, Flurry's whip went up, and with a swift backhander the cane and the looped thong caught Bernard across his broad shoulders.

"Oh, Mr. Shute!" shrieked Miss Sally, as I stared dumbfounded; "did that branch hurt you?"

"All right! Nothing to signify!" he called out as he bucketed past, tugging at his horse's head. "Thought someone had hit me at first. Come on, we'll catch 'em up this way!"

He swung perilously into the main ride and was gone,

totally unaware of the position that Miss Sally's quickness had saved.

Flurry rode straight up to his cousin, with a pale, dangerous face.

"I suppose you think I'm to stand being ridden over and having my hounds killed to please you," he said; "but you're mistaken. You were very smart, and you may think you've saved him his licking, but you needn't think he won't get it. He'll have it in spite of you, before he goes to his bed this night!"

A man who loses his temper badly because he is badly in love is inevitably ridiculous, far though he may be from thinking himself so. He is also a highly unpleasant person to argue with, and Miss Sally and I held our peace respectfully. He turned his horse and rode away.

Almost instantly the three couple of hounds opened in the underwood near us with a deafening crash, and not twenty yards ahead the hunted fox, dark and wet with mud, slunk across the ride. The hounds were almost on his brush; Moonlighter reared and chafed; the din was redoubled, passed away to a little distance, and suddenly seemed stationary in the middle of the laurels.

"Could he have got into the old ice-house?" exclaimed Miss Sally, with reviving excitement. She pushed ahead, and turned down the narrowest of all the rides that had that day been my portion. At the end of the green tunnel there was a comparatively open space; Flurry's mare was standing in it, riderless, and Flurry himself was hammering with a stone at the padlock of a door that seemed to lead into the heart of a laurel clump. The hounds were baying furiously somewhere back of the entrance, among the laurel stems.

"He's got in by the old ice drain," said Flurry, addressing himself sulkily to me, and ignoring Miss Sally. He had not the least idea of how absurd was his scowling face, draped by the luxuriant hart's-tongues that overhung the doorway.

The padlock yielded, and the opening door revealed a low, dark passage, into which Flurry disappeared, lugging a couple of hounds with him by the scruff of the neck; the remaining two couple bayed implacably at the mouth of the drain. The croak of a rusty bolt told of a second door at the inner end of the passage.

"Look out for the steps, Flurry, they're all broken," called out Miss Sally in tones of honey.

There was no answer. Miss Sally looked at me; her face was serious, but her mischievous eyes made a confederate of me.

"He's in an *awful* rage!" she said. "I'm afraid there will certainly be a row."

A row there certainly was, but it was in the cavern of the ice-house, where the fox had evidently been discovered. Miss Sally suddenly flung Moonlighter's reins to me and slipped off his back.

"Hold him!" she said, and dived into the doorway under the overhanging branches.

Things happened after that with astonishing simultaneousness. There was a shrill exclamation from Miss Sally, the inner door was slammed and bolted, and at one and the same moment the fox darted from the entry, and was away into the wood before one could wink.

"What's happened?" I called out, playing the refractory Moonlighter like a salmon.

Miss Sally appeared at the doorway, looking half scared and half delighted.

"I've bolted him in, and I won't let him out till he promises to be good! I was only just in time to slam the door after the fox bolted out!"

"Great Scott!" I said helplessly.

Miss Sally vanished again into the passage, and the imprisoned hounds continued to express their emotions in the echoing vault of the ice-house. Their master remained mute as the dead, and I trembled.

"Flurry!" I heard Miss Sally say. "Flurry, I—I've locked you in!"

This self-evident piece of information met with no response.

"Shall I tell you why?"

A keener note seemed to indicate that a hound had been kicked.

"I don't care whether you answer me or not, I'm going to tell you!"

There was a pause; apparently telling him was not as simple as had been expected.

"I won't let you out till you promise me something. Ah, Flurry, don't be so cross! What do you say?—Oh, that's a ridiculous thing to say. You know quite well it's not on his account!"

There was another considerable pause.

"Flurry!" said Miss Sally again, in tones that would have wiled a badger from his earth. "Dear Flurry——"

At this point I hurriedly flung Moonlighter's bridle over a branch and withdrew.

My own subsequent adventures are quite immaterial, until the moment when I encountered Miss Sally on the steps of the hall door at Castle Knox.

"I'm just going in to take off these wet things," she said airily.

This was no way to treat a confederate.

"Well?" I said, barring her progress.

"Oh—he—he promised. It's all right," she replied, rather breathlessly.

There was no one about; I waited resolutely for further information. It did not come.

"Did he try to make his own terms?" I said, looking hard at her.

"Yes, he did." She tried to pass me.

"And what did you do?"

"I refused them!" she said, with the sudden stagger of a sob in her voice, and she escaped into the house.

Now what on earth was Sally Knox crying about?

THE HOUSE OF FAHY

Nothing could shake the conviction of Maria that she was by nature and by practice a house dog. Every one of Shreelane's many doors had, at one time or another, slammed upon her expulsion, and each one of them had seen her stealthy, irrepressible return to the sphere that she felt herself so eminently qualified to grace. For her the bone, thriftily interred by Tim Connor's terrier, was a mere diversion; even the fruitage of the ashpit had little charm for an accomplished *habitué* of the kitchen. She knew to a nicety which of the doors could be burst open by assault, at which it was necessary to whine sycophantically; and the clinical thermometer alone could furnish a parallel for her perception of mood in those in authority. In the case of Mrs. Cadogan she knew that there were seasons when instant and complete self-effacement was the only course to pursue; therefore when, on a certain morning in July, on my way through the downstairs regions to my office, I saw her approach the kitchen door with her usual circumspection, and, on hearing her name enunciated indignantly by my cook, withdraw swiftly to a city of refuge at the back of the hayrick, I drew my own conclusions.

Had she remained, as I did, she would have heard the disclosure of a crime that lay more heavily on her digestion than her conscience.

"I can't put a thing out o' me hand but he's watching me to whip it away!" declaimed Mrs. Cadogan, with all the disregard of her kind for the accident of sex in the brute creation. " 'Twas only last night I was back in the scullery when I heard Bridget let a screech, and there was me brave dog up on the table eating the roast beef that was after coming out from the dinner!"

"Brute!" interjected Philippa, with what I well knew to be a simulated wrath.

"And I had planned that bit of beef for the luncheon," continued Mrs. Cadogan in impassioned lamentation, "the way we wouldn't have to inthrude on the cold turkey! Sure he has it that dhragged, that all we can do with it now is run it through the mincing machine for the Major's sandwiches."

At this appetizing suggestion I thought fit to intervene in the deliberations.

"One thing," I said to Philippa afterwards, as I wrapped up a bottle of Yanatas in a cardigan jacket and rammed it into an already apoplectic Gladstone bag, "that I do draw the line at, is taking that dog with us. The whole business is black enough as it is."

"Dear," said my wife, looking at me with almost clairvoyant abstraction, "I could manage a second evening dress if you didn't mind putting my tea-jacket in your portmanteau."

Little, thank Heaven! as I know about yachting, I knew enough to make pertinent remarks on the incongruity of an ancient sixty-ton hireling and a fleet of smart evening dresses; but none the less I left a pair of indispensable boots behind, and the tea-jacket went into my portmanteau.

It is doing no more than the barest justice to the officers of the Royal Navy to say that, so far as I know them, they cherish no mistaken enthusiasm for a home on the rolling deep when a home anywhere else presents itself. Bernard Shute had unfortunately proved an exception to this rule. During the winter, the invitation to go for a cruise in the yacht that was in process of building for him hung over me like a cloud; a timely strike in the builder's yard brought a respite, and, in fact, placed the completion of the yacht at so safe a distance that I was betrayed into specious regrets, echoed with an atrocious sincerity by Philippa. Into a life pastorally compounded of Petty Sessions and lawn-tennis parties, retribution fell when it was least expected. Bernard Shute hired a yacht in Queenstown, and one short week after-wards the worst had happened, and we were packing our things for a cruise in her, the only alleviation being the knowledge that, whether by sea or land, I was bound to return to my work in four days.

We left Shreelane at twelve o'clock, a specially depressing hour for a start, when breakfast had died in you, and lunch is still remote. My last act before mount-ing the dogcart was to put the collar and chain on Maria and immure her in the potato-house, whence, as we drove down the avenue, her wails rent the heart of Philippa and rejoiced mine. It was a very hot day, with a cloudless sky; the dust lay thick on the white road, and on us also as, during two baking hours, we drove up and down the long hills and remembered things that had been left behind, and grew hungry enough to eat sand-wiches that tasted suspiciously of roast beef.

The yacht was moored in Clountiss Harbour; we drove through the village street, a narrow and unlovely thoroughfare, studded with public-houses, swarming with children and poultry, down through an ever-growing smell of fish, to the quay.

Thence we first viewed our fate, a dingy-looking schooner, and the hope that I had secretly been nour-ishing that there was not wind enough for her to start, was dispelled by the sight of her topsail going up. More than ever at that radiant moment—as the reflection of the white sail quivered on the tranquil blue, and the still water flattered all it reproduced, like a fashionable photographer—did I agree with George Herbert's advice, "Praise the sea, but stay on shore".

"We must hail her, I suppose," I said drearily. I assailed the *Eileen Oge*, such being her inappropriate name, with desolate cries, but achieved no more result beyond the assembling of some village children round us and our luggage.

"Mr. Shute and the two ladies was after screeching here for the boat a while ago," volunteered a horrid little girl, whom I had already twice frustrated in the attempt to seat an infant relative on our bundle of rugs. "Timsy Hallahane says 'twould be as good for them to stay ashore, for there isn't as much wind outside as 'd out a candle."

With this encouraging statement the little girl devoted herself to the alternate consumption of gooseberries and cockles.

All things come to those who wait, and to us arrived at length the gig of the *Eileen Oge,* and such, by this time, were the temperature and the smells of the quay that I actually welcomed the moment that found us leaving it for the yacht.

"Now, Sinclair, aren't you glad we came?" remarked Philippa, as the clear green water deepened under us, and a light briny air came coolly round us with the motion of the boat.

As she spoke there was an outburst of screams from the children on the quay, followed by a heavy splash.

"Oh stop!" cried Philippa in an agony; "one of them has fallen in! I can see its poor little brown head!"

" 'Tis a dog, ma'am," said briefly the man who was rowing stroke.

"One might have wished it had been that little girl," said I, as I steered to the best of my ability for the yacht.

We had traversed another twenty yards or so, when Philippa, in a voice in which horror and triumph were strangely blended, exclaimed, "She's following us!"

"Who? The little girl?" I asked callously.

"No," returned Philippa; "worse."

I looked round, not without a prevision of what I was to see and beheld the faithful Maria swimming steadily after us, with her brown muzzle thrust out in front of her, rippling through the reflections like a plough.

"Go home!" I roared, standing up and gesticulating in fury that I well knew to be impotent. "Go home, you brute!"

Maria redoubled her efforts, and Philippa murmured uncontrollably: "Well, she *is* a dear!"

187

Had I had a sword in my hand I should undoubtedly have slain Philippa; but before I could express my sentiments in any way, a violent shock flung me endways on top of the man who was pulling stroke. Thanks to Maria, we had reached our destination all unawares; the two men, respectfully awaiting my instructions, had rowed on with disciplined steadiness, and, as a result, we had rammed the *Eileen Oge* amidships, with a vigour that brought Mr. Shute tumbling up the companion to see what had happened.

"Oh, it's you, is it?" he said, with his mouth full. "Come in; don't knock! Delighted to see you, Mrs. Yeates; don't apologize. There's nothing like a hired ship after all—it's quite jolly to see the splinters fly—show's you're getting your money's worth. Hullo, who's this?"

This was Maria, feigning exhaustion, and noisily treading water at the boat's side.

"What, poor old Maria? Wanted to send her ashore, did he? Heartless ruffian!"

Thus was Maria installed on board the *Eileen Oge*, and the element of fatality had already begun to work.

There was just enough wind to take us out of Clountiss Harbour, and with the last of the out-running tide we crept away to the west. The party on board consisted of our host's sister, Miss Cecilia Shute, Miss Sally Knox, and ourselves; we sat about in conventional attitudes in deck chairs and on adamantine deck bosses, and I talked to Miss Shute with feverish brilliancy, and wished the patience-cards were not in the cabin; I knew the supreme importance of keeping one's mind occupied, but I dared not face the cabin. There was a long, almost imperceptible swell, with queer little sea-birds that I have never seen before—and trust I never shall again—dotted about on its glassy slopes. The coast-line looked low and grey and dull, as, I think, coast-lines always do when viewed from the deep. The breeze that Bernard promised us we should find outside was barely enough to keep us moving. The burning sun of four o'clock focused its heat on the deck; Bernard stood up among us, engaged in what he was pleased to call "handling the stick", and beamed almost as offensively as the sun.

"Oh, we're slipping along," he said, his odiously healthy face glowing like copper against the blazing blue sky. "You're going a great deal faster than you think, and the men say we'll pick up a breeze once we're round the Mizen."

I made no reply; I was not feeling ill, merely thoroughly disinclined for conversation. Miss Sally smiled wanly, and closing her eyes, laid her head on Philippa's knee. Instructed by a dread freemasonry, I knew that for her the moment had come when she could no longer bear to see the rail rise slowly above the horizon, and with an equal rhythmic slowness sink below it. Maria moved restlessly to and fro, panting and yawning, and occasionally rearing herself on her hind-legs against the side, and staring forth with wild eyes at the headachy sliding of the swell. Perhaps she was meditating suicide; if so I sympathized with her, and since she was obviously going to be sick I trusted that she would bring off the suicide with as little delay as possible. Philippa and Miss Shute sat in unaffected serenity in deck chairs, and stitched at white things—tea-clothes for the *Eileen Oge*, I believe, things in themselves a mockery—and talked untiringly, with that singular indifference to their marine surroundings that I have often observed in ladies who are not sea-sick. It always stirs me afresh to wonder why they have not remained ashore; nevertheless, I prefer their tranquil and total lack of interest in seafaring matters to the blatant Vikingism of the average male who is similarly placed.

Somehow, I know not how, we crawled onwards, and by about five o'clock we had rounded the Mizen, a gaunt spike of a headland that starts up like a boar's tusk above the ragged lip of the Irish coast, and the *Eileen Oge* was beginning to swing and wallow in the long sluggish rollers that the American liners know and despise. I was very far from despising them. Down in the west, resting on the sea's rim, a purple bank of clouds lay awaiting the descent of the sun, as seductively and as malevolently as a damp bed at a hotel awaits a traveller.

The end, so far as I was concerned, came at tea-time. The meal had been prepared in the saloon, and thither it became incumbent on me to accompany my hostess and my wife. Miss Sally, long past speech, opened, at the suggestion of tea, one eye, and disclosed a look of horror. As I tottered down the companion I respected her good sense. The *Eileen Oge* had been built early in the 'sixties, and head-room was not her strong-point; neither, apparently, was ventilation. I began by dashing my forehead against the frame of the cabin door, and then, shattered morally and physically, entered into the atmosphere of the pit. After which things, and the sight of a plate of rich cakes, I retired in good order to my cabin, and began upon the Yanatas.

I pass over some painful intermediate details and resume at the moment when Bernard Shute woke me from a drugged slumber to announce that dinner was over.

"It's been raining pretty hard," he said, swaying easily with the swing of the yacht; "but we've got a clinking breeze, and we ought to make Lurriga Harbour to-night. There's good anchorage there, the men say. They're rather a lot of swabs, but they know this coast, and I don't. I took 'em over with the ship all standing."

"Where are we now?" I asked, something heartened by the blessed word "anchorage".

"You're running up Sheepskin Bay—it's a thundering big bay; Lurriga's up at the far end of it, and the night's as black as the inside of a cow. Dig out and get something to eat, and come on deck—— What! no dinner?" —I had spoken morosely, with closed eyes—"Oh, rot! you're on an even keel now. I promised Mrs. Yeates I'd make you dig out. You're as bad as a soldier officer that we were ferrying to Malta one time in the old *Tamar*. He got one leg out of his berth when we were going down the Channel, and he was too sick to pull it in again till we got to Gib!"

I compromised on a drink and some biscuits. The ship was certainly steadier, and I felt sufficiently restored to climb weakly on deck. It was by this time past ten o'clock, and heavy clouds blotted out the last of the afterglow, and smothered the stars at their birth. A wet warm wind was lashing the *Eileen Oge* up a wide estuary; the waves were hunting her, hissing under her stern, racing up to her, crested with the white glow of phosphorus, as she fled before them. I dimly discerned in the greyness the more solid greyness of the shore. The mainsail loomed out into the darkness, nearly at right angles to the yacht, with the boom creaking as the following wind gave us an additional shove. I know nothing of yacht sailing, but I can appreciate the grand fact that in running before a wind the boom is removed from its usual sphere of devastation.

I sat down beside a bundle of rugs that I had discovered to be my wife, and thought of my whitewashed office at Shreelane and its bare but stationary floor, with a yearning that was little short of passion. Miss Sally had long since succumbed; Miss Shute was tired, and had turned in soon after dinner.

"I suppose she's overdone by the delirious gaiety of the afternoon," said I acridly, in reply to this information.

Philippa cautiously poked forth her head from the rugs, like a tortoise from under its shell, to see that Bernard, who was standing near the steersman, was out of hearing.

"In all your life, Sinclair," she said impressively, "you never knew such a time as Cecilia and I have had down there! We've had to wash *everything* in the cabins, and re-make the beds, and *hurl* the sheets away—they were covered with black finger-marks—and while we were doing that, in came the creature that calls himself the steward, to ask if he might get something of his that he had left in Miss Shute's 'birthplace'! and he rooted out

191

from under Cecilia's mattress a pair of socks and half a loaf of bread!'"

"Consolation to Miss Shute to know her berth has been well aired," I said, with the nearest approach to enjoyment I had known since I came on board; "and has Sally made any equally interesting discoveries?"

"She said she didn't care what her bed was like; she just dropped into it. I must say I am sorry for her," went on Philippa; "she hated coming. Her mother made her accept."

"I wonder if Lady Knox will make her accept *him*!" I said. "How often has Sally refused him, does anyone know?"

"Oh, about once a week," replied Philippa; "just the way I kept on refusing you, you know!"

Something cold and wet was thrust into my hand, and the aroma of damp dog arose upon the night air; Maria had issued from some lair at the sound of voices, and was now, with palsied tremblings, slowly trying to drag herself on to my lap.

"Poor thing, she's been so dreadfully ill," said Philippa. "Don't send her away, Sinclair. Mr. Shute found her lying on his berth not able to move; didn't you, Mr. Shute?"

"She found out that she was able to move," said Bernard, who had crossed to our side of the deck; "it was somehow borne in upon her when I got at her with a boot-tree. I wouldn't advise you to keep her in your lap, Yeates. She stole half a ham after dinner, and she might take a notion to make the only reparation in her power."

I stood up and stretched myself stiffly. The wind was freshening, and though the growing smoothness of the water told that we were making shelter of some kind, for all that I could see of land we might as well have been in mid-ocean. The heaving lift of the deck under my feet, and the lurching swing when a stronger gust filled the ghostly sails, were more disquieting to me in suggestion than in reality, and, to my surprise, I found

192

something almost enjoyable in rushing through darkness at the pace which we were going.

"We're a small bit short of the mouth of Lurriga Harbour yet, Sir," said the man who was steering, in reply to a question from Bernard. "I can see the shore well enough; sure I know every yard of wather in the bay——"

As he spoke he sat down abruptly and violently; so did Bernard, so did I. The bundle that contained Philippa collapsed upon Maria.

"Main sheet!" bellowed Bernard, on his feet in an instant, as the boom swung in and out again with a terrific jerk. "We're ashore!"

In response to this order three men in succession fell over me while I was still struggling on the deck, and something that was either Philippa's elbow or the acutest angle of Maria's skull, hit me in the face. As I found my feet the cabin skylight was suddenly illuminated by a wavering glare. I got across the slanting deck somehow, through the confusion of shouting men and the flapping thunder of the sails, and saw through the skylight a gush of flame rising from a pool of fire around an overturned lamp on the swing-table. I avalanched down the companion and was squandered like an avalanche on the floor at the foot of it. Even as I fell, McCarthy the steward dragged the strip of carpet from the cabin floor and threw it on the blaze; I found myself, in some unexplained way, snatching a railway rug from Miss Shute and applying it to the same purpose, and in half a dozen seconds we had smothered the flame and were left in total darkness. The most striking feature of the situation was the immovability of the yacht.

"Great Ned!" said McCarthy, invoking I know not what heathen deity, "it is on the bottom of the say we are? Well, whether or no, thank God we have the fire quinched!"

We were not, so far, at the bottom of the sea, but during the next ten minutes the chances seemed in favour of our getting there. The yacht had run her bows

193

upon a sunken ridge of rock, and after a period of feminine indecision as to whether she were going to slide off again, or roll over into deep water, she elected to stay where she was, and the gig was lowered with all speed, in order to tow her off before the tide left her.

My recollection of this interval is but hazy, but I can certify that in ten minutes I had swept together an assortment of necessaries and knotted them into my counterpane, had broken the string of my eye-glass, and lost my silver matchbox; had found Philippa's curling-tongs and put them in my pocket; had carted all the luggage on deck; had then applied myself to the manly duty of reassuring the ladies, and had found Miss Shute merely bored, Philippa enthusiastically anxious to be allowed to help to pull the gig, and Miss Sally radiantly restored to health and spirits by the cessation of move-ment and the probability of an early escape from the yacht.

The rain had, with its usual opportuneness, begun again; we stood in it under umbrellas, and watched the gig jumping on its tow-rope like a dog on a string, as the crew plied the labouring oar in futile endeavour to move the *Eileen Oge.* We had run on the rock at half-tide, and the increasing slant of the deck as the tide fell brought home to us the pleasing probability that at low water—viz., about 2 a.m.—we should roll off the rock and go to the bottom. Had Bernard Shute wished to show himself in the most advantageous light to Miss Sally he could scarcely have bettered the situation. I looked on in helpless respect while he whom I had known as the scourge of the hunting field, the terror of the shooting party, rose to the top of a difficult position and kept there, and my respect was, if possible, increased by the presence of mind with which he availed himself of all critical moments to place a protecting arm round Miss Knox.

By about 1 a.m. the two gaffs with which Bernard had contrived to shore up the slowly heeling yacht began to show signs of yielding, and, in approved ship-

wreck fashion, we took to the boats, the yacht's crew
in the gig remaining in attendance on what seemed likely
to be the last moments of the *Eileen Oge*, while we, in
the dinghy, sought for the harbour. Owing to the tilt of
the yacht's deck, and the roughness of the broken water
round her, getting into the boat was no mean feat of
gymnastics. Miss Sally did it like a bird, alighting in the
inevitable' arms of Bernard; Miss Shute followed very
badly, but, by innate force of character, successfully;
Philippa, who was enjoying every moment of her ship-
wreck, came last, launching herself into the dinghy with
my silver shoe-horn clutched in one hand, and in the
other the tea-basket. I heard the hollow clank of its tin
cups as she sprang, and appreciated the heroism with
which Bernard received one of its corners in his waist.
How or when Maria left the yacht I know not, but when
I applied myself to the bow oar I led off with three
crabs, owing to the devotion with which she thrust her
head into my lap.

I am no judge of these matters, but in my opinion we
ought to have been swamped several times during that
row. There was nothing but the phosphorus of breaking
waves to tell us where the rocks were, and nothing to
show where the harbour was except a solitary light, a
mast-head light, as we supposed. The skipper had
assured us that we could not go wrong if we kept "a
westerly course with a little northing in it"; but it seemed
simpler to steer for the light, and we did so. The dinghy
climbed along over the waves with an agility that was
safer than it felt; the rain fell without haste and without
rest, the oars were as inflexible as crowbars, and somewhat resembled them in shape and weight; nevertheless,
it was Elysium when compared with the afternoon
leisure of the deck of the *Eileen Oge*.

At last we came, unexplainably, into smooth water, and
it was at about this time that we were first aware that
the darkness was less dense than it had been, and that
the rain had ceased. By imperceptible degrees a greyness touched the back of the waves, more a dreariness

195

than a dawn, but more welcome than thousands of gold and silver. I looked over my shoulder and discerned vague bulky things ahead; as I did so, my oar was suddenly wrapped in seaweed. We crept on; Maria stood up with her paws on the gunwale, and whined in high agitation. The dark objects ahead resolved themselves into rocks, and without more ado Maria pitched herself into the water. In half a minute we heard her shaking herself on shore. We slid on; the water swelled under the dinghy and lifted her keel on to grating gravel.

"We couldn't have done it better if we'd been the Hydrographer Royal," said Bernard, wading knee-deep in a light wash of foam, with the painter in his hand; "but all the same, that masthead light is someone's bedroom candle!"

We landed, hauled up the boat, and then feebly sat down on our belongings to review the situation, and Maria came and shook herself over each of us in turn. We had run into a little cove, guided by the philanthropic beam of a candle in the upper window of a house about a hundred yards away. The candle still burned on, and the anaemic daylight exhibited to us our surroundings, and we debated as to whether we could at 2.45 a.m. present ourselves as objects of compassion to the owner of the candle. I need hardly say that it was the ladies who decided on making the attempt, having, like most of their sex, a courage incomparably superior to ours in such matters; Bernard and I had not a grain of genuine compunction in our souls, but we failed in nerve.

We trailed up from the cove, laden with emigrants' bundles, stumbling on wet rocks in the half-light, and succeeded in making our way to the house.

It was a small two-storied building, of that hideous breed of architecture usually dedicated to the rectories of the Irish Church; we felt that there was something friendly in the presence of a pair of carpet slippers in the porch, but there was a hint of exclusiveness in the fact that there was no knocker and that the bell was broken. The light still burned in the upper window, and with a faltering hand I flung gravel at the glass. This summons was appallingly responded to by a shriek; there was a flutter of white at the panes, and the candle was extinguished.

"Come away!" exclaimed Miss Shute, "it's a lunatic asylum!"

We stood our ground, however, and presently heard a footstep within, a blind was poked aside in another window, and we were inspected by an unseen inmate; then someone came downstairs, and the hall door was opened by a small man with a bald head and a long sandy beard. He was attired in a brief dressing-gown, and on his shoulder sat, like an angry ghost, a large white cockatoo. Its crest was up on end, its beak was a good two inches long and curved like a Malay kris; its claws gripped the little man's shoulder. Maria uttered in the background a low and thunderous growl.

"Don't take any notice of the bird, please," said the little man nervously, seeing our united gaze fixed upon this apparition; "he's extremely fierce if annoyed."

The majority of our party here melted away to either side of the hall door, and I was left to do the explaining. The tale of our misfortunes had its due effect, and we were ushered into a small drawing-room, our host holding open the door for us, like a nightmare footman with bare shins, a gnome-like bald head, and an unclean spirit swaying on his shoulder. He opened the shutters, and we sat decorously round the room, as at an afternoon party, while the situation was further expounded on both sides. Our entertainer, indeed, favoured us with the leading items of his family history, among them the facts that he was a Dr. Fahy from Cork, who had taken someone's rectory for the summer, and had been prevailed on by some of his patients to permit them to join him as paying guests.

"I said it was a lunatic asylum," murmured Miss Shute to me.

"In point of fact," went on our host, "there isn't an

197

empty room in the house, which is why I can only offer your party the use of this room and the kitchen fire, which I make a point of keeping burning all night."

He leaned back complacently in his chair, and crossed his legs; then, obviously remembering his costume, sat bolt upright again. We owed the guiding beams of the candle to the owner of the cockatoo, an old Mrs. Buck, who was, we gathered, the most paying of all the patients, and also, obviously, the one most feared and cherished by Dr. Fahy. "She has a candle burning all night for the bird, and her door open to let him walk about the house when he likes," said Dr. Fahy; "indeed, I may say her passion for him amounts to dementia. He's very fond of me, and Mrs. Fahy's always telling me I should be thankful, as whatever he did we'd be bound to put up with it!"

Dr. Fahy had evidently a turn for conversation that was unaffected by circumstance; the first beams of the early sun were lighting up the rep chair covers before the door closed upon his brown dressing-gown, and upon the stately white back of the cockatoo, and the demoniac possession of laughter that had wrought in us during the interview burst forth unchecked. It was most painful and exhausting, as such laughter always is; but by far the most serious part of it was that Miss Sally, who was sitting in the window, somehow drove her elbow through a pane of glass, and Bernard, in pulling down the blind to conceal the damage, tore if off the roller.

There followed on this catastrophe a period during which reason tottered and Maria barked furiously. Philippa was the first to pull herself together, and to suggest an adjournment to the kitchen fire that, in honour of the paying guests, was never quenched, and, respecting the repose of the household, we proceeded thither with a stealth that convinced Maria we were engaged in a rat hunt. The boots of paying guests littered the floor, the débris of their last repast covered the table; a cat in some unseen fastness crooned a war song to Maria, who feigned unconsciousness and fell to scientific research in the scullery.

We roasted our boots at the range, and Bernard, with all a sailor's gift for exploration and theft, prowled in noisome purlieus and emerged with a jug of milk and a lump of salt butter. No one who has not been a burglar can at all realize what it was to roam through Dr. Fahy's basement story, with the rookery of paying guests asleep above, and to feel that, so far, we had repaid his confidence by breaking a pane of glass and a blind, and putting the scullery tap out of order. I have always maintained there was something wrong with it before I touched it, but the fact remains that when I had filled Philippa's kettle, no human power could prevail upon it to stop flowing. For all I know to the contrary it is running still.

It was in the course of our furtive return to the drawing-room that we were again confronted by Mrs. Buck's cockatoo. It was standing in malign meditation on the stairs, and on seeing us it rose, without a word of warning, upon the wing, and with a long screech flung itself at Miss Sally's golden-red head, which a ray of sunlight had chanced to illumine. There was a moment of stampede as the selected victim, pursued by the cockatoo, fled into the drawing-room; two chairs were upset (one, I think, broken), Miss Sally enveloped herself in a window curtain, Philippa and Miss Shute effaced themselves beneath a table; the cockatoo, foiled of its prey, skimmed, still screeching, round the ceiling. It was Bernard who, with a well-directed sofa-cushion, drove the enemy from the room. There was only a chink of the door open, but the cockatoo turned on his side as he flew, and swung through it like a woodcock.

We slammed the door behind him, and at the same instant there came a thumping on the floor overhead, muffled, yet peremptory.

"That's Mrs. Buck!" said Miss Shute, crawling from under the table; "the room over this is the one that had the candle in it."

We sat for a time in awful stillness, but nothing further happened, save a distant shriek overhead, that told the cockatoo had sought and found sanctuary in his owner's room. We had tea *sotto voce*, and then, one by one, despite the amazing discomfort of the drawing-room chairs, we dozed off to sleep.

It was at about five o'clock that I woke with a stiff neck and an uneasy remembrance that I had last seen Maria in the kitchen. The others, looking, each of them, about twenty years older than their age, slept in various attitudes of exhaustion. Bernard opened his eyes as I stole forth to look for Maria, but none of the ladies awoke. I went down the evil-smelling passage that led to the kitchen stairs, and, there on a mat, regarding me with intelligent affection, was Maria; but what—oh what was the white thing that lay between her forepaws?

The situation was too serious to be coped with alone. I fled noiselessly back to the drawing-room and put my head in; Bernard's eyes—blessed be the light sleep of sailors!—opened again, and there was that in mine that summoned him forth. (Blessed also be the light step of sailors!)

We took the corpse from Maria, withholding perforce the language and the slaughtering that our hearts ached to bestow. For a minute or two our eyes communed.

"I'll get the kitchen shovel," breathed Bernard; "you open the hall door!"

A moment later we passed like spirits into the open air, and on into a little garden at the end of the house. Maria followed us, licking her lips. There were beds of nasturtiums, and of purple stocks, and of marigolds. We chose a bed of stocks, a plump bed, that looked like easy digging. The windows were all tightly shut and shuttered, and I took the cockatoo from under my coat and hid it, temporarily, behind a box border. Bernard had brought a shovel and a coal scoop. We dug like badgers. At eighteen inches we got down into shale and stones, and the coal scoop struck work.

"Never mind," said Bernard; "we'll plant the stocks on top of him."

It was a lovely morning, with a new-born blue sky and a light northerly breeze. As we returned to the house, we looked across the wavelets of the little cove and saw, above the rocky point round which we had groped last night, a triangular white patch moving slowly along.

"The tide's lifted her!" said Bernard, standing stock-still. He looked at Mrs. Buck's window and at me. "Yeates!" he whispered, "let's quit!"

It was now barely six o'clock, and not a soul was stirring. We woke the ladies and convinced them of the high importance of catching the tide. Bernard left a note on the hall table for Dr. Fahy, a beautiful note of leave-taking and gratitude, and apology for the broken window (for which he begged to enclose half-a-crown). No allusion was made to the other casualties. As we neared the strand he found an occasion to say to me:

"I put in a postscript that I thought it best to mention that I had seen the cockatoo in the garden, and hoped it would get back all right. That's quite true, you know! But look here, whatever you do, you must keep it all dark from the ladies——"

At this juncture Maria overtook us with the cockatoo in her mouth.

OCCASIONAL LICENSES

"It's out of the question," I said, looking forbiddingly at Mrs. Moloney through the spokes of the bicycle that I was pumping up outside the grocer's in Skebawn.

"Well, indeed, Major Yeates," said Mrs. Moloney, advancing excitedly and placing on the nickel plating a hand that I had good and recent cause to know was warm, "sure I know well that if th' angel Gabriel came down from heaven looking for a license for the races, your honour wouldn't give it to him without a charackther, but as for Michael! Sure, the world knows what Michael is!"

I had been waiting for Philippa for already nearly half an hour, and my temper was not at its best.

"Character or no character, Mrs. Moloney," said I with asperity, "the magistrates have settled to give no occasional licenses, and if Michael were as sober as——"

"Is it sober! God help us!" exclaimed Mrs. Moloney with an upward rolling of her eye to the Recording Angel; "I'll tell your honour the truth. I'm his wife now fifteen years, and I never seen the sign of dhrink on Michael only once, and that was when he went out o' good-nature helping Timsy Ryan to whitewash his house, and Timsy and himself had a couple o' pots o' porther, and look, he was as little used to it that his head got light, and he walked away out to dhrive in the cows and it no more than eleven o'clock in the day! And the cows, the craytures, as much surprised, goin' hither and over the four corners of the road from him! Faith, ye'd have to laugh. 'Michael,' says I to him,'ye're dhrunk!' 'I am,' says he, and the tears rained from his eyes. I

202

turned the cows from him. 'Go home,' I says, 'and lie down on Willy Tom's bed——' "

At this affecting point my wife came out of the grocer's with a large parcel to be strapped to my handlebar, and the history of Mr. Moloney's solitary lapse from sobriety got no further than Willy Tom's bed.

"You see," I said to Philippa, as we bicycled quietly home through the hot June afternoon, "we've settled we'll give no licenses for the sports. Why, even young Sheehy, who owns three pubs in Skebawn, came to me and said he hoped the magistrates would be firm about it, as these one-day licenses were quite unnecessary, and only led to drunkenness and fighting, and every man on the Bench has joined in promising not to grant any."

"How nice, dear!" said Philippa absently. "Do you know Mrs. McConnell can only let me have three dozen cups and saucers; I wonder if that will be enough?"

"Do you mean to say you expect three dozen people?" said I.

"Oh, it's always well to be prepared," replied my wife evasively.

During the next few days I realized the true inwardness of what it was to be prepared for an entertainment of this kind. Games were not at a high level in my district. Football, of a wild, guerilla species, was waged intermittently, blended in some inextricable way with Home Rule and a brass band, and on Sundays gatherings of young men rolled a heavy round stone along the roads, a rudimentary form of sport, whose fascination lay primarily in the fact that it was illegal, and, in lesser degree, in betting on the length of each roll. I had had a period of enthusiasm, during which I thought I was going to be the apostle of cricket in the neighbourhood, but my mission dwindled to single wicket with Peter Cadogan, who was indulgent but bored, and I swiped the ball through the dining-room window, and someone took one of the stumps to poke the laundry fire. Once a year, however, on that festival of the Roman Catholic Church which is familiarly known as "Pether and Paul's day", the district was wont to make a spasmodic effort at athletic sports, which were duly patronized by the gentry and promoted by the publicans, and this year the honour of a steward's green rosette was conferred upon me. Philippa's genius for hospitality here saw its chance, and broke forth into unbridled tea-party in connection with the sports, even involving me in the hire of a tent, the conveyance of chairs and tables, and other large operations.

It chanced that Flurry Knox had on this occasion lent the fields for the sports, with the proviso that horse-races and a tug-of-war were to be added to the usual programme; Flurry's participation in events of this kind seldom failed to be of an inflaming character. As he and I planted arch spars for the high jump, and stuck furze-bushes into hurdles (locally knows as "hurrls"), and skirmished hourly with people who wanted to sell drink on the course, I thought that my next summer leave would singularly coincide with the festival consecrated to Saint Peter and Saint Paul. We made a grand stand of quite four feet high, out of old fish-boxes, which smelt worse and worse as the day wore on, but was, none the less, as sought after by those for whom it was not intended as is the royal enclosure at Ascot; we broke gaps in all the fences to allow carriages on to the ground, we armed a gang of the worst blackguards in Skebawn with cart-whips, to keep the course, and felt that organization could go no further.

The momentous day of Pether and Paul opened badly, with heavy clouds and every indication of rain, but after a few thunder showers things brightened, and it seemed within the bounds of possibility that the weather might hold up. When I got down to the course on the day of the sports the first thing I saw was a tent of that peculiar filthy grey that usually enshrines the sale of porter, with an array of barrels in a crate beside it; I bore down on it in all the indignant majesty of the law, and in so doing, came upon Flurry Knox, who was engaged in flogging boys off the grand stand.

"Sheehy's gone one better than you!" he said, without taking any trouble to conceal the fact that he was amused.

"Sheehy!" I said; "why, Sheehy was the man who went to every magistrate in the country to ask them to refuse a license for the sports."

"Yes, he took the trouble to prevent anyone else having a look in," replied Flurry; "he asked every magistrate but one, and that was the one that gave him the license."

"You don't mean to say that it was you?" I demanded in high wrath and suspicion, remembering that Sheehy bred horses, and that my friend Mr. Knox was a person of infinite resource in the matter of a deal.

"Well, well," said Flurry, rearranging a disordered fish-box, "and me that's a churchwarden, and sprained my ankle a month ago with running downstairs at my grandmother's to be in time for prayers! Where's the use of a good character in this country?"

"Not much when you keep it eating its head off for want of exercise," I retorted; "but if it wasn't you, who was it?"

"Do you remember old Moriarty out at Castle Ire?"

I remembered him extremely well as one of those representatives of the people with whom a paternal Government had leavened the effete ranks of the Irish magistracy.

"Well," resumed Flurry, "that license was as good as a five-pound note in his pocket."

I permitted myself a comment on Mr. Moriarty suitable to the occasion.

"Oh, that's nothing," said Flurry easily; "he told me one day when he was half screwed that his Commission of the Peace was worth a hundred and fifty a year to him in turkeys and whisky, and he was telling the truth for once."

At this point Flurry's eye wandered, and following its direction I saw Lady Knox's smart 'bus cleaving its way through the throng of country people, lurching over

205

the ups and downs of the field like a ship in a sea. I was too blind to make out the component parts of the white froth that crowned it on top, and seethed forth from it when it had taken up a position near the tent in which Philippa was even now propping the legs of the tea-table, but from the fact that Flurry addressed himself to the door, I argued that Miss Sally had gone inside.

Lady Knox's manner had something more than its usual bleakness. She had brought, as she promised, a large contingent, but from the way that the strangers within her gates melted impalpably and left me to deal with her single-handed, I drew the further deduction that all was not well.

"Did you ever in your life see such a gang of women as I have brought with me?" she began with her wonted directness, as I piloted her to the grand stand, and placed her on the stoutest looking of the fish boxes. "I have no patience with men who yacht! Bernard Shute has gone off to the Clyde, and I had counted on his being a man at my dance next week. I suppose you'll tell me you're going away too."

I assured Lady Knox that I would be a man to the best of my ability.

"This is the last dance I shall give," went on her ladyship, unappeased; "the men in this country consist of children and cads."

I admitted that we were but a poor lot. "But," I said, "Miss Sally told me——"

"Sally's a fool!" said Lady Knox, with a falcon eye at her daughter, who happened to be talking to her distant kinsman, Mr. Flurry of that ilk.

The races had by this time begun with a competition known as the "Hop, Step, and Lep"; this, judging by the yells, was a highly interesting display, but as it was conducted between two impervious rows of onlookers, the aristocracy on the fish-boxes saw nothing save the occasional purple face of a competitor, starting into view above the wall of backs like a jack-in-the-box. For me, however, the odorous sanctuary of the fish-boxes was not to be. I left it guarded by Slipper with a cart-whip of flail-like dimensions, as disreputable an object as could be seen out of low comedy, with someone's old white cords on his bandy legs, butcher-boots three sizes too big for him, and a black eye. The small boys fled before him; in the glory of his office he would have flailed his own mother off the fish-boxes had occasion served.

I had an afternoon of decidedly mixed enjoyment. My stewardship blossomed forth like Aaron's rod, and added to itself the duties of starter, handicapper, general referee, and chucker-out, besides which I from time to time strove with emissaries who came from Philippa with messages about water and kettles. Flurry and I had to deal single-handed with the foot-races (our brothers in office being otherwise engaged at Mr. Sheehy's), a task of many difficulties, chiefest being that the spectators all swept forward at the word "Go!" and ran the race with the competitors, yelling curses, bless-ings, and advice upon them, taking short cuts over anything and everybody, and mingling inextricably with the finish. By fervent applications of the whips, the course was to some extent purged for the quarter-mile, and it would, I believe, have been a triumph of handi-capping had not an unforeseen disaster overtaken the favourite—old Mrs. Knox's bath-chair boy. Whether, as was alleged, his braces had or had not been tampered with by a rival was a matter that the referee had sub-sequently to deal with in the thick of a free fight; but the painful fact remained that in the course of the first lap what were described as "his galluses" abruptly severed their connection with the garments for whose safety they were responsible, and the favourite was obliged to seek seclusion in the crowd.

The tug-of-war followed close on this *contretemps*, and had the excellent effect of drawing away, like a blister, the inflammation set up by the grievances of the bath-chair boy. I cannot at this moment remember of how many men each team consisted; my sole aim was to keep the numbers even, and to baffle the volunteers who, in an ecstasy of sympathy, attached themselves to the tail of the rope at moments when their champions weakened. The rival forces dug their heels in and tugged, in an uproar that drew forth the innermost line of customers from Mr. Sheehy's porter tent, and even attracted "the quality" from the haven of the fish-boxes, Slipper, in the capacity of Squire of Dames, pioneering Lady Knox through the crowd with the cart-whip, and with language whose nature was providentially veiled, for the most part, by the din. The tug-of-war continued unabated. One team was getting the worst of it, but hung doggedly on, sinking lower and lower till they gradually sat down; nothing short of the trump of judgement could have conveyed to them that they were breaking rules, and both teams settled down by slow degrees on to their sides, with the rope under them, and their heels still planted in the ground, bringing about complete deadlock. I do not know the record duration for a tug-of-war, but I can certify that the Cullinagh and Knockranny teams lay on the ground at full tension for half an hour, like men in apoplectic fits, each man with his respective adherents howling over him, blessing him, and adjuring him to continue.

With my own nauseated eyes I saw a bearded country-man, obviously one of Mr. Sheehy's best customers, fling himself on his knees beside one of the combatants, and kiss his crimson and streaming face in a rapture of encouragement. As he shoved unsteadily past me on his return journey to Mr. Sheehy's, I heard him informing a friend that "he cried a handful over Danny Mulloy, when he seen the poor brave boy so shtubborn, and, indeed, he couldn't say why he cried."

"For good-nature ye'd cry," suggested the friend.

"Well, just that, I suppose," returned Danny Mulloy's admirer resignedly; "indeed, if it was only two cocks ye seen fightin' on the road, yer heart'd take part with one o' them!"

I had begun to realize that I might as well abandon the

tug-of-war and occupy myself elsewhere, when my wife's much harassed messenger brought me the portentous tidings that Mrs. Yeates wanted me at the tent at once. When I arrived I found the tent literally bulging with Philippa's guests; Lady Knox, seated on a hamper, was taking off her gloves, and loudly announcing her desire for tea, and Philippa, with a flushed face and a crooked hat, breathed into my ear the awful news that both the cream and the milk had been forgotten.

"But Flurry Knox says he can get me some," she went on; "he's gone to send people to milk a cow that lives near here. Go out and see if he's coming."

I went out and found, in the first instance, Mrs. Cadogan, who greeted me with the prayer that the devil might roast Julia McCarthy, that legged it away to the races like a wild goose, and left the cream after her on the servants' hall table. "Sure, Mister Flurry's gone looking for a cow, and what cow would there be in a backwards place like this? And look at me shivering to keep the kettle simpering on the fire, and not as much coals undher it as 'd redden a pipe!"

"Where's Mr. Knox?" I asked.

"Himself and Slipper's galloping the counthry like the deer. I believe it's to the house above they went, sir."

I followed up a rocky hill to the house above, and there found Flurry and Slipper engaged in the patriarchal task of driving two brace of coupled and spancelled goats into a shed.

"It's the best we can do," said Flurry briefly; "there isn't a cow to be found, and the people are all down at the sports. Be d——d to you, Slipper, don't let them go from you!" as the goats charged and doubled like football players.

"But goats' milk!" I said, paralysed by horrible memories of what tea used to taste like at Gib.

"They'll never know it!" said Flurry, cornering a venerable nanny; "here, hold this divil, and hold her tight!"

I have no time to dwell upon the pastoral scene that

followed. Suffice it to say, that at the end of ten minutes of scorching profanity from Slipper, and incessant warfare with the goats, the latter had reluctantly yielded two small jugfuls, and the dairymaids had exhibited a nerve and skill in their trade that won my lasting respect.

"I knew I could trust *you*, Mr. Knox!" said Philippa, with shining eyes, as we presented her with the two foaming beakers. I suppose a man is never a hero to his wife, but if she could have realized the bruises on my legs, I think she would have reserved a blessing for me also.

What was thought of the goats' milk I gathered symptomatically from a certain fixity of expression that accompanied the first sip of the tea, and from observing that comparatively few ventured on second cups. I also noted that after a brief conversation with Flurry, Miss Sally poured hers secretly on to the grass. Lady Knox had throughout the day preserved an aspect so threatening that no change was perceptible in her demeanour. In the throng of hungry guests I did not for some time notice that Mr. Knox had withdrawn until something in Miss Sally's eye summoned me to her, and she told me she had a message from him to me.

"Couldn't we come outside?" she said.

Outside the tent, within less than six yards of her mother, Miss Sally confided to me a scheme that made my hair stand on end. Summarized, it amounted to this: That, first, she was in the primary stage of a deal with Sheehy for a four-year-old chestnut colt, for which Sheehy was asking double its value on the assumption that it had no rival in the country; that, secondly, they had just heard it was going to run in the first race; and, thirdly and lastly, that as there was no other horse available, Flurry was going to take old Sultan out of the bus and ride him in the race; and that Mrs. Yeates had promised to keep mamma safe in the tent, while the race was going on, and "you know, Major Yeates, it would be delightful to beat Sheehy after his getting the better of you all about the license!"

With this base appeal to my professional feelings, Miss Knox paused, and looked at me insinuatingly. Her eyes were greeny-grey, and very beguiling.

"Come on," she said; "they want you to start them!"

Pursued by visions of the just wrath of Lady Knox, I weakly followed Miss Sally to the farther end of the second field, from which point the race was to start. The course was not a serious one: two or three natural banks, a stone wall, and a couple of "hurrls". There were but four riders, including Flurry, who was seated composedly on Sultan, smoking a cigarette and talking confidentially to Slipper. Sultan, although something stricken in years and touched in the wind, was a brown horse who in his day had been a hunter of no mean repute; even now he occasionally carried Lady Knox in a sedate and gentlemanly manner, but it struck me that it was trying him rather high to take him from the pole of the bus after twelve miles on a hilly road, and hustle him over a country against a four-year-old. My acutest anxiety, however, was to start the race as quickly as possible, and to get back to the tent in time to establish an *alibi*; therefore I repressed my private sentiments, and, tying my handkerchief to a stick, determined that no time should be fashionably frittered away in false starts.

They got away somehow; I believe Sheehy's colt was facing the wrong way at the moment when I dropped the flag, but a friend turned him with a stick, and with a cordial and timely whack, speeded him on his way on sufficiently level terms, and then somehow, instead of returning to the tent, I found myself with Miss Sally on the top of a tall narrow bank, in a precarious line of other spectators, with whom we toppled and swayed, and, in moments of acuter emotion, held on to each other in unaffected comradeship.

Flurry started well, and from our commanding position we could see him methodically riding at the first fence at a smart hunting canter, closely attended by James Canty's brother on a young black mare, and by

211

an unknown youth on a big white horse. The hope of Sheehy's stable, a leggy chestnut, ridden by a cadet of the house of Sheehy, went away from the friend's stick like a rocket, and had already refused the first bank twice before old Sultan decorously changed feet on it and dropped down into the next field with tranquil precision. The white horse scrambled over it on his stomach, but landed safely, despite the fact that his rider clasped him round the neck during the process; the black mare and the chestnut shouldered one another at the hole the white horse had left, and the whole party went away in a bunch and jumped the ensuing hurdle without disaster. Flurry continued to ride at the same steady hunting pace, accompanied respectfully by the white horse and by Jerry Canty on the black mare. Sheehy's colt had clearly the legs of the party, and did some showy galloping between the jumps, but as he refused to face the banks without a lead, the end of the first round found the field still a sociable party personally conducted by Mr. Knox.

"That's a dam nice horse," said one of my hangers-on, looking approvingly at Sultan as he passed us at the beginning of the second round, making a good deal of noise but apparently going at his ease; "you might depind your life on him, and he have the crabbedest jock in the globe of Ireland on him this minute."

"Canty's mare's very sour," said another; "look at her now, baulking the bank! she's as cross as a bag of weasels."

"Begob, I wouldn't say but she's a little sign lame," resumed the first; "she was going light on one leg on the road a while ago."

"I tell you what it is," said Miss Sally, very seriously, in my ear, "that chestnut of Sheehy's is settling down. I'm afraid he'll gallop away from Sultan at the finish, and the wall won't stop him. Flurry can't get another inch out of Sultan. He's riding him well," she ended in a critical voice, which yet was not quite like her own. Perhaps I should not have noticed it but for the fact

212

that the hand that held my arm was trembling. As for me, I thought of Lady Knox, and trembled too.

There now remained but one bank, the trampled remnant of the furze hurdle, and the stone wall. The pace was beginning to improve, and the other horses drew away from Sultan; they charged the bank at full gallop, the black mare and the chestnut flying it perilously, with a windmill flourish of legs and arms from their riders, the white horse racing up to it with a gallantry that deserted him at the critical moment, with the result that his rider turned a somersault over his head and landed, amidst the roars of the onlookers, sitting on the fence facing his horse's nose. With creditable presence of mind he remained on the bank, towed the horse over, scrambled on to his back again, and started afresh. Sultan, thirty yards to the bad, pounded doggedly on, and Flurry's cane and heels remained idle; the old horse, obviously blown, slowed cautiously coming in at the jump. Sally's grip tightened on my arm, and the crowd yelled as Sultan, answering to a hint from the spurs and a touch at his mouth, heaved himself on to the bank. Nothing but sheer riding on Flurry's part got him safe of it, and saved him from the consequences of a bad peck on landing; none the less, he pulled himself together and went away down the hill for the stone wall as stoutly as ever. The high-road skirted the last two fields, and there was a gate in the roadside fence beside the place where the stone wall met it at right angles. I had noticed this gate, because during the first round Slipper had been sitting on it, demonstrating with his usual fervour. Sheehy's colt was leading, with his nose in the air, his rider's hands going like a circular saw, and his temper, as a bystander remarked, "up on end"; the black mare, half mad from spurring, was going hard at his heels, completely out of hand; the white horse was steering steadily for the wrong side of the flag, and Flurry, by dint of cutting corners and of saving every yard of ground, was close enough to keep his antagonists' heads over their shoulders, while their right arms rose and fell in unceasing flagellation.

"There'll be a smash when they come to the wall! If one falls they'll all go!" panted Sally. "Oh!—Now! Flurry! Flurry!——"

What had happened was that the chestnut colt had suddenly perceived that the gate at right angles to the wall was standing wide open, and, swinging away from the jump, he had bolted headlong out on to the road, and along it at top speed for his home. After him fled Canty's black mare, and with her, carried away by the spirit of stampede, went the white horse.

Flurry stood up in his stirrups and gave a view-halloa as he cantered down to the wall. Sultan came at it with the send of the hill behind him, and jumped it with a skill that intensified, if that were possible, the volume of laughter and yells around us. By the time the black mare and the white horse had returned and ignominiously bundled over the wall to finish as they might, Flurry was leading Sultan towards us.

"That blackguard, Slipper!" he said, grinning; "everyone'll say I told him to open the gate! But look here, I'm afraid we're in for trouble. Sultan's given himself a bad over-reach; you could never drive him home to-night. And I've just seen Norris lying blind drunk under a wall!"

Now Norris was Lady Knox's coachman. We stood aghast at his "horror on horror's head", the blood trickled down Sultan's heel, and the lather lay in flecks on his dripping, heaving sides, in irrefutable witness to the iniquity of Lady Knox's only daughter. Then Flurry said:

"Thank the Lord, here's the rain!"

At the moment I admit that I failed to see any cause for gratitude in this occurrence, but later on I appreciated Flurry's grasp of circumstances.

That appreciation was, I think, at its highest development about half an hour afterwards, when I, an unwilling conspirator (a part with which my acquaintance with

Mr. Knox had rendered me but too familiar) unfurled Mrs. Cadogan's umbrella over Lady Knox's head, and hurried her through the rain from the tent to the bus, keeping it and my own person well between her and the horses. I got her in, with the rest of her bedraggled and exhausted party, and slammed the door.

"Remember, Major Yeates," she said through the window, "you are the only person here in whom I have any confidence. I don't wish *anyone* else to touch the reins!" this with a glance towards Flurry, who was standing near.

"I'm afraid I'm only a moderate whip," I said.

"My dear man," replied Lady Knox testily, "those horses could drive themselves!"

I slunk round to the front of the bus. Two horses, carefully rugged, were in it, with the inevitable Slipper at their heads.

"Slipper's going with you," whispered Flurry, stepping up to me; "she won't have me at any price. He'll throw the rugs over them when you get to the house, and if you hold the umbrella well over her she'll never see. I'll manage to get Sultan over somehow, when Norris is sober. That will be all right."

I climbed to the box without answering, my soul being bitter within me, as is the soul of a man who has been persuaded by womankind against his judgement.

"Never again!" I said to myself, picking up the reins; "let her marry him or Bernard Shute, or both of them if she likes, but I won't be roped into this kind of business again!"

Slipper drew the rugs from the horses, revealing on the near side Lady Knox's majestic carriage horse, and on the off, a thick-set brown mare of about fifteen hands.

"What brute is this?" said I to Slipper, as he swarmed up beside me.

"I don't rightly know where Misther Flurry got her," said Slipper, with one of his hiccoughing crows of laughter; "give her the whip, Major, and"—here he broke into song:

215

"Howld to the shteel,
    Honamaundhiaoul; she'll run off like an eel!'"

"If you don't shut your mouth," said I, with pent-up ferocity, "I'll chuck you off the bus."

Slipper was but slightly drunk, and taking this delicate rebuke in good part, he relapsed into silence.

Wherever the brown mare came from, I can certify that it was not out of double harness. Though humble and anxious to oblige, she pulled away from the pole as if it were red hot, and at critical moments had a tendency to sit down. However, we squeezed without misadventure among the donkey carts and between the groups of people, and bumped at length in safety out on to the high-road.

Here I thought it no harm to take Slipper's advice, and I applied the whip to the brown mare, who seemed inclined to turn round. She immediately fell into an uncertain canter that no effort of mine could frustrate; I could only hope that Miss Sally would foster conversation inside the bus and create a distraction; but judging from my last view of the party, and of Lady Knox in particular, I thought she was not likely to be successful. Fortunately the rain was heavy and thick, and a rising west wind gave every promise of its continuance. I had little doubt but that I should catch cold, but I took it to my bosom with gratitude as I reflected how it was drumming on the roof of the bus and blurring the windows.

We had reached the foot of a hill, about a quarter of a mile from the racecourse; the Castle Knox horse addressed himself to it with dignified determination, but the mare showed a sudden and alarming tendency to jib.

"Belt her, Major!" vociferated Slipper, as she hung back from the pole chain, with the collar half-way up her ewe-neck, "and give it to the horse, too! He'll dhrag her!"

I was in the act of "belting" when a squealing whinney struck upon my ear, accompanied by a light pattering gallop on the road behind us; there was an answering roar from the brown mare, a roar, as I realized with a sudden-drop of the heart, of outraged maternal feeling, and in another instant a pale, yellow foal sprinted up beside us, with shrill whickerings of joy. Had there at this moment been a bog-hole handy, I should have turned the bus into it without hesitation; as there was no accommodation of the kind, I laid the whip severely into everything I could reach, including the foal. The result was that we topped the hill at a gallop, three abreast, like a Russian troika; it was like my usual luck that at this identical moment we should meet the police patrol, who saluted respectfully.

"That the divil may blisther Michael Moloney!" ejaculated Slipper, holding on to the rail; "didn't I give him the foaleen and a halther on him to keep him! I'll howld you a pint 'twas the wife let him go, for she being vexed about the license! Sure the one's a March foal, and he'd run from here to Cork!"

There was no sign from my inside passengers, and I held on at a round pace, the mother and child galloping absurdly, the carriage horse pulling hard, but behaving like a gentleman. I wildly revolved plans of how I would make Slipper turn the foal in at the first gate we came to, of what I should say to Lady Knox supposing the worst happened and the foal accompanied us to her hall door, and of how I would have Flurry's blood at the earliest possible opportunity, and here the fateful sound of galloping behind us was again heard.

"It's impossible!" I said to myself; "she can't have twins!"

The galloping came nearer, and Slipper looked back.

"Murdher alive!" he said in a stage whisper; "Tom Sheehy's afther us on the butcher's pony!"

"What's that to me?" I said, dragging my team aside to let him pass; "I suppose he's drunk, like everyone else!"

Then the voice of Tom Sheehy made itself heard.

"Shtop! Shtop thief!" he was bawling; "give up my mare! How will I get me porther home!"

That was the closest shave I have ever had, and nothing could have saved the position but the torrential nature of the rain and the fact that Lady Knox had on a new bonnet. I explained to her at the door of the bus that Sheehy was drunk (which was the one unassailable feature of the case), and had come after his foal, which, with the fatuity of its kind, had escaped from a field and followed us. I did not mention to Lady Knox that when Mr. Sheehy retreated, apologetically, dragging the foal after him in a halter belonging to one of her own carriage horses, he had a sovereign of mine in his pocket, and during the narration I avoided Miss Sally's eye as carefully as she avoided mine.

The only comments on the day's events that are worthy of record were that Philippa said to me that she had not been able to understand what the curious taste in the tea had been till Sally told her it was turf-smoke, and that Mrs. Cadogan said to Philippa that night that "the Major was that dhrinched that if he had a shirt between his skin and himself he could have wrung it", and that Lady Knox said to a mutual friend that though Major Yeates had been extremely kind and obliging, he was an uncommonly bad whip.

"OH LOVE! OH FIRE!"

It was on one of the hottest days of a hot August that I walked over to Tory Lodge to inform Mr. Flurry Knox, M.F.H., that the limits of human endurance had been reached, and that either Venus and her family, or I and mine, must quit Shreelane. In a moment of impulse I had accepted her and her numerous progeny as guests in my stableyard, since when Mrs. Cadogan had given warning once or twice a week, and Maria, lawful autocrat of the ashpit, had had—I quote the kitchenmaid— "tin battles for every male she'd ate".

The walk over the hills was not of a nature to lower the temperature, moral or otherwise. The greasy path was as slippery as glass, the rocks radiated heat, the bracken radiated horseflies. There was no need to nurse my wrath to keep it warm.

I found Flurry seated in the kennel-yard in a long and unclean white linen coat, engaged in clipping hieroglyphics on the ears of a young out-going draft, an occupation in itself unfavourable to argument. The young draft had already monopolized all possible forms of remonstrance, from snarling in the obscurity behind the meal sack in the boiler-house, to hysterical yelling as they were dragged forth by the tail; but through these alarms and excursions I denounced Venus and all her works, from slaughtered Wyandottes to broken dishes. Even as I did so I was conscious of something chastened in Mr. Knox's demeanour, some touch of remoteness and melancholy with which I was quite unfamiliar; my indictment weakened and my grievances became trivial when laid before this grave and almost religiously gentle young man.

"I'm sorry you and Mrs. Yeates should be vexed by

her. Send her back when you like. I'll keep her. Maybe it'll not be for so long after all."

When pressed to expound this dark saying, Flurry smiled wanly and snipped a second line in the hair of the puppy that was pinned between his legs. I was almost relieved when a hard try to bite on the part of the puppy imparted to Flurry's language a transient warmth; but the reaction was only temporary.

"It'd be as good for me to make a present of this lot to old Welby as to take the price he's offering me," he went on, as he got up and took off his highly scented kennel-coat; "but I couldn't be bothered fighting him. Come on in and have something. I drink tea myself at this hour."

If he had said toast and water it would have seemed no more than was suitable to such a frame of mind. As I followed him to the house I thought that when the day came that Flurry Knox could not be bothered with fighting old Welby things were becoming serious, but I kept this opinion to myself and merely offered an admiring comment on the roses that were blooming on the front of the house.

"I put up every stick of that trellis myself with my own hands," said Flurry, still gloomily; "the roses were trailing all over the place for the want of it. Would you like to have a look at the garden while they're getting tea? I settled it up a bit since you saw it last."

I acceded to this almost alarmingly lady-like suggestion, marvelling greatly.

Flurry certainly was a changed man, and his garden was a changed garden. It was a very old garden, with unexpected arbours madly overgrown with flowering climbers, and a flight of grey steps leading to a terrace, where a moss-grown sundial and ancient herbaceous plants strove with nettles and briars; but I chiefly remembered it as a place where washing was wont to hang on blackcurrant bushes, and the kennel terrier matured his bones and hunted chickens. There was now rabbit wire on the gate, the walks were cleaned, the beds weeded. There was even a bed of mignonette, a row of sweet peas, and a blazing party of sunflowers, and Michael, once second in command in many a filibustering expedition, was now on his knees, ingloriously tying carnations to little pieces of cane.

We walked up the steps to the terrace. Down below us the rich and southern blue of the sea filled the gaps between scattered fir-trees; the hillside above was purple with heather; a bay mare and her foal were moving lazily through the bracken, with the sun glistening on it and them. I looked back at the house, nestling in the hollow of the hill, I smelled the smell of the mignonette in the air, I regarded Michael's labouring back among the carnations, and without any connection of ideas I seemed to see Miss Sally Knox, with her golden-red hair and slight figure, standing on the terrace beside her kinsman.

"Michael! Do ye know where's Misther Flurry?" squalled a voice from the garden gate, the untrammelled voice of the female domestic at large among her fellows. "The tay's wet, and there's a man over with a message from Aussolas. He was tellin' me the owld hairo beyant is giving out invitations——"

A stricken silence fell, induced, no doubt, by hasty danger signals from Michael.

"Who's 'the old hero beyant'?" I asked, as we turned towards the house.

"My grandmother," said Flurry, permitting himself a smile that had about as much sociability in it as skim milk; "she's giving a tenants' dance at Aussolas. She gave one about five years ago, and I declare you might as well get the influenza into the country, or a mission at the chapel. There won't be a servant in the place will be able to answer their name for a week after it, what with toothache and headache, and blathering in the kitchen!"

We had tea in the drawing-room, a solemnity which I could not but be aware was due to the presence of a new carpet, a new wall-paper, and a new piano. Flurry made no comment on these things, but something told me that I was expected to do so, and I did.

"I'd sell you the lot to-morrow for half what I gave for them," said my host, eyeing them with morose respect as he poured out his third cup of tea.

I have all my life been handicapped by not having the courage of my curiosity. Those who have the nerve to ask direct questions on matters that do not concern them seldom fail to extract direct answers, but in my lack of this enviable gift I went home in the dark as to what had befallen my landlord, and fully aware of how my wife would despise me for my shortcomings. Philippa always says that she never asks questions, but she seems none the less to get a lot of answers.

On my own avenue I met Miss Sally Knox riding away from the house on her white cob; she had found no one at home, and she would not turn back with me, but she did not seem to be in any hurry to ride away. I told her that I had just been over to see her relative, Mr. Knox, who had informed me that he meant to give up the hounds, a fact in which she seemed only convention-ally interested. She looked pale, and her eyelids were slightly pink; I checked myself on the verge of asking her if she had hay-fever, and inquired instead if she had heard of the tenants' dance at Aussolas. She did not answer at first, but rubbed her cane up and down the cob's clipped toothbrush of a mane. Then she said:

"Major Yeates—look here—there's a most awful row at home!"

I expressed incoherent regret, and wished to my heart that Philippa had been there to cope with the situation.

"It began when mamma found out about Flurry's racing Sultan, and then came our dance——"

Miss Sally stopped; I nodded, remembering certain episodoes of Lady Knox's dance.

"And—mamma says—she says——"

I waited respectfully to hear what mamma had said; the cob fidgeted under the attentions of the horseflies, and nearly trod on my toe.

"Well, the end of it is," she said with a gulp, "she said such things to Flurry that he can't come near the house again, and I'm to go over to England to Aunt Dora, next week. Will you tell Philippa I came to say good-bye to her? I don't think I can get over here again."

Miss Sally was a sufficiently old friend of mine for me to take her hand and press it in a fatherly manner, but for the life of me I could not think of anything to say, unless I expressed my sympathy with her mother's point of view about detrimentals, which was obviously not the thing to do.

Philippa accorded to my news the rare tribute of speechless attention, and then was despicable enough to say that she had foreseen the whole affair from the beginning.

"From the day that she refused him in the ice-house, I suppose," said I sarcastically.

"That *was* the beginning," replied Philippa.

"Well," I went on judicially, "whenever it began, it was high time for it to end. She can do a good deal better than Flurry."

Philippa became rather red in the face.

"I call that a thoroughly commonplace thing to say," she said. "I dare say he has not many ideas beyond horses, but no more has she, and he really does come and borrow books from me——"

"*Whitaker's Almanack*," I murmured.

"Well, I don't care, I like him very much, and I know what you're going to say, and you're wrong, and I'll tell you why——"

Here Mrs. Cadogan came into the room, her cap at rather more than its usual warlike angle over her scarlet forehead, and in her hand a kitchen plate, on which a note was ceremoniously laid forth.

"But this is for you, Mrs. Cadogan," said Philippa, as she looked at it.

"Ma'am," returned Mrs. Cadogan with immense dignity, "I have no learning, and from what the young

223

man's afther telling me that brought it from Aussolas,
I'd sooner yerself read it for me than thim gerrls."

My wife opened the envelope, and drew forth a gilt-
edged sheet of pink paper.

"Miss Margaret Nolan presents her compliments to
Mrs. Cadogan," she read, "and I have the pleasure of
telling you that the servants of Aussolas is inviting you
and Mr. Peter Cadogan, Miss Mulrooney, and Miss
Gallagher"—Philippa's voice quavered perilously—"to
a dance on next Wednesday. Dancing to begin at seven
o'clock, and to go on till five.—Yours affectionately,
Maggie Nolan."

"How affectionate she is!" snorted Mrs. Cadogan;
"them's Dublin manners, I dare say!"

"P.S.," continued Philippa; "steward, Mr. Denis
O'Loughlin; stewardess, Mrs. Mahony."

"Thoughtful provision," I remarked; "I suppose Mrs.
Mahony's duties will begin after supper."

"Well, Mrs. Cadogan," said Philippa, quelling me
with a glance. "I suppose you'd all like to go?"

"As for dancin'," said Mrs. Cadogan, with her eyes
fixed on a level with the curtain-pole, "I thank God I'm
a widow, and the only dancin' I'll do is to dance to my
grave."

"Well, Perhaps Julia, and Annie, and Peter——"
suggested Philippa, considerably overawed.

"I'm not one of them that holds with loud mockery
and harangues," continued Mrs. Cadogan, "but if I had
any wish for dhrawing down talk I could tell you,
ma'am, that the like o' them has their share of dances
without going to Aussolas! Wasn't it only last Sunday
week I wint follyin' the turkey that's layin' out in the
plantation, and the whole o' thim hysted their sails and
back with them to their lovers at the gate-house, and
the kitchenmaid having a Jew-harp to be playing for
them!"

"That was very wrong," said the truckling Philippa,
"I hope you spoke to the kitchenmaid about it."

"Is it spake to thim?" rejoined Mrs. Cadogan. "No,

but what I done was to dhrag the kitchenmaid round the passages by the hair o' the head!"

"Well, after that, I think you might let her go to Aussolas," said I venturously.

The end of it was that everyone in and about the house went to Aussolas on the following Wednesday, including Mrs. Cadogan. Philippa had gone over to stay at the Shutes, ostensibly to arrange about a jumble sale, the real object being (as a matter of history) to inspect the Scotch young lady before whom Bernard Shute had dumped his affections in his customary manner. Being alone, with every prospect of a bad dinner, I accepted with gratitude an invitation to dine and sleep at Aussolas and see the dance; it is only on very special occasions that I have the heart to remind Philippa that she had neither part nor lot in what occurred—it is too serious a matter for trivial gloryings.

Mrs. Knox had asked me to dine at six o'clock, which meant that I arrived, in blazing sunlight and evening clothes, punctually at that hour, and that at seven o'clock I was still sitting in the library, reading heavily bound classics, while my hostess held loud conversations downstairs with Denis O'Loughlin, the red-bearded Robinson Crusoe who combined in himself the offices of coachman, butler, and, to the best of my belief, valet to the lady of the house. The door opened at last, and Denis, looking as furtive as his prototype after he had sighted the footprint, pushed in his head and beckoned to me.

"The misthress says will ye go to dinner without her," he said very confidentially; "sure she's greatly vexed ye should be waitin' on her. 'Twas the kitchen chimney cot fire, and faith she's afther giving Biddy Mahony the sack, on the head of it! Though, indeed, 'tis little we'd regard a chimney on fire here any other day."

Mrs. Knox's woolly dog was the sole occupant of the dining-room when I entered it; he was sitting on his mistress's chair, with all the air of outrage peculiar to a small and self-important dog when routine has been

225

interfered with. It was difficult to discover what had caused the delay, the meal, not excepting the soup, being a cold collation; it was heavily flavoured with soot, and was hurled on to the table by Crusoe in spasmodic bursts, contemporaneous, no doubt, with Biddy Mahony's fits of hysterics in the kitchen. Its most memorable feature was a noble lake trout, which appeared in two jagged pieces, a matter lightly alluded to by Denis as the result of " a little argument" between himself and Biddy as to the dish on which it was to be served. Further conversation elicited the interesting fact that the combatants had pulled the trout in two before the matter was settled. A brief glance at my attendant's hands decided me to let the woolly dog justify his existence by consuming my portion for me when Crusoe left the room.

Old Mrs. Knox remained invisible till the end of dinner, when she appeared in the purple velvet bonnet that she was reputed to have worn since the famine, and a dun-coloured woollen shawl fastened by a splendid diamond brooch, that flashed rainbow fire against the last shafts of sunet. There was a fire in the old lady's eye, too, the light that I had sometimes seen in Flurry's in moments of crisis.

"I have no apologies to offer that are worth hearing," she said, "but I have come to drink a glass of port wine with you, if you will so far honour me, and then we must go out and see the ball. My grandson is late, as usual."

She crumbled a biscuit with a brown and preoccupied hand; her claw-like fingers carried a crowded sparkle of diamonds upwards as she raised her glass to her lips.

The twilight was falling as we left the room and made our way downstairs. I followed the little figure in the purple bonnet through dark regions of passages and doorways, where strange lumber lay about; there was a rusty suit of armour, an upturned punt, mouldering pictures, and finally, by a door that opened into the yard, a lady's bicycle, white with the dust of travel. I

supposed this latter to have been imported from Dublin
by the fashionable Miss Maggie Nolan, but on the other
hand it was well within the bounds of possibility that it
belonged to old Mrs. Knox. The coach-house at Aussolas was on a par with the rest of the establishment, being
vast, dilapidated, and of unknown age. Its three double
doors were wide open, and the guests overflowed through
them into the cobble-stoned yard; above their heads the
tin reflectors of paraffin lamps glared at us from among
the Christmas decorations of holly and ivy that fes-
tooned the walls. The voices of a fiddle and a concertina, combined, were uttering a polka with shrill and
hideous fluency, to which the scraping and stamping of
hobnailed boots made a ponderous bass accompaniment.

Mrs. Knox's donkey-chair had been placed in a commanding position at the top of the room, and she made
her way slowly to it, shaking hands with all varieties of
tenants and saying right things without showing any
symptom of that flustered boredom that I have myself
exhibited when I went round the men's messes on
Christmas Day. She took her seat in the donkey-chair,
with the white dog in her lap, and looked with her
hawk's eyes round the array of faces that hemmed in
the space where the dancers were solemnly bobbing and
hopping.

"Will you tell me who that tomfool is, Denis?" she
said, pointing to a young lady in a ball dress who was
circling in conscious magnificence and somewhat painful
incongruity in the arms of Mr. Peter Cadogan.

"That's the lady's-maid from Castle Knox, yer honour,
ma'am," replied Denis, with something remarkably like
a wink at Mrs. Knox.

"When did the Castle Knox servants come?" asked
the old lady, very sharply.

"The same time yer honour left the table, and——
Pillilew! What's this?

There was a clatter of galloping hoofs in the court-
yard, as of a troop of cavalry, and out of the heart of it
Flurry's voice shouting to Denis to drive out the colts

227

and shut the gates before they had the people killed. I noticed that the colour had risen to Mrs. Knox's face, and I put it down to anxiety about her young horses. I may admit that when I heard Flurry's voice, and saw him collaring his grandmother's guests and pushing them out of the way as he came into the coach-house, I rather feared that he was in the condition so often defined to me at Petty Sessions as "not dhrunk, but having dhrink taken". His face was white, his eyes glittered, there was a general air of exaltation about him that suggested the solace of the pangs of love according to the most ancient convention.

"Hullo!" he said, swaggering up to the orchestra, "what's this humbugging thing they're playing? A polka, is it? Drop that, John Casey, and play a jig."

John Casey ceased abjectly.

"What'll I play, Masther Flurry?"

"What the devil do I care? Here, Yeates, put a name on it! You're a sort of musicianer yourself!"

I know the names of three or four Irish jigs; but on this occasion my memory clung exclusively to one, I suppose because it was the one I felt to be peculiarly inappropriate.

"Oh, well, 'Haste to the Wedding', I said, looking away.

Flurry gave a shout of laughter.

"That's it!" he exclaimed. "Play it up, John! Give us 'Haste to the Wedding'. That's Major Yeates's fancy!"

Decidedly Flurry was drunk.

"What's wrong with you all that you aren't dancing?" he continued, striding up the middle of the room. "Maybe you don't know how. Here, I'll soon get one that'll show you!"

He advanced upon his grandmother, snatched her out of the donkey-chair, and, amid roars of applause, led her out, while the fiddle squealed its way through the inimitable twists of the tune, and the concertina surged and panted after it. Whatever Mrs. Knox may have thought of her grandson's behaviour, she was evidently going to make the best of it. She took her station opposite to him, in the purple bonnet, the dun-coloured shawl, and the diamonds, she picked up her skirt at each side, affording a view of narrow feet in elastic-sided cloth boots, and for three repeats of the tune she stood up to her grandson, and footed it on the coach-house floor. What the cloth boots did I could not exactly follow; they were, as well as I could see, extremely scientific, while there was hardly so much as a nod from the plumes of the bonnet. Flurry was also scientific, but his dancing did not alter my opinion that he was drunk; in fact, I thought he was making rather an exhibition of himself. They say that that jig was twenty pounds in Mrs. Knox's pocket at the next rent day; but though this statement is open to doubt, I believe that if she and Flurry had taken the hat round there and then she would have got in the best part of her arrears.

After this the company settled down to business. The dances lasted a sweltering half-hour, old women and young dancing with equal and tireless zest. At the end of each the gentlemen abandoned their partners without ceremony or comment, and went out to smoke, while the ladies retired to the laundry, where families of tea-pots stewed on the long bars of the fire, and Mrs. Mahony cut up mighty "barm-bracks", and the tea-drinking was illimitable.

At ten o'clock Mrs. Knox withdrew from the revel; she said that she was tired, but I have seldom seen any-one look more wide awake. I thought that I might unobtrusively follow her example, but I was intercepted by Flurry.

"Yeates," he said seriously, "I'll take it as a kind-ness if you'll see this thing out with me. We must keep them pretty sober, and get them out of this by daylight. I—I have to get home early."

I at once took back my opinion that Flurry was drunk; I almost wished he had been, as I could then have deserted him without a pang. As it was, I addressed

229

myself heavily to the night's enjoyment. Wan with heat,
but conscientiously cheerful, I danced with Miss Maggie
Nolan, with the Castle Knox lady's-maid, with my own
kitchenmaid, who fell into wild giggles of terror whenever I spoke to her, with Mrs. Cadogan, who had
apparently postponed the interesting feat of dancing to
her grave, and did what she could to dance me into
mine. I am bound to admit that though an ex-soldier
and a major, and therefore equipped with a ready-made
character for gallantry, Mrs. Cadogan was the only one
of my partners with whom I conversed with any comfort.

At intervals I smoked cigarettes in the yard, seated on
the old mounting-block by the gate, and overheard much
conversation about the price of pigs in Skebawn; at
intervals I plunged again into the coach-house, and led
forth a perspiring wallflower into the scrimmage of a
polka, or shuffled meaninglessly opposite to her in the
long double line of dancers who were engaged with
serious faces in executing a jig or a reel, I neither knew
nor cared which. Flurry remained as undefeated as ever;
I could only suppose it was his method of showing that
his broken heart had mended.

"It's time to be making the punch, Masther Flurry,"
said Denis, as the harness-room clock struck twelve;
"sure the night's warm, and the men's all gaping for it,
the craytures!"

"What'll we make it in?" said Flurry, as we followed
him into the laundry.

"The boiler, to be sure," said Crusoe, taking up a
stone of suger, and preparing to shoot it into the laundry
copper.

"Stop, you fool, it's full of cockroaches!" shouted
Flurry, amid sympathetic squalls from the throng of
country-women. "Go get a bath!"

"Sure yerself knows there's but one bath in it," retorted Denis, "and that's within in the Major's room.
Faith, the tinker got his own share yesterday with the
same bath, sthriving to quinch the holes, and they as

thick in it as the stars in the sky, and 'tis weeping still, afther all he done!"

"Well, then, here goes for the cockroaches!" said Flurry. "What doesn't sicken will fatten! Give me the kettle, and come on you, Kitty Collins, and be skimming them off!"

There were no complaints of the punch when the brew was completed, and the dance thundered on with a heavier stamping and a louder hilarity than before. The night wore on; I squeezed through the unyielding pack of frieze coats and shawls in the doorway, and with feet that momentarily swelled in my pumps I limped over the cobblestones to smoke my eighth cigarette on the mounting-block. It was a dark, hot night. The old castle loomed above me in piled-up roofs and gables, and high up in it somewhere a window sent a shaft of light into the sleeping leaves of a walnut-tree that overhung the gateway. At the bars of the gate two young horses peered in at the medley of noise and people; away in an outhouse a cock crew hoarsely. The gaiety in the coach-house increased momently, till, amid shrieks and bursts of laughter, Miss Maggie Nolan fled coquettishly from it with a long yell, like a train coming out of a tunnel, pursued by the fascinating Peter Cadogan brandishing a twig of mountain ash, in imitation of mistletoe. The young horses stampeded in horror, and immediately a voice proceeded from the lighted window above, Mrs. Knox's voice, demanding what the noise was, and announcing that if she heard any more of it she would have the place cleared.

An awful silence fell, to which the young horses' fleeing hoofs lent the final touch of consternation. Then I heard the irrepressible Maggie Nolan say: "Oh God! Merry-come-sad!" which I take to be a reflection on the mutability of all earthly happiness.

Mrs. Knox remained for a moment at the window, and it struck me as remarkable that at 2.30 a.m. she should still have on her bonnet. I thought I heard her speak to someone in the room, and there followed a laugh, a laugh that was not a servant's, and was puzzlingly familiar. I gave it up, and presently dropped into a cheerless doze.

With the dawn there came a period when even Flurry showed signs of failing. He came and sat down beside me with a yawn; it struck me that there was more impatience and nervousness than fatigue in the yawn.

"I think I'll turn them all out of this after the next dance is over," he said; "I've got a lot to do, and I can't stay here."

I grunted in drowsy approval. It must have been a few minutes later that I felt Flurry grip my shoulder.

"Yeates!" he said; "look up at the roof. Do you see anything up there, by the kitchen chimney?"

He was pointing at a heavy stack of chimneys in a tower that stood up against the grey and pink of the morning sky. At the angle where one of them joined the roof smoke was oozing busily out, and, as I stared, a little wisp of flame stole through.

The next thing I distinctly remember is being in the van of a rush through the kitchen passages, everyone shouting "Water! Water!" and not knowing where to find it, then up several flights of the narrowest and darkest stairs it has ever been my fate to ascend, with a bucket of water that I snatched from a woman, spilling as I ran. At the top of the stairs came a ladder leading to a trap-door, and up in the dark loft above was the roar and the wavering glare of flames.

"My God! That's sthrong fire!" shouted Denis, tumbling down the ladder with a brace of empty buckets; "we'll never save it! The lake won't quinch it!"

The flames were squirting out through the bricks of the chimney, through the timbers, through the slates; it was barely possible to get through the trap-door, and the booming and crackling strengthened every instant.

"A chain to the lake!" gasped Flurry, coughing in the stifling heat as he slashed the water at the blazing rafters; "the well's no good! Go on, Yeates!"

The organizing of a double chain out of the mob that thronged and shouted and jammed in the passages and yard was no mean feat of generalship; but it got done somehow. Mrs. Cadogan and Biddy Mahony rose magnificently to the occasion, cursing, thumping, shoving; and stable buckets, coal buckets, milk pails, and kettles were unearthed and sent swinging down the grass slope to the lake that lay in glittering unconcern in the morning sunshine. Men, women and children worked in a way that only Irish people can work in an emergency. All their cleverness, all their good-heartedness, and all their love of a ruction came to the front; the screaming and the exhortations were incessant, but so were also the buckets that flew from hand to hand up the loft. I hardly know how long we were at it, but there came a time when I looked up from the yard and saw that the billows of reddened smoke from the top of the tower were dying down, and I bethought me of old Mrs. Knox.

I found her at the door of her room, engaged in tying up a bundle of old clothes in a sheet; she looked as white as a corpse, but she was not in any way quelled by the situation.

"I'd be obliged to you, all the same, Major Yeates, to throw this over the balusters," she said, as I advanced with the news that the fire had been got under. " 'Pon my honour, I don't know when I've been as vexed as I've been this night, what with one thing and another! 'Tis a monstrous thing to use a guest as we've used you, but what could we do? I threw all the silver out of the dining-room window myself, and the poor peahen that had her nest there was hurt by an entrée dish, and half her eggs were——"

There was a curious sound not unlike a titter in Mrs. Knox's room.

"However, we can't make omelettes without breaking eggs—as they say——" she went on rather hurriedly; "I declare I don't know what I'm saying! My poor old head is confused——"

Here Mrs. Knox went abruptly into her room and shut the door. Obviously there was nothing further to do for my hostess, and I fought my way up the dripping back staircase to the loft. The flames had ceased, the supply of buckets had stopped, and Flurry, standing on a ponderous crossbeam, was poking his head and shoulders out into the sunlight through the hole that had been burned in the roof. Denis and others were pouring water over charred beams, the atmosphere was still stifling, everything was black, everything dripped with inky water. Flurry descended from his beam and stretched himself, looking like a drowned chimney-sweep.

"We've made a night of it, Yeates, haven't we?" he said, "but we've bested it anyhow. We were done for only for you!" There was more emotion about him than the occasion seemed to warrant, and his eyes had a Christy Minstrel brightness, not wholly to be attributed to the dirt on his face. "What's the time?—I must get home."

The time, incredible as it seemed, was half-past-six. I could almost have sworn that Flurry changed colour when I said so.

"I must be off," he said; "I had no idea it was so late."

"Why, what's the hurry?" I asked.

He stared at me, laughed foolishly, and fell to giving directions to Denis. Five minutes afterwards he drove out of the yard and away at a canter down the long stretch of avenue that skirted the lake, with a troop of young horses flying on either hand. He whirled his whip round his head and shouted at them, and was lost to sight in a clump of trees. It is a vision of him that remains with me, and it always carries with it the bitter smell of wet charred wood.

Reaction had begun to set in among the volunteers. The chain took to sitting in the kitchen, cups of tea began mysteriously to circulate, and personal narratives of the fire were already foreshadowing the amazing legends that have since gathered round the night's adventure. I left to Denis the task of cleaning the house, and went up to change my wet clothes, with a feeling that I had not been to bed for a year. The ghost of a waiter who had drowned himself in a bog-hole would have presented a cheerier aspect than I, as I surveyed myself in the prehistoric mirror in my room, with the sunshine falling on my unshorn face and begrimed shirt-front.

I made my toilet at considerable length, and, it being now nearly eight o'clock, went downstairs to look for something to eat. I had left the house humming with people; I found it silent as Pompeii. The sheeted bundles containing Mrs. Knox's wardrobe were lying about the hall; a couple of ancestors who in the first alarm had been dragged from the walls were leaning drunkenly against the bundles; last night's dessert was still on the dining-room table. I went out on to the hall-door steps, and saw the entrée dishes in a glittering heap in a nasturtium bed, and realized that there was no breakfast for me this side of lunch at Shreelane.

There was a sound of wheels on the avenue, and a brougham came into view, driving fast up the long open stretch by the lake. It was the Castle Knox brougham, driven by Norris, whom I had last seen drunk at the athletic sports, and as it drew up at the door I saw Lady Knox inside.

"It's all right, the fire's out," I said, advancing genially and full of reassurance.

"What fire?" said Lady Knox, regarding me with an iron countenance.

I explained.

"Well, as the house isn't burned down," said Lady Knox, cutting short my details, "perhaps you would kindly find out if I could see Mrs. Knox."

Lady Knox's face was many shades redder than usual. I began to understand that something awful had happened, or would happen, and I wished myself safe at Shreelane, with the bedclothes over my head.

"If 'tis for the misthrss you're looking, me lady,"

235

said Denis's voice behind me, in tones of the utmost respect, "she went out to the kitchen garden a while ago to get a blasht o' the fresh air afther the night. Maybe your ladyship would sit inside in the library till I call her?"

Lady Knox eyed Crusoe suspiciously.

"Thank you, I'll fetch her myself," she said.

"O, sure, that's no throuble——" began Denis.

"Stay where you are!" said Lady Knox, in a voice like the slam of a door.

"Bedad, I'm best plased she went," whispered Denis, as Lady Knox set forth alone down the shrubbery walk.

"But *is* Mrs. Knox in the garden?" said I.

"The Lord preserve your innocence, sir!" replied Denis, with seeming irrelevance.

At this moment I became aware of the incredible fact that Sally Knox was silently descending the stairs; she stopped short as she got into the hall, and looked almost wildly at me and Denis. Was I looking at her wraith? There was again a sound of wheels on the gravel; she went to the hall door, outside which was now drawn up Mrs. Knox's donkey-carriage, as well as Lady Knox's brougham, and, as if overcome by this imposing spectacle, she turned back and put her hands over her face.

"She's gone round to the garden, asthore," said Denis in a hoarse whisper; "go in the donkey-carriage. 'Twill be all right!" He seized her by the arm, pushed her down the steps and into the little carriage, pulled up the hood over her to its furthest stretch, snatched the whip out of the hand of the broadly grinning Norris, and with terrific objurgations lashed the donkey into a gallop. The donkey-boy grasped the position, whatever it might be; he took up the running on the other side, and the donkey-carriage swung away down the avenue, with all its incongruous air of hooded and rowdy invalidism.

I have never disguised the fact that I am a coward, and therefore when, at this dynamitical moment, I caught a glimpse of Lady Knox's hat over a laurustinus as she

236

returned at high speed from the garden, I slunk into the house and faded away round the dining-room door.

"This minute I seen the misthress going down through the plantation beyond," said the voice of Crusoe outside the window, "and I'm afther sending Johnny Regan to her with the little carriage, not to put any more delay on yer ladyship. Sure you can see him making all the haste he can. Maybe you'd sit inside in the library till she comes."

Silence followed. I peered cautiously round the window curtain. Lady Knox was looking defiantly at the donkey-carriage as it reeled at top speed into the shades of the plantation, strenuously pursued by the woolly dog. Norris was regarding his horses' ears in expressionless respectability. Denis was picking up the entrée dishes with decorous solicitude. Lady Knox turned and came into the house; she passed the dining-room door with an ominous step, and went on into the library.

It seemed to me that now or never was the moment to retire quietly to my room, put my things into my portmanteau, and——

Denis rushed into the room with the entrée dishes piled up to his chin.

"She's diddled!" he whispered, crashing them down on the table. He came at me with his hand out. "Three cheers for Masther Flurry and Miss Sally," he hissed, wringing my hand up and down, "and 'twas yerself called for 'Haste to the Weddin'' last night, long life to ye! The Lord save us! There's the misthress going into the library!"

Through the half-open door I saw old Mrs. Knox approach the library from the staircase with a dignified slowness; she had on a wedding garment, a long white burnous, in which she might easily have been mistaken for a small, stout clergyman. She waved back Crusoe, the door closed upon her, and the battle of giants was entered upon. I sat down—it was all I was able for—and remained for a full minute in stupefied contemplation of the entrée dishes.

Perhaps of all conclusions to a situation so portentous, that which occurred was the least possible. Twenty minutes after Mrs. Knox met her antagonist I was summoned from strapping my portmanteau to face the appalling duty of escorting the combatants, in Lady Knox's brougham, to the church outside the back gate, to which Miss Sally had preceded them in the donkey-carriage. I pulled myself together, went downstairs, and found that the millennium had suddenly set in. It had apparently dawned with the news that Aussolas and all things therein were bequeathed to Flurry by his grandmother, and had established itself finally upon the considerations that the marriage was past praying for, and that the diamonds were intended for Miss Sally.

We fetched the bride and bridegroom from the church; we fetched old Eustace Hamilton, who married them; we dug out the champagne from the cellar; we even found rice and threw it.

The hired carriage that had been ordered to take the runaways across country to a distant station was driven by Slipper. He was shaved; he wore an old livery coat and a new pot hat; he was wondrous sober. On the following morning he was found asleep on a heap of stones ten miles away; somewhere in the neighbourhood one of the horses was grazing in a field with a certain amount of harness hanging about it. The carriage and the remaining horse were discovered in a roadside ditch, two miles farther on; one of the carriage doors had been torn off, and in the interior the hens of the vicinity were conducting an intensive search after the rice that lurked in the cushions.

THE PUG-NOSED FOX

"5 Turkies and their Mother
 5 Ducks and the Drake
 5 Hins and the Cock
        CATHARINE O'DONOVAN, Skeagh"

A leaf from a copy-book, with these words written on
it, was placed in my hand as I was in the act of dragging
on a new pair of gloves in the stableyard. There was
something rhythmic in the category, suggestive of burnt-
offerings and incantations; some touch of pathos, pointing to tragedy; something, finally, that in the light of
previous events recalled to me suddenly and unpleasantly
my new-born position of Deputy M.F.H.

Not, indeed, that I was in need at that moment of circumstances to remind me of it. A new hunting-cap,
pressing implacably upon my forehead, an equally new
red coat, heavy as a coat of mail, a glittering horn, red
hot from the makers, and so far totally unresponsive to
my apoplectic wooings; these things in themselves, without the addition of a poultry bill, were sufficient to bring
home to me my amazing folly in having succumbed to
the wiles of Mr. Florence McCarthy Knox, and accepted
the charge of his hounds, during his absence with the
Irish Yeomanry at the South African War.

I had yielded in a burst of patriotic emotion to the
spirit of volunteering that was in the air. It would be,
Flurry had assured me, a purely nominal position.

"They'll only go out one day a week, and Jerome
Hickey and Michael'll do all the work. I do secretary
for myself, but that'll be no trouble to you. There's
nothing at all to do but send out the cards of the meets.

It'll be a comfort to me to think you were running the show."

I suggested other names that seemed to me infinitely more comfortable, but found them blocked by intricate and insuperable objections, and when I became aware that Mr. Knox had so engineered his case as to get my wife on his side it seemed simpler to give in.

A week afterwards I saw Flurry off at the station. His last words to me were:

"Well, good-bye, Major. Be fighting my grandmother for her subscription, and whatever you do, don't give more than half a crown for a donkey. There's no meat on them."

Upon this touching farewell the train steamed out, and left me standing, shelterless, a reluctant and incapable Master of Hounds.

Exhaustive as Flurry's instructions had been on the subject of the cuisine and other details of kennel management, he had not even hinted at the difficulties that are usually composed by means of a fowl fund. My first experience of these had taken place about a week ago, when from the breakfast-table I had perceived a donkey and cart rambling, unattended, in the shrubberies, among the young hydrangeas and azaleas. The owner, a most respectable-looking old man, explained that he had left it there because he was "delicate" to bring it up to the house, and added that he had come for compensation for "a beautiful milking goat" that the hounds had eaten last March, "and she having two kids that died after her".

I asked why he had not long since been to Mr. Knox about it, and was favoured with an interminable history of the claimant's ill-health during the summer, consequent on his fretting after the goat; of how he had been anointed four times, and of how the donkey was lame this long while where a branch bet her in the thigh one day she ran into the wood from the hounds. Fearing that the donkey was about to be included in the bill, I made haste to settle for the goat and her offspring, a matter of fifteen shillings.

Next day two women took up a position on the steps at luncheon-time, a course which experience has taught me indicates affairs too exalted and too personal to be transmitted via the kitchen. They were, according to their own showing, ruined proprietors of poultry yards, in proof of which they pointed to a row of decapitated hens, laid forth on the grass like the bag at a fashionable shoot. I was irritably aware of their triumph in the trophy.

"Sure he didn't make off with anny of them only three, but he snapped the heads off all that was in it, and faith, if Masther Flurry was at home, he'd give us the blood of his arm before he'd see our little hins desthroyed on us this way."

I gave them thirty-two and sixpence as an alternative compensation, not, I admit, without an uneasy sense of something unusual in Peter Cadogan's expression, as he assiduously raked the gravel hard by.

It was Michael Leary, Flurry's Michael, who placed the matter of a fowl fund upon a basis. Catharine O'Donovan and her list of casualties had been dismissed at a cost of ten shillings, a price so inadequate, and so cheerfully accepted, as to confirm my dawning suspicions.

"Is it what would they get from Mr. Flurry?" replied Michael when I put the matter to him; "it isn't ten shillings, no, nor thirty-two shillings that they'd get from him, but a pelt of a curse after their heels! Why wouldn't they keep their hens inside in the house with themselves at night, the same as annyone that'd have sense, and not to leave them out enticing the fox this way."

Michael was in a bad temper, and so, for the matter of that, was I, quite irrespective of dealings in poultry. Our red coats, our horses, and the presence of the hounds, did not betoken the chase, they merely indicated that the Hunt was about to be photographed. The local photographer, backed by Mrs. Sinclair Yeates, had extorted from me the privilege of "a sitting", a figurative expression, involving a ride of five miles to a covert, selected by my wife as being typical of the country, accompanied by the fourteen and a half couple of half-bred harriers who figured in Hound Lists as "Mr. Knox's Foxhounds".

It was a blazing day in late August, following on forty-eight hours of blanketing sea-fog; a day for flannels and a languid game of croquet. Lady Jane, the grey mare lent to me by Flurry, had been demoralized by her summer at grass, and was in that peculiarly loathsome frame of mind that is a blend of laziness and bumptiousness. If I left her to her own devices she drowsed, stumbling, through the dust; if I corrected her, she pranced and pulled, and kicked up behind like a donkey. My huntsman, Doctor Jerome Hickey, who was to have been in the forefront of the photograph, was twenty miles off in an open boat, on his way to an island at the far end of his dispensary district, with fifteen cases of measles ahead of him. I envied him; measles or no, he had on a turned down collar. As a result of his absence I rode in solitary dignity at the head of the pack, or, to speak more correctly, I preceded Michael by some thirty yards of unoccupied road, while the pack, callous to flogging, and disdainful of my cajoleries, clave to the heels of Michael's horse.

In this order we arrived at the tryst, a heathery hill side, flanked by a dense and rambling wood. A sea-gull scream from the hillside announced the presence of my wife, and summoned me to join her and the photographer at the spot where they were encamped. I put the mare at a suitable place in the wall by the roadside. She refused it which was no more than I had expected. I sampled my new spurs on her fat sides, with the result that she charged the wall, slantways, at the exact spot where Philippa had placed her bicycle against it, missed the bicycle by a hair's-breadth, landed in the field with a thump, on all four feet, and ended with two most distressing bucks. It was a consolation to me, when I came in touch again with the saddle, to find that one of the new spurs had ploughed a long furrow in her shoulder.

The photographer was a young man from Belfast, a new-comer to the neighbourhood; Philippa is also a photographer, a fact that did not tend as much as might have been expected to the harmony of the occasion.

"Mrs. Yeates has selected this hillock," said Mr. McOstrich, in tones of acrid resignation, indicating as he spoke a sugar-loaf shaped knoll, thickly matted with furze and heather. "She considers the background characteristic. My own suggestion would have been the grass field yonder."

It is an ancient contention of my wife that I, in common with all other men, in any dispute between a female relative and a tradesman, side with the trades-man, partly from fear, partly from masculine clannish-ness, and most of all from a desire to stand well with the tradesman. Nothing but the remembrance of this preposterous reproach kept me from accepting Mr. McOstrich's point of view, and, while I hesitated, Michael was already taking up his position on the hillock, perhaps in obedience to some signal from Philippa, perhaps because he had realized the excellent concealment afforded by the deep heather to his horse's fetlocks, whose outline was of a somewhat gouty type. It was part of Flurry Knox's demoniac gift for horse-flesh that he should be able to buy screws and make them serve his exacting purposes. Michael's horse, Moses, had, at a distance, the appearance of standing upon four champagne bottles, but he none the less did the work of two sound horses and did it well.

I goaded Lady Jane through the furze, and established myself beside Michael on the sugar-loaf, the hounds disposed themselves in an interval of bracken below, and Mr. McOstrich directed his camera upon us from an opposite slope.

"Show your teeth, please," said Mr. McOstrich to Michael. Michael already simmering with indignation

243

at the senseless frivolity of the proceedings, glowered at his knuckles, evidently suspicious of an ill-timed pleasantry.

"Do you hear, Whip?" repeated Mr. McOstrich, raising his bleak northern voice, "show your teeth, please!"

"He only wants to focus us," said I, foreseeing trouble, and hurriedly displaying my own new front row in a galvanic smile.

Michael murmured to Moses' withers something that sounded like a promise to hocus Mr. McOstrich when occasion should serve, and I reflected on the hardship of having to feel apologetic towards both Michael and the photographer.

Only those who have participated in "Hunt Groups" can realize the combined tediousness and tension of the moments that followed. To keep thirty hounds headed for the camera, to ensure that your horse has not closed its eyes and hung its head in a doze of boredom, to preserve for yourself that alert and workmanlike aspect that becomes a sportsman, and then, when these things have been achieved and maintained for what feels like a month, to see the tripod move in spider strides to a fresh position and know that all has to be begun over again. After several of these tentative selections of a site, the moment came when Mr. McOstrich swung his black velvet pall in the air and buried his head under its portentous folds. The hounds, though uneasy, had hitherto been comparatively calm, but at this manifestation their nerve broke, and they unanimously charged the glaring monster in the black hood with loud and hysterical cries.

Had not Michael perceived their intention while there was time awful things might have happened. As it was, the leaders were flogged off with ignominy, and the ruffled artist returned from the rock to which he had fled. Michel and I arranged ourselves afresh upon the hillock; I squared my shoulders, and felt my wonted photographic expression of hang-dog desperation settle down upon me.

"The dogs are not in the picture, Whip!" said Mr. McOstrich in the chill tone of outraged dignity.

I perceived that the hounds, much demoralized, had melted away from the slope in front of us, and were huddling in a wisp in the intervening hollow. Blandishments were of no avail; they wagged and beamed apologetically, but remained in the hollow. Michael, in whose sensitive bosom the term "Whip" evidently rankled, became scarlet in the face and avalanched from the hilltop upon his flock with a fury that was instantly recognized by them. They broke in panic, and the astute and elderly Venus, followed by two of the young entry, bolted for the road. They were there met by Mr. McOstrich's carman, who most creditably headed the puppies with yells and his driving-whip, but was outplayed by Venus, who, dodging like a football professional, doubled under the car horse, and fled irrevocably. Philippa, who had been flitting from rock to rock with her kodak, and unnerving me with injunctions as to the angle of my cap, here entered the lists with a packet of sandwiches, with which, in spite of the mustard, she restored a certain confidence to the agitated pack, a proceeding observed from afar with trembling indignation by Minx, her fox-terrier. By reckless expenditure of sandwich the hounds were tempted to their proper position below the horses, but, unfortunately, with their sterns to the camera, and their eyes fastened on Phillipa.

"Retire, madam!" said Mr. McOstrich, very severely. "*I* will attract the dogs!"

Thus rebuked, Madam scrambled hastily over the crest of the hillock and sank in unseemly laughter into the deep heather behind it.

"Now, very quiet, please," continued Mr. McOstrich, and then unexpectedly uttered the words, "Pop! Pop! Pop!" in a high soprano.

Michael clapped his hand over his mouth, the superseded siren in the heather behind me wallowed in fresh convulsions; the hounds remained unattracted.

Then arose, almost at the same moment, a voice from

245

the wood behind us, the voice of yet a third siren, more potent than that of either of her predecessors, the voice of Venus hunting a line. For the space of a breath the hounds hung on the eager hacking yelps, in the next breath they were gone.

Matters now began to move on a serious scale, and with a speed that could not have been foreseen. The wood was but fifty yards from our sugar-loaf. Before Michael had got out his horn, the hounds were over the wall, before the last stern had disappeared the leaders had broken into full cry.

"Please God it might be a rabbit!" exclaimed Michael, putting spurs to his horse and bucketing down through the furze towards the wood, with blasts of the horn that were fraught with indignation and rebuke.

An instant later, from my point of vantage on the sugar-loaf, I saw a big and very yellow fox cross an open space of heather high up on the hill above the covert. He passed and vanished; in half a dozen seconds Venus, plunging through the heather, came shrieking across the open space and also vanished. Another all too brief an interval, and the remainder of the pack had stormed through the wood and were away in the open after Venus, and Michael, who had pulled up short on the hither side of the covert wall, had started up the hill side to catch them.

The characteristic background chosen by Philippa, however admirable in a photograph, afforded one of the most diabolical rides of my experience. Uphill, over courses of rock masked in furze bushes, round the head of a boggy lake, uphill again through deep and purple heather, over a horrid wall of long slabs half buried in it; past a ruined cabin, with thorn bushes crowding low over the only feasible place in the bank, and at last, the top of the hill, and Michael pulling up to take observations.

The best pack in the kingdom, schoolmastered by a regiment of whips, could not have precipitated themselves out of covert with more academic precision than had been shown by Flurry Knox's irregulars. They had already crossed the valley below us, and were running up a long hill as if under the conventional tablecloth; their cry, floating up to us, held all the immemorial romance of the chase.

Michael regarded me with a wild eye; he looked as hot as I felt, which was saying a good deal, and both horses were puffing.

"He's all the ways for Temple Braney!" he said. "Sure I know him well—that's the pug-nosed fox that's in it these last three seasons, and it's what I wish——"

(I regret that I cannot transcribe Michael's wish in its own terms, but I may baldly summarize it as a desire minutely and anatomically specified that the hounds were eating Mr. McOstrich.)

Here the spurs were once more applied to Moses' reeking sides, and we started again, battering down the twists of a rocky lane into the steaming, stuffy valley. I felt as guilty and as responsible for the whole affair as Michael intended that I should feel; I knew that he even laid to my charge the disastrous appearance of the pug-nosed Temple Braney fox. (Whether this remarkable feature was a freak of nature, or of Michael's lurid fancy, I have never been able to ascertain.)

The valley was boggy, as well as hot, and the deep and sinuous ditch that by courtesy was supposed to drain it, was blind with rushes and tall fronds of *Osmunda regalis* fern. Where the landing was tolerable, the take-off was a swamp, where the take-off was sound the landing was feasible only for a frog; we lost five panting minutes, closely attended by horse-flies, before we somehow floundered across and began the ascent of the second hill. To face tall banks, uphill, is at no time agreeable, especially when they are enveloped in a jungle of briars, bracken, and waving grass, but a merciful dispensation of cow-gaps revealed itself; it was one of the few streaks of luck in a day not conspicuous for such.

At the top of the hill we took another pull. This

afforded to us a fine view of the Atlantic, also of the surrounding country and all that was therein, with, however, the single unfortunate exception of the hounds. There was nothing to be heard save the summery rattle of a reaping-machine, the strong and steady rasp of a corncrake, and the growl of a big steamer from a band of fog that was advancing, ghost-like, along the blue floor of the sea. Two fields away a man in a straw hat was slowly combing down the flanks of a haycock with a wooden rake, while a black and white cur slept in the young after-grass beside him. We broke into their sylvan tranquillity with a heated demand whether the hounds had passed that way. Shrill clamour from the dog was at first the only reply; its owner took off his hat, wiped his forehead with his sleeve, and stared at us.

"I'm as deaf as a beetle this three weeks," he said, continuing to look us up and down in a way that made me realize, if possible, more than before, the absurdity of looking like a Christmas card in the heat of a summer's day.

"Did ye see the *Hounds*?" shouted Michael, shoving the chestnut up beside him.

"It's the neurology I got," continued the haymaker, "an' the pain does be whistlin' out through me ear till I could mostly run into the say from it."

"It's a pity ye wouldn't," said Michael, whirling Moses round, "an' stop in it! Whisht! Look over, sir! Look over!"

He pointed with his whip along the green slopes. I saw, about half a mile away, two boys standing on a fence, and beyond them some cattle galloping in a field: three or four miles farther on the woods of Temple Braney were a purple smear in the hazy heat of the landscape. My heart sank; it was obvious even to my limited capacities that the pug-nosed fox was making good his line with a straightness not to be expected from one of his personal peculiarity, and that the hounds were still running as hard as ever on a scent as steamingly hot as the weather. I wildly thought of removing my coat and

248

leaving it in charge of the man with neuralgia, but was restrained by the reflection that he might look upon it as a gift, flung to him in a burst of compassion, a misunderstanding that, in view of his affliction, it would be impossible to rectify.

I picked up my lathered reins and followed Michael at a gloomy trot in the direction of the galloping cattle. After a few fields a road presented itself, and was eagerly accepted by the grey mare, on whom the unbridled gluttonies of a summer's grass were beginning to tell.

'She's bet up, sir," said Michael, dragging down a rickety gate with the handle of his whip. "Folly on the road, there's a near way to the wood from the cross."

Moses here walked cautiously over the prostrate gate.

"I'm afraid you'll kill Moses," said I, by no means pleased at the prospect of being separated from my Intelligence Department.

"Is it him?" replied Michael, scanning the country ahead of him with hawk eyes. "Shure he's as hardy as a throut!"

The last I saw of the trout was his bottle fetlocks disappearing nimbly in bracken as he dropped down the far side of a bank.

I "follied on the road" for two stifling miles. The heavy air was pent between high hedges hung with wisps of hay from passing carts (hay-carrying in the south-west of Ireland conforms to the leisure of the farmer rather than to the accident of season); phalanxes of flies arose as if at the approach of royalty, and accompanied my progress at a hunting jog, which, as interpreted by Lady Jane, was an effective blend of a Turkish bath and a churn.

The "near way" from the cross-roads opened seductively with a lane leading to a farmhouse, and presently degenerated into an unfenced but plausible cart track through the fields. Breaches had been made in the banks for its accommodation, and I advanced successfully towards the long woods of Temple Braney, endeavouring, less successfully, to repel the attentions of two young

249

horses, who galloped, squealed, and bucked round me and Lady Jane with the imbecile pleasantry of their kind. The moment when I at length slammed in their faces the gate of the wood was one of sorely needed solace.

Then came the sudden bath of coolness and shade, and the gradual realization that I did not in the least know what to do next. The air was full of the deeply preoccupied hum of insects, and the interminable monologue of a wood pigeon; I felt as if I ought to apologize for my intrusion. None the less I pursued a ride that crossed the wood, making perservering efforts to blow my horn, and producing nothing but gramophonic whispers, fragmentary groans, and a headache. I was near the farther side of the wood when I saw fresh hoof-tracks on a path that joined the ride; they preceded me to a singularly untempting bank, with a branch hanging over it ,and a potato-field beyond it. A clod had been newly kicked out of the top of it; I could not evade the conviction that Michael had gone that way. The grey mare knew it too, and bundled on to and over the bank with surprising celerity, and dropped skilfully just short of where the potato beds began. An old woman was digging at the other side of the field, and I steered for her, making a long tack down a deep furrow between the "lazy-beds".

"Did you see the hounds, ma'am?" I called out across the intervening jungle of potato stalks.

"Sir!"

She at all events was not deaf. I amended my inquiry.

"Did you see any dogs, or a man in a red coat?"

"Musha, bad cess to them, then I did!" bawled the old woman, "look at the thrack o' their legs down thro' me little pratie garden! 'Twasn't but a whileen ago that they come leppin' out o' the wood to me, and didn't I think 'twas the Divil and all his young ones, an' I thrun meself down in the thrinch the way they wouldn't see me, the Lord save us!"

My heart warmed to her; I also would gladly have lain

250

down among the umbrageous stalks of the potatoes, and concealed myself for ever from Michael and the hounds.

"What way did they go?" I asked, regretfully dismissing the vision, and feeling in my pocket for a shilling.

"They went wesht the road, your Honour, an' they screeching always; they crossed out the field below over-right the white pony, and faith ye couldn't hardly see Michael Leary for the shwcat! God help ye asthore, yourself is getting hardship from them as well as another!"

The shilling here sank into her earthy palm, on which she prayed passionately that the saints might be surprised at my success. I felt that as far as I was concerned the surprise would be mutual; I had had nothing but misfortune since ten o'clock that morning, and there seemed no reason to believe that the tide had turned.

The pony proved to be a white mule, a spectral creature, standing in malign meditation trace-high in bracken; I proceeded in its direction at a trot, through clumps of bracken and coarse grass, and as I drew near it uttered a strangled and heart-broken cry of greeting. At the same moment Lady Jane fell headlong on to her nose and the point of her right shoulder. It is almost superfluous to observe that I did the same thing. As I rolled on my face in the bracken, something like a snake uncoiled itself beneath me and became taut; I clutched at it, believing it to be the reins, and found I was being hung up, like clothes on a line, upon the mule's tethering rope. Lady Jane had got it well round her legs, and had already fallen twice in her efforts to get up, while the mule, round whose neck the tether rope had been knotted, was backing hard, like a dog trying to pull its head through its collar.

In sunstroke heat I got out my knife, and having cut the rope in two places, an operation accomplished in the depths of a swarm of flies and midges, I pulled the mare on to her legs. She was lame on the off fore, and the rope had skinned her shins in several places; my own

251

shoulder and arm were bruised, and I had broken a stirrup leather. Philippa and the photographer had certainly provided me with a day of varied entertainment, and I could not be sure that I had even yet drained the cup of pleasure to the dregs.

I led Lady Jane out into the road, and considered the position. We were about nine miles from home, and at least five from any place where I could hire a car. To walk, and lead the mare, was an alternative that, powerless as events had proved me to be in the hands of misfortune, I still refused to consider. It was then given me to remember old McRory.

My acquaintance with old McRory was of the slightest. He was, it was understood, a retired Dublin coal merchant, with an enormous family, and a reputation for great riches. He had, within the last year or so, taken the derelict house of Temple Braney, and having by strenuous efforts attained that dubious honour, the Commission of the Peace, it had happened to me to sit on the Bench with him on one or two occasions. Of his family I knew little, save that whenever I saw an unknown young man buying cigarettes at Mr. Dannaher's in Skebawn, I was informed that it was one of the young McRory's, a medical student, and "a bit of a lad, but nothing at all to the next youngest". The Misses McRory were only occasionally viewed, whirling in large companies on glittering bicycles, and the legend respectfully ran that they had forty blouses apiece. Perhaps the most definite information about them was supplied by our cook. Mrs. Cadogan, who assured Philippa that wild pigs in America wouldn't be treated worse than what Mrs. McRory treated her servants. All these things together made an unpromising aggregate, but the fact remained that Temple Braney House was within a quarter of a mile of me, and its charity my only hope.

The lodge gates of Temple Braney were wide open, so was the door of the lodge; the weedy drive was scored with fresh wheel-tracks, as also, for the matter of that, was the grass on either side. I followed it for a short distance, in the roomy shade of splendid beech-trees, servants of the old regime, preserving their dignity through the vicissitudes of the new. Near the house was a second open gate, and on a species of arch over it I was amazingly greeted by the word "Welcome" in white letters on a blazing strip of turkey-red. This was an attention that I had not anticipated; did it mean a school feast?

I made a cautious survey, but saw nobody, and nerved by the increasing lameness of Lady Jane, I went on to the house and rang the bell. There was no response; the hall door was wide open, and from an inner hall two lanky red setter puppies advanced with their tails between their legs, barking uncertainly, and acutely conscious of the fact that upon the collar of each was fastened a flaunting though much chewed bow of white satin ribbon. Full of foreboding I rang again. The bell tinkled vigorously in some fastness of the house, but nothing else happened. I decided to try the stable-yard, and, attended by the decorated puppies, set forth to find it.

It was a large quadrangle, of which one side was formed by a wing of the house; had there been a few more panes of glass in the windows and slates in the roof it might have been imposing. A cavernous coach-house stood open, empty save for the wheelless body of an outside car that was seated on the floor, with wings outspread like a hatching hen. Every stable-door gaped wide. Odds and ends of harness lay about, but neither horse nor human being was visible. A turkey-cock, in transports of wrath, stormed to and fro in front of his household, and to some extent dispelled the sentiment of desertion and stampede that pervaded the place. I led the limping mare into a stable wherein were two loose-boxes. A sickly smell greeted me, and I perceived that in one of the boxes was a long low cage, alive with the red-currant-jelly eyes and pink noses of a colony of ferrets, and in the other was a pile of empty wine-boxes and several bicycles. Lady Jane snorted

253

heavily, and I sought elsewhere for a refuge for her. I found it at length in a long stable with six empty stalls, and proceeded to tie her up in one of them.

It was while I was thus engaged that a strange succession of sounds began overhead, heavy, shapeless sounds in which were blended the suggestions of shove and thump. There was a brief interval of silence, during which Lady Jane and I listened with equal intentness; then followed a hoarse bellow, which resolved itself into the inquiry.

"Is there anyone there?"

Here was the princess of the enchanted palace waking up with a vengeance. More and angrier bellows followed; I went stealthily out into the yard, and took stock of the windows above the stable. One of them was open, and it was from this that the voice issued, loudly demanding release. It roared a string of Christian names, which I supposed to be those of the McRory family, it used most unchristian language, and it finally settled down into shouts for help, and asseverations that it was smothering. I admit that my first and almost overwhelming impulse was to steal a bicycle and wing my way to my far-away and peaceful home, leaving Michael, the hounds, and the smothering gentleman to work out their own salvation. Unfortunately for me, the voice of conscience prevailed. There was a ladder near at hand leaning against the wall, and I put it to the window, and went up it as fast as my top boots would allow me, with a vision before me of old McRory in apoplexy as the probable reward of my labours. I thrust my head in, blocking the light in so doing; the shouting ceased abruptly, and after the glare of sunshine outside I could at first see nothing. Then was revealed to me a long and darksome room, once, probably, a loft, filled with broken chairs and varieties of primeval lumber. In the middle of the floor lay an immense feather bed, and my bewildered eyes discovered, at one end of it, a crimson face, the face, not of old McRory, but that of a young gentleman of my acquaintance, one Mr. Tomsy Flood

254

of Curranhilty. The mysteries were deepening. I straddled the window-sash, and arrived in the room with a three-cornered tear in the shoulder of my coat, inflicted by a nail in the frame, and one spur draped with ancestral cobweb.

"Take me out of this!" howled Mr. Flood hysterically, accepting my pantomime entrance without question. "Can't you see I'm smothering in this darned thing?"

Fluff hung from his black moustache and clung to his eyebrows, his hair was full of feathers; earthquake throes convulsed the feather-bed, and the fact was suddenly revealed to me that Mr. Flood was not under it, as I had at first imagined, but in it, stitched in, up to the chin. The weaned child, or any other conventional innocent, could not have failed for an instant to recognize the handiwork of practical humorists of a high order. I asked no questions, but got out my knife once more, and beginning with due precaution somewhere near Mr. Flood's jugular vein, proceeded to slit open the end of the "tick". The stitches were long and strong, and as each one yielded, the feathers burst forth in stifling puffs, and Tomsy Flood's allusion to the young McRorys were mercifully merged in spluttering. I did not laugh, not at least till I found that I had to drag him out like a mummy, accompanied by half the contents of the bed, and perceived that he was in full evening clothes, and that he was incapable of helping himself because the legs of his trousers were sewn together and his coat-sleeves sewn to his sides; even then, I only gave way in painful secrecy behind the mighty calves of his legs legs as I cut the stitches out. Tomsy Flood weighed about fifteen stones and was not in a mood to be trifled with, still less to see the humour of the position. The medical students had done their work with a surgical finish, and by the time that I had restored to Tomsy the use of his arms and legs, the feathers had permeated to every recess of my being, and I was sneezing as if I had hay fever.

Having at length, and with considerable difficulty, got

Mr. Flood on to his legs, I ventured, with the tact demanded by the situation, a question as to whether he had been dining at Temple Braney.

"Dining?" queried Mr. Flood, with an obvious effort of memory. "Yes, I was, to be sure! Amn't I staying in the house?" Then, with an equally obvious shock of recollection, "Sure I'm best man at the wedding to-day!"

The scattered elements of the situation began to fall symmetrically into line, from the open gates to the white bows on the puppies' collars. My chief concern, however, bearing in mind Tomsy Flood's recent potations and provocations, was to let him down as easily as possible, and, reserving my conclusions to myself, to escape, swiftly and silently, while yet there was time. There was always that stall-full of bicycles; I could borrow clothes from Tomsy, and leave this accursed tomfoolery of hunting kit to be fetched with the mare. I could write a beautifullly explanatory note when I got home——

"Hadn't you better get out of your evening things as quickly as you can?" I suggested.

Mr. Flood regarded me with heavy and bloodshot eyes of imperfect intelligence.

"Oh, I've time enough. Ye wouldn't get a pick of breakfast here before ten o'clock in the day. Now that I come to look into you," he continued, "you're as big a show as myself! Is it for the wedding that you have the red coat on you?"

I do not now remember with what lies I composed Tomsy Flood, but I got him out of the room at last by a door into a passage of seemingly interminable length; he took my arm, he treated me as his only friend, he expressed his full confidence that I would see fair play when he got a hold of Stanley McRory. He also gave it as his private opinion that his cousin, Harry Flood, was making a hare of himself marrying that impudent little Pinkie McRory, that was as vulgar as a bag of straddles, in spite of the money. Indeed, the

256

whole family had too many airs about them for his fancy. They take the English *Times,* if you please, and they all dress for dinner—every night, I tell ye! I call that rot, y'know!"

We were all this time traversing the house by labyrinthine passages, flights of stairs, and strange empty lobbies; we progressed conversationally and with maddening slowness, followed by a fleecy train of feathers that floated from us as we went. And all the time I was trying to remember how long it took to get married. In my own case it seemed as if I had been in the church for two hours at least.

A swing-door suddenly admitted us to the hall, and Tomsy stood still to collect his faculties.

"My room's up there," he began, pointing vaguely up the staircase.

At this identical moment there was a loud and composite crash from behind a closed door on our right, followed by minor crashes, and noises as of chairs falling about.

"That's the boys!" said Tomsy, a sudden spark kindling in his eye; "they're breakfasting early, I suppose."

He dropped my arm unexpectedly, and flung the door open with a yell.

The first object that met my eyes was the original sinner, Venus, mounted on a long and highly adorned luncheon table, crunching and gulping cold chicken as fast as she could get it down; on the floor half a dozen of her brethren tore at a round of beef amid the débris of crockery and glass that had been involved in its overthrow. A cataract of cream was pouring down the tablecloth, and making a lake on the carpet for the benefit of some others; and President, the patriarch of the pack, was apparently seated on the wedding-cake, while he demolished a cold salmon. I had left my whip in the stable, but even had this paralysing sight left me the force to use it, its services would not have been needed. The leaders of the revel leaped from the table, mowing down colonies of wine-glasses in the act, and fled through

257

the open window, followed by the rest of the party, with a precipitancy that showed their full consciousness of sin—the last scramblers over the sill yelping in agonized foretaste of the thong that they believed was overtaking them.

At such a moment of catastrophe the craving for human sympathy is paramount.

I turned even to the fuddled and feathered Tomsy Flood as to a man and a brother, and was confronted in the doorway by the bride and bridegroom.

Behind them, the hall was filling, with the swiftness of an evil dream, with glowing faces and wedding bonnets; there was a turmoil of wheels and hoofs at the door, and through it all, like "horns of Elfland faintly blowing", Michael's blasts of summons to his pirates. Finally, the towering mauve bonnet and equally towering wrath of Mrs. McRory, as she advanced upon me and Tomsy Flood. I thought of the wild pigs in America, and wished I were with them.

Lest I should find myself the object of a sympathy more acute than I deserve, it may be well to transcribe a portion of a paragraph from the *Curranhilty Herald* of the following week:

". . . After the ceremony a reception was held at Temple Braney House, where a sumptuous collation had been provided by the hospitable Mr. and Mrs. McRory. The health of the happy pair having been drunk, that of the bridesmaids was proposed, and Mr. T. Flood, who had been prevented by a slight indisposition from filling the office of best man, was happily sufficiently recovered to return thanks for them in his usual sprightly vein. Major Sinclair Yeates, R.M., M.F.H., who, in honour of the festive occasion had donned sporting attire, proposed the health of the bride's mother in felicitous terms. . . ."

A ROYAL COMMAND

When I heard that Bernard Shute of Clountiss, Esquire, late Lieutenant, R.N., was running an agricultural show, to be held in his own demesne, I did not for a moment credit him with either philanthropy or public spirit. I recognized in it merely another outbreak of his exasperating health and energy. He bombarded the country with circulars, calling upon farmers for exhibits, and upon all for subscriptions; he made raids into neighbouring districts on his motor car, turning vague promises into bullion, with a success in mendicancy fortunately given to few. It was in a thoroughly ungenerous spirit that I yielded up my guinea and promised to attend the show in my thousands: peace at twenty-one shillings was comparatively cheap, and there was always the hope that it might end there.

The hope was fallacious: the show boomed; it blossomed into a grandstand, a brass band, an afternoon tea tent; finally, fortune, as usual, played into Bernard's hands and sent a celebrity. There arrived in a neighbouring harbour a steam-yacht, owned by one of Mr. Shute's dearest friends, one Captain Calthorpe, and having on board a coloured potentate, the Sultan of X——, who had come over from Cowes to see Ireland and the Dublin Horse Show. The dearest friend—who, as it happened, having been for three days swathed in a wet fog from the Atlantic, was becoming somewhat pressed for entertainment for his charge—tumbled readily into Bernard's snare, and paragraphs appeared with all speed in the local papers proclaiming the intention of H.H. the Sultan of X—— to be present at the Clountiss Agricultural Show. Following up this coup, Bernard achieved for his function a fine, an even sumptuous day, and the weather and the Sultan between them filled the grandstand beyond the utmost hopes (and possibly the secret misgivings) of its constructors.

Having with difficulty found seats on the topmost corner for myself, my wife, and my two children, I had leisure to speculate upon its probable collapse. For half an hour, for an hour, for an hour and a half, we sat on on its hot bare boards and surveyed the wide and empty oval of grass that formed the arena of the show. Five "made-up" jumps of varying dimensions and two vagrant fox-terriers were its sole adornment. A dark rim of spectators encircled it, awaiting developments, i.e., the arrival of the Sultan, with tireless patience, and the egregious Slipper, attired in a gala costume of tall hat, frock-coat, white breeches, and butcher boots, gleanings, no doubt, from bygone jumble sales, swaggered and rolled to and fro, selling catalogues and cards of the jumping. Away under the tall elms near the gate, amid the rival clamour of the cattle sheds and the poultry hens, was stationed the green and yellow band of the "Sons of Liberty"; at intervals it broke into an excruciating shindy of brass instruments, through which the big drum drove a ferocious and unfaltering course. Above the heads of the people, at the far end of the arena, tossing heads and manes moving ceaselessly backwards and forwards, told where the "jumping horses" were waiting, eaten by flies, inconsolably agitated by the band, becoming momently more jaded and stale from the delay. I thanked Heaven that neither my wife nor Bernard Shute had succeeded in inducing me to snatch my string of two from the paddock in which they were passing the summer, to take part in this purgatorial procession.

The grandstand, a structure bare as a mountain top to the assaults of sun and wind, was canopied with parasols and prismatic with millinery. The farmers, from regions unknown to me, had abundantly risen to the occasion; so also had their wives and daughters; and fashionable ladies, with comfortable brogues and a vigorous taste

260

in scent, closed us in on every side. Throughout that burning period of delay went the searching catechisms of my two sons (aged respectively four and seven) as to the complexion, disposition, and domestic arrangements of the Sultan. Philippa says that I ought to have known that they were thoroughly overstrung; possibly my description of the weapons that he wore and the cannibal feasts that he attended were a trifle lurid, but it seemed simpler to let the fancy play on such details than to decide, for the benefit of an interested *entourage* of farmers' daughters, whether the Sultan's face was the colour of my boots or of their mother's, and whether he had a thousand or a million wives. The inquiry was interrupted by the quack of a motor horn at the entrance gate.

"Here he is!" breathed the grandstand as one man. There was a flocking of stewards towards the gate, and the Sons of Liberty, full of anxiety to say the suitable thing, burst into the melancholy strains of "My Old Kentucky Home Far Away". To this somewhat "hearse-like" air the group of green-rosetted stewards advanced across the arena, escorting the yacht party, in whose midst moved a squat figure, clad in grey flannel, and surmounted by a massive and snowy turban. My elder son became very pale; the younger turned an ominous crimson, and the corners of his mouth went down, slowly, but, as I well knew, fatally. The inevitable bellow that followed in the inevitable routine had scarcely died away in the heart of Philippa's boa, when Mr. Shute's red face and monstrous presidential rosette presented themselves on the stairs at my elbow.

"Mrs. Yeates!" he began, in a gusty whisper, "Cecilia implores you to come and fling yourself to the Lion! She says she simply can't and won't tackle him single-handed, and she trusts to you to see her through! He talks French all right, and I know your French is top-hole! Do come——"

Incredible as it may appear, my wife received this

suggestion with a reluctance that was obviously but half-hearted. Such it is to have the social gift.

I presently found myself alone with my offspring, both in tears, and deaf to my assurances that neither the Sultan nor his lion would eat their mother. Consolation, however, came with the entry of the "jumping horses" into the arena, which followed with all speed upon that of the Sultan. The first competitor bucketed up to the starting-point, and at the same moment the discovery was made that there was no water in the water-jump, a space of perhaps a foot in depth by some five feet wide. Nothing but a thin paste of mud remained, the water having disappeared, unnoticed, during the hot hours of the morning.

Swift in expedient, the stewards supplied the deficiency with quick-lime, which was scattered with a lavish hand in the fosse, and shone like snow through the barrier of furze bushes on the take-off side. If, as I suppose, the object was to delude the horses into the belief that it was a water-jump, it was a total failure; they immediately decided that it was a practical joke, dangerous, and in indifferent taste. If, on the other side, a variety entertainment for the public was aimed at, nothing could have been more successful. Every known class of refusal was successfully exhibited. One horse endeavoured to climb the rails into the grandstand; another, having stopped dead at the critical point, swung round, and returned in consternation to the starting-point, with his rider hanging like a locket round his neck. Another, dowered with a sense of humour, unusual among horses, stepped delicately over the furze-bushes, and, amidst rounds of applause, walked through the lime with a stoic calm. Yet another, a ponderous war-horse of seventeen hands, hung, trembling like an aspen, on the brink, till a sympathizer, possibly his owner, sprang irrepressibly from his seat on the stand, climbed through the rails, and attacked him from behind with a large umbrella. It was during this three-cornered conflict that the green-eyed filly forced herself into the front rank of events. A chorus of "Hi! Hi! Hi!" fired at the rate of about fifty per second, volleyed in warning from the crowd round the starting-point, and a white-legged chest-nut, with an unearthly white face and flying flounces of tawny mane and tail, came thundering down at the jump. Neither umbrella nor war-horse turned her by a hair's-breadth from her course, still less did her rider, a lean and long-legged country boy, whose single object was to keep on her back. Picking up her white stockings, she took off six feet from the jump, and whizzed like a driven grouse past the combatants and over the furze bushes and the lime. Beneath her creamy forelock, I caught a glimpse of her amazing blue-green eyes.

She skimmed the hurdle, she flourished over the wall, flinging high her white heels with a twist that showed more consideration for their safety than that of her rider. She ramped over the big double bank, while the roars of approval swelled with each achievement, and she ended a faultless round by bolting into the heart of the crowd, which fled hilariously, and as hilariously hived in round her again.

From my exalted seat I could see the Sultan clapping his hands in sweet accord with Philippa. Somewhere near me a voice yelled:

"Cripes! She's a monkey! When she jumped the wall she went the height of a tree over it!"

To which another voice replied that "It'd be a good bird that'd fly the height she wouldn't lep, and John Cullinane'd be apt to get first with her at the Skebawn Show." I remembered casually that John Cullinane was a neighbour of mine.

"Well, I wouldn't fancy her at all," said a female voice. "I'd say she has a very maleecious glance."

"Ah! ye wouldn't feel that when the winkers'd be on her," said the first speaker; "she'd make a fine sweeping mare under a side-car."

Meantime, the war-horse, much embittered by the umbrella, floundered through the lime, and, continuing his course, threw down the hurdle, made a breach in the wall that would, as my neighbour put it, give three hours' work to seven idlers, and came to a sudden conclusion in front of the bank, while his rider slowly turned a somersault that, by some process of evolution, placed him sitting on the fence, facing the large and gloomy countenance of his horse.

It was after this performance that my wife looked round to see if her sons were enjoying themselves, and waved her handkerchief. The snowy turban of the Sultan moved round too, and beneath its voluminous folds the round, black discs of a pair of field-glasses were directed at us. The effect was instant. With a simultaneous shriek of terror, my children flung themselves upon me and buried their faces in my breast. I shall never forget the farmers' daughters that, in this black hour, their sympathy was prompt and practical.

"Oh! Fie, fie! Oh! the creatures! 'Twas the spy-glasses finished them altogether! Eat a sweetie now, lovey! that's the grand man! Pappy'll not let the dirty fella near ye!"

A piece of the brown sugar-stick known as "Peggy's leg" accompanied these consolations, and a tearful composure was graduallly restored; but "Pappy" had arrived at the conclusion that he had had about as much as he could stand. In shameful publicity I clambered down the steep tiers of seats, with one child under my arm, the other adhering to my coat-tail. Philippa made agitated signals to me; I cut her dead, and went to ground in the tea tent.

A couple of days later my duty took me to the farthest end of my district—a matter that involved a night's absence from home. I left behind me an infant family restored to calm, and a thoroughly domesticated wife and mother, pledged to one o'clock dinner with the children and tea in the woods. I returned in time for luncheon next day, bicycling from the station, as was my wont. It was a hot day, and as I walked my bicycle up the slope of the avenue, the shade of the beech-trees was passing pleasant; the dogs galloped to meet me over the soft after-grass, and I thought about flannels and an idle afternoon.

In the hall I met Margaret, the parlour-maid, engaged, with the house-maid, in carrying the writing-table out of my smoking-room. They were talking loudly to each other, and I noticed that their eyes were very bright and their complexions considerably above par. I am a man of peace, but the veriest dove will protect its nest, and I demanded with some heat the cause of this outrage.

"The mistress told us to clear this room for the servant of the—the gentleman that's coming to lunch to-morrow, sir," replied Margaret with every appearance of offence.

She and Hannah staggered onwards with my table, and the contents of the drawers rolled and rattled.

"Put down that table," I said firmly. "Where is the mistress?"

"I believe she's dressing, sir," replied Margaret; "she only came home about an hour ago. She was out all night on the sea, I believe."

Instant on the heels of these astonishing statements the swing door to the kitchen was flung open, and Mrs. Cadogan's angry voice was projected through it.

"Hannah! go tell the mistress the butcher's below, and he says he never heard tell of the like, and would she lend him one o' the Major's spears? How would the likes o' him have a spear! Such goings on!"

"What the devil is all this about?" I said with equal anger. "No one is to touch my spears!"

"Thanks be to God, the Major's come home!" exclaimed the ruler of the kitchen, advancing weightily into the hall. "There's no fear I'd put a hand on your spears, sir, nor the butcher neither, the poor, decent, man! He says he's supplying the gentry for twenty-five years, and he was never asked to do the like of a nasty thing like that!"

"Like *what*?" I said, with growing wrath and bewilderment.

"It's what the mistress said," rejoined Mrs. Cadogan,

the flush of injury mounting to her cap-frill. "That what-shall-I-call-him—that King, wouldn't ate mate without it'd be speared! And it's what I say," she went on, perorating loudly and suddenly, "what's good enough for Christians and gentry is good enough for an owld blackamoor!"

It was now sufficiently obvious that Philippa had, with incredible perfidy, taken advantage of my absence to embroil herself in the entertainment of barbaric royalty. "Tell the butcher to wait," was all I could trust myself to say, as I started in search of my wife.

"Wait, Sinclair! I'm coming down!" cried an urgent voice from the upper landing, and Philippa, attired in what I may perhaps describe as a tempestuous dressing-gown, came swiftly downstairs and swept me before her into the drawing-room.

"My dear," she said breathlessly, "let me break it to you as gently as possible. The Shutes called for me in the motor after you left yesterday, and we went on board Bernard's yacht and sailed round to tea with Captain Calthorpe and the Sultan. We were becalmed coming back, and we were out all night—we had nothing to eat but the men's food—not that I wanted anything!" She gave a nauseated shudder of reminiscence. "There was an awful swell. It rained too. Cecilia and I tried to sleep in the cabin with all our clothes on; I never spent a more horrible night. The yacht crawled in with the tide at about ten o'clock this morning, and I got back here half-dead, and was just going up to bed when Captain Calthorpe arrived on a car and said that the Sultan wanted to lunch here to-morrow. He says we *must* have him—it's a kind of Royal command—in fact, I suppose you *ought* to wear your frock-coat!"

"I'm dashed if I do!" I said, with decision.

"Well, be that as it may," resumed Philippa, discreetly evading this point, "that green-eyed thing that got the first prize for jumping is to be here to meet him. He wants to buy it for his State carriage. I did my best to get out of it, and I told Captain Calthorpe it would be impossible to manage about the food. I forgot to tell you," faltered Philippa, with a wan giggle, "that he says he must have speared mutton!"

"I call it an infernal liberty of Calthorpe's!" I said, with indignation fanned by the spectacle of Philippa's sleepless black-rimmed eyes and pallid face, "dumping his confounded menagerie upon us in this way! And I may tell you that those spears of mine are poisoned!"

"Oh! don't be so horrid, Sinclair," said Philippa, "inventing difficulties like that!"

I arose the following morning with a heart of lead— of boiling lead—as I went down to the smoking-room to look for cigarettes and found that they, in common with every other thing that I wanted, had been tidied into oblivion. From earliest dawn I had heard the thumping of feet, and the swish of petticoats, and the plying of brooms; but for me the first shot of the engagement was not fired till eight-thirty, when, as I was moodily stropping my razor, I was told that John Cullinane was below, and would be thankful to see me. As I shaved, I could see John Cullinane standing about in front of the house, in his Sunday clothes, waiting for me; and I knew that he would so wait, patiently, inexorably, if I did not come down till noonday.

I interviewed him, unsympathetically, on the hall door steps, and told him, firstly, that, as I knew nothing of his filly, I could not "say a good word" to the Sultan for her; and, secondly, that I certainly would not mention to the Sultan that, in my opinion, she was a cheap mare at £80. John Cullinane then changed the conversation by remarking that he had brought over a small donkey for a present for the young gentlemen; to which, with suitable politeness, I responded that my children already had a donkey, and that I could not think of depriving him of his, and the interview closed.

Breakfast was late, and for the most part uneatable, the excitement of the household having communicated itself to the kitchen-range.

"If I was to put my head under it, it wouldn't light for me!" Mrs. Cadogan said to Philippa.

As a matter of fact, judging by a glimpse vouchsafed to me of her face as I struggled forth from the cellar with a candle and the champagne, one might have expected it to cause a conflagration anywhere.

My smoking-room had been dedicated to the Sultan's personal attendant, a gentleman who could neither lunch with his master nor with my servants; I was therefore homeless, and crept, an outcast, to the drawing-room to try to read the newspaper undisturbed. Sounds from above told me that trouble was brewing in the nursery: I closed the door.

At about eleven-thirty an outside car drove up to the house, and I saw a personable stranger descend from it, with a black bag in his hand, a forerunner, no doubt, of the Sultan, come over to see that the preparations were *en règle*. I saw no reason for my intervention, and, with a passing hope that Providence might deliver him over to Mrs. Cadogan, I returned to my paper. The door was flung open.

"Sinclair, dear," said my wife, very apologetically, here is Mr. Werner, the piano-tuner, from Dublin. He says he can't come again—he thinks he can finish it by luncheon-time. I quite forgot that he was coming——"

Mr. Werner's spectacled and supercilious face regarded me over her shoulder; he evidently had a low opinion of me, I do not know why. With one Cenci-like glance of reproach at Philippa, I rose and left the room. As I put on my cap I heard the first fierce chords break forth, followed by the usual chromatic passages, fluent and searching, which merged in their turn into a concentrated attack upon a single note. I hurried from the house.

It was a perfect August morning; the dogs lay on the hot gravel and panted politely as I spoke to them, but did not move. Rejected by all, I betook myself to a plantation near the front gate to see how the work of clearing a ride was progressing. The cross-cut saw and a bill-hook lay on the ground, but of workmen there was no sign. From the high road came the sound of wheels and of rapid trotting, also something that seemed like cheering.

"Good heavens!" I thought, my blood running cold, "here they are!"

I broke through the tall bracken and the larches to an opening from which the high road was visible. My two workmen were lying on their stomachs across the coping of the demesne wall, and a line of countrymen, with their best clothes on and crape "weepers" on their hats, sat on the opposite fence and applauded what was apparently a trotting match between a long-legged bay colt and John Cullinane's chestnut filly, owners up.

I joined the entertainment, my two men melting like snow from the top of the wall, and it was explained to me that there had been a funeral in the locality, and that these were a few of the neighbours that had been at it and were now waiting to see the black gentleman. An outside car rested on its shafts by the side of the road, and a horse with harness on it browsed voraciously on the shrubs inside my gate. Far away down the road I saw the receding figures of my two children, going forth to the picnic that had been arranged to allay their panic and to remove them from the sphere of action. Any Irish person will readily believe that one of them was mounted on "the small little donkey", the bribe which I had that morning irrevocably repudiated. I knew that John Cullinane saw them too, but I was too broken to interfere; I turned my back and walked rapidly away.

The rhythmic rasp of the cross-cut told me that work at the clearing had been resumed; I said to myself vindictively that I would see that it continued, and returned to the ride. The bill-hook was doing nothing, and picking it up I fell to snicking and chopping, with soothing destructiveness, among the briars and ash-saplings. Notwithstanding heat and horseflies, the time passed not disagreeably, and I was, at all events, out of range of the piano. I had paused for the fifteenth time to wipe a heated brow, and extract a thorn from my finger, when the familiar voice of the Shutes' motor-horn roused me to the appalling fact that it was nearly luncheon-time, and that I was far from fit to receive royalty. As I hurriedly emerged from the wood, there was a sound of hard galloping, and I beheld the green-eyed filly flying riderless up the avenue. She crossed the croquet ground, thoroughly, from corner to corner, and disappeared into the shrubbery in the direction of the flower garden. I ran as I have seldom run, dimly aware of a pursuing party of mourners on the avenue behind me, and, as I ran, I cursed profusely the Sultan, Calthorpe, and chiefly Bernard Shute and all his works.

The chase lasted for twenty minutes, and was joined in by not less than five-and-thirty people. The creamy mane of the filly floated like a banner before us through the shrubberies, with the dogs in full cry behind her; through it all went the reiterations of the piano, the monotonous hammerings, the majestic chords, the pyrotechnic scales; they expressed as fully as he himself could have desired the complete indifference of the tuner. The filly was ubiquitous; at one moment she was in the flower garden, the next, a distant uproar among the poultry told that she had traversed the yard, whence she emerged, *ventre-a-tèrre*, delivered herself of three bucks at sight of her original enemy the motor, at the hall door, and was away again for the croquet ground. At every turn I encountered a fresh pursuer; it was Bernard Shute and the kitchen-maid who slammed the flower-garden gate in her face; it was Philippa, in her very best dress, abetted by John Cullinane, very dusty and waving a crushed and weepered hat, who, with the best intentions, frustrated a brilliant enveloping movement directed by me; finally the cross-cut saw men, the tuner's car-driver, and a selection from the funeral, came so near cornering her that she charged the sunk fence, floated across its gulf with offensive ease, and scurried away, with long and defiant squeals, to assault my horses at the farther end of the paddock.

When we, i.e., Philippa, Bernard, and I, pulled ourselves together on the top of the steps, it was two o'clock. By the special favour of Providence the Sultan was late, but the position was desperate. Philippa had trodden on the front of her dress and torn it. Bernard had greened the knees of his trousers; I do not know what I looked like, but when Cecilia Shute emerged, cool and spotless, from the hall, where she had judiciously remained during the proceedings, she uttered a faint shriek and covered her face with her hands.

"I know," I said, with deadly calm, stuffing my tie inside my waistcoat, "I can't help it——"

"Here they are!" said Bernard.

The sound of wheels was indeed in the avenue. We fled as one man into the back hall, and Philippa, stumbling over her torn flounce, fell on her knees at the feet of Mr. Werner, the tuner, who stood there, his task finished, awaiting with cold decorum the reward of his labours. The wheels stopped. What precisely happened during that crowded moment I cannot pretend to explain, but as we dragged my wife to her feet I found that she had knelt on my eyeglass, with the result that may be imagined.

All was now lost save honour. I turned at bay, and dimly saw, silhouetted in the open doorway, a short figure in a frock-coat, with a species of black turban on its head. I advanced, bowed, and heroically began:

"Sire! J'ai l'honneur——"

"Yerrah my law! Major!" said the bewildered voice of Slipper. "Don't be making game of me this way! Sure I have a tallagram for you." He removed the turban, which I now perceived to be a brown tweed cap, swathed in a crape "weeper", and handed me the telegram. "I got it from the boy that was after breaking his bike on the road, an' I coming from the funeral."

The telegram was from Calthorpe, and said, with suitable regrets, that the Sultan had been summoned to London on instant and important business.

I read it to the back hall, in a voice broken by many emotions.

"I saw the gentleman you speak of waiting for the Dublin train at Sandy Bay Station this morning," remarked the tuner, condescending for a moment to our level.

"Then why did you not tell us so?" demanded Philippa, with sudden indignation.

"I was not aware, madam, that it was of any importance," replied Mr. Werner, returning to his normal altitude of perpetual frost.

Incredible as it may seem, it was apparent that Philippa was disappointed. As for me, my heart was like a singing bird.

POISSON d'AVRIL

The atmosphere of the waiting-room set at naught at a single glance the theory that there can be no smoke without fire. The stationmaster, when remonstrated with, stated, as an incontrovertible fact, that any chimney in the world would smoke in a south-easterly wind, and further, said there wasn't a poker, and that if you poked the fire the grate would fall out. He was, however, sympathetic, and went on his knees before the smouldering mound of slack, endeavouring to charm it to a smile by subtle proddings with the handle of the ticket-punch. Finally, he took me to his own kitchen fire and talked politics and salmon-fishing, the former with judicious attention to my presumed point of view, and careful suppression of his own, the latter with no less tactful regard for my admission that for three days I had not caught a fish, while the steam rose from my wet boots, in witness of the ten miles of rain through which an outside car had carried me.

Before the train was signalled I realized for the hundredth time the magnificent superiority of the Irish mind to the trammels of officialdom, and the inveterate supremacy in Ireland of the Personal Element.

"You might get a foot-warmer at Carrig Junction," said a species of lay porter in a knitted jersey, ramming my suitcase upside down under the seat. "Sometimes they're in it, and more times they're not."

The train dragged itself rheumatically from the station, and a cold spring rain—the time was the middle of a most inclement April—smote it in flank as it came into the open. I pulled up both windows and began to smoke; there is, at least, a semblance of warmth in a thoroughly vitiated atmosphere.

273

It is my wife's habit to assert that I do not read her letters, and being now on my way to join her and my family in Gloucestershire, it seemed a sound thing to study again her latest letter of instructions.

"I am starting to-day, as Alice wrote to say we must be there two days before the wedding, so as to have a rehearsal for the pages. Their dresses have come, and they look too delicious in them——"

(I here omit profuse particulars not pertinent to this tale.)

"It is sickening for you to have had such bad sport. If the worst comes to the worst couldn't you buy one?——"

I smote my hand upon my knee. I had forgotten the infernal salmon! What a score for Philippa! If these contretemps would only teach her that I was not to be relied upon, they would have their uses, but experience is wasted upon her; I have no objection to being called an idiot, but, that being so, I ought to be allowed the privileges and exemptions proper to idiots. Philippa had, no doubt, written to Alice Hervey, and assured her that Sinclair would be only too delighted to bring her a salmon, and Alice Hervey, who was rich enough to find much enjoyment in saving money, would reckon upon it, to its final fin in mayonnaise.

Plunged in morose meditations, I progressed through a country parcelled out by shaky and crooked walls into a patchwood of hazel scrub and rocky fields, veiled in rain. About every six miles there was a station, wet and windswept; at one the sole occurrence was the presentation of a newspaper to the guard by the station-master; at the next the guard read aloud some choice excerpts from the same to the porter. The personal element was potent on this branch of the Munster and Connaught Railway. Routine, abhorrent to all artistic minds, was sheathed in conversation; even the engine-driver, a functionary ordinarily as aloof as the Mikado, alleviated his enforced isolation by sociable shrieks to every level crossing, while the long row of public-houses that formed, as far as I could judge, the town of Carrig, received a special and, as it seemed, humorous salutation.

The time-table decreed that we were to spend ten minutes at Carrig Junction; it was fifteen before the crowd of market people on the platform had been assimilated; finally, the window of a neighbouring carriage was flung open, and a wrathful English voice asked how much longer the train was going to wait. The stationmaster, who was at the moment engrossed in conversation with the guard and a man who was carrying a long parcel wrapped in newspaper, looked round, and said gravely:

"Well now, that's a mystery!"

The man with the parcel turned away, and convulsively studied a poster. The guard put his hand over his mouth.

The voice, still more wrathfully, demanded the earliest hour at which its owner could get to Belfast.

"Ye'll be asking me next when I take me Breakfast," replied the station-master, without haste or palpable annoyance.

The window went up again with a bang, the man with the parcel dug the guard in the ribs with his elbow, and the parcel slipped from under his arm and fell on the platform.

"Oh my! oh my! Me fish!" exclaimed the man, solicitously picking up a remarkable good-looking salmon that had slipped from its wrapping of newspaper.

Inspiration came to me, and I, in my turn, opened my window and summoned the stationmaster.

Would his friend sell me the salmon? The stationmaster entered upon the mission with ardour, but without success.

No; the gentleman was only just after running down to the town for it in the delay, but why wouldn't I run down and get one for myself? There was half a dozen more of them below at Coffey's, selling cheap; there would be time enough, the mail wasn't signalled yet.

I jumped from the carriage and doubled out of the station at top speed, followed by an assurance from the guard that he would not forget me.

Congratulating myself on the ascendancy of the personal element, I sped through the soapy limestone mud towards the public-houses. En route I met a heated man carrying yet another salmon, who, without preamble, informed me that there were three or four more good fish in it, and that he was after running down from the train himself.

"Ye have whips o' time!" he called after me. "It's the first house that's not a public-house. Ye'll see boots in the window—she'll give them for tenpence a pound if ye're stiff with her!"

I ran past the public-houses.

"Tenpence a pound!" I exclaimed inwardly, "at this time of year! That's good enough."

Here I perceived the house with boots in the window, and dived into its dark doorway.

A cobbler was at work behind a low counter. He mumbled something about Herself, through lengths of waxed thread that hung across his mouth, a fat woman appeared at an inner door, and at that moment I heard, appallingly near, the whistle of the incoming mail. The fat woman grasped the situation in an instant, and with what appeared but one movement, snatched a large fish from the floor of the room behind her and flung a newspaper round it.

"Eight pound weight!" she said swiftly. "Ten shillings!"

A convulsive effort of mental arithmetic assured me that this was more than tenpence a pound, but it was not the moment for stiffness. I shoved a half-sovereign into her fishy hand, clasped my salmon in my arms, and ran.

Needless to say it was uphill, and at the steepest gradient another whistle stabbed me like a spur; above the station roof successive and advancing puffs of steam warned me that the worst had probably happened, but

276

still I ran. When I gained the platform my train was already clear of it, but the personal element held good. Every soul in the station, or so it seemed to me, lifted up his voice and yelled. The stationmaster put his fingers in his mouth and sent after the departing train an unearthly whistle, with a high trajectory and a serrated edge. It took effect; the train slackened, I plunged from the platform and followed it up the rails, and every window in both trains blossomed with the heads of deeply interested spectators. The guard met me on the line, very apologetic and primed with an explanation that the gentleman going for the boat-train wouldn't let him wait any longer, while from our rear came an exultant cry from the stationmaster.

"Ye *told* him ye wouldn't forget him!"

"There's a few countrywomen in your carriage, sir," said the guard, ignoring the taunt, as he shoved me and my salmon up the side of the train, "but they'll be getting out in a couple of stations. There wasn't another seat in the train for them!"

My sensational return to my carriage was viewed with the utmost sympathy by no less than seven shawled and cloaked countrywomen. In order to make room for me, one of them seated herself on the floor with her basket in her lap, another, on the seat opposite to me, squeezed herself under the central elbow flap that had been turned up to make room. The aromas of wet cloaks, turf smoke, and salt fish formed a potent blend. I was excessively hot, and the eyes of the seven women were fastened upon me with intense and unwearying interest.

"Move west a small piece, Mary Jack, if you please," said a voluminous matron in the corner, "I declare we're as throng as three in a bed this minute!"

"Why then, Julia Casey, there's little throubling yourself," grumbled the woman under the flap. "Look at the way meself is! I wonder is it to be putting humps on themselves the gentry has them things down on top o'

277

them! I'd sooner be carrying a basket of turnips on me back than to be scrooged this way!"

The woman on the floor at my feet rolled up at me a glance of compassionate amusement at this rustic ignorance, and tactfully changed the conversation by supposing it was at Coffey's I got the salmon.

I said it was.

There was a silence, during which it was obvious that one question burnt in every heart.

"I'll go bail she axed him tinpence!" said the woman under the flap, as one who touches the limits of absurdity.

"It's a beautiful fish!" I said defiantly. "Eight pounds weight. I gave her ten shillings for it."

What is described in newspapers as "sensation in court" greeted this confession.

"Look!" said the woman under the flap, darting her head out of the hood of her cloak, like a tortoise, " 'tis what it is, ye haven't as much roguery in your heart as'd make ye a match for her!"

"Divil blow the ha'penny Eliza Coffey paid for that fish!" burst out the fat woman in the corner. "Thim lads o' hers had a creel full o' thim snatched this morning before it was making day!"

"How would the gentleman be a match for her?" shouted the woman on the floor through a long-drawn whistle that told of a coming station. "Sure a Turk itself wouldn't be a match for her! That one has a tongue that'd clip a hedge!"

At the station they climbed out laboriously, and with groaning. I handed down to them their monster baskets, laden, apparently, with ingots of lead; they told me in return that I was a fine *grauver* man, and it was a pity there weren't more like me; they wished, finally, that my journey might well thrive with me, and passed from my ken, bequeathing to me, after the agreeable manner of their kind, a certain comfortable mental sleekness that reason cannot immediately dispel. They also left me in possession of the fact that I was about to present the irreproachable Alice Hervey with a contraband salmon.

The afternoon passed cheerlessly into evening, and my journey did not conspicuously thrive with me. Somewhere in the dripping twilight I changed trains, and again later on, and at each change the salmon moulted some more of its damp raiment of newspaper, and I debated seriously the idea of interring it, regardless of consequences, in my portmanteau. A lamp was banged into the roof of my carriage, half an inch of orange flame, poised in a large glass globe, like a gold-fish, and of about as much use as an illuminant. Here also was handed in the dinner basket that I had wired for, and its contents, arid though they were, enabled me to achieve at least some measure of mechanical distension, followed by a dreary lethargy that was not far from drowsiness.

At the next station we paused long; nothing whatever occurred, and the rain drummed patiently upon the roof. Two nuns and some schoolgirls were in the carriage next door, and their voices came plaintively and in snatches through the partition; after a long period of apparent collapse, during which I closed my eyes to evade the cold gaze of the salmon through the netting, a voice in the next carriage said resourcefully:

"Oh, girls, I'll tell you what we'll do! We'll say the Rosary!"

"Oh, that will be lovely!" said another voice; "well, who'll give it out? Theresa Condon, you'll give it out."

Theresa Condon gave it out, in a not unmelodious monotone, interspersed with the responses, always in a lower cadence; the words were indistinguishable, but the rise and fall of the western voices was lulling as the hum of bees. I fell asleep.

I awoke in total darkness; the train was motionless, and complete and profound silence reigned. We were at a station, that much I discerned by the light of a dim lamp at the far end of a platform glistening with wet. I struck a match and ascertained that it was eleven o'clock, precisely the hour at which I was to board the mail train. I jumped out and ran down the platform;

there was no one in the train; there was no one even on the engine, which was forlornly hissing to itself in the silence. There was not a human being anywhere. Every door was closed, and all was dark. The name-board of the station was faintly visible; with a lighted match I went along it letter by letter. It seemed as if the whole alphabet were in it, and by the time I got to the end I had forgotten the beginning. One fact I had, however, mastered, that it was not the junction at which I was to catch the mail.

I was undoubtedly awake, but for a moment I was inclined to entertain the idea that there had been an accident, and that I had entered upon existence in another world. Once more I assailed the station-house and the appurtenances thereof, the ticket-office, the waiting-room, finally, and at some distance, the goods store, outside which the single lamp of the station commented feebly on the drizzle and the darkness. As I approached it a crack of light under the door became perceptible, and a voice was suddenly uplifted within.

"Your best now agin that. Throw down your Jack!"

I opened the door with pardonable violence, and found the guard, the stationmaster, the driver, and the stoker, seated on barrels round a packing case, on which they were playing a game of cards.

To have too egregiously the best of a situation is not, to a generous mind, a source of strength. In the perfection of their overthrow I permitted the driver and stoker to wither from their places, and to fade away into the outer darkness without any suitable send-off; with the guard and the stationmaster I dealt more faithfully, but the pleasure of throwing water on drowned rats is not a lasting one. I accepted the statements that they thought there wasn't a Christian in the train, that a few minutes here or there wouldn't signify, that they would have me at the junction in twenty minutes, and it was often the mail was late.

Fired by this hope I hurried back to my carriage, preceded at an emulous gallop by the officials. The guard thrust in with me the lantern from the card table, and fled to his van.

"Mind the goods, Tim!" shouted the stationmaster, as he slammed my door, "she might be coming any time now!"

The answer travelled magnificently back from the engine.

"Let her come! She'll meet her match!" A war-whoop upon the steam whistle fittingly closed the speech, and the train sprang into action.

We had about fifteen miles to go, and we banged and bucketed over it in what was, I should imagine, record time. The carriage felt as if it were galloping on four wooden legs, my teeth chattered in my head, and the salmon slowly churned its way forth from its news-paper, and moved along the netting with dreadful stealth.

All was of no avail.

"Well," said the guard, as I stepped forth on to the deserted platform of Loughranny, "that owld Limited Mail's th' unpunctualest thrain in Ireland! If you're a minute late she's gone from you, and maybe if you were early you might be half an hour waiting for her!"

On the whole the guard was a gentleman. He said he would show me the best hotel in the town, though he feared I would be hard set to get a bed anywhere because of the *Feis* (a Feis, I should explain, is a Festi-val, devoted to competitions in Irish songs and dances). He shouldered my portmanteau, he even grappled suc-cessfully with the salmon, and, as we traversed the empty streets, he explained to me how easily I could catch the morning boat from Rosslare, and how it was, as a matter of fact, quite the act of Providence that my original scheme had been frustrated.

All was dark at the uninviting portals of the hotel favoured by the guard. For a full five minutes we waited at them, ringing hard: I suggested that we should try elsewhere.

"He'll come," said the guard, with the confidence of

the Pied Piper of Hamelin, retaining an implacable thumb upon the button of the electric bell. "He'll come. Sure it rings in his room!"

The victim came, half awake, half dressed, and with an inch of dripping candle in his fingers. There was not a bed there, he said, nor in the town either.

I said I would sit in the dining-room till the time for the early train.

"Sure there's five beds in the dining-room," replied the boots, "and there's mostly two in every bed."

His voice was firm, but there was a wavering look in his eye.

"What about the billiard-room, Mike?" said the guard, in wooing tones.

"Ah, God bless you! we have a mattress on the table this minute!" answered the boots, wearily, "and the fellow that got the first prize for reels asleep on top of it!"

"Well, and can't ye put the palliasse on the floor under it, ye omadhawn?" said the guard, dumping my luggage and the salmon in the hall, "sure there's no snugger place in the house! I must run away home now, before Herself thinks I'm dead altogether!"

His retreating footsteps went lightly away down the empty street.

"Annything don't throuble *him*!" said the boots bitterly.

As for me, nothing save the personal element stood between me and destitution.

It was in the dark of the early morning that I woke again to life and its troubles. A voice, dropping, as it were, over the edge of some smothering over-world, had awakened me. It was the voice of the first prize for reels, descending through a pocket of the billiard-table.

"I beg your pardon, sir, are ye going on the five to Cork?"

I grunted a negative.

"Well, if ye were, ye'd be late," said the voice.

I received this useful information in indignant silence, and endeavoured to wrap myself again in the vanishing skirts of a dream.

"I'm going on the six-thirty meself," proceeded the voice, "and it's unknown to me how I'll put on me boots. Me feet is swelled the size o' three-pound loaves with the dint of the little dancing-shoes I had on me in the competition last night. Me feet's delicate that way, and I'm a great epicure about me boots."

I snored aggressively, but the dream was gone. So, for all practical purposes, was the night.

The first prize for reels awoke, presenting an astonishing spectacle of grass-green breeches, a white shirt, and pearl-grey stockings, and accomplished a toilet that consisted of removing these and putting on ordinary garments, completed by the apparently excruciating act of getting into his boots. At any other hour of the day I might have been sorry for him. He then removed himself and his belongings to the hall, and there entered upon a resounding conversation with the boots, while I crawled forth from my lair to renew the strife with circumstances and to endeavour to compose a telegram to Alice Hervey of explanation and apology that should cost less than seven and sixpence. There was also the salmon to be dealt with.

Here the boots intervened, opportunely, with a cup of tea, and the intelligence that he had already done up the salmon in straw bottle-covers and brown paper, and that I could travel Europe with it if I liked. He further informed me that he would run up to the station with the luggage now, and that maybe I wouldn't mind carrying the fish myself; it was on the table in the hall.

My train went at six-fifteen. The boots had secured for me one of many empty carriages, and lingered conversationally till the train started; he regretted politely my bad night at the hotel, and assured me that only for Jimmy Durkan having a little drink taken— Jimmy Durkan was the first prize for reels—he would have turned him off the billiard-table for my benefit. He finally confided to me that Mr. Durkan was engaged to his sister, and was a rising baker in the town of Limerick; "indeed," he said, "any girl might be glad to get him. He dances like whalebone, and he makes grand bread!"

Here the train started.

It was late that night when, stiff, dirty, with tired eyes blinking in the dazzle of electric lights, I was conducted by the Herveys' beautiful footman into the Herveys' baronial hall, and was told by the Herveys' imperial butler that dinner was over, and the gentlemen had just gone into the drawing-room. I was in the act of hastily declining to join them there when a voice cried:

"Here he is!"

And Philippa, rustling and radiant, came forth into the hall, followed in shimmers of satin, and flutterings of lace, by Alice Hervey, by the bride-elect, and by the usual festive rout of exhilarated relatives, male and female, whose mission it is to keep things lively before a wedding.

"Is this a wedding present for me, Uncle Sinclair?" cried the bride elect, through a deluge of questions and commiserations, and snatched from under my arm the brown-paper parcel that had remained there from force of direful habit.

"I advise you not to open it!" I exclaimed; "it's a salmon!"

The bride-elect, with a shriek of disgust, and without an instant of hesitation, hurled it at her nearest neighbour, the head bridesmaid. The head bridesmaid, with an answering shriek, sprang to one side, and the parcel that I had cherished with a mother's care across two countries and a stormy channel, fell, with a crash, on the flagged floor.

Why did it crash?

"A salmon!" screamed Philippa, gazing at the parcel, round which a pool was forming, "why, that's whisky! Can't you smell it?"

284

The footman here respectfully interposed, and kneeling down, cautiously extracted from folds of brown paper a straw bottle-cover full of broken glass and dripping with whisky.

"I'm afraid the other things are rather spoiled, sir," he said seriously, and drew forth, successively, a very large pair of high-low shoes, two long grey worsted stockings, and a pair of grass-green breeches.

They brought the house down, in a manner doubtless familiar to them when they shared the triumphs of Mr. Jimmy Durkan, but they left Alice Hervey distinctly cold.

"You know, darling," she said to Philippa afterwards, "I don't think it was very clever of dear Sinclair to take the wrong parcel. I *had* counted on that salmon."

"THE MAN THAT CAME TO BUY APPLES"

It had been freezing hard all the way home, and the Quaker skated perilously once or twice on the northerly stretches. As I passed the forge near my gate I issued an order for frost-nails, and while I did so the stars were kindling like diamonds over the black ridge of Shreelane Hill.

The overture to the Frost Symphony had begun, with its usual beauties and difficulties, and its leading theme was given forth in a missive from Flurry Knox, that awaited me on the hall table. Flurry's handwriting was an unattractive blend of the laundress's bill, and the rambling zigzags of the temperature chart, but he exhibited no more of it than was strictly necessary in getting to the point. Would I shoot at Aussolas the following day? There were a lot of cock in, and he had whipped up four guns in a hurry. There was a postscript, "Bernard Shute is coming. Tell Mrs. Yeates he didn't kill anyone yet this season."

Since his marriage, Flurry had been promoted to the position of agent to his grandmother, old Mrs. Knox of Aussolas, and through the unfathomable maze of their dealings and fights with each other, the fact remained that he has secured to himself the Aussolas shooting at about half its market value. So Mrs. Knox said. Her grandson, on the other hand, had often informed me that the privilege "had him beggared, what with beaters and all sorts, and his grandmother's cattle turned into the woods destroying all the covert—let alone her poaching." Into the differences of such skilled combatants the prudent did not intrude themselves, but they accepted without loss of time such invitations to shoot at Aussolas as came their way. Notwithstanding the buccaneerings of Flurry's grandmother, the woods of

Aussolas, in decent weather, were usually good for fifteen to twenty couple of cock.

I sent my acceptance before mentioning to Philippa that Bernard Shute was to be of the party. It was impossible to make Philippa understand that those who shot Bernard's pheasants at Clountiss could hardly do less than retaliate when occasion served. I had once, in a moment of regrettable expansion, entertained my wife with an account of how an entire shooting party had successively cast themselves upon their faces, while the muzzle of Bernard's gun had followed, half-way round the compass, a rabbit that had broken back. No damage had ensued, not even to the rabbit, but I had supplied Philippa with a fact that was an unfortunate combination of a thorn in her pillow and a stone in her sling.

The frost held; it did more than hold, it gripped. As I drove to Aussolas the fields lay rigid in the constraining cold; the trees were as dead as the telegraph poles, and the whistle of the train came thin and ghostly across four miles of silent country. Everything was half alive, with the single exception of the pony, which, filled with the idiotic exaltation that frost imparts to its race, danced upon its frost-nails, shied with untiring inventiveness, and made three several and well-conceived attempts to bolt. Maria, with her nose upon my gaiter, shuddered uninterruptedly throughout the drive, partly because of the pinching air, partly in honour of the sovereign presence of the gun-case.

Old Mrs. Knox was standing on the steps as I walked round to the hall door of Aussolas Castle. She held a silver bowl in her hand; on her head, presumably as a protection against the cold, was a table-napkin; round her feet a throng of hens and pigeons squabbled for the bits that she flung to them from the bowl, and a furtive and distrustful peacock darted a blue neck in among them from the outskirts.

" 'Good-morrow, old Sir Thomas Erpingham,' " was Mrs. Knox's singular greeting, " 'a good soft pillow for that good grey head were better than a churlish turf of France!' "

My friendship with Mrs. Knox was now of several

287

years' standing, and I knew enough of her to gather that I stood rebuked for being late.

"Flurry arrived only half an hour ago! my first intimation of a shooting party," she continued, in the dictatorial voice that was always a shock when taken in connection with her beggarwoman's costume, "a nice time of day to begin to look for beaters! And the other feather-bed sportsmen haven't arrived yet. In old times they would have had ten couple by this time, and then Mr. Flurry complains of the shooting!"

She was here interrupted by the twitching of the table-napkin from her head by her body-woman, who had advanced upon her from the rear, with the reigning member of the dynasty of purple velvet bonnets in her hand. The bonnet was substituted for the table-napkin, much as a stage property is shoved on from the wings, and two bony hands, advancing from behind, tied the strings under Mrs. Knox's chin, while she uninterruptedly fed the hens, and denounced the effeteness of modern cock-shooters. The hands descended and fixed a large pin in the uppermost of her mistress's shawls.

"Mullins, have done!" exclaimed Mrs. Knox, suddenly tearing herself from her captor, "you're an intolerable nuisance!"

"Oh, very well, ma'am, maybe you'd sooner go out with your head naked and soak the cold!" returned Mullins, retiring with the honours of war and the table-napkin.

"Mullins and I get on famously," observed Mrs. Knox, crushing an empty egg-shell with her yellow diamonded fingers and returning it to its original donors, "we're both mad, you know!"

Comment on this might have been difficult, but I was preserved from it by the approach across the frozen gravel of a short, red-bearded man, Mrs. Knox's gardener, wood-ranger, and ruling counsellor, John Kane. He held in his hands two large apples of arsenical hue, and, taking off his hat to me with much dignity, addressed himself to the lady of the house.

"He says he'd sooner walk barefoot to Cork than to give three and fippence for the likes of them!"

"I'm sure I've no objection if he does," responded Mrs. Knox, turning the silver bowl upside down over the scrimmaging hens and pigeons, "I dare say it would be no novelty to him."

"And isn't that what I told him!" said John Kane, his voice at once ascending to the concert pitch of altercation, "I said to him if the Lord Left'nant and the Pope was follying me around the yard of Aussolas offering three and a penny for them apples they'd not get them! Sure the nuns gave us that much for windfalls that was only fit to be making cherubs with!"

I might have been struck by the fitness, as well as the ingenuity, of this industry, but in some remote byway of my brain the remembrance awoke of a "black-currant cherub" prescribed by Mrs. Cadogan for sore throats, and divined by Philippa to be a syrup. I turned away and lit a cigarette in order to conceal my feelings from John Kane, round whose red beard the smoke of battle hung almost palpably.

"What's between you?" asked his mistress sharply.

"Three and a penny he's offering, ma'am!" declaimed her deputy, "for sheep's noses that there isn't one in the country has but yourself! And not a brown farthing more would he give!—the consecrated blagyard!"

Anything less like a sheep's nose than Mrs. Knox's hooked beak, as she received this information, could hardly be imagined.

"You're half a fool, John Kane!" she snapped, "and the other half's not sensible! Go back and tell him Major Yeates is here and wants to buy every apple I have!" She dealt me a wink that was the next thing to a dig in the ribs. As she spoke a cart drawn by a cheerful-looking grey pony, and conducted by a tall, thin man, came into view from the direction of the yard. It rattled emptily, and proclaimed, as was intended, the rupture of all business relations.

"See here, sir," said John Kane to me in one hoarse breath, "when he's over-right the door I'll ask him the three and fippence again, and when he refuses, your Honour will say we should split the difference——"

The cart advanced, it passed the hall door with a

289

dignity but little impaired by the pony's apprehensive interest in the peacock, and the tall man took off his hat to Mrs. Knox with as gloomy a respect as if she had been a funeral.

John Kane permitted to the salutation the full time due to it, in the manner of one who counts a semibreve rest, while the cart moved implacably onwards. The exact, the psychic moment arrived.

"Honomaundhiaoul! Sullivan!" he shouted, with a full-blown burst of ferocity, hurtling down the steps in pursuit, " will ye take them or lave them?"

To manifest, no doubt, her complete indifference to the issue, Mrs. Knox turned and went into the house, followed by the majority of the hens, and left me to await my cue. The play was played out with infinite credit to both artists, and at the full stretch of their lungs; at the pre-ordained moment I intervened with the conventional impromptu, and suggested that the difference should be split. The curtain immediately fell, and somewhere in the deep of the hall a glimpse of the purple bonnet told me that Mrs. Knox was in the auditorium.

When I rejoined her I found Flurry with her, and something in the atmosphere told that here also was storm.

"Well, take them! Take them all!" Mrs. Knox was saying in high indignation. "Take Mullins and the maids if you like! I dare say they might be more use than the men!"

"They'll make more row, anyhow," said Flurry sourly. "I wonder is it them that put down all the rabbit-traps I'm after seeing in the coach-house this minute!"

"It may be *they*, but it is certainly not *them*," retorted Mrs. Knox, hitting flagrantly below the belt; "and if you want beaters found for you, you should give me more than five minutes' warning——" She turned with the last word, and moved towards the staircase.

"I beg your pardon, ma'am," said John Kane, very respectfully, from the hall door, "that Sullivan brought this down for your Honour."

He placed on the table a bottle imperfectly wrapped in newspaper.

"Tell Sullivan," said Flurry, without an instant's hesitation, "that he makes the worst potheen in the country, and I'll prosecute him for bringing it here, unless he comes out to beat with the rest of you."

Remembering my official position, I discreetly examined the barrels of my gun.

"You'll give him no such message!" screamed Mrs. Knox over the dark rail of the staircase. "Let him take himself and his apples off out of this!" Then, in the same breath, and almost the same key, "Major Yeates, which do you prefer, curry, or Irish stew?"

The *cuisine* at Aussolas was always fraught with dark possibilities, being alternately presided over by bibulous veterans from Dublin, or aboriginal kitchen-maids off the estate. Feeling as fair Rosamund might have felt when proffered the dagger or the bowl, I selected curry.

"Then curry it shall be," said Mrs. Knox, with a sudden and awful affability. In this gleam of stormy sunshine I thought it well to withdraw.

"Did you ever eat my grandmother's curry?" said Flurry to me, later, as we watched Bernard Shute trying to back his motor into the coach-house.

I said I thought not.

"Well, you'd take a splint off a horse with it," said Mrs. Knox's grandson.

The Aussolas woods were full of birds that day. Birds bursting out of holly-bushes like corks out of soda-water bottles, skimming low under the branches of fir-trees, bolting across rides at a thousand miles an hour, swinging away through prohibitive tree-tops, but to me had befallen the inscrutable and invincible accident of being "off my day", and, by an unequal unkindness, Fate had allotted to me the station next Flurry. Every kind of bird came my way except the easy ones, and, as a general thing, when I had done no more than add a little pace to their flight, they went down to Flurry, who never in my experience had been off his day, and they seldom went farther afield. The beaters, sportsmen every man of them, had a royal time. They flailed the bushes and whacked the tree trunks; the discordant chorus of "Hi cock! Hi cock! Cock! Cock! Prrrr!"

rioted through the peaceful woods, and every other minute a yell of "Mark!" broke like a squib through the din. The clamour, the banging of the guns, and the expectancy, kept the nerves tingling; the sky between the grey branches was as blue as Italy's; despite fingers as icy as the gun-barrels, despite the speechless reproach of Maria, slinking at my heels in unemployed dejection, I enjoyed every breath of the frosty day. After all, hit or miss, a good day with the cock comes very near a good day with the hounds, without taking into consideration the comfortable fact that in the former the risk is all on the side of the birds.

Little Bosanquet, the captain of coastguards, on my left, was doing remarkably well; so apparently was Murray, the D.I. of Police; how Bernard Shute was faring I know not, but he was certainly burning a lot of powder. At the end of the third beat I found myself beside Murray. His face was redder than usual, even his freckles conveyed an impression of impartially sprinkled cayenne pepper.

"Did you see Shute just now?" he demanded in a ferocious whisper. "A bird got up between us, and he blazed straight at me! Straight bang in my face, I tell you! Only that I was in a dead line with the bird he'd have got me!"

"I suppose that was about the safest place," I said. "What did you do?"

"I simply told him that if ever he puts a grain into me I shall let him have it back, both barrels."

"Everyone says that to Bernard sooner or later," said I pacifically; "he'll settle down after lunch."

"We'll all settle down into our graves," grumbled Murray; "that'll be the end of it."

After this it was scarcely composing to a husband and father to find Mr. Shute occupying the position on my right hand as we embarked upon the last beat of the Middle Wood. He was still distinctly unsettled, and most distressingly on the alert. Nothing escaped his vigilance, the impossible wood pigeon, clattering out of the wrong side of a fir-tree, received its brace of cartridges as instantly as the palpable rabbit, fleeing down

292

the ride before him, and with an equal immunity. Between my desire to keep the thickest tree trunks between me and him, and the companion desire that he should be thoroughly aware of my whereabouts, my shooting, during that beat, went still more to pieces; a puff of feathers, wandering softly down through the radiant air, was the sum total of my achievements.

The end of the beat brought us to the end of the wood, and out upon an open space of sedgy grass and bog that sterteched away on the right to the shore of Aussolas Lake; opposite to us, a couple of hundred yards away, was another and smaller wood, clothing one side of a high promontory near the head of the lake. Flurry and I were first out of the covert.

"We'll have time to run through the rhododendron wood before lunch," he said, looking at his watch. "Here! John Kane!" He put two fingers in his mouth and projected a whistle that cleft my head like a scimitar.

John Kane emerged, nymph-like, from a laurel bush in our immediate vicinity.

" 'Tis only lost time to be beating them rosydandhrums, Master Flurry," he said volubly, "there wasn't a bird in that bit o' wood this winter. Not a week passes but I'm in it, making up the bounds fence against the cattle, and I never seen a one!"

"You might be more apt to be looking out for a rabbit than a cock, John," said Flurry expressionlessly, "but isn't it down in the lower paddocks you have the cattle and the young horses this hard weather?"

"Oh it is, sir, it is, of course, but indeed it's hard for me to know where they are, with the misthress telling this one and that one to put them in their choice place. Sure she dhrives me to and fro in my mind till I do have a headache from her!"

A dull rumble came to us across the march, and, as if Mrs. Knox had been summoned by her henchman's accusation, there laboured into view on the road that skirted the marsh a long and dilapidated equipage, silhouetted with its solitary occupant, against the dull shine of the frozen lake.

"Tally-ho! Here comes the curry for you, Major!

You'll have to eat it, I tell you!" He paused. "I'm dashed if she hasn't got Sullivan's pony! Well, she'd steal the horns off a cow!"

It was indeed the grey pony that paced demurely in the shafts of Mrs. Knox's phaeton, and at its head marched Sullivan; fragments of loud and apparently agreeable conversation reached us, as the procession moved onwards to the usual luncheon tryst at the head of the lake.

"Come now, John Kane," said Flurry, eyeing the *cortège*, "you're half your day sitting in front of the kitchen fire. How many of my rabbits went into that curry?"

"Rabbits, Master Flurry?" echoed John Kane almost pityingly, "there's no call for them trash in Aussolas kitchen! And if we wanted them itself, we'd not get them. I declare to me conscience there's not a rabbit in Aussolas demesne this minute, with the way your Honour has them ferreted—let alone the foxes!——"

"I suppose it's scarcely worth your while to put the traps down," said Flurry benignly; "that's why they were in the coach-house this morning."

There was an undissembled titter from a group of beaters in the background; Flurry tucked his gun under his arm and walked on.

"It'd be no more than a charity if ye'd eat the lunch now, sir," urged John Kane at his elbow, in fluent remonstrance, "and leave Sullivan go home. Sure it'll be black night on him before the misthress will be done with him. And as for that wood, it's hardly we can go through it with the threes that's down since the night of the big wind, and briars, and all sorts. Sure the last time I was through it me pants was in shreds, and I was that tired when I got home I couldn't stoop to pick a herrin' off a tongs, and as for the floods and the holes in the western end——" John Kane drew a full breath, and with a trawling glance gathered Bernard and me into his audience. "I declare to ye, gintlemen, me boots when I took them off was more than boots. They resimbled the mouth of a hake!"

"Ah, shut your own mouth," said Flurry.

The big rhododendron was one of the glories of Aussolas. Its original progenitor had been planted by Flurry's great-grandmother, and now, after a century of unchecked licence, it and its descendants ran riot among the pine stems on the hillside above the lake, and, in June, clothed a precipitous half-acre with infinite varieties of pale mysterious mauve. The farm road by which Mrs. Knox had traversed the marsh, here followed obediently the spurs of the wood and the creeks of the shore, in their alternate give and take. From the exalted station that had been given me on the brow of the hill, I looked down on it between the trunks of the pine-trees, and saw, instead of mysterious mauve blossome, the defiant purple of Mrs. Knox's bonnet, glowing, motionless, in a sheltered and sunny angle of the road just where it met the wood. She was drawn up in her phaeton with her back to a tumble-down erection of stones and branches, that was supposed to bar the way into the wood, beside her was the great flat boulder that had for generations been the table for shooting lunches. How, in any area of less than a quarter of a mile. Sullivan had contrived to turn the phaeton, was known only to himself, but he had accomplished it, and was now adding to the varied and unforeseen occupations of his day the task of unpacking the luncheon basket. As I waited for the whistle that was the signal for the beat to begin, I viewed the proceedings up to the point where Sullivan, now warming artistically to his work, crowned the arrangement with the bottle of potheen.

It was at that moment that I espied John Kane break from a rhododendron bush beside the phaeton, with a sack over his shoulder. This, as far as I could see through the branches, he placed upon Mrs. Knox's lap, the invaluable Sullivan hurrying to his aid. The next instant I saw Murray arrive and take up his allotted station upon the road; John Kane retired into the evergreen thicket as abruptly as he had emerged from it, Flurry's whistle sounded, and the yells of "Hi cock" began again.

We moved forward very slowly, in order to keep

station with Murray, who had to follow on the road the outer curve of the wood, while we struck straight across it. It was a wood of old and starveling trees, strangled by ivy, broken by combat with each other in the storms that rushed upon them up the lake; it was two years since I had last been through it, and I remembered well the jungle of ferns and the undergrowth of briars that had shredded the pants of John Kane, and had held in their thorny depths what Flurry had described as "a dose of cock". To-day the wood seemed strangely bare, and remarkably out of keeping with John Kane's impassioned indictment; the ferns, even the bracken, had almost disappeared, the briar brakes were broken down, and laced with black paths, and in the frozen paste of dead leaves and peat mould the hoof-marks of cattle and horses bore witness against them, like the thumb-prints of a criminal. In the first ten minutes not a gun had been let off; I anticipated pleasantly, if inadequately, the remarks that Flurry would address to John Kane at the conclusion of the beat. To foreshadow John Kane's reply to Flurry was a matter less simple. Bernard Shute was again the next gun on my left, and kept, as was his wont, something ahead of his due place in the line; of this I did not complain, it made it all the easier to keep my eye on him. The idle cartridges in his gun were obviously intolerable to him; as he crossed a little glade he discharged both barrels into the firmament, where far above, in tense flight and as steady as a constellation, moved a wedge of wild geese. The wedge continued its course unshaken, but, as if lifted by the bang, the first woodcock of the beat got up in front of me, and swung away into the rhododenrons. "Mark!" I shouted, loosing an ineffectual cartridge after him. Mr. Shute was equal to the occasion, and let fly his usual postman's knock with both barrels. In instant response there arose from behind the rhododendrons the bray of a donkey, fraught with outrage and terror, followed by crashing of branches and the thunderous galloping of many hoofs, and I had a glimpse of a flying party of cattle and horses, bursting from the rhododendron bushes and charging down a

296

grassy slope in the direction of the road. Every tail was in the air, the cattle bellowed, and the donkey, heading the flight, did not cease to proclaim his injuries.

"How many of them have you hit?" I shouted.

"I believe I got 'em all, bar the cock!" returned Mr. Shute, with ecstasy scarcely tempered by horror.

I hastened to the brow of the hill, and thence beheld Mrs. Knox's livestock precipitate themselves on to the road, and turn as one man in the direction of home. With a promptitude for which I have never been given sufficient credit, I shoved my gun into the branches of a tree and ran back through the wood at my best pace. In that glimpse of the rout I had recognized the streaming chestnut mane and the white legs of the venerable Trinket, the most indomitable old rogue that had ever reared up generations of foals in the way they should not go, and I knew by repute that once she was set going it would take more to stop her than the half-demolished barricade at the entrance to the wood.

As I ran I seemed to see Trinket and her disciples hurling themselves upon Mrs. Knox's phaeton and Sullivan's pony, with what results no man could tell. They had, however, first to circumnavigate the promontory; my chance was by crossing it at the neck to get to the phaeton before them. The going was bad, and the time was short; I went for all I was worth, and Maria, mystified, but burning with zeal, preceded me with kangaroo leaps and loud and hysterical barks. A mossy wall ringed the verge of the hill; I followed Maria over it, and the wall, or a good part of it, followed me down the hill. I plunged onward amid the coiling stems and branches of the big rhododendrons, an illuminative flash of the purple bonnet giving me my bearings. A sort of track revealed itself, doubling and dodging and dropping down rocky slides, as if in flight before me. It was near the foot of the hill that a dead branch extended a claw, and with human malignity plucked the eye-glass from my eye and snapped the cord: the eye-glass, entering into the spirit of the thing, aimed for the nearest stone and hit it. It is the commonest of disasters for the short-sighted, yet custom cannot stale it; I made the usual comment, with the usual fervour and futility, and continued to blunder forward in all the discomfort of half-sight. The trumpeting of the donkey heralded the oncoming of the stampede; I broke my way through the last of the rhododendrons and tumbled out on to the road twenty yards ahead of the phaeton.

Sullivan's pony was on its hind legs, and Sullivan was hanging on to its head. Mrs. Knox was sitting erect in the phaeton with the reins in her hand.

"Get out, ma'am! Get out!" Sullivan was howling, as I scrambled to my feet.

"Don't be a fool!" replied Mrs. Knox, without moving.

The stampede was by this time confronted by the barrier. There was not, however, a moment of hesitation: Trinket came rocketing out over it as if her years were four, instead of four-and-twenty; she landed with her white nose nearly in the back seat of the phaeton, got past with a swerve and a slip up, and went away for her stable with her tail over her back, followed with stag-like agility by her last foal, her last foal but one, and the donkey, with the young cattle hard on their flying heels. Bernard, it was very evident, had peppered them impartially all round. Sullivan's pony was alternately ramping heraldically, and wriggling like an eel in the clutches of Sullivan, and I found myself snatching blindly at whatever came to my hand of his headstall. What I caught was a mingled handful of forelock and browband; the pony twitched back his head with the cunning that is innate in ponies, and the headstall, which was a good two sizes too large, slid over its ears as though they had been buttered, and remained, bit and all, in my hand. There was a moment of struggle, in which Sullivan made a creditable effort to get the pony's head into chancery under his arm; foreseeing the issue, I made for the old lady, with the intention of dragging her from the carriage. She was at the side furthest from me, and I got one foot into the phaeton and grasped at her.

At that precise moment the pony broke away, with a jerk that pitched me on to my knees on the mat at her feet. Simultaneously I was aware of Sullivan, at the opposite side, catching Mrs. Knox to his bosom as the phaeton whirled past him, while I, as sole occupant, wallowed prone upon a heap of rugs. That ancient vehicle banged in and out of the ruts with an agility that ill befitted its years, while, with extreme caution, and the aid of the side rail, I gained the seat vacated by Mrs. Knox, and holding on there as best I could, was aware that I was being seriously run away with by the apple-man's pony, on whom my own disastrous hand had bestowed his freedom.

The flying gang in front, enlivened no doubt by the noise in their rear, maintained a stimulating lead. We were now clear of the wood and the frozen ditches of the causeway awaited me on either side in steely parallel lines; out in the open the frost had turned the ruts to iron, and it was here that the phaeton, entering into the spirit of the thing, began to throw out ballast. The cushions of the front seat were the first to go, followed, with a bomb-like crash, by a stone hot-water jar, that had lurked in the deeps of the rugs. It was in negotiating a stiffish outcrop of rock in the track that the back seat broke loose and fell to earth with a hollow thump; with a corresponding thump I returned to my seat from a considerable altitude, and found that in the interval the cushion had removed itself from beneath me, and followed its fellows overboard. Near the end of the causeway we were into Trinket's rearguard, one of whom, a bouncing young heifer, slammed a kick into the pony's ribs as he drew level with her, partly as a witticism, partly as a token of contempt. With that the end came. The pony wrenched to the left, the off front wheel jammed in a rut, came off, and the phaeton rose like a live thing beneath me and bucked me out on to the road.

A succession of crashes told that the pony was making short work of the dashboard; for my part, I lay something stunned, and with a twisted ankle, on the crisp whitened grass of the causeway, and wondered dully why I was surrounded by dead rabbits.

By the time I had pulled myself together Sullivan's pony was continuing his career, accompanied by a fair proportion of the phaeton, and on the road lay an inexplicable sack, with a rabbit, like Benjamin's cup, in its mouth.

Not less inexplicable was the appearance of Minx, my wife's fox-terrier, whom I had last seen in an arm-chair by the drawing-room fire at Shreelane, and now, in the role of the faithful Saint Bernard, was licking my face lavishly and disgustingly. Her attentions had the traditional reviving effect. I sat up and dashed her from me, and in so doing beheld my wife in the act of taking refuge in the frozen ditch as the cavalcade swept past, the phaeton and pony bringing up the rear like artillery.

"What has happened? Are you hurt?" she panted, speeding to me.

"I am; very much hurt," I said, with what was, I think, justifiable ill-temper, as I got gingerly on to my feet, almost annoyed to find that my leg was not broken.

"But, dearest Sinclair, *has* he shot you? I got so frightened about you that I bicycled over to—— Ugh! Good gracious!"—as she trod on and into a mound of rabbits—"what are you doing with all those horrible things?"

I looked back in the direction from which I had come, and saw Mrs. Knox advancing along the cause-way arm-in-arm with the now inevitable Sullivan (who, it may not be out of place to remind the reader, had come to Aussolas early in the morning, with the pure and single intention of buying apples). In Mrs. Knox's disengaged arm was something that I discerned to be the bottle of potheen, and I instantly resolved to mini-mize the extent of my injuries. Flurry, and various items of the shooting party, were converging upon us from the wood by as many and various short cuts. "I don't quite know what I am doing with the rabbits," I replied, "but I rather think I am giving them away."

As I spoke something darted past Mrs. Knox, some-thing that looked like a bundle of rags in a cyclone, but was, as a matter of fact, my faithful water-spaniel, Maria. She came on in zigzag bounds, in short maniac

300

rushes. Twice she flung herself by the roadside and rolled, driving her snout into the ground like the coulter of a plough. Her eyes were starting from her head, her tail was tucked between her legs. She bit, and tore frantically with her claws at the solid ice of a puddle.

"She's mad! She's gone mad!" exclaimed Philippa, snatching up a weapon something that looked like a frying-pan, but was, I believe, the step of the phaeton.

Maria was by this time near enough for me to discern a canary-coloured substance masking her muzzle.

"Yes, she's quite mad," I replied, possessed by a spirit of divination. "She's been eating the rabbit curry."

A CONSPIRACY OF SILENCE

It has not often been my lot to be associated with a being of so profound and rooted a pessimism as Michael Leary, Huntsman and Kennelman to Mr. Flurry Knox's Foxhounds. His attitude was that of the one and only righteous man in a perfidious and dissolute world. With, perhaps, the exception of Flurry Knox, he believed in no one save himself. I was thoroughly aware of my inadequacy as Deputy Master, and cherished only a hope that Michael might look upon me as a kind of Parsifal, a fool perhaps, yet at least "a blameless fool"; but during my time of office there were many distressing moments in which I was made to feel not only incapable, but culpable.

Michael was small, sandy, green-eyed, freckled, and, I believe, considerably junior to myself; he neither drank nor smoked, and he had a blistering tongue. I have never tried more sincerely to earn anyone's good opinion.

It was a pleasant afternoon towards the middle of December, and I was paying my customary visit to the kennels to see the hounds fed. What Michael called

301

"the troch" was nearly empty; the greedier of the hounds were flitting from place to place in the line, in the undying belief that others were better off than they. I was studying the row of parti-coloured backs, and trying for the fiftieth time to fit each with its name, when I was aware of a most respectable face, with grey whiskers, regarding me from between the bars of the kennel door.

With an effort not inferior to that with which I had just discriminated between Guardsman and General, I recognized my visitor as Mr. Jeremiah Flynn, a farmer, and a cattle dealer on a large scale, with whom I had occasionally done business in a humble way. He was a District Councillor, and a man of substance; he lived twenty miles away, at a place on the coast called Knockeenbwee, in a flat-faced, two-storied house of the usual type of hideousness. Once, when an unkind fate had sent me to that region, I had heard the incongruous tinkle of a piano proceeding from Mr. Flynn's mansion, as I drove past fighting an umbrella against the wet wind that swept in from the Atlantic.

"I beg your pardon, Major Yeates," began Mr. Flynn, with an agreeable smile, which I saw in sections between the bars; "I had a little business over this side of the country, and I took the liberty of taking a stroll around to the kennels to see the hounds."

I made haste to extend the hospitality of the feeding-yard to my visitor, who accepted it with equal alacrity, and went on to remark that it was wonderful weather for the time of year. Having obeyed this primary instinct of mankind, Mr. Flynn embarked upon large yet able compliments on the appearance of the hounds. His manners were excellent; sufficiently robust to accord with his grey frieze coat and flat-topped felt hat, and with just the extra touch of deference that expressed his respect for my high qualities and position.

"Ye have them in great form, Michael," he remarked, surveying the hounds' bloated sides with a knowledge-able eye; "and upon me word, there's our own poor Playboy, and a fine dog he is too!"

"He is; and a fine dog to hunt rabbits!" said

Michael, without a relaxation of his drab countenance.

"I dare say, Major, you didn't know that it was in my place that fellow was rared?" continued Mr. Flynn.

Owing to his providentially distinctive colouring of lemon and white, Playboy was one of the hounds about whose identity I was never in doubt. I was able to bestow a suitable glance upon him, and to recall the fact of his having come from a trencher-fed pack, of which Mr. Flynn was the ruling spirit, kept by the farmers in the wildernesses beyond and around Knockeenbwee.

"Ah! Mr. Knox was too smart for us over that hound!" pursued Mr. Flynn pleasantly; "there was a small difference between himself and meself in a matter of a few heifers I believe—a trifle of fifteen shillings it was, I believe."

"Five and thirty," said Michael to the lash of his thong, in which he was making a knot.

"And I had to give him the pup before we could come to terms," ended my visitor.

Whether at fifteen or thirty-five shillings Playboy had been a cheap hound. Brief, and chiefly ornamental, as my term of office had been, I had learnt to know his voice in covert, and had learned also to act upon it in moments of solitary and helpless ignorance as to what was happening. This, however, was not the moment to sing his praises; I preserved a careful silence.

"I rared himself and his sister," said Mr. Flynn, patting Playboy heavily, "but the sister died on me. I think 'twas from all she fretted after the brother when he went, and 'twas a pity. Those two had the old Irish breed in them; sure you'd know it by the colour, and there's no more of them now in the country only the mother, and she had a right to be shot this long time."

"Come, hounds," said Michael, interrupting this rhapsody, "open the door, Bat."

The pack swept out of the feeding-yard and were away on their wonted constitutional in half a minute.

"Grand training, grand training!" said Mr. Flynn admiringly, "they're a credit to you, Major! It's impossible to have hounds anyway disciplined running wild through the country the way our little pack is. Indeed it came into my mind on the way here to try could I coax you to come over and give us a day's hunting. We're destroyed with foxes. Such marauding I never saw! As for turkeys and fowl, they're tired of them, and it's my lambs they'll be after next."

The moment of large and general acquiescence in Mr. Flynn's proposal narrowed itself by imperceptible degrees to the moment, not properly realized till it arrived, the horrid moment of getting up at a quarter to seven on a December morning in order to catch the early train for Knockeenbwee.

In the belief that I was acting in the interest of sport I had announced at the last meet that there was to be a by-day at Knockeenbwee. To say that the fact was received without enthusiasm is to put it mildly. I was assured by one authority that I should have to hunt the hounds from a steam launch; another, more sympathetic, promised a drag, but tempered the encouragement by saying that the walls there were all made of slates, and that by the end of the run the skin would be hanging off the horses' legs like the skins of bananas. Nothing short of a heart-to-heart talk with my whip, Dr. Jerome Hickey, induced him to promise his support. Michael, from first to last, remained an implacable thunder-cloud. The die, however, was cast, and the hospitality of Mr. Flynn accepted. The eve of the by-day arrived, and the Thunder-cloud and the hounds were sent on by road to Knockeenbwee, accompanied by my ancient ally Slipper, who led my mare, and rode Philippa's pony, which had been commandeered for the occasion.

Next morning at 9.45 a.m. the train stopped by signal at the flag-station of Moyny, a cheerless strip of platform, from which a dead straight road retreated to infinity across a bog. An outside car was being backed hard into the wall of the road by a long, scared rag of a chestnut horse as Dr. Hickey and I emerged from the station, and its driver was composing its anxieties as to the nature of trains by beating it in the face with his whip. This, we were informed, was Mr. Flynn's equipage, and, at a favourable moment in the conflict, Dr. Hickey and I mounted it.

"It's seldom the thrain stands here," said the driver apologetically, as we started a strong canter, "and this one's very frightful always."

The bog ditches fleeted by at some twelve miles an hour; they were the softest, blackest, and deepest that I have ever seen, and I thanked heaven that I was not in my red coat.

"I suppose you never met the Miss Flynns?" murmured Dr. Hickey to me across the well of the car.

I replied in the negative.

"Oh, they're very grand," went on my companion, with a wary eye on the humped back of the driver. "I beleive they never put their foot outside the door unless they're going to Paris. Their father told me last week that lords in the streets of Cork were asking who they were."

"I suppose that was on their way to Paris," I suggested.

"It was not," said the driver, with stunning unexpectedness, " 'twas when they went up on th' excursion last month for to have their teeth pulled. G'wout o' that!" This to the horse, who had shied heavily at a goat.

Dr. Hickey and I sank into a stricken silence, five minutes of which, at the pace we were travelling, sufficed to bring us to a little plantation, shorn and bent by the Atlantic wind, low whitewashed walls, an economical sweep of gravel, and an entrance gate constructed to fit an outside car to an inch. From the moment that these came within the range of vision the driver beat the horse with the handle of his whip, a prelude, as we discovered, to the fact that a minor gate, obviously and invitingly leading to the yard, lolled open on one hinge at the outset of the plantation. There was a brief dissension, followed by a hand gallop to the more fitting entrance; that we should find it too fitting was a foregone conclusion, and Dr. Hickey whirled his legs on to the seat at the moment when impact between his side of the car and the gate post became inevitable. The bang that followed was a hearty one, and the driver transmitted it to me in great perfection with his elbow as he lurched on to me, there was a second and hollower bang as the well of the car, detached by the shock, dropped on the axle and turned over, flinging from it in its somersaults a harlequinade assortment of herrings, loaves of bread, and a bandbox. It was, I think, a loaf of bread that hit the horse on the hocks, but under all the circumstances even a herring would have been ample excuse for the two sledge-hammer kicks which he instantly administered to the foot-board. While the car still hung in the gateway, a donkey, with a boy sitting on the far end of its back, was suddenly mingled with the episode. The boy was off the donkey's back and the driver was off mine at apparently one and the same moment, and the car was somehow backed off the pillar; as we scraped through the boy said something to the driver in a brogue that was a shade more sophisticated than the peasant tune. It seemed to me to convey the facts that Miss Lynie was waiting for her hat, and that Maggie Kane was dancing mad for the soft sugar. We proceeded to the house leaving the ground strewn with what appeared to be the elemental stage of a picnic.

"I suppose you're getting him into form for the hunt, Eugene?" said Dr. Hickey, as the lathered and panting chestnut came to a stand some ten yards beyond the hall door.

"Well, indeed, we thought it no harm to loosen him under the car before Master Eddy went riding him," replied Eugene, "and begannies I'm not done with him yet! I have to be before the masther at the next train."

He shed us and our belongings on the steps, and drove away at a gallop.

The meet had been arranged for half-past eleven. It was half-past ten when Dr. Hickey and I were incarcerated in a dungeon-cold drawing-room by a breathless being in tennis shoes, with her hair down her back, doubtless Maggie Kane, hot from the war-dance brought on by the lack of soft sugar. She told us in a gusty whisper that the masther would be in shortly, and the

306

ladies was coming down, and left us to meditate upon our surroundings.

A cascade of white paper flowed glacially from the chimney to the fender; the gloom was Cimmerian, and unalterable, owing to the fact that the blind was broken; the cold of a never-occupied room ate into our vitals. Footsteps pounded overhead and crept into the hall. The house was obviously full of people, but no one came near us. Had it not been for my companion's biographical comments on the photographs with which the room was decked, all of them, it appeared, suitors of the Misses Flynn, I think I should have walked back to the station. At eleven o'clock the hurrying feet overhead were stilled, there was a rustling in the hall as of a stage storm, and the daughters of the house made their entry, wonderfully attired in gowns suggestive of a theatre, or a tropical garden party, and in picture hats. As I viewed the miracles of hairdressing, black as the raven's wing, the necklaces, the bracelets, and the lavish top-dressing of powder, I wondered wildly if Dr. Hickey and I should not have been in evening clothes.

We fell to a laboured conversation, conducted on the highest social plane. The young ladies rolled their black eyes under arched eyebrows, and in almost unimpeachable English accents supposed I found Ireland very dull. They asked me if I often went to the London Opera. They declared that when at home, music was their only resource, and made such pointed reference to their Italian duets that I found myself trembling on the verge of asking them to sing. Dr. Hickey, under whose wing I had proposed to shelter myself, remained sardonically aloof. A blessed diversion was created by the entrance, at racing speed, of Maggie Kane, bearing a trayful of burning sods of turf; the cascade was torn from the chimney, and the tray was emptied into the grate. Blinding smoke filled the room, and Maggie Kane murmured an imprecation upon "jack-dahs", their nests, and all their works.

The moment seemed propitious for escape; I looked at my watch, and said that if they would kindly tell me the way to the yard I would go round and see about things.

The arched eyebrows went up a shade higher; the Misses Flynn said they feared they hardly knew the way to the stables.

Dr. Hickey rose. "Indeed it isn't easy to find them," he said, "but I dare say the Major and myself will be able to make them out."

When we got outside he looked down his long nose at me.

"Stables indeed!" he said, "I hate that dirty little boasting!"

Mr. Flynn's yard certainly did not at the first glance betray the presence of stables. It consisted of an indeterminate assembly of huts, with a long corrugated iron shed standing gauntly in the midst; swamp of varying depths and shades occupied the intervals. From the shed proceeded the lamentable and indignant clamours of the hounds, against its door leaned Michael in his red coat, enacting, obviously, the role of a righteous man constrained to have his habitation in the tents of Kedar. A reverential knot of boys admired him from the wall of a neighbouring pigsty; countrymen of all ages, each armed with a stick and shadowed by a cur more or less resembling a fox-hound, stood about in patient groups; two or three dejected horses were nibbling, unattended, at a hayrick. Of our host there was no sign.

At the door of the largest hut Slipper was standing.

"Come in and see the mare, Major," he called to me in his bantam-cock voice as I approached. "Last night when we got in she was clean dead altogether, but this morning when I was giving the feed to the pony she retched out her neck and met her teeth in me poll! Oh, she's in great heart now!"

In confirmation of this statement a shrewish squeal from Lady Jane proceeded from the interior.

"Sure I slep' in the straw last night with herself and the pony. She'd have him ate this morning only for me."

The record of his devotion was here interrupted by a tremendous rattling in the farm lane; it heralded the entrance of Mr. Flynn on his outside car, drawn at full gallop by the young chestnut horse.

"Oh, look at me, Major, how late I am!" shouted Mr. Flynn jovially, as he scrambled off the car. "I declare you could light a candle at me eye with the shame that's in it, as they say! I was back in Curranhilty last night buying stock, and this was the first train I could get. Well, well, the day's long and drink's plenty!"

He bundled into a darksome hole, and emerged with a pair of dirty spurs and a malacca crop as heavy as a spade handle.

"Michael! Did they tell you we have a fox for you in the hill north?"

"I wasn't speaking to any of them," replied Michael coldly.

"Well, your hounds will be speaking to him soon! Here, hurry, boys, pull out the horses!"

His eye fell on the chestnut, upon whose reeking back Eugene was cramming a saddle, while the boy who had met us at the entrance gate was proffering to it a tin basin of oats.

"What are you doing with the young horse?" he roared.

"I thought Master Eddy would ride him, sir," replied Eugene.

"Well, he will not," said Mr. Flynn, conclusively; "the horse has enough work done, and let you walk him about easy till he's cool. You can folly the hunt then."

Two more crestfallen countenances than those of the young gentlemen he addressed it has seldom been my lot to see. The saddle was slowly removed. Master Eddy, red up to the roots of his black hair, retired silently with his basin of oats into the stable behind Slipper. Even had I not seen his cuff go to his eyes I should have realized that life would probably never hold for him a bitterer moment.

The hounds were already surging out of the yard with a following wave composed of every living thing in sight. As I took Lady Jane from the hand of Slipper, Philippa's pony gave a snort. Some touch of Philippa's criminal weakness for boys assailed me.

309

"That boy can ride the pony if he likes," I said to Slipper.

I followed the hounds and their *cortège* down a deep and filthy lane. Mr. Flynn was just in front of me, on a broad-beamed white horse, with string-halt; three or four of the trencher-fed aliens slunk at his heels, the mouth of a dingy horn protruded from his coat pocket. I trembled in spirit as I thought of Michael.

We were out at length into large and furzy spaces that slanted steeply to the cliffs; like smuts streaming out of a chimney the followers of the hunt belched from the lane and spread themselves over the pale green slopes. From this point the proceedings became merged in total incoherence. Accompanied, as it seemed, by the whole population of the district, we moved *en masse* along the top of the cliffs, while hounds, curs, and boys strove and scrambled below us, over rocks and along ledges which, one might have thought, would have tried the head of a seagull. Two successive bursts of yelling notified the capture and slaughter of two rabbits; in the first hour and a half I can recall no other achievement.

It was, however, evident that hunting, in its stricter sense, was looked on as a mere species of side show by the great majority of the field; the cream of the entertainment was found in the negotiation of such jumps as fell to the lot of the riders. These were neither numerous nor formidable, but the storm of cheers that accompanied each performance would have dignified the win of a Grand National favourite.

To Master Eddy, on Philippa's pony, it was apparent that the birthday of his life had come. Attended by Slipper and a howling company of boon companions, he and the pony played a glorified game of pitch and toss, in which, as it seemed to me, heads never turned up. It certainly was an adverse circumstance that the pony's mane had, the day before, been hogged to the bone, so that at critical moments the rider slid, unchecked, from saddle to ears, but the boon companions, who themselves jumped like antelopes, stride for stride with the pony, replaced him unfailingly with timely snatches at whatever portion of his frame first offered itself.

310

Music, even, was not wanting to our progress. A lame fiddler, on a donkey, followed in our wake, filling Michael's cup of humiliation to the brim by playing jigs during our frequent moments of inaction. The sun pushed its way out of the grey sky, the sea was grey, with a broad and flashing highway to the horizon, a frayed edge of foam tracked the broken coast-line, sea-gulls screamed and swooped, and the grass on the cliff summits was wondrous green. Old Flynn, on his white horse, moving along the verge, and bleating shrilly upon his horn to the hounds below, became idyllic.

I believe that I ought to have been in a towering passion, and should have swept the hounds home in a flood of blasphemy; as a matter of fact I enjoyed myself. Even Dr. Hickey admitted that it was as pleasant a day for smoking cigarettes as he had ever been out.

It must have been nearly three o'clock when one of Mr. Flynn's hounds, a venerable lady of lemon and white complexion, poked her lean head through furze-bushes at the top of the cliff, and came up on the level ground.

"That's old Terrible, Playboy's mother," remarked Dr. Hickey, "and a great stamp of an old hound too, but she can't run up now. Flynn tells me when she's beat out she'll sit down and yowl on the line, she's that fond of it."

Meantime Terrible was becoming busier and looking younger every moment, as she zigzagged up and across the trampled field towards the hillside. Dr. Hickey paused in the lighting of what must have been his tenth cigarette.

"If we were in a Christian country," he said, "you'd say she had a line——"

Old Flynn came pounding up on his white horse, and rode slowly up the hill behind Terrible, who silently pursued her investigations. Fifty or sixty yards higher up, my eye lighted on something that might have been a rusty can, or a wisp of bracken, lying on the sunny side of a bank. As I looked, it moved, and slid away over the top of the bank. A yell, followed by a frenzied tootling on Mr. Flynn's ancient horn, told that he had seen it too, and, in a bedlam of shrieks, chaos was upon us. Through an inextricable huddle of foot people the hounds came bursting up from the cliffs, fighting every foot of ground with the country-boys, yelping with the contagion of excitement, they broke through, and went screaming up the hill to old Terrible, who was announcing her find in deep and continuous notes.

How Lady Jane got over the first bank without trampling Slipper and two men under foot is known only to herself; as I landed, Master Eddy and the pony banged heavily into me from the rear, the pony having once and for all resolved not to be sundered by more than a yard from his stable companion of the night before. I can safely say that I have never seen hounds run faster than did Mr. Knox's and the trencher-feds, in that brief scurry from the cliffs at Knockeenbwee. By the time we had crossed the second fence the foot people were gone, like things in a dream. In front of me was Michael, and, in spite of Michael's spurs, in front of Michael was old Flynn, holding the advantage of his start with a most admirable jealousy. The white horse got over the ground in bucks like a rabbit, the string-halt lending an additional fire to his gait; on every bank his great white hindquarters stood up against the sky, like the gable end of a chapel. Had I time to think of anything, I should have repented acutely of having lent Master Eddy the pony, who was practically running away. Twice I replaced his rider in the saddle with one hand, as he landed off a fence under my stirrup. Master Eddy has lost his cap and whip, his hair was full of mud, pure ecstasy stretched his grin from ear to ear, and broke from him in giggles of delight.

Providentially, it was, as I have said, only a scurry. It seemed that we had run across the neck of a promontory, and in ten minutes we were at the cliffs again, the company reduced to old Flynn, his son, and the Hunt establishment. Below us Moyny Bay was spread forth, enclosing in its span a big green island; between us and the island was a good hundred yards of mud, plumplooking mud, with channels in it. Deep in this the hounds were wading; some of them were already ashore on the island, struggling over black rocks thatched with yellow seaweed, their voices coming faintly back to us against the wind. The white horse's tail was working like a fan, and we were all, horses and men, blowing hard enough to turn a windmill.

"That's better fun than to be eating your dinner!" puffed Mr. Flynn, purple with pride and heat, as he lowered himself from the saddle. "There isn't a hound in Ireland would take that stale line up from the cliff only old Terrible!"

"What will we do now, sir?" said Michael to me, presenting the conundrum with colourless calm, and ignoring the coat-tail trailed for his benefit, "we'll hardly get them out of that island to-night."

"I suppose you know you're bare-footed, Major?" put in Hickey, my other Job's comforter, from behind. "Your two fore-shoes are gone."

A December day is not good for much after half-past three. For half an hour the horns of Michael and old Flynn blew their summons antiphonally into the immensities of sea and sky, and summoned only the sunset, and after it the twilight; the hounds remained unresponsive, invisible.

"There's rabbits enough in that island to keep ten packs of hounds busy for a month," said Mr. Flynn; "the last time I was there I thought 'twas the face of the field was running from me. And what was it after all but the rabbits!"

"*My* hounds wouldn't hunt rabbits if they were throwing after them," said Michael ferociously.

"Oh, I suppose it's admiring the view they are!" riposted Mr. Flynn; "I tell ye now, Major, there's a man on the strand below has a flat-bottomed boat, and here's Eugene just come up. I'll send him over with the horn as soon as there's water enough, and he'll flog them out of it."

The tide crept slowly in over the mud, and a young moon was sending a slender streak of light along it through the dusk before Eugene had accomplished his mission.

The boat returned at last across the channel with a

precarious cargo of three hounds, while the rest splashed and swam after her.

"I have them all, only one," shouted Eugene as he jumped ashore, and came scrambling up the steep slants and shaley ledges of the cliff.

"I hope it isn't Terrible ye left after ye?" roared Mr. Flynn.

"Faith, I don't know which is it it is. I seen him down from me floating in the tide. It must be he was clifted. I think 'tis one of Major Yeates's. We have our own whatever."

A cold feeling ran down my back. Michael and Hickey silently conned over the pack in the growing darkness, striking matches and shielding them in their hands as they told off one hound after another, hemmed in by an eager circle of countrymen.

"It's Playboy's gone," said Michael, with awful brevity. "I suppose we may go home now, sir?"

"Ah! hold on, hold on," put in Mr. Flynn, "are ye sure now, Eugene, it wasn't a sheep ye saw? I wouldn't wish it for five pounds that the Major lost a hound by us."

"Did ye ever see a sheep with yalla spots on her?" retorted Eugene.

A shout of laughter instantly broke from the circle of sympathizers. I mounted Lady Jane in gloomy silence; there was nothing for it but to face the long homeward road, minus Flurry Knox's best hound, and with the knowledge that while I lived this day's work would not be forgotten to me by him, by Dr. Hickey, and by Michael.

It was Hickey who reminded me that I was also minus two fore-shoes, and that it was an eighteen-mile ride. On my responding irritably that I was aware of both facts, and would get the mare shod at the forge by the station, Mr. Flynn, whose voluble and unceasing condolences had not been the least of my crosses, informed me that the smith had gone away to his father-in-law's wake, and that there wasn't another forge between that and Ske-awn.

The steps by which the final disposition of events was

314

arrived at need not here be recounted. It need only be said that every star went out of its course to fight against me; even the special luminary that presided over the Curranhilty and Skebawn branch railway was hostile; I was told that the last train did not run except on Saturdays. Therefore it was that, in a blend of matchlight and moonlight, a telegram was written to Philippa, and, at the hour at which Dr. Hickey, the hounds, and Michael were nearing their journey's end, I was seated at the Knockeenbwee dinner-table, tired, thoroughly annoyed, devoured with sleep, and laboriously discoursing of London and Paris with the younger Miss Flynn.

A meal that had opened at six with strong tea, cold mutton, and bottled porter, was still, at eight o'clock, in slow but unceasing progress, suggesting successive inspirations on the part of the cook. At about seven we had had mutton chops and potatoes, and now, after an abysmal interval of conversation, we were faced by a roast goose and a rice pudding with currants in it. Through all these things had gone the heavy sounds and crashes that betokened the conversation of the drawing-room into a sleeping place for me. There was, it appeared, no spare room in the house; I felt positively abject at the thought of the trouble I was inflicting. My soul abhorred the roast goose, and was yet conscious that the only possible acknowledgement of the hospitality that was showered upon me, was to eat my way unflinchingly through all that was put upon my plate.

It must have been nine o'clock before we turned our backs upon the pleasures of the table, and settled down to hot whisky-punch over a fierce turf fire. Then ensued upon my part one of the most prolonged death-grapples with sleep that it has been my lot to endure. The conversation of Mr. Flynn and his daughters passed into my brain like a narcotic; after circling heavily round various fashionable topics it settled at length upon croquet, and it was about here that I began to slip from my moorings and drift softly towards unconsciousness. I pulled myself up on the delicious verge of a dream to agree with the statement that "croquet was a fright! You'd boil a leg of mutton while you'd be waiting for your turn!"

315

Following on this came a period of oblivion, and then an agonized recovery. Where were we? Thank heaven, we were still at the croquet party, and Miss Lynie's narrative was continuing.

"That was the last place I saw Mary. Oh, she was mad! She was mad with me! 'I was born a lady,' says she, 'and I'll die a lady!' I never saw her after that day."

Miss Lynie, with an elegantly curved little finger, finished her wine-glass of toddy and awaited my comment.

I was, for the instant, capable only of blinking like an owl, but was saved from disaster by Mr. Flynn.

"Indeed ye had no loss," he remarked. "She's like a cow that gives a good pail o' milk and spoils all by putting her leg in it!"

I said, "Quite so—exactly", while the fire, old Flynn, and the picture of a Pope over the chimney-piece, swam back into their places with a jerk.

The tale, or whatever it was, wound on. Nodding heavily. I heard how "Mary", at some period of her remarkable career, had been found "bawling in the kitchen" because Miss Flynn had refused to kiss her on both cheeks when she was going to bed, and of how, on that repulse, Mary had said that Miss Flynn was "squat". I am thankful to say that I retained sufficient control of my faculties to laugh ironically.

I think the story must then have merged into a description of some sort of entertainment, as I distinctly remember Miss Lynie saying that they "played 'Lodging-houses'—it was young Scully from Ennis made us do it—a very vulgar game I call it."

"I don't like that pullin' an' draggin'," said Mr. Flynn.

I did not feel called upon to intrude my opinion upon the remarkable pastime in question, and the veils of sleep once more swathed me irresistibly in their folds. It seemed very long afterwards that the clang of a fire-iron pulled me up with what I fear must have been an audible snort. Old Flynn was standing up in front of the fire; he had obviously reached the climax of a narrative, he awaited my comment.

316

"That—that must have been very nice," I said desperately.

"Nice!" echoed Mr. Flynn, and his astounded face shocked me into consciousness; "sure she might have burned the house down!"

What the catastrophe may have been I shall never know, nor do I remember how I shuffled out of the difficulty; I only know that at this point I abandoned the unequal struggle, and asked if I might go to bed.

The obligations of a troublesome and self-inflicted guest seal my lips as to the expedients by which the drawing-room had been converted into a sleeping-place for me. But though gratitude may enforce silence, it could not enforce sleep. The paralysing drowsiness of the parlour deserted me at the hour of need. The noises in the kitchen ceased, old Flynn pounded up to bed, the voices of the young ladies overhead died away, and the house sank into stillness, but I grew more wakeful every moment. I heard the creeping and scurrying of rats in the walls, I counted every tick, and cursed every quarter told off by a pragmatical cuckoo clock in the hall. By the time it had struck twelve I was on the verge of attacking it with the poker.

I suppose I may have dozed a little, but I was certainly aware that a long tract of time had elapsed since it had struck two, when a faint but regular creaking of the staircase impressed itself upon my ear. It was followed by a stealing foot in the hall; a hand felt over the door, and knocked very softly. I sat up in my diminutive stretcher-bed and asked who was there. The handle was turned, and a voice at the crack of the door said "It's me!"

Even in the two monosyllables I recognized the accents of the son of the house.

"I want to tell you something," pursued the voice.

I instantly surmised all possibilities of disaster; Slipper drunk and overlaid by Lady Jane, Philippa's pony dead from over-exertion, or even a further instalment of the evening meal, only now arrived at completion.

"What's the matter? Is anything wrong?" I demanded, raising myself in the trough of the bed.

"There is not; but I want to speak to you."

317

I had by this time found the matches, and my candle revealed Eddy Flynn, fully dressed save for his boots, standing in the doorway. He crept up to my bedside with elaborate stealth.

"Well, what is it?" I asked, attuning my voice to a conspirator's whisper.

"Playboy's above stairs!"

"Playboy!" I repeated incredulously, "what do you mean?"

"Eugene cot him. He's above in Eugene's room now," said the boy, his face becoming suddenly scarlet.

"Do you mean that he wasn't killed?" I demanded, instantly allocating in my own mind half a sovereign to Eugene.

"He wasn't in the island at all," faltered Master Eddy, "Eugene cot him below on the cliffs when the hounds went down in it at the first go off, and he hid him back in the house here."

The allotment of the half-sovereign was abruptly cancelled. I swallowed my emotions with some difficulty.

"Well," I said, after an awkward pause, "I'm very much obliged to you for telling me. I'll see your father about it in the morning."

Master Eddy did not accept this as a dismissal. He remained motionless, except for his eyes, that sought refuge anywhere but on my face.

There was a silence for some moments; he was almost inaudible as he said:

"It would be better for ye to take him now, and to give him to Slipper. I'd be killed if they knew I let on he was here." Then, as an afterthought, "Eugene's gone to the wake."

The inner aspect of the affair began to reveal itself, accompanied by a singularly unbecoming sidelight on old Flynn. I perceived also the useful part that had been played by Philippa's pony, but it did not alter the fact that Master Eddy was showing his gratitude like a hero. The situation was, however, too delicate to admit of comment.

"Very well," I said, without any change of expression, "will you bring the dog down to me?"

318

"I tried to bring him down with me, but he wouldn't let me put a hand on him."

I hastily got into the few garments of which I had not divested myself before getting into the misnamed stretcher-bed, aware that the horrid task was before me of burglariously probing the depths of Eugene's bedroom, and acutely uncertain as to Playboy's reception of me.

"There's a light above in the room," said Master Eddy, with a dubious glance at the candle in my hand.

I put it down, and followed him into the dark hall.

I have seldom done a more preposterous thing than creep up old Flynn's stairs in the small hours of the morning, in illicit search for my own property; but, given the dual determination to recover Playboy and to shield my confederate, I still fail to see that I could have acted otherwise.

We reached the first landing; it vibrated reassuringly with the enormous snores of Mr. Flynn. Master Eddy's cold paw closed on my hand and led me to another and steeper flight of stairs. At the top of these was a second landing, or rather passage, at the end of which a crack of light showed under a door. A dim skylight told that the roof was very near my head; I extended a groping hand for the wall, and without any warning found my fingers closing improbably, awfully, upon a warm human face. I defy the most hardened conspirator to have refrained from some expression of opinion.

"Good Lord!" I gasped, starting back, and knocking my head hard against a rafter. "What's that?"

"It's Maggie Kane, sir!" hissed a female voice. "I'm after bringing up a bone for the dog to quieten him!"

That Maggie Kane should also be in the plot was a complication beyond my stunned intelligence; I grasped only the single fact that she was an ally, endued with supernatural and sympathetic forethought. She placed in my hand a tepid and bulky fragment, which, even in the dark, I recognized as the mighty drumstick of last night's goose; at the same moment Master Eddy opened the door, and revealed Playboy, tied to the leg of a low wooden bedstead.

He was standing up, his eyes gleamed green as emeralds, he looked as big as a calf. He obviously regarded himself as the guardian of Eugene's bower, and I failed to see any recognition of me in his aspect, in point of fact he appeared to be on the verge of an outburst of suspicion that would waken the house once and for all. We held a council of war in whispers that perceptibly increased his distrust; I think it was Maggie Kane who suggested that Master Eddy should proffer him the bone while I unfastened the rope. The strategy succeeded, almost too well in fact. Following the alluring drumstick Playboy burst into the passage, towing me after him on the rope. Still preceded by the light-footed Master Eddy, he took me down the attic stairs at a speed which was the next thing to a headlong fall, while Maggie Kane held the candle at the top. As we stormed past old Flynn's door I was aware that the snoring had ceased, but "the pace was too good to inquire". We scrimmaged down the second flight into the darkness of the hall, fetching up somewhere near the clock, which, as if to give the alarm, uttered three loud and poignant cuckoos. I think Playboy must have sprung at it, in the belief that it was the voice of the drumstick; I only know that my arm was nearly wrenched from its socket, and that the clock fell with a crash from the table to the floor, where, by some malevolence of its machinery, it continued to cuckoo with jocund and implacable persistence. Something that was not Playboy bumped against me. The cuckoo's note became mysteriously muffled, and a door, revealing a fire-lit kitchen, was shoved open. We struggled through it, bound into a sheaf by Playboy's rope, and in our midst the cuckoo clock, stifled but indomitable, continued its protest from under Maggie Kane's shawl.

In the kitchen we drew breath for the first time, and Maggie Kane put the cuckoo clock into a flour bin; the house remained still as the grave. Master Eddy opened the back door; behind his head the Plough glittered wakefully in a clear and frosty sky. It was uncommonly cold.

Slipper had not gone to the wake, and was quite sober.

320

I shall never forget it to him. I told him that Playboy had come back, and was to be taken home at once. He asked no inconvenient questions, but did not deny himself a most dissolute wink. We helped him to saddle the pony, while Playboy crunched his hard-earned drumstick in the straw. In less than ten minutes he rode quietly away in the starlight, with Playboy trotting at his stirrup, and Playboy's rope tied to his arm.

I did not meet Mr. Flynn at breakfast; he had started early for a distant fair. I have, however, met him frequently since then, and we are on the best of terms. We have not shirked allusions to the day's hunting at Knockeenbwee, but Playboy has not on these occasions been mentioned by either of us.

I understand that Slipper has put forth a version of the story, in which the whole matter is resolved into a trial of wits between himself and Eugene. With this I have not interfered.

THE BOAT'S SHARE

I was sitting on the steps of Shreelane House, smoking a cigarette after breakfast. By the calendar the month was November, by the map it was the south-west of Ireland, but by every token that hot sun and soft breeze could offer it was the Riviera in April.

Maria, my wife's water spaniel, elderly now, but unimpaired in figure, and in character merely fortified in guile by the castigations of seven winters, reclined on the warm limestone flags beside me. Minx, the nursery fox-terrier, sat, as was her practice, upon Maria's ribs, nodding in slumber. All was peace.

Peace, I say, but even as I expanded in it and the sunshine, there arose to me from the kitchen window in the area the voice of Mrs. Cadogan, uplifted in passionate questioning.

"Bridgie!" it wailed. "Where's me beautiful head and me lovely feet?"

The answer to this amazing inquiry shrilly from the region of the scullery.

"Bilin' in the pot, ma'am."

I realized that it was merely soup in its elemental stage that was under discussion, but Peace spread her wings at the cry: it recalled the fact that Philippa was having a dinner party that same night. In a small establishment such as mine, a dinner party is an affair of many aspects, all of them serious. The aspect of the master of the house, however, is not serious, it is merely contemptible. Having got out the champagne, and reverentially decanted the port, there remains for him no further place in the proceedings, no moment in which his presence is desired. If, at such a time, I wished to have speech with my wife, she was not to be found; if I abandoned the search and stationed myself in the hall, she would pass me, on an average, twice in every three minutes, generally with flowers in her hands, always with an expression so rapt as to abash all questionings, I therefore sat upon the steps and read the paper, superfluous to all save the dogs, to whom I at least offered a harbourage in the general stress.

Suddenly, and without a word of warning, Minx and Maria were converted from a slumbrous mound into twin comets—comets that trailed a continuous shriek of rage as they flew down the avenue. The cause of the affront presently revealed itself, in the form of a tall woman, with a shawl over her head, and a basket on her arm. She advanced unfalteringly, Minx walking on her hind legs beside her, as if in a circus, attentively smelling the basket, while Maria bayed her at large in the background. She dropped me a curtsy fit for the Lord Lieutenant.

"Does your Honour want any fish this morning?" Her rippling grey hair gleamed like silver in the sunlight, her face was straight-browed and pale, her grey eyes met mine with respectful self-possession. She might have been Deborah the prophetess, or the Mother of the Gracchi; as a matter of fact I recognized her as a certain Mrs. Honora Brickley, mother of my present kitchenmaid, a lady whom, not six months before, I had fined in a matter of trespass and assault.

"They're lovely fish altogether!" she pursued, "they're leppin' fresh!"

Here was the chance to make myself useful. I called down the area and asked Mrs. Cadogan if she wanted fish. (It may or may not be necessary to mention that my cook's name is locally pronounced "Caydogawn").

"What fish is it, sir?" replied Mrs. Cadogan, presenting at the kitchen window a face like a harvest moon.

" 'Tis pollock, ma'am!" shouted Mrs. Brickley from the foot of the steps.

" 'Sha! thim's no good to us!" responded the harvest moon in bitter scorn. "Thim's not company fish!"

I was here aware of the presence of my wife in the doorway, with a menu-slate in one hand, and one of my best silk pocket handkerchiefs, that had obviously been used as a duster, in the other.

"Filleted with white sauce——" she murmured to herself, a world of thought in her blue eyes, "or perhaps quenelles——"

Mrs. Brickley instantly extracted a long and shapely pollock from her basket, and, with eulogies of its beauty, of Philippa's beauty, and of her own magnanimity in proffering her wares to us instead of to a craving market in Skebawn, laid it on the steps.

At this point a series of yells from the nursery, of the usual bloodcurdling description, lifted Philippa from the scene of action as a wind whirls a feather.

'Buy them!" came back to me from the stairs.

I kept to myself my long-formed opinion that eating pollock was like eating boiled cotton wool with pins in it, and the bargain proceeded. The affair was almost concluded, when Mrs. Brickley, in snatching a fish from the bottom of her basket to complete an irresistible half-dozen, let it slip from her fingers. It fell at my feet, revealing a mangled and gory patch on its side.

"Why, then, that's the best fish I have!" declared Mrs. Brickley in response to my protest. "That's the very one her honour Mrs. Yeates would fancy! She'd always like to see the blood running fresh!'

This flight of sympathetic insight did not deter me from refusing the injured pollock, coupled with a regret that Mrs. Brickley's cat should have been interrupted in its meal.

Mrs. Brickley did not immediately reply. She peeped down the area, she glanced into the hall.

'Cat is it!' she said, sinking her voice to a mysterious whisper. "Your Honour knows well, God bless you, that it was no cat done that!"

Obedient to the wholly fallacious axiom that those who ask no questions will be told no lies, I remained silent.

"Only for the luck of God being on me they'd have left meself no betther than they left the fish!" continued Mrs. Brickley. "Your Honour didn't head what work was in it on Hare Island Strand last night? Thim Keohanes had the wooden leg pulled from undher me husband with the len'th o' fightin'! Oh! Thim's outlawed altogether, and the faymales is as manly as the men! Sure the polis theirselves does be in dhread of thim women! The day-and-night-screeching porpoises!"

Seven years of Resident Magistracy had bestowed upon me some superficial knowledge of whither all this tended. I rose from the steps, with the stereotyped statement that if there was to be a case in court I could not listen to it beforehand. I then closed the hall door, not, however, before Mrs. Brickley had assured me that I was the only gentlemen, next to the Lord Almighty, in whom she had any confidence.

The next incident in the affair occurred at about a quarter to eight that evening. I was tying my tie when my wife's voice summoned me to her room in tones that presaged disaster. Philippa was standing erect, in a white and glittering garment. Her eyes shone, her cheeks glowed. It is not given to everyone to look their best when they are angry, but it undoubtedly is becoming to Philippa.

"I ask you to look at my dress," she said in a level voice.

324

"It looks very nice——" I said cautiously, knowing there was a trap somewhere. "I know it, don't I?"

"Know it!" replied Philippa witheringly, 'did you know that it had only one sleeve?"

She extended her arms; from one depended vague and transparent films of whiteness, the other was bare to the shoulder. I rather preferred it of the two.

"Well, I can't say I did," I said helplessly, "is that a new fashion?"

There was a spectral knock at the door, and Hannah, the housemaid, slid into the room, purple of face, abject of mien.

"It's what they're afther tellin' me, ma'am," she panted. " 'Twas took to sthrain the soup!"

"They took my sleeve to strain the soup!" repeated Philippa, in a crystal clarity of wrath.

"She said she got it in the passage, ma'am, and she thought you were afther throwin' it," murmured Hannah, with a glance that implored my support.

"Who are you speaking of?" demanded Philippa, looking quite six feet high.

The situation, already sufficiently acute, was here intensified by the massive entry of Mrs. Cadogan, bearing in her hand a plate, on which was a mound of soaked brownish rag. She was blowing hard, the glare of the kitchen range at highest power livid in her face.

"There's your sleeve, ma'am!" she said, "and if I could fall down dead this minute it'd be no more than a relief to me! And as for Bridgie Brickley!" continued Mrs. Cadogan, catching her wind with a gasp, "I thravelled many genthry's kitchens, but thanks be to God, I never seen the like of her! Five weeks to-morrow she's in this house, and there isn't a day but I gave her a laceratin'! Sure the hair's droppin' out o' me head, and the skin rollin' off the soles o' me feet with the heart scald I get with her! The big, low, dirty buccaneer! And I declare to you, ma'am, and to the Major, that I have a pain switching out through me hips this minute that'd bring down a horse!"

"Oh God!" said Hannah, clapping her hands over her mouth.

My eye met Philippa's; some tremor of my inward agony declared itself, and found its fellow on her quivering lips. In the same instant, wheels rumbled in the avenue.

"Here are the Knoxes!" I exclaimed, escaping headlong from the room with my dignity as master of the house still intact.

Dinner, though somewhat delayed by these agitations, passed off reasonably well. Its occasion was the return from the South African war of my landlord and neighbour, Mr. Florence McCarthy Knox, M.F.H., J.P., who had been serving his country in the Yeomanry for the past twelve months. The soup gave no hint of its cannibalistic origin, and was of a transparency that did infinite credit to the services of Philippa's sleeve; the pollock, chastely robed in white sauce, held no suggestion of a stormy past, nor, it need scarcely be said, did they foreshadow their influence on my future. As they made their circuit of the table I aimed a communing glance at my wife, who, serene in pale pink and conversation with Mr. Knox, remained unresponsive.

How the volcano that I knew to be raging below in the kitchen could have brought forth anything more edible than molten paving stones I was at a loss to imagine. Had Mrs. Cadogan sent up Bridget Brickley's head as an *entremet* it would not, indeed, have surprised me. I could not know that as the gong sounded for dinner Miss Brickley had retired to her bed in strong hysterics, announcing that she was paralysed, while Mrs. Cadogan, rapt by passion to an ecstasy of achievement, coped single-handed with the emergency.

At breakfast time next morning Philippa and I were informed that the invalid had at an early hour removed herself and her wardrobe from the house, requisitioning for the purpose my donkey-cart and the attendance of my groom, Peter Cadogan; a proceeding on which the comments of Peter's aunt, Mrs. Cadogan, left nothing to be desired.

The affair on the strand at Hare Island ripened, with infinite complexity of summonses and cross-summonses, into an imposing Petty Sessions case. Two separate deputations presented themselves at Shreelane, equipped with black eyes and other conventional injuries, one of them armed with a creelful of live lobsters to underline the argument. To decline the bribe was of no avail: the deputation decanted them upon the floor of the hall and retired, and the lobsters spread themselves at large over the house, and to this hour remain the nightmare of the nursery.

The next Petty Sessions day was wet; the tall windows of the Court House were grey and streaming, and the reek of wet humanity ascended to the ceiling. As I took my seat on the bench I perceived with an inward groan that the services of the two most eloquent solicitors in Skebawn had been engaged. This meant that Justice would not have run its course till heaven knew what dim hour of the afternoon, and that that course would be devious and difficult.

All the pews and galleries (any Irish court-house might, with the addition of a harmonium, pass presentably as a dissenting chapel) were full, and a line of flat-capped policemen stood like churchwardens near the door. Under the galleries, behind what might have answered to choir-stalls, the witnesses and their friends hid in darkness, which could, however, but partially conceal two resplendent young ladies, barmaids, who were to appear in a subsequent Sunday drinking case. I was a little late, and when I arrived Flurry Knox, supported by a couple of other magistrates, was in the chair, imperturbable of countenance as was his wont, his fair and delusive youthfulness of aspect unimpaired by his varied experiences during the war, his roving, subtle eye untamed by four years of matrimony.

A woman was being examined, a square and ugly countrywoman, with wispy hair, a slow, dignified manner, and a slight and impressive stammer. I recognized her as one of the bodyguard of the lobsters. Mr. Mooney, solicitor for the Brickleys, widely known and respected as "Roaring Jack", was in possession of that much-enduring organ, the ear of the Court.

"Now, Kate Keohane!" he thundered, "tell me what time it was when all this was going on?"

"About duskish, sir. Con Brickley was slashing the f-fish at me mother the same time. He never said a word but to take the shtick and fire me dead with it on the sthrand. He gave me plenty of blood to dhrink too," said the witness with acid decorum. She paused to permit this agreeable fact to sink in, and added, "his wife wanted to f-fasten on me the same time, an' she havin' the steer of the boat to sthrike me."

These were not precisely the facts that Mr. Mooney, as solicitor for the defence, wished to elicit.

"Would you kindly explain what you mean by the steer of the boat?" he demanded, sparring for wind in as intimidating a manner as possible. The witness stared at him.

"Sure 'tis the shtick, like, that they pulls here and there to go in their choice place."

"We may presume that the lady is referring to the tiller," said Mr. Mooney, with a facetious eye at the Bench. "Maybe now, ma'am, you can explain to us what sort of a boat is she?"

"She's that owld that if it wasn't for the weeds that's holding her together she'd bursht up in the deep."

"And who owns this valuable property?" pursued Mr. Mooney.

"She's between Con Brickley and me brother, an' the saine is between four, an' whatever crew does be in it should get their share, and the boat has a man's share."

I made no attempt to comprehend this, relying with well-founded confidence on Flurry Knox's grasp of such enigmas.

"Was Con Brickley fishing the same day?"

"He was not, sir. He was at Lisheen Fair; for as clever as he is, he couldn't kill two birds under one slat!"

Kate Keohane's voice moved unhurried from sentence to sentence and her slow pale eyes turned for an instant to the lair of the witnesses under the gallery.

"And you're asking the Bench to believe that this decent man left his business in Lisheen in order to slash fish at your mother?" said Mr. Mooney truculently.

"B'lieve me, sorra much business he laves afther him wherever he'll go!" returned the witness, "himself and

328

his wife had business enough on the sthrand when the fish was dividing, and it's then themselves put every name on me."

"Ah, what harm are names!" said Mr. Mooney, dallying elegantly with a massive watch-chain. "Come now, ma'am! will you swear you got any ill-usage from Con Brickley or his wife?" He leaned over the front of his pew, and waited for the answer with his massive red head on one side.

"I was givin' blood like a c-cow that ye'd shtab with a knife!" said Kate Keohane, with unshaken dignity. "If it was yourself that was in it ye'd feel the smart as well as me. My hand and word on it, ye would! The marks is on me head still, like the prints of dog-bites!"

She lifted a lock of hair from her forehead, and exhibited a sufficiently repellant injury. Flurry Knox leaned forward.

"Are you sure you haven't that since the time there was that business between yourself and the postmistress at Munig? I'm told you had the name of the office on your forehead where she struck you with the office stamp! Try now, sergeant, can you read Munig on her forehead?"

The Court, not excepting its line of churchwardens, dissolved into laughter; Kate Keohane preserved an offended silence.

"I suppose you want us to believe," resumed Mr. Mooney sarcastically, "that a fine hearty woman like you wasn't defending yourself!" Then with a turkey-cock burst of fury, "On your oath now! What did you strike Honora Brickley with? Answer me that now! What had you in your hand?"

"I had nothing only the little rod I had afther the ass," answered Miss Keohane, with childlike candour. "I done nothing to them; but as for Con Brickley he put his back to the cliff and he took the flannel wrop that he had on him, and he threwn it on the sthrand, and he said he should have Blood, Murder, or F-fish!"

She folded her shawl across her breast, a picture of virtue assailed, yet unassailable.

"You may go down now," said "Roaring Jack" rather hastily, "I want to have a few words with your brother."

Miss Keohane retired, without having moulted a feather of her dignity, and her brother Jer came heavily up the steps and on to the platform, his hot, wary, blue eyes gathering in the Bench and the attorneys in one bold comprehensive glance. He was a tall, dark man of about five and forty, clean-shaved, save for two clerical inches of black whiskers, and in feature of the type of a London clergyman who would probably preach on Browning.

"Well, sir!" began Mr. Mooney stimulatingly, "and are you the biggest blackguard from here to America?"

"I am not," said Jer Keohane tranquilly.

"We had you here before us not so very long ago about kicking a goat, wasn't it? You got a little touch of a pound, I think?"

This delicate allusion to a fine that the Bench had thought fit to impose did not distress the witness.

"I did, sir."

"And how's our friend the goat?" went on Mr. Mooney, with the furious facetiousness reserved for hustling tough witnesses.

"Well, I suppose she's something west of the Skelligs by now," replied Jer Keohane with great composure.

An appreciative grin ran round the court, the fact that the goat had died of the kick and been "given the cliff" being regarded as an excellent jest.

Mr. Mooney consulted his notes:

"Well, now, about this fight," he said pleasantly, "did you see your sister catch Mrs. Brickley and pull her hair down to the ground and drag the shawl off of her?"

"Well," said the witness airily, "they had a little bit of a scratch on account o' the fish. Con Brickley had the shteer o' the boat in his hand and says he, 'is there any man here that'll take the shteer from me?' The man was dhrunk, of course," added Jer charitably.

"Did you have any talk with his wife about the fish?"

"I couldn't tell the words that she said to me!" replied the witness, with a reverential glance at the Bench, "and she over-right three crowds o' men that was on the sthrand."

330

Mr. Mooney put his hands in his pockets and surveyed the witness.

"You're a very refined gentleman upon my word! Were you ever in England?"

"I was part of three years."

"Oh, that accounts for it, I suppose!" said Mr. Mooney, accepting this lucid statement without a stagger, and passing lightly on. "You're a widower, I understand, with no objection to consoling yourself?"

No answer.

"Now, sir! Can you deny you made proposals of marriage to Con Brickley's daughter last Shraft?"

The plot thickened. Con Brickley's daughter was my late kitchenmaid.

Jer Keohane smiled tolerantly.

"Ah! That was a thing o' nothing!"

"Nothing!" said Mr. Mooney, with the roar of a tornado, "do you call an impudent proposal of marriage to a respectable man's daughter nothing! That's English manners, I suppose!"

"I was goin' home one Sunday," said Jer Keohane, conversationally to the Bench, "and I met the gerr'l and her mother. I spoke to the gerr'l in a friendly way, and asked her why wasn't she gettin' marrid, and she commenced to peg stones at me and dhrew several blows of an umbrella on me. I had only three bottles o' porther taken. There now was the whole of it."

Mrs. Brickley, from under the gallery, groaned heavily and ironically.

I found it difficult to connect these coquetries with my impressions of my late kitchenmaid, a furtive and touzled being, who, in conjunction with a pail and scrubbing brush, had been wont to melt round corners and into doorways at my approach.

"Are we trying a breach of promise case?" interpolated Flurry, "if so, we ought to have the plaintiff in."

"My purpose, sir," said Mr. Mooney, in a manner discouraging to levity, "is to show that my clients have received annoyance and contempt from this man and his sister such as no parents would submit to."

A hand came forth from under the gallery and plucked

at Mr. Mooney's coat. A red monkey-face appeared out of the darkness, and there was a hoarse whisper whose purport I could not gather. Con Brickley, the defendant, was giving instructions to his lawyer.

It was perhaps as a result of these that Jer Keohane's evidence closed here. There was a brief interval, enlivened by coughs, grinding of heavy boots on the floor, and some mumbling and groaning under the gallery.

"There's great duck-shooting out on a lake on this island," commented Flurry to me, in a whisper. "My grand-uncle went there one time with an old duck-gun he had, that he fired with a fuse. He was three hours stalking the ducks before he got the gun laid. He lit the fuse then, and it set to work sputtering and hissing like a goods-engine till there wasn't a duck within ten miles. The gun went off then."

This useful sidelight on the matter in hand was interrupted by the cumbrous ascent of the one-legged Con Brickley to the witness-table. He sat down heavily, with his slouch hat on his sound knee, and his wooden stump stuck out before him. His large monkey-face was immovably serious; his eye was small, light grey, and very quick.

McCaffery, the opposition attorney, a thin, restless youth, with ears like the handles of an urn, took him in hand. To the pelting cross-examination that beset him Con Brickley replied with sombre deliberation, and with a manner of uninterested honesty, emphasizing what he said with slight, very effective gestures of his big, supple hands. His voice was deep and pleasant; it betrayed no hint of so trivial a thing as satisfaction when, in the teeth of Mr. McCaffery's leading questions, he established the fact that the "little rod" with which Miss Kate Keohane had beaten his wife was the handle of a pitchfork.

"I was counting the fish the same time," went on Con Brickley, in his rolling basso profundissimo, "and she said, 'Let the divil clear me out of the sthrand, for there's no one else will put me out!' says she."

"It was then she got the blow, I suppose!" said

McCaffery venomously; "you had a stick yourself, I dare say?"

"Yes. I had a stick. I must have a stick," deep and mellow pathos was hinted at in the voice, "I am sorry to say. What could I do to her? A man with a wooden leg on a sthrand could do nothing!"

Something like a laugh ran round the back of the court. Mr. McCaffery's ears turned scarlet and became quite decorative. On or off a strand Con Brickley was not a person to be scored off easily.

His clumsy yet impressive descent from the witness-stand followed almost immediately, and was not the least telling feature of his evidence. Mr. Mooney surveyed his exit with the admiration of one artist for another, and rising, asked the Bench's permission to call Mrs. Brickley.

Mrs. Brickley, as she mounted to the platform, in the dark and nun-like severity of her long cloak, the stately blue cloth cloak that is the privilege of the Munster peasant woman, was an example of the rarely blended qualities of picturesqueness and respectability. As she took her seat in the chair, she flung the deep hood back on to her shoulders, and met the gaze of the Court with her grey head erect; she was a witness to be proud of.

"Now, Mrs. Brickley," said "Roaring Jack" urbanely, "will you describe this interview between your daughter and Keohane."

"It was the last Sunday in Shrove, your Worship, Mr. Flurry Knox, and gentlemen," began Mrs. Brickley nimbly, "meself and me little gerr'l was comin' from mass, and Jer Keohane come up to us and got on in a most unmannerable way. He asked me daughter would she marry him. Me daughter told him she would not, quite friendly like. I'll tell ye no lie, gentlemen, she was teasing him with the umbrella the same time, an' he raised his shtick and dhrew a sthroke on her in the back, an' the little gerr'l took up a small pebble of a stone and fired it at him. She put the umbrella up to his mouth, but she called him no names. But as for him, the names he put on her was to call her 'a nasty long slopeen of a proud thing, and a slopeen of a proud tinker'."

333

"Very lover-like expressions!" commented Mr. Mooney, doubtless stimulated by ladylike titters from the barmaids; "and had this romantic gentleman made any previous proposals for your daughter?"

"Himself had two friends over from across the water one night to make the match, a Saturday it was, and they should land the lee side o' the island, for the wind was a fright," replied Mrs. Brickley, launching her tale with the power of easy narration that is bestowed with such amazing liberality on her class; "the three o' them had dhrink taken, an' I went to shlap out the door agin them. Me husband said then we should let them in, if it was a Turk itself, with the rain that was in it. They were talking in it then till near the dawning, and in the latther end all that was between them was the boat's share."

"What do you mean by 'the boat's share'?" said I.

" 'Tis the same as a man's share, me worshipful gintleman," returned Mrs. Brickley splendidly; "it goes with the boat always, afther the crew and the saine has their share got."

I possibly looked as enlightened as I felt by this exposition.

"You mean that Jer wouldn't have her unless he got the boat's share with her?" suggested Flurry.

"He said it over-right all that was in the house, and he reddening his pipe at the fire," replied Mrs. Brickley, in full-sailed response to the helm. " 'D'ye think,' says I to him, 'that me daughter would leave a lovely situation, with a kind and tendher masther, for a mean, hungry blagyard like yerself,' says I, 'that's livin' always in this backwards place!' says I."

This touching expression of preference for myself, as opposed to Mr. Keohane, was received with expressionless respect by the Court. Flurry, with an impassive countenance, kicked me heavily under cover of the desk. I said that we had better get on to the assault on the strand. Nothing could have been more to Mrs. Brickley's taste. We were minutely instructed as to how Katie Keohane drew the shawleen forward on Mrs. Brickley's head to stifle her; and how Norrie Keohane was fast in her hair. Of how Mrs. Brickley had then given a stroke upwards between herself and her face (whatever that might mean) and loosed Norrie from her hair. Of how she then sat down and commenced to cry from the use they had for her.

" 'Twas all I done," she concluded, looking like a sacred picture. "I gave a sthroke of a pollock on them." Then, an afterthought, "an' if I did, 'twas myself was at the loss of the same pollock!'"

I fixed my eyes immovably on my desk. I knew that the slightest symptom of intelligence on my part would instantly draw forth the episode of the fish-buying on the morning of the dinner party, with the rape of Philippa's sleeve, and the unjust aspersion on Miss Brickley following in due sequence, ending with the paralytic seizure and dignified departure of the latter to her parents' residence in Hare Island. The critical moment was averted by a question from Mr. Mooney.

"As for language," replied Mrs. Brickley, with clear eyes a little uplifted in the direction of the ceiling, "there was no name from heaven and hell but she had it on me, and wishin' the divil might burn the two heels off me, and the like o' me wasn't in sivin parishes! And that was the clane part of the discoorse, yer Worships!' "

Mrs. Brickley here drew her cloak more closely about her, as though to enshroud herself in her own refinement, and presented to the Bench a silence as elaborate as a drop scene. It implied, amongst other things, a generous confidence in the imaginative powers of her audience.

Whether or no this was misplaced, Mrs. Brickley was not invited further to enlighten the Court. After her departure the case droned on in inexhaustible rancour, and trackless complications as to the shares of the fish. Its ethics and its arithmetic would have defied the allied intellects of Solomon and Bishop Colenso. It was somewhere in that dead hour of the afternoon, when it is too late for lunch and too early for tea, that the Bench, wan with hunger, wound up the affair by impartially binding both parties in sheaves "to the Peace".

As a sub-issue I arranged with Mr. Knox to shoot duck on the one-legged man's land on Hare Island as soon as should be convenient, and lightly dismissed from my mind dealings, official and otherwise, with the house of Brickley.

But even as there are people who never give away old clothes, so are there people, of whom is Flurry Knox, who never dismiss anything from their minds.

THE LAST DAY OF SHRAFT

It was not many days after the Keohane and Brickley trial that my wife's elderly stepbrother, Maxwell Bruce, wrote to us to say that he was engaged in a tour through the Irish-speaking counties, and would look us up on his way from Kerry. The letter began *"O Bean uasal"*, and broke into eruptions of Erse at various points, but the excerpts from Bradshaw were, fortunately, in the vernacular.

Philippa assured me she could read it all. During the previous winter she had had five lessons and a half in the Irish language from the National schoolmaster, and believed herself to be one of the props of the Celtic movement. My own attitude with regard to the Celtic movement was sympathetic, but a brief inspection of the grammar convinced me that my sympathies would not survive the strain of triphthongs, eclipsed consonants, and synthetic verbs, and that I should do well to refrain from embittering my declining years by an impotent and humiliating pursuit of the most elusive of pronuciations. Philippa had attained to the height of being able to greet the schoolmaster in Irish, and, if the day happened to be fine, she was capable of stating the fact; other aspects of the weather, however remarkable, she epitomized in a brilliant smile, and the schoolmaster was generally considerate enough not to press the matter.

My stepbrother-in-law neither hunted, shot, nor fished, yet as a guest he never gave me a moment's anxiety. He possessed the attribute, priceless in guests, of a good partable hobby, involving no machinery, accessories or paraphernalia of any kind. It did not even involve the personal attendance of his host. His mornings were spent in proffering Irish phrases to bewildered beggars at the hall door, or to the respectfully bored Peter Cadogan in the harness-room. He held *conversaziones* in the servants' hall after dinner, while I slept balmily in front of the drawing-room fire. When not thus engaged, he sat in his room making notes, and writing letters to the Archimandrites of his faith. Truly an ideal visitor, one to whom neglect was a kindness, and entertainments an abomination; certainly not a person to take to Hare Island to shoot ducks with Flurry Knox.

But it was otherwise ordained by Philippa. Hare Island was, she said, and the schoolmaster said, a place where the Irish language was still spoken with a purity worthy of the Isles of Aran. Its folk-lore was an unworked mine, and it was moreover the home of one Shemus Ruadth, a singer and poet (and, I may add, a smuggler of tobacco) of high local renown: Maxwell should on no account miss such a chance. I mentioned that Hare Island was at present going through the measles phase of its usual rotation of epidemics. My wife wavered, in a manner that showed me that I had been on the verge of a family picnic, and I said I had heard that there was whooping-cough there too. The children had had neither. The picnic expired without a sound, but my stepbrother-in-law had made up his mind.

It was a grey and bitter December morning when Maxwell and I, accompanied by Peter Cadogan, stood waiting on the beach at Yokahn for Flurry to arrive. Maria, as was her wont, was nosing my gun as if she expected to see a woodcock fly out of it; that Minx was beside her was due to the peculiar inveteracy of Minx. How she had achieved it is of no consequence; the distressing fact remained that she was there, seated, shuddering, upon a space of wet stone no larger than a sixpence, and had to be accepted as one of the party. It struck me that Mr. Cadogan had rather overdressed the part of dog-boy and bag-bearer, being attired in a striped blue flannel suit that had once been mine, a gaudy new cap, and yellow boots. The social possibilities of Hare Island had faded from my mind; I merely experienced the usual humiliation of perceiving how discarded garments can, in a lower sphere, renew their youth and blossom as the rose. I was even formulating a system of putting my old clothes out at grass, as it were, with Peter Cadogan, when a messenger arrived with a note from Flurry Knox in which he informed me, with many regrets, that he was kept at home on unexpected business, but he had arranged that we should find a boat ready to take us to the island, and Con Brickley would look after us when we got there. The boat was even now nearing the beach, rowed by two men, who, in beautiful accord with our "binding to the Peace", proved to be the widower, Jer Keohane, and his late antagonist, the one-legged Con Brickley. In view of this millennial state of affairs it seemed alarmingly probable that the boat which had come for us was that on which, as on a pivot, the late battle had turned. A witness had said, on oath, that "if it wasn't for the weeds that's holding her together she'd bursht up in the deep". I inspected her narrowly, and was relieved to see that the weeds still held their ground.

A mile of slatey water tumbled between us and the island, and an undue proportion of it, highly flavoured by fish, flowed in uneasy tides in the bottom of the boat, with a final disposition towards the well-laden stern. There were no bottom boards, and, judging by the depth of the flood over the keel, her draught appeared to be equal to that of a racing yacht. We sat precariously upon strips of nine-inch plank, our feet propped against the tarred sides just out of the wash; the boat climbed and wallowed with a three-cornered roll, the dogs panted in mingled nausea and agitation, and the narrow blades of the oars dipped their frayed edges in the waves in short and untiring jerks.

My brother-in-law, with a countenance leaden magenta from cold, struggled with the whirling leaves of a phrase book. He was tall and thin, of the famished vegetarian type of looks, with unpractical prominent eyes, and a complexion that on the hottest day in summer imparted

338

a chill to the beholder; in this raw December wind it was a positive suffering even to think of his nose, and my eyes rested, in unconscious craving for warmth, upon the changeless, impartial red of Con Brickley's monkey-face.

We landed with a rush on the steep shingle of a sheltered cove. The island boasted a pier, built with "Relief" money, but it was two miles from the lake where I was to shoot, and this small triangle of beach, tucked away in a notch of the cliff, was within ten minutes' walk of it. At the innermost angle of the cove, where the notch ended in a tortuous fissure, there was a path that zigzagged to the top of the cliff, a remarkably excellent path, and a well-worn one, with steps here and there. I commented on it to Mr. Brickley.

"Why, thin, it was in this same place that I losht the owld leg, sir," he replied in his sombre voice. "I took a ship on a dark night and me landlord was that much sorry for me that he made a good pat' in it." He was pitching himself up the steps on his crutches as he spoke, an object of compassion of the most obvious and silencing sort. Why, then, should Peter Cadogan smile furtively at the widower?

At the top of the fissure, where it melted into a hollow between low, grassy hills, stood the Brickleys' cottage, long, low, and whitewashed, deep in shelter, with big stones, hung in halters of hay-rope, lying on its thatch, to keep the roof on in the Atlantic gales. A thick fuchsia hedge surrounded it; from its open door preceeded sounds of furious altercation; apparently a man and woman hurling invective and personalities at each other in Irish, at the tops of their voices. Con Brickley sprang forward on his crutch, a girl at the door vanished into the house, and a sudden silence fell. With scarcely a perceptible interval, Mrs. Brickley appeared in the doorway, a red shawl tied over her rippling grey hair, her manner an inimitable blend of deference and hospitality.

"Your Honour's welcome, Major Yeates," she said with a curtsy. A door banged at the back of the cottage. "That was a poor man from across the water that came apalogizin' to me for dhrawin' me name down in a little disagreement that he had about a settin' o' goose eggs."

I suppose that it was contrition that caused the apologist to stumble heavily as he came round the corner of the house, and departed at a tangent through an opening in the fuchsia hedge. Feeling that comment on the incident was too delicate a matter for my capacities, I introduced Maxwell and his aspirations to the lady of the house. Any qualms that I might have had as to how to dispose of him while I was shooting were set at rest by Mrs. Brickley's instant grasp of the situation. I regret to say that I can neither transcribe nor translate the rolling periods in which my brother-in-law addressed himself to her. I have reason to believe that he apostrophized her as "O worthy woman of cows!" invoking upon her and her household a comprehensive and classic blessing, dating from the time of Cuchulain.

Mrs. Brickley received it without a perceptible stagger, and in the course of the next few minutes, Miss Bridget Brickley (who, it may be remembered, had but recently renounced the office of kitchenmaid in my house) emerged, beautifully dressed, from the cottage, and was dispatched, at full speed, to summon Shemus Ruadth, the poet, as well as one or two of "the neighbours" reputed to speak Irish of the purest kind. If to make a guest feel himself to be the one person in the world whose welfare is of any importance is the aim of hostesses, they can study the art in its perfection under the smoky rafters of Irish cabins. If it is insincere, it is equally to be respected: it is often amiable to be insincere.

My own share of the day's enjoyment opened plausibly enough, though not, possibly, as cloudlessly as Maxwell's. Attended by Maria, Peter Cadogan, and the widower, and by a smell of whisky that floated to me on the chill breeze when the widower was to windward, I set forth, having—as I fatuously imagined—disposed of Minx and of her intention to join the shooting-party, by tying a sout piece of cord to her collar, and placing its other end in my brother-in-law's hand. I had, by Flurry's advice, postponed the shooting of the lake till the last thing before leaving the island, and turning my back upon it, I tramped inland along half-thawed marshes in search of snipe, and crept behind walls after plover, whose elusive whistling was always two fields ahead. After an unfruitful hour or so the entertainment began to drag, and another plan of campaign seemed advisable: I made a *cache* of my retinue behind a rock, one of the many rocks that stood like fossilized mammoths upon the ragged hill stopes, and, with Maria at my heels, accomplished a long and laborious détour. At length, through the crannies of a wall, I perceived, just within shot, a stand of plover, hopping, gobbling, squealing, quite unaware of my proximity. I cautiously laid my gun at the top of the wall. As I cocked it, a white form appeared on a fence behind the birds, poised itself for an instant with elf-like ears spread wide, then, volleying barks, the intolerable Minx burst like a firework into the heart of the plover. In lightning response to her comrade's tally-ho Maria rocketed over the wall; the plover rose as one man, and, as I missed with both barrels, swirled out of range and sight. By way, I suppose, of rounding off the jest effectively, Maria rushed in scientific zigzags through the field, in search of the bird that she well knew I had not shot, deaf as the dead to words of command, while Minx, stark mad with excitement, circled and shrieked round Maria. To take off Maria's collar and thrash her heavily with the buckle end of it was futile, except as a personal gratification, but I did it. To thrash Minx was not only absurd but impossible; one might as well have tried to thrash a grasshopper.

I whistled for Peter and the widower without avail, and finally, in just indignation, went back to look for them. They were gone. Not a soul was in sight. I concluded that they had gone on towards the lake, and having sacrificed a sandwich to the capture of Minx I coupled her to Maria by means of the cord that still trailed from her collar, and again set forth. The island was a large one, three or four miles long by nearly as many wide; I had opened my campaign along its western shores, where heather struggled with bog, and stones, big and little, bestrewed any patch sound enough to carry them. Here and there were places where turf had been cut for fuel, leaving a drop like a sunk fence with black

water at its foot, a matter requiring a hearty jump on to
what might or might not be sound landing. When two
maniacs are unequally yoked together by their necks,
heartiness and activity are of less importance than
unanimity, and it was in unanimity that Maria and Minx
chiefly failed. At such moments, profoundly as I detested
Minx, my sympathies reluctantly were hers. Conscious,
as are all little dogs, of her superior astuteness, she yet
had to submit to Maria's choice of pace, to Maria's professional quarterings and questings of obviously barren
tracts of bogland. In bursts of squealing fury she hung
from Maria's ear, she tore mouthfuls of brown wool
from her neck, she jibbed with all her claws stuck into
the ground; none the less she was swept across the
ditches, and lugged over the walls, in seeming oneness of
purpose, in total and preposterous absurdity. At one
juncture a snipe, who must, I think, have been deaf,
remained long enough within their sphere of action for
me to shoot him. The couple, unanimous for once,
charged down upon the remains: the corpse was secured
by Maria, but was torn piecemeal from her jaws by
Minx. They then galloped emulously back to me for
applause, still bitterly contesting every inch of the snipe,
and, having grudgingly relinquished the fragments,
waited wild-eyed and panting, with tongues hanging like
aprons to their knees.

It was towards the close of the incident that I was
aware of a sibilant whispering near me, and found that I
was being observed from the rear with almost passionate
interest, by two little girls and a pair of goats. I addressed
the party with an inquiry as to whether they had seen
Jer Keohane.

The biggest little girl said that she had not seen him,
but, in a *non sequitur* full of intelligence, added that she
had seen Peter Cadogan a while ago, sitting down under
a wall, himself and Pidge.

"What's Pidge?" said I cautiously. "Is it a dog?"

"Oh Christians!" said the smaller child, swiftly covering her mouth with her pinafore.

The elder, with an untrammelled grin, explained that

"Pidge" was the name by which my late kitchenmaid was known in the home circle.

I postponed comment till Peter should be delivered into my hand, then, rightly concluding that the tendance of Hare Island goats would ensure the qualities necessary for dealing with even Maria and Minx, I engaged the pair as dog-boys.

My progress from this point to the lake might have been taken from the Old Testament, or the Swiss Family Robinson. In front of me paced the goats, who had sociably declined to be left out of the expedition; behind me strove the dogs, with the wiry and scarlet fingers of their attendants knotted in Mrs. Brickley's invaluable piece of string. It proved to be a thoroughly successful working arrangement; I even shot a plover, which was retrieved *en másse* by all except the goats.

In complete amity we reached the lake, a reedy strip of water that twisted in and out between low hills, its indeterminate shores cloaked with reeds. It was now past three o'clock, and the cold grey afternoon was already heaping into the west the pile of dark clouds that was to be its equivalent for sunset. I crept warily forward round the flank of the nearest hill, leaving the dogs and their keepers in death grapple, and the goats snatching mouthfuls of grass beside them, in the petulant, fractious manner of goats that so ill assorts with their Presbyterian grey beards.

The frost had been preceded by a flood, and the swamp bordering the lake was very bad going; the tussocks were rotten, the holes were delusively covered with lids of white ice, and to traverse these in the attitude of a man with acute lumbago was no light matter. But the ducks were there. I could hear them quacking and splashing beyond the screen of reeds, and, straightening my back for an observation, caught sight of four or five swimming in a line, well within range. There was not an instant to lose; balancing precariously on a tussock, I flung up my gun and fired. Terrific quacking followed, interspersed by distant and heartrending yells from the dogs, but the inexplicable feature of the case was that the ducks did not rise from the water. Had I slain the whole crowd?

343

There was a sound as if the marsh behind me was being slashed with a flail; a brown body whizzed past me, closely followed by a white one. "From his mountain home King James had rushing come", in other words, my retrievers had hurled themselves upon their prey.

Maria's performance was faultless; in half a minute she had laid a bird at my feet, a very large pale drake, quite unlike any wild drake that I had ever——

Out of the silence that followed came a thin, shrill voice from the hill:

"Thim's Mrs. Brickley's ducks!"

In confirmation of this appalling statement I perceived the survivors already landing on the far side of the lake, and hurrying homeward up the hill with direful clamours, while a wedge-shaped ripple in the grey water with a white speck at its apex, told of Minx in an ecstasy of pursuit.

"Stop the dog!" I shouted to my maids-of-honour, "run round and catch her!"

Maria here, in irrepressible appropriation of the mission, bolted between my legs, and sent me staggering backwards into a very considerable boghole.

I will not labour the details. After some flounderings I achieved safety and the awe-stricken comments of the maids-of-honour, as wet as I have ever been in my life, and about five times as cold. One of my young ladies captured Minx in the act of getting ashore; the other collected the slaughtered drake and shrouded him in her pinafore, with a grasp of the position that did credit to both heart and head, and they finally informed me that Mrs. Brickley's house was only a small piece–een away.

I had left Mrs. Brickley's house a well-equipped sportsman, creditably escorted by Peter Cadogan and the widower. I returned to it a muddy and dripping outcast, attended by two little girls, two goats, and her own eight ducks whom my hand had widowed. My sodden clothes clung clammily about me; the wind, as it pierced them, carried with it all the iciness of the boghole. I walked at top speed to get up some semblance of a circulation; I should have run were it not for the confusion that such a proceeding would have caused to my *cortège*. As it was, the ducks fled before me in waddling panic, with occasional help from their wings, and panting and pattering in the rear told that the maids-of-honour, the goats, and the dogs were maintaining with difficulty their due places in the procession. As I neared the cottage I saw a boy go quickly into it and shut the door; I passed into the yard within the fuchsia hedge and heard someone inside howling and droning a song in Irish, and as I knocked, with frozen knuckles, the house gave the indefinable feeling of being full of people. There was no response; I lifted the latch. The door opened into the frieze-covered backs of several men, and an evenly blended smell of whisky, turf smoke, and crowded humanity steamed forth.

The company made way for me, awkwardly; I noticed a tendency amongst them to hold on to each other, and there was a hilarious light in Mrs. Brickley's eye as she hustled forward to meet me. My brother-in-law was sitting at a table by the window writing in a notebook by the last light of the waning day; he gave me a glance laden with affairs to which I was superfluous. A red-eyed, red-headed man, evidently the singer, was standing in the middle of the room; it must have been in conformity with some irresistible law of nature that his hair stood out round his head in the orthodox poetic aureole.

In spite of the painful publicity of the moment there was but one course open to me. I tendered to my hostess the corpse of the drake, with abject apologies and explanations. To say that Mrs. Brickley accepted them favourably is quite inadequate. She heaped insults upon the drake, for his age, for his ugliness, for his temerity in getting in my way; she, in fact, accepted his slaughter in the light of a personal favour and an excellent jest combined, and passed rapidly on to explain that the company consisted of a few of the neighbours that was gathered to talk to the gentleman, and to be singing "them owld songs" for him; their number and their zeal being entirely due to the deep personal regard entertained for me by Hare Island. She further mentioned that it was Shrove

Tuesday, and that people should "jolly themselves" before Lent. I was hurriedly conveyed to what is known as "back in the room", a blend of best parlour and bedroom, with an immense bed in the corner. A fire was lighted, by the simple method of importing most of the kitchen fire, bodily, in a bucket, and placing it on the hearth, and I was conjured to "sthrip" and to put on a new suit of clothes belonging to my host while my own were being dried. He himself valeted me, inaugurating the ceremony with a tumbler of hot whisky and water. The suit of new clothes was of the thickest blue cloth, stiff as boards, and they smelt horribly of stale turf smoke. The discovery that the trousers consisted of but a leg and a half was startling; I had forgotten this aspect of the case, but now, in the proprietor's presence, it was impossible to withdraw from the loan. I could, at all events, remain *perdu*. Through all these preparations I was aware of highly incensed and fruitless callings for "Pidge"; of Peter Cadogan no tidings were forthcoming, and although a conventional sense of honour withheld me from disclosing the information I might have given about the young lady, it did not deter me from mentally preparing a warm reception for her squire.

I sat by the fire in regal seclusion, with my clothes steaming on a chair opposite to me, and the strong glow of the red turf scorching the skin that was unprotected. Maria and Minx, also steaming, sat in exquisite serenity in front of the blaze, retiring every now and then to fling themselves, panting, on a cold space of floor. The hot whisky and water sent its vulgar and entirely acceptable consolations into the frozen recesses of my being, a feeling of sociability stole upon me; I felt magnanimously pleased at the thought that Maxwell, at least, had had a perfectly successful day; I glowed with gratitude towards Con Brickley and his wife.

Judged by the usual test of hostesses, that is to say, noise, the *conversazione* in Maxwell's honour was a high success. Gabble and hum, harangue and argument, and, through all, Maxwell's unemotional educated voice in discussion with the poet. Scraps of English here and there presently told me that the talk had centred itself upon

346

the tragedy of the drake. I had the gratification of hearing Mrs. Brickley inform her friends that "if that owld dhrake was shot, itself, he was in the want of it, and divil mend him, going parading there till he had the Major put asthray! Sure that's the gintleman that's like a child! and Pidge could tell ye the same."

"Faith and thrue for ye," said another apologist, also female, "and ye wouldn't blame him if he didn't leave duck nor dhrake livin' afther him, with the annoyance he got from thim that should be tinding him, and he bloated with the walk and all!"

(I may, in my own interest, explain that this unattractive description merely implied that I was heated from excessive exercise.)

"And as for the same Pidge," broke in Mrs. Brickley with sudden fire, "when I ketch her it isn't to bate her I'll go, no! but to dhrag her by the hair o' the head round the kitchen."

These agreeable anticipations were interrupted by other voices. Someone named Paddy was called upon to sing the song about Ned Flaherty's drake.

"Sing up, Paddy boy, for the gentleman! Arrah, what ails ye, Paddy! Don't be ashamed at all!"

"'Tis a lovely song, your honour, sir (this to my brother-in-law).

"Is it an ancient song?" I heard Maxwell inquire with serious eagerness.

"It is, your honour; 'twas himself made it up lasht year, and he sings it beautiful! Oh! Paddy's a perfect modulator!"

With curiosity stimulated by this mysterious encomium I rose softly and half opened the door in order to obtain a view of the modulator. A lamp with a glaring tin reflector was on the table beside Maxwell; it illumined Paddy, the modulator, an incredibly freckled youth, standing in front of my brother-in-law, with eyes fixed on the ground and arms hanging limply at his sides, like a prisoner awaiting sentence. It illumined also the artistic contempt on the elder poet's countenance, and further revealed to me the fact that from twenty-five to thirty men and women were packed into the small kitchen.

The modulator opened with a long-drawn and nasal cadenza, suggestive of the droning preliminary canter of a bagpipe, which merged into the statement that

> The poor little fella',
> His legs they were yella',
> His bosom was blue, he could swim like a hake;
> But some wicked savage,
> To grease his white cabbage,
> Murdered Ned Flaherty's beautiful dhrake!

Riotous applause followed on this startingly appropriate requiem. Maxwell coldly laid down his stylograph with the manner of a reporter during an unimportant speech; the poet took a clay pipe out of his pocket and examined its contents with an air of detachment; Paddy, with a countenance of undiminished gloom, prepared the way for the next verse with some half-dozen jig-steps, ending with a sledge-hammer stamp on the earthen floor. Fresh thunders of approval greeted the effort. It seemed to me that Con Brickley's hospitality had been a trifle excessive; I even meditated a hint to that effect, but neither my host nor my hostess was visible. They were apparently holding an overflow meeting in a room at the other end of the house, and I noticed that although there was a steady flow of passers in and out between it and the kitchen, the door was carefully closed after each opening.

Suddenly the lamp on Maxwell's table flared up smokily as the door of the house was burst open. The second verse of the drake's elegy ceased at its first line. A woman whom I recognized as Kate Keohane, sister of the widower, drove her way into the kitchen, sweeping back the people on either side of her with her arms, as though she were swimming. Her face was scarlet.

"Is Jer Keohane within here?" she shouted.

"He is not!" replied several voices.

Instantly the door of the inner room flew open, and like a stag (or a tom-cat, either simile would serve) answering the challenge of a rival, Mrs. Brickley came forth.

"Is it yer brother you're wantin', ma'am?" she said
with lofty politeness. "Ye can search out the house for
him if ye like. It's little he troubles my house or myself
now, thanks be to God, and to the magistrates that took
my part before all that was in the coort-house! Me that
he had goin' in dhread o' me life, with him afther me
always in me thrack like a lap-dog!"

"And who has him enticed now but your own
daughther?" shrieked Miss Keohane with lightning
rapidity. "Isn't Ellen, the chapel-woman, afther tellin'
me she seen herself and himself shneakin' down behind-
side the chapel, like they'd be goin' aisht to the far
sthrand, and she dhressed out, and the coat she stole
from Mrs. Yeates on her and a bundle in her hand! Sure
doesn't the world know she has her passage paid to
Ameriky this two months!"

"Ye lie!" panted Mrs. Brickley, catching her antagonist by the arm, not in attack, but in the awful truce of
mutual panic.

Miss Keohane flung her off, only the better to gather
force for the prolonged and direful howl of which she
delivered herself.

"If she didn't come here with him it's to Ameriky she's
taken him! Look in yer box an' ye'll see where she got
the passage money! She has the boat's share taken from
ye in spite of yer teeth!" Miss Keohane here dropped
upon her knees. "An' I pray," she continued, lyrically,
"that the divil may melt her, the same as ye'd melt the
froth off porther——"

Groans, hoots, and drunken laughter overwhelmed the
close of this aspiration. Oblivious of my costume, I
stepped forward, with the intention of attracting Maxwell's attention, and withdrawing him and myself as
swiftly and unobtrusively as possible from a position that
threatened to become too hot to hold us.

Even as I did so, I saw in the dark blue space of the
open door a face that was strangely familiar, a face at
once civilized and martial, whose gaze was set incredulously upon me.

"Here's the polis!" squeaked a little girl.

The poet blew out the lamp. The house was in an

349

instant full of the voiceless and strenuous shoving and trampling of people trying to escape. I heard the table go over with a crash, and could only suppose that Maxwell had gone with it, and Maria and Minx, convinced that a cat-hunt was at the root of the matter, barked deafeningly and unceasingly.

In a blinding flash of insight I realized that my brother-in-law and I had been taken red-handed in a "shebeen", that is to say, a house in which drink is illictly sold without a license.

The police-sergeant was egregiously tactful. During the conversation that I held with him in the inner room he did not permit his eye to descend lower than the top button of Mr. Brickley's coat, a consideration that but served to make me more conscious of the humiliating deficiency below, nor did it deviate towards the empty tumbler, with the incriminating spoon in it, that stood on the table.

He explained to me and to Maxwell, whose presence I felt to be my sole link with respectability, that the raid had been planned in consequence of information received after the trial.

"I was going to you, sir, to sign the warrant, but Mr. Knox and Dr. Hickey signed it for us. It was Mr. Knox advised us to come here to-day. We've found three half-barrels of porter under the bed in the room over there, and about two gallons of potheen hid under fishing nets. I'll have about thirty summonses out of it."

The sergeant's maner was distressingly apologetic. I said nothing, but my heart burned within me as I recognized the hand of Flurry Knox.

"In case you might be looking for your man Cadogan, sir," went on the sergeant, "we seen him in a boat, with two other parties, a man and a woman, going to the mainland when we were coming over. The man that was pulling the other oar had the appearance of having drink taken."

A second flash, less blinding than the first, but equally illuminative, revealed to me that the brown boots, the flannel suit, had been a wedding garment, the predetermined attire of the best man, and a third recalled the

350

fact that Shrove Tuesday was the last day between this and Easter on which a marriage could take place.

Maxwell and I went back with the police, and Maxwell explained to me at some length the origin of the word "shebeen". As I neared the mainland, which tomorrow would ring with Flurry's artistic version of the day's events, the future held but one bright spot, the thought of putting Peter Cadogan to fire and sword.

But even that was denied to me. It must have been at the identical moment that my cook, Mrs. Cadogan (aunt of the missing Peter), was placing her wedding ring in the Shrove Tuesday pancakes that evening, that my establishment was felled as one man by tidings that still remain pre-eminent among the sensations of Shreeland. They reached me, irrepressibly, with the coffee.

Hard on the heels of the flushed parlour-maid followed the flat and heavy tread of Mrs. Cadogan, who, like the avenging deities, was habitually shod with felt.

"And now, sir, what do ye say to Pether Cadogan!" she began, launching the enigma into space from the obscurity of the deep doorway. "What do ye say to him now? The raving scamp!"

I replied that I had a great deal to say to him, and that if I might so far trespass on his leisure as to request his presence in the hall, I would say it.

"Hall is it!" echoed Peter's aunt in bitter wrath. "It's my heart's grief that he ever stood in Shreeland hall to dhraw disgrace on me and on yer Honour! God forgive me, when I heard it I had to spit! Himself and Bridget Brickley got married in Skebawn this evenin', and the two o' them is gone to Ameriky on the thrain to-night, and it's all I'll say for her, whatever sort of a thrash she is, she's good enough for him!" There was a pause while one might pant twice.

"I'll tell ye no lie. If I had a gun in me hand, I'd shoot him like a bird! I'd down the brat!"

The avenging deity retired.

What part the widower proposed to play in the day's proceedings will never be clearly known. He was picked up next day in Hare Island Sound, drifting seaward in the boat whose "share" had formed the marriage portion of Mrs. Peter Cadogan. Both oars were gone; there remained to him an empty bottle of "potheen", and a bucket. He was rowing the boat with the bucket.

"A HORSE! A HORSE!"

PART I

"Old Jimmy Porteous!" I ejaculated, while a glow of the ancient enthusiasm irradiated my bosom, "Philippa, I say! Do you see this? Jimmy Porteous is to command this district!"

"No, darling, *not* with an egg!" replied Philippa, removing the honey spoon from the grasp of her youngest child, just too late to avert disaster, "we *don't* eat honey with eggs."

The heavy hand of experience has taught me that at moments such as these the only possible course is to lie to, head to wind, till the squall passes, and then begin from the beginning again. I readdressed myself to my newspaper, while the incident went, like a successful burlesque, with a roar, sustained from the foot of the stairs to the point when the nursery door slammed upon it.

Philippa resumed her seat at the breakfast table.

"Yes, dear, what were you saying?" she said, yielding me the laborious but vague attention that is the best any husband can expect from any wife on such occasions.

I repeated my statement, and was scandalized to find that Philippa had but the most shadowy remembrance of Jimmy Porteous, who, in the days when I first joined my regiment had been its senior subaltern, and, for me and my fellows, one of the most revered of its law-givers. As a captain he left us, and proceeded to do something brilliant on somebody's staff, and, what time I got my company, had moved on in radiance into a lofty existence in the War Office and newspaper paragraphs.

I recalled these things to my wife, coupling them with

the information that she would have to call on Lady Porteous, when the door opened, and the face of Flurry Knox, unshaven and blue, with the miserable mother-o'-pearl blueness of fair people in cold weather, appeared in the opening.

He had looked in, he said, on his way home from the fair, to try would we give him a cup of tea, and he went on to remark that the wind was cold enough to cut the horns off a cow.

I asked him if he had seen my beasts there, and if they had been sold.

"Oh, they were, they were," he said tolerantly; "it was a wonderful good fair. The dealers were buying all before them. There was a man said to me, 'If you had a little dog there, and he to be a calf, you'd have sold him'."

It was one of Flurry Knox's ruling principles in life to disparage the livestock of his friends; it was always within the bounds of possibility that the moment might arrive when he might wish to buy them.

"I met a man from Sir Thomas Purcell's country yesterday," said Flurry presently; 'he says there's been the father and mother of a row down there between old Sir Thomas and Hackett, that's the man has the harriers. Sir Thomas is wild because they say the soldiers are giving Hackett as good a subscription as himself, and he says Hackett has all the foxes killed."

"But surely—harriers don't hunt foxes?" said Philippa ingenuously.

Flurry looked at her for a moment in silence. "Is it Hackett's harriers!" he said compassionately; "sure he flogs them off hares."

"Talking of soldiers, they've just sent a man who used to be in my regiment to command this district," I said, plucking my own topic from the tangle of inter-hunt squabbles; "a great man to hounds he used to be, too."

"Would he buy the Dodger?" asked Flurry swiftly. "Would he give a price?"

"I dare say he would if he liked the horse. If I got a chance I might tell him," I said, magnanimously.

"I tell you what, Major," said Flurry, with an eye on his ally, Philippa, "you and me and Mrs. Yeates will go up and have a day with Sir Thomas's hounds, and you'll say the word for me to the General!"

Looking back at it all now, I recognize that here was the moment for firmness. I let the moment slip, and became immersed in tracking General Sir James Porteous, K.C.B., through the pages of an elderly Army List. By the time I had located him in three separate columns, I found that Philippa and Flurry had arranged unalterably the details of what my wife is pleased to call a ramp—i.e., an expedition that, as its name implies, suggests a raid made by tramps.

"——Why, my gracious! aren't they cousins of my own? They'll be only delighted! Sure, Sally had measles there three years ago, and 'twas as good as a play for them——put us up, is it? Of course they will! The whole lot of us. D'ye think Sally'd stay at home?—No, you'll not take your own horses at all. Hire from Flavin; I'll see he does you well."

"And you know, Sinclair"—thus the other conspirator—"it would be an excellent chance for you to meet your beloved Jimmy Porteous!"

It was not Mr. Knox's habit to let the grass grow under his feet. Before I had at all grasped the realities of the project, my wife heard from Mrs. Sally Knox to say that she had arranged it all with the Butler-Knoxes, and that we were to stay on for a second night in order to go to a dance at which we should meet the General. At intervals during the following week I said to Philippa that it was preposterous and monstrous to dump ourselves upon the Butler-Knoxes, unknown people whom we had but once met at a function at the Bishop's. My remembrance of them, though something blurred by throngs of the clergy and their wives, did not suggest the type of person who might be expected to keep open house for stray fox-hunters. I said all this to Philippa, who entirely agreed with me, and continued her preparations, after the manner of experienced wives.

It was raining hard one afternoon in the following week when a four-wheeled inside car—an admirable vehicle, which I wish in no way to disparage—disgorged its burden at the door of Garden Mount House. One item of the burden was experiencing a sensation only too familiar, such a sensation as a respectable seaman might feel on being pressed into a crew of buccaneers. The house loomed over us, large, square, and serious, in the wet moonlight of the January evening; the husky, over-fed bark of an elderly dog was incessant in the hall. If by laying hold of the coat-tails of the leading pirate, as he got out to ring the bell; I could then and there have brought the expedition to a close, I would thankfully have done so.

The door was opened by a melancholy old gentleman with a grey moustache and whiskers; he might have been Colonel Newcome in his decadence, but from the fact that he wore an evening coat and grey trousers, I gathered that he was the butler, and for anyone skilled in Irish households, he at once placed the establishment —rich, godly, low church, and consistently and conten-tedly dull. As we entered the hall there arose from some fastness in the house a shrill clamour that resolved itself into the first line of a hymn.

Flurry dug me in the ribs with his elbow. "They've found!" he whispered, "you needn't look so frightened. It's only Lucy and Louisa having the choir practice!"

To these strains Colonel Newcome ushered us into the drawing-room. There was no one in it. It was a large double drawing-room, and nothing but heavy maroon curtains now separated us from the choir practice. The hymn continued, a loud and long-drawn proclamation, and, pending its conclusion, my wife and Mrs. Flurry Knox swiftly and stealthily circumnavigated the room, and appraised all its contents, from a priceless Battersea basket filled with dusty bulbs to a Chippendale card-table with a sewing machine clamped on to it, while Flurry, in a stage whisper, dilated to me upon the super-fluous wealth that Providence had seen fit to waste upon the Butler-Knoxes. The household, as I had gradually learnt, consisted of an elderly bachelor, Mr. Lucius Butler-Knox (commonly known as "Looshy"), his un-married sister, Miss Louisa, his widowed sister, Mrs. Hodnett, and a corpulent, grey-muzzled black-and-tan terrier. Their occupations were gardening, and going to what they called "the city", i.e., the neighbouring county town, to attend charitable committee meetings; they kept a species of philanthropic registry office for servants; their foible was hospitality, disastrously coupled with the fact that they dined at half-past six. It was one of the mysteries of kinship that Flurry Knox and our host and hostess should posses a nearer relative in common than Adam. That he should have established their respectable home as his hostelry and house of call was one of the mysteries of Flurry Knox.

The hymn ceased, the raiders hastily formed into line, the maroon drapery parted, and the ladies of the house, flushed with song, and importing with them a potent sample of the atmosphere of the back drawing-room, were upon us, loud in hospitable apologies, instant in offers of tea; the situation opened and swallowed us up.

The half-past six o'clock dinner came all too swiftly. Glared upon by an unshaded lamp that sat like a ball of fire in the centre of the table, we laboured in the trough of a sea of the thickest ox-tail soup; a large salmon followed; with the edge of dubious appetite already turned, we saw the succeeding items of the menu spread forth on the table like a dummy hand at bridge. The boiled turkey, with its satellite ham, the roast saddle of mutton, with its stable companion the stack of cutlets; the succeeding course, where a team of four wild duck struggled for the lead with an open tart and a sago pudding. Like Agag, we went delicately, and, like Agag, it availed us nothing.

I watched my *vis-à-vis*, little Mrs. Flurry, furtively burying a slab of turkey beneath mashed potatoes as neatly as a little dog buries a bone; her green kitten's eyes met mine without a change of expression, and turned to her glass, which Colonel Newcome had filled with claret. "The beaded bubbles, winking at the brim", had a greyish tinge.

"Cousin Lucius!" observed Mrs. Flurry, in a silence that presently happened to fall, "can you remember who painted that picture of our great-grandfather—the one over the door I mean?"

Mr. Butler-Knox, a small, grey-bearded, elderly gentleman, wholly, up to the present, immersed in carving, removed the steam of the ducks from his eye-glasses, and concentrated them upon the picture.

"It's by Maclise, isn't it?" went on Sally, leaning forward to get a nearer view.

In that moment, when all heads turned to the picture, I plainly saw her draw the glass of claret to the verge of the table, it disappeared beneath it and returned to its place empty. Almost simultaneously, the black-and-tan terrier sprang from a lair near my feet, and hurried from the room, shaking his ears vigorously. Mrs. Flurry's eyes wavered from the portrait to mine, and her face became slowly and evenly pink, like an afterglow.

It was but one of the many shameless acts of my party during the age-long evening. At ten o'clock we retired to rest, for my own part, thoroughly overfed, not in the least sleepy, worn with conversation, and oppressed by the consciousness of flippant, even brutal, ingratitude.

The weather had cleared next morning to mild greyness, that softened even the asperity of half-past eight breakfast. I lumbered stiffly downstairs in a pair of new butcher boots, and found with thankfulness that our hosts, exhausted possibly by their efforts, had kept their rooms.

Marshalled in order upon the sideboard stood the remains of all the more enduring items of last night's dinner, cold indeed, but firm and undefeated; hot dishes of ancient silver roasted before the noble brass-mounted fireplace; there was vats of lethargic cream, a clutch of new-laid eggs, a heap of hot scones.

"It's easy seen it wasn't cracking blind nuts made Lucy Hodnett and Louisa the size they are!" remarked Flurry, as the party, feeling more piratical than ever, embarked upon this collation. "Mrs. Yeates, do you think I am bound to dance with the pair of them to-night? *You* are, Major, anyway! But I might get off with Louisa."

"Oh, Sinclair's card is full", said my wife, who was engaged in trying to decipher the marks on the cream jug without upsetting the cream; "he and the General are plighted to one another for the evening."

"I wonder if the claret has stained the carpet!" said Mrs. Flurry, diving under the table. "It has! How awful!" Mrs. Flurry's voice indicated the highest enjoyment. "Never mind, they'll never see it! They're too fat to get under the table!"

"If they did, it'd be the first time old Looshy's claret ever put anyone there!" said Flurry.

We have never known the precise moment in this speech at which "Old Looshy's" butler entered the room; we only know that while Mrs. Flurry, much hampered by habit and boots, was in the act of struggling from beneath the table, he was there, melancholy and righteous, with a telegram on a salver.

It was from Flavin, the livery stableman, and its effect upon the spirits of the company was that of a puncture in a tyre.

"Regret horses not available; am trying to procure others; will send by next train if possible."

We said that there was no answer, and we finished our breakfasts in a gravity scarcely lightened by Flurry's almost religious confidence in Flavin's infallibility, and in his power of making horses out of rushes, like the fairies, if need be.

I was, I may admit, from the first thoroughly pessimistic. I almost went up and got into ordinary clothes; I at least talked of doing so, as a means of preparing Philippa for the worst. I said it was a mere waste of time to send the Butler-Knox coachman to the station, as had been arranged, and I did my best to dissuade Flurry from his intention of riding to the meet by way of the station to help in unboxing animals that could not possibly be there.

In abysmal dejection my wife and I surveyed the departing forms of Mr. and Mrs. Florence Knox; the former on the Dodger, a leggy brown four-year-old, the planting of whom upon General Poreous had been the germ of the expedition; while Sally skipped and sidled upon a narrow, long-tailed chestnut mare, an undefeated jumper, and up to about as much much weight as would go by parcel post for ninepence. There then ensued a period of total desolation, in which we looked morosely at old photograph books in the drawing-room, and faced the prospect of a long day with the Butler-Knoxes, while heavy footsteps overhead warned us that our entertainers were astir, and that any moment the day's conversation might begin.

I was engaged, not, I fancy, for the first time, in telling Philippa that I had always said that the entire expedition was a mistake, when Colonel Newcome again entered the room.

"The master sent me to ask you, sir, if you'd like to have the pony-phaeton to drive down to the station to meet the half-past ten train. Flavin might be sending the horses on it, and it'd save you time to meet them there."

We closed with the offer; at its worst, the pony-carriage could be smoked in, which the drawing-room could not; at its best, it might save half an hour in getting to the meet. We presently seated ourselves in it, low down behind an obese piebald pony, with a pink nose, and a mane hogged to the height of its ears. As I took up the whip it turned and regarded us with an un-blinkered eye, pink-lidded and small as a pig's.

"You should go through Fir Grove, sir," said the boy who had brought the equipage to the door, "it's half a mile of a short cut, and that's the way Tom will come with the horses. It's the first gate-lodge you'll meet on the road."

The mud was deep, and the piebald pony plodded through it at a sullen jog. The air was mild and chilly, like an uninteresting woman; the foreknowledge of fiasco lay heavily upon us; it hardly seemed worth while to beat the pony when he sank into a walk; it was the most heartbroken forlorn hope that ever took the field.

The gate-lodge of Fir Grove fulfilled the assignation made for it by the stable boy, and met us on the road. The gates stood wide open, and the pony turned in as by an accustomed route, and crawled through them with that simulation of complete exhaustion that is the gift of lazy ponies. Loud narrative in a male voice proceeded from the dark interior of the lodge, and, as we passed, a woman's voice said, in horrified rejoinder:

"The Lord save us! She must be Anti-Christ!"

Here, apparently, the speaker became aware of our proximity, and an old woman looked forth. Her face was apprehensive.

"Did ye see the police, sir?" she asked.

We replied in the negative.

"Please God, she'll not come our way!" she said, and banged the door.

We moved on, heavily, in the deep gravel of the avenue.

"Isn't this rather awful? Shall we go on?" said Philippa.

I replied with truth that there was no room to turn. On either side of the narrow drive laurels and rhododendrons were crammed as thickly as they could be planted, their dark foliage met overhead; if the inexpressible "she" referred to by the lodge-keeper did come our way, retreat would be out of the question. The tunnel ran uphill, and I drove the pony up it as one drives a hoop, by incessant beating; had I relaxed my efforts he would probably, like a hoop, have lain down. Presently, and still uphill, we turned a corner, the tunnel ceased, and we were face to face with a large pink house.

As we advanced, feeling to the full the degradation of making a short cut past a strange house in tall hats and a grovelling pony-carriage, we beheld figures rushing past the windows of one of the rooms on the ground floor, as if in headlong flight. Was this the fulfilment of the dark sayings of the lodge-keeper, and was "she" "coming our way"? The bouncing strains of a measure, known, I believe, as "Whistling Rufus", came forth to us hilariously as we drew nearer. The problem changed, but I am not sure that the horror did not deepen.

Divining the determination of the piebald pony to die, if necessary, rather than pass a hall door without stopping at it, yet debarred by the decencies from thrashing him past the long line of windows, I administered two or three rousing tugs to his wooden mouth. At the third tug the near rein broke. The pony stopped dead. Simultaneously the hall door was flung open, and a young and lovely being, tall, and beautifully dressed, fluttered out on to the steps and peered at us through long-handled eyeglasses.

"Oh! I thought you were the police!" exclaimed the being, with unaffected disappointment.

The position seemed, from all points, to demand an apology. I disengaged myself from the pony carriage and proffered it; I also volunteered any help that a mere man, not a policeman, might be capable of rendering.

The young lady aimed her glasses at the piebald, motionless in sullen stupor, and replied irrelevantly:

"Why! That's the Knoxes' pony!"

I made haste to explain our disaster and the position generally, winding up with a request for a piece of string.

"You're staying at the Butler-Knoxes!" exclaimed the lady of the house. "How funny that is! Do you know you're coming to our dance to-night, to meet your old friend the General! I know all about it, you see!" She advanced with a beaming yet perturbed countenance upon Philippa, "I'm so glad to meet you. Do come in! We've got an infuriated cook at bay in the kitchen, and things are rather disorganized, but I think we can rise to a bit of string! The pony's all right—he'll sleep there for months, he always does."

We followed her into a hall choked with the exiled furniture of the drawing-room and saw through an open door the whirling forms of two or three couples of young men and maidens.

"They're polishing the floor," said our hostess, swiftly shutting the door, "they make a hideous noise, but it keeps them quiet—if you know what I mean. It's most disastrous that my husband has gone out hunting," she pursued; "this odious cook only arrived two days ago, and——"

At this juncture a door at the end of the hall burst open, disclosing a long passage and a young and crimson housemaid.

"She's coming, my lady! She's coming! Mr. Ralph's sent me on to get the door open!" she panted.

At the same moment a loud and wrathful voice arose in the passage and a massive form, filling it from wall to wall, appeared; the capitulating cook, moving down

361

upon us with the leisurely and majestic truculence of a traction-engine. As she came she chanted these words in measured cadence:

> "Lady Flora,
> Gets her brother
> To do her dirty work."

By this time this rune had been repeated three times she was in the hall, shepherded by a tall young man, obviously the brother referred to, and by the butler, the vista being filled in the rear by a wavering assortment of female domestics. As the cook tacked to weather a sofa, there was something about her that woke a vague and unpleasant chord of memory. Her ranging eye met mine, and the chord positively twanged as I recognized the formidable countenance of a female, technically known as a 'job-cook", who for two cyclonic weeks had terrorized our household while Mrs. Cadogan was on leave. I backed convulsively into Lady Flora, in futile and belated attempt to take cover, but even as I did so the chanting ceased and I knew the worst had happened.

"Is that my darlin' Major Yeates?" shouted the cook, tacking again and bearing down on me full-sailed. "Thanks be to God, I have the gentleman that'll see I get justice! And Mrs. Yeates, a noble lady, that'd never set foot in my kitchen without she'd ask my leave! Ah, ha! As Shakespeare says, I'd know a rale lady as soon as I'd put an eye on her, if she was boiling cabbage!"

She caught my reluctant hand and waved it up and down, and the muffled triumphings of "Whistling Rufus" in the drawing-room filled up the position.

Through them came a sound of wheels on the gravel, and through this again a strangled whisper from behind:

"Take her out to the steps; I hear the car with the police!"

Holding the fervid hand of the job-cook, I advanced with her through the furniture, skew-wise, as in the visiting figure of the Lancers; there was an undoubted effort on her part to keep time with the music, and she did not cease to inform the company that Major and Mrs. Yeates were the real old nobility, and that they would see she got her rights.

Followed closely by the shepherd and the butler, we moved forth on to the steps. The police were not there. There was nothing there save a complicated pattern of arcs and angles on the gravel, as of a four-wheeled vehicle that has taken an uncommonly short turn. At the bend of the avenue the pony-carriage, our link with the world without, was disappearing from view, the piebald pony heading for home at a pig-like but determined gallop. The job-cook clasped her hands on my arm and announced to the landscape that she would live and die with the Major.

PART II

A quarter of an hour later Philippa and I stood in the high road, with the sense of deliverance throbbing in every grateful nerve, and viewed the car, with the job-cook and the policeman, swing heavily away towards the railway station.

Mine was the strategy that had brought about our escape, mine were the attractions that had lured the cook to mount the policemen's car with me, and still more inalienably mine was the searing moment when, still arm-in-arm with the cook, we drove away from the deeply apreciative party on the doorsteps, Philippa and a policeman were on the opposite side of the car; the second policeman, very considerately, walked.

We were close to the station, the cook had sung herself to sleep, and Philippa and I had relapsed into the depths of abysmal despondency, when our incredulous eyes beheld the Butler-Knoxes' coachman coming towards us at a trot, riding a bay horse and leading a grey, on which was a side-saddle. Flavin, the horse dealer, had, after all, been as good as Flurry's word—the hirelings were here, and all was right with the world.

The car slackened to a walk, we slid from it silently, and it and its burden passed into that place of shadows to which all extraneous affairs of life betake themselves on a hunting morning, when the hour is come, and the horse.

Looshy's coachman delivered to me the bay horse, a large and notable-looking animal, with a Roman nose adorned with a crooked blaze, a tranquil eye, and two white stockings. In his left hand he held a compact iron-grey mare, hogged and docked, who came up to the bank by the roadside to be mounted, as neatly as a man-'o-war boat comes alongside. Hirelings of so superior a class it had never before been my privilege to meet, and I made up my mind that they were either incurably vicious or broken winded.

"It's easy known that this mare's carried a lady before, sir," said the coachman, a young man with a soul for higher things than driving the Butler-Knox covered car, "and the big horse is the best I ever seen come out of Flavin's! He's in grand condition, he's as slick as a mouse! Only for Mr. Flurry being there we'd hardly have got them," he continued, while he lengthened my stirrup-leathers, "the chap Flavin sent with them had drink taken, and the porters had the box shunted and himself in it, stretched, and the bottle of whisky with him!"

Flavin's man and his bottle of whisky were now negligible incidents for me. Philippa was already under way, and the time was short. The bay horse, arching his neck and reaching pleasantly at his bit, went away at a rhythmic and easy trot, the grey mare flitted beside him with equal precision; it was, perhaps, rather fast for riding to a meet, but we were late, and were they not hirelings?

We followed our guides, the telegraph posts, for some four miles of level road; they dropped down a deepening valley to a grey and brimming river, and presently came slate roofs and whitewashed houses, staring at each other across an empty village street. We had arrived at Kilbarron, the scene of the meet, and the meet was not.

"They've gone on! They've gone on!" screamed an old woman from a doorway, "away up over the hill!"

Evidently every other live thing had followed the hunt, and we did not spare Mr. Flavin's horses in doing the same. We reached the top of the long hill in a remarkably brief space of time, and, having done so, realized that we were not too late. A couple of fields away a row of figures, standing like palings along the top of a bank, with their backs to us, told that the hounds were still in view; even as we sighted them, the palings plunged *en masse* from their standpoint with that composite yell that in Ireland denotes the breaking (and frequently the heading) of a fox, and vanished. Whatever was happening, it was not coming our way. I turned my hireling at the bank by the roadside, he came round with a responsive swing, and in two large and orderly bounds he was over. Before I had time to look round, the grey mare, with the faintest hint of a buck, galloped emulously past me.

"Perfection!" panted Philippa, putting her hat straight.

As we came up on to the next bank, recently vacated by its human palisade, we found that fortune had smiled upon us. Just below, on our right, was a long strip of gorse covert; three big fields beyond it, gliding from us like a flock of seagulls, were the clamouring hounds, and in the space between us and them bucketed the hunt, in the first fine frenzy of getting away. Flavin's bay immediately caught hold, not implacably, but with the firmness of superior knowledge; the grey mare, having ascertained that Philippa was not going to interfere, thought better of going on alone, and took the time from her stable companion. The field was already sorting itself into the usual divisions of the forward, the cunning, and the useless; our luck stood to us; the forward division, carried away by the enthusiasm of a good start and a sympathetic fall of ground, succeeded in less than a quarter of a mile in hustling the hounds over the line, and brought about a check. We joined the rearguard, and worked our way towards the front, unobtrusively, because Sir Thomas Purcell's comments on the situation were circling like a stock-whip among the guilty, and were not sparing the innocent. At this moment we found Flurry Knox beside us.

'Sir Thomas is giving the soldiers their tea in a mug!" he said; "and they were in the want of it! How are those horses doing with you?" he went on, looking our steeds up and down. "They look up to your weights, anyhow!

I suppose you didn't see your friend, the General? He was at the meet in a motor."

"In a motor!" repeated Philippa. 'I thought he was such a wonderful rider."

'He knows how to get a motor along, anyhow," replied Flurry, his attentive eyes following the operations of the hounds; "maybe he has the gout. You'd say he had by the colour of his face. Hullo! Boys! They're away again! Come on, Mrs. Yeates! Knock your two guineas' worth out of Flavin!"

Short as it was, the burst had been long enough to tranquillize my anxieties as to our hirelings' wind, and when we started again we found them almost excessively ready for the stone-faced bank that confronted us at the end of the field. Some twenty of us, including the chidden but wholly unabashed soldiers, went at it in line, and, after the manner of stone-faced banks, it grew very tall as we approached it. Flavin's bay strode unfalteringly over it; it was as though he grasped it and flung it behind him. The grey mare, full of jealousy and vainglory, had a hard try to fly the whole thing, but retained sufficient self-control to change feet at the last possible instant; with or without a scramble or a peck, we all arrived somehow in the next field, and saw, topping the succeeding fence, the bulky chestnut quarters of Sir Thomas Purcell's horse and the square scarlet back of Sir Thomas. Away to the left, on an assortment of astute crocks, three of the Misses Purcell followed the first whip, at as considerable a distance from their parent as was consistent with a good place. Their voices came confusedly to us; aparently each was telling the others to get out of her way.

For a quarter of an hour the hounds ran hard over the clean pastureland, whose curves rose before us and glided astern like the long rollers under an Atlantic liner. Innocent of rocks or pitfalls, unimpeachable as to surface, it was a page of fair print as compared with the black letter manuscript to which the country of Mr. Flurry Knox's hounds might be likened. Never before have I crossed fences as sound, as seductive, it was like jumping large and well-upholstered Chesterfield sofas;

Chesterfieldian also were the manners of Flavin's bay.
I found myself in the magnificent position of giving a
lead to Flurry and the Dodger, of giving several leads to
the soldiery; once, when a wide and boggy stream
occurred, the Misses Purcell and the crocks looked to me
as their pioneer. The hustle and the hurry never relaxed;
the hounds had fastened on the line and were running it
as though it were a footpath; but for the check at the
start, no fox could have held his lead for so long at such
a pace, and whatever the pace, the tails of the horses of
Sir Thomas and the first whip never failed to disappear
over the bank just ahead.

For me, in the unwonted glory of heading the despera-
does of the first flight, life and the future were contained
in the question of how much longer I could count on my
hireling. I was just able to spare a hasty thought or two
to Philippa and the grey, and I remembered that it was
after a heavy drop into a road that I noticed, with the
just and impotent wrath of a husband, that her hair was
beginning to come down.

It was just then that I first saw the motor. The fox
had run the road for some little distance; we clattered
and splashed along it, until an intimidating roar from
Sir Thomas and the sight of his right arm in the air,
brought us, bumping and tugging, to a standstill. The
hounds were for a moment at fault, swarming, with their
heads down, over every inch of the road, and beyond
them, about a hundred yards from us, was a resplendent
scarlet motor, whose nearer approach was summarily
interdicted by the first whip. I am short-sighted, but I
caught an impression of two elderly gentlemen, one of
whom, wearing a white moustache and a tall hat, was
responding warmly to the fulminations of Sir Thomas.
If this were my ancient brother-in-arms, Jimmy Porteous, following hounds in a motor, times were indeed
changed. I dismissed the possibility from my mind. Just
then I caught sight of Flurry's face; it had in it the
fearful joy of a schoolboy who had seen a squib put into
the tail pocket of the schoolmaster, and awaits the result. Mrs. Flurry, in the heroic act of plucking a hairpin
from her own unshaken golden-red plaits, and yielding

it to Philippa, met his eye with a glance that was so expressionless as to amount to a danger signal.

At this moment the hounds jostled over the wall with a clatter of falling stones; they spread themselves in the field like the opening of a fan, they narrowed to the recovered line like the closing of one; Sir Thomas's chestnut hoisted himself and his fifteen-stone burden out of the road with the heave of an earthquake. The riders shoved after him, and we were swept again into the current of the hunt.

As we thundered away up the field threatening shouts from the checked motorists followed us; apparently, after the manner of their kind, they had not a moment to spare, and the delay had annoyed them. The next fence arrived, and they, and all else, were forgotten.

There was a wood ahead of us, cresting a long upland, and for it the hounds were making, at a pace that brutally ignored the rise of ground, and the fact that in these higher levels the fields were smaller, and the fences had to be faced up a hill that momentarily grew steeper.

"Hold on, Mrs. Yates, till I take down that pole for you!" Flurry's voice followed us up the hill, and there was that in it that told he was making heavy weather of it. He was leading the dripping Dodger, and I have seldom seen a redder face than his as he laboured past Philippa and dragged away the shaft of a cart that barred a gap. 'Bad luck to this for a close country!" he puffed. "You're not off one fence before you're on top of the next!" Flavin's horses were certainly lathering pretty freely, but were otherwise making no remark on the situation, and neither of them had so far made a mistake of any kind. I saw the first whip regard the bay with obvious respect, and turn with a confidential comment to the nearest Miss Purcell. It hall-marked my achievements.

Philippa and I were among the first into the wood; even Flurry had been left three fields behind, and the glory of our position radiated from us, as we stood at the end of the main ride, sublimely surveying the arrival of the rest of the streaming hunt. Sir Thomas and the hounds had dived out of sight into the recesses of the wood; a period of inaction ensued, and for a few balmy minutes peace with honour was ours.

Balmy, however, as were the minutes, there crept into them an anxiety as to what the hounds were doing. A great and complete silence had fallen as far as they and Sir Thomas were concerned, and Philippa and I, conscious of our high estate as leaders of the hunt, melted away from the crowd to investigate matters. We followed a path that took us across the wood, and the deeper we went the deeper was the silence, and the more acute became our fears that we had been left behind. Sir Thomas had an evil reputation for slipping his field and getting away alone.

"There's the horn!" cried Philippa. "It's outside the wood! They *have* gone away. Hurry!"

We were squeezing along the farther edge of the covert looking for a way out, and I too heard the note, faint, yet commanding. I hurried. That is to say, with my hat over my eyes, and my cheek laid against the bay's neck, I followed my wife up an alley that was barely wide enough for a woodcock.

On our left was an impassable hedge of small trees, crowning a heavy drop into the field outside the wood; our faces were rowelled by the branches of young spruce firs. It was all very well for Philippa, riding nearly two hands lower than I, to twist her way in and out through them like a squirrel, but for me, on a 16.2 horse, resolved on following his stable companion through a keyhole if necessary, it was anything but well. My eyes were tightly shut, my arm was in front of them, and my eye-glass was hanging down my back, when I felt the bay stop.

"Here's a way out," said my wife's voice, apparently from the middle of a fir-tree, "there's a sort of cattle-track here."

There followed a scramble and a slide, then Philippa's voice again, enjoining me to keep to the right.

She has since explained that she really meant the left, and that, in any case, I might have known that she always said right when she meant left; be that as it may, when the bay and I had committed ourselves to the steep descent

369

—half water-course, half cattle-track—I was smitten in the face by a holly branch. Before I had recovered from its impact, a stout beechen bough, that it had masked, met me violently across the waistcoat and held me in mid-air, as the gorilla is reputed to grasp and hold the traveller, while my horse moved firmly downward from beneath me. After a moment of suspense, mental and physical, I fell to earth, like the arrow in the song, I knew not where, and tobogganed painfully down something steep and stony, with briers in it.

As I rose to my feet, the mellow note of the horn that had beguiled us from the wood, again sounded; nearer now, and with a harsher cadence, and I perceived, at the farther end of the field in which I had arrived, a bullock, with his head over a gate, sending a long and lamentable bugle note to the companions from whom he had been separated. Simultaneously the hounds opened far back in the wood behind me, and I knew that the flood-tide of luck had turned against us.

Flavin's bay had not waited for me. He was already well away, going with head and tail high held, a gentleman at large, seeking for entertainment at a lively and irresponsible trot. Pursuing him, with more zeal than discretion, was Philippa on the grey mare; he broke into a canter, and I had the pleasure of seeing them both swing through a gateway and proceed at a round gallop across the next field. I followed them at the best imitation of the same pace that my boots permitted, and squelched through the mire of the gateway in time to see the bay horse jump a tall bank, and drop with a clatter into a road. At the same moment the drumming and hooting of a motor-car broke upon my ear, and three heads, one of them wearing a tall hat, slid at high speed along the line of the fence. At sight of this apparition the bay horse gave a massive buck, and fled at full speed up a lane. To my surprise and gratification, the motor-car instantly stopped, and one of its occupants—the wearer of the tall hat—sprang out and gave chase to my horse.

My attention was here abruptly transferred to my wife, who, having followed the chase, whether by her own wish or that of the grey mare I have never been able to discover, was now combating the desire of the latter to jump the bank at the exact spot calculated to land them both in the lap of the motor-car. The dispute ended in a slanting and crab-like rush at a place twenty yards lower down, and it was then that the figure of our host, Mr. Lucius Butler-Knox, rose, amazingly, in the motor-car, making semaphore gestures of warning.

The mare jumped crookedly on to the bank, hung there for half a second, and launched herself into space, the launch being followed, appropriately, by a mighty splash. Neither she nor Philippa reappeared.

Throughout these events I had not ceased to run, and the next thing I can distinctly recall is scrambling, thoroughly blown, on to the fence, whence a moving scene presented itself to me. The grey mare and Philippa had, with singular ingenuity, selected between them the one place in the fence where disaster was inevitable; and I now beheld my wife prone in two feet of yellow water, the overflow of a flooded ditch that had turned a hollow by the roadside into a sufficiently imposing pond. Mr. Butler-Knox and the chauffeur were already rendering all the assistance possible, short of wetting their feet, and were hauling her ashore; while the grey mare, recumbent in deeper water, surveyed the operation with composure, and made no attempt to move. When I joined the party —a process involving a wide circuit of the flood— Philippa had sunk, dripping, upon a heap of stones by the roadside, in laughter as inexplicable as it was unsuitable. There was, at all events, no need to ask if she were hurt.

"The most appalling thing that you ever knew in your life has happened!" she wailed, and instantly fell again into unseemly convulsions.

Whatever the just might be, it did not appeal to the chauffeur, who withdrew in silence to his motor, coldly wiping the vicarious duckweed from his knees with a silk pocket-handkerchief. Still less did it appeal to me. Any fair-minded person will admit that I had cause to be excessively angry with Philippa. That a grown woman, the mother of two children, should mistake the bellow of a bullock for the note of a horn was bad enough; but that when, having caused a serious accident by not knowing her right hand from her left, and having, by further insanities, driven one valuable horse adrift into the country, probably broken the back of another, laid the seeds of heart disease in her husband from shock and over-exertion, and of rheumatic fever in herself; when, I repeat, after all these outrages, she should sit in a soaking heap by the roadside, laughing like a maniac, I feel that the sympathy of the public will not be withheld from me.

The mystery of Mr. Butler-Knox's appearance in the motor-car passed by me like a feather in a whirlwind; I strode without a word into the yellow flood in which the mare was lying, and got hold of her reins with the handle of my crop; I might as well have tried to draw out Behemoth with a hook. Her hindquarters were well fixed in the hidden ditch, she made not the slightest effort to stir, and continued to recline, contentedly, not to say defiantly.

"That's a great sign of fine weather," said a voice behind me in affable comment, "when a horse will lie down in wather that way."

I turned upon my consoler, and saw a young countryman with a furlined coat hanging upon his arm.

"I got this thrown in the bohereen above," he said, "the other gentleman, that's follying the bay horse, stripped it off him, and God knows it's itself that's weighty!"

"My dear Major!" began Looshy, addressing me agitatedly from the bank, as a hen might address a refractory duckling, "there has been a most unfortunate mistake."

"There has! There has! It's all Flurry's fault!" gasped Philippa, staggering towards me like a drunken woman.

"I fear the General is terribly annoyed," continued Looshy, wiping his grey beard and mopping his collar to remove the muddy imprint of Philippa's arm; "he rushed into Garden Mount in search of his horses when he found they were not at the meet nor at the station—he left Lady Porteous with my sisters and took me to identify you; I mentioned your name, but he did not seem to grasp it—indeed his language was—er—was such that I thought it unwise to press the point."

I dropped the reins and began, slowly, to wade out of the pool.

"I understand he has but just paid £300 for these horses—it was an unpardonable mistake of Flurry's," went on Looshy, "he found the General's horses at the station and thought that they were Flavin's."

"Dear Flurry!" sobbed Philippa, shamelessly, reeling against me and clutching my arm.

"Begor' he have the horse!" said the young countryman, looking up the hill.

A stout figure in a red coat and tall hat was approaching by way of the bohereen, followed by a man leading a limping horse.

"I think," said Looshy nervously, "that Mrs. Yeates had better have my seat in the motor-car and hurry home. I will walk—I should really prefer it. The General will be quite happy now that he has found his horses and his old friend."

The chauffeur, plying a long-necked oil-can, smiled sardonically.

SHARPER THAN A FERRET'S TOOTH

"My dear Philippa," said Miss Shute gloomily, "I have about as much chance of spending next winter in Florence as I have of spending it in the moon. I despair of ever getting Bernard married. I look upon him as hopeless."

"I don't agree with you at all," replied Philippa, "don't you remember how demented he was about Sally Knox? And when we all thought he was on the verge of suicide, we discovered that he was deep in a flirtation with that American girl. It seems to me he's ready to be devoted to anyone who takes him in hand. He has none of that deadly helpless fidelity about him."

"I ought never to have allowed him to take up gardening," said Miss Shute, despondently pursuing her own line of thought, "it only promotes intimacies with dowagers."

"Yes, and it makes men elderly, and contented, and stay-at-homes," agreed Philippa; "it's one of the worst signs! But I can easily make Sybil Hervey think she's a gardener. She's a thoroughly nice, coercible girl. Alice has always been so particular about her girls. Of course with their money they've been run after a good deal, but they're not in the least spoilt."

"I don't think," I murmured privately to Maria, who was trying to hypnotize me into letting her crawl on to the sofa beside me, "that we'll borrow half a crown to get drunk with her."

Maria wagged her tail in servile acquiescence.

"Nonsense!" said my wife largely.

A month from the date of this conversation, Sybil Hervey, my wife's pretty, young, and well-dowered niece, was staying beneath our roof. I had not changed my mind about the half-crown, though Maria, perfidious as ever, feigned for her the impassioned affection that had so often imposed upon the guileless guest within my gates.

"Why, this dog has taken the most extraordinary fancy to me!" Sybil Hervey (who was really a very amiable girl) would say, and Maria, with a furtive eye upon her owners, would softly draw the guest's third piece of cake into the brown velvet bag that she called her mouth.

This was all very well from Maria's point of view, but a friendship with Maria had not been the object of Miss Hervey's importation. I evade, by main strength, the quotation from Burns proper to this state of affairs, and proceed to say that the matrimonial scheme laid by my wife and Miss Shute was not prospering. Sybil Hervey, the coercible, the thoroughly nice, shied persistently at the instructive pages of Robinson's *English Flower Garden*, and stuck in her toes and refused point blank to weed seedlings for her Aunt Philippa. Nor was a comprehensive garden party at Clountiss attended with any success; far otherwise. Miss Shute unfortunately thought it incumbent on her to trawl in deep waters, and to invite even the McRory family to her entertainment, with the result that her brother, Bernard—I quote my wife verbatim—made a ridiculous spectacle of himself by walking about all afternoon with a fluffy-haired, certainly-rather-pretty little abomination, a creature who was staying with the McRorys. Worse even than this, Sybil had disappointed, if not disgraced, her backers, by vanishing from the ken of ungentle men with Mr. De Lacy McRory, known to his friends as "Curly".

I have before now dealt, superficially, and quite inadequately, with the McRorys. It may even be permitted to me to recall again the generic description of each young male McRory. "A bit of a lad, but nothing at all to the next youngest." Since that time the family had worn its way, unequally and in patches, into the tolerance of the neighbourhood. It was said, apologetically, that the daughters danced, and played tennis and golf so well, and the sons did the same and were such excellent shots, and that Mrs. McRory bought, uncomplainingly, all that was offered to her at bazaars, and could always be counted on for a whole row of seats at local concerts. As for old McRory, people said that he was certainly rather awful, but that he was better than his family in that he knew that he was awful, and kept out of the way. As a matter of history, there were not many functions where a McRory of some kind, in accordance with its special accomplishment, did not find, at all events, standing room; fewer still where they did not form a valued topic of conversation.

Curly McRory was, perhaps, the pioneer of his family in their advance to cross what has been usefully called "the bounder-y line". He played all games well, and he was indisputably good-looking, he knew how to be discreetly silent; he also apparently knew how to talk to Sybil, what time her accredited chaperon, oblivious of her position, played two engrossing sets of tennis.

After this fiasco came a period of stagnation, during which Mr. De Lacy McRory honoured us with his first visit to Shreelane, bicycling over to see me, on business connected with the golf club; in my regretted absence he asked for Mrs. Yeates, and stayed for tea. Following upon this Sybil took to saying, "I will", in what she believed to be a brogue, instead of "Yes", and was detected in fruitless search for the McRorys of Temple Braney in the pages of Burke's *Irish Landed Gentry*.

It was at this unsatisfactory juncture that Mrs. Flurry Knox entered into the affair with an invitation to us to spend three days at Aussolas Castle, one of which was to be devoted to the destruction of a pack of grouse, fabled by John Kane, the keeper, to frequent a mountain back of Aussolas: the Shutes were also to be of the party. I seemed to detect in the arrangement a hand more diplomatic than that of Providence, but I said nothing.

The Flurry Knoxes were, for the moment, in residence at Aussolas, while old Mrs. Knox made her annual pilgrimage to Buxton. They were sent there to keep the servants from fighting, and because John Kane had said that there was no such enemies to pigs as servants on board wages. (A dark saying, bearing indirectly on the plenishing of pig-buckets.)

Between servants and pigs, as indeed in most affairs of life, little Mrs. Flurry held the scales of justice with a remarkably steady hand, and under her regime one could at all events be reasonably sure of having one's boots cleaned, and of getting a hot bath in the morning. We went to Aussolas, and Flurry and Bernard Shute and I put in a blazing September day on the mountain, wading knee deep in matted heather and furze, in pursuit of the mythical grouse, and brought home two hares and a headache (the latter being my contribution to the bag). The ladies met us with tea; Sybil, in Harris tweed and admirable boots, looked, I must admit, uncommonly smart. Even Flurry was impressed, and it was palpable to the most superficial observer that Bernard was at length beginning, like a baby, to "take notice". After tea he and she moved away in sweet accord to wash teacups in a bog-hole, from whence their prattle came prosperously to the ears of the three diplomatists, seated, like the witches in *Macbeth*, upon the heath, and, like them, arranging futures for other people. Bearing in mind that one of the witches had (in a previous incarnation as Miss

Sally Knox) held Bernard in her thrall, and still retained him in a platonic sphere of influence, any person of experience would have said that the odds were greatly against Mr. Shute.

The hot bath that was the *fine fleur* of Mrs. Flurry's regime at Aussolas failed conspicuously next morning. It was the precursor of a general slump. When, at a liberal nine-thirty, I arrived in the dining-room, of neither host, hostess, nor breakfast was there any sign. The host, it appeared, had gone to a fair; having waited for a hungry half-hour we were coming to the conclusion that the hostess had gone with him, when the door opened and Mrs. Flurry came swiftly into the room. Her face was a book, where men might read strange matters; it was also of a hue that suggested the ardent climate of the kitchen; in her hand she carried a toast-rack, and following hard on her heels came three maids, also heavily flushed, bearing various foods, and all, apparently, on the verge of tears. This *cortège* having retired, Mrs. Flurry proceeded to explain. The butler, Johnny, a dingy young man, once Mrs. Knox's bath chair-attendant, had departed at 8 a.m., accompanied by Michael the pantry-boy, to dig a grave for a cousin. To those acquainted with Aussolas there was nothing remarkable in this, but Sybil Hervey's china-blue eyes opened wide, and I heard her ask Bernard in a low voice if he thought it was anything agrarian. The annoyance of the cook at the defection of the butler and pantry-boy was so acute that she had retired to her room and refused to send in breakfast.

"That was no more than I should have expected from the servants here," said Mrs. Flurry vindictively, "but what was just a little too much was finding the yard-boy cramming the toast into the toast-rack with his fingers."

At this my wife's niece uttered the loud yell which all young women with any pretension to smartness have by them for use in emergencies, and exclaimed:

'Oh, *don't!*"

"You needn't be frightened," said Mrs. Flurry, giving Miss Hervey the eighth part of a glance of her greeny-grey eyes; "I made this stuff myself, and you may all think yourselves lucky to get anything," she went on, "as one of the herd of incapables downstairs said, 'to get as much milk as 'd do the tea itself, that was the stratagem'!"

Hard on the heels of the quotation there came a rushing sound in the hall without, a furious grappling with the door-handle, and the cook herself, or rather the Tragic Muse in person, burst into the room. Her tawny hair hung loose about her head; her yellow-brown eyes blazed in an ashen and extremely handsome face; she shook a pair of freckled fists at the universe. I cannot pretend to do more than indicate the drift of her denunciation. Brunhilde, ascending the funeral pyre, with full orchestral accompaniment, could not more fully and deafeningly have held her audience, and the theme might have been taken out of the darkest corner of any of the sagas.

The burying-ground of her clan was—so she had been informed by a swift runner—even now being broken into by the butler and the pantry-boy, and the graves of her ancestors were being thrown open to the four winds of the world, to make room for the scuff of the country (whatever that might mean). Here followed the most capable and comprehensive cursings of the butler and the pantry-boy that it has ever been my lot to admire, delivered at lightning speed, and with gestures worthy of the highest traditions of classic drama, the whole ending with the statement that she was on her way to the graveyard now to drink their blood.

"I trust you will, Kate," cordially responded Mrs. Flurry, "don't wait a moment!"

The Tragic Muse, startled into an instant of silence, stared wildly at Mrs. Flurry, seemed to scent far off the possibility that she was not being taken seriously, and whirled from the room, a vampire on the warpath.

"I meant every word I said to her!" said Sally, looking round upon us defiantly, "I was very near offering her your motor, Mr. Shute! The sooner she kills Johnny and Michael the better pleased I shall be! And I may tell you all," she added, "that we shall have no luncheon to-day, and most probably no dinner!"

"Oh, that's all right!" said Philippa, seeing her chance,

and hammering in her wedge with all speed, "now there's nothing for it but sandwiches and a picnic!"

The lake at Aussolas was one of a winding chain of three, connected by narrow channels cut through the bog for the passage of boats that carried turf to the lake-side dwellers. The end one of these, known as Braney's Lake, was a recognized place for picnics; a ruined oratory on a wooded point supplying the pretext, and a reliable spring well completing the equipment. The weather was of the variety specially associated in my mind with Philippa's picnics, brilliantly fine, with a falling glass, and twelve o'clock saw us shoving out from the Aussolas turf quay, through the reeds and the rocks.

We were a party of six, in two boats; diplomacy, whose I know not, had so disposed matters that Bernard Shute and Sybil Hervey were dispatched together in a dapper punt, and I, realizing to the full the insignificance of my position as a married man, found myself tugging at a tough and ponderous oar, in a species of barge known to history as "The Yellow-Boat-that-was-painted-black". My wife and Mrs. Flurry took turns in assisting my labours by paddling with a scull in the bow, while Miss Shute languidly pulled the wrong string at intervals, in the stern. Why, I grumbled contentiously, should, as it were, fish be made of Bernard and flesh be made of me (which was a highly figurative way of describing a performance that would take a stone off my weight ere all was done). Why, I repeated, should not Bernard put his broad back into it in the heavy boat with me, and leave the punt for the ladies? My wife tore herself from *sotto voce* gabblings with Sally in the bow to tell me that I was thoroughly unsympathetic, what time she dealt me an unintentional but none the less disabling blow in the spine, in her effort to fall again into stroke. Mrs. Flurry, in order to take turns at the oar with Philippa, had seated herself on the luncheon basket in the bow, thereby sinking the old tub by the head, and, as we afterwards found, causing her to leak in the sun-dried upper seams. To us travelled the voice of Bernard, lightly propelling his skiff over the ruffled and sparkling blue water.

"He's telling her about all the alterations he's going to make at Clountiss!" hissed Sally down the back of Philippa's neck.

"Almost actionable!" responded my wife, and in her enthusiasm her oar again took me heavily between the shoulder blades.

We laboured out of the Aussolas lake, and poled down the narrow channel into the middle lake, where shallows, and a heavy summer's growth of reeds, did not facilitate our advance. The day began to cloud over; as we wobbled out of the second channel into Braney's lake the sun went in, a sharp shower began to whip the water, and simultaneously Miss Shute announced that her feet were wet, and that she thought the boat must be leaking. I then perceived that the water was up to the bottom boards, and was coming in faster than I could have wished. A baler was required, and I proceeded with confidence to search for the rusty mustard tin, or cracked jam-crock, that fills that office. There was nothing to be found.

"There are plenty of cups in the luncheon basket," said Sally, tranquilly; "Flurry once had to bale this old boat out with one of his grandmother's galoshes."

Philippa and I began to row with some vigour, while Sally wrestled with the fastening of the luncheon basket in the bow. The lid opened with a jerk and a crack. There was one long and speechless moment, and then Sally said in a very gentle voice:

"They've sent the washing-basket, with all the clean clothes!"

Of the general bearings of this catastrophe there was no time to think; its most pressing feature was the fact that there were no cups with which to bale the boat. I looked over my shoulder and saw Bernard dragging the punt ashore under the ruined oratory, a quarter of a mile away; there was nothing for it but to turn and make for the shore on our right at the best pace attainable. Sally and Philippa double-banked the bow oar, and the old boat, leaking harder at each moment, wallowed on towards a landing stage that suddenly became visible amid the reeds—the bottom boards were by this time awash, and Miss Shute's complexion and that of her holland dress matched to a shade.

"Could you throw the washing overboard?" I suggested over my shoulder, labouring the while at my massy oar.

"My — new — nightgowns!" panted Mrs. Flurry, never!"

Just then big rocks began to show yellow in the depths, the next moment the boat scraped over one, and, almost immediately afterwards, settled down quietly and with dignity in some three feet of brown water and mud.

Only those who have tried to get out of a submerged boat can form any idea of what then befell. Our feet and legs turned to lead, the water to glue, all that was floatable in the boat rose to the surface, and lay about there impeding our every movement. We had foundered in sight of port and were not half a dozen yards from the landing stage, but to drag myself and three women, all up to our waists in water, and the ladies hopelessly handicapped by their petticoats, over the gunwale of a sunken boat, and to flounder ashore with them in mud, over unsteady rocks, and through the ever-hampering reeds, was infinitely more difficult and exhausting than it may seem.

Clasping a slimy post to my bosom with one arm, I was in the act of shoving Miss Shute up on to the landing stage, when I heard the unmistakable Dublin light tenor voice of a McRory hail me, announcing that he was coming to our rescue. More distant shouts, and the rapid creaking of hard-pulled oars told that Bernard and Sybil were also speeding to our aid. The three diplomats, dripping on the end of the pier, looked at each other bodefully, and Philippa murmured:

"The w t has happened!"

After that the worst continued to happen, and at a pace that overbore all resistance. Mr. De Lacy McRory, tall and beautiful, in lily-white flannels, took the lead into his own hands and played his game faultlessly. Philippa was the object of his chief solicitude. Sally and Miss Shute had their share of a manly tenderness that resolutely ignored the degrading absurdity of their appearance; his father's house, and all that was therein was laid at our feet. Captive and helpless, we slopped and squelched beside him through the shrubberies of Temple Braney House, with the shower, now matured into a heavy downpour, completing our saturation, too spiritless to resent the heavy pleasantries of Bernard, the giggling condolences of Sybil.

We have never been able to decide at which moment the knife of humiliation cut deepest, whether it was when we stood and dripped on the steps, while Curly McRory summoned in trumpet tones his womenkind, or when, still dripping, we stood in the hall and were presented to Mrs. McRory and a troop of young men and maidens, vociferous in sympathy and hospitality; or when, having progressed like water-carts through the house, we found ourselves installed, like the plague of frogs, in the bed-chambers of the McRorys, face to face with the supreme embarrassment of either going to bed, or of arraying ourselves in the all too gorgeous garments that were flung before us with a generous abandon worthy of Sir Walter Raleigh.

I chose the latter course, and, in process of time, found myself immaculately clothed in what is, I believe, known to tailors as "a lounge suit", though not for un-told gold would I have lounged, or by any carelessness endangered the perfection of the creases of its dark-grey trousers.

The luncheon gong sounded, and, like the leading gentleman in any drawing-room drama, I put forth from my dressing-room, and at the head of the stairs met my wife and Miss Shute. They were, if possible, grander than I, and looked as if they were going to a wedding.

"We had the choice of about eighty silk blouses," breathed Philippa, gathering up a long and silken train. "Sally has to wear Madame's clothes, nothing else were short enough. We're in for it, you know," she added, "a luncheon is inevitable, and goodness knows when we can get away, especially if this rain lasts——" her voice broke hysterically; I turned and saw Mrs. Flurry shuf-fling towards us in velvet slippers, holding up with both hands a flowing purple brocade skirt. I pointed repressively downwards, to where, in the window seat of the hall below, were visible the crisped golden curls of Mr. De Lacy McRory, and the shining rolls and undulations of Miss Sybil Hervey's *chevelure*. Their heads were in close proximity, and their voices were low and confidential.

"This must be put a stop to!" said Philippa, rustling swiftly downstairs.

We all moved processionally in to lunch, arm in arm with the McRorys. To Philippa had fallen old McRory, who was the best of the party (in being so awful that he knew he was awful). He maintained an unbroken silence throughout the meal, but whistled jigs secretly through his teeth, a method of keeping up his courage of which I believe he was quite unconscious. Of the brilliance of the part that I played with Mrs. McRory it would ill become me to speak; what is more worthy of record is the rapid and Upas-like growth of intimacy between Curly McRory and my wife's niece. She had probably never before encountered a young man so anxious to be agreeable, so skilled in achieving that end. The fact that he was Irish accounted, no doubt, in her eyes for all that was unusual in his voice and manners, and his long eyelashes did the rest. Sybil grew momently pinker and prettier as the long, extraordinary meal marched on.

Of its component parts I can only remember that there was a soup tureen full of custard, a mountainous dish of trifle, in whose veins ran honey, instead of jam, and to whose enlivenment a bottle at least of whisky had been dedicated; certainly, at one period, Philippa had on one side of her plate a cup of soup, and on the other a cup of tea. Cecilia Shute was perhaps the member of our party who took it all hardest. Pale and implacable, attired in a brilliant blue garment that was an outrage alike to her convictions and her complexion, she sat between two young McRorys, who understood no more of her language than she did of theirs, and was obliged to view with the frigid tranquility boasted of by Doctor Johnson, the spectacle of her brother devoting himself enthusiastically to that McRory cousin whom Philippa had described as a fluffy-haired abomination. Everything, in fact, was occurring that was least desired by the ladies of my party, with the single exception of my niece by marriage; and the glowing satisfaction of the McRory family was not hid from us, and did not ameliorate the position.

When luncheon was at length brought to a close nothing could well have been blacker than the outlook. The rain, and the splendour of our borrowed plumes, put a return by boat out of the question. It was a good seven miles round by road, and the McRory family fleet and tireless bicylists, had but one horse, which was lame. A telegram to Aussolas had been dispatched an hour ago, but as Mrs. Flurry was gloomily certain that every servant there had gone to the funeral, the time of our release was unknown.

I do not now distinctly remember what occurred immediately after lunch, but I know there came a period when I found myself alone in the hall, turning over the pages of a dreary comic paper, uncertain what to do, but determined on one point, that neither principalities nor powers should force me into the drawing-room, where sat the three unhappy women of my party, being entertained within an inch of their lives by Mrs. McRory. Sybil and Bernard and their boon companions had betaken themselves to that distant and dilapidated wing of the house in which I had once unearthed Tomsy Flood, there to play squash racquets in one of the empty rooms. I was consequently enacting the part laid down for me by my lounge suit; I was lounging, as a gentleman should, without for an instant disturbing the creases of my trousers.

At times I was aware of the silent and respectful surveillance of Mr. McRory in the inner hall, but I thought it best for us both to feign unconsciousness of his presence. Through a swing door that, true to its definition, swung wheezily to the cabbage-laden draughts from the lower reigions, I could hear the tide of battle rolling through the disused wing. The squash racquets seemed to be of a most pervading character; the thunder of rushing feet, blent with the long, progressive shriek of an express train, would at intervals approach almost to the swing door, but I remained unmolested. I had entered upon my second cigarette, and a period of comparative peace, when I heard a stealing foot, and found at my elbow a female McRory, of about twelve years as years go, but dowered with the accumulated experience of six elder sisters.

"Did Pinkie and Mr. Shute come in this way to hide?" she began, looking at me as if "Pinkie", whoever she might be, was in my pocket. "We're playing hid'n-go-seek, and we can't find them."

I said I knew nothing of them.

The McRory child looked at me with supernal intelligence from under the wing of dark hair that was tied over one ear.

"They're not playing fair anyhow, and there's Curly and Miss Hervey that wouldn't play at all!" She eyed me again. "He took her out to show her the ferrets and they never came back. I was watching them; she said one of the ferrets bit her finger, and Curly kissed it!"

"I suppose you mean he kissed the ferret," I said repressively, while I thought of Alice Hervey, mother of Sybil, and trembled.

"Ah, go on! what a fool you're letting on to be!" replied the McRory child, with elegant sarcasm. She swung round on her heel and sped away again upon the trail, cannoning against old McRory in the back hall.

"I tell you, that's the lady!" soliloquized old McRory, from the deep of the back hall. I gathered that he was referring to the social capacity of his youngest daughter and thought he was probably right.

It was at this moment that deliverance broke like a sunburst upon us; I saw through the windows of the hall a dogcart and an outside car whirl past the door and onwards to the yard. The former was driven by Flurry Knox, the car by Michael the Aussolas pantry-boy, apparently none the worse for his encounter with the vampire cook. I snatched an umbrella, and, regardless of the lounge suit, followed with all speed the golden path of the sunburst.

Flurry, clad in glistening yellow oilskins, met me in

the yard, wearing an expression of ill-concealed exulta-
tion worthy of Job's comforters at their brightest.

"D'ye know who opened your wire?" he began,
regarding me with an all-observant eye from under his
sou'wester, while the raindrops ran down his nose. "I
can tell you there's the Old Gentleman to pay at Aussolas—or the old lady, and that's worse! That's a nice suit
—you ought to buy that from Curly."

"Who opened my telegram?" I said. I was not at all
amused.

"'When she got there, the cupboard was bare',"
returned Flurry. "Not a servant in the house, not a bit in
the larder! If it wasn't that by the mercy of Providence
I found the picnic basket that you bright boys had left
after you, she'd have torn the house down!"

"I suppose you mean that your grandmother has come
back," I said stonily.

"She fought with her unfortunate devil of a doctor at
Buxton," said Flurry, permitting himself a grin of
remembrance, "he told her she was too old to eat late
dinner, and she told him she wasn't going to be a slave
to her stomach or to him either, and she'd eat her dinner
when she pleased, and she landed in at Aussolas by the
midday train without a word."

"What did she say when she opened my telegram?"
I faltered.

"She said 'Thank God I'm not a fool!'" replied her
grandson.

The proposition was unanswerable, and I took it so to
speak, lying down.

"Here!" said Flurry, summoning the pantry-boy,
"These horses must go in out of the rain. I'll look over
there for some place I can put them."

"I see Michael got back from the funeral," I said,
following Flurry across the wide and wet expanse of the
yard, "I suppose the cook killed Johnny?"

"Ah, not at all," said Flurry, "anyway, my grandmother had the two of them up unpacking her trunks
when I left. Here, this place looks like a stable——"

He opened a door, in front of which a cascade from

a broken watershoot was splashing noisily. The potent smell of ferrets greeted us.

Seated on the ferrets' box were Mr. De Lacy McRory, and Sybil, daughter of Alice Hervey. Apparently she had again been bitten by the ferret, but this time the bite was not on her finger.

OWENEEN THE SPRAT

I was labouring in the slough of Christmas letters and bills, when my wife came in and asked me if I would take her to the Workhouse.

"My dear," I replied, ponderously, but, I think, excusably, "you have, as usual, anticipated my intention, but I think we can hold out until after Christmas."

Philippa declined to pay the jest the respect to which its age entitled it, and replied inconsequently that I knew perfectly well that she could not drive the outside car with the children and the Christmas tree. I assented that they would make an awkward team, and offered, as a substitute for my services, those of Denis, the stopgap.

Those who live in Ireland best know the staying powers of stopgaps. Denis, uncle of Michael Leary the whip, had been imported into the kennels during my ministry, to bridge a hiatus in the long dynasty of the kennel-boys, and had remained for eighteen months, a notable instance of the survival of what might primarily have been considered the unfittest. That Denis should so long have endured his nephew's rule was due not so much to the tie of blood, as to the privileged irresponsibility of a stopgap. Nothing was expected of him, and he pursued an unmolested course, until the return of Flurry Knox from South Africa changed the general conditions. He then remained submerged until he drifted into the gap formed in my own establishment by Mr. Peter Cadogan's elopement.

Philippa's workhouse-tea took place on Christmas

Eve. We were still hurrying through an early luncheon when the nodding crest of the Christmas tree passed the dining-room windows. My youngest son immediately upset his pudding into his lap; and Philippa hustled forth to put on her hat, an operation which, like the making of an omelette, can apparently only be successfully performed at the last moment. With feelings of mingled apprehension and relief I saw the party drive from the door, the Christmas tree seated on one side of the car, Philippa on the other, clutching her offspring, Denis on the box, embossed, like a wood-pigeon, in the boughs of the spruce fir. I congratulated myself that the Quaker, now white with the snows of many winters, was in the shafts. Had I not been too deeply engaged in so arranging the rug that it should not trail in the mud all the way to Skebawn, I might have noticed that the lamps had been forgotten.

It was, as I have said, Christmas Eve, and as the afternoon wore on I began to reflect upon what the road from Skebawn would be in another hour, full of drunken people, and, what was worse, of carts steered by drunken people. I had assured Philippa (with what I believe she describes as masculine *esprit de corps*) of Denis's adequacy as a driver, but that did not alter the fact that in the last rays of the setting sun, I got out my bicycle and set forth for the Workhouse. When I reached the town it was dark, but the Christmas shoppers showed no tendency to curtail their operations on that account, and the streets were filled with an intricate and variously moving tide of people and carts. The paraffin lamps in the shops did their best, behind bunches of holly, oranges, and monstrous Christmas candles, and partially illumined the press of dark-cloaked women, and more or less drunken men, who swayed and shoved and held vast conversations on the narrow pavements. The red glare of the chemist's globe transformed the leading female beggar of the town into a being from the Brocken; her usual Christmas family, contributed for the festival by the neighbours, as to a Christmas number, were grouped in forunate ghastliness in the green light. She extracted from me her recognized tribute, and pursued by her assurance that she would forgive me now till Easter (i.e., that further alms would not be exacted for at least a fortnight), I made my way onward into the outer darkness, beyond the uttermost link in the chain of public-houses.

The road that led to the Workhouse led also to the railway station; a quarter of a mile away the green light of a signal-post stood high in the darkness, like an emerald. As I neared the Workhouse I recognized the deliberate footfall of the Quaker, and presently his long pale face entered the circle illuminated by my bicycle-lamp. My family were not at all moved by my solicitude for their safety, but, being in want of an audience, were pleased to suggest that I should drive home with them. The road was disgustingly muddy; I tied my bicycle to the back of the car with the rope that is found in the wells of all outside cars. It was not till I had put out the bicycle lamp that I noticed that the car-lamps had been forgotten, but Denis, true to the convention of his tribe, asseverated that he could see better without lights. I took the place vacated by the Christmas tree, the Quaker pounded on at his usual stone-breaking trot, and my offspring, in strenuous and entangled duet, declaimed to me the events of the afternoon.

It was without voice or warning that a row of men was materialized out of the darkness, under the Quaker's nose; they fell away to right and left, but one, as if stupefied, held on his way in the middle of the road. It is not easy to divert the Quaker from his course; we swung to the right, but the wing of the car, on my side, struck the man full in the chest. He fell as instantly and solidly as if he were a stone pillar, and, like a stone, he lay in the mud. Loud and inebriate howls rose from the others, and, as if the answer, came a long and distant shriek from an incoming train. Upon this, without bestowing an instant's further heed to their fallen comrade, the party took to their heels and ran to the station. It was all done in a dozen seconds; by the time the Quaker was pulled up we were alone with our victim, and Denis was hoarsely suggesting to me that it would be better to drive away at once. I have often since then regretted that I did not take his advice.

The victim was a very small man; Denis and I dragged him to the side of the road, and propped him up against the wall. He was of an alarming limpness, but there was a something reassuring in the reek of whisky that arose as I leaned over him, trying to diagnose his injuries by the aid of a succession of lighted matches. His head lay crookedly on his chest; he breathed heavily, but peacefully, and his limbs seemed uninjured. Denis at my elbow, did not cease to assure me, tremulously, that there was nothing ailed the man, that he was a stranger, and that it would be as good for us to go home. Philippa, on the car, strove as best she might with the unappeasable curiosity of her sons and with the pigheaded anxiety of the Quaker to get home to his dinner. At this juncture a voice, fifty yards away in the darkness, uplifted itself in song:

"Heaven's refle-hex! Kill-ar-ney!"

it bawled hideously.

It fell as balm upon my ear, in its assurance of the proximity of Slipper.

"Sure I know the man well," he said, shielding the flame of a match in his hand with practised skill. "Wake up, me *bouchaleen*!" He shook him unmercifully. "Open your eyes, darlin'!"

The invalid here showed signs of animation by uttering an incoherent but, as it seemed, a threatening roar. It lifted Denis as a feather is lifted by a wind, and wafted him to the Quaker's head, where he remained in strict attention to his duties. It also lifted Philippa.

"Is he very bad, do you think?" she murmured at my elbow. "Shall I drive for the doctor?"

"Arrah, what dochtor?" said Slipper magnificiently. "Give me a half-crown, Major, and I'll give him what meddyceen will answer him as good as any docthor! Lave him to me!" He shook him again. "I'll regulate him!"

The victim here sat up, and shouted something about going home. He was undoubtedly very drunk. It seemed to me that Slipper's ministrations would be more suitable to the situation than mine, certainly than Philippa's. I administered the solatium; then I placed Denis on the box of the car with the bicycle-lamp in his hand, and drove my family home.

After church next day we met Flurry Knox. He approached us with the green glint in his eye that told that game was on foot, whatever that game might be.

"Who bailed you out, Mrs. Yeates?" he said solicitously. "I heard you and the Major and Denis Leary were all in the lock-up for furious driving and killing a man! I'm told he was anointed last night."

Philippa directed what she believed to be a searching glance at Flurry's face of friendly concern.

"I don't believe a word of it!" she said dauntlessly, while a very becoming warmth in her complexion betrayed an inward qualm. "Who told you?"

"The servants heard it at first Mass this morning; and Slipper had me late for church telling me about it. The fellow says if he lives he's going to take an action against the Major."

I listened with, I hope, outward serenity. In dealings with Flurry Knox the possibility that he might be speaking the truth could never be safely lost sight of. It was also well to remember that he generally knew what the truth was.

I said loftily, that there had been nothing the matter with the man but Christmas Eve, and inquired if Flurry knew his name and address.

"Of course I do," said Flurry, "he's one of those mountainy men that live up in the hill behind Aussolas. Oweneen the Sprat is the name he goes by, and he's the crossest little thief in the Barony Never mind, Mrs. Yeates, I'll see you get fair play in the dock!"

"How silly you are!" said Philippa; but I could see that she was shaken.

Whatever Flurry's servants may have heard at first Mass was apparently equalled, if not excelled, by what Denis heard at second. He asked me next morning, with a gallant attempt at indifference, if I had had any word of "the man-een".

" 'Twas what the people were saying on the roads last

night that he could have the law on us, and there was more was saying that he'd never do a day's good. Sure they say the backbone is cracked where the wheel of the car went over him! But didn't yourself and the misthress swear black and blue that the wheel never went next or nigh him? And didn't Michael say that there wasn't a Christmas this ten years that that one hadn't a head on him the size of a bullawawn with the len'th o' dhrink?"

In spite of the contributory negligence that might be assumed in the case of anyone with this singular infirmity, I was not without a secret uneasiness. Two days afterwards I received a letter, written on copybook paper in a clerkly hand. It had the Aussolas post-mark, in addition to the imprint of various thumbs, and set forth the injuries inflicted by me and my driver on Owen Twohig on Christmas Eve, and finally, it demanded a compensation of twenty pounds for the same. Failing this satisfaction the law was threatened, but a hope was finally expressed that the honourable gentleman would not see a poor man wronged; it was, in fact, the familiar mixture of bluff and whine, and, as I said to Philippa, the Man-een (under which title he had passed into the domestic vocabulary) had of course got hold of a letter writer to do the trick for him.

In the next day or so I met Flurry twice, and found him so rationally interested, and even concerned, about fresh versions of the accident that had cropped up, that I was moved to tell him of the incident of the letter. He looked serious, and said he would go up himself to see what was wrong with Oweneen. He advised me to keep out of it for the present, as they might open their mouths too big.

The moon was high as I returned from this interview; when I wheeled my bicycle into the yard I found that the coach-house in which I was wont to stable it was locked; so also was the harness-room. Attempting to enter the house by the kitchen door I found it also was locked; a gabble of conversation prevailed within, and with the mounting indignation of one who hears but cannot make himself heard, I banged ferociously on the door. Silence fell, and Mrs. Cadogan's voice implored heaven's protection.

"Open the door!" I roared.

A windlike rush of petticoats followed, through which came sibilantly the words, "Glory be to goodness! 'Tis the masther!"

The door opened, I found myself facing the entire strength of my establishment, including Denis, and augmented by Slipper.

"They told me you were asking afther me, Major," began Slipper, descending respectfully from the kitchen table, on which he had been seated.

I noticed that Mrs. Cadogan was ostentatiously holding her heart, and that Denis was shaking like the conventional aspen.

"What's all this about?" said I, looking round upon them. "Why is the whole place locked up?"

"It was a little unaisy they were," said Slipper, snatching the explanation from Mrs. Cadogan with the determination of the skilled leader of conversation; "I was telling them I seen two men below in the plantation, like they'd be watching out for someone, and poor Mr. Leary here got a reeling in his head after I telling it——"

"Indeed the crayture was as white, now, as white as a masheroon!" broke in Mrs. Cadogan, "and we dhrew him in here to the fire till your Honour came home."

"Nonsense!" I said angrily, "a couple of boys poaching rabbits! Upon my word, Slipper, you have very little to do coming here and frightening people for nothing."

"What did I say," demanded Slipper, dramatically facing his audience, "only that I seen two men in the plantation. How would I know what business they had in it?"

"Ye said ye heard them whishling to each other like curlews through the wood," faltered Denis, "and sure that's the whishle them Twohigs has always——"

"Maybe it's whistling to the girls they were!" suggested Slipper, with an unabashed eye at Hannah.

I told him to come up with me to my office, and stalked from the kitchen, full of the comfortless wrath that has failed to find a suitable victim.

The interview in the office did not last long, nor was it in any way reassuring, Slipper, with the manner of the confederate who had waded shoulder to shoulder with me through gore, could only tell me that though he believed that there was nothing ailed the Man-een, he wouldn't say but what he might be sevarely hurted. That I wasn't gone five minutes before near a score of the Twohigs come leathering down out of the town in two ass-butts (this term indicates donkey-carts of the usual dimensions), and when Oweneen felt them coming, he let the most unmarciful screech, upon which Slipper, in just fear of the Twohigs, got over the wall, and executed a strategic retreat upon the railway station, leaving the Twohigs to carry away their wounded to the mountains. That for himself he had been going in dread of them ever since, and for no one else in the wide world would he have put a hand to one of them.

I preserved an unshaken front towards Slipper, and I was subsequently sarcastic and epigrammatic to Philippa on the subject of the curlews who were rabbiting in the plantation, but something that I justified to myself as a fear of Philippa's insatiable conscientiousness, made me resolve that I would, without delay, go "back in the mountain", and interview Oweneen the Sprat.

New Year's Day favoured my purpose, bringing with it clear frost and iron roads, a day when even the misanthropic soul of a bicycle awakens into sympathy and geniality. I started in the sunny vigour of the early afternoon, I sailed up the hill with the effortless speed of a seagull, I free-wheeled down them with the dive of a swallow, and, as it seemed to me with a good deal of its grace. Had Oweneen the Sprat had the luck to have met me when, at the seventh milestone from Shreelane, I realized that I had beaten my own best time by seven minutes, he could practically have made his own terms. At that point, however, I had to leave the high road, and the mountain lane that ensued restored to me the judicial frame of mind. In the first twenty yards my bicycle was transformed from a swallow to an opinionated and semi-paralysed wheelbarrow; struggling in a species of dry watercourse I shoved it up the steep gradients of a large and brown country of heather and bog, silent save for the contending voices of the streams. A family of goats, regarding me from a rocky mound, was the first hint of civilization; a more reliable symptom presently advanced in the shape of a lean and hump-backed sow, who bestowed on me a side glance of tepid interest as she squeezed past.

The bohireen dropped, with a sudden twist to the right, and revealed a fold in the hillside, containing a half-dozen or so of little fields, crooked, and heavily walled, and nearly as many thatched cabins, flung about in the hollows as indiscriminately as the boulders upon the wastes outside. A group of children rose in front of me like a flight of starlings, and scudded with bare-footed nimbleness to the shelter of the houses, in a pattering, fluttering stampede. I descended upon the nearest cabin of the colony. The door was shut; a heavy padlock linking two staples said Not at Home, and the nose of a dog showed in a hole above the sill, sniffing deeply and suspiciously. I remembered that the first of January was a holy-day, and that every man in the colony had doubtless betaken himself to the nearest village. The next cottage was some fifty yards away, and the faces of a couple of children peered at me round the corner of it. As I approached they vanished, but the door of the cabin was open, and blue turf smoke breathed placidly outwards from it. The merciful frost had glazed the inevitable dirty pool in front of the door, and had made practicable the path beside it; I propped my bicycle against a rock, and projected into the dark interior an inquiry as to whether there was anyone in.

I had to repeat it twice before a small old woman with white hair and a lemon-coloured face appeared; I asked her if she could tell me where Owen Twohig lived.

"Your Honour's welcome," she replied, tying the strings of her cap under her chin with wiry fingers, and eyeing me with concentrated shrewdness. I repeated the question.

She responded by begging me to come in and rest myself, for this was a cross place and a backwards place, and I should be famished with the cold—"sure them little wheels dhraws the wind".

I ignored this peculiarity of bicycles, and, not without exasperation, again asked for Owen Twohig.

"Are you Major Yeates, I beg your pardon?" I assented to what she knew as well as I did.

"Why then 'tis here he lives indeed, in this little house, and a poor place he have to live in. Sure he's my son, the crayture——" her voice at once ascended to the key of lamentation—"faith, he didn't rise till today. Since Christmas Eve I didn't quinch light in the house with him stretched in the bed always, and not a bit passed his lips night or day, only one suppeen of whisky in its purity. Ye'd think the tongue would light out of his mouth with the heat, and ye'd see the blaze of darkness in his face! I hadn't as much life in me this morning as that I could wash my face!"

I replied that I wanted to speak to her son, and was in a hurry.

"He's not within, asthore, he's not within at all. He got the lend of a little donkey, and he went back the mountain to the bone-setter, to try could he straighten the leg with him."

"Did Dr. Hickey see him?" I demanded.

"Sure a wise woman came in from Finnaun, a' Stephen's Day," pursued Mrs. Twohig swiftly, "and she bet three spits down on him, and she said it's what ailed him he had the Fallen Palate, with the dint o' the blow the car bet him in the poll, and that onyone that have the Fallen Palate might be spechless for three months with it. She took three ribs of his hair then, and she was pulling them till she was in a passpiration, and in the latther end she pulled up the palate." She paused and wiped her eyes with her apron. "But the leg is what has him destroyed altogether; she told us we should keep sheep's butter rubbed to it in the place where the thrack o' the wheel is down in it."

The blush of a frosty sunset was already in the sky, and the children who had fled before me had returned, reinforced by many others, to cluster in a whispering swarm round my bicycle, and to group themselves attentively in the rear of the conversation.

"Look here, Mrs. Twohig," I said, not as yet angry, but in useful proximity to it, "I've had a letter from your son, and he and his friends have been trying to frighten my man, Denis Leary; he can come down and see me if he has anything to say, but you can tell him from me that I'm not going to stand this sort of thing!"

If the Widow Twohig had been voluble before, this pronouncement had the effect of bringing her down in spate. She instantly, and at the top of her voice, called heaven to witness her innocence, and the innocence of her "little boy"; still at full cry, she sketched her blameless career, and the unmerited suffering that had ever pursued her and hers; how, during the past thirty years, she had been drooping over her little orphans, and how Oweneen, that was the only one she had left to do a hand's turn for her, would be "under clutches" the longest day that he'd live. It was at about this point that I gave her five shillings. It was a thoroughly illogical act, but at the moment it seemed inevitable, and Mrs. Twohig was good enough to accept it in the same spirit. I told her that I would send Dr. Hickey to see her son (which had, it struck me, a somewhat stemming effect upon her eloquence), and I withdrew, still in magisterial displeasure. I must have been half-way down the lane before it was revealed to me that a future on crutches was what Mrs. Twohig anticipated for her son.

By that night's post I wrote to Hickey, a strictly impartial letter, stating the position, and asking him to see Owen Twohig, and to let me have his professional opinion upon him. Philippa added a postscript, asking for a nerve-tonic for the parlour-maid, a Dublin girl, who, since the affair of the curlews in the plantation, had lost all colour and appetite, and persisted in locking the hall door day and night, to the infinite annoyance of the dogs.

Next morning, while hurrying through an early breakfast, preparatory to starting for a distant Petty Sessions, I was told that Denis wished to speak to me at the hall door. This, as I before have had occasion to point out, boded affairs of the first importance. I proceeded to the hall door, and there found Denis, pale as the Lily Maid of Astolat, with three small fishes in his hand.

"There was one of thim before me in my bed lasht night!" he said in a hoarse and shaken whisper, "and there was one in the windy in the harness-room, down on top o' me razor, and there was another nelt to the stable door with the nail of a horse's shoe."

I made the natural suggestion that someone had done it for a joke.

"Thim's no joke, sir," replied Denis, portentously, "thim's Sprats!"

"Well, I'm quite aware of that," I said, unmoved by what appeared to be the crushing significance of the statement.

"Oweneen the *Sprat*!" murmured Philippa, illuminatingly, emerging from the dining-room door with her cup of tea in her hand, "it's Hannah, trying to frighten him!"

Hannah, the housemaid, was known to be the humorist of the household.

"He have a brother a smith, back in the mountain," continued Denis, wrapping up the sprats and the nail in his handkerchief; "'twas for a token he put the nail in it. If he dhraws thim mountainy men down on me, I may as well go under the sod. It isn't yourself or the misthress they'll folly; it's meself." He crept down the steps as deplorably as the Jackdaw of Rheims, "and it's what Michael's after telling me, they have it all through the country that I said you should throw Twohig in the ditch, and it was good enough for the likes of him, and I said to Michael 'twas a lie for them, and that we cared him as tender as if he was our mother itself, and we'd have given the night to him only for the misthress that was roaring on the car, and no blame to her; sure the world knows the mother o' children has no courage!"

This drastic generality was unfortunately lost to my wife, as she had retired to hold a court of inquiry in the kitchen.

The inquiry elicited nothing beyond the fact that since Christmas Day Denis was "using no food", and that the kitchen, so far from indulging in practical jokes at his expense, had been instant throughout in sympathy, and in cups of strong tea, administered for the fortification of the nerves. All were obviously deeply moved by the incident of the sprats, the parlour-maid indeed having already locked herself into the pantry, through the door of which, on Philippa's approach, she gave warning hysterically.

The matter remained unexplained, and was not altogether to my liking. As I drove down the avenue, and saw Denis carefully close the yard gates after me, I determined that I would give Murray, the District Inspector of Police, a brief sketch of the state of affairs. I did not meet Murray, but, as it happened, this made no difference. Things were already advancing smoothly and inexorably towards their preordained conclusion.

I have since heard that none of the servants went to bed that night. They, including Denis, sat in the kitchen, with locked doors, drinking tea and reciting religious exercises; Maria, as a further precaution, being chained to the leg of the table. Their fears were in no degree allayed by the fact that nothing whatever occurred, and the most immediate result of the vigil was that my bath next morning boiled as it stood in the can, and dimmed the room with clouds of steam—a circumstance sufficiently rare in itself, and absolutely without precedent on Sunday morning. The next feature of the case was a letter at breakfast time from a gentleman signing himself "Jas. Fitzmaurice". He said that Dr. Hickey having gone away for a fortnight's holiday, he (Fitzmaurice) was acting as his locum tenens. In that capacity he had opened my letter, and would go and see Twohig as soon as possible. He enclosed prescription for tonic as requested.

It was a threatening morning, and we did not go to church. I noticed that my wife's housekeeping *séance* was unusually prolonged, and even while I smoked and read the papers, I was travelling in my meditations to the point of determining that I would have a talk with the priest about all this infernal nonsense. When Philippa at length rejoined me, I found that she also had arrived at a conclusion, impelled thereto by the counsels of Mrs. Cadogan, abetted by her own conscience.

Its result was that immediately after lunch, long before the Sunday roast beef had been slept off, I found myself carting precarious parcels—a jug, a bottle, a pudding-dish—to the inside car, in which Philippa had already placed herself, with a pair of blankets and various articles culled from my wardrobe (including a pair of boots to which I was sincerely attached). Denis, pale yellow in complexion and shrouded in gloom, was on the box, the Quaker was in the shafts. There was no rain, but the clouds hung black and low.

It was an expedition of purest charity; so Philippa explained to me over again as we drove away. She said nothing of propitiation or diplomacy. For my part I said nothing at all, but I reflected on the peculiar gifts of the Dublin parlour-maid in valeting me, and decided that it might be better to allow Philippa to run the show on her own lines, while I maintained an attitude of large-minded disapproval.

The blankets took up as much room in the car as a man; I had to hold in my hand a jug of partly jellied beef tea. A sourer Lady Bountiful never set forth upon an errand of mercy. To complete establishment—in the words of the *Gazette*—Maria and Minx, on the floor of the car, wrought and strove in ceaseless and objectless agitation, an infliction due to the ferocity of a female rival, who terrorized the high road within hail of my gates. I thanked heaven that I had at least been firm about not taking the children; for the dogs, at all events, the moment of summary ejectment would arrive sooner or later.

Seven miles in an inside car are seven miles indeed. The hills that had run to meet my bicycle and glided away behind it, now sat in their places to be crawled up and lumbered down, at such a pace as seemed good to the Quaker, whose appetite for the expedition was, if possible, less than that of his driver. Appetite was, indeed, the last thing suggested by the aspect of Denis. His drooping shoulders and deplorable countenance proclaimed apology and deprecation to the mountain tops, and more especially to the mountainy men. Looking back on it now, I recognize the greatness of the tribute to my valour and omnipotence that he should have consented thus to drive us into the heart of the enemy's country.

A steep slope, ending with a sharp turn through a cutting, reminded me that we were near the mountain bohireen that was our goal. I got out and walked up the hill, stiffly, because the cramp of the covered car was in my legs. Stiff though I was, I had outpaced the Quaker, and was near the top of the hill, when something that was apparently a brown croquet-ball rolled swiftly round the bend above me, charged into the rock wall of the cutting with a clang, and came on down the hill with a weight and venom unknown to croquet-balls. It sped past me, missed the Quaker by an uncommonly near shave, and went on its way, hotly pursued by the two dogs, who, in the next twenty yards, discovered with horror that it was made of iron, a fact of which I was already aware.

I have always been as lenient as the law, and other circumstances, would allow towards the illegal game of "bowling". It consists in bowling an iron ball along a road, the object being to cover the greatest possible distance in a given number of bowls. It demands considerable strength and skill, and it is played with a zest much enhanced by its illegality and by its facilities as a medium for betting. The law forbids it, on account of its danger to the unsuspecting wayfarer, in consideration of which a scout is usually posted ahead to signal the approach of the police, and to give warning to passers-by. The mountainy men, trusting to their isolation, had neglected this precaution, with results that came near being serious to the Quaker, and filled with wrath, both personal and official, I took the hill at a vengeful run, so as to catch the bowler red-handed. At the turn in the cutting I met him face to face. As a matter of fact he nearly ran into my arms, and the yelp of agony with which he dodged my impending embrace is a life-long possession. He was a very small man; he doubled like a rabbit, and bolted back towards a swarm of men who were following the fortunes of the game. He flitted over the wall by the roadside, and was away over the rocky hillside at a speed that even in my best days would have left me nowhere.

The swarm on the road melted; a good part of it was quietly absorbed by the lane up which I had dragged my bicycle two days before, the remainder, elaborately uninterested and respectable, in their dark blue Sunday clothes, strolled gravely in the opposite direction. A man on a bicycle met them, and dismounted to speak to the leaders. I wondered if he were a policeman in plain clothes on the prowl. He came on to meet me, leading his bicycle, and I perceived that a small black leather bag was strapped to the carrier. He was young, and apparently very hot.

"I beg your pardon," he said in the accents of Dublin, "I understand you're Major Yeates. I'm Dr. Hickey's 'locum', and I've come out to see the man you wrote to me about. From what you said I thought it better to lose no time."

I was rather out of breath, but I expressed my sense of indebtedness.

"I think there must be some mistake," went on the 'locum'. "I've just asked these men on the road where Owen Twohig lives, and one of them—the fellow they call Skipper, or some such name—said Owen Twohig was the little chap that's just after sprinting up the mountain. He seemed to think it was a great joke. I suppose you're sure Owen was the name?"

"Perfectly sure," I said heavily.

The eyes of Dr. Fitzmaurice had travelled past me, and were regarding with professional alertness something farther down the road. I followed their direction, dreamily, because in spirit I was far away, tracking Flurry Knox through deep places.

On the hither side of the rock cutting the covered car had come to a standstill. The reins had fallen from Denis's hands; he was obviously having the "wakeness"

402

appropriate to the crisis. Philippa, on the step below him, was proffering to him the jug of beef tea and the bottle of port. He accepted the latter.

'He knows what's what!" said the "locum".

THE WHITEBOYS

PART I

It has been said by an excellent authority that children and dogs spoil conversation. I can confidently say that had Madame de Sévigné and Dr. Johnson joined me and my family on our wonted Sunday afternoon walk to the kennels they would have known what it was to be ignored. This reflection bears but remotely on the matter in hand, but is, I think, worthy of record. I pass on to a certain still and steamy afternoon in late September, when my wife and I headed forth in the accustomed way, accompanied by, or (to be accurate), in pursuit of, my two sons, my two dogs, and a couple of hound puppies, to view that spectacle of not unmixed attractiveness, the feeding of the hounds.

Flurry Knox and Michael were superintending the operation when we arrived, coldly observing the gobbling line at the trough, like reporters at a public dinner. It was while the last horrid remnants of the repast were being wolfed that my wife hesitatingly addressed Mr. Knox's first whip and kennel huntsman.

"Michael," she said, lowering her voice, "you know the children's old donkey that I spoke to you about last week—I'm afraid you *had* better——"

"Sure he's boiled, ma'am," said Michael with swift and awful brevity, "that's him in the throch now!"

Philippa hastily withdrew from the vicinity of the trough, murmuring something incoherent about cannibals or parricides, I am not sure which, and her eldest son burst into tears that were only assuaged by the tactful intervention of the kennel-boy with the jawbone of a horse, used for propping open the window of the boiler-house.

"Never mind, Mrs. Yeates," said Flurry consolingly, "the new hounds that I'm getting won't be bothered with donkeys as long as there's a sheep left in the country, if the half I hear of them is true!" He turned to me. "Major, I didn't tell you I have three couple of O'Reilly's old Irish hounds bought. They're the old white breed y'know, and they say they're terrors to hunt."

"They'd steal a thing out of your eye," said Michael, evidently reverting to an interrupted discussion between himself and his master. "There's a woman of the O'Reillys married back in the country here, and she says they killed two cows last season."

"If they kill any cows with me, I'll stop the price of them out of your wages, Michael, my lad!" said Flurry to his henchman's back. "Look here, Major, come on with me to-morrow to bring them home!"

It was, I believe, no more than fifty miles across country to the mountain fastness of the O'Reillys, and a certain chord of romance thrilled at the thought of the old Irish breed of white hounds, with their truly national qualities of talent, rebelliousness, and love of sport. Play-boy was one of the same race—Playboy, over whose recapture, it may be remembered, I had considerably distinguished myself during my term of office as M.F.H.

I went. At one o'clock next day two lines of rail had done their uttermost for us, and had ceded the task of conveying us to Fahoura to the inevitable outside car. And still there remained a long flank of mountain to be climbed; the good little slave in the shafts made no com-plaint, but save for the honour and glory of the thing we might as well have walked; certainly of the seven Irish miles of road, thrown over the pass like a strap over a trunk, our consciences compelled us to tramp at least three. A stream, tawny and translucent as audit ale, foamed and slid among its brown boulders beside us at the side of the road; as we crawled upwards the fields became smaller, and the lonely white-washed cottages ceased. The heather came down to the wheel marks, and a pack of grouse suddenly whizzed across the road like a shot fired across our bows to warn us off.

At the top of the pass we stood, and looked out over half a county to the pale peaks of Killarney.

"There's Fahoura now, gentlemen," said the carman, pointing downwards with his whip to a group of white-washed farm buildings that had gathered themselves incongruously about a square grey tower. 'I'm told old Mr. O'Reilly's sick this good while."

"What ails him?" said Flurry.

"You wouldn't know," said the carman, "sure he's very old, and that 'fluenzy has the country destroyed; there's people dying now that never died before."

"That's bad," said Flurry sympathetically, "I had a letter from him a week ago, and he only said he was parting the hounds because he couldn't run with them any more."

"Ah, don't mind him!" said the carman, "it's what it is he'd sooner sell them now, than to give the nephew the satisfaction of them, after himself'd be dead."

"Is that the chap that's been hunting them for him?" said Flurry, while I, for the hundredth time, longed for Flurry's incommunicable gift of being talked to.

"It is, sir; Lukey O'Reilly——" the carman gave a short laugh. "That's the lad! They say he often thried to go to America, but he never got south of Mallow; he gets that drunk sayin' good-bye to his friends!"

"Maybe the old fellow will live a while yet, just to spite him," suggested Flurry.

"Well, maybe he would, faith!" agreed the carman, "didn't the docthor say to meself that maybe it's walking the road I'd be, and I to fall down dead!" he continued complacently, "but sure them docthors, when they wouldn't know what was in it, they should be saying something!"

We here turned into the lane that led to Mr. O'Reilly's house.

We pulled up at the gate of a wide farmyard, with out-crops of the brown mountain rock in it, and were assailed in the inevitable way by the inevitable mongrel collies. Blent with their vulgar abuse was the mellow baying of hounds, coming, seemingly, from the sky. The carman pointed to the tower which filled an angle of the yard, and I saw, about twenty feet from the ground, an arrow-slit, through which protruded white muzzles, uttering loud and tuneful threats.

"The kitchen door's the handiest way," said Flurry, "but I suppose for grandeur we'd better go to the front of the house."

He opened a side gate, and I followed him through a wind-swept enclosure that by virtue of two ragged rosebushes, and a walk edged with white stones, probably took rank as a garden. At the front door we knocked; a long pause ensued, and finally bare feet thudded down a passage, a crack of the door was opened, and an eye glistened for a moment in the crack. It was slammed again, and after a further delay it was reopened, this time by a large elderly woman with crinkled black and grey hair and one long and comamnding tooth in the front of her mouth.

"Why then I wasn't looking to see ye till to-morrow, Mr. Knox!" she began, beaming upon Flurry, "but sure ye're welcome any day and all day, and the gentleman too!"

The gentleman was introduced, and felt himself being summed up in a single glance of Miss O'Reilly's nimble brown eyes. With many apologies, she asked us if we would come and see her brother in the kitchen, as he did not feel well enough to walk out to the parlour, and she couldn't keep him in the bed at all.

The kitchen differed more in size than in degree from that of the average cabin. There was the same hummocky earthen floor, the same sallow white-washed walls, the same all-pervading turf smoke—the difference was in the master of the house. He was seated by the fire in an angular arm-chair, with an old horse-blanket over his knees, and a stick in his hand, and beside him lay an ancient white hound, who scarcely lifted her head at our entrance. The old man laboured to his feet, and, bent as he was, he towered over Flurry as he took his hand.

"Your father's son is welcome, Mr. Florence Knox, and your friend——' He was short of breath, and he lowered his great frame into his chair again. "Sit down, gentlemen, sit down!" he commanded. "Joanna! These gentlemen are after having a long drive——"

The clink of glasses told that the same fact had occurred to Miss O'Reilly, and a botle of port, and another of what looked like water, but was in effect old potheen, were immediately upon the table.

"How well ye wouldn't put down a glass for me!" thundered old O'Reilly, "I suppose it's saving it for my wake you are!"

"Or her own wedding, maybe!" said Flurry, shamelessly ogling Miss O'Reilly, "we'll see that before the wake, I'm thinking!"

"Well, well, isn't he the dead spit of his father!" said Miss O'Reilly to the rafters.

"Here, woman, give me the kettle," said her brother, "I'll drink my glass of punch with Mr. Florence Knox, the way I did with his father before him! The doctor says I might carry out six months, and I think myself I won't carry out the week, but what the divil do I care! I'm going to give Mr. Knox his pick of my hounds this day, and that's what no other man in Ireland would get, and be dam we'll wet our bargain!"

"Well, well," said Miss O'Reilly, remonstratingly, bringing the kettle, "and you that was that weak last night that if you got Ireland's crown you couldn't lift the bedclothes off your arms!"

"Them hounds are in my family, seed and breed, this hundred years and more," continued old O'Reilly, silencing his sister with one black glance from under his thick grey brows, "and if I had e'er a one that was fit to come after me they'd never leave it!" He took a gulp of the hot punch. "Did ye ever hear of my brother Phil that was huntsman to the Charlevilles long ago, Mr. Knox? Your father knew him well. Many's the good hunt they rode together. He wasn't up to forty years when he was killed, broke his neck jumping a hurl, and when they went to bury him it's straight in over the churchyard wall they took him! They said he never was one to go round looking for a gate!"

"May the Lord have mercy on him!" murmured Miss O'Reilly in the background.

"Amen!" growled the old man, taking another pull at his steaming tumbler, as if he were drinking his brother's health. "And look at me here," he went on, reddening slowly through the white stubble on his cheeks, "dying as soft as any owld cow in a boghole, and all they'll be saying afther me is asking would they get their bellyful of whisky at my wake! I tell you this—and let you be listening to me, Joanna!—what hounds Mr. Knox doesn't take, I'll not leave them afther me to be disgraced in the counthry, running rabbits on Sunday afternoons with them poaching blackguards up out of the town! No! But they'll have a stone round their neck and to be thrown below in the lough!"

I thought of the nephew Luke, whose friends had so frequently failed to see him off, and I felt very sorry for old O'Reilly.

"They will, they will, to be sure!" said Miss O'Reilly soothingly, "and look at you now, the way you are! Didn't I know well you had no call to be drinking punch, you that was coughing all night. On the face of God's earth, Mr. Knox, I never heard such a cough! 'Tis like a sheep's cough! I declare it's like the sound of the beating of the drum!"

"Well, Mr. O'Reilly," said Flurry, ignoring these remarkable symptoms, but none the less playing to her lead, "I suppose we might have a look at the hounds now."

"Go, tell Tom to open the tower door," said old O'Reilly to his sister, after a moment's silence. He handed her a key. "And shut the gate you."

As soon as she had gone he got on to his feet. "Mr. Knox, sir," he said, "might I put as much trouble on you as to move out this chair to the door? I'll sit there the way I can see them. Maybe the other gentleman would reach me down the horn that's up on the wall. He's near as tall as meself."

Flurry did as he asked, and helped him across the room.

"Close out the half door if you please, Mr. Knox, and

give me the old rug that's there, my feet is destroyed with the rheumatics."

He dropped groaningly into his chair, and I handed him the horn, an old brass one, bent and dinted.

Already the clamour of the hounds in the tower had broken out like bells in a steeple, as they heard the footsteps of their jailer on the stone steps of their prison.

Then Tom's voice, shouting at them in Irish to stand back, and then through the narrow door of the tower the hounds themselves, a striving torrent of white flecked with pale yellow, like one of their own mountain streams. There were about seven couples of them, and in a moment they overran the yard like spilt quicksilver.

"Look at them now, Mr. Knox!" said their owner, "they'd take a line over the hob of hell this minute!"

Pending this feat they took a very good line into what was apparently the hen-house, judging by the hysterics that proceeded from within. Almost immediately one of them reappeared with an egg in his mouth. Old O'Reilly gave a laugh and an attempt at a holloa. "Ah ha! That's Whiteboy! The rogue!" he said, and putting the horn to his lips he blew a thin and broken note, that was cut short by a cough. Speechlessly he handed the horn to Flurry, but no further sumomns was needed; the hounds had heard him. They converged upon the doorway with a rush, and Flurry and I were put to it to keep them from jumping in over the half-door.

I had never seen hounds like them before. One or two were pure white, but most had some touch of faded yellow or pale grey about them; they were something smaller than the average foxhound, and were strongly built, and active as terriers. Their heads were broad, their ears unrounded, and their legs and feet were far from complying with the prescribed bedpost standard; but wherein, to the unprofessional eye, they chiefly differed from the established pattern was in the human lawlessness of their expression. The old hound by the fire had struggled up at the note of the horn, and stood staring in perplexity at her master, and growling, with all the arrogance of the favourite, at her descendants, who yelped, and clawed, and strove, and thrust their muzzles over the half-door.

Flurry regarded them in silence.

"There's not a straight one among them," he whispered in my ear through the din.

"There they are for you now, Mr. Knox," said old O'Reilly, still panting after his fit of coughing. "There isn't another man in Ireland would get them but yourself, and you've got them, as I might say, a present!"

Flurry and I went out into the yard, and the door was closed behind us.

The examination—I may say the cross-examination—of the hounds that followed was conducted by Flurry and Michael to the accompaniment of a saga from Tom, setting forth their miraculous merits and achievements, to which, at suitable points, the carman shouted "Selah," or words to that effect, through the bars of the gate. At the end of half an hour, Flurry had sorted out six of them; these were then coupled, and by dint of the exertions of all present, were bestowed in a cart with sides like a crate, in which pigs went to the fair.

We did not see our host again. His sister told us that he had gone to bed and wasn't fit to see anyone, but he wished Mr. Knox luck with his bargain, and he sent him this for a luck-penny. She handed Flurry the dinted horn.

"I'm thinking it's fretting after the hounds he is," she said, turning her head away to hide the tears in her brown eyes. I have never until then known Flurry completely at a loss for an answer.

PART II

A fortnight afterwards—to be precise, it was October the 10th—I saw the white hounds in the field. I had gone through the dreary routine of the cub-hunter. The alarm clock had shrilled its exulting and age-long summons in the pitchy dark. I had burnt my fingers with the spirit-lamp, and my mouth with hot cocoa; I had accomplished my bathless toilet, I had groped my way through the puddles in the stable yard, and got on to my horse by the light of a lantern, and at 5.30 a.m. I was over the worst, and had met Flurry and the hounds, with Michael and Dr. Jerome Hickey, at the appointed cross-roads. The meet was nine miles away, in a comparatively unknown land, to which Flurry had been summoned by tales of what appeared to be an absolute epidemic of foxes, accompanied by bills for poultry and threats of poison. It was still an hour before sunrise, but a pallor was in the sky, and the hounds, that had at first been like a gliding shoal of fish round the horses' feet, began to take on their own shapes and colours.

The white Irish hounds were the first to disclose themselves, each coupled up with a tried old stager. I had been away from home for the past ten days, and knew nothing of their conduct in their new quarters, and finding Flurry uncommunicative, I fell back presently to talk about them to Michael.

"Is it settling down they are?" said Michael derisively. "That's the fine settling down! Roaring and screeching every minute since they came into the place! And as for fighting! They weren't in the kennel three days before they had Rampant ate, and nothing only his paws left before me in the morning! I didn't give one night in my bed since, with running down to them. The like o' them trash isn't fit for a gentleman's kennels. Them O'Reillys had them rared very pettish; it'd be as good for me to be trying to turn curlews as them!"

The indictment of "The Whiteboys" (a title sarcastically bestowed by Dr. Hickey), their sheep-killing, their dog-hunting, with the setting forth of Michael's trials, talents, and unrequited virtues, lasted, like an Arabian Nights' tale, till the rising of the sun, and also until our arrival at the place we were first to draw. This was a long and deep ravine, red with bracken, bushy with hazel and alders; a black stream raced downwards through it, spreading at the lower end into bog, green, undefined, entirely treacherous; a place that instantly assures the rider that if the hounds get away on its farther side he will not be with them.

A couple of men were waiting for us at the lower end of the ravine.

"They're in it surely!" they said, shoving down a stone gap for our benefit; "there isn't a morning but we'll see the owld fellow and his pups funning away for themselves down by the river. My little fellows, when they does be going to school in the morning, couldn't pass his nest for the fume that'd be from it."

The first ten minutes proved that the foxes were certainly there, and during the following half-hour pandemonium itself raged in the ravine. There were, I believe, a brace and a half of cubs on foot; they were to me invisible, but they were viewed about twice in every minute by Flurry and his subordinates, and continuously by a few early rising countrymen, who had posted themselves along the edges of the ravine. The yells of the latter went up like steam whistles, and the hounds, among whom were five couple of newly entered puppies, were wilder than I had ever known them. They burst through the bracken and strove in the furze, in incessant full cry and still the cubs doubled and dodged, and made détours round the valley, and Flurry and Michael roared themselves inside out, without producing the smallest effect upon anything save their own larynges. No less than three times a fox was frantically holloaed away, and when, by incredible exertions on all our parts, the hounds, or a fair proportion of them, had been got together on to the line, a fresh outburst of yells announced that, having run a ring, he had returned to the covert.

Each of these excursions involved:
1. Scrambling at best speed down a rocky hillside.
2. Coercing a diffident horse across a noisy stream, masked by briars, out of bog, on to rock.
3. Reverse of the first proceedings.
4. Arrival, blown and heated, at the boggy end of the valley, to find the original conditions prevailing as before.

I should, perhaps, have already mentioned that I was riding a young horse, to whom I was showing hounds for the first time. My idea had been to permit him, strictly as an onlooker, to gather some idea of the rudiments of the game. He was a good young horse, with the large gravity of demeanour that is often the result of a domestic bringing up in the family of a small farmer; and when the moment came, and I was inexorably hustled into acting as third whip, he followed in the wake of Dr. Hickey with an anxious goodwill that made even his awkwardness attractive.

Throughout these excursions I noticed, as far as I was able to notice anything, the independent methods of the O'Reilly draft. They ignored the horn, eluded Michael, and laughed at Hickey and me; they hunted with bloodthirsty intentness and entirely after their own devices. Their first achievement was to run the earth-stopper's dog, and having killed him, to eat him. This horrid feat they accomplished, secure from interruption, in the briary depths of the ravine, and while the main body of the pack were industriously tow-rowing up and down the stream after their lawful fox, a couple of goats were only saved from "The Whiteboys" by miracles of agility and courage on the part of the countrymen. The best that could be said for them was that, "linking one virtue to a thousand crimes", whenever the hounds got fairly out of covert, the Whiteboys were together, and were in front.

It was about eight o'clock, and the fierce red and grey sunrise had been overridden by a regiment of stormy clouds, when one of the foxes met his fate, amid earpiercing whoops, and ecstatic comments from the onlookers who had descended from the hill-tops with the speed of ski-runners.

"Aha! that's the lad had many a fat duck under his rib!"

"He had, faith! I'l go bail 'twas him that picked me wife's fashionable cocks!"

"Well, I'm told that if ye'll see a fox taking a hen or a goose, and ye'll call to him in Irish, that he'll drop it," remarked an older man to me, as we waited while Flurry and Hickey, in their capacity of butler and footman to the hounds' repast, snatched the few remaining morsels from the elder revellers and endeavoured to force them upon the deeply reluctant young entry, who, having hunted with the innocent enthusiasm *débutante*, thought as little of the ensuing meal as the *débutante* thinks of supper at her first ball.

"I wonder why the deuce Michael can't get those Irish hounds," said Flurry, catching at the word and looking round. "I only have Lily here."

(Lily, I should say, was the romantic name of one of the Whiteboys.)

"I believe I seen a two-three of the white dogs running east a while ago," said the elderly farmer, "and they yowling!"

"They're likely killing a sheep now," murmured Hickey to me.

At the same moment I chanced to look up towards the western end of the ravine, and saw what seemed to be five seagulls gliding up a rift of grass that showed green between rocks and heather.

"There are your white hounds, Flurry," I called out, "and they're hunting."

"Well, well," said the farmer, "they're afther wheeling round the length of the valley in the minute! They're nearly able to fly!"

A distant holloa from Michael, whose head alone was visible above a forest of furze, rose like a rocket at the end of the sentence, and every hound sprang to attention.

Once more we traversed the valley at full speed, and tackled the ladder of mud that formed the cattle track up the ravine; slough up to the horses' knees, furze bushes and briars meeting over their heads and ours, hounds and country boys jostling to get forward, with pistol shots behind from Hickey's thong, and the insistent doubling of Flurry's horn in front. Up that green rift I went on foot, and, as it were, hand in hand with my admirable young horse. The rift, on closer acquaintance, proved to be green with the deceitful verdure of swampy grass (in Ireland, it may be noted, water runs uphill, and the subtlest bog holes lie in wait for their prey on the mountain tops). As we ascended, the wind that had risen with the sun fought us every inch of the way, and by the time I had won to level ground I was speechless, and blowing like the bellows of a forge. A country boy, whose grinning purple face remains a fond and imperishable memory, caught me by the leg and rammed me into my saddle; just in front of me Flurry, also speechless, with his foot not as yet in his off stirrup, was getting up to his hounds. These were casting themselves uncertainly over a sedgy and heathery slope, on which, in this wind, the hottest scent would soon be chilled to its marrow. Of Michael and the Whiteboys nothing was to be seen.

At a little distance a young man was grasping by the ears and nose a donkey with a back-load of bracken, and a misplaced ardour for the chase.

"Did ye see the fox?" bellowed Flurry.

"I did! I did!"

"Which way did he go?"

"Yerrah! aren't yer dogs after ateing him below!" shouted the young man, waltzing strenuously with the donkey.

"Well, there's a pair of you!" replied Flurry, cracking his whip viciously at the donkey's tail, and thereby much stimulating the dance, "and if I was given my choice of ye it's the ass I'd take! Here, come on out of this Hickey!" He shoved ahead. "Put those hounds on to me, can't you!"

During this interchange of amenities Lily had wandered aside, and now, far to the left of the rest of the pack, was thoughtfully nosing along through tufts of rushes; she worked her way down to a fence, and then, mute as a wraith, slid over it and slipped away across a grass field, still in jealous silence.

"Hark forrad to Lily, hounds!" roared Flurry, with electrical suddenness. "Put them on to her, Jerome!"

"Well, those white hounds are the divil!" said Dr. Hickey, with a break of admiration in his voice, as the hounds, suddenly driving ahead, proclaimed to heaven that they had got the line. They were running up a fierce north-westerly wind, and their cry came brokenly back to us through it like the fragments of the chimes through the turmoil of Tschaikowsky's "1812" symphony. The young horse began to realize that there was something

415

in it, and, with a monster and frog-like leap, flew over the ensuing heathery bank, landing, shatteringly, on all fours. We were travelling downhill, a fact that involved heavy drops, but involved also the privilege, rare for me, of seeing the hounds comfortably. Lily, leading the rest by half a field, was going great guns, so were Flurry and Hickey, so, I may say with all modesty, were the young horse and I. After an eventful and entirely satisfactory ten minutes of racing over the class of country that has, on a low average, seventeen jumps to the mile, we skated down a greasy path, and found ourselves in a deep lane, with the hounds at fault, casting themselves eagerly right and left. It was here that we came upon Michael, a dolorous spectacle, leading his mare towards us. She was dead lame.

"What happened her?" shouted Flurry through the rioting wind.

"The foot's dropping off her, sir," replied Michael, with his usual optimism.

"Well, get away home with her as quick as you can," interrupted Flurry, accepting the diagnosis with the usual discount of 90 per cent. "What way did those white hounds go?"

"The last I seen o' them they were heading west over the hill beyond for Drummig. It might be he was making for an old fort that's back in the land there behind Donovan's farm. There was a fellow driving a bread van above in the road there that told me if the hounds got inside the fort we'd never see them again. He said there were holes down in it that'd go from here to the sea."

"What the devil good were you that you didn't stop those hounds?" said Flurry, cutting short this harangue with a countenance as black as the weather. "Here, come on!" he called to Hickey and me, "the road'll be the quickest for us."

It was about a mile by the road to Donovan's farm, and as Hickey and I pounded along in the rear of the disgusted hounds, big pellets of rain were flung in our faces, and I began to realize, not for the first time, that to turn up the collar of one's coat is more of a protest than a protection.

The farmhouse of Donovan of Drummig was connected with the high road by the usual narrow and stony lane; as we neared the entrance of the lane we saw through the swirls of rain a baker's van bumping down it. There were two men on the van, and in the shafts was a raking young brown horse, who, having espied the approach of the hounds, was honouring them with what is politically known as a demonstration. One of the men held up his hand, and called out a request to "hold on awhile till they were out on to the road."

"Did you see any hounds?" shouted Flurry, holding back the hounds, as the van bounded round the corner and into the main road, with an activity rare in its species.

"We did, sir," returned the men in chorus, clinging to the rail of their knifeboard seat, like the crew of a racing yacht, "they have him back in the fort above this minute! Ye can take your time, faith!"

The van horse reared and backed, and Flurry turned in his saddle to eye him as he ramped ahead in response to a slash from the driver; so did Dr. Hickey, and so also did Lily, who, with her white nose in the air, snuffed inquisitively in the wake of the departing van.

"You'd say she knew a good one when she saw him," said Hickey as we turned the hounds into the lane.

"Or a good loaf of bread," I suggested.

"It's little bread that lad carries!" answered Hickey, thonging the reluctant Lily on; "I'll go bail there's as much bottled porter as bread in that van! He supplies half the shebeens in the country."

As we splashed into the farmyard a young man threw open a gate at its farther side, shouting to Flurry to hurry on. He waved us on across a wide field, towards a low hill or mound, red with wet withered bracken, and crested by a group of lean fir-trees, flinging their arms about in the wild gusts of wind and rain.

"The fox wasn't the length of himself in front of them!" shouted the young man, running beside us, "and

417

he as big as a donkey! The whole kit of them is inside in the fort together!'"

Flurry turned his horse suddenly.

'Two and a half couple underground is enough for one while," he said, riding back into the farmyard. "Have you any place I could shove these hounds into?"

The door of a cow-house was open, and as if in anticipation of his wishes, the hounds jostled emulously into the darkness within. Again, guided by the young man, we faced the storm and rain. What Flurry's intentions were we neither knew nor dared to ask, and, as we followed him over the soaked fields, a back more expressive of profound and wrathful gloom it has never been my lot to contemplate.

The place in which the fox and the Irish hounds had entombed themselves was one of the prehistoric earthen fortresses that abound in the south-west of Ireland. The fort at Drummig was like a giant flat-topped molehill; the spadework of a forgotten race had turned it into a place of defence, and, like moles, they had burrowed into its depths. The tongue of the young man who guided us did not weary in the recital of the ways, and the passages, and the little rooms that were within in it. He said that a calf belonging to himself was back in it for a week, and she came out three times fatter than the day she went in. He also, but with a certain diffidence, mentioned fairies.

Round and about this place of mystery went Flurry, blowing long and dreary blasts at the mouths of its many holes, uttering "Gone away" screeches, of a gaiety deplorably at variance with his furious countenance. A more pessimistic priest never trumpeted round the walls of a more impracticable Jericho.

Hickey led the dripping horses to and fro in the lee of the fort, and I was deputed to listen at a rabbit hole from which the calf was said to have emerged. After a period of time which I was too much deadened by misery to compute, Flurry appeared, and told me that he was going home. Judging from his appearance, he had himself been to ground; what he said about the white hounds

418

and the weather was very suitable, but would not read as well as it sounded.

We returned to the farmyard with the wind and rain chivying us from behind.

"I asked a man, one time," said Dr. Hickey, as side by side, and at a well-maintained distance, we followed our leader across the field, "why his father had committed suicide, and he said, 'well, your honour, it was an ease like for his temper'. I'm thinking, Major, it'd be no harm for us to keep an eye on Flurry."

I stooped my head to let the water flow out of the brim of my hat.

"You needn't neglect me either," I said.

While Hickey was getting the hounds out of the cow-house, my young horse shivered with cold, and gave an ominous cough. I reflected upon the twelve long miles that lay between him and home, and asked our saturated guide if I could get a warm drink for him. There was no difficulty about that; to be sure I could and welcome. I abandoned my comrades; regret, if it were felt, was not expressed by Flurry. When the hounds had paddled forth from the cow-house I put my horse into it, and before they had accomplished half a mile of their direful progress, I was standing with my back to a glowing turf fire, with my coat hanging on a chair, and a cup of scalding tea irradiating the inmost recesses of my person.

My hostess, Mrs. Jeremiah Donovan, was a handsome young woman, tall, fair, and flushed, agonized with hospitality, shy to ferocity. The family dog was lifted from the heart with a side kick worthy of an international football match; her offspring, clustered, staring, in the chimney-corner, were dispersed with a scorching whisper, of which the words, "ye brazen tinkers", gave some clue to its general trend. Having immured them in an inner room she withdrew, muttering something about another "goleen o' turf", and I was left alone with an excellent cake of soda-bread and two boiled eggs.

Presently a slight and mouse-like rattle made me aware that one of the offspring, aged about five, had escaped from captivity, and was secretly drawing my whip to him along the floor by the thong.

"What have ye the whip for?" said the offspring, undaunted by discovery.

"To bate the dogs with," I replied, attuning my speech to his as best I could.

"Is it the big white dogs?" pursued the offspring.

I paused midway in a mouthful of soda-bread.

"Did you see the white dogs?" I asked very gently.

"God knows I did!" said the offspring, warming to his work, "an' they snapped the bit o' bread out of Joola's hand within the cow-house! And Joola said they were a fright!"

I sat still and waited while one might count five, fearful of scaring the bird that had perched so near me.

"Are the white dogs here now?" I ventured, wooingly.

"They are not."

The crook of my crop was beginning to prove dangerously engrossing, and the time was short.

"Where did they go?" I persevered.

"Jimmy Mahony and me uncle Lukey took them away in the van," said the offspring with clearness and simplicity, slashing with my whip at a member of the guild of Brazen Tinkers whom I assumed to be the already injured Julia.

As I bestowed at parting a benefaction upon Jeremiah Donovan, I said that I hoped he would let Mr. Knox know if any of the white hounds came out of the fort. He assured me that he would do so. He was, like his wife, a thoroughly good fellow, and he had wisped the young horse until one would have said he had never been out of the stable.

The storm had blown itself away, and the rain was nearly over. I rode home quietly, and in peace and good-will towards all men; after all, there was no hurry. This was a thing that was going to last me for the rest of my life, and Flurry's.

I overtook Michael on the way home. Michael said that sure he knew all through it was a drag, and if Mr. Flurry had been said by him, he'd have had neither cut, shuffle, nor deal with them O'Reillys. In the course

420

of his life Michael has never been known to be in the wrong.

Dr. Hickey told me (but this was some time afterwards) that often he had to get out of his bed to laugh when he thought of Flurry getting Jeremiah Donovan to screech in Irish down the holes in the fort, for fear old O'Reilly's hounds had no English. It is hardly necessary to say that Dr. Hickey also had been convinced by the way the hounds ran that it was a drag, but had omitted to mention the fact at the time.

Flurry was lost to home and country for three days. It was darkly said that he had gone to Fahoura to break every bone in young O'Reilly's body, and, incidentally, to bring back the white hounds. At the end of the three days he telegraphed for a man and a saddle to meet the afternoon train. There was nothing in the telegram about hounds. Next day I met him riding a young brown horse, with a wildish eye, and a nasty rub from a misfitting collar.

"I got him in a sort of a swap," said Flurry tranquilly.

"I suppose he got that rub in the bread-van?" I remarked drawing a bow at a venture.

"Well, that might be, too," assented Flurry, regarding me with an eye that was like a stone wall with broken glass on the top.

THE AUSSOLAS MARTIN CAT

Flurry Knox and I had driven some fourteen miles to a tryst with one David Courtney, of Fanaghy. But, at the appointed cross-roads, David Courtney was not. It was a gleaming morning in mid-May, when everything was young and tense and thin and fit to run for its life, like a Derby horse. Above us was such of the spacious bare country as we had not already climbed, with nothing on it taller than a thorn-bush from one end of it to the other. The hill-top blazed with yellow furze, and great silver balls of cloud looked over its edge. Nearly as white were the little white-washed houses that were tucked in and out of the grey rocks on the hillside.

"It's up there somewhere he lives," said Flurry, turning his cart across the road; "which'll you do, hold the horse or go look for him?"

I said I would go to look for him. I mounted the hill by a wandering bohireen resembling nothing so much as a series of bony elbows; a white-washed cottage presently confronted me, clinging, like a sea-anemone, to a rock. I knocked at the closed door, I tapped at a window held up by a great, speckled foreign shell, but without success. Climbing another elbow, I repeated the process at two successive houses, but without avail. All was as deserted as Pompeii, and, as at Pompeii, the live rock in the road was worn smooth by feet and scarred with wheel tracks.

An open doorway faced me; I stooped beneath its lintel and asked of seeming vacancy if there were "anyone inside". There was no reply. I advanced into a clean kitchen, with a well-swept earthen floor, and was suddenly aware of a human presence very close to me.

A youngish woman, with a heavy mop of dark hair, and brown eyes staring at the opposite wall, was sitting at the end of a settle behind the door. Every bit of her was trembling. She looked past me as if I did not exist. Feeling uncertain as to whether she or I were mad, I put to her my question as to where David Courtney lived, without much expectation of receiving an answer.

Still shaking from head to foot, and without turning her eyes, she replied:

"A small piece to the north. The house on the bare rock."

The situation showed no symptom of expansion; I faltered thanks to her profile and returned to Flurry.

The house of David Courtney produced David Courtney's large and handsome wife, who told us that Himself was gone to a funeral, and all that was in the village was gone to it, but there was a couple of the boys below in the bog.

"What have they done with those cubs?" asked Flurry.

Mrs. Courtney shot at him a dark-blue side-glance, indulgent and amused, and, advancing to the edge of her rock terrace, made a trumpet of her hands and projected a long call down the valley.

"Mikeen! Con! Come hither!"

From a brown patch in the green below came a far-away response, and we presently saw two tall lads coming towards us, running up the hill as smoothly and easily as a couple of hounds. Their legs were bare and stained with bog-mould, they were young and light and radiant as the May weather.

I did not withhold my opinion of them from their proprietor.

"Why, then, I have six more as good as them!" replied Mrs. Courtney, her hands on her hips.

We took the horse from the shafts and pushed him, deeply suspicious, into a darksome lair, in one corner of which glimmered a pale object, either pig or calf. When this was done we followed Mikeen and Con up through blossoming furze and blue-grey rock to the ridge of the hill, and there came face to face with the vast blue dazzle of the Atlantic, with a long line of cliffs standing it off, in snowy lather, as far as eye could follow them into the easterly haze.

"That's the cliff over-right you now," said one of the boys, pointing downwards, with a hand dark with bog-stuff, to a grey and green wedge thrust out into the blue. "It's there where she have her den. She have a pat' down for herself in it—it's hardly a bird could walk it—the five pups was following her, and two o' them rolled down into the strand, and our dogs held them. Ourselves was below in the cove gathering seaweed."

"Make a note of it now, Major," said Flurry, "and if ever you see hounds pointing this way, don't spare spurs to get to the cliff before them!"

"Why don't you get them out and blow up the place?"

"Is it get them out of that hole!" said one of the boys. "If all the foxes in Europe was inside in it you couldn't get them out!"

"We mightn't want them either," said Flurry, his eye

ranging the face of the cliff, and assimilating its uncompromising negations.

"Then there's plenty that would!" returned Mikeen, looking at us with an eye as blue and bright as the sea. "There was a man east here that cot a fox and her five young ones in the one night, and he got three half-crowns for every lad o' them!"

"He'd be turned out of hell for doing that," said Flurry, very severely.

We went back to the cottage on the rock, and the matter entered upon its more serious phase. I took no part in the negotiations, and employed myself in converse with Mrs. Courtney, who—it may not be out of place to recall—informed me, amongst other domestic details, that the farm wouldn't carry all the children she had, and that nowadays, when the ger'rls would be going to America, it's white nightdresses and flannelette nightdresses she should give them; and further, that she thought, if she lived to be as old as a goat, she'd never see them so tasty.

On the way home I asked Flurry what he was going to do with the two cubs, now immured in a market basket under the seat of the dog-cart.

Flurry was ambiguous and impenetrable; there were certain matters in which Flurry trusted nobody, knowing the darkness of his own heart and the inelasticity of other people's points of view.

"That woman, you know, that told you the way," he remarked, with palpable irrelevance, " 'Kitty the Shakes', they call her—they say she mightn't speak to anyone once in three months, and she shakes that way then. It's a pity that was the house you went into first."

"Why so?" said I.

"That's the why!" said Flurry.

It was during the week following this expedition that Philippa and I stayed for a few days at Aussolas, where Flurry and Mrs. Flurry were now more or less permanently in residence. The position of guest in old Mrs. Knox's house was one often fraught with more than the normal anxieties proper to guests. Her mood

424

was like the weather, a matter incalculable and beyond control; it governed the day, and was the *leitmotif* in the affairs of the household. I hope that it may be given to me to live until my mood also is as a dark tower full of armed men.

On the evening of our arrival my wife, whose perception of danger is comparable only to that of the wild elephant, warned me that Mrs. Knox was rheumatic, and that I was on no account to condole with her. Later on the position revealed itself. Mrs. Knox's Dublin doctor had ordered her to Buxton with as little delay as possible; furthermore, she was to proceed to Brighton for the summer, possibly for the winter also. She had put Aussolas on a house agent's books, "out of spite", Flurry said sourly; "I suppose she thinks I'd pop the silver, or sell the feather beds."

It was a tribute to Mrs. Knox's character that her grandson treated her as a combatant in his own class, and did not for an instant consider himself bound to allow her weight for either age or sex.

At dinner that night Mrs. Knox was as favourable to me as usual; yet it was pointed out to me by Mrs. Flurry that she was wearing two shawls instead of one, always an indication to be noted as a portent of storm. At bridge she played a very sharp-edged game, in grimness scarcely mitigated by two well-brought-off revokes on the part of Philippa, who was playing with Flurry; a gross and unprincipled piece of chivalry on my wife's part that was justly resented by Mr. Knox.

Next morning the lady of the house was invisible, and Mullins, her maid, was heard to lament to an unknown sympathizer on the back stairs that the divil in the wild woods wouldn't content her.

In the grove at Aussolas, on a height behind the castle, romantically named Mount Ida, there is a half-circle of laurels that screens, with pleasing severity, an ancient bench and table of stone. The spot commands a fair and far prospect of Aussolas Lake, and, nearer at hand, it permitted a useful outlook upon the kitchen garden and its affairs. When old Mrs. Knox first led me thither to admire the view, she mentioned that it was a place to which she often repaired when the cook was on her trail with inquiries as to what the servants were to have for dinner.

Since our expedition to Fanaghy the glory of the weather had remained unshaken, and each day there was a shade of added warmth in the sunshine and a more caressing quality in the wind. Flurry and I went to Petty Sessions in the morning, and returned to find that Mrs. Knox was still in her room, and that our respective wives were awaiting us with a tea-basket in the classic shades of Mount Ida. Mrs. Knox had that mysterious quality of attraction given to some persons, and some dogs, of forming a social vortex into which lesser beings inevitably swim; yet I cannot deny that her absence induced a sneaking sensation of holiday. Had she been there, for example. Mrs. Flurry would scarcely have indicated, with a free gesture, the luxuriance of the asparagus beds in the kitchen garden below, nor promised to have a bundle of it cut for us before we went home; still less would she and Philippa have smoked cigarettes, a practice considered by Mrs. Knox to be, in women, several degrees worse than drinking.

To us there, through the green light of young beech leaves and the upstriking azure glare of myriads of bluebells, came the solid presence of John Kane. It would be hard to define John Kane's exact status at Aussolas; Flurry had once said that, whether it was the house, or the garden, or the stables, whatever it'd be that you wanted to do, John Kane'd be in it before you to hinder you; but that had been in a moment of excusable irritation, when John Kane had put a padlock on the oat loft, and had given the key to Mrs. Knox.

John Kane now ascended to us, and came to a standstill, with his soft black hat in his hands; it was dusty, so were his boots, and the pockets of his coat bulked large. Among the green drifts and flakes of the pale young beech leaves his bushy beard looked as red as a squirrel's tail.

"I have the commands here, Master Flurry," he began, "and it's to yourself I'd sooner give them. As for them ger'rls that's inside in the kitchen, they have every pup

426

in the place in a thrain at the back door, and, if your tobacco went asthray, it's me that would be blemt."

"The commands"—i.e. some small parcels—were laid on the stone table, minor pockets yielded an assortment of small moneys that were each in turn counted and placed in heaps by their consort parcels.

"And as for the bottle the misthress wrote down for me," said John Kane, his eye rounding up his audience like a sheep-dog, "I got me 'nough with the same bottle. But sure them's the stupidest people in Hennessy's! 'Twas to Hennessy himself I gave the misthress's paper, and he was there looking at it for a while. 'What have she in it?' says he to me. 'How would I know,' says I, 'me that have no learning?' He got the spy-glass to it then, and 'twas shortly till all was in the shop was gethered in it looking at it. 'Twould take an expairt to read it!' says one fella——"

'True for him!" said Flurry.

"—'She have it written in Latin!' says Hennessy. 'Faith she's able to write it that way, or anny other way for yee!' says I. 'Well, I'll tell ye now what ye'll do,' says Hennessy. 'There's a boy in the Medical Hall, and he's able to read all languages. Show it to him,' says he. I showed it then to the boy in the Medical Hall. Sure, the very minute he looked at it—'Elliman's Embrocation', says he." John Kane waved his hand slightly to one side; his gestures had throughout been supple and restrained. "Sure them's the stupidest people in Hennessy's!"

My sympathies were with the house of Hennessy; I, too, had encountered Mrs. Knox's handwriting, and realized the high imaginative and deductive qualities needed in its interpreter. No individual word was decipherable, but, with a bold reader, groups could be made to conform to a scheme based on probabilites.

"You can tell the mistress what they were saying at Hennessy's about her," said Flurry.

"I will, your honour," replied John, accepting the turn in the conversation as easily as a skilful motorist changes gear. "I suppose you'll have a job for me at Tory Lodge when I get the sack from the misthress?"

"No, but they tell me I'm to be put on the Old Age Pension Committee," returned Flurry, "and I might get a chance to do something for you if you'd give over dyeing that beard you have."

"I'm sorry to say it's the Almighty is dyeing my beard for me, sir," replied John Kane, fingering a grey streak on his chin, "and I think He's after giving yourself a touch, too!" He glanced at the side of Flurry's head, and his eye travelled on to mine. There was an almost flagrant absence of triumph in it.

He put aside a beechen bough with his hand; "I'll leave the things on the hall table for you, sir," he said, choosing the perfect moment for departure, and passed out of sight. The bough swung into place behind him; it was like an exit in a pastoral play.

"She never told me about the embrocation," said Sally, leaning back against the mossed stones of the bench and looking up into the web of branches. "She never will admit that she's ill."

"Poor old Mrs. Knox!" said Philippa compassionately, "I thought she looked so ill last night when she was playing bridge. Such a tiny fragile thing, sitting wrapped up in that great old chair——"

Philippa is ineradicably romantic, yet my mind, too, dwelt upon the old autocrat lying there, ill and undefeated, in the heart of her ancient fortress.

"Fragile!" said Flurry, "you'd best not tell her that. With my grand-mother no one's ill till they're dead, and no one's dead till they're buried!"

Away near the house the peacock uttered his defiant screech, a note of exclamation that seemed entirely appropriate to Aussolas; the turkey-cock in the yard accepted the challenge with effusion, and from further away the voice of Mrs. Knox's Kerry bull, equally instant in taking offence, ascended the gamut of wrath from growl to yell. Blended with these voices was another— a man's voice, in loud harangue, advancing down the long beech walk to the kitchen garden. As it approached, the wood-pigeons bolted in panic, with distracted clappings of wings, from the tall firs by the garden wall in which they were wont to sit arranging plans of campaign with regard to the fruit. We sat in tense silence. The latch of the garden gate clicked, and the voice said in stentorian tones:

"—My father 'e kept a splendid table!"

"I hear wheels!" breathed Sally Knox.

A hawthorn tree and a laburnum tree leaned over the garden gate, and from beneath their canopy of cream and pale gold there emerged the bath-chair of Mrs. Knox, with Mrs. Knox herself seated in it. It was propelled by Mullins—even at that distance the indignation of Mullins was discernible—and it progressed up the central path. Beside it walked the personage whose father had kept a splendid table. Parenthetically it may be observed that he did credit to it.

"Glory be to Moses! Look at my grandmother!" said Flurry under his breath. "How fragile she is! Who the dickens has she got hold of?"

"He thinks she's deaf, anyhow," said Sally.

"That's where he makes the mistake!" returned Flurry.

"I don't see your glawss, Mrs. Knox," shouted the stout gentleman.

"That's very possible," replied the incisive and slightly cracked voice of Mrs. Knox, "because the little that is left of it is in the mortar on the wall, to keep thieves out, which it fails to do."

The pair passed on, and paused, still in high converse, at the asparagus beds; Mullins, behind the bath-chair, wiped her indignant brow.

"You'll go home without the asparagus," whispered Flurry, "she has every stick of it counted by now!"

They moved on, heading for the further gate of the garden.

"I'll bet a sovereign he's come after the house!" Flurry continued, following the *cortège* with a malevolent eye.

Later, when we returned to the house, we found a motor-bicycle, dusty and dwarfish, standing beside the hall door steps. Within was the sound of shouting. It was then half-past seven.

"Is it possible that she's keeping him for dinner?" said Sally.

"Take care he's not staying for the night!" said Flurry. "Look at the knapsack he has on the table!"

"There's only one room he can possibly have," said Mrs. Flurry, with a strange and fixed gaze at her lord, "and that's the James the Second room. The others are cleared for the painters."

"Oh, that will be all right," replied her lord, easily.

When I came down to dinner I found the new arrival planted on his short, thick legs in front of the fireplace, still shouting at Mrs. Knox, who, notwithstanding the sinister presence of the two shawls of ill omen, was listening with a propitious countenance. She looked very tired, and I committed the *gaucherie* of saying I was sorry to hear she had not been well.

"Oh, that was nothing!" said Mrs. Knox, with a wave of her tiny, sunburnt, and bediamonded hand. "I've shaken that off, 'like dewdrops from the lion's mane!' This is Mr. Tebbutts, from—er—England, Major Yeates."

Mr. Tebbutts, after a bewildered stare, presumably in search of the lion, proclaimed his gratification at meeting me, in a voice that might have been heard in the stable yard.

At dinner the position developed apace. The visitor was, it appeared, the representative of a patriarchal family, comprising samples of all the relationships mentioned in the table of affinities, and *fortissimo*, and at vast length, he laid down their personal histories and their various requirements. It was pretty to see how old Mrs. Knox, ill as she looked, and suffering as she undoubtedly was, mastered the bowling .

Did the Tebbutts ladies exact bathing for their young? The lake supplied it.

("It's all mud and swallow-holes!" said Flurry in an audible aside.)

Did the brothers demand trout fishing? the schoolboys rabbit shooting? the young ladies lawn tennis and society?—all were theirs, especially the latter. "My grandson and his wife will be within easy reach in their own house, Tory Lodge!"

430

The remark about the swallow-holes had not been lost upon the Lady of the Lake.

Mrs. Knox had her glass of port at dessert, an act equivalent to snapping her rheumatic fingers in our faces, and withdrew, stiff but erect, and still on the best of terms with her prospective tenant. As I held the door open for her, she said to me:

" 'Twas whispered in heaven, 'twas muttered in hell'."

By an amazing stroke of luck I was enabled to continue:

" 'And echo caught softly the sound as it fell!' " with a glance at Mr. Tebbutts that showed I was aware the quotation was directed at his missing aspirates.

As the door closed, the visitor turned to Flurry and said impressively:

"There's just one thing, Mr. Knox, I should like to mention, if you will allow me. Are the drains quite in order?"

"God knows," said Flurry, pulling hard at a badly lighted cigarette and throwing himself into a chair by the turf fire.

Mrs. Knox's health has held out against them for about sixty years," I remarked.

"Well, as to that," replied Mr. Tebbutts, "I feel it is only right to mention that the dear old lady was very giddy with me in the garden this afternoon."

Flurry received this remarkable statement without emotion.

"Maybe she's taken a fancy to you!" he said brutally. "If it wasn't that it was whipped cream."

Mr. Tebbutts' bulging eyes sought mine in complete mystification; I turned to the fire, and to it revealed my emotions. Flurry was not at all amused.

"Well—er—I understood her maid to say she 'ad bin ailing," said the guest after a pause. "I'd have called it a kind of megrim myself, and, as I say, I certainly perceived a sort of charnel-'ouse smell in the room I'm in. And look 'ere, Mr. Knox, 'ere's another thing. 'Ow about rats? You know what ladies are; there's one of my sisters-in-law, Mrs. William Tebbutts, who'd just scream

431

the 'ouse down if she 'eard the 'alf of what was goin' on behind the panelling in my room this evening."

"Anyone that's afraid of rats had better keep out of Aussolas," said Flurry, getting up with a yawn.

"Mr. Tebbutts is in the James the Second room, isn't he?" and I, idly. "Isn't that the room with the powdering-closet off it?"

"It is," said Flurry. "Anything else you'd like to know?"

I recognized that someone had blundered, presumably myself, and made a move for the drawing-room.

Mrs. Knox had retired when we got there; my wife and Mrs. Flurry followed suit as soon as might be; and the guest said that, if the gentlemen had no objection, he thought he'd turn in too.

Flurry and I shut the windows—fresh air is a foible of the female sex—heaped turf on the fire, drew up chairs in front of it, and composed ourselves for that sweetest sleep of all, the sleep that has in it the bliss of abandonment, and is made almost passionate by the deep underlying knowledge that it can be but temporary.

How long we had slumbered I cannot say; it seemed but a moment when a door opened in our dreams, and the face of Mr. Tebbutts was developed before me in the air like the face of the Cheshire cat, only without the the grin.

"Mr. Knox! Gentlemen!" he began, as if he were addressing a meeting. The thunder had left his voice; he stopped to take breath. He was in his shirt and trousers, and the laces of his boots trailed on the floor behind him. "I've 'ad a bit of a start upstairs. I was just winding up my watch at the dressing-table when I saw some kind of an animal gloide past the fireplace and across the room——"

"What was it like?" interrupted Flurry, sitting up in his chair.

"Well, Mr. Knox, it's 'ard to say what it was like. It wasn't a cat, nor yet it wasn't what you could call a squirrel——"

Flurry got on to his feet.

"By the living Jingo!" he said, turning to me an

432

awestruck countenance; "he's seen the Aussolas Martin Cat!"

I had never before heard of the Aussolas Martin Cat, and it is indisputable that a slight chill crept down my backbone.

Mr. Tebbutts' eyes bulged more than ever, and his lower lip fell.

"What way did it go?" said Flurry; "did it look at you?"

"It seemed to disappear in that recess by the door," faltered the seer of the vision; "it just vanished!"

"I don't know if it's for my grandmother or for me," said Flurry in a low voice, "but it's a death in the house anyway."

The colour in Mr. Tebbutts' face deepened to a glossy sealing-wax red.

"If one of you gents would come upstairs with me," he said, "I think I'll just get my traps together. I can be back at the 'otel in 'alf an 'our——"

Flurry and I accompanied Mr. Tebbutts to the James the Second room. Over Mrs. Knox's door there were panes of glass, and light came forth from them. (It is my belief that Mrs. Knox never goes to bed.) We trod softly as we passed it, and went along the uncarpeted boards of the musicians' gallery, above the entrance hall.

There certainly was a peculiar odour in the James the Second room, and the adjective "charnel-'ouse" had not been misapplied.

I thought about a dead rat, and decided that the apparition had been one of the bandit tribe of tawny cats that inhabited the Aussolas stables. And yet legends of creatures that haunted old houses and followed old families came back to me; of one in particular, a tale of medieval France, wherein "a yellow furry animal" ran down the throat of a sleeping lady named Sagesse.

Mr. Tebbutts, by this time fully dressed, was swiftly bestowing a brush and comb in his knapsack. Perhaps he too had read the legend about Madame Sagesse. Flurry was silently, and with a perturbed countenance, examining the room; rapping at the panelling and

433

peering up the cavernous chimney; I heard him sniff as he did so. Possibly he also held the dead-rat theory. He opened the flap in the door of the powdering-closet, and, striking a match, held it through the opening. I looked over his shoulder, and had a glimpse of black feathers on the floor, and a waft of a decidedly "charnel-'ouse" nature.

"Damn!" muttered Flurry to himself, and slammed down the flap.

"I think, sir," said Mr. Tebbutts, with his knapsack in his hand and his cap on his head, "I must ask you to let Mrs. Knox know that this 'ouse won't suit Mrs. William Tebbutts. You might just say I was called away rather sudden. Of course, you won't mention what I saw just now—I wouldn't wish to upset the pore old lady——"

We followed him from the room, and treading softly as before, traversed the gallery, and began to descend the slippery oak stairs. Flurry was still looking furtively about him, and the thought crossed my mind that in the most hard-headed Irishman there wanders a vein of superstition.

Before we had reached the first landing, the violent ringing of a handbell broke forth in the room with the light over the door, followed by a crash of fire-irons; then old Mrs. Knox's voice called imperatively for Mullins.

There was a sound of rushing, slippered feet, a bumping of furniture; with a squall from Mullins the door flew open, and I was endowed with a never-to-be-forgotten vision of Mrs. Knox, swathed in hundreds of shawls, in the act of hurling the tongs at some unseen object.

Almost simultaneously there was a scurry of claws on the oak floor above us, Mrs. Knox's door was slammed, and something whizzed past me. I am thankful to think that I possess, as a companion vision to that of Mrs. Knox, the face of Mr. Tebbutts with the candlelight on it as he looked up from the foot of the stairs and saw the Aussolas Martin Cat in his track.

"Look out, Tebbutts!" yelled Flurry. "It's you he's after!"

Mr. Tebbutts here passed out of the incident into the night, and the Aussolas Martin Cat was swallowed up by a large hole in the surbase in the corner of the first landing.

'He'll come out in the wine-cellar," said Flurry, with the calm that was his in moments of crisis, "the way the cat did."

I pulled myself together.

"What's happened to the other Fanaghy cub?" I inquired with, I hope, equal calmness.

"He's gone to blazes," replied Flurry; "there isn't a wall in this house that hasn't a way in it. I knew I'd never have luck with them after you asking the way from Kitty the Shakes."

As is usual in my dealings with Flurry, the fault was mine.

While I reflected on this, the stillness of the night was studded in a long diminishing line by the running pant of the motor-bicycle.

THE FINGER OF MRS. KNOX

A being stood in a dark corner under the gallery of the hall at Aussolas Castle; a being who had arrived noiselessly on bare feet, and now revealed its presence by hard breathing.

"Come in, Mary," comanded old Mrs. Knox without turning her head; "make up the fire."

"I will, ma'am," murmured the being, advancing with an apologetic eye upon me, and an undulating gait suggestive of a succession of incipient curtsies.

She was carrying an armful of logs, and, having stacked them on the fire in a heap calculated to set alight any chimney less roomy than the Severn Tunnel, she retired by way of the open hall door with the same deferential stealth with which she had entered.

"The hen-woman," explained Mrs. Knox casually, "the only person in this place who knows a dry log from a wet one."

Like all successful rulers, Mrs. Knox had the power of divining in her underlings their special gifts, and of wresting them to the sphere in which they shone, no matter what their normal functions might be. She herself pervaded all spheres.

"There's no pie but my grandmother has a finger in it," was Flurry Knox's epitome of these high qualities; a sour tribute from one freebooter to another.

"If the mistress want a thing she mus' have it!" was the comment of John Kane, the gamekeeper, as he threw down the spade with which he was digging out a ferret, and armed himself with a holly-bush wherewith to sweep the drawing-room chimney.

As Mrs. Knox and I sat by the hen-woman's noble fire, and gossiped, the cook panted in with the tea-tray; the butler, it appeared, had gone out to shoot a rabbit for dinner. All these things pointed to the fact that Mrs. Knox's granddaughter-in-law, Mrs. Flurry, was not, at the moment, in residence at Aussolas. The Jungle was creeping in; Sally Knox, by virtue, I suppose, of her English mother, spasmodically endeavoured to keep it out, but with her departure the Wild triumphed.

It was an October afternoon, grey and still; the hall door stood open, as indeed it always did at Aussolas, and on the topmost of the broad limestone steps Mrs. Knox's white woolly dog sat, and magisterially regarded lake and wood and lawn. The tawny bracken flowed like a sea to the palings that bounded the lawn; along its verge squatted the rabbits, motionless for the most part, sometimes languidly changing their ground, with hops like the dying efforts of a mechanical toy. The woolly dog had evidently learned in many fruitless charges the futility of frontal attack; a close and menacing supervision from the altitude of the steps was all that was consistent with dignity, but an occasional strong shudder betrayed his emotion. The open door framed also a pleasing view of my new car, standing in beautiful repose at the foot of the steps, splashed with the mud of a twenty-mile run

436

from an outlying Petty Sessions Court; her presence added, for me, the touch of romance.

It was twilight in the back of the hall by the fireplace; the flames of the logs, branching like antlers, made a courteous and not too searching inquisition into dark corners, and lighted with a very suitable evasiveness Mrs. Knox's Witch of Endor profile. She wore her usual velvet bonnet; the rest of her attire recalled to my memory the summary of it by her kinswoman, Lady Knox, "A rag bag held together by diamond brooches". Yet, according to her wont, her personality was the only thing that counted; it reduced all externals to a proper insignificance.

The object of my visit had ostensibly been to see her grandson, but Flurry was away for the night.

"He's sleeping at Tory Lodge," said Mrs. Knox. "He's cubbing at Drumvoortneen, and he has to start early. He tried to torment me into allowing him to keep the hounds in the yard here this season, but I had the pleasure of telling him that old as I might be, I still retained possession of my hearing, my sense of smell, and, to a certain extent, of my wits."

"I should have thought," I said discreetly, "that Tory Lodge was more in the middle of his country."

"Undoubtedly," replied Flurry's grandmother; "but it is not in the middle of my straw, my meal, my buttermilk, my firewood, and anything else of mine that can be pilfered for the uses of a kennel!" She concluded with a chuckle that might have been uttered by a scald-crow.

I was pondering a diplomatic reply, when the quiet evening was rent by a shrill challenge from the woolly dog.

"Thy sentinel am I!" he vociferated, barking himself backwards into the hall, in proper strategic retreat upon his base.

A slow foot ascended the steps, and the twilight in the hall deepened as a man's figure appeared in the doorway; a middle-aged man, with his hat in one hand, and in the other a thick stick, with which he was making respectfully intimidating demonstrations to the woolly dog.

437

"Who are you?" called out Mrs. Knox from her big chair.

"I'm Casey, your ladyship," replied the visitor in a deplorable voice, "from Killoge."

"Cornelius Casey?" queried Mrs. Knox.

"No, but his son, your Honour ma'am, Stephen Casey, one of the tenants."

"Well, come in, Stephen," said Mrs. Knox affably, supplementing her spectacles with a gold-rimmed single eyeglass, and looking at him with interest. "I knew your father well in old times, when he used to stop the earths in Killoge Wood for the Colonel. They tell me that's all cut down now?"

"There's not the boiling of a kettle left in it afther Goggin, my lady!" said Casey eagerly. Mrs. Knox cut him short.

"Many a good hunt the Colonel had out of Killoge, and I too, for the matter of that!" she added, turning to me; "my cousin Bessie Hamilton and I were the only huntresses in the country in those days, and people thought us shocking tomboys, I believe. Now, what with driving motors and riding astride, the gentlemen are all ladies, and the ladies are gentlemen!"

With another scald-crow chuckle she turned to Casey. "Did your father ever tell you of the great hunt out of Killoge into the Fanaghy cliffs?"

"He did, your ladyship, he did!" responded Casey, with a touch of life in his lamentable voice. "Often he told me that it knocked fire from his eyes to see yourself facing in at the Killoge river."

"I was riding Bijou, the grandmother of old Trinket, in that run," said Mrs. Knox, leaning back in her chair, with a smile that had something of the light of other days in it.

I remembered the story that Colonel Knox had run away with her after a hunt, and wondered if that had been the occasion when she had knocked fire from the eyes of Cornelius Casey.

Her thin old hand drooped in momentary languor over the arm of her chair; and the woolly dog thrust his nose under it, with a beady eye fixed upon the hot cakes.

"Here!" said Mrs. Knox, sitting up, and throwing a buttery bun on the floor. "Be off with you! Well, Casey," she went on, "what is it you want with me?"

"Great trouble I got, Mrs. Knox, your Honour ma'am," replied Casey from the door-mat, "great trouble entirely." He came a step or two nearer. He had a long, clean-shaved face, with mournful eyes like a sick blood-hound, and the enviable, countryman's thatch of thick, strong hair, with scarcely a touch of grey in it.

"That Goggin, that has the shop at Killoge Cross, has me processed. I'm pairsecuted with him; and the few little bastes I has, and me donkey and all——" his voice thinned to a whimper, "he's to drive them to-morrow ——"

"I suppose that's Goggin, the Gombeen?" said Mrs. Knox; "how were you fool enough to get into dealings with him?"

The statement of Casey's wrongs occupied quite ten minutes, and was generous in detail. His land was bad, ever and always. The grass that was in it was as bare as that you could pick pins in it. He had no pushing land at all for cattle. Didn't he buy a heifer at Skebawn fair and the praisings she got was beyant all raves, and he had her one month, and kinder company he never had, and she giving seven pints at every meal, and wasn't that the divil's own produce? One month, indeed, was all he had her till she got a dropsy, and the dropsy supported her for a while, and when it left her she faded away. And didn't his wife lose all her hens in one week?" They fell dead on her like hailstones!" He ceased, and a tear wandered down the channels in his long cheek.

"How much do you owe Goggin?" asked Mrs. Knox sharply.

What Casey owed to Goggin had, as might have been expected, but a remote relation to the sum that Goggin was now endeavouring to extract from Casey. At the heart of the transaction was a shop account, complicated by loans of single pounds (and in my mind's eye I could see, and with my mind's nose I could smell, the dirty crumpled notes). It was further entangled by per-contra accounts of cribs of turf, scores of eggs, and a day's work now and again. I had, from the judgement seat, listened to many such recitals, so, apparently, had Mrs. Knox, judging by the ease with which she straightened Casey's devious narrative at critical points, and shepherded him to his facts, like a cunning old collie steering a sheep to its pen. The conclusion of the matter was that Goggin was, on the morrow, to take possession of Casey's remaining stock, consisting of three calves, a donkey, and a couple of goats, in liquidation of a debt of £15, and that he, Stephen Casey, knew that Mrs. Knox would never be satisfied to see one of her own tenants wronged.

"I have no tenants," replied Mrs. Knox tartly; "the Government is your landlord now, and I wish you joy of each other!"

"Then I wish to God it was yourself we had in it again!" lamented Stephen Casey; "it was better for us when the gentry was managing their own business. They'd *give* patience, and they'd *have* patience."

"Well, that will do now," said Mrs. Knox; "go round to the servants' hall and have your tea. I'll see what I can do."

There was silence while Stephen Casey withdrew. As the sound of his hobnailed tread died away the woolly dog advanced very stiffly to the hall door, and, with his eyes fixed on the departing visitor, licked his lips hungrily.

"When those rascals in Parliament took our land from us," said Mrs. Knox, flinging a sod of turf on to the huge fire with practised aim, "we thought we should have some peace, now we're both beggared and bothered!" She turned upon me a countenance like that of an ancient and spectacled falcon. "Major Yeates! You have often offered me a drive in your motor-car. Will you take me to Killoge to-morrow morning?"

It was a brisk and windy morning, with the sharpness of 9 a.m. in it, when Mullins, Mrs. Knox's tirewoman, met me at the hall door of Aussolas with her arms full of shawls, and a countenance dark with doom and wrath. She informed me that it was a shame for me to be enticing the mistress out of her bed at this hour of the

440

morning, and that she would get her death out of it. I was repudiating this soft impeachment (which had indeed some flavour of the Restoration drama about it), when the companion of my flight appeared.

"How would anyone know the minute——" continued Mullins, addressing the universe, "that this what's-this-I'll-call-it wouldn't turn into a bog-hole?" She put this conundrum while fiercely swaddling her mistress in cloak upon cloak. I attempted no reply, and Mrs. Knox, winking both eyes at me over the rim of the topmost shawl, was hoisted into the back of the car; as we glided away I had, at all events, the consolation of knowing that, in the event of an accident, Mrs. Knox in her cloaks would float from the car as softly and bulkily as a bumble bee.

As we ran out of the gates on to the high road I remembered that my passenger's age was variously reckoned at from ninety to a hundred, and thought it well to ask her if fifteen miles an hour would be too fast for pleasure.

"You can't go too fast to please me," replied Mrs. Knox, through the meshes of a Shetland shawl. "When I was a girl I rode a fourteen-hand pony to the fourteenth milestone on the Cork road in a minute under the hour! I think you should be able to double that!"

I replied to this challenge with twenty miles an hour, which, with a head wind and a bad road, I considered to be fast enough for any old lady. As a matter of fact it was too fast for her costume. We had run some eight or nine miles before, looking back, I noticed that a change of some sort had occurred.

"Oh, the red one blew away long ago!" screamed Mrs. Knox against the wind; "it doesn't matter, I shall get it back—I'll ask Father Scanlan to speak about it at Mass next Sunday. There's a veil gone too—how frantic Mullins will be!"

A skirl of laughter came from the recesses of the remaining shawls.

We were running now on a level road under the lee of a long line of hills; a strip of plantation, gay with the yellows and greens of autumn, clung to a steep slope ahead of us, and, at the top of it, some ragged pines

441

looked like blots against the sky. As we neared it, a faint and long-drawn call came from the height; presently among the tree-trunks we saw hounds, like creatures in a tapestry hunting scene, working up and up through the brown undergrowth. I slackened speed.

" 'Pon my honour, we've hit off the Hunt!" exclaimed Mrs. Knox.

As she spoke there was a responsive yelp from a tract of briars in the lower part of the wood; two or three couples jostled downwards to their comrade, and a full chorus, led by the soprano squeals of the Hunt terrier, arose and streamed along the wood above the road. I came to a full stop, and, just in front of us, a rabbit emerged very quietly from the fence of the wood, crept along in the ditch, and disappeared in a hole in the bank. The hounds still uttered the classic paeans of the chase; hoofs clattered in a steep lane on the hillside, and Flurry Knox charged on to the road a little ahead of us.

"Forrad, forrad, forrad!" he shouted as he came.

"Rabbit, rabbit, rabbit!" cackled his grandmother at him in malevolent imitation.

I let the car go, and as we flew past him he asked me, sideways out of a very red face, what the devil I was doing there. It was evident that Mrs. Knox's observation had been accepted in the spirit in which it was offered.

"That will do my young gentleman no harm!" said Mrs. Knox complacently, as we became a speck in the distance.

It was about ten o'clock when we ran down a valley between steep hills to Killoge cross-roads. The hillsides were set thick with tree stumps, like the crowded headstones of a cemetery, with coarse grass and briars filling the spaces between them. Here and there a slender, orphaned ash sapling, spared because despised, stood among the havoc, and showed with its handful of yellow leaves what the autumn colours might once have been here. A starkly new, cemented public-house, with "J. Goggin" on the name board, stood at the fork of the roads. Doubtless into it had flowed the blood-money of the wood; it represented the alternative offered to the community by Mr. Goggin. I slowed up and looked about me.

"I suppose this is—or was—Killoge Wood?" I said to my passenger.

Mrs. Knox was staring through her spectacles at the devastated hillside.

"Ichabod, Ichabod!" she murmured, and leaned back in her place.

A man got up from a heap of stones by the roadside and came slowly towards the car.

"Well, Stephen," began Mrs. Knox irritably, "what about the cattle? He looks as if he were walking behind his own coffin!" she continued in a loud aside to me.

Stephen Casey removed his hat, and with it indicated a group composed of three calves—and nothing can look as dejected as an ill-fed, underbred calf—two goats, and a donkey, attended by a boy with a stick, and a couple of cur dogs.

"Himself and the sheriff's man is after driving them, my lady," replied their proprietor, and proceeded to envelope the name of Goggin in a flowing mantle of curses.

"There, that will do for the present," said Mrs. Knox peremptorily, as Casey, with tears streaming down his face, paused to catch his wind. "Where's Goggin?"

"The two of them is inside in the shop," answered the miserable Casey, still weeping copiously.

I drove over to the public-house, thinking that if Casey could not put up a better fight than this it would be difficult to do much for him. The door of the pub was already filled by the large and decent figure of Mr. Goggin, who advanced to meet us, taking off his hat reverentially; I remembered at once his pale and pimpled face, his pink nose, his shabby grey and yellow beard. He had been before me in a matter of selling drink on Sunday, and had sailed out of court in stainless triumph, on sworn evidence that he was merely extending hospitality to some friends that had come to make a match for a niece of his own, and were tired after walking the land and putting a price on the cattle.

"Well, Goggin," said Mrs. Knox, waving towards the

443

hillside a tiny hand in a mouldy old black kid glove, "you've done a great work here! You've destroyed in six months what it took the Colonel and the Lord Almighty eighty years to make. That's something to be proud of!"

Goggin, again, and with even deeper reverence, removed his hat, and murmured something about being a poor man.

"It was your own grandfather that planted those trees for the Colonel," continued Mrs. Knox, diving, as it were, into an ancient armoury and snatching a rusty weapon from the wall.

"That's the case ma'am," replied Mr. Goggin solemnly. "The Lord have mercy on his soul!"

"You'll be wanting mercy on your own soul in the next world, if you meet the Colonel there!" said Mrs. Knox unhesitatingly.

"I mightn't have the honour of meeting the Colonel there, ma'am!" tittered Goggin sycophantically.

"You might not indeed," responded Mrs. Knox, "but you might find your grandfather making up a good fire for you with the logs out of Killoge Wood!"

"Ha, ha! That's good, faith!" said a fat voice from the porter-flavoured depths of the pub. I recognized among other half-seen faces the round cheeks and bristling moustache of little M'Sweeny, the sheriff's officer, at Goggin's elbow.

"And what's this I hear about Stephen Casey?" went on Mrs. Knox, in shrill and trenchant tones, delivering her real attack now that she had breached the wall. "You lent him five pounds two years ago, and now you're driving all his stock off! What do you call that, I'd thank you to tell me?"

In the discussion that followed I could almost have been sorry for Goggin, so entirely overweighted was he by Mrs. Knox's traditional prestige, by my official position, by knowledge of the unseen audience in the pub, and by the inherrent rottenness of his case. Nevertheless, the defence put forward by him was a very creditable work of art. The whole affair had its foundation in a foolish philanthropy, the outcome of generous instincts exploited to their utmost, only, indeed, kept within bounds by Mr. Goggin's own financial embarrassments. These he primarily referred back to the excessive price extorted from him by Mrs. Knox's agent for the purchase of his land under the Act; and secondarily to the bad debts with which Stephen Casey and other customers had loaded him in their dealings with his little shop. There were moments when I almost had to accept Mr. Goggin's point of view, so well-ordered and so mildly stated were his facts. But Mrs. Knox's convictions were beyond and above any possibility of being shaken by mere evidence; she has often said to me that if all magistrates were deaf there would be more justice done. She herself was not in the least deaf, but she knew Mr. Goggin, which did as well.

"Fifteen pounds' worth of stock to pay a debt that was never more than £7! What do you call that, Major Yeates?"

She darted the question at me.

I had, some little time before, felt my last moment of sympathy with Goggin expire, and I replied with considerable heat that, if Mrs. Knox would forgive my saying so, I called it damned usury.

From this point the Affaire Casey went out swiftly on an ebb tide. It was insinuated by someone, M'Sweeny, I think, that an instalment of five pounds might be accepted, and the eyes of Goggin turned, tentatively, to Mrs. Knox. It has always been said of that venerable warrior that if there were a job to be done for a friend she would work her fingers to the bone, but she would never put them in her pocket. I observed that the eye of Goggin, having failed in its quest of hers, was concentrating itself upon me: I suddenly, and without premeditation, found myself promising to be responsible for the five pounds.

Before the glow of this impulse had time to be succeeded by its too familiar reaction, the broken yet persistent cry of hounds came to my ear. It advanced swiftly, coming, seemingly, from higher levels, into the desolated spaces that had once been Killoge Wood. From the inner depths of Mrs. Knox's wrappings the face of the woolly dog amazingly presented itself; from the companion

445

depths of the public-house an equally unexpected party of *convives* burst forth and stood at gaze. Mrs. Knox tried to stand up, was borne down by the sheer weight of rugs and the woolly dog, glared at me for a tense moment, and hissed, "They're coming this way! Try to get a view!"

Before the words had passed her lips someone in the group at the door vociferated, "Look at him above! Look at him!"

I looked "above", but could see nothing. Not so the rest of the group.

"Now! look at him going west the rock! Now! He's passing the little holly-tree—he's over the fence——"

I bore, as I have so often borne, the exasperation of, as it were, hearing instead of seeing a cinematograph, but I saw no reason why I should submit to the presence of Mr. M'Sweeny, who had sociably sprung into the motor beside me in order to obtain a better view.

"Look at him over the wall!" howled the cinematograph. "Look at the size he is! Isn't he the divil of a sheep!"

It was at this moment that I first caught sight of the fox, about fifty yards on the farther side of Casey's assortment of livestock and their guardian cur dogs, gliding over the wall like a cat, and slipping away up the road. At this point Mr. M'Sweeny, finding the disadvantage of his want of stature, bounded onto the seat beside me and uttered a long yell.

"Hi! At him! Tiger, good dog! Hi! Rosy!"

I cannot now say whether I smote M'Sweeny in the legs before he jumped, or if I merely accelerated the act; he appeared to be running before he touched the ground, and he probably took it as a send-off, administered in irrepressible fellow-feeling.

Tiger and Rosy were already laying themselves out down the road, and their yelps streamed back from them like the sparks from an engine. The party at the door was suddenly in full flight after them with a swiftness and unanimity that again recalled the cinematograph. They caught away with them Stephen Casey and his animals; and I had an enlivening glimpse of the donkey

446

at the top of the hunt, braying as it went; of Goggin trying in vain to stem the companion flight of the calves. The bend of the road hid them all from us; the thumping of heavy feet, the sobbing bray of the donkey, passed rapidly into remoteness, and Mrs. Knox and I were left with nothing remaining to us of the situation save the well-defined footmarks of M'Sweeny on the seat beside me (indelible, as I afterwards discovered).

"Get on, Major Yeates!" screamed Mrs. Knox, above the barking of the woolly dog. "We must see it out!"

I started the car, and just before we in our turn rounded the corner I looked back, and saw the leading hounds coming down the hillside. I slackened and saw them drop into the road and there remain, mystified, no doubt, by the astonishing variety of scents, from goat to gombeen man, that presented themselves. Of Flurry and his followers there was no sign.

"Get on, get on," reiterated Mrs. Knox, divining, no doubt, my feelings; "we shall do no more harm than the rest!"

I gave the car her head, knowing that whatever I did Flurry would have my blood. In less than two minutes we were all but into Stephen Casey's goats, who, being yoked together in body but not in spirit, required the full width of the road for their argument. We passed Stephen Casey and the gombeen man cornering the disputed calves in the sympathetic accord that such an operation demands. As we neared M'Sweeny, who brought up the rear, the body of the hunt, still headed by the donkey, swept into a field on the left of the road. The fox, as might have been expected, had passed from the ken of the cur dogs, and these, intoxicated by the incitements of their owners, now flung themselves, with the adaptability of their kind, into the pursuit of the donkey.

I stopped and looked back. The leading hounds were galloping behind the car; I recognized at their heads Rattler and Roman, the puppies I had walked, and for a moment was touched by this mark of affection. The gratification was brief. They passed me without a glance, and with anticipatory cries of joy flung themselves into the lead and joined in the chase of the donkey.

"They'll kill him!" exclaimed Mrs. Knox, restraining with difficulty the woolly dog; "what good is Flurry that he can't keep with his hounds!"

Galloping hoofs on the road behind us clattered a reply, accompanied by what I can only describe as imprecations on the horn, and Flurry hurtled by and swung his horse into the field over a low bank with all the dramatic fury of the hero rushing to the rescue of the leading lady. It recalled the incidents that in the palmy days of the Hippodrome gloriously ended in a plunge into deep water, amid a salvo of firearms.

In Flurry's wake came the rest of the pack, and with them Dr. Jerome Hickey. "A great morning's cubbing!" he called out, snatching off his old velvet cap. "Thirty minutes with an old fox, and now a nice burst with a jackass!"

For the next three or four minutes shrieks, like nothing so much as forked lightning, lacerated the air, as the guilty hounds began to receive that which was their due. It seemed possible that my turn would come next; I looked about to see what the chances were of turning the car and withdrawing as soon as might be, and decided to move on down the road in search of facilities. We had proceeded perhaps a hundred yards without improving the situation, when my eye was caught by something moving swiftly through the furze-bushes that clothed a little hill on the right of the road. It was brownish red, it slid into the deep furze that crested the hill, and was gone.

Here was a heaven-sent peace-offering!

"Tally-ho!" I bellowed, rising in my place and waving my cap high in air. "Tally-ho, over!"

The forked lightning ceased.

"What way is he?" came an answering bellow from Flurry.

"This way, over the hill!"

The hounds were already coming to the holloa. I achieved some very creditable falsetto screeches; I leaped from the car, and cheered and capped them over the fence; I shouted precise directions to the master and whip, who were now, with the clamours proper to their calling, steeplechasing into the road and out of it again, followed by two or three of the field, including the new District Inspector of the Royal Irish Constabulary (recently come from Meath with a high reputation as a goer). They scrambled and struggled up the hillside, through rocks and furze (in connection with which I heard the new D.I. making some strenuous comments to his Meath hunter), the hounds streamed and screamed over the ridge of the hill, the riders shoved their puffing horses after them, topped it, and dropped behind it. The furzy skyline and the pleasant blue and white sky above it remained serene and silent.

I returned to my car, and my passenger, who, as I now realized, had remained very still during these excitements.

"That was a bit of luck!" I said happily, inflated by the sense of personal merit that is the portion of one who has viewed a fox away. As I spoke, I became aware of something fixed in Mrs. Knox's expression, something rigid, as though she were repressing emotion; a fear flashed through my mind that she was overtired, and that the cry of the hounds had brought back to her the days when she too had known what a first burst away with a fox out of Killoge Wood had felt like.

"Major Yeates," she said sepulchrally, and yet with some inward thrill in her voice, "I think the sooner we start for home the better."

I could not turn the car, but, rather than lose time, I ran it backwards towards the cross-roads; it was a branch of the art in which I had not become proficient, and as, with my head over my shoulder, I dodged the ditches, I found myself continually encountering Mrs. Knox's eye, and was startled by something in it that was both jubilant and compassionate. I also surprised her in the act of wiping her eyes. I wondered if she were becoming hysterical, and yearned for Mullins as the policeman (no doubt) yearns for the mother of the lost child.

On the road near the public-house we came upon M'Sweeny, Goggin, and Casey, obviously awaiting us. I stopped the car, not without reluctance.

"That will be all right, Goggin," said Mrs. Knox, airily; "we're in a hurry to get home now."

The three protagonists looked at one another dubiously, and simultaneously cleared their throats.

"I beg your pardon, Mrs. Knox, ma'am," began Mr. Goggin very delicately. "Mr. M'Sweeny would be thankful to speak a word to you before you go."

"Well, let him speak and be quick about it," returned Mrs. Knox, who seemed to have recovered remarkably from her moment of emotion.

"You must excuse me, Major Yeates," said Mr. M'Sweeny, chivalrously selecting me as the person to whom the present business end of the transaction, "but I'm afraid I must trouble you about that little matter of five pounds that we arranged a while ago—I couldn't go back without it was settled——"

Mr. Goggin coughed, and looked at his boots; Stephen Casey sighed heavily.

At the same moment I thought I heard the horn.

"I'm afraid I haven't got it with me," I said, pulling out a handful of silver and a half-sovereign. "I suppose eighteen and sixpence wouldn't be any use to you?"

Mr. M'Sweeny smiled deprecatingly, as at a passing jest, and again I heard the horn, several harsh and prolonged notes.

Mrs. Knox leaned forward and poked me in the back with some violence.

"Goggin will lend it to you," she said, with the splendid simplicity of a great mind.

It must be recorded of Goggin that he accepted this singular inversion of the position like a gentleman. We moved on to his house and he went in with an excellent show of alacrity to fetch the money wherewith I was to stop his own mouth. It was while we were waiting that a small wet collie, reddish-brown in colour, came flying across the road, and darted in at the open door of the house. Its tongue was hanging out, it was panting heavily.

"I seen her going over the hill, and the hounds after her; I thought she wouldn't go three sthretches before they'd have her cot," said M'Sweeny pleasantly. "But I declare she gave them a nice chase. When she seen the Doctor beating the hounds, that's the time she ran."

I turned feebly in my place and looked at Mrs. Knox.

"It was a very natural mistake," she said, again wiping her eyes; "I myself was taken in for a moment—but only for a moment!" she added, with abominable glee.

I gave her but once glance, laden with reproach, and turned to M'Sweeny.

"You'll get the five pounds from Goggin," I said, starting the car.

As we ran out of Killoge, at something near thirty miles an hour, I heard scald-crow laughter behind me in the shawls.

THE FRIEND OF HER YOUTH

It has come to this with me, I am not the country-house visitor that I once was. It is a sign of age, I suppose, and of growing unamiability; so, at any rate, my wife tells me. For my part, I think it indicates a power of discriminating between the things that are good enough, and the infinitely more numerous things that are the reverse.

"Do you mean to say this isn't good enough?" said Philippa, putting down the novel that, at 11 a.m., she was shamelessly readling, and indicating our surroundings with a swing of her open parasol.

It was a perfect morning in August. She and I were seated in incredible leisure, in comfortable basket chairs, on a space of sward that sank in pleasant curves to the verge of the summer sea. We looked across three miles of burnished water to the Castle Manus hills, that showed mistily through grey veils of heat; in the middle distance a forty-ton cutter yacht drowsed at anchor; at the end of the sward a strand, theatrical in the perfection of its pale sand and dark rocks, laid itself out to attract the bather.

"I think it is very good," I replied, "but it won't last.

451

At any minute old Derryclare will come and compel me to go out trawling, or mending nets, or cutting up bait, or mucking out the dinghy——"

"You may be thankful if he lets you off with that!" said Philippa, flitting from her first position and taking up one in advance of mine.

Following the direction of her eyes, I perceived, as it were at the back of the stage, two mysterious, shrouded figures pursuing a swift course towards the house through a shrubbery of immense hydrangea bushes. Their heads resembled monster black door-handles, round their shoulders hung flounces of black muslin; in gauntleted hands they bore trays loaded with "sections" of honey; even at a distance of fifty yards we could see their attendant *cortège* of indignant bees.

"Taken thirty pounds this morning!" shouted the leading door-handle, speeding towards the house. "Splendid heather honey!"

"You ought to show some interest," said my wife malignly. "Go in and look at it. He's our host!"

"Not if he were all the hosts of Midian!" I said, but I felt shaken.

I rose from my chair.

"I'm going to the motor-house," I said firmly.

"Very well, I shall bathe," replied Philippa.

"I suppose you are aware that your old friend, Mr. Chichester, is at present in possession of the bathing cove," I returned, "and it might be as well to ascertain the opinion of your hostess on the subject of mixed bathing."

"Did you observe that Lord Derryclare was wearing your new motor-gloves?" said Philippa as I moved away.

I magnanimously left the last word with her.

The Derryclares were in the habit of hurling themselves, at intervals, out of civilization, and into the wilderness, with much the same zest with which those who live in the wilderness hurl themselves into civilization. In the wilderness, twenty miles from a railway station, they had built them a nest, and there led that variety of the simple life that is founded on good servants, old clothes, and a total indifference to weather.

452

Wandering friends on motor tours swooped occasionally out of space; married daughters, with intervals between visits to be filled in, arrived without warning, towing reluctant husbands (who had been there before). Lost men, implicated with Royal Commissions and Congested Districts, were washed in at intervals; Lady Derryclare said she never asked anyone; people came.

It is true that she had asked us, but the invitation had been given on our wedding-day, and had been put away with our duplicate wedding presents; we had now disinterred it, because I had bought a motor, and was still in the stage of enthusiasm when the amateur driver will beat up visits for his wife to pay. I do not know how Chichester got there; he, like Lady Derryclare, dated from the benighted period before Philippa knew me, and I may admit that, in common with most husbands, I am not attracted by the male friends of my wife's youth. If Chichester had been the type she fancied, was I merely a Super-Chichester?

Chichester was an elderly young man, worn smooth by much visiting in country houses, and thoroughly competent in the avocations proper to his career. He knew the best "stands" at half the shoots in Ireland, and could tell to half a crown the value set upon each by the keeper; if you gave him a map he could put a pudgy finger upon the good cooks as promptly as an archbishop upon his cathedral towns; he played a useful and remunerative game of bridge; to see his eye, critical, yet alight with healthful voracity, travelling down the array of dishes on the sidetable at breakfast, and arranging unhesitatingly the order in which they were to be attacked, was a lesson to the heedless who blunt the fine edge of appetite with porridge.

He faced me at lunch, plump and pink and shining after his bathe; he was clean-shaved (the only reliable remedy for a greying moustache, as I did not fail to point out to Philippa); it increased his resemblance to a well-fed and *passé* schoolboy. Old Derryclare, whose foible it was to believe that he never had any luncheon, was standing at the sideboard, devouring informally a slice of bread and honey. One of his eyes was bunged up by bee-stings, and the end of his large nose shone red from the same cause.

"Bill," he said, addressing his eldest son, "don't you forget to take those sections on board this afternoon."

"No fear!" responded Bill, helping himself to a beaker of barley-water with hands that bore indelible traces of tar and motor grease.

Bill was a vigorous youth, of the type that I have heard my friend Slipper describe as "a hardy young splinter"; he was supposed to be preparing for a diplomatic career, and in the meantime was apparently qualifying for the engine-room of a tramp steamer (of which, it may be added, his father would have made a most admirable skipper).

"Great stuff, honey, with a rice-pudding," went on Bill. "Mrs. Yeates, do you know I can make a topping rice-pudding?"

I noticed that Chichester, who was seated next to Philippa, suddenly ceased to chew.

"I can do you a very high-class omelette, too," continued Bill, bashing a brutal spoon into the fragile elegance of something that looked as if it were made of snow and spun glass. "I'm not so certain about my mutton-chops and beefsteak, but I've had the knives sharpened, anyhow!"

Chichester turned his head away, as from a jest too clownish to be worthy of attention. His cheek was large, and had a tender, beefy flush in it.

"In my house," he said to Philippa, "I never allow the knives to be sharpened. If meat requires a sharp knife it is not fit to eat."

"No, of course not!" replied Philippa, with nauseating hypocrisy.

"The principle on which my wife buys meat," I said to the table at large, "is to say to the butcher, 'I want the best meat in your shop; but don't show it to me!'"

"Mrs. Yeates is quite right," said Chichester seriously; "you should be able to trust your butcher."

The door flew open, and Lady Derryclare strode in, wrestling as she came with the strings of a painting apron, whose office had been no sinecure. She was tall

454

and grey-haired, and was just sufficiently engrossed in her own pursuits to be an attractive hostess.

"It was perfectly lovely out there on the *Sheila*," she said, handing the apron to the butler, who removed it from the room with respectful disapproval. "If only she hadn't swung with the tide! I found my sketch had more and more in it every moment—turning into a panorama, in fact! Yachts would be perfect if they had long solid legs and stood on concrete."

I said that I thought a small island would do as well.

Lady Derryclare disputed this, and argued that an island would involve a garden, whereas the charm of a yacht was that one hideous bunch of flowers on the cabin table was all that was expected of it, and that kind people ashore always gave it vegetables.

I said that these things did not concern me, as I usually neither opened my eyes nor touched food while yachting. I said this very firmly, being not without fear that I might yet find myself hustled into becoming one of the party that was to go aboard the *Sheila* that very night. They were to start on the top of the tide, that is to say, at 4 a.m. the following morning, to sail round the coast to a bay some thirty miles away, renowned for its pollack-fishing, and there to fish. Pollack-fishing, as a sport, does not appeal to me; according to my experience, it consists in hauling up coarse fish out of deep water by means of a hook baited with red flannel. It might appear poor-spirited, even effeminate, but nothing short of a press-gang should get me on board the *Sheila* that night.

"Every expedition requires its martyr," said Lady Derryclare, helping herself to some of the best cold salmon it has been my lot to encounter, "it makes it so much pleasanter for the others; someone they can despise and say funny things about."

"The situation may produce its martyr," I said.

Lady Derryclare glanced quickly at me, and then at Chichester, who was now expounding to Philippa the method, peculiar to himself, by which he secured mountain mutton of the essential age.

At nine-thirty that night I sat with my hostess and my

wife, engaged in a domestic game of poker-patience. Shaded lights and a softly burning turf fire shed a mellow radiance; an exquisite completeness was added by a silken rustle of misty rain against the south window.

"Do you think they'll start in this weather?" said Philippa sympathetically.

"Seventy-five, and one full house, ten, that's eighty-five," said Lady Derryclare abstractedly. "Start? You may be quite sure they'll start! Then we three shall have an empty house. That ought to count at least twenty!"

Lady Derryclare was far too good a hostess not to appreciate the charms of solitude; that Philippa and I should be looked upon as solitude was soothing to the heart of the guest, the heart that, however good the hostess, inevitably conceals some measure of apprehension.

"Has Mr. Chichester been on board the *Sheila*?" I inquired, with elaborate unconcern.

"*Never!*" said Lady Derryclare melodramatically.

"I believe he has done some yachting?" I continued.

"A five-hundred-ton steam yacht to the West Indies!" replied Lady Derryclare. "Bathrooms and a *chef*——"

There was a thumping of heavy feet outside the door, and the yacht party entered, headed by Lord Derryclare with a lighted lantern. They were clad in oilskins and sou'westers; Bill had a string of onions in one hand and sponge-bag in the other; Chichester carried a large gold-mounted umbrella.

"You look as if you were acting a charade," said Lady Derryclare, shuffling the cards for the next game, the game that would take place when the pleasure-seekers had gone forth into the rain. "The word is Fare-well, I understand?"

It occurred to me that to fare well was the last thing that Chichester was likely to do; and, furthermore, that the same thing had occurred to him.

" 'Fare thee well, my own Mary Anne!' " sang Lord Derryclare, in a voice like a bassoon, and much out of tune. "It's a dirty night, but the glass is rising, and" (here he relapsed again into song) "'we are bound for the sea, Mary Anne! We are bound for the sea!'"

"Then we're to meet you on Friday?" said Philippa, addressing herself to Chichester in palpable and egregious consolation.

"Dear lady," replied Chichester tartly, "in the south of Ireland it is quite absurd to make plans. One is the plaything of the climate!"

"All aboard," said Lord Derryclare, with a swing of his lantern.

As they left the room the eye of Bill met mine, not without understanding.

"Now D's perfectly happy," remarked Lady Derryclare, sorting her suits; "but I'm not quite so sure about the supercargo."

The game progressed pleasantly, and we heard the rain enwrap the house softly, as with a mantle.

The next three days were spent in inglorious peace, not to say sloth. On one of them, which was wet, I cleared off outstanding letters and browsed among new books and innumerable magazines: on the others, which were fine, I ran the ladies in the car back into the hills, and pottered after grouse with a venerable red setter, while Lady Derryclare painted, and Philippa made tea. When not otherwise employed, I thanked heaven that I was not on board the *Sheila*.

On Thursday night came a telegram from the yacht:

"Ronnie's flotilla in; luncheon party to-morrow; come early.—BILL."

At nine o'clock the next morning we were on the road; there was a light northerly breeze, enough to dry the roads and to clear the sky of all save a few silver feathers of cloud; the heather was in bloom on the hills, the bogs were bronze and green, the mountains behind them were as blue as grapes; best of all, the car was running like a saint, floating up the minor hills, pounding unfalteringly up the big ones. She and I were still in the honeymoon stage, and her most normal virtues were to me miraculous; even my two ladies, though, like their sex, grossly utilitarian, and incapable, as I did not fail to assure them, of appreciating the poesy of mechanism, were complimentary.

In that part of Ireland in which my lot is cast signposts do not exist. The residents, very reasonably, consider them to be superfluous, even ridiculous, in view of the fact that everyone knows the way, and as for strangers, "haven't they tongues in their heads as well as another?" It all tends to conversation and an increased knowledge of human nature. Therefore it was that when we had descended from the hills, and found ourselves near the head of Dunerris Bay, at a junction of three roads, any one of which might have been ours, our only course was to pause there and await enlightenment.

It came, plentifully, borne by an outside car, and bestowed by no less than four beautifully dressed young ladies. I alighted and approached the outside car, and was instructed by the driver as to the route, an intricate one, to Eyries Harbour. The young ladies offered supplementary suggestions; they were mysteriously acquainted with the fact that the *Sheila* was our destination, and were also authorities on the movements of that section of the British Navy that was known to the family of Sub-Lieutenant the Hon. Ronald Cunningham as "Ronnie's Flotilla".

"We met the yacht gentlemen at tea on Mr. Cunningham's torpedo-boat yesterday afternoon," volunteered the prettiest of the young ladies, with a droop of her eyelashes.

The party then laughed, and looked at each other, as those do who have together heard the chimes at midnight.

"Why, we're going to lunch with them to-day at the hotel at Ecclestown! And with you too!" broke in another, with a sudden squeal of laughter.

I said that the prospect left nothing to be desired.

"Mr. Chichester invited us yesterday!" put in a third from the other side of the car.

"I don't think it's pollack he'll order for luncheon," said the fourth of the party from under the driver's elbow, a flapper, with a slow, hoarse voice, and a heavy cold in her head.

458

"Shut up, Katty, you brat!" said the eldest, with light-ning utterance.

The quartette again dissolved into laughter. I said "Au revoir", and withdrew to report my progress to my deeply interested passengers.

As the outside car disappeared from view at a corner, the Flapper waved a large pocket-handkerchief to me.

"You seem to have done wonderfully well in the time," said Lady Derryclare kindly.

For half an hour or more we ran west along the southern shore of the great bay; Ecclestown, where Chichester's luncheon-party was to take place, was faintly visible on the further side. So sparkling was the sea, so benign the breeze that even I looked forward without anxiety, almost with enjoyment, to the sail across the bay.

There is a bland and peaceful suggestion about the word village that is wholly inapplicable to the village of Eyries, a collection of dismal, slated cabins, grouped round a public-house, like a company of shabby little hens round a tawdry and bedraggled cock. The road that had conveyed us to this place of entertainment com-mitted suicide on a weedy beach below, its last moments much embittered by chaotic heaps of timber, stones, and gravel. A paternal Board was building a pier, and "mountains of gold was flying into it, but the divil a much would ever come out of it".

This I was told by the publican as I bestowed the car in an outhouse in his yard, wherein, he assured me, "neither chick nor child would find it".

The *Sheila* was anchored near the mouth of the har-bour; there was a cheerful air of expectancy about her, and her big mainsail was hosted; her punt, propelled by Bill, was already tripping towards us over the little waves; the air was salt, and clean, and appetizing. Bill appeared to be in robust health; he had taken on a good many extra tones of sunburn, and it was difficult, on a cursory inspection, to decide where his neck ended and his brown flannel shirt began.

"—Oh, a topping time!" he said, as we moved out over the green, clear water, through which glimmered to us the broken pots and pans of Eyries that lay below. "Any amount of fish going. We've had to give away no end."

"I should like to hear what you've been giving Mr. Chichester to eat?" said Lady Derryclare suavely.

"Well, there was the leg of mutton that we took with us; he ate that pretty well; and a sort of a hash next day, fair to middling."

"And after that?" said his mother, with polite interest.

"Well, after that," said Bill, leaning his elbows on his sculls and ticking off the items on his fingers, "we had boiled pollack and fried pollack, and pollack *réchauffé aux fines herbes*—onions, you know——"

Bill broke off artistically, and I recalled to myself a saying of an American sage, "Those that go down to the sea in ships see the works of the Lord, but those that go down to the sea in cutters see hell".

"He went ashore yesterday," said Bill, resuming his narrative and the sculls, "and came aboard with a pig's face and a pot of jam that he got at the pub, and I say! —that pig's face!—Phew! My aunt!"

"'Look in my face; my name is Might-have-been'," quoted Lady Derryclare.

Philippa shuddered aloud.

"But he's going to come level to-day," went on Bill; "he's standing us all lunch at the Ecclestown Hotel, Ronnie's skipper and all. He spent a good half-hour writing out a menu, and Ronnie took it over last night. We had tea on board Ronnie's ship, you know."

We said we knew all about the tea-party and the guests.

"Oh, you do, do you?" said Bill; "then you know a good deal! Chichester can tell you a bit more about the dark one if you like to ask him!"

"He seems to have outgrown his fancy for fair people," I said.

Philippa put her nose in the air.

"He's gorgeously dressed for the occasion," continued Bill.

"More than you are!" said his mother.

"Oh, my one don't care. No more does Ronnie's. What they enjoyed was the engine-room."

"It seems to me," said Lady Derryclare to Philippa, "that we are rather superfluous to this entertainment."

Chichester stood at the gangway and helped the ladies on to the narrow, hog-backed deck of the *Sheila*. He was indeed beautifully dressed, but to the critical eye it seemed that the spotless grey flannel suit hung a shade easier, and that the line of his check was less freshly rounded. His nose had warmed to a healthful scarlet, but his eye was cold, and distinctly bleak. He was silent, not, it was obvious to me, because he had nothing to say, but because he might have more to say than would be convenient. In all senses save the literal one he sugegsted the simple phrase, "Fed up". I felt for him. As I saw the grim deck-bosses on which we might have to sit, and the dark mouth of the cabin in which we might have to eat, and tripped over a rope, and grasped at the boom, which yielded instead of supporting me, I thought with a lover's ardour of the superiority—whether as means of progression or as toy—of the little car, tucked away in the Eyries publican's back-yard, where neither chick nor child would find her.

"You ought to have come with us, Yeates," said Derryclare, emerging from the companion-hatch with a fishing-line in his hand. "Great sport! we got a hundred and fifty yesterday—beats trout-fishing! Doesn't it, Chichester?"

Chichester smiled sarcastically and looked at his watch.

"Quite right," said his lordship, twisting his huge hairy paw, and consulting the nickel timekeeper on his wrist. "Time to be off—mustn't keep our young ladies waiting. We'll slip across in no time with this nice breeze. Regular ladies' day. Now then, Bill! get that fores'l on her—we'll up anchor and be off!"

There are few places in creation where the onlooker can find himself more painfully and perpetually *de trop* than on the deck of a small yacht. I followed the ladies to the saloon. Chichester remained on deck. As I carefully descended the companion-ladder I saw him looking again at his watch, and from it across the bay to the hazy white specks, some four miles away, in one of which assiduous waiters were even now, it might be, setting forth the repast that was to indemnify him for three days of pollack.

"P'ff; I wonder if they ever open the windows?" said Lady Derryclare, fitting herself skilfully into the revolving chair at the end of the cabin table. "Do sit down—these starting operations are always lengthy."

I took my seat, that is to say, I began to sit down in the air, well outside the flap of the table, and gradually inserted myself underneath it. The bunch of flowers, foretold by Lady Derryclare, confronted us, packed suffocatingly into its vase, and even the least astute of the party (I allude to myself) was able unhesitatingly to place it as an attention from the fair ones of the outside car. Behind my shoulders, a species of trough filled the interval between the back of the seat and the sloping side of the yacht; in it lay old tweed caps, old sixpenny magazines, fieldglasses, cans of tobacco, and a well-worn box of patience cards. Above and behind it a rack made of netting was darkly charged with signal-flags, fishing-rods, and minor offal.

"Think of them all, smoking here on a wet night," said Lady Derryclare with abhorrence; "with the windows shut and no shade on the lamp! Let nothing tempt any of you to open the pantry door; we might see the pig's face. Unfortunate George Chichester!"

"I shouldn't pity him too much," said I. "I expect he wouldn't take five pounds for his appetite this moment!"

The rhythmic creak of the windlass told that the anchor was coming up. It continued for some moments, and then stopped abruptly.

"Now then, all together!" said Lord Derryclare's voice.

A pause, punctuated by heavy grunts of effort—then Bill's voice.

"What the blazes is holding it? Come on, Chichester, and put your back into it!"

Chichester's back, ample as it would seem, had no appreciable effect on the situation.

462

"You ought to go and help them, Sinclair," said my wife, with that readiness to offer a vicarious sacrifice that is so characteristic of wives.

I said I would wait till I was asked. I had not to wait long.

I took my turn at the warm handle-bar of the windlass, and grunted and strove as strenuously as my predecessors. The sun poured down in undesired geniality; the mainsail lurched and flapped; the boom tugged at its tether; the water jabbered and gurgled past the bows.

"I think we're in the *consommé*!" remarked Bill, putting his hands in his pockets.

"Here," said Lord Derryclare, with a very red face; "confound her! we'll sail her off it!"

Chichester sat down in a deck-chair as remote as possible from his kind, and once again consulted his watch. Bill took the tiller; ropes were hauled, slacked, made fast; the boom awoke to devastating life; the *Sheila* swung, tilted over to the breeze, and made a rush for freedom. The rush ended in a jerk, the anchor remained immovable, and the process was repeated in the opposite direction, with a vigour that restored Chichester abruptly to the bosom of society—in point of fact, my bosom. He said nothing, or at least nothing to signify, as I assisted him to rise, but I felt as if I were handling a live shell.

During the succeeding quarter of an hour the *Sheila*, so it seemed to my untutored mind, continued to sail in tangents towards all the points of the compass, and at the end of each tangent was brought up with an uncompromising negative from the anchor. By that time my invariable yacht-headache was established, and all the other men in the ship were advancing, at a varying rate of progress, into a frame of mind that precluded human intercourse, and was entirely removed from perceiving any humour in the situation.

Through all these affairs the sound of conversation ascended steadily through the main hatch. Lady Derryclare and my wife were playing patience in the cabin, and were at the same time discussing intricate matters in connection with District Nurses, with that strange power of doing one thing and talking about another that I have

463

often noticed in women. It was about this period that the small, rat-like head of Bill's kitchen-maid, Jimmy, appeared at the fore-hatch (accompanied by a reek of such potency that I immediately assigned it to the pig's face), and made the suggestion about the congested diver. That the diver, however congested, was a public official, engaged at the moment in laying the foundations of the Eyries Pier, did not, this being Ireland, complicate the situation. The punt, with Bill, hot and taciturn, in the stern, sprang forth on her errand, smashing and bouncing through the sharpened edges of the little waves. As I faced that dainty and appetizing breeze, I felt the first pang of the same hunger that was, I knew, already gnawing Chichester like a wolf.

"We must have fouled some old moorings," said Derryclare, coming up from the cabin, with a large slice of bread and honey in his hand, and an equanimity somewhat restored by a working solution of the problem. "Damn nuisance, but it can't be helped. Better get something to eat, Chichester; you won't get to Ecclestown before three o'clock at the best."

"No, thank you," said Chichester, without raising his eyes from the four-day-old paper that he was affecting to read.

I strolled discreetly away, and again looked down through the skylight into the cabin. The ladies were no longer there, and, in defiance of all nautical regulations, a spirit-lamp with a kettle upon it was burning on the table, a sufficient indication to a person of my experience that Philippa and Lady Derryclare had abandoned hope of the Ecclestown lunch and were making tea. The prospect of something to eat, of any description, was not unpleasing; in the meantime I took the fieldglasses, and went forward to follow, pessimistically, the progress of the punt in its search for the diver.

There was no one on the pier. Bill landed, went up the beach, and was lost to sight in the yard of the public-house.

"It must be he's at his dinner," said Jimmy at my elbow, descrying these movements with a vision that appeared to be equal to mine plus the field-glasses. There was an interval, during which I transferred my attention to Ecclestown; its white hotel basked in sunshine, settled and balmy, as of the land of Beulah. Its comfortable aspect suggested roast chicken, tingling glasses of beer, even of champagne. A torpedo-boat, with a thread of smoke coming quietly from its foremost funnel, lay in front of the hotel. It seemed as though it were enjoying an after-luncheon cigarette.

"They're coming out now!" said Jimmy, with excitement; "it must be they were within the house looking at the motor."

I turned the field-glasses on Eyres; a fair proportion of its population was emerging from the yard of the public-house, and the length to which their scientific interest had carried them formed a pleasing subject for meditation.

"There's the ha'past-one mail-car coming in," said Jimmy; "it's likely he'll wait for the letters now."

The mirage of the Ecclestown lunch here melted away, as far as I was concerned, and with a resignation perfected in many Petty Sessions courts, I turned my appetite to humbler issues. To those who have breakfasted at eight, and have motored over thirty miles of moorland, tea and sardines at two o'clock are a mere affair of outposts, that leave the heart of the position untouched. Yet a temporary glow of achievement may be attained by their means, and the news brought back by Bill, coupled with a fresh loaf, that the diver was coming at once, flattered the hope that the game was still alive. Bill had also brought a telegram for Chichester.

"Who has the nerve to tell Mr. Chichester that there's something to eat here?" said Lady Derryclare, minutely examining the butter.

"Philippa is obviously indicated," I said malignly. 'She is the Friend of his Youth!"

"You're all odious," said Philippa, sliding from beneath the flap of the table with the light of the lion-tamer in her eye.

What transpired between her and the lion we shall never know. She returned almost immediately with a heightened colour, and the irrelevant information that

465

the diver had come on board. The news had the lifting power of a high explosive. We burst from the cabin and went on deck as one man, with the exception of my wife, who, with a forethought that did her credit, turned back to improvise a cosy for the teapot.

The diver was a large person, of few words, with a lowering brow and a heavy moustache. He did not minimize the greatness of his condescension in coming aboard the yacht; he listened gloomily to the explanations of Lord Derryclare. At the conclusion of the narrative he moved in silence to the bows and surveyed the situation. His boat, containing the apparatus of his trade, was alongside; a stalwart underling, clad in a brown jersey, sat in the bows; in the stern was enthroned the helmet, goggling upon us like a decapitated motorist. It imparted a thrill that I had not experienced since I read Jules Verne at school.

"Here, Jeremiah," said the diver.

The satellite came on deck with the single sinuous movement of a salmon.

The diver motioned him to the windlass. "We'll take a turn at this first, he said.

They took each a handle, they bent to their task, and the anchor rose at their summons like a hot knife out of butter.

Every man present, with the exception of the diver and the satellite, made the simple declaration that he was damned, and it was in the period of paralysis following on this that a fresh ingredient was added to the situation.

A giant voice filled the air, and in a windy bellow came the words:

"Nice lot you are!"

We faced about and saw "Ronnie's torpedo-boat" executing a sweeping curve in the mouth of Eyries Harbour.

"Couldn't wait any longer!" proceeded the voice of the megaphone. "We've got to pick up the others outside. Thanks awfully for luncheon! Top-hole!"

T.B. No. 1000 completed the curve and headed for the open sea with a white mane of water rising above her bows. There was something else white fluttering at the stern. I put up the field-glasses, and with their aid perceived upon the deck a party of four ladies, one of whom was waving a large pocket-handkerchief. The glasses were here taken out of my hand by Chichester, but not before I had identified the Flapper.

What Chichester said of Ronnie was heard only by me, and possibly by Jimmy, who did not count. I think it may have saved his life, being akin to opening a vein. That I was the sole recipient of these confidences was perhaps due to the fact that the Sheila, so swiftly and amazingly untethered, here began to fall away to leeward, with all the wilful helplessness of her kind, and instant and general confusion was the result. There were a few moments during which ropes, spars, and human beings pursued me wherever I went. Then I heard Lord Derryclare's voice—"Let go that anchor again!"

The sliding rattle of the chain followed, the anchor plunged; the *status quo* was re-established.

Chichester went ashore with the diver to catch the outgoing mail-car. The telegram that had arrived with Bill was brought into action flagrantly, and was as flagrantly accepted. (It was found, subsequently, on his cabin floor, and was to the effect that the cartridges had been forwarded as directed.) The farewells were made, the parting regrets very creditably accomplished, and we stood on the deck and saw him go, with his suitcase, his rods, his guncase, heaped imposingly in the bow, his rug, and his coats, the greater and the less, piled beside him in the stern.

The wind had freshened; the diver and Jeremiah drove the boat into it with a will, and the heavy oars struck spray off the crests of the waves. We saw Chichester draw forth the greater coat, and stand up to put it on. The boat lurched, and he sat down abruptly, only to start to his feet again as if he had been stung by a wasp. He thrust his hand into the pocket, and Philippa clutched my arm.

"Could it have been into the pocket of *his* coat that I put the teapot——?" she breathed.

HARRINGTON'S

Breakfast was over; Philippa was feeding the dogs. Philippa's cousin, Captain Andrew Larpent, R.E., was looking out of the window with that air of unemployment that touches the conscience of a host like a spur. Andrew did not smoke, a serious matter in a male guest, which means that there are, for him, no momen.s of lethargy, and that when he idles, his idleness stands stark in the foreground against a clear sky, a reproach and a menace to his entertainers.

It was a cold day about the middle of September, and there was an unrest among the trees that commemorated a night of storm; the gravel was wet, the lawn-tennis ground was strewn with sycamore leaves.

"I suppose you'll say I'm drunk," said Andrew, "but the fact remains that I see two natives coming up the drive."

In the green tunnel that was the avenue of Shreelane were two dark figures; both were dressed in frock-coats, of which the tails fluttered meagrely in the wind; their faces were black; with the half-hearted blackness of a leg in a black silk stocking; one of them wore a tall hat.

"This is what comes of leaving Calcutta without paying your bills," I suggested; "or perhaps it's a missionary deputation——"

The natives advanced into the middle distance.

"It's the sweep!" exclaimed Philippa. "It's my beloved Cantillon!"

She flung open the window.

"Oh, Cantillon!" she cried, invoking the gentleman in the top-hat as if he were an idol. "I've been longing to see you!"

The leading native halted beneath the window and curtsied.

"I partly guessed it, my lady!" he replied modestly, and curtsied again.

"Then why didn't you come before?" screamed Philippa, suppressing with difficulty the indignation of the dogs.

"I had the toothache, my lady, and a howlt in my poll," returned the sweep, in dignified narrative. "I may say my hands was crackin' with the stren'th of pain, and these four days back there was the rumour of passpiration all over me, with respex to ye——"

"I'll see you in the kitchen," said Philippa, shutting the window abruptly. "My poor friends," she continued, "this means a cold luncheon for you, and a still colder reception for me from Mrs. Cadogan, but if I let Cantillon escape me now, I may never see him again—which is unthinkable!"

I presume that white is the complementary colour of a sweep. In half an hour after the arrival of Mr. Cantillon the sitting-rooms were snowed over with sheets, covering alike floor and furniture, while he and his disciple moved from room to room on tiptoe, with ostentatious humility, leaving a round black spoor upon the snow. My writing-table was inaccessible, so also was the piano, which could usually be trusted to keep Andrew quiet for an hour of the morning. Perhaps it would be more accurate to say it kept him occupied. Captain Larpent had not been many years in the service of his country, yet it was already told of him that "From Birr to Bareilly", undeterred by hardships, his intrepid piano had accompanied him, and that house-rents fell to zero within a half-mile radius of his vicinity. Daily the walls of Shreelane shook to the thunder of his practising; nightly his duets with my wife roared like a torrent over my sleeping head. Sometimes also he sang, chiefly in German (a language I do not understand), and with what seemed to me superfluous energy. But this, I am told, means "temperament".

Haunting as a waltz refrain the flavour of soot stole through the menu at dinner; it was whispered in the soup, it was muttered in the savoury, and in the coffee it abandoned subterfuge and shouted down all opposition.

Next morning, at breakfast, Philippa asked if the car wanted exercise, because it seemed to her a day marked out by Providence for calling on the chicken farmers. We might start early, take sandwiches, show Andrew something of the country—the programme was impulsively sketched in, but none the less I divined that an indignant household had demanded a day of atonement in which to obliterate the memory of the sweep.

It was, as well as I remember, in the preceding spring that the chicken farmers had come before the swallow dared, and had taken—in addition to the winds of March—a small farm about midway in the wilderness between us and the Derryclares. They were two young women who had recently been commended to our special attention by Lady Derryclare; they were, she said, pioneers, and were going to make their fortunes, and would incidentally set an example to the district. Philippa had met them on the Derryclare's yacht.

"One of them is very pretty," she explained to Andrew, "and the other is a doctor."

"I wonder which of them does most damage?" said Andrew. "I think I'll stay at home."

None the less he came.

It was not until the car was at the door that I found we were to be favoured with the society of my eldest son, Anthony, in consequence of the facts that (1) the day before had been his ninth birthday, (2) that he had not cried when he met the sweep in the passage, and (3) that for lack of the kitchen fire he had had no birthday cake. Minx also was one of us, but as she came as a stowaway, this did not transpire till later, when explanations were superfluous.

It was at the moment of departure that I perceived a donkey-cart, modestly screening itself behind the evergreens on the way to the yard, and one of Flurry Knox's men approached me with Mr. Knox's compliments, and would I lend him the loan of the long ladder? Some two years ago, in a moment of weakness, I had provided myself with a ladder wherewith to attain to the eaveshoots of Shreelane, since when I had found myself in the undesired position of public benefactor. How life

without a long ladder had hitherto been possible for my
neighbours I was at a loss to imagine, and as I was also
at a loss for any valid excuse for refusing to lend it, the
ladder enjoyed a butterfly existence of country-house
visiting. Its visits to Mr. Knox had been especially
lengthy and debilitating. It is, as Mrs. Cadogan is wont
to say, the last straw that puts the hump on the camel.
The blood suddenly mounted to my brain, and with it
came inspiration.

"You can tell Mr. Knox that the eaveshoots of this
house are leaking like sieves, and I want the ladder myself."

In the glow of satisfaction kindled by the delivery of
this message I started the caravan. The western breeze
fanned my brow agreeably, the car purred her satisfaction with our new and only stretch of steam-rolled road,
and Anthony was still in the condition of being good (a
condition, nevertheless, by no means to be relied on,
and quite distinct from goodness).

We ran west, we ran north; we skirted grey and
sounding bays of the Atlantic; we climbed high among
heathery, stone-besprinkled moors; we lunched by the
roadside in the lee of a rick of turf, and Anthony, by
this time emerging from the condition of being good,
broke the thermos, and flashed his birthday electric
torch in Minx's face until she very properly bit him,
and Philippa slurred over the incident with impartial
chocolate, and said it was time to start.

The region in which the chicken farmers had established themselves suggested the nurture of snipe and seagulls rather than chickens. It was an indeterminate patch-
work of stony knobs of hill and pockets of bog, among
which the road humped and sagged, accepting pessimistically the facts of nature. Hardy, noisy hill-streams
scurried beside it, or over it, as seemed good to them;
finally a sharp turn, a high horizon of sea, and a steep
downhill grade, ending on the shore of a small, round
lake. There was a little pink box of a house on its
farther side, with a few bunches of trees round it, and
among them a pigmy village of prim wooden huts.

"That's the place," said Philippa, who had been there

471

with Lady Derryclare. "And those are the last cry in hen-houses. Now remember, both of you, one of them is a doctor, Scotch, and a theosophist, or something mysterious of that sort; and the pretty one was engaged to a gunner and it was broken off—why, I don't know—drink, I fancy, or mad—so you had better be careful——"

"I shall be guarded in my condolences," I said, turning in at the little gate, with the sensation of being forcibly fed.

"As far as one can gather," said Andrew, "there remains no topic in heaven or earth that——"

"Music and poultry," said Philippa in a breath, as I drew up at the hall door.

Andrew rang the bell, and a flock of white ducks hurried up from among the trees and gathered round him with loud cries of welcome. There was no other reply to his summons, and at the second essay the bell-wire came out by the roots with generous completeness.

"The ladies is gone to th' oxtion!" cried a voice from among the hen-coops, and the ducks lifted up their voices in ardent reply.

"Where is the auction?" Philippa called, when a comparative silence had fallen.

"In Harrington's, beyond at the mines!" replied the oracle, on a well-sustained high G.

"Put the cards on the hall table," said Philippa, "we might go back that way."

Several things combine in the spell that an auction casts upon my wife, as upon many others of her sex; the gamble, the competition, the lure of the second-hand, the thrill of possible treasure-trove. We proceeded along the coast road towards the mines, and I could hear Philippa expounding to her first-born the nature and functions of auctions, even as the maternal carnivore instructs her young in the art of slaughter. The road with which we were now dealing ran, or, it would be more accurate to say, walked, across the stony laps of the hills. The cliffs were on our right; the sea was still flustered after the storm, like a dog that has fought and is ready to fight again. We toiled over the shoulder of a headland, and there caught sight of Harrington's.

On a green plateau, high above the sea, were a couple

of iron sheds and a small squat tower; landward of them was a square and hideous house, of the type that springs up, as if inevitably, in the neighbourhood of mines, which are, in themselves, among the most hideous works of man. One of the sheds had but half a roof; a truck lay on its side in a pool of water; defeat was written starkly over all.

"Copper, and precious little of it," I explained to Andrew; "and they get some gold too—just enough to go to their heads, and ruin them."

"Did they put it in their mouths—where you have it, Father?" inquired Anthony, who was hanging on my words and on the back of my seat.

"Suppose you shut yours," I replied, with the brutality that is the only effective defence against the frontal attacks of the young.

We found the yard at Harrington's thronged with a shabby company of carts, cars, and traps of many varieties; donkey-carts had made their own of the road outside, even the small circle of gravel in front of the hall door was bordered by bicycles; apparently an auction was a fashionable function in the region of the Lug-na-Coppal copper-mines. Dingy backs bulged from the open door of the hall, and over their heads as we arrived floated the voice of the auctioneer, demanding in tragic incredulity if people thought his conscience would permit him to let an aneroid barometer go for half a crown. Without a word Philippa inserted herself between the backs, followed by her son, and was lost to view.

"Thank you, madam!" said the voice, with a new note of cheer in it. "Five shillings I am bid! Any advance on five shillings?"

"That's a good weather-glass!" hissed a farmer's daughter with a plumed hat, to a friend with a black shawl over her head. "An' I coming into the house to-day I gave it a puck, and it knocked a lep out o' the needle. It's in grand working order."

"I'm told it was the last thing in the house poor Mr. Harrington left a hand on, the day he made away with himself, the Lord save us!" remarked a large matron, casually, to Andrew and me.

473

"I thought the coroner's jury found that he fell down the shaft?" I returned, accepting the conversational opening in the spirit in which it was offered.

The matron winked at me with a mixture of compassion and confederacy.

"Ah, the poor fellow was insured, and the jury were decent men, they wouldn't wish to have anything said that'd put the wife out of the money."

"The right men in the right place, evidently," said Andrew, who rather fancies his dry humour. "But apart from the climate and the architecture, was there any reason for suicide?"

"I'm told he was a little annoyed," said an enormous old farmer, delicately.

"It was the weather preyed on him," said the matron. "There was a vessel was coming round to him with coal and all sorts, weather-bound she was, in Kinsale, and in the latther end she met a rock, and she went down in a lump, and his own brother that was in her was drownded."

"There were grounds for annoyance, I admit," said Andrew.

The big farmer, who had, perhaps, been one of the jury, remarked non-committally that he wouldn't say much for the weather we were getting now, and there was one of them planets was after the moon always.

We moved on to the yard, in which prospective buyers were prowling among wheelbarrows, coils of rope, ladders, and the various rubbish proper to such scenes, and Andrew discoursed of the accessories that would be needed for the repair of my eaveshoots, with the large-mindedness of the Government official who has his own spurs and another man's horse. He was in the act of assuring me that I should save half a man's wages by having a second long ladder, when someone in the house began to play on a piano, with knowledge and vigour. The effect on Captain Larpent was as when a hound, outside a covert, hears the voice of a comrade within. The room from which the music came was on the ground floor, the back door was open, and Andrew walked in.

"That is one of those young ladies who have come

474

here to make their fortunes with poultry," observed a melancholy-looking clergyman at my elbow, "Miss Longmuir, I expect; she is the musician. Her friend, Dr. Catherine Fraser, is here also. Wonderful young ladies —no wish for society. I begged them to come and live near my church—I offered them a spare corner of the churchyard for their hen-coops—all of no avail."

I said that they seemed hard to please.

"Very, very," assented the clergyman; "yet I assure you there is nothing cynical about them. They are merely recluses."

He sighed, on what seemed to be general grounds, and moved away.

I followed Andrew into the house and found myself in the kitchen. The unspeakable dreariness of an auction was upon it. Pagodas of various crockeries stood high on the tables, and on benches round the walls sat, rook-like, an assembly of hooded countrywomen. A man with a dingy pale face was standing in front of the cold fire-place, addressing the company. On my arrival he removed his hat with stately grace, and with an effort, I recognized Cantillon the sweep, in mufti—that is to say, minus some of his usual top-dressing of soot.

"It's what I was saying, Major Yeates," he resumed. "I'm sweeping those chimneys thirty years, and five managers I seen in this house, and there wasn't one o' them that got the price of their ticket to Cork out o' that mine. This poor man was as well liked as anyone in the world, but there was a covey of blagyards in it that'd rob Saint Pether, let alone poor Mr. Harrington!"

The company assented with a groan of general application, and the ensuing pause was filled by the piano in the next room, large and heavy chords, suggestive of the hand of Andrew.

"God! Mrs. Harrington was a fine woman!" croaked one of the rooks on the bench.

"She was, and very stylish," answered another. "Oh, surely she was a crown!'"

"And very plain," put in a third, taking up the encomium like a part in a fugue, "as plain as the grass on the hills!"

I moved on, and met my wife in a crowd at the door of the dining-room, and in an atmosphere which I prefer not to characterize.

"I've got the barometer!" she said breathlessly. "No one bid for it, and I got it for five shillings! A lovely old one. It's been in the house for at least fifty years, handed from one manager to another."

"It doesn't seem to have brought them luck," I said. "What have you done with Anthony? Lost him, I hope!"

"There have been moments when I could have spared him," Philippa admitted, "especially when it came to his bidding against me, from the heart of the crowd, for a brass tea-kettle, and running the price up to the skies before I discovered him. Then I found him upstairs, auctioning a nauseous old tail of false hair, amidst the yells of country girls; and finally he tried to drop out of the staircase window—ten feet at least—with a stolen basket of tools round his neck. I just saw his hands on the edge of the window-sill."

"I think it's time to go home," I said grimly.

"Darling, *not* till I've bought the copper coal-scuttle. come and look at it!"

I followed her, uttering the impotent growls of a husband. As we approached the drawing-room the music broke forth again, this time in power. Three broad countrywomen, in black hooded cloaks and brown kid gloves, were seated on a sofa; two deeply engrossed backs at the piano accounted for the music. There is no denying the fact that a piano duet has some inescapable association with the schoolroom, no matter how dashing the execution, how superior the performers.

"Poor old 'Semiramide'!" whispered Philippa; "I played that overture when I was twelve!" Over her shoulder I had a view of Andrew's sleek black poll and brown neck, and an impression of fluffy hair, and a slight and shapely back in a Norfolk jacket.

"He seems to have discovered an interest in common after all," I said. "That's the pretty one, isn't it?"

I here became aware that the hall was filling with

476

people, and that Mr. Armstrong, the auctioneer, with his attendant swarm of buyers, was at my elbow.

"That's a sweet instrument," he said dispassionately, "and, I may say, magnificently played. Come, ladies and gentlemen, we'll not interrupt the concert. It might be as good for me to take the yard next, before the rain comes."

He led away his swarm like a queen bee; "Semiramide" stormed on; some people strayed into the room and began to examine the furniture. The afternoon had grown overcast and threatening, and I noticed that a tall man in dark clothes and a yachting cap had stationed himself near the treble's right hand. He was standing between her and the light, rather rudely, it seemed to me, but the players did not appear to notice.

"That was rather a free and easy fellow," I said to Philippa as we were borne along to the back door by the tide of auction. "I'm rather fond of him——"

"Who? Do you mean Mr. Armstrong?" said Philippa.

"No, the tall chap in the yachting cap."

"I didn't notice him——" began Philippa, but at this moment we were shot into the yard by pressure from behind. Mr. Armstrong took his stand on a packing-case, the people hived in round him, and I saw my wife no more.

Coils of fencing wire and sheets of corrugated iron were proffered, and left the audience cold; a faint interest was roused when the auctioneer's clerk held up one of a party of zinc pails for inspection.

"You'd count the stars through that one!" said a woman beside me.

"You can buy it for a telescope, ma'am!" said Mr. Armstrong swiftly.

"Well, well, hasn't he a very fine delivery!" said my neighbour, regarding Mr. Armstrong as if he were a landscape.

"Hannah," said the woman on my other hand, in a deep and reproachful contralto, speaking as if I did not exist, "did ye let the kitchen chairs go from you?"

"There wasn't one o' them but had a leg astray," apologized Hannah—"they got great hardship. When

477

Harrington'd have a drop taken he'd throw them here and there."

"Ladies! Ladies!" reproved Mr. Armstrong. "Is this an oxtion or is it a conversassiony? John! show that ladder."

"A big lot of use a forty-foot ladder'd be to the people round this place!" said a superior young farmer in a new suit of clothes; "there isn't a house here, unless it's my father's, would have any occasion for it."

Hannah dug me hard in the ribs with her elbow and put out her tongue.

"Five shillings I am bid for a forty-foot ladder!" said Mr. Armstrong to the heavens; "I'd get a better price at a jumble sale!"

"Look at the poker they have in it by the way of a rung!" continued the young farmer. "I wouldn't be bothered buying things at oxtions; if it was only gettin' marr'ed you were you'd like a new woman!"

"Seven and six!"

To my own astonishment I heard my voice saying this.

"Seven and six I am bid," said the auctioneer, seizing me with his eye. "Ten shillings may I say? Thank you, sir——"

The clergyman had entered the lists against me.

I advanced against him by half-crowns; the audience looked on as at a battle of giants. At twenty-five shillings I knew that he was weakening; at thirty shillings the ladder was mine.

I backed out of the crowd with the victor's laurels on my brow, and, as I did so, a speck of rain hit me in the eye. The sea was looking cold and angry, and the horizon to windward was as thick as a hedge. It was obviously time to go, and I proceeded in the direction of the car.

As I left the yard a remarkable little animal, which for a single wild instant I took for a fox or a badger, came running up the road. It was reddish brown, with white cheeks and a white throat; it advanced hesitatingly and circled round me with agitated and apologetic whimpers.

"Minx!" I said incredulously.

478

The fox or badger flung itself on its side and waved a forepaw at me.

"It's hunting rabbits below on the cliffs she was," said a boy in a white flannel jacket, who was sitting on the wall.

"Oh, there you are," said Philippa's voice behind me; "I wanted to remind you to remember the aneroid. It's on the dining-room table. I'm feeling rather unhappy about that child," she went on, "I can't find him any-where."

"*I'll* go in and find him," I said, with a father's ferocity.

"I hope he's there," said Philippa uncomfortably. "Good gracious! Is that Minx?"

I left the boy to explain, and made for the house, getting through the crowd in the doorway by the use of tongue and elbows, and making my way upstairs, strode hastily through the dark and repellent bedrooms of Har-rington's. Anthony was not there.

In the dining-room I heard Andrew's voice. I went in and found him sitting at the dinner-table with two ladies, one of whom was holding his hand and examining it attentively.

She had pale eyelashes, and pale golden hair, very firmly and repressively arranged; she was big and fresh and countrified-looking, and her eyes were water-green. She looked like an Icelander or a Finn, but I recognized her as the second chicken farmer, Dr. Fraser.

"I was looking for Anthony," I said, withholding with difficulty an apology for intrusion. "We've got to get away, Andrew——"

"I was having my fortune told," said Andrew, looking foolish.

"I saw your little boy going across the field there, about half an hour ago," said Dr. Fraser, looking up at me with eyes of immediate understanding. "The white terrier was with him."

"Towards the cliffs!" I said, feeling glad that Philippa was not there.

"No, to the right—towards the tower." She went to the window. "There was someone with him," she added quickly. "There he is now—that man in a yachting cap, by the tower——"

"I don't see anyone," I said, refixing my eyeglass.

Miss Fraser continued to stare out of the window. "You're short-sighted," she said, without looking at me. "Perhaps if the window were open——"

Before I could help her she had opened it, and the west wind rushed in, with big drops in it.

"I must be blind," I said, "I can see no one."

"Nor can I—now," she said, drawing back from the window.

She sat down at the table as if her knees had given way, and her strong white hand fell slackly on Philippa's purchase, the old aneroid barometer, and rested there. The other girl looked at her anxiously.

"Hold up, Cathie!" she said, as one speaks to a horse when it stumbles.

Her friend's eyes were fixed, and empty of expression, and the fresh pervading pink of her face had paled.

"Perhaps we had better go and look for that kid," said Andrew, getting up, and I knew that he too was aware of something uncomfortable in the atmosphere. Before we could get out of the room, Dr. "Cathie" spoke.

"I see tram-lines," she said gropingly, "and water—I wonder if he's asleep——"

She sighed. Andrew and I, standing aghast, saw her colour begin to return.

Her friend's eye indicated to us the door. We closed it behind us, and shoved our way through the hall.

"I say!" said Andrew, as we got outside, "I thought she was going to chuck a fit, or have hysterics, or something. Didn't you?"

I did not answer. Cantillon, the sweep, was hurrying towards me with tidings in his face.

"Mrs. Yeates is after going to the cliff looking for the young gentleman—but sure what I was saying——"

I did not wait to hear what Cantillon's observations had been, because I had caught sight of Philippa, away in a field near the edge of the cliffs. She was running, and the boy with the white flannel jacket was in front of her. It seemed ridiculous to hurry, when I knew that Anthony had been accompanied by a large man in a yachting cap (in itself a guarantee of competency).

None the less, I ran, with the wind and the heavy raindrops in my face, across country, not round by the road, and ran the faster for seeing my wife and her companion sinking out of sight over the edge of the cliff, as by an oblique path. My way took me past the tower; there was a little plateau there, with a drooping wire fence round it, and I had a glimpse of the square black mouth of the disused shaft.

"Near the tower," the girl had said; but she had also said there was a man with him.

I ran on, but fear had sprung out of the shaft and came with me.

A hard-trodden path led from the tower to the cliff; it fell steeper and steeper till, at a hairpin turn, it became rocky steps, slanting in sharp-cut zigzags down the face of the cliff. On the right hand the rocks leaned out above my head, yellow and grey and dripping, and tufted with sea pinks; on the left there was nothing except the wind. A couple of hundred feet below the sea growled and bellowed, plunging among broken rocks. I did not give room to the thought of Anthony's light body, tossed about there.

At a corner far below I had a glimpse of Philippa and the boy in the white jacket; he was leading her down—holding her hand—my poor Philippa, whose nightmare is height, who has *vertige* on a step-ladder. She must have had a sure word that Anthony had gone down this dizzy path before her. A mass of rock rose up between us, and they were gone, and in that gusty and treacherous wind it was impossible to make better speed.

The damnable iteration of the steps continued till my knees shook and my brain was half numb. They ceased at last at the mouth of a tunnel, half-way down the vertical face of the cliff; there was a platform outside it, over the edge of which two rusty rails projected into space above a narrow cove, where yellow foam, far below, churned and blew upwards in heavy flakes. Philippa and her guide had vanished. I felt for my match-box, and plunged into the dark and dripping tunnel.

I pushed ahead, at such speed as is possible for a six-foot man in a five-foot passage, splashing in the stream that gurgled between the tram-rails, and stumbling over the sleepers. Soon the last touches of daylight glinted in the water, they died, and it was pitch dark. I struck a match, sheltering it with my cap from the drips of the roof, and shouted, and stood still, listening. There was no sound, except the muffled roar of the sea outside; the match kindled broad sparkles of copper ore in the rock, but other response there was none.

Match by match I got ahead, shouting at intervals, stooping, groping, clutching at the greasy baulks of timber that supported the roof and sides, till a cold draught blew out my match. My next revealed a cross-gallery, with a broken truck blocking one entrance. There remained two ways to choose between. It was certain that the tram-rails must lead to the shaft, but which way had Philippa gone? And Anthony—I stood in maddening blackness; some darkness is a negative thing, this seemed an active, malevolent pressure. I counted my matches, and shouted, and still my voice came back to me, baffled, and without a hope in it. There were not half a dozen matches left.

A faint, paddling sound became audible above the dripping from the roof; I struck another of my matches, and something low and brown came panting into the circle of light. It was Minx, coming to me along the gallery of the tram-rails. She paused just short of the cross-ways, staring as though I were a stranger, and again a circling wind blew out my match. A fresh light showed her, still motionless; her back was up, not in the ordinary ridge, but in patches here and there; she was looking at something behind me; she made her mouth as round as a shilling, held up her white throat, and howled, thinly and carefully, as if she were keening. I cannot deny that I stiffened as I stood, and that second being that inhabits us, the being that is awake when we are asleep (and is always afraid), took charge for a moment; the other partner, who is, I try to think, my real self, pulled himself together with a certain amount of bad language, thrust Minx aside, and went ahead along the gallery of the tram-lines.

It needed only a dozen steps, and what Minx had or had not seen became a negligible matter. A white light, that turned the flame of my match to orange, began to irradiate the tunnel like moonrise, defining theatrically the profiles of rock, and the sagging props and beams. It came from an electric lamp, Anthony's electric lamp, standing on a heap of shale. The boy in the flannel jacket was holding a lighted candle-end in his fingers, and bending low over Philippa, who was kneeling between the tram-lines in the muddy water, holding Anthony in her arms. He was motionless and limp, and I felt that sickening drop of the heart that comes when the thing that seems too bad to think of becomes in an instant the thing that is.

"Tram-lines and water——" said a level voice in my brain. "I wonder if he is asleep——"

I wondered too.

Philippa looked up, with eyes that accepted me without comment.

"Only stunned, I think," she said hoarsely. "He opened his eyes an instant ago."

"The timber fell on him," said the country boy. "Look where he have the old prop knocked. 'Twas little but he was dead."

Anthony stirred uneasily.

"Oh, Mother, you're holding me too tight!" he said fractiously.

From somewhere ahead vague noises came, rumblings, scrapings, bangings like falling stones.

"It must be they're putting a ladder down in the shaft," said the boy.

Anthony had broken his collar-bone. So Dr. Fraser said; she tied him up with her knitted scarf by the light of the electric torch; I carried him up the ladder, and have an ineffaceable memory of the lavender glare of daylight that met us, and of the welcome that was in the everyday rain and the wet grass. In the relief of the upper air I even bore with serenity that didactics of

483

Andrew, who assured me that he had seen from the first that the shaft was the centre of the position, though he had never been in the slightest degree uneasy, because Dr. Fraser had seen someone with Anthony.

Dr. Fraser said nothing; no more did I.

"See now," said Cantillon the sweep, who, in common with the rest of the auction, was standing round the car to view our departure, "it pinched me like death when they told me the Major had that laddher bought!"

Being at the time sufficiently occupied in preparing to get away, I did not inquire why Cantillon should have taken the matter so much to heart.

"But after all," he proceeded, having secured the attention of his audience by an effective opening, "wasn't it the mercy of God them chaps Mr. Knox has at the kennels had it lent to the Mahonys, and them that's here took it from the Mahony's in a hurry the time Mr. Harrington died! And through all it was the Major's ladder."

Andrew had the ill-breeding to laugh.

"Sure it'd be no blame for a gentleman not to know the like of it," said Cantillon with severity. "Faith, I mightn't know it meself only for the old poker I stuck in it one time at Mr. Knox's when a rung broke under me——"

It is a valuable property of the motor-car that it can, at a moment's notice, fill an inconvenient interval with loud noises. I set the engine going and jumped into the car.

Something, covered by a rug, cracked and squashed under my foot. It was the aneroid.

When we reached a point in the road where it skirts the cliff I stopped the car, and flung the aneroid, like a quoit, over the edge, through the wind and the rain, into oblivion.

THE MAROAN PONY

I had taken ten minutes to work the car over the bridge at Poundlick, so intricate was the crowd of people and carts, so blind and deaf to any concerns save their own; a crowd that offered sometimes the resistance of the feather bed, sometimes that of the dead wall, an intractable mass, competent to reduce the traffic of Piccadilly to chaos, and the august Piccadilly police to the point of rushing to the nearest lunatic asylum and saying, "Let us in! We are mad!"

The town of Poundlick is built at so accommodating a tilt that it is possible to stand on the bridge at its foot, and observe the life of its single street displayed like a poster on the hillside; even to compare the degrees of custom enjoyed by its public-houses, and to estimate the number of cur dogs to the square yard of pavement. I speak of an ordinary day. But this hot 20th of September was far from being ordinary.

The Poundlick Races are, I believe, an ancient and annual function but, being fifteen miles from anywhere, I had hitherto been content to gauge their attractions by their aftermath of cases in the Petty Sessions Court next following the fixture. There is, however, no creature more the sport of circumstances than a married man with a recent motor; my attendance, and that of the car at the Poundlick Races had been arranged to the last sandwich before I had time to collect objections (and this method, after all, saves some wear and tear).

The races are held on the banks of the Arrigadheel River, within hail of the town, and are reached—as everything in Ireland is reached—by a short cut. We—that is to say, my wife, her cousin, Captain Andrew Larpent, R.E., and I—were gathered into the jovial crowd that straggled, and hustled, and discoursed over the marshy meadows of the river, and ploughed through the brown mud in the gaps without a check in pace or conversation. The committee had indeed "knocked" walls, and breached banks, but had not further interfered with the course of nature, and we filed at length on to the course across a tributary of the river, paying a penny each for the facilities offered by a narrow and bounding plank and the muddy elbow of a young man who stood in mid-stream; an amenity accepted with suitable yells by the ladies (of whom at least ninety per cent remarked "O God!" in transit).

The fact that there are but four sound and level fields with a ten-mile radius of Poundlick had simplified the labours of the committee in the selection of a course. Rocky hills rose steeply on two sides of the favoured spot, the Arrigadheel laid down the law as to its boundaries, and within these limitations an oval course had been laid out by the simple expedient of breaking gaps in the banks. The single jump-race on the programme was arranged for by filling the gaps with bundles of furze, and there was also a water-jump, more or less forced upon the committee by the intervention of a ditch pertaining to one of the fences. A section of the ditch had been widened and dammed, and the shallow trough of pea-soup that resulted had been raised from the rank of a puddle by a thin decoration of cut furze-bushes.

The races had not begun, but many horses were galloping about and over the course, whether engaged in unofficial competitions or in adding a final bloom to their training, I am unable to say. We wandered deviously among groups of country people, anchored in conversation, or moving, still in conversation, as irresistibly as a bog slide. Whether we barged into them, or they into us, was a matter of as complete indifference to them as it would have been to a drove of their own bony cattle.

"These are the sort of people I love," said Philippa, her eyes ranging over the tented field and its throngs, and its little red and green flags flapping in the sunshine. "Real Primitives, like a chorus in *Acis and Galatea*!"

She straightened her hat with a gasp, as a couple of weighty female primitives went through us and passed on. (In all circumstances and fashions, my wife wears a large hat, and thereby adds enormously to the difficulties of life.) Among the stalls of apples and biscuits, and adjacent to the drink tent, a roulette table occurred, at which the public were invited to stake on various items of the arms of the United Kingdom. The public had accepted the invitation in considerable numbers, and I did not fail to point out to Philippa the sophisticated ease with which Acis flung his penny upon "Harp", while Galatea, planking twopence upon the Prince of Wales' plumes, declared that the last races she was at she got the price of her ticket on "Feather".

We passed on, awaking elusive hopes in the bosoms of two neglected bookmakers, who had at intervals bellowed listlessly to the elements, and now eagerly offered me Rambling Katty at two to one.

"Boys, hurry! There's a man dead, north!" shrieked a boy, leaping from the top of a bank. "Come north till we see him!"

A rush of boys went over us; the roulette table was deserted in a flash, and its proprietor and the bookmakers exchanged glances expressive of the despicable frivolity of the rustics of Poundlick.

"We ought to try to find Dr. Fraser," said Philippa, hurrying in the wake of the stampede.

"I did not know that the chicken farmers were to be among the attractions," I said to Andrew, realizing, not for the first time, that I am but an infant crying in the night where matters of the higher diplomacy are toward.

Andrew made no reply, as is the simple method of some men when they do not propose to give themselves away, and we proceeded in the direction of the catastrophe.

The dead man was even less dead than I had expected. He was leaning against a fence, explaining to Dr. Catherine Fraser that he felt all the noise of all the wars of all the worlds within his head.

Dr. Fraser, who was holding his wrist, while her friend, Miss Longmuir, kept the small boys at bay, replied that she would like a more precise description. The sufferer, whose colour was returning, varied the metaphor, and said that the sound was for all the world like the quacking of ducks.

"You'd better go home and keep quiet," said Dr. Fraser, accepting the symptom with professional gravity.

I asked my next-door neighbour how the accident had occurred.

"Danny Lyons here was practising this young mare of Herlihy's for Lyney Garrett, that's to ride her in the first race," said my neighbour, a serious man with bushy black whiskers, like an old-fashioned French waiter, "and sure she's as loose as a hare, and when she saw the flag before her on the fénce, she went into the sky, and Danny dhruv in the spur to keep the balance, and with that then the sterrup broke."

"It's little blagyarding she'd have if it was Lyney was riding her!" said someone else.

"Ah, Lyney's a tough dog," said my neighbour; "in the ring of Ireland there isn't a nicer rider."

"There might be men as good as him in Poundlick!" said an ugly little black-muzzled fellow, suddenly and offensively, "and horses too! As good as any *he'll* throw his leg over!"

Dr. Fraser's patient stood up abruptly.

"Oh, oh, oh!" said the man with the bushy whiskers, placing himself in front of the invalid. "Let you be said by the lady, Danny, and go home! Have behaviour now, Peter Lynch!"

The matter hung for a moment; a bell began to ring in the middle of the course, and the onlookers flung the situation from them like a squeezed lemon, and swept *en masse* towards the summons, bearing with them the invalid.

"Off the stage I have never seen people clear out so fast," remarked Andrew. "Now that we've seen Dr. Fraser's Lightning Cure, I suppose we may as well go too."

His eyes, by a singular coincidence, met those of Miss Longmuir, which were very pretty eyes, dark and soft.

"I must go and hunt up our pony," she said, with a

very businesslike air; "we've entered her for the third race, you know."

She put back her hair as it blew across her forehead, and the gold in it glinted in the sun.

"How sporting of you!" we heard Andrew say, as they walked away together.

My wife and Dr. Fraser and I turned as one man, and went in the opposite direction.

We steered for an island of furze and grey boulders that had been flung into the valley like a vedette from the fortified hillside, and was placed, considerately, at the apex of the oval course. Half a dozen men were already grouped upon the boulders, like cormorants. We clambered to a higher *étage*, and there spread forth ourselves and our belongings upon the warm slabs. The sun was hot, yet not too hot, the smell of trodden turf was pleasant in the air, the river sparkled and gurgled beside us; the chimneys of Poundlick sent up languid spires of blue smoke; its yellow and pink and white houses became poetic in the September haze. The first delicate pangs of hunger were stealing upon us, and I felt reasonably certain that nothing necessary to our welfare had been forgotten. I lit a cigarette and pulled my cap over my eyes, and listened to a lark, spiring like the smoke into the blue, while my wife clattered in the luncheon basket. It was a moment of entire well-being, overshadowed only by the prospect of having to take an interest in the racing.

I said as much to Dr. Fraser, who was dismembering a cold chicken with almost awful surgical dexterity.

"You must wake up for our race," she said. "I'll call you in time."

"Must I? I hope you're going to ride."

"Heaven forfend!" replied Dr. Fraser. "Nothing more spirited than a weight-carrying bicycle! I'm not in the least horsy. Meg was dying to ride, but as we bought the pony from the great Lyney, and he had won any number of races on her, he was distinctly indicated."

"Quite right too," I said, with dowager-like propriety. "And I should wish it to be clearly understood that if,

489

at the last moment, your friend Mr. Lyney should be too drunk to ride, I will not take his place."

"He doesn't drink," said Dr. Fraser, who has an unsympathetic way of keeping to the point. "He's been a great friend of mine ever since I mended a broken finger for him."

There was a stir among the cormorants on the lower tier of boulders, a shot was fired at the far end of the course, everyone began to shout, and an irregularly shaped mass was detached from the crowd, and resolved itself into a group of seven horses, pounding towards us at a lumbering canter. One of the riders had a green jacket, the others were in shirt sleeves, with coloured scarves over their shoulders; all were bareheaded. As they neared the first jump, I found myself on my feet on my boulder, with two unknown men hanging on to me to steady themselves.

"That's no throuble to them!" shouted one of my *attachés*, as each horse in turn galloped over or through the barrier of furze in the gap.

"Which is Lyney Garrett?" I asked.

"That's him on the chestnut mare—the jock that have the dhress on him." He pointed to the wearer of the green jacket.

"Ah ha! Lyney's the boy! Look at him now, how he'll stoop and leave the horse to go for herself! He'll easy the horse, and he'll easy himself!"

"That Rambling Katty he's riding's a nice loose mare —she has a good fly in her," said another.

"Lyney's built for it. If there's any sort of a spring in a horse at all, he'll make him do it."

"He'd make a donkey plough!" flung in another enthusiast.

As they neared the flags at the turn of the oval—and an uncommonly sharp turn it was—the pace improved, each man trying to get the inside station; I could already see, written on the countenance of a large young grey horse, his determination to pursue an undeviating course of his own.

"Now, Lyney! Spare him in the angle!" shouted my

neighbour, hanging on to my sleeve and rocking perilously.

Lyney, a square-shouldered young man, pale and long-jawed, bored determinedly on to the first flag, hit it with his right knee, wrenched Rambling Katty round the second flag, and got away for the water-jump three lengths ahead of anyone else.

"Look at that for ye—how he goes round the corner on one leg!" roared his supporter. "He'd not stop for the Lord Leftenant!"

The remaining riders fought their way round the flags, with strange tangents and interlacing curves; all, that is to say, save the grey horse, who held on unswervingly and made straight for the river. The spectators, seated on the low bank at its edge, left their seats with singular unanimity. The majority fled, a little boy turned a somersault backwards into the water, but three or four hardier spirits tore off their coats, swung them like flails in front of the grey, and threw their caps in his face, with a wealth of objurgation that I have rarely heard equalled.

"The speed was in him and he couldn't turn", explained one of my neighbours, at the top of his voice, as the grey, yielding to public opinion, returned to the course and resumed the race.

"That horse is no good," said a dapper young priest, who had joined our crowd on the rock. "Look at his great flat feet! You'd bake a cake on each of them!"

"Well, that's the case indeed, Father," replied a grizzled old farmer, "but he's a fine cool horse, and a great farming horse for ever. Be gance! He'd plough the rocks!"

"Well, he'll get a nice view of the race, anyway," said the young priest, "he has it all before him."

"They don't seem to be getting any delay with the water-jump," said someone else regretfully.

"Ah, what's in it but the full of a few tin cans!" said my adherent.

"Well, for all, it knocked a good lep out o' Rambling Katty; she went mountains over it!"

"Look south! Look south! They're coming on again, and only five o' them in it——"

The cheering was hotter this time, and it was entirely characteristic that it was the riders who were shouted for and not the horses.

"They'll win now this turn—there's three o' them very thick, that's a nice tidy race," said the old farmer.

"Good boy, Kenny! Go on, Kenny!" bellowed someone on a lower ledge.

"Who's second, coming up to the flag now—" panted Philippa, who was hanging on to the collar of my coat and trying to see over my shoulder.

"That's Jimmy Kenny," responded the man below, turning a black-muzzled face up towards us, his light eyes gleaming between their black lashes in the sunshine, like aquamarines. I recognized Peter Lynch, whom we had met earlier in the day.

"It's young Kenny out of the shop," explained the old farmer to me; "he rides very nate."

No one was found to endorse his opinion. The horses came on, sweating and blowing, the riders, by this time very red in the face, already taking to their whips. By some intricate process of jostling, young Kenny got the inside place at the first flag.

"Now is he nate! What was I saying!" exulted the old farmer.

"Lyney! Lyney!" roared the faithful gallery, as the leaders hustled round the second flag and went away up the course.

"Up, Kenny!" replied the raucous tenor of Peter Lynch in solitary defiance.

Last of all, the grey horse, who would plough the rocks, came on indomitably, and made, as before, a bee-line for the river. Here, however, he was confronted by a demonstration hurriedly arranged by his friends, who advanced upon him waving tall furze-bushes, with which they beat him in the face. The grey horse changed his mind with such celerity that he burst his girth; someone caught him by the head, while his rider hung precariously upon his neck; someone else dragged off the saddle, replanted his jockey upon his broad bare back, and speeded him on his way by bringing the saddle

492

down upon his hind-quarters with an all-embracing thump.

"It's only the age he wants," said a partisan. "If they'd keep him up to the practice, he'd be a sweeper yet!"

Tumult at the end of the course, and a pistol-shot, here announced that the race was over.

"Lyney have it!" shouted some men, standing on the fence by the water-jump.

"What happened Kenny?" bawled Peter Lynch.

"He was passing the flag and he got clung in the pole, and the next man knocked him down out of the pole!" shouted back the field telegraph.

"Oh pity!" said the old farmer.

"He didn't get fair play!" vociferated Peter Lynch, glowering up at the adherents of Lyney with a very green light in his eye.

The young priest made a slight and repressive gesture with his hand.

"That'll do now, Peter," he said, and turned to the old farmer. "Well, Rambling Katty's a hardy bit of stuff," he went on, brushing the rock-lichen from his black coat.

"She is that, Father," responded my late adherent, who, to my considerable relief, had now ceased to adhere. "And nothing in her but a fistful of bran!"

"She's the dryest horse that came in," said the young priest, descending actively from the rock.

With the knowledge that the committee would allow an hour at least for the effects of a race to pass off before launching another, we climbed to the summit of the island, and began upon the luncheon basket; and, as vultures drop from the blue empyrean, so did Andrew and Miss Longmuir arrive from nowhere and settle upon the sandwiches.

"Oh, I can't eat our own game, can I?" said the latter, with a slight shudder, as I placed the chicken before her. "No—really—not even for your sake!" She regarded me very pleasingly, but I notice that it is only since my hair began to turn grey over my ears that these things are openly said to me. "I had to feed four dozen of the brutes before we started this morning, and I shall have to do it all over again when we get home!"

"I don't know how you stand it, I should let 'em starve," said Andrew, his eyes travelling from her white forehead to her brown hands. "*I* don't consider it is work for ladies."

"You can come and help the ladies if you like," said Miss Longmuir, glancing at him as she drove her white teeth into a sandwich.

"Do you mean that?" said Andrew in a low voice.

"She's blown him to pieces before he's left the covert," I said to myself, and immediately withdrew into blameless conversation with my wife and Dr. Fraser.

We had gone pretty well down through the luncheon basket, and had arrived at a second and even more balmy—being well-fed—period of peace, before it occurred to Miss Longmuir to look at her watch, and to spoil the best cigarette of the day with agitations concerning the non-appearance of her pony. I suggested that she and Captain Larpent should go in search of it, and for a brief interval the disturbing element was eliminated. It returned, with added agitation, in a quarter of an hour.

"Cathie! I can't find Nancy anywhere! We've been all round the course!" cried Miss Longmuir from below. "And John Sullivan is nowhere to be found either, and I can't get near Lyney, he's riding in the trotting race."

"You'll find the pony is somewhere about all right," I said, with the optimism of combined indolence and indifference.

"That seems probable," said Andrew, "but the point is, she's somewhere where we're not."

"The point is, she ought to be here," said Miss Longmuir, with a very bright colour in her cheeks as she looked up at us.

"Heavens! They're very angry!" I murmured to Dr. Fraser.

"Well, what do you want us to do?" inquired Dr. Fraser lethargically.

"You might take some faint shadow of interest in the fact that Nancy is lost," replied Miss Longmuir.

"I think we'd better organize a search-party," said Philippa (who does not smoke).

We rose stiffly, descended from our sun-warmed boulders, and took up the White Man's burden.

A sweeping movement as inaugurated, whose objects were to find the pony or her attendant, John Sullivan, or Lyney.

"Should you know the pony if you saw her?" I said confidentially to Dr. Fraser, as she and I set forth together.

"We've not had it very long," she replied dubiously. "Luckily it's an easy colour. John Sullivan calls it maroan—a sort of mixture of roan and maroon."

We advanced from field to field, driving like twin darning-needles through the groups of people, but neither John Sullivan nor the maroan pony transpired.

"Come on, come on! The stepping match is starting!" shouted someone.

Dr. Fraser and I were caught in the tightening mesh of the crowd, as in the intricacies of a trammel net; an irregular thumping of hoofs, and a row of bare and bobbing heads passing above the heads of the crowd, indicated that the stepping match was under way. Lyney's dour face and green jacket were in the lead, and, as before, had he been Diana of the Ephesians, he could not have been more passionately called upon. As it was obviously useless for us to do so at this juncture, we climbed on to a bank near the winning post, and watched the race. Lyney was riding a long-backed yellow animal with a face as cross as his own, and a step as fast as the tick of a watch.

"Any other man than Lyney wouldn't carry that old pony round," said one man.

"She has a score o' years surely, but she's as wicked as a bee," said another.

"Lyney's very knacky; he couldn't be bate," said the first man.

"Well, well, look at Jimmy Kenny and his father, and the two o' them riding!" went on the commentator.

495

"Faith, I'd give the father the sway. Jimmy's riding uneven. When the nag is rising, he's falling."

"Sure he has his two elbows into his ears! Go on, Lyney boy!"

The horses pounded past, splashing through the shallow flood of the water-jump, and trampling over such furze-bushes as had withstood the vicissitudes of the steeplechase. They passed from our view, and Dr. Fraser and I agreed that we should be justified in staying where we were till the finish. Three times they passed us, enveloped in a travelling roar of encouragements, and with each passing the supporters of Lyney and Kenny bayed and howled more emulously. The competitors, now, to all practical intent, reduced to the Kennys, *père et fils*, and Lyney, again disappeared on their last round, and the volleys of incitement became a dropping fire of criticism.

"Kenny's mare is the one, the others is too crippled."

"She'll not bate Lyney! Divil blast the bate she have in her! she's too dropped and too narra!"

"What horse is first?"

"I'd know; only one, I think."

"Look at young Kenny coming up on the father now!"

"Ah, there's more in the owld fella, never fear him!"

"Come on, Lyney! Come on, Kenny! Lyney! Lyney!"

Lyney won. The bee-like wickedness of the yellow mare apparently served her as well as youth, and despite the fact that she was but little over fourteen hands and was carrying twelve stone, she finished a dozen lengths in front. The interest of the race was at once transferred to the struggle for second place between the Kennys.

"Come on, Tom! Come on, Jimmy! Begor' the father have it!" yelled the crowd, as Kenny *père*, flourishing his whip over his grey head, finished half a length in front of his son.

"Them two tight wheels at the corner, 'twas there he squeezed the advantage of the son."

"No, but the father had a drop taken, 'twas that that gave him the heart."

Dr. Fraser and I got off our fence and steered for Lyney.

He was in the act of throwing the reins on the pony's neck and himself off her back as we arrived.

"Here!" he said to the owner, "take your old skin!" —he tossed his whip on to the ground—"and your old whip too!"

The owner took the "old skin" by her drooping and dripping head, and picked up the whip, in reverential submission, and the ring of admirers evidently accepted this mood of the hero as entirely befitting his dignity.

Dr. Fraser advanced through them with the effortless impressiveness of a big woman, and made her inquiries about the pony. Lyney dropped the hero manner.

"I don't at all doubt but John Sullivan's gone up to Lynch's for her, Doctor; you needn't be uneasy at all," he said, with a respect that must have greatly enhanced our position in the eyes of the crowd. "I told him he shouldn't bring her too soon for fear she'd sour on us. We have an hour yet."

Soothed by this assurance we moved on, and even, in this moment of unexpected leisure, dallied with the roulette table. I had, in fact, lost ninepence, when the remainder of the search-party bore down upon us at speed.

"The pony is *not* here!" said Miss Longmuir, regarding our outspread coppers with an eye of burning indignation, "and Sullivan's brother doesn't know where he is—says he went up to the town two hours ago. I'm going up to look for him, but of course if you'd rather stay and play roulette——" Her voice shook. I need hardly say that we went.

On our arrival at the town of Poundlick we found it to be exclusively inhabited by grandmothers. Lynch's public-house was garrisoned by a very competent member of the force, who emerged from the kitchen with an infant in her arms, and another attached to her clothing. She knew nothing of the pony, she knew nothing of John Sullivan. There was certainly a young lad that came in, and he having drink taken, and wherever he got it, it wasn't in this house, and what did he do but to

497

commence jumping the counter, you'd think he'd jump the house. She paused, and I murmured to Dr. Fraser that she was like a Holbein, and Dr. Fraser replied that she did not believe one word she said, which was rather my own idea, only more so. It appeared that her son Peter had, an hour ago, expelled the young lad from the house (lest its fair fame should be sullied), and as for Peter, the dear knew where he was, she didn't see him since.

Miss Longmuir and Andrew here left the shop, very purposefully; we pursued, and saw them open the gate of Lynch's yard and stride in. The yard was a small one, littered with cases of bottles, and congested by the outside cars and carts of race-goers; such level spaces as it possessed had been dug out of the side of the hill, and slatternly stables and outhouses were perched on the different levels. Through a low-browed doorway might be seen the horses of race-goers, standing "ready dight", like the steeds of Branksome Hall, with heads hanging, in resigned depression, before empty racks and mangers. But of the maroon pony there was no sign.

Fierce as terriers on a rat-hunt, Miss Longmuir and Andrew dashed in and out of the dark sheds and outhouses, till there remained unexplored but one hovel, whose open door revealed only semi-darkness, edged with fern-litter. None the less, the leading terrier determined to make good the ground. A sharp yelp told of a find, and Miss Longmuir emerged, holding aloft a new check horse-sheet, with the initials "M.L." large upon it.

"They must have taken her down to the racecourse, after all——" I began.

"Thoughtless of them to take her without her saddle or bridle," said Andrew bitingly. "Here they are behind the door!"

The silence that followed this discovery was broken by Philippa.

"I hear someone snoring!" she said in a conspirator's whisper. "Do come away. I'm sure it's a drunken man."

"Quite so," said Andrew, who had been pursuing his researches. "Allow me to introduce Mr. John Sullivan."

In the dark corner behind the door lay a stout youth, comfortably extended, with his flushed face half hidden in the dry and tawny bracken, and his open mouth framing long and quiet snores. He was obviously at peace with all the world.

Some heartless assaults on the part of Captain Larpent had no appreciable result, so inveterate was the peace, so potent the means by which it had been invoked. The ladies had retired during the interview, and, as we rejoined them in the yard, we all became aware of muffled and thunderous sounds near at hand; they were suggestive of a ponderous and chaotic clog-dance, and proceeded from an outhouse, built against the bank that formed the upper side of the yard, with its gable askew to the other buildings.

" 'Lots of things is coor'us,' as Anthony said when I told him about Jonah and the Whale," remarked Philippa, who, throughout, had not taken the affair as seriously as it deserved. "I supose the party that John Sullivan was at is going on up there."

Miss Longmuir darted round the gable of the house, a wild and summoning cry followed, the call of the terrier who has run his rat to ground.

We found her at the foot of a low flight of irregular stone steps (in telling the story I have formed the habit of saying that there were ten of them) that led to a door-way in a loft. In the doorway, with a cabbage leaf in her mouth, was the maroan pony, looking down at us with an expression of mild surprise.

We all said unanimously, and with equal futility, "How—on—earth——?"

After which Andrew, who dislikes miracles, arranged that she had, of course, got into the loft from the back, where the ground was high. Unfortunately the theory did not work, an inspection of the loft revealing nothing but four walls, a large store of dried bracken, and a donkey-panier filled with cabbages.

"These mountainy ponies climb like monkeys," said Philippa, with her inevitable effort to shelter the discomfited, as Andrew returned with the ruins of his theory, "she must have walked up the steps!"

Miss Longmuir, snatching out her watch, said she didn't care how the pony got there, the point was to get her down as quickly as possible. "If people would only *do* something and not talk!" she added, under her breath.

"If she walked up she can walk down," said Andrew firmly.

He mounted the steps and took the pony by the halter. The pony immediately backed thunderously out of sight, taking Andrew with her. Miss Longmuir flew up the steps to his assistance, and unseen sarabands pummelled the floor of the loft.

"Go up and help them, you great lazy thing!" said Philippa to me.

"There's no room for anyone else," I protested.

Here the combatants reappeared in the doorway, gradually, with endearments on one side, and suspicious snortings on the other. The steps were broad and not too intimidating; the pony advanced almost to the sill, repented in haste, and in her retreat flung Andrew against the panier of cabbages. A donkey's panier is made to resist shocks; in this case it apparently gave more than it took; Andrew said nothing, but he dragged the basket over the sill and hurled it down the steps with considerable emotion. I joined the party in the loft, and Philippa collected the cabbages, and laid them in rows upon the steps as if it were a harvest festival, in the hope of luring the pony to the descent. The lure was rejected with indignation, and I proceeded to offer a few plain truths. That the floor would come down before the mare did. That it would take six men, and planks, and cart-loads of straw, to get her out. Finally, that her race was due to start in twenty minutes.

"We're done," said Miss Longmuir tragically, addressing Philippa and Dr. Fraser from the top of the steps, as if they were a stage mob. "These brutes have beaten us! Don't you remember that Lyney's father said, "Let ye keep out from them lads in Poundlick'? And after all our trouble, and the training, and everything——" She turned abruptly away from the door.

Dr. Fraser stood still, with her hand to her forehead, as though she were trying to remember something. Then she too came up into the loft. The pony had now backed into the pile of bracken; Andrew, whose back teeth were evidently set tight, was tugging at her halter, and she was responding by throwing her nose in the air and showing the whites of her eyes.

"Meg," said Dr. Fraser, at the doorway, "I've remembered something that I was once told——" She peered into the darkness of the loft. "May I try?" she said, advancing quietly to the pony's head.

"By all means," said Andrew, as chillingly as was possible for a man who was very red in the face and was draped with cobwebs.

Looking back now to the affair, I cannot remember that Dr. Fraser did anything in the least remarkable. She took hold of the halter with one hand and with the other patted the pony's neck, high up, near the ears. She also spoke to it, the sort of things anyone might say. For the life of me I could not see that she did more than anyone else had done, but Nancy lowered her head and put her ears forward.

Dr. Fraser gave the halter a gentle pull, and said, "Come on, old girl!" and the pony started forward with a little run.

At the doorway she stopped. We held our breaths. Dr. Fraser patted her again and placidly descended the first step; the maroon pony placed a trembling foot upon the threshold, steadied herself, poked her nose forward, and dropped her forefeet on to the second step.

"She'll come down on top of her!" said Andrew, starting forward.

"Don't touch her!" exclaimed Miss Longmuir, grasping his arm.

With the tense caution of an old dog, the pony let herself down from step to step, planting her little hoofs cunningly on the rough-set stones, bracing herself with the skill learned on the rocky staircases of her native hills. Dr. Fraser kept a step in advance of her. Thus, with slow clattering, and in deep gravity, they joined Philippa in the yard.

Five people cannot advantageously collaborate in putting a saddle and bridle on a pony, but we tried, and in the grim hustle that resulted no one asked questions or made comments. Amongst us the thing was done,

and there were still seven minutes in hand when Andrew
shot out of the yard on her back. Hard on her heels
followed Philippa and Miss Longmuir, with scarcely
inferior velocity. I returned to the remaining member
of the party and found that she had seated herself on
the steps.

She said she was tired, and she looked it.

"I dare say getting that beast down the steps was
rather a strain?" I said, spreading the pony's rug for
her to sit on.

"Oh, that was nothing. Please don't wait for me."

I said in my best ironic manner that doctors were of
course impervious to fatigue, and indeed superior to all
human ills.

She laughed. "I admit that I was rather nervous that
the thing wouldn't work, or would break down half-
way."

"What thing?" I demanded. "The pony?"

"No. The secret. It *is* a secret, you know. My grandfather gave Rarey thirty pounds for it. I've never had
much to say to horses, but I have started a jibbing
hansom horse in Oxford Street with it." she laughed
again apologetically.

"You needn't believe it unless you like. I must say I
was afraid it mightn't include a flight of steps!" She
paused and put back her abundant fair hair. "How hot
it was up in that loft! I wonder if you could get me a
glass of water?"

I told her that I was old enough to believe anything,
but added that after what she had told me I would get
a second glass of water, with sal volatile in it, for myself.

The Holbein grandmother was standing at the back
door of the house with the baby still on her arm. She
and the baby fetched the glass of water. She said wasn't
the pony a Fright for ever after the way he came down
them steps, but why wouldn't the lady take him out
through the other door into the field above?

I made no reply, but while Dr. Fraser was drinking
the water, I went up into the loft, and cleared away the
bracken that had been piled in front of the "door into
the field above". I opened the door, and walked out into

the field, and viewed the small hoof-prints that led to the door of the loft.

I returned to Dr. Fraser, and very gently broke the news to her.

Of course Lyney and the maroan pony won the race. Had this not been a foregone conclusion it is possible that John Sullivan might have scored less heavily in the matter of free drinks.

As I was conducting my exhausted but triumphant party off the course, the Poundlick sergeant of police met me and asked me if I would sign a few summonses for him, as he was after taking some parties into custody for fighting.

"Drunk, I suppose?"

The sergeant admitted it, and said the dispute had arisen between the Kennys and the Lynches on the one side, and the partisans of Lyney Garrett on the other, out of "circumstances connected with the last race". The sergeant's eye rested for an instant, with what may be described as a respectful twinkle, upon Miss Long-muir.

"It was mostly heavy offers and small blows, Major," he concluded.

"Look here, sergeant," I said oracularly, "take them all to the water-jump. Build up the furze in front of it. Make them jump it. Anyone that gets over it may be considered sober. Anyone that falls in will be sober enough when he gets out."

I have not, in my judicial career, delivered a judgement that gave more satisfaction to the public.

MAJOR APOLLO RIGGS

PART I

The leave of Captain Andrew Larpent, R.E., was expiring, dying hard, "in rings of strenuous flight" (and my motor), on the road between Shreelane and Licknavar, which is the home of the chicken farmers. Philippa, who regards a flirtation with an enthusiasm that is as disinterested as it is inexplicable, assured me that the state of affairs was perfectly unmistakable. She further said that the male determination to deny and ignore these things was partly sympathetic secretiveness, partly the affectation of despising gossip, and mainly stupidity. She took a long breath after all this, and, seeing Andrew approaching along the garden path in apparently romantic meditation, enjoined me to be nice to the poor thing, and departed.

The sun was bright, with the shallow brightness of early October, and the Virginian creeper made a conflagration on the weather-slated end of the house. The poor thing deposited himself beside me on the garden seat. I noticed that his eye rested upon a white chicken with a brilliant scarlet comb; it was one of several, purchased from the chicken farmers. I would not for worlds have admitted it to Philippa, but there was undoubtedly sentiment in the glance.

"I hear they're having beastly weather at the Curragh," he said, leaning back and looking gloomily up into the melting blue sky. "Stunning that red stuff looks on the house!" He surveyed it, and sighed; then, suddenly, sentiment faded from his glance. "D'you know, old boy, that chimney up there is well out of the perpendicular. It'll be down about your ears some day."

I replied that it had maintained that angle for the ten years of my tenancy.

"It won't do it much longer," returned my guest. "Look at that crack in the plaster!"

"Which crack?" I said coldly. (Mr. Flurry Knox is my landlord, and it is my misfortune to have a repairing lease.)

"Take your choice," said Andrew, scanning the chimneys with the alert and pitiless eye of the Royal Engineer. "My money's on the northern one, under the jackdaw."

"Oh, confound you and the jackdaws!" I said pettishly. "The chimney draws all right."

But the matter did not end there. Before luncheon, Andrew and I had made a tour of the roof, and he had demonstrated unanswerably, and with appalling examples from barracks that he had repaired in Central India, and built in Wei-hai-Wei, that nothing but habit and family feeling induced any one of the chimney stacks to stand up.

At luncheon he told Philippa that he hoped she would insure the children before the next westerly gale. Philippa replied by asking if he, or anyone else, had ever heard of a chimney falling, unless it had been struck by lightning, in which case it wouldn't matter if it were straight or crooked; and though this was manifestly worthless as an argument, neither Andrew nor I could remember an instance in support of our case. That the case had now become mine as well as Andrew's was the logical result of illogical opposition, and at Philippa's door I deposit the responsibility for a winter of as varied discomforts as it has been our lot to endure.

The matter matured rapidly. In the mellow moment that comes with coffee and cigarettes I began, almost pleasurably, to lay out the campaign.

"I can't see any point in wasting money on a contractor," said Andrew airily. "Any of your local masons could do it if I explained the job to him. A fortnight ought to see it through."

It was at this point that I should have sat heavily upon Andrew. I was not without experience of the local mason and his fortnights; what could Andrew know of such? I had a brief and warning vision of Captain Larpent, seated at an office table adorned with sheets of perfect ground-plans and elevations, issuing instructions to a tensely intelligent sapper sergeant. I saw the sergeant, supreme in scientific skill (and invariably sober), passing on the orders to a scarcely less skilled company of prompt subordinates—but my "worser angel" obliterated it. And that very afternoon, on our way to Aussolas, we chanced to meet upon the road the local mason himself, William Shanahan, better known to fame as "Walkin' Aisy". He was progressing at a rate of speed that accorded with his sub-title, and, as I approached him, a line of half-forgotten verse came back:

Entreat her not, her eyes are full of dreams

Nevertheless, I stopped the car.

In answer to inquiries, he mused, with his apostolic countenance bent upon the ground; after a period of profound meditation, he asked me why wouldn't I get one of the big fellas out from the town? I have never known Walkin' Aisy to accept a job without suggesting that someone else could do it better than he (in which he was probably quite right). This may have been humility, due to the fact that his father had been that despised thing, "a dry-wall builder"; it may have been from coquetry, but I am inclined to think it was due to a mixture of otherworldliness and sloth.

On pressure he said that he had still a small piece en of work to finish, but he might be able to come down to-morrow to travel the roof and see what would be wanting to us, and on Monday week, with the help of God, he would come in it. His blue eyes wavered towards the horizon. The interview closed.

" 'Fair and young were they when in hope they began that long journey'," cooed Philippa, as we moved away. The quotation did not, as I well knew, refer to our visit to the Knoxes.

At Aussolas I aired my project to my landlord. Flurry is not a person to whom it is agreeable to air a project.

"Rebuild the chimneys, is it? Oh, with all my heart. Is there anything the matter with them?"

Andrew explained the imminence of our peril, and Flurry listened to him with his inscrutable eye on me.

"Well, it'll be some fun for you during the winter, Major, but be careful when you're cutting the ivy!"

I was betrayed into asking why.

"Because there's only it and the weather-slating keeping the walls standing."

"If I may presume to contradict one so much younger than myself," said old Mrs. Knox, "Shreelane is as well built a house as there is in the county." Her voice was, as ever, reminiscent of a bygone century and society; it was also keen-edged, as became a weapon of many wars, ancient and modern. She turned to me. "In the storm of '39 I remember that my father said that if Shreelane fell not a house in Ireland would stand. Everyone in the house spent that night in the kitchen."

"Maybe that was nothing new to them," suggested Flurry.

Mrs. Knox regarded her grandson steadfastly and continued her story. It has already been noted that when he and she were of the same company they considered no other antagonist worthy of their steel.

"It was my great-grandfather who built Shreelane in honour of his marriage," she went on. "He married a Riggs of Castle Riggs, a cousin of the celebrated Major Apollo—and thereby hangs a tale!" She blinked her eyes like an old rat, and looked round at each of us in turn. I felt as if I were being regarded through a telescope, from the standpoint of a distant century.

"They knew how to build in those days," she began again. "The basement story of Shreelane is all vaulted."

"I dare say the kitchen would make a nice vault," said Flurry.

His grandmother looked hard at him, and was silent, which seemed to me a rather remarkable occurrence.

On the following day, Andrew and Walkin' Aisy "travelled the roof", and I accompanied them—that is to say, I sat on the warm lead, with my back against the sunny side of a chimney, and smoked torpidly, while Andrew preached, firmly and distinctly, from the top of a ladder. Walkin' Aisy stood at the foot of the ladder, submissive, with folded hands, and upturned bearded face, looking like an elderly saint in the lower corner of a stained-glass window. At the conclusion of the lecture he said that surely the chimneys might fall any minute, but, for all, they might stand a hundred years; a criticism almost stupefying in its width of outlook.

The following day Captain Larpent departed to the Curragh, and, as is often the way of human beings with regard to their guests, we partly breathed more freely, and partly regretted him. On the whole it was restful.

A fortnight passed, and I had almost forgotten about the chimneys; I was in the act of making an early start for an absence of a couple of days at the farther side of my district when I encountered Walkin' Aisy at the hall door.

"I'm here since six o'clock this morning, but I had no one to tend me," he began.

I was familiar with this plaint, and proffered him the yard boy.

"The young fella's too wake," replied Walkin' Aisy, in his slow and dreamy voice, "and they takes him from me." His mild eyes rested upon me in saddened reverie. "And there should be morthar mixed," he resumed slowly, "and there's not a pick of gravel in the yard."

I said, as I pulled on my gloves, that he could have Johnny Brien from the garden to minister to him, and that there was no hurry about the mortar.

"Well, it's what I was saying to the gardener," returned Walkin' Aisy very slowly, "I have no business coming here at all till those chimneys is taken down. The sahmint that's on them is very strong. It's what the gardener said, that quarry-men would be wanting."

"Why the devil didn't you say this at first?" I demanded, not without heat. "You and Captain Larpent told me that the old cement had no more hold than the sugar on a cake."

"Well, the Captain knows best," replied Walkin' Aisy gently, "we should do what he says."

"Well, get the chimneys down; I don't care who does it."

I drove away, and from the turn of the drive saw Walkin' Aisy, in motionless trance, looking after the car as if it were a chariot of fire.

The well-known routine followed; the long and airless day in the court-house, the roar of battle of the rival solicitors, the wearisome iteration of drunks and trespasses, the intricacies of family feuds; the stodgy and solitary dinner at the hotel, followed by the evening in the arid smoking-room, the stale politics of its habitués, the stagnant pessimism of the proprietor, the same thing over again next day and the day after.

It was not until the afternoon of the third day that I found myself serenely gliding homeward, with the wind behind me, and before me the prospect of that idleness that, like the only thirst worth having, has been earned. I was in the straight for the hall door when I saw my wife dart from the house, gesticulating, and waving her handkerchief as if to check my approach. She was followed, at no great interval, by an avalanche of rubble and bricks from the roof, that fell like a portent from heaven, and joined itself to a considerable heap by the steps.

"You never know when it's coming!" she cried breathlessly. "I've been watching for you. It's impossible to make them hear from below, and I can't find any of the men—they're all on the roof."

The restoration had begun, but that fact might not have occurred to a stranger. Next day, and for many days—six weeks, to be exact—the house shook as from the blows of a battering-ram, in response to the efforts of the quarrymen to remove from the chimneys the cement that had no more hold on them than the sugar on a cake, and at frequent and uncertain intervals various debris rumbled down the roof and fell heavily below. There were days when it fell in front of the house, there were days when it fell in the flower garden; where it fell, there it lay, because there was no one to take it away; all were absorbed in tending Walkin' Aisy, and the murmurs of their inexhaustible conversation came to us down the chimneys like the hoarse cooing of wood pigeons. There were also days when by reason of storms and rain nothing was done, and black and evil floods descended into the rooms down the ruins of the chimneys, and through the slates broken by the feet of the quarrymen. At Christmas the kitchen chimney alone remained in action, and we ate our Christmas dinner in fur coats and a fireless dining-room. Philippa refrained from any allusion to the quotation from Longfellow that she had made after that first interview with Walkin' Aisy. She even denied herself the gratification of adding its context:

509

"Faded and old were they when in disappointment it ended," but I knew that she was thinking it.

PART II

It was somewhere towards the end of March that one chimney stack re-entered the list of combatants, trim in new cement, and crowned with tall and hideous chimney-pots. They all smoked, a thing that had never occurred before, but Walkin' Aisy said that the chimneys were cold, and that they wouldn't do it when they'd come to themselves; and (this was a little later on) that any chimney would smoke in an east wind. It was true that a period of east wind and drought had set in. The pump in the yard went dry; carts had to be sent half a mile for water, and it was reported to me that the masons had as much water put astray, mixing mortar and all sorts, as would drown a herring.

Other unpleasant things occurred. The housemaid gave half an hour's warning, and married one of the quarrymen, and Mrs. Cadogan then revealed that it wasn't once or twice during the winter that she had given that particular quarryman the full of the poker, to put him out from under her feet when she'd be dishing up the dinner. Shreelane was twice drawn blank by Flurry Knox's hounds, and their master said that as long as I had every idle blackguard in the country tending Walkin' Aisy, and making short cuts through the covert, how would I have foxes there? I ignored the conundrum, and hoped that the quarryman's yellow dog would remain where I had last seen him, in the ashpit, till Flurry had left the premises.

It was some little time after this that Captain Larpent advanced upon us on a week's leave from the Curragh; he wrote to say that I evidently wanted a Clerk of the Works, and that he would see if he couldn't get a move on Shanahan. I was away when he arrived, and on my return Philippa met me in the hall.

"Meg Longmuir is here!" she said, not without a touch of defiance. "Doctor Catherine had to go to

510

Scotland, so I asked Meg here for a few days. She'll play duets with Andrew. She's up on the roof with him now."

"Better have a string band up there at once," I said, "and open it as a public recreation ground."

"And the Flurry Knoxes and Bernard Shute are coming to dinner," continued my wife, ignoring this *jeu d'esprit*; "the smoking-room chimney is all right, and we can have the oil stove and some music in the drawing-room."

With this agreeable prospect in store, we sat down to dinner. We were too many for general conversation, and the table was round, which is unfavourable for *tête-à têtes*. Yet it was not round enough to frustrate Miss Meg Longmuir's peculiar gift for duets, and I was presently aware that she was unwarrantly devoting herself to Bernard Shute, leaving Captain Larpent derelict, and that the latter was, after the manner of derelicts, becoming a danger to navigation, and was laying down laws and arguing about them acridly with Mr. Knox. I realized too late that there should have been champagne. Whisky and soda is all very well, but it will not warm wet blankets.

Meg Longmuir, however, was doing remarkably well without either; she wore something intricate that was either green or blue or both, and glittered. I recognized it as the panoply of war, and knew that the tomahawk was concealed in its folds. So also was Andrew's scalp; I don't know why I felt some pleasure in remembering that it had a bald patch on it.

After the ladies had gone, Bernard, to whose head Miss Longmuir had mounted as effectively as if she had been the missing champagne, rejoined the lesser world of men by asking Flurry why he had shut up the season so early, and suggested a by-day, if only for the sake of giving the horses something to do.

Flurry put the end of his cigarette into his finger-glass, and lit another at the flaming tongue of my tame Chinese dragon.

"I didn't know you had one that would carry a lady," he said.

"Oh, rot!" said Bernard helplessly.

"I haven't one that will carry myself," went on Flurry. "There's five lame legs among three of them this minute. Anyway the hounds are in sulphur."

The discussion progressed with the prolixity proper to such themes; I think it was Andrew who suggested the paper-chase. He had, he said, ridden in paper-chases in Egypt, and he gave us details of the stark mud walls and fathomless water-courses that were commonplaces of these events. We were left with the impression that none of us had ever seen obstacles so intimidating, and, more than that, if we had seen them we should have gone home in tears.

"I think we'd better make a hare of *you*," said Flurry, fixing expressionless eyes upon Captain Larpent. "It mightn't be hard."

The double edge of this suggestion was lost upon Andrew, who accepted it as a tribute, but said he was afraid he didn't know the country well enough.

"That's your Egyptian darkness," said Flurry with unexpected erudition.

Andrew glanced sideways and suspiciously at him over the bridge of his sunburnt nose, and said rather defiantly that if he could get hold of a decent horse he wouldn't mind having a try.

"I suppose you ride about 11.6?" asked Flurry, after a moment or two of silence. His manner had softened; I thought I knew what was coming. "I've a little horse that I was thinking of parting . . ." he began.

A yell, sharp and sudden as a flash of lightning, was uttered outside the door, followed by a sliding crash of crockery, and more yells. We plunged into the hall, and saw Julia, the elderly parlourmaid, struggling on the floor amid ruins of coffee cups and their adjuncts.

"The rat! He went in under me foot!" she shrieked. "He's in under me this minute!"

Here the rat emerged from the ruins. Simultaneously the drawing-room door burst open, and the streaming shrieks of Minx and her son and daughter were added to those of the still prostrate Julia.

The chase swept down the passage to the kitchen

stairs, the pack augmented by Bob, the red setter, and closely followed by the dinner party. A rat is a poor performer on a staircase, and, at the door leading into the turf-house, the dogs seemed to be on top of him. The bolt-hole under the door, that his own teeth had prepared, gave him an instant of advantage; Flurry had the door open in a second, someone snatched the passage lamp from the wall, but it was abviously six to four on the rat.

The turf-house was a large space at the very root of the house, vaulted and mysterious, bearing Shreelane on its back like the tortoise that supports the world. Barrels draped with cobwebs stood along one wall, but the rat was not behind them, and Minx and her family drove like hawks into a corner, in which, beneath a chaotic heap of broken furniture and household debris, the rat had gone to ground. We followed, treading softly in the turf-mould of unnumbered winters. We tore out the furniture, which yielded itself in fragments; the delirium of the terriers mounting with each crash, and being, if possible, enhanced by the well-meant but intolerable efforts of the red setter to assist them. Finally we worked down to an old door, lying on its face on something that raised it a few inches from the ground.

"Now! Mind yourselves!" said Flurry, heaving up the door and flinging it back against the wall.

The rat bolted gallantly, and darted into an old box, of singular shape, that lay, half open, among the debris, and there, in a storm of tattered paper, met his fate. Minx jumped out of the box very deliberately, with the rat across her jaws, and a scarlet bite in her white muzzle. With frozen calm, and a menacing eye directed at the red setter, she laid it on the turf mould, and stiffly withdrew. Her son and daughter advanced in turn, smelt it respectfully and retired. There was no swagger; all complied with the ritual of fox-terrier form laid down for such occasions.

I was then for the first time aware that the ladies, in all the glitter and glory of their evening dresses, had each mounted herself upon a barrel; in the theatrical gloom of the vaulted turf-house they suggested the resurrection of Ali Baba's Forty Thieves.

"Look where he had his nest in among the old letters!" said Flurry to Philippa, as she descended from her barrel to felicitate Minx and to condole with the rat. "That box came out of the rumble of an old coach, the Lord knows when!"

"There's some sort of a ring in the floor here," said Andrew, who was rooting with a rusty crowbar in the turf-mould where the door had lain. "Bring the light, someone——"

The lamp revealed a large iron ring which was fixed in a flat stone; we scraped away the turf-mould and found that the stone was fastened down with an iron bar, passing through a staple at either end, and padlocked.

"As long as I'm in this place," said Flurry, "I never saw this outfit before."

"There's a seal over the keyhole," said Andrew, turning over the padlock.

"That means it was not intended it should be opened," said Meg Longmuir quickly.

I looked round, and, bad as the light was, I thought her face looked pale.

Andrew did not answer her. He poised the crowbar scientifically, and drove it at the padlock. It bróke at the second blow, releasing the bar.

"No trouble about that!" he said, addressing himself to the gallery ,and not looking at Miss Longmuir. "Now, then, shall we have the flag up?"

There were only two dissentients; one was Flurry, who put his hands in his pockets, and said he wasn't going to destroy his best evening pants; the other was Miss Longmuir who said that to break an old seal like that was to break luck. She also looked at Andrew in a way that should have gone far to redress the injuries inflicted during dinner. Apparently it did not suffice. Captain Larpent firmly inserted the end of the bar under the edge of the flag. Bernard Shute took hold of the ring.

"All together!" said Andrew.

There was a moment of effort, the flag came up abruptly, and, as abruptly, Bernard sat down in the turf-mould with the flag between his legs. The crowbar slipped forward, and vanished with a hollow-sounding splash down a black chasm; Andrew, thrown off his balance, also slipped forward, and would have followed it, head first, had not Flurry and I caught him.

The chasm was a well, nearly full; the water twinkled at us, impenetrably black; it made me think of the ink in the hollowed palm of a native who had told my fortune, up at Peshawar.

"That was about as near as makes no difference!" said Bernard. "You've cut your cheek, Larpent."

"Have I?" said Andrew vaguely, putting up a rather shaky hand to his face. "I think my head took the edge of the well."

We covered the hole with the old door, and Andrew was taken away to have his wound attended to. It was not a severe wound, but the process was lengthy, and involved the collaboration of all the ladies. It seemed to the three neglected males, waiting for a fourth to play bridge, that this mobilization of ministering angels was somewhat overdone.

Andrew came down to breakfast next morning with a headache, and said he had slept badly. Had he discovered the source of the Nile in the turf-house the night before, my wife and Miss Longmuir could not have been more adulatory and sympathetic, nor could the projects based upon the discovery have been more ambitious. I went forth to my work and to my labour without so much as a dog to wave me farewell; all were in the turf-house, surrounded by visionary force-pumps, bath-rooms, and even by miraged fountains in the garden.

When I drove the car into the yard on my return that afternoon, I was confronted by a long chestnut face with a white blaze, looking at me out of the spare loose-box —the face, in fact, of "the little horse" of whom Flurry had spoken to Andrew. There was also, added to the more familiar heaps of mortar, gravel, and stones, a considerable deposit of black and evil-smelling sludge. It seemed, as was not uncommonly the case, that a good many things had been happening during my absence. The stone floor of the hall was stencilled with an intricate pattern of black paw-marks, and was further decorated with scraps of torn paper; a cold stench pervaded the smoking-room (which was situated above the turf-house); far away, a sound as of a gramophone in the next world indicated that Captain Andrew's *affaire de cœur* was finding an outlet in song.

I followed the sounds to the drawing-room, and found Andrew and Miss Longmuir at the piano, in a harmony obviously world-forgetting, though not likely to be by the world forgot. Philippa was sitting by the oil stove, and was, I hope, deriving some satisfaction from inhaling its fumes, its effect upon the temperature being negligible.

Andrew's song was a Hungarian ditty, truculent and amorous, and very loud; under cover of it my wife told me that he, assisted by Walkin' Aisy and the quarrymen, and attended by Miss Longmuir, had baled out the newly discovered well, and that the quarrymen had exacted whisky to sustain them during the latter stages of the process, and that the sludge would be ideal for the roses. They believed the well was filling again beautifully, but they had to leave it because Flurry came over with the horse for Andrew for the paper-chase, and Andrew and Meg went out schooling.

"What paper-chase?" I interpolated coldly.

"Oh, they've got one up for Monday," said Philippa airily. "The children have been tearing up paper all day. I found—rather with horror—that Flurry had given them those old letters out of the turf-house to tear up— I said you and I would ride, of course"—she looked at me with apprehension veiled by defiance, and I said it was thoughtful of her. "But I want to tell you about old Mrs. Knox," she said, hurrying on. "She told Flurry that the well had never been used since the time of the Famine, when they got up a soup-kitchen here, and the day after they opened the well she said the servants flew in a body out of the house, like wild geese!"

516

"I don't wonder, if it smelt as it does now," I said. "Was that why they flew?"

"Flurry said he didn't know what lifted them. But Flurry never says he doesn't know unless he *does* know and doesn't want to tell!"

The following day was Saturday, and for the first time for many weeks a Sabbath stillness prevailed on the roof. Walkin' Aisy was absent; no explanation was forthcoming, and I diagnosed a funeral in the neighbourhood. It was on Sunday afternoon that I was roused from my usual meditation—consequent upon Sunday roast beef—by the intelligence that Mrs. William Shanahan wanted to speak to me. Mrs. Shanahan was a fair freckled woman, with a loud voice and a red face and the reputation of ruling Walkin' Aisy with a rod of iron. It appeared that Walkin' Aisy was confined to his bed; that he had had a reel in his head after getting home on Friday, and whatever work it was that young gentleman gave him to do, he wasn't the better of it.

"And he was as wake in himself and as troubled in his mind as that he couldn't walk to Mass. I told him he should mind the chickens while I'd be out, and when I came in the dog had three of me chickens dead on the floor, and where was himself, only back in the room, and he kneeling there with the two hands up, sayin' his prayers! 'What ails ye,' says I, 'ye old gommoch, that ye'd let the dog kill me chickens?' 'Sure, I was sayin' me prayers,' says he; 'That the Lord mightn't hear your prayers!' says I. God forgive me, I had to say it!'"

I recalled to her the question of the chimneys, pointing out that the gable chimney was half down, and could not be left as it was.

To this Mrs. Walkin' Aisy replied at great length that William's father had given him an advice not to go in it, and that the father was dark these scores of years, and it was what he blamed for it was the work he done in Shreelane House in the time of the Famine. It was after that the sight went bandy with him.

She declined to offer any opinion as to when Walkin' Aisy would return to work, and withdrew, leaving me to consider my position under the Employers' Liability

Act in the event of her husband's demise, and to wish, not for the first time, that Andrew (now strolling at his ease with Miss Longmuir, reviewing a course for the paper-chase), had been at Jericho, or any other resort of the superfluous, before he interfered with the tranquil progress of the chimneys towards dissolution.

There were strange lapses at dinner—delays, omissions, disasters, and Julia the parlour-maid had a trembling hand and a general suggestion of nerve-storm. After dinner it was reported to Philippa that Anthony was not well, and after a prolonged absence she returned with the information that he had had a nightmare, and that there was a rumour in the house that all the servants were going to give warning the following morning. Their reason for this was obscure, but was somehow connected with Mrs. Walkin' Aisy's visit, and the fact that the swing-door leading to the turf-house had opened and shut twice, of its own volition. We did not mention these matters to our guests, and retired to rest in perturbation. I admit that at some time during the night, which was a still one, I heard the turf-house door groan on its hinges, and slam. I went downstairs and found nothing; it was certainly unusual, however, that Bob, the red setter, had abandoned his lair in the smoking-room, and was spending the night on the mat outside my dressing-room door.

Next morning Philippa, considering that a thrust was better than a parry, held a court of inquiry in the lower regions, and, according to her own report, spoke seriously on the grave responsibility incurred by those who frightened other people about nonsense. Julia's version of the proceedings, I heard at a later date. She said that "the misthress spoke to us lovely, and the Priest couldn't speak better than her. She told us that the divils in hell wasn't worse than us."

PART III

It has been said of Ireland that the inevitable never happens, and that the impossible invariably occurs.

When on Monday morning I learned that Flurry was to be one of the hares, and beheld him mounted on his best horse, as covered with bags as a postman on Christmas Day, I recalled the epigram. Another confirmation of the law of the unexpected was the fact that Meg Longmuir, on the "maroon pony", was his fellow hare, very smart, much elated, and quite unaware that she had been substituted for Sally Knox at the last moment, in order that she might be as a millstone hung round the neck of Flurry. That this arrangement was not what Captain Larpent had desired was sufficiently apparent to the naked eye: why Flurry submitted to it was less obvious.

About a dozen riders had been whipped up to take part in this preposterous affair, and we were standing about on the grass in front of Shreelane, cutting up the turf as much as the hardness of the ground would permit, and making as much noise as a pack of hounds at feeding time. The April sun glared hot, the better part of a north-easterly gale was blowing, the horses had overeaten themselves with the bread of idleness, and were fat and frisky.

"Is he any good?" said Flurry to me in a low voice, with his eye on Andrew, who was sitting, shrouded in gloom and remoteness, on the chestnut horse.

"Ask Miss Longmuir," I said. "She was schooling with him on Saturday."

"I'll have plenty to do minding her, without asking her questions that she couldn't answer," returned Flurry. He resumed his survey of Andrew. "I wonder will he be able to hold that horse in a snaffle? He catches hold an odd time."

"Stand by!" said Doctor Hickey, his watch in his hand. "Fifteen seconds more before the hares start!"

"Well, if Larpent goes as big as he talks, he'll do," said Flurry, gathering up the reins.

The ten minutes of grace ebbed slowly away, and preposterous though I still held the affair to be, I do not deny that I was aware of an inward simmering of impatience.

"I'll have the face worn off my watch looking at it

519

if you don't let us start soon!" said Miss Larkie McRory to Hickey.

She was mounted on a long-legged animal that had been summarized by Flurry as "the latter end of a car-horse", and was certainly in need of all the time it could get.

"Don't excite yourself now, or I'll be having to order you a cooling draught!" returned the Doctor, but I perceived that he, in common with everyone else, was edging his horse towards the point of departure.

"Go!"

In the riot of the breakaway, I was able to think of nothing but of keeping Daniel from bucking me over his head, but during the hustle at the avenue gates I observed Andrew riding off Bernard, and getting to the front with pale and ferocious determination. The "scent" took us along the road; we followed it over a stony bank and across two fields, at steeplechase pace, and then it ceased. By this time any lingering sense of absurdity had ceased also. We cast ourselves feverishly, like hounds; we galloped great circles; someone found the paper again, and yelled like a maniac. We all yelled in response, a variety of yells, from "Tally Ho" to "Cooee", as, like Bedlam let loose, we rushed to the discoverer. We were up on high land now, and the wind was whirling in our ears, snatching our voices away to infinity, and blowing up the temperatures of horses and riders like a bellows. It had caught away the torn paper and flung it to leeward, into furze brakes, against the sides of the banks, and checks were many, and the horses, convinced that the hounds were somewhere ahead, pulled double. In the bare fields, with their scanty April grass, everything showed up; we were deceived by white stones, by daisies, by dandelion puff-balls, by goose-feathers; most of all we were deceived by country-people, whom, I have no doubt, Flurry had instructed to mislead us.

We had had a long check, consequent on a false trail, when, three fields away, Andrew held up his hat.

"Look at him now, running mute!" giggled Sally Knox in my ear, as we battered down a road. "He's too cross to shout. He's frantic because he's not the hare, and Meg Longmuir was sent with Flurry! And poor Flurry, who's going such a nice safe line!"

"I suppose we may thank Miss Longmuir for the safe line?" I responded with some difficulty, because Daniel was enjoying himself on the road, according to the idiotic manner of horses.

"No! You may thank the chestnut horse!" ejaculated Flurry Knox's wife, as she hoisted out of the road over a loose wall.

Remembering that Andrew was intended to buy the chestnut horse, the deduction was a simple one. It was also quite clear that, disappointing as it might be, and contrary to the most cherished convention, Andrew was going as big as he talked, and even bigger.

"'Them that's in love is like no one'!" I quoted to Mrs. Flurry, as Captain Larpent, taking the shortest way to a drift of paper on a hill-side, charged a tall, furze-tufted fence, and got over with a scramble. We followed, less heroically, by a gap, and ascended the hill, with the torn paper scurrying in front of us in the gusty wind. We had now been going for thirty-five minutes, and were all, horses and riders, something blown; Miss Larkie's car-horse could have been heard down-wind for half a mile, and I would have backed Daniel to out-roar any lion in the den.

Nothing but the checks held us together. Doctor Hickey, and Irving, the District Inspector, were taking the matter seriously, and were riding hard to catch Andrew, for the honour of the country. Bernard Shute and two or three other heavyweights were afoot, dragging their dripping horses over a bank with an uphill take off; Miss McRory and the car-horse were making an extremely gradual progress in the rear, and Philippa had pulled back to give her leads, with an unselfishness that was not only futile, but was also a reproach to me and my fellow-men.

We had been going in a big ring, and from the top of the hill we could again see Shreelane, below us among its trees. It was there also that we caught the first sight of the hares, now heading for home and safety. The wind had strengthened to half a gale, and the wild and composite yell with which the hounds viewed their quarry was blown back into their throats. The maroon pony had fulfilled her mission as a handicap; twice we saw Flurry dismount and pull down a gap; once, at a bank, he got behind her and whipped her over like a peg-top. Another field took them to the high road. A puff of white paper fluttered out, and Miss Longmuir looked back and flourished a defiant whip; they turned, and galloped in a cloud of dust along the road for Shreelane.

It was not a nice hill to get down in a hurry, and I should think the chestnut horse dreams of it now, somewhere in the level English Midlands, after he has overeaten himself on fat English oats. For my part, I remembered a humble but useful path, that links a little group of cottages with the rest of the world.

The paper lay thick on the road in the shelter of the fences; everyone began to ride for a finish, and after a quarter of a mile of pounding in the dust at the heel of the hunt, I considered that Daniel and I had satisfied the demands of honour, and ignobly turned in at the back way to the stable-yard, permitting the chase to sweep on to the front gates without me.

In the stable-yard I found several objects of interest. The hares were there, dismounted, very hot, and uncaptured; Mrs. Knox was there, seated in her phaeton; there was a cluster of servants at the back door; there were McRorys, leaning on bicycles; there was Cecilia Shute, in her motor, with unknown rank and fashion billowing in motor veils beside her.

All were gazing at a mass of sooty bricks and shattered chimney-pots that lay, scattered wide, in and about the black dredgings of the turf-house well.

"That's the gable chimney," said Flurry coolly; "it got tired of waiting for Walkin' Aisy. We heard the roar of it as we came in the front gate!" He turned his mail-bag upside down so that its ultimate dregs were blown far and wide. "How did the chestnut horse go with——?"

As if in reply, hoofs clattered outside the yard, and

the white nose of the chestnut shot into the opening of the yard gate. He plunged past me, with Andrew lying back and tugging at the snaffle. The Shreelane yard was fairly spacious, but I began to think that the thing wasn't as funny as it looked. The horse swerved at Mrs. Knox's phaeton, swerved again as Flurry turned him from his stable door with a flourish of the mail-bag. Andrew wrenched his head straight for the open back gate, and might have got him out without disaster, had not the widespread ruin of the chimney intervened. The chestnut once more tried to swerve, his legs went from under him, and he fell, striking fire from the cobblestones of the yard. Andrew stuck to him to the last instant, but was shot clear, and was flung, head first, into the heap of stones and black mud.

It seemed long, long hours between this catastrophe, and a sufficient subsidence of things in general, for me to be able, without inhumanity, to envisage a whisky and soda. Old Mrs. Knox watched me with approval.

"I'm tired of looking at young men drinking tea," she commented. (It was Mrs. Knox's pleasing idiosyncrasy to look upon me as a young man.) "They were like a pack of curates at a school-feast! Not that I was ever at a school-feast, thank God!" she added, with an abandoned chuckle.

We were sitting in a corner of the dining-room, surrounded by empty cups and crumby plates; tides of tea and of talkers had ebbed and flowed, but Mrs. Knox had sat on—to hear my personal report of Andrew, she said.

"Upon my honour, he escaped very well! A dislocated shoulder is nothing, and the young lady is there to 'tend the wounded Deloraine'!"

She paused, and put her head on one side, as if waiting for the prompter. "How does it go? 'She thought some spirit of the sky had done the bold mosstrooper wrong!'"

She paused again, and looked at me; the evening light shone on her spectacles, and made them impenetrable.

"Now I'm going to give you a piece of advice; 'And I'll not take it!' said Major Yeates, R.M.!"

I protested that I had said nothing of the kind. She prodded me in the knee with a goblin finger.

"*Close that well!* Put on the flagstone, and seal it down again!" She fumbled in her shawls, and pulled out a thin old gold chain. "Here's the seal, the same one that my father sealed it with at the time of the Famine!"

I said that I was ready to do anything that she told me, but it would be interesting to know why.

Mrs. Knox detached the seal from her chain, to which it was knotted by something that I darkly suspected to be a bit of bootlace. It was a cornelian seal, made in the grand manner; massively wrought, the gold smooth from age.

"I dare say you never heard of Major Apollo Riggs? He drove up to this house one fine day in a coach-and-four. Next day the coach-and-four drove away, but Major Apollo Riggs was not in it!"

"He found himself a success at Shreelane?" I suggested.

"Not so much with his host as his hostess!" returned Mrs. Knox portentously.

"A duel?" I asked.

"He was never seen again, my dear!" replied Mrs. Knox. (There are moments, in Ireland, when this term of affection is used not so much affectionately as confidentially.)

At this point the door opened. Mrs. Knox put the goblin finger on her lips, as Philippa, still in her habit, slid into the room.

"The patient and Meg are extremely self-sufficing," she said, dropping into a chair. "His face is turning all colours of the rainbow, and one eye has disappeared, but the other is full of expression and is fixed on Meg!"

"There's not much colour about *you*," I said. "You ought to have a whisky and soda."

"Nonsense!" said Philippa, waving me away; "we've got most of the black stuff out of his hair; even his waistcoat pocket was full of it! And bits of the torn paper had stuck to it, like confetti."

"That suggests a wedding," I observed.

"Quite," said Philippa. "But the absurd thing was

that one of the confetti—obviously a bit of those old letters that the children tore up—had the word 'Apollo' on it! It was stuck on to him like a label."

Mrs. Knox clasped her hands, and lay back in her chair.

"I said it was, of course, a tribute to his beauty, but Meg was not at all amused. She thought it was *lèse majesté*."

"She'll get over that in time," I said, putting the seal in my pocket.

THE BOSOM OF THE McRORYS

Since the day when fate had shipwrecked us at the end of the Temple Braney shrubbery, and flung us, dripping, into the bosom of the McRorys, we had been the victims of an indissoluble friendship with the family. This fulfilled itself in many ways.

Gratitude, what is known as Common Gratitude (which is merely a hollow compliance with the voice of conscience), impelled us to lunch Mr. and Mrs. McRory, heavily and elaborately (but without anyone to meet them); to invite the whole family to a lawn-tennis party (and the whole family came); and, at other people's tennis parties, to fawn upon them (when it was no longer possible to elude them). It was a despicable position, and had I at all foreseen, when the picnic sank at Temple Braney pier, that the result would have been dinner-parties, I should unhesitatingly have left Philippa to drown.

The intimacies imposed by common gratitude had, under the healing hand of time, become less acute, and might, indeed, have ceased to affect us, had not fate again intervened, and cemented the family friendship in the most public way possible. There befell a Harvest Festival in Skebawn Church, with a bishop, and an anthem, and a special collection. To it the McRorys, forsaking their own place of worship, came in power, and my wife, very superfluously, indicated to Mrs. McRory a seat in our pew. The pew is a front one, and Mrs. McRory became at once a figure-head to the rest of the congregation—a buxom figure-head, upholstered tightly in royal blue satin, that paled the ineffectual fires of the pulpit dahlias, and shouted in a terrible major chord with the sunflowers in the east window. She creaked mysteriously and rhythmically with every breath; a large gold butterfly, poised on an invisible spring, quivered and glittered above her bonnet. It was while waiting for the service to begin that Philippa was inspired to whisper to Mrs. McRory some information, quite immaterial, connected with the hymns. The next moment I perceived that Mrs. McRory's butterfly had fixed its antennae into some adjunct of my wife's hat that was at once diaphanous and sinewy, with the result that the heads of the two ladies were locked together. A silent struggle ensued; the butterfly's grappling-irons held, so also did the hat-trimming, and Philippa and Mrs. McRory remained brow to brow in what seemed to be a prolonged embrace. At this point Philippa showed signs of collapse; she said that Mrs. McRory's nose, glowing like a ruby within two inches of her own, made her hysterical. I affected unconsciousness, while my soul thirsted for an axe with which to decapitate one or both of the combatants, and subsequently to run amok among the congregation, now, as the poet says, "abashlessly abandoned to delight". The butterfly's vitals slowly uncoiled, and were drawn out into a single yet indomitable strand of gold wire; the bishop was imminent, when a female McRory in the pew behind (known to the Fancy as "Larkie") intervened with what were, I believe, a pair of manicure scissors, and the incident closed.

It was clear that our blood brotherhood with the McRorys was fore-ordained and predestined. We evaded two invitations to dinner, but a third was inescapable, even though an alarming intimacy was fore-shadowed by the request that we should come "in a very quiet way".

"Do they expect us to creep in in tennis shoes?" I demanded.

"I think it only means a black tie," said Philippa, with the idea that she was soothing me.

"If I have to go to a McRory free-and-easy, I shall not act as such," I returned, slamming myself into my dressing-room, and dragging forth ceremonial attire.

As, with a docility that I was far from feeling, I followed my wife into the drawing-room at Temple Braney, and surveyed the semicircle of McRorys and unknown notabilities (summarized as "Friends from Dublin") that silently awaited us, I felt that neither freedom nor ease would be my lot. But few things in life are quite as bad as one expects them to be—always excepting seasickness. In its dreary circuit of the room, my eye met that of my old friend Miss Bobby Bennett, of the Curranhilty Hunt, niece of its Master, and consultant and referee of all its affairs. My friendship with Miss Bennett was of an ideal nature; when we met, which was seldom, we were delighted to see one another; in the intervals we forgot one another with, I felt sure, an equal completeness. Her social orbit was incalculable; she resembled a fox of whom I heard an earth-stopper say that you "couldn't tell any certain place where he wouldn't puck out". Whether it was at Punchestown, or at a Skebawn parish tea, or judging cakes and crochet at an agricultural show, whenever she appeared it was with the same air of being on top of the situation and of extracting the utmost from it.

To me befell the onerous task of taking the lady of the house in to dinner, but upon my other hand sat Miss Bennett (squired by a friend from Dublin of apparently negligible quality), and before I had recovered from the soup—a hell-broth of liquid mustard that called itself mulligatawny—I found that to concentrate upon her was no more than was expected of me by both ladies. Mrs. McRory's energies were indeed fully engrossed by the marshalling of a drove of heated females, who hurried stertorously and spasmodically round the table, driven as leaves before the wind by fierce signals from their trainer. Opposite to me sat that daughter of the house whose manicure scissors had terminated the painful episode of the butterfly. I had always maintained that she was the prettiest of the McRorys, and it was evident that Irving, the new District Inspector of R.I.C., who sat beside her, shared my opinion. He was a serious, lanky young man, and at such moments as he found himself deprived of Miss McRory's exclusive attention, he accepted no alternative, and devoted himself austerely to his food.

Miss Bennett's intention was, I presently discovered, to hunt with Flurry Knox's hounds on the following day: she had brought over a horse, and it became clear to me that her secondary intention was to return without it.

"Larkie McRory's going to take up hunting," she said in her low swift voice. "The new D.I. hunts, you know."

Miss Bennett's astute grey eyes rested upon the young lady in question, and returned to me laden with inference.

"He's got a horse from a farmer for her to ride to-morrow—goodness knows what sort of a brute it is! —I hope she won't break her neck. She's the best of the lot. If the old man had sense he'd buy my mare for her—he's full of money—and I'd let her go cheap, too, as I have a young one coming on."

It is worthy of mention that I have never known Miss Bennett's stable composed of anything save old ones to go cheap and young ones coming on. I asked her what she would give me if I didn't tell Mr. McRory that her mare was touched in the wind.

"I'll give you in charge for defamation of character," replied Miss Bennett, with speed comparable only to the dart of an ant-eater's tongue. "Anything else you'd like to know? But look at Larkie now, I ask you! Quick!"

I did as desired, and was fortunate enough to see Miss McRory putting a spoonful of salt in Mr. Irving's champagne, what time he was engaged in repulsing one of Mrs. McRory's band of flaming ministers, who, with head averted in consultation with a collaborator, was continuously offering him melted butter, regardless of the fact that he had, at the moment, nothing in front of him but the tablecloth.

"There's Miss Larkie's Dublin manners for you," said Miss Bennett, and passed on to other themes.

I should say theme, because, broadly speaking, Miss Bennett had but one, and all roads sooner or later led to it. During the slow progress of the meal I was brought up to date in the inner gossip of the Curranhilty country. I learned that Mrs. Albert Dougherty had taken to riding astride because she thought it was smart, and it was nothing but the grab she got of the noseband that saved her from coming off every time she came down a drop. I asked for that Mr. Tomsy Flood whose career had twice, at vital points, been intersected by me.

"Ah, poor Tomsy! He took to this, y'know," Miss Bennett slightly jerked her little finger, "and he wouldn't ride a donkey over a sod of turf. They sent him out to South Africa, to an ostrich farm, and when the people found he couldn't ride they put him to bed with a setting of ostrich eggs to keep them warm, and he did that grand, till someone gave him a bottle of whisky, and he got rather lively and broke all the eggs. They say it's a lay-preacher he's going to be now!"

Across a dish of potatoes, thrust at me for the fourth time, I told Miss Bennett that it was all her fault, and that she had been very unkind to Tomsy Flood. Miss Bennett gave me a look that showed me what she still could do if she liked, and replied that she supposed I was sorry that she hadn't gone to South Africa with him.

"I suppose we'll be going there soon," she went on. "Uncle says if Home Rule comes there won't be a fox or a Protestant left in Ireland in ten years' time; and he said, what's more, that if *he* had to choose it mightn't be the Protestants he'd keep! But that was because the Dissenting Minister's wife sent in a claim of five pounds to the fowl fund, and said she'd put down poison if she didn't get it."

Not thus did Philippa and old McRory, at their end of the table, fleet the time away. Old McRory, as far as I could judge, spoke not at all, but played tunes with his fingers on the tablecloth, or preoccupied himself with what seemed to be an endeavour to plait his beard into a point. On my wife's other hand was an unknown gentleman, with rosy cheeks, a raven moustache, and a bald head, who was kind enough to solace her isolation with facetious stories, garnished with free and varied gestures with his knife, suggestive of sword-practice, all concluding alike in convulsive tenor laughter. I was aware, not unpleasantly, that Philippa was bearing the brunt of the McRory beanfeast.

When at length my wife's release was earned, and the ladies had rustled from the room in her wake, with all the conscious majesty of the Mantle Department, I attempted some conversation with my host, but found it was more considerate to leave him to devour unmolested the crystallized fruits and chocolates that were not, I felt quite sure, provided by Mrs. McRory for the master of the house. I retired upon the D.I., my opinion of whom had risen since I saw him swallow his salted champagne without a change of countenance. That he addressed me as "sir" was painful, but at about my age these shocks have to be expected, and are in the same category as lumbago, and what my dentist delicately alludes to as "dentures".

The young District Inspector of Irish Constabulary had wisdom beyond his years: we talked profoundly of the state of the country until the small voice of old McRory interrupted us.

"Major," it said, "if you have enough drink taken we might join the ladies."

Most of the other gallants had already preceded us, and as I crossed the hall I heard the measured pounding of a waltz on the piano: it created an impulse, almost as uncontrollable as that of Spurius Lartius and Herminius, to dart back to the dining-room.

"That's the way with them every night," said old McRory dispassionately. "They mightn't go to bed now at all."

Old McRory had a shadowy and imperceptible quality that is not unusual in small fathers of large families; it always struck me that he understood very thoroughly the privileges of the neglected, and pursued an unnoticed, peaceful, and, observant path of his own in the background. I watched him creep away in his furtive, stupefied manner like a partly chloroformed ferret. " 'Oh, well is thee, thou art asleep!'—or soon will be," I said to myself, as I turned my back on him and faced the music.

I was immediately gratified by the spectacle of Philippa, clasped to the heart of the gentleman who had been kind to her at dinner, and moving with him in slow and crab-like sidlings round the carpet. Her eyes met mine with passionate appeal; they reminded me of those of her own fox-terrier, Minx, when compelled to waltz with my younger son.

The furniture and the elder ladies had been piled up in corners, and the dancing element had been reinforced by a gang of lesser McRorys and their congeners, beings who had not been deemed worthy of a place at the high table. Immured behind the upright piano sat Mrs. McRory, thumping out the time-honoured "Blue Danube" with the plodding rhythm of the omnibus horse. I furtively looked at my watch; we had dined at seven-thirty, and it was now but a quarter to ten o'clock. Not for half an hour could we in decency withdraw, and, finding myself at the moment beside Miss Larkie McRory, it seemed to me that I could do no less than invite her to take the carpet with me.

I am aware that my dancing is that of ten years ago, which places it in the same scrap-heap class as a battleship of that date, but Miss McRory told me that she preferred it, and that it exactly suited her step. It would be as easy to describe the way of a bird in the air as to define Miss McRory's step; scrap-heap or no, it made me feel that I walked the carpet like a thing of life. We were occasionally wrecked upon reefs of huddled furniture, and we sustained a collision or two of first-rate magnitude: after these episodes my partner imperceptibly steered me to a corner, in which I leaned heavily against whatever was most stable, and tried to ignore the fact that the floor was rocking and the walls were waving, and that it was at least two years since I had exceeded in this way.

It was in one of these intervals that Miss McRory told me that she was going hunting next day, and that he—her long hazel-grey eyes indicated Mr. Irving, now slowly and showily moving a partner about the room—had got a horse for her to ride, and she had never hunted before. She hoped to goodness she wouldn't fall off, and (here she dealt me the fraction of a glance) she hoped I'd pick her up now and again. I said that the two wishes were incompatible, to which she replied that she didn't know what incompatible meant; and I told her to ask Mr. Irving whether he had found that salt and champagne were compatible.

"I thought you only wore that old eyeglass for show," replied Miss McRory softly, and again looked up at me from under her upcurled Irish eyelashes; "it was out of spite he drank it! A girl did that to my brother Curly at a dance, and he poured it down her back."

"I think Mr. Irving treated you better than you deserved," I replied paternally, adventuring once more into the tide of dancers.

When, some five minutes afterwards, I resigned my partner to Irving, D.I., I felt that honour had been satisfied, and that it was now possible to leave the revel. But in this I found that I had reckoned, not so much without my host, as without my fellow-guest. Philippa, to my just indignation, had blossomed into the success of the evening. Having disposed of the kind-hearted gentleman (with the pink cheeks and the black moustache), she was immediately claimed by Mr. De Lacey McRory, the eldest son of the house, and with him exhibited a proficiency in the latest variant of the waltz that she had hitherto concealed from me. The music, like the unseen orchestra of a merry-go-round, was practically continuous. Scuffles took place at intervals behind the upright piano, during which music-books fell heavily upon the keys, and one gathered that a change of artist was taking place, but the fundamental banging of the bass was maintained, and the dancing ceased not. The efforts of the musicians were presently reinforced by a young lady in blue who supplied a shrill and gibbering *obligato* upon a beribboned mandoline, and even, at some passionate moments, added her voice to the *ensemble*.

"Will this go on much longer?" I asked of Miss Bennett, with whom I had withdrawn to the asylum of a bow window.

"D'ye mean Miss Cooney O'Rattigan and her mandoline?" replied Miss Bennett. "I can tell you it was twice worse this afternoon when she was singing Italian to it. I never stayed here before, and please goodness I never will again; the wardrobe in my room is crammed with Mrs. McRory's summer clothes, and the chest of drawers is full of apples! Ah, but after all," went on Miss Bennett largely, "what can you expect from a cob but a kick? Didn't Tomsy Flood find a collection of empty soda-water bottles in his bed the time he stayed here for the wedding, when you found him stitched up in the feather bed!"

I said that the soda-water bottles had probably prepared him for the ostrich eggs, and Miss Bennett asked me if it were true that I had once found a nest of young mice in the foot of my bed at Aussolas, because that was the story she had heard. I was able to assure her that, on the contrary, it had been kittens, and passing from these pleasing reminiscences I asked her to come forth and smoke a cigarette in the hall with me, as a preliminary to a farther advance in the direction of the motor. I have a sincere regard for Miss Bennett, but her dancing is a serious matter, with a Cromwellian quality in it, suggestive of jack boots and the march of great events.

The cigarettes were consolatory, and the two basket-chairs by the fire in the back-hall were sufficiently comfortable; but the prospect of home burned like a beacon before me. The clock struck eleven.

"They're only beginning now!" said Miss Bennett, interpreting without resentment my glance at it. "Last night it was near one o'clock in the morning when they had high tea, and then they took to singing songs, and playing 'Are you there, Mike?' and cock-fighting."

I rose hastily, and began to search for my overcoat and cap, prepared to plunge into the frosty night, when Miss Bennett offered to show me a short way through the house to the stable-yard, where I had left the car.

"I slipped out that way after dinner," she said, picking up a fur-lined cloak and wrapping it about her. "I wanted to make sure the mare had a second rug on her this cold night."

I followed Miss Bennett through a wheezy swing-door; a flagged passage stretched like a tunnel before us, lighted by a solitary candle planted in its own grease in a window. A long battle-line of bicycles occupied one side of the passage; there were doors, padlocked and cobwebbed, on the other. A ragged baize door at the end of the tunnel opened into darkness that smelt of rat-holes, and was patched by a square or two of moonlight.

"This is a sort of lobby," said Miss Bennett. "Mind! There's a mangle there—and there are oars on the floor somewhere——"

As she spoke I was aware of a distant humming noise, like bees in a chimney.

"That sounds uncommonly like a motor," I said.

"That's only the boiler," replied Miss Bennett; "we're at the back of the kitchen here."

She advanced with confidence, and flung open a door. A most startling vista was revealed, of a lighted room with several beds in it. Children's faces, swelled and scarlet, loomed at us from the pillows, and an old woman, with bare feet and a shawl over her head, stood transfixed, with a kettle in one hand and a tumbler in the other.

Miss Bennett swiftly closed the door upon the vision.

"My gracious heavens!" she whispered, "what on earth children are those? I'm sure it's mumps they have, whoever they are. And how secret the McRorys kept it!—and did you see it was punch the old woman was giving them?"

"We might have asked her the way to the yard," I

534

said, inwardly resolving to tell Philippa it was scarlatina; "and she might have given us a light."

"It was this door I should have tried," said my guide, opening another with considerable circumspection.

Sounds of hilarity immediately travelled to us along a passage; I followed Miss Bennett, feeling much as if I were being led by a detective into Chinatown, San Francisco. A square of light in the wall indicated one of those inner windows that are supposed to give light mutually to room and passage, and are, as a matter of fact, an architect's confession of defeat. Farther on a door was open, and screams of laughter and singing proceeded from it. I admit, without hesitation, that we looked in at the window, and thus obtained a full and sufficient view of the *vie intime* of the Temple Braney kitchen. A fat female, obviously the cook, was seated in the midst of a remarkably lively crowd of fellow-retainers and camp-followers, thumping with massive knuckles on a frying-pan, as though it were a banjo, and squalling to it something in an unknown tongue.

"She's taking off Miss Cooney O'Rattigan!" hissed Miss Bennett, in ecstasy. "She's singing Italian, by way of! And look at those two brats of boys, Vincent and Harold, that should have been in their beds two hours ago!"

Masters Vincent and Harold McRory were having the time of their lives. One of them, seated on the table, was shovelling tipsy-cake into his ample mouth with a kitchen spoon; the other was smoking a cigarette, and capering to the squalls of the cook.

As noiselessly as two bats Miss Bennett and I flitted past the open door, but a silence fell with a unanimity that would have done credit to any orchestra.

"They saw us," said Miss Bennett, scudding on, "but we'll not tell on them—the creatures!"

An icy draught apprised us of an open door, and through it we escaped at length from the nightmare purlieus of the house into the yard, an immense quadrangle, where moonlight and black shadows opposed one another in a silence that was as severe as they. Temple Braney House and its yard dated from what may be called the Stone Age in Ireland, about the middle of the eighteenth century, when money was plenty and labour cheap, and the Barons of Temple Braney, now existent only in guide-books, built, as they lived, on the generous scale.

We crossed the yard to the coach-house in which I had left my motor: its tall arched doorway was like the mouth of a cave, and I struck a match. It illuminated a mowing-machine, a motor-bicycle, and a flying cat. But not my car. The first moment of bewilderment was closed by the burning of my fingers by the match.

"Are you sure it was here you left it?" said Miss Bennett, with a fatuity of which I had not believed her capable.

The presence of a lady was no doubt a salutary restraint, but as I went forth into the yard again, I felt as though the things I had to leave unsaid would break out all over me like prickly heat.

"It's the medical student one," said Miss Bennett with certainty, "the one that owns the motor-bike."

The yard and the moonlight did not receive this statement with a more profound silence than I.

"I'm sure he won't do it any harm," she went on, making the elementary mistake of applying superficial salves to a wound whose depths she was incapable of estimating. "He's very good about machinery—maybe it's only round to the front door he took it."

As Miss Bennett offered these consolations I saw two small figures creep from the shadows of the house. Their white collars shone in the moonlight, and, recognizing them as the youngest members of the inveterate clan of McRory, I hailed them in a roar that revealed very effectively the extent of my indignation. It did not surprise me that the pair, in response to this, darted out of the yard gate with the speed of a pair of minnows in a stream.

I pursued, not with any hope of overtaking them, but because they were the only clue available, and in my wake, over the frosty ground, in her satin shoes, followed that sound sportswoman, Miss Bennett.

The route from the stable-yard to the front of Temple

Braney House is a long and circuitous one, that skirts a plantation of evergreens. At the first bend the moonlight displayed the track of a tyre in the grass; at the next bend, where the edge was higher, a similar economy of curve had been effected, and that the incident had been of a fairly momentous nature was suggested by the circumstance that the tail lamp was lying in the middle of the drive. It was as I picked it up that I heard a familiar humming in the vicinity of the hall door.

"He didn't go so far, after all," said Miss Bennett, somewhat blown, but holding her own, in spite of the satin shoes.

I turned the last corner at a high rate of speed, and saw the dignified Georgian façade of the house pale and placid in the moonlight; through the open hall door a shaft of yellow light fell on the ground. The car was nowhere to be seen, yet somewhere, close at hand, the engine throbbed and drummed to me—*a cri de cœur*, as I felt it, calling to me through the accursed jingle of the piano that proceeded from the open door.

"Where the devil——?" I began.

Even as I spoke I escried the car. It was engaged, apparently, in forcing its way into the shrubbery that screened one end of the house. The bonnet was buried in a holly-bush, the engine was working, slowly but industriously. The lamps were not lighted, and there was no one in it.

"Those two imps made good use of their legs, never fear them!" puffed Miss Bennett; "the 'cuteness of them—cutting away to warn the brother!"

"What's this confounded thing?" I said fiercely, snatching at something that was caught in the handle of the brake.

Miss Bennett snatched it in her turn, and held it up in the moonlight, while I stilled the fever of the engine.

"Dublin for ever!" she exclaimed. "What is it but the streamers of Miss Cooney's mandoline! There's the spoils of war for you! And it's all the spoils you'll get —the whole pack of them's hid in the house by now!"

From an unlighted window over the hall door a voice added itself to the conversation.

"God help the house that holds them!" it said, addressing the universe.

The window was closed.

"That's old McRory!" said Miss Bennett in a horrified whisper.

Again I thought of Chinatown, sleepless, incalculable, with its infinite capacity for sheltering the criminal.

.   .   .   .

"—But, darling," said Philippa, some quarter of an hour later, as we proceeded down the avenue in the vaulted darkness of the beech-trees (and I at once realized that she had undertaken the case for the defence), "you've no reason to suppose that they took the car any farther than the hall door."

"It is the last time that it will be taken to *that* hall door," I replied going dead slow, with my head over the side of the car, listening to unfamiliar sounds in its interior—sounds that did not suggest health. "I should like to know how many of your young friends went on the trip——"

"My dear boy," said Philippa pityingly, "I ask you if it is likely that there would have been more than two, when one of them was the lady with the mandoline! And," she proceeded with cat-like sweetness, "I did not perceive that you took a party with you when you retired to the hall with your old friend Miss Bennett, and left me to cope single-handed with the mob for about an hour!"

"Whether there were two or twenty-two of them in the car," I said, treating this red herring with suitable contempt, "I've done with your McRorys."

I was, very appropriately, in the act of passing through Temple Braney entrance gates as I made this pronouncement ,and it was the climax of many outrages that the steering-gear, shaken by heaven knows what impacts and brutalities, should suddenly have played me false. The car swerved in her course—fortunately a slow one—and laid her bonnet impulsively against the Temple Braney gate pillar, as against a loved one's shoulder.

As we regained our composure, two tall forms

538

appeared in the light of the head lamps, and one of them held up his hand. I recognized a police patrol.

"That's the car right enough," said one of them. He advanced to my side. "I want your name, please. I summons you for furious driving on the high road, without lights, a while ago, and refusing to stop when called on to do so. Go round and take the number, McCaffery."

When, a few days later, the story flowed over and ran about the country, some things that were both new and interesting came to my ears.

Flurry Knox said that Bobby Bennett had sold me her old mare by moonlight in the Temple Braney yard, and it was a great credit to old McRory's champagne.

Mrs. Knox, of Aussolas, was told that I had taken Mrs. McRory for a run in the car at one o'clock in the morning, and on hearing it said *"De gustibus non est disputandum."*

Someone, unknown, repeated this to Mrs. McRory, and told her it meant "You cannot touch pitch without being disgusted."

Mrs. Cadogan, my cook, reported to Philippa that the boy who drove the bread-cart said that it was what the people on the roads were saying that the Major was to be fined ten pounds; to which Mrs. Cadogan had replied that it was a pity the Major ever stood in Temple Braney, but she supposed that was laid out for him by the Lord.

PUT DOWN ONE AND CARRY TWO

The promise of that still and moonlit December night, wherein we had beanfeasted with the McRorys, was shamelessly broken. The weather next morning was a welter of wind and mist, with rain flung in at intervals. The golden fox on the stable weathercock was not at peace for a moment, facing all the southern points of the compass as if they were hounds that held it at bay. For my part, I do not know why people go out hunting on such days, unless it be for the reason that many people go to church, to set an example to others.

Philippa said she went because she had done her hair for riding before she could see out of the window—a fiction beneath the notice of any intelligent husband. I went because I had told my new groom, Wilson (an English disciplinarian), that I was going, and I was therefore caught in the cogs of the inexorable wheel of stable routine. I also went because I nourished a faint hope that I might be able to place before the general public, and especially before Flurry Knox, an authentic first version of the McRory episode. Moreover, I had a headache; but this I was not going to mention, knowing that the sun never sets upon the jests consecrated to after-dinner headaches.

As we rode away from Shreelane, and felt the thick small rain in our faces, and saw the spray blown off the puddles by the wind, and heard the seagulls, five miles inland, squealing in the mist overhead, I said that it was preposterous to think of hunting at Lonen Hill in such weather, and that I was going home. Philippa said that we might as well go on to the meet, to exercise the horses, and that we could then come straight home. (I have a sister who has said that I am a lath painted to look like iron, and that Philippa is iron painted to look like a lath.)

The meet was in shelter, the generous shelter of Lonen Hill, which interposed itself between us and the weather. There is just space for the road, between the shore of Lough Lonen and the southern face of the hill, that runs precipitously up into the sky for some six hundred feet, dark with fir-trees, and heather, and furze, fortified with rock—a place renowned as a fastness for foxes and woodcock (whose fancies as to desirable winter residences generally coincide). One would have thought that only a pack of monkeys could deal with such a covert, but hounds went through it, and so did beaters—or said they did.

We found the hounds waiting in an old quarry under the side of the hill, and, a little farther on, a very small and select company of waterproofs was huddled under

540

the branches of a fir-tree that hung over the road. As we neared them I recognized Miss Bennett's firm and capable back: she was riding the black mare that she had come over to "pass on" to old McRory. It was Philippa who pointed out that she was accompanied by Miss Larkie McRory, seated on a stout and shaggy animal, whose grey hindquarters were draped by the folds of its rider's voluminous black mackintosh, in a manner that recalled the historic statue of the Iron Duke. Farther on, Mrs. Flurry and her mother, the redoubtable Lady Knox, were getting out of a motor and getting themselves on to their horses.

"There's room under the umbrella for Mrs. Yeates!" called out Miss Bennett hospitably, "but the Major must find one for himself, and a very big one, too!"

"We could make room for him here," said Miss Larkie McRory, "if he liked to come."

I maintained, I hope, an imperturbable demeanour, and passed on.

"Who is that?" said Lady Knox, approaching me, on her large and competent iron grey.

I informed her, briefly, and without prejudice.

"Oh, one of that crew," said Lady Knox, without further comment.

Lady Knox is not noted for receptive sympathy, yet this simple statement indicated so pleasingly our oneness of soul in the matter of the McRorys that I was on the verge of flinging overboard the gentleman-like scruples proper to a guest, and giving her the full details of last night's revel. At this moment, however, her son-in-law came forth from the quarry with his hounds, and his coadjutors, Dr. Hickey and Michael, and moved past us.

"Yeates!" he called out, "I'd be obliged to you if you'd take that point up on the hill, on the down-wind side, where he often breaks." He looked at me with a serious, friendly face. "He won't break *down*, you know —it's only motors do that."

This witticism, concocted, no doubt, in the seclusion of the quarry, called for no reply on my part (or, to be accurate, no suitable reply presented itself). There was an undoubted titter among the waterproofs; I moved

541

away upon my mission at a dignified trot: a trot is seldom dignified, but Daniel has dignity enough for himself and his rider.

Daniel stands sixteen hands two inches in his stockings, of which he wears one white one, the rest of his enormous body being that of unlovely bluish-dun colour to which a dark bay horse turns when clipped. His best friend could not deny that he "made a noise"; his worst enemy was fain to admit that he was glad to hear it in front of him at a nasty place. Someone said that he was like a Settled Religious Faith, and no lesser simile conveys the restful certainty imparted by him. It was annoying, no doubt, to hear people say, after I had accomplished feats of considerable valour, that that horse couldn't make a mistake, and a baby could ride him; but these were mere chastenings, negligible to the possessor of a Settled Religious Faith.

I trotted on through the rain, up a steep road seamed with water-courses, with Lonen Hill towering on my left, and a lesser hill on my right. Looking back, I saw Flurry dismount, give his horse to a boy, and clamber on to the wall of the road: he dropped into the wood, and the hounds swarmed over after him, looking like midgets beside the tremendous citadel that they were to attack. Hickey and Michael, equally dwarfed by the immensities of the position, were already betaking themselves through the mist to their allotted outposts in space. Five-and-twenty couple of hounds would have been little enough for that great hillside; Flurry had fifteen, and with them he began his tough struggle through the covert, a solitary spot of red among pine-stems, and heather, and rocks, cheering his fifteen couple with horn and voice, while he climbed up and up by devious ways, seemingly as marvellously endowed with wind as the day itself. I cantered on till, at the point where the wood ended, it became my melancholy duty to leave the road and enter upon the assault of the hill. I turned in at a gap beside the guardian thornbush of a holy well, on whose branches votive rags fluttered in the wind, and addressed Daniel to his task of carrying thirteen stone up an incline approximating to a rise of one in three.

542

A path with the angles of a flash of lightning indicated the views of the local cow as to the best method of dealing with the situation. Daniel and I accepted this, as we had done more than once before, and we laboured upwards, parallel with the covert, while the wind, heavy with mist, came down to meet us, and shoved against us like a living thing. We gained at length a shelf on the hillside, and halting there in the shelter of a furzy hummock, I applied myself to my job. From the shelf I commanded a long stretch of the boundary wall of the wood, including a certain gap which was always worthy of special attention, and for a quarter of an hour I bent a zealous and travelling gaze upon the wall, with the concentration of a professor of a Higher Thought Society.

As is not unusual in such cases, nothing happened. At rare intervals a hint of the cry of hounds was carried in the wind, evanescent as a whiff from a summer garden. Once or twice it seemed to swing towards me, and at such moments the concentration of my eyeglass upon the gap was of such intensity that had the fox appeared I am confident that he would instantly have fallen into a hypnotic trance. As time wore on I arrived at the stage of obsession, when the music of the hounds and the touches of the horn seemed to be in everything, the wind, the streams, the tree branches, and I could almost have sworn hounds were away and running hard, until some vagrant voice in the wood would dispel the mirage of sound. This was followed by the reactionary period of pessimism, when I seemed to myself merely an imbecile, sitting in heavy rain, staring at a stone wall. Half an hour, or more, passed.

"I'm going out of this," I said to myself defiantly, "there's reason in the roasting of eggs."

It seemed, however, my duty to go up rather than down, and I coerced Daniel into the bed of a stream, as offering the best going available. It led me into a cleft between the hillside and the wall of the covert, which latter was, like a thing in a fairy tale, changing very gradually from a wall into a bank. I ascended the cleft, and presently found that it too was changing its nature, and becoming a flight of stairs. Daniel clattered slowly and carefuly up them, basing his feet, like Sir Bedivere, on "juts of slippery crag that rang sharp-smitten with the dint of armed heels."

We had reached the top in safety when I heard a thin and wavering squeal behind me, and looking back saw Miss Larkie McRory ascending the rocky staircase on the grey cob, at a speed that had obviously and legitimately drawn forth the squeal.

"Oh, gracious! The brute! I can't stop him!" she cried as she rushed upon me.

The grey cob here bumped into Daniel's massive stern, rebounded, and subsided, for the excellent reason that no other course was open to it. Miss McRory's reins were clutched in a looped confusion, that summoned from some corner of my brain a memory of the Sultan's cipher on the Order of the Medjidie: her hat was hanging down her back, and there was a picturesqueness about her hair that promised disaster later on. Her hazel eyes shone, and her complexion glowed like a rose in rain.

"Mr. Irving's fit to be tied!" she continued. "His horse jumped about like a mad thing when he saw those awful steps——!"

Sounds of conflict and clattering came from below. I splashed onwards in the trough between the hill and the fence, and had emerged into a comparatively open space with my closely attendant McRory, when the impassioned face of Mr. Irving's Meath mare shot into view at the top of the steps. The water in the trough was apparently for her the limit of what should or could be endured. She made a crooked spring at the hillside, slipped, and, recognizing the bank as the one civilized feature in a barbarous country, bounced sideways on to the top of it, pivoted there, and sat down backwards into a thicket of young ash and hazel trees. A succession of short yells from Miss McRory acclaimed each phase of the incident; Mr. Irving's face, as he settled down amongst the branches, was as a book where men might read strange matters, not of an improving nature.

It was probably the reception accorded to the bay mare by the branches and briars in which she had seated herself that caused her to return to the top of the bank in a kangaroo-bound, as active as it was unexpected. Horses can do these things when they choose, but they seldom choose. From the top of the bank she dropped into the trough, and joined us, with her nerves still in a state of acute indignation, and less of her rider in the saddle than is conventional, but a dinge in his pot-hat appeared to be the extent of the damage. Miss McRory's eye travelled from it to me, but she abstained from comment. It was the eye of a villain and a conspirator. I had by no means forgotten the injuries inflicted on me by her brothers, nor did I forget that Flurry had said that there wasn't one of the family but was as clever as the devil and four times as unscrupulous. Yet, taken in conjunction with the genuineness of her complexion, and with the fact that Irving was probably twenty years my junior, "I could'nt" —as the song says "help smiling at McRory O'More" (behind the back of young Mr. Irving, D.I.).

It transpired that Irving, from some point of vantage below, shared, it would appear, with Miss McRory, had seen the hounds running out of the top of the wood, and had elected to follow me. He did not know where anyone was, had not heard a sound of the horn and gave it as his opinion that Flurry was dead, and that trying to hunt in this country was simply farcical. He bellowed these things at me in his consequential voice as we struggled up the hill against the immense weight of wind, in all the fuss, anxiety, and uncertainty out of which the joys of hunting are born. It was as we topped the ultimate ridge that, through the deafening declamations of the wind, I heard, faint as a bar of fairy music, distant harmonies as of hounds running.

The wind blew a hole in the mist, and we had a bird's-eye view of a few pale-green fields far below: across one of them some pigmy forms were moving; they passed over a dark line that represented a fence, and proceeded into the heart of a cloud.

"That's about the limit," shouted Irving, dragging at his mare's mouth, as she swerved from a hole in the track. "It's only in this God-forsaken country that a fox'd go away in the teeth of a storm like this!"

To justify to Mr. Irving the disregard of the Lonen Hill

foxes for the laws of the game was not my affair. It seemed to me that in piloting him and Miss McRory I was doing rather more than humanity had any right to expect. I have descended Lonen Hill on various occasions, none of them agreeable, but never before with an avalanche travelling hard on my heels—a composite avalanche that slid, and rushed, and dropped its hind-legs over the edge at bad corners, and was throughout vocal with squeals, exclamations, inquiries as to facts of which Providence could alone be cognizant, and thunder-ous with objurgations. The hillside merged at length into upland pasture, strange little fields, composed partly of velvet patches, like putting-greens, predominantly of nightmare bunkers of rocks and furze. We rushed down-wards through these, at a pace much accelerated by the prevalence of cattle gaps; the bay mare, with her head in the air, zigzagging in bounds as incalulable as those of a grasshopper; the grey cob, taking sole charge of Miss McRory, tobogganing with her hind feet, propping with her fore, and tempering her enthusiasm with profound understanding of the matter. Finally, a telegraph-post loomed through the fog upon us, and a gate discovered itself, through which we banged in a bunch on to the high road. A cottage faced us, with a couple of women and an old man standing outside it.

To them we put the usual question, with the usual vehemence (always suggestive of the King's Troopers in romance, hotly demanding information about a flying rebel).

"I didn't see a fox this long while," replied the old man deliberately, "but there was a few jocks went west the road a while ago."

The King's Troopers, not specially enlightened, turned their steeds and went in pursuit of the jocks. A stone gap, flung in ruins among black hoof-marks, soon gave a more precise indication, and we left the road, with pro-found dubiety on my part as to where we were going and how we were going to get there. The first fence decided the matter for Irving, D.I. It was a bank on which slices of slaty stone had been laid, much as in Germany slabs of cold sausage are laid upon bread. The Meath mare looked at it but once, and fled from it at a tangent; the grey pony, without looking at it, followed her. Daniel selected an interval between the slabs, and took me over without comment. Filled by a radiant hope that I had shaken off both my companions, I was advancing in the line of the hoof-tracks, when once more I heard behind me on the wind cries as of a storm-driven seagull, and the grey cob came up under my stirrup, like a runaway steam pinnace laying itself beside a man-o'-war. Miss McRory was still in the saddle, but minus reins and stirrup; the wind had again removed her hat, which was following her at full stretch of its string, like a kite. Had it not been for her cries I should have said, judging by her face, that she was thoroughly enjoying herself.

Having achieved Daniel's society the cob pulled up, and her rider, not without assistance from me, restored her hat, reins, and stirrup to their proper spheres. I looked back, and saw Irving's mare, still on the farther side of the fence, her nose pointing to the sky, as if invoking the protection of heaven, and I knew that for better or worse Miss McRory was mine until we reached the high road. No doubt the thing was to be: as one of our own poets had sung of Emer and Cuchulain, "all who read my name in Erin's story would find its loving letters linked with" those of McRory. The paraphrase even rhymed—another fingermark of Fate. Yet it was hard that, out of all the possible, and doubtless eager, squires of the hunting-field I should have been chosen.

The hoof-tracks bent through a long succession of open gaps to a farmyard, and there were swallowed in the mire of a lane. I worked the lane out for every inch it was worth, with the misty rain pricking my face as it were with needles, and the intention to go home at the earliest possible opportunity perfecting itself in my heart. But the lane, instead of conducting us to the high road, melted disastrously into a turf bog. I pulled up, and the long steady booming of the sea upon the rocks made a deep undertone to the wind. There was no voice of hound or horn, and I was on the point of returning to the farm-house when the mist, in its stagey, purposeful way, again lifted, and laid bare the skyline of a low hill on our left. A riderless horse was limping very slowly along it, led by something that seemed no higher than a toadstool. Obviously we were on the line of the hunt, and obviously, also, it was my duty to inquire into the matter of the horse. I turned aside over a low bank, hotly followed by the grey cob, and the wail to which I was now becoming inured. As Miss McRory arrived abruptly at my side, she cried that she would have been off that time only for the grab she got of his hair. (By which I believe she meant the mare's mane.)

Fortune favoured us with broken-down fences; we overtook the horse, and found it was Flurry Knox's brown mare hobbling meekly in tow of a very small boy. In one of her hind fetlocks there was a clean, sharp cut that might have been done with a knife.

In answer to my questions the small boy pointed ahead. I polished my eyeglass, and, with eyes narrowed against the wind, looked into the south-west, and there saw, unexpectedly, even awfully near, the Atlantic Ocean, dingy and angry, with a long line, as of battle-smoke, marking its assault upon the cliffs. Between the cliffs and the hill on which we were standing a dark plateau, striped with pale grey walls, stretched away into the mist.

"There's the huntsman for ye," squeaked the little boy, who looked about six years old.

I descried at a distance of perhaps a quarter of a mile a figure in a red coat, on foot, in the act of surmounting one of the walls, accompanied by a hovering flock of country boys.

'The dogs is out before him," pursued the little boy at the full pitch of his lungs. "I seen the fox, too. I'll go bail he has himself housed in the Coosheen Grohogue by now."

"Gracious!" said Miss McRory.

I said he probably had a simpler telegraphic address, and that, no matter where he was, it was now my duty to overtake Mr. Knox and offer him my horse; "and you," I added, "had better get this little boy to show you the way to the road."

Miss McRory replied confidently that she'd sooner stay with me.

I said, as well as I remember, that her preference was highly flattering, but that she might live to regret it.

Miss McRory answered that she wished I wouldn't be spying at her through that old glass of mine; she knew well enough she was a show, and her hair was coming down, and she'd as soon trust herself to the cat as to that little urchin.

As I made my way downwards over the knife-edged ridges of rock and along their intervening boggy furrows, I should myself have been grateful for the guidance of the cat. Even the grey cob accepted the matter as serious, and kept the brake hard on, accomplishing the last horrid incident of the descent—a leap from the slant of the hill on to the summit of a heathery bank—without frivolity, even with anxiety. We had now arrived at the plateau above the cliffs—a place of brown, low-growing ling, complicated by boggy runnels, and heavily sprinkled with round stones. The mist was blowing in thicker than ever, Flurry and his retinue were lost as though they had never been, and the near thunder of the breakers, combined with the wind, made an impenetrable din round me and Miss McRory.

After perhaps a mile, in the course of which I got off several times to pull down loose walls for the benefit of my companion, I discovered the rudiments of a lane, which gradually developed into a narrow but indubitable road. The rain had gone down the back of my neck and into my boots: I determined that if Flurry had to finish the run on all-fours, I would stick to the lane until it took me to a road. What it took me to was, as might have been foreseen in any County Cork bohereen, a pole jammed across it from wall to wall and reinforced by furze-bushes —not a very high pole, but not one easy to remove. I pulled up and looked dubiously from it to Miss McRory.

"D'ye dare me?" she said.

"I bet you sixpence you take a toss if you do," I replied firmly, preparing to dismount.

"Done with you!" said Miss McRory, suddenly smiting the grey cob with a venomous little cutting whip (one that probably dated from the sixties, and had for a handle an ivory greyhound's head with a painted silver collar round its neck).

I have seldom seen a pole better and more liberally dealt with, as far as the grey cob's share of the transaction went, and seldom, indeed, have I seen a rider sail more freely from a saddle than Miss McRory sailed. She alighted on her hands and knees, and the cob, with the sting of the whip still enlivening her movements, galloped on up the lane and was lost in the mist.

"Well, you won your sixpence," said Miss McRory dauntlessly, as I joined her. "I suppose you're delighted."

I assured her with entire sincerity that I was very much the reverse, and proceeded at high speed in pursuit of the cob. The result of this excursion—a fairly prolonged one —was the discovery that the lane led into a road, and that it was impossible to decide in which direction the fugitive had gone. I returned in profound gloom to my young lady, and found her rubbing herself down with a bunch of heather.

"So you couldnt' ketch her!" she called out as I approached. "What'll we do now?" She was evidently highly amused. "I'll tell the Peeler it was your fault. You dared me!"

My reply need not be recorded; I only know it was by no means up to the standard to which Miss McRory was accustomed.

I took what seemed to be the only possible course, and established her seated sideways on my saddle, with her foot—and it is but fair to say, a very small foot—in the leather instead of the stirrup, and her right hand knotted in Daniel's mane. I held the off stirrup, and splashed beside her in the ruts and mud. The mist was thicker than ever, the wind was pushing it in from the sea in great masses, and Miss McRory and I progressed onward in a magic circle of some twenty yards in diameter, occupied only by herself and me, with Daniel thrown in as chaperon.

On arriving at the road I relied on the wind for guidance, and turning to the right, let it blow us in what was, I trusted, our course. It was by this time past three o'clock, we were at least nine or ten miles from home, and one of my boots had begun to rub my heel. There was nothing for it but to keep on as we were going, until we met something, or someone, or died.

It is worthy of record that in these afflicting circumstances Miss Larkie McRory showed a staying power, attained, probably, in the long and hungry bicycle picnics of her tribe, that was altogether commendable. Not for an instant did she fail to maintain in me the belief that she found me one of the most agreeable people she had ever met, a little older, perhaps, than Irving, D.I., but on that very account the more to be confided in. It was not until the pangs of hunger recalled to me the existence of my sandwiches that I discovered she had no food with her, nor, as far as could be gathered, had she had any breakfast.

"Sure they were all snoring asleep when I started. I just got a cup o' tea in the kitchen——"

This, I suppose, was a point at which I might suitably have said something incisive about the feats of her brethren on the previous night, but with deplorable weakness I merely offered her my sandwiches. Miss McRory replied that she'd fall off in a minute if she were to let go the mane, and why wouldn't I eat them myself? I said if there were any shelter left in Ireland I would wait till I got there, and we could then decide who should eat them.

Æons of mist and solitude ensued. I must have walked for an hour or more, without meeting anyone except one old woman, who could only speak Irish, and I had begun to feel as if my spur were inside my boot instead of outside, when I became aware of something familiar about the look of the fences. It was not, however, until I felt shelter rising blessedly about us, and saw the thorn bush with the rags hanging from it, that I realized that our luck had turned, and we had blundered our way back to the holy well under the side of Lonen Hill. The well was like a tiny dripping cave, about as big as a beehive, with a few inches of water in it; a great boulder stood guard over it, and above it stooped the ancient and twisted thorn bush. It seemed indicated as a place of rest, none the less that my heel was by this time considerably galled by my boot.

Miss McRory glissaded from my saddle into my arms, and was assisted by me to deposit herself on a flat stone beside the well, stiff, wet, but still undefeated. We shared my sandwiches, we drank whisky mixed with the water of the holy well, and Miss McRory dried her face with her handkerchief, and her complexion looked better than ever. Daniel, slowly and deliberately, ate the rags off the thorn bush. I have been at many picnics that I have enjoyed less.

By the time we had got to the gingerbread biscuits I had discovered that Mr. Irving thought she had talked too much to me after dinner last night, and that it was a wonder to her how men could be so cross about nothing. I said I was sorry she called it nothing, at which she looked up at me and down again at the gingerbread, and did not reply. After this I felt emboldened to ask her why she had been called so inappropriate a name as "Larkie".

Miss McRory agreed that it was indeed a silly old name, and that it was a friend of one of her brothers, a Mr. Mulcahy, who had said that she and her sister were "Lorky little gurls with lorge dork eyes". He had that way of speaking," she added, "because he thought it was grand, and he always kept his watch at English time. He said he ran over to London so often it wasn't worth while to change it."

She herself had never been out of Ireland, and she supposed she'd never get the chance.

I said that when she married Mr. Mulcahy she could keep her watch at Irish time, so as to equalize things.

Miss McRory suggested that I should give her a watch as a wedding present, and that, English or Irish time, it would be all hours of the night before we were home.

I realized with a slight shock that the position had indeed become inverted when one of the House of McRory had to remind me, after about four hours in her undiluted society, of the flight of time. It was now past four, which was bad enough, and a still greater shock awaited me in the discovery that I was dead lame, the interval of repose having been fatal to my damaged heel.

I have always asserted, and shall continue to do so to my dying day, that the way out of the difficulty was suggested by Miss McRory. I mounted Daniel, Miss McRory ascended the boulder by the holy well, announcing that she was as stiff as fifty crutches, and that once she got up she'd be there for life. The thing was done, somehow, thanks to the incomparable forbearance of Daniel, and with Miss McRory seated behind me on his broad back, and her arms clasped round my waist, I once more, and very cautiously, took the road.

Daniel continued to conduct himself like a gentleman, but considering how precarious was the position of Miss McRory, it was unnerving to feel her shaken by silent and secret laughter.

"You'll fall off," I warned her.

She replied by a further paroxysm, and asked me what size I took in stays—she supposed about forty inches.

Dusk was now an accomplished fact: thickened with fog and rain, it was even turning to darkness as we descended the long hill, but humanly speaking, the end was in sight. There was, I knew, a public-house a couple of miles farther on, where a car might be hired, and there I proposed to bid a long farewell to Miss Larkie McRory, and to send her home by herself, to have rheumatic fever, as I assured her.

We moved on and on, at a careful foot-pace: we were out in the wind again, and it was very cold. It was also quite dark. Silence fell upon us, and, after a time, the sustained pressure of Miss McRory's hat-brim against my shoulder suggested that it was the silence of exhaustion, if not of sleep. I thought of her with compassion. I believe I formulated her to myself as a poor little girl, and found myself asserting with defiance to imaginary detractors that no one could say she hadn't pluck, and that, in spite of her family, she really had a soul to be saved.

Again we found ourselves in shelter, and a greater darkness in the darkness told that we were in the lee of a wooded hill. I knew where I was now, and I said to Miss McRory that the pub was just round the corner, and she replied at once that that was where they always were, in Dublin anyway. She also said she thought she heard horses' hoofs coming up behind us. I pushed on.

We turned the corner, and were immediately struck blind by the twin glare of the lamps of a motor, that lay motionless, as in ambush, at the side of the road. Even the equanimity of Daniel was shattered; he swung to one side, he drifted like a blown leaf, and Miss McRory clung to me like a knapsack. As we curveted in the full glare of the limelight, I was aware of a figure in a pot-hat and a vast fur coat standing near the motor. Even as I recognized Lady Knox three or four muddy hounds trailed wearily into the glare, and a voice behind me shouted, " 'Ware horse!"

Flurry came on into the light: there was just room in me for a subconscious recognition of the fact that he was riding the missing grey cob, and that this was a typical thing, and one that might have been expected.

At the hunt dinner that took place soon afterwards someone sang a song, one that I have ceased to find amusing. The first verse runs as follows:

> Throttin' to the fair,
>   Me and Moll Moloney,
> Sittin', I declare,
>   On a single pony——

By a singular coincidence, the faces of all those present turned towards me.

THE COMTE DE PRALINES

"I had forgotten how nice London is!" purred Philippa, as we moved beautifully across the threshold of Bill Cunningham's club, and were conducted to the lift with a tender deference that was no more than was due to our best clothes.

The ladies' tea-room at Bill's club was a pleasant place, looking forth, high above the noise, upon trees that were yellow in the hazy October afternoon. In a very agreeable bow-window were Lady Derryclare and the tea-table, and with her were her son, and a small and ornamental young man, who was introduced to us as Mr. Simpson-Hodges.

"Front name John, known to a large circle of admirers as 'Mossoo'," supplemented Bill, whose hands were so clean that I found it difficult to recognize him.

"So called because of the incredible circumstance that he can speak French, in spite of the best public-school education," said Lady Derryclare. "When I think of the money that has been wasted on you! You good-for-nothing creature!"

"It's more his looks," pursued Bill, "his dark foreign beauty——"

"These humorists!" said Mr. Simpson-Hodges indulgently, showing a set of white teeth under a diminutive black moustache. "Please, Lady Derryclare, let's talk of something pleasant."

"Ask him about the chickens you made him get from the chicken farmers for the dance his regiment gave," said Bill to his mother.

"Oh, that was rather a bad business," said Mr. Simpson-Hodges apologetically, with an eye on Philippa, who, in a new hat, was looking about five-and-twenty. "I'm sure no one wants to hear about it."

"Mossoo ran the supper and he ordered three brace," said Bill, "but they never turned up till the week after the show! The postman was viewed coming up to the mess towing something after him on a long painter. The painter was superfluous. The chickens would have followed him at a trot if he had been kind to them. They kept them for the drag, I believe. Didn't you, Mossoo? He's one of the whips, you know."

"They'd have been quite useful," admitted Mr. Simpson-Hodges.

"How interesting to be a whip!" said Philippa, looking at him with egregious respect.

"Rather too interesting, sometimes," replied Simpson-Hodges, expanding to the glance in a way not unfamiliar to me. "Last time we were out the fellow with the drag started from the cross-roads where we were going to meet, and was asinine enough to take it a bit down the road before he went into the country, and, as it happened, we were bringing the hounds up to the meet by that particular road. They simply put down their heads and ran it heel for all they were worth! The first whip and I galloped our best, but we couldn't get to their heads, and we all charged into the middle of the meet full-cry!"

"Oh! I wish I had been there!" said Philippa ardently.

"We wished we were anywhere else," replied Mr. Simpson-Hodges; "the Brigadier was there, and everybody. We heard all about it afterwards, I can tell you!"

"That ought to have happened in Mr. Knox's country, Major Yeates!" said Lady Derryclare, whose interest in fox-hunting was more sympathetic than technical.

"We don't run drags, Lady Derryclare," I said reproachfully, but Lady Derryclare had already entered upon another topic.

Simpson-Hodges, however, did not end there.

A week afterwards Philippa and I crept home, third-class, with full trunks and empty pockets, sustained only by the aphorism, evolved by my wife, that economies, and not extravagances, are what one really regrets. It was approaching the end of November before we next heard of Simpson-Hodges. The Derryclares had come down for their first woodcock shoot, and Bill swooped over one morning in the big Daimler and whirled us back with him over the forty intervening miles of bog and mountain, to shoot, and to dance on the carpet after dinner, and to act charades; to further, in short, the various devices for exercising and disciplining a house party. Mr. John Simpson-Hodges was there, no less ornamental than in London, and as useful as he was ornamental. He shot well, he danced beautifully, and he made of the part of a French count in a charade so surprising a work of art that people said—as is the habit of people—that he ought to be making a hundred a week on the stage.

Before we left the Derryclares Philippa told me that she had arranged with "those boys"—by which she referred to Mr. Cunningham and the French count—to come over next week and have a hunt with Flurry Knox's hounds. Something whispered to me that there was more in this than met the eye, but as they were to provide their own mounts the position was unassailable, and I contented myself with telling her that a predilection for the society of the young was one of the surest signs of old age.

It was not till we were all seated at breakfast on the morning of the meet (which was to be at Castle Knox) that it was suggested, with all the spontaneity of a happy thought, by Bill, that "Mossoo" should be introduced to the members of the Hunt as a Frenchman who was unable to speak English.

"Call him the Comte de Pralines," said Philippa, with suspicious promptitude.

"You can call him Napoleon Buonaparte if you like," I said defiantly, "*I* shall stay at home!"

"All the Curranhilty people will be there," said Philippa softly.

The thought of introducing the Comte de Pralines to Miss Bobbie Bennett was certainly attractive.

"I refuse to introduce him to Lady Knox," I said with determination, and knew that I had yielded.

A meet at Castle Knox always brought out a crowd; there were generally foxes, and always luncheon, and there was a touch of the G.O.C. about Lady Knox that added a pleasing edge of anxiety, and raised the meet to something of the nature of a full-dress parade. I held to my point about Lady Knox, and did nothing more compromising than tremble in the background, while Bill Cunningham presented the Comte de Pralines to the lady of the house, supplementing the presentation with the statements that this was his first visit to Ireland, and that he spoke no English.

The Comte de Pralines, in the newest of pink coats, and the whitest of breeches, and the most glittering of boots and spurs, stood on the step below Lady Knox, with the bridle of his hireling over his arm, and his shining silk hat in his hand. Still with his hat in his hand, and looking, as Miss Larkie McRory whispered to me, "as pretty as a Christmas card", the Count rippled forth a stream of mellifluous French, commenting upon the beauty of the day, of the place, of the scene.

Lady Knox's face deepened to so apoplectic a crimson, and her eyes became so fixed that I, watching the scene apprehensively, doubted if it were not my duty to rush at her and cut open her hunting-stock. When the Count ceased, having, as far as I could gather, inquired as to when she had last been to Auteuil, and if she had ever hunted in France, Lady Knox paused, and said very slowly:

"Er—*j'espère que nous aurons un bon jour aujourd'-hui.*" Then, rapidly, to me, "Take your friend in for a drink, Major Yeates."

My heart bled for her, and also quaked for myself, but I was in it now, up to my chin.

During the next ten minutes Bill Cunningham, feebly abetted by me, played the game remorselessly, sparing neither age nor sex. In the hall, amidst the sloe-gins and the whiskies and sodas (to which the Count, for a foreigner, took remarkably kindly), introductions slipped between cup and lip, poisoning the former and paralysing the latter. The victims took it variously; some sought refuge in bright smiles and large foreign gestures; some, in complete mental overthrow, replied in broken English to Mossoo's sugared periods; all were alike in one point, they moved as swiftly as might be, and as far as possible, out of the immediate neighbourhood of the Comte de Pralines. Philippa, who, without any solid attainment, can put up a very good bluff in French, joined spasmodically in these encounters, alternately goading Mossoo to fresh outrages, and backing out when the situation became too acute. I found her, affecting to put her sandwiches into the case on her saddle, and giving way to her feelings, with her face pressed against her mare's shoulder.

" I introduced him to Bobbie Bennett," she said brokenly; "and he asked her if she spoke French. She looked at me as if she were drowning, and said, '*Seulement trés petit!*'"

I said, repressively, that Lady Knox could see her, and

558

that people would think, firstly, that she was crying, and secondly, that she was mad.

"But I *am* mad, darling!" replied my wife, turning a streaming face to me.

I informed her of my contempt for her, and, removing myself from her vicinity, collected myself for the introduction of the Count to Flurry Knox and Dr. Hickey. By this time most of the field were mounted, and the Comte de Pralines bent to his horse's mane as he uncovered with grave courtesy on his presentation to the Master and the first whip, and proceeded to express the profundity of his gratification at meeting an Irish Master of Hounds. The objects of the attention were palpably discomposed by it; Flurry put a finger to his cap, with a look at me expressive of No Surrender; Dr. Hickey, in unconscious imitation of the Count, bowed low, but forgot about his cap.

"He has no English, I'm told," said Flurry, eyeing the Count suspiciously.

I stopped myself on the verge of bowing assent, so infectious was the grace of the Pralines manner.

"Is he come to buy horses for the German Army?" went on Flurry. (It need hardly be said that this occurred before the war.)

I explained that he was French.

"You wouldn't know what these foreigners might be up to," returned Mr. Knox, quite unconvinced. "I'm going on now——"

He too moved expeditiously out of the danger zone.

The field straggled down the avenue, and progressed over tracts of tussocky grass in the wake of the hounds, towards the plantation that was the first draw. The keeper was outside the wood, with the assurance that there was a score of foxes in it, and that they had the country ate.

"Maybe they'll eat the hounds, so," said Flurry. "Let you all stay outside. You can be talking French now for a bit——"

I looked round to see who were availing themselves of this permission. The Count had by this time been introduced to Miss Larkie McRory; Philippa was apparently acting as interpreter, and Miss McRory was showing no disposition to close the interview. The field had withdrawn, and had formed itself into a committee meeting on the Count.

It was warm and sunny in the shelter of the wood. Although the time was November there were still green leaves on some of the trees; it was a steamy day after a wet night, and I thought to myself that if the hounds *did* run—— Here came a challenge from the wood, answered multitudinously, and the next minute they were driving through the laurels towards the entrance gates, with a cry that stimulated even the many-wintered Daniel to capers quite unbefitting his time of life, or mine. The Castle Knox demesne is a large one, and being surrounded by a prohibitively high and coped wall, it is easier to find a fox there than to get away with one. Mighty galloping on the avenue followed, with interludes in the big demesne fields, where every gate had been considerately left open, and in which every horse with any pretentions to *savoir faire* stiffened his neck, and put up his back, and pulled. The hounds, a choir invisible, carried their music on through the plantations, with whimpering, scurrying pauses, with strophe and antistrophe of soprano and bass. Sometimes the cry bore away to the demesne wall, and someone would shout "They're away!" and the question of the front gate versus the western gate would divide us like a sword. Twice, in the undergrowth, above the sunk fence that separated us from the wood, the quick, composed face of the fox showed itself; at last, when things were getting too hot in the covert, he sprang like a cat over the ditch, and flitted across the park with that gliding gait that dissimulates its own speed, while I and my fellows offered a painful example of the discordance of the human voice when compared with that of the hound, and five or six couple pitched themselves out of the wood and stretched away over the grass.

It was fortunate for the Comte de Pralines that his entirely British view-holloa was projected for the most part into my ear (the drum of which it nearly split) and was merged in the general conversation as we let ourselves go.

"For God's sake, Major Yeates!" said Michael, the second whip, thundering up beside me as we neared the covert on the furthest side of the park, "come into the wood with me and turn them hounds! Mr. Flurry's back on another fox with the body of the pack, and he's very near his curse!"

I followed Michael into the covert, and was myself followed by a section of the field, who might, with great advantage, have remained outside. In the twinkling of an eye Michael was absorbed into the depths of the wood; so also were the six couple, but not so my retinue, who pursued me like sleuth-hounds, as I traversed the covert at such speed as the narrow rides permitted. I made at length the negative discovery that it contained nothing save myself and my followers, a select party, consisting of the Comte de Pralines, Miss McRory, Miss Bobbie Bennett, Lady Knox's coachman on a three-year-old, and a little boy in knickerbockers, on a midget pony with the bearing of a war-horse and a soul to match. We had come to a baffled pause at the cross-ways when, faint and far away, an indisputable holloa was borne to us.

"They've gone out the west gate," said the coachman, from among the tree-trunks into which he had considerately manœuvred the kicking end of the three-year-old. "It must be they ran him straight out into the country——"

We made for the west gate, reached it without sight or sound of Flurry or anyone else, and, on the farm road outside it, pulled up to listen.

The holloa was repeated; half a mile ahead a gesticulating figure signalled to us to come on. I wish to put it on record that I said I could not hear the hounds. The Comte de Pralines (excitable, like all Frenchmen) spurred his hireling at the opposite bank, saying ,as he shot past me:

"It's no damned use humbugging here any longer!"

As I turned Daniel to follow him, my eyes met those of Miss Larkie McRory, alight with infernal intelligence; they challenged, but at the same time they offered conıederacy. I jumped into the field after the Count; Miss McRory followed.

"I'll tell Lady Knox on you!" she murmured, as she pounded beside me on the long-legged spectre, who, it may be remembered, had been described as "the latther end of a car-horse."

The holloa had come to us from the side of a smooth green hill, and between us and it was a shallow valley, neatly fenced with banks that did credit to Sir Valentine Knox's farming. The horses were fresh, the valley smiled in the conventional way, and spread sleek pastures before us; we took the down grade at a cheerful pace, and the bank's a shade faster than was orthodox, and the coachman's three-year-old made up in enthusiasm what he lacked in skill, and the pony, who from the first was running away, got over everything by methods known only to itself. The Comte de Pralines held an undeviating line for the spot whence the holloa had proceeded, when we reached it there was no one to be seen, but there was another holloa further on. The pursuit of this took us on to a road, and here the Castle Knox coachman, who had scouted on ahead, yelled something to the effect that he saw a rider out before him, accompanying the statement by an application of the spurs to the dripping but undaunted three-year-old. A stretching gallop up the road ensued, headed by the little boy and the coachman, who had both secured a commanding lead. The pace held for about a hundred yards, when the road bent sharply to the left, more sharply indeed than was anticipated by the leaders, who, as their mounts skidded as it were on one wheel round the corner, sailed from their saddles with singular unanimity and landed in the ditch. At the same moment the rider we had been following came into view; he was a priest, in immaculate black coat and top-hat, seated on a tall chestnut horse, and proceeding at a tranquil footpace on his own affairs.

He had seen the fox, he admitted (I am inclined to think he had headed him), and he had heard a man shouting, but no hounds had come his way. He was entirely sympathetic, and, warm as I was at the moment, a chill apprehension warned me that we might presently need sympathy.

"It's my belief," said Miss Bennett, voicing that which I had not put into words, "we've been riding after the fox, and the hounds didn't leave the covert at all!"

An elaborate French oath from the Count fell, theatrical as a drop-scene, on the close of the first act. Miss Larkie McRory looked at him admiringly, and allowed just the last rays of her glance to include me.

It was when we had retraced our steps to the bend of the road that we had a full view of the Castle Knox coverts, crowning in gold and brown those pleasant green slopes, easy as the descent to Avernus, down which we had galloped with such generous ardour some fifteen minutes ago. Outside the west gate, through which we had emerged from the demesne, were three motionless figures in scarlet; Lady Knox and her grey horse were also recognizable; a few hounds were straying undecidedly in the first of the grass fields that we had traversed.

A note of the horn leaped to us across the valley, an angry and peremptory note. One of the scarlet figures started at a canter and turned the hounds. Another and longer blast followed. As if in obedience to its summoning, the coachman's three-year-old came ramping, riderless, down the road; he passed us with his head high in air and his flashing eye fixed upon the distant group, and, with a long shrill neigh, put his tail over his back and directed his flight for his owner and her grey horse.

"God help poor Tierney!" said Miss Bennett, in a stricken voice, "and ourselves too! I believe they saw us all the time, and we galloping away on the line of the fox!"

"I'm going home," I said. "Will you kindly make my apologies to the Master?"

"I'll kindly do no such thing," replied Miss Bennett. I'll let Flurry Knox cool off a bit before I meet him again, and that won't be this side of Christmas, if *I* can help it! Good-bye, dear friends!"

She turned her mare, and set her face for her own country.

There now remained only the Count, Miss McRory and myself, and to remove ourselves from the field of vision of the party at the gate was our first care. We had, no doubt, been thoroughly identified, nevertheless the immediate sensation of getting a furzy hill between us and Flurry was akin to that of escaping from the rays of a burning-glass. In shelter we paused and surveyed each other.

The Comte de Pralines, with his shiny hat very much on the back of his head, put down his reins, shoved his crop under his knee, and got out his cigarette case.

"Well," he began philosophically, striking a match, "our luck ain't in——!"

He broke off, the match went out, and a lively glow suffused his unsheltered countenance.

"Vous voyez, mon cher——" he resumed, very rapidly. *"J'ai appris quelques petits mots——"*

"What a lovely English accent he has!" interrupted Miss McRory rapturously; "it's a lot nicer than his French one. To look at him you'd never think he was so clever. It's a pity he wouldn't try to pick up a little more."

"Now, that's hitting a man when he's down," said the Comte de Pralines. "I want someone to be kind to me. I've had a poor day of it; no one would talk to me. I stampeded them wherever I went."

"I didn't notice Miss McRory stampeding to any great extent," I said.

"Wait awhile!" rejoined Miss McRory. "Maybe the stampeding will be going the other way when you and he meet Lady Knox!"

"I shan't wait an instant," said the Comte de Pralines, "you and Major Yeates will explain."

The horses had been moving on, and the covert was again in sight, about a quarter of a mile away on our left. There was nothing to be seen, but hounds were hunting again in the demesne; their cry drove on through the woods inside the grey demesne wall; they were hunting in a body, and they were hunting hard.

At each moment the cry was becoming more remote,

but it was still travelling on inside the wall. The fear of
Flurry fell from us as a garment, and the only question
that presented itself was whether to return to the west
gate or to hold on outside. It was a long-accepted theory
at Castle Knox that the demesne wall was not negotiable,
and that the foxes always used the gates, like Christians;
bearing this in mind, I counselled the front gate and the
outside of the wall. A couple of lanes favoured us; we
presently found ourselves in a series of marshy fields,
moving along abreast of the invisible hounds in the wood.
They were in the thickest and least accessible part of it,
and Flurry's voice and horn came faintly as from a
distance.

I explained that it was impossible to ride that part of
the wood, but that, if they held on as they were going,
the front gate would make it all right for us, and of
course Flurry would——

"Oh! look, look, look!" shrieked Miss McRory,
snatching at my arm and pointing with her whip.

A short way ahead of us a huge elm-tree had fallen
upon the wall; the greenish-yellow leaves still clinging to
its branches showed that the catastrophe was recent. It
had broken down the wall to within five or six feet of
the ground, and was reclining in the breach it had made,
with its branches sprawling in the field. I followed the
line of Miss Larkie's whip, and was just in time to see a
fox float like a red leaf from one of these to the ground,
and glide straight across our front. He passed out of
sight over a bank, and the Count stood up in his stirrups,
put his finger in his ear, and screamed in a way that must
have been heard in the next county. I contributed with a
not ineffective bellow, and Miss McRory decorated the
occasion with long thin squeals.

The hounds, inside the wall, answered in an agony
that was only allayed by the discovery that the trunk of
the tree formed as handy a bridge for them as for the
fox. They came dropping like ripe fruit through the
branches, and, under our rejoicing eyes, swarmed to the
fox's line, and flung on, in the fullest of full-cry, over
the bank on which we had last seen him. I had not failed
to assure Flurry Knox that anything less suggestive of

565

"sneaking away with the hounds" than the manner of our departure could hardly be conceived, but Mr. Knox has not withdrawn the phrase.

It may be conceded that Flurry had grounds for annoyance. Had I had the fox in one hand and the ordnance map in the other, I could hardly have improved on the course steered by our pilot. Uphill for a bit, when the horses were fresh, with gradients just steep enough to temper Daniel's well-sustained tug-of-war, yet not so steep as to make a three-foot bank look like a house, or to guarantee a big knee at each "stone gap". Then high and dry country, with sheep huddled in defensive positions in the corners of the fields, and grass like a series of putting-greens, minus the holes, and fat, comely banks, and thin walls, from which the small round stones rattled harmlessly as Miss McRory's car-horse swept through them. Down into a long valley, with little sky-blue lakes, set in yellow sedge; and there was a helpful bog road there, that nicked nicely with the bending line of the hounds through the accompanying bog, and allayed a spasm of acute anxiety as to whether we should ever get near them again. Then upwards once more, deviously, through rougher going, with patches of low-growing furze sprouting from blackened tracts where the hillside had been set on fire, with the hounds coming to their noses among brakes of briars and bracken; finally, in the wind and sun of the hill-top, a well-timed check.

We looked back for the first time, half in fear that we might find Flurry hot on our track, half in hope that he and his horn were coming to our help; but neither in the green country nor in the brown valley was there any sign or sound of him. There was nothing to be seen but a couple of men standing on a fence to watch us, nothing to be heard except cur dogs vociferating at every cottage.

"Fifteen couple on," said the Count professionally. "How many does Knox usually have out?"

"All he's got," I said, mopping my brow.

"I don't see the two that have no hair on their backs," said Miss McRory, whose eyes, much enhanced by the radiant carmine of her cheeks, beamed at us through wisps and loops of hair. "I know them, they're always scratching, the poor things!"

That Miss McRory and her steed kept, as they did, their place in what is known to history as the Great Castle Knox Run is a matter that I do not pretend to explain. Some antiquarian has unearthed the fact that the car-horse had three strains of breeding, and had twice been second in a point-to-point; but I maintain that credit must be ascribed to Miss Larkie, about whom there is something inevitable; some street-boy quality of being in the movement.

We were now on a heathery table-land, with patches of splashy, rushy ground, from which the snipe flickered out as the hounds cast themselves through it. Presently, on the top of a hard, peaty bank, a hound spoke, hesitatingly, yet hopefully, and plunged down on the other side; the pack crowded over, and drove on through the heather. Daniel changed feet on a mat of ling with a large stone in it, and therefrom ramped carefully out over a deep cut in the peat, unforeseen, and masked by tufts of heather. The hireling of the Comte de Pralines had, up to this, done his work blamelessly, if without originality; he had an anxiousness to oblige that had been matured during a dread winter when he had been the joint property of three subalterns, but he reserved to himself a determination to drop economically off his banks, and boggy slits were not in his list of possibilities.

How the matter occurred I do not know, but, when I looked round, his head alone was visible, and the Count was standing on his in the heather. Miss McRory's car-horse, who had pulled up in the act of following the Count, with a suddenness acquired, no doubt, in the shafts of a Cork covered-car, was viewing the scene with horror from the summit of the bank. The hounds were by this time clear of the heather, and were beginning to run hard; it was not until I was on the further side of the next bank that I cast another fleeting look back; this time the Count was standing on his feet, but the hireling was still engulfed, and Miss McRory was still on the wrong side of the slit. After that I forgot them, wholly and heartlessly, as is invariable in such cases.

As a matter of fact, I had no attention to spare for anyone but myself, even though we went, for the first twenty minutes or so, as on rubber tyres, through bland dairy farms wherein the sweet influences of the dairy-cow had induced gaps in every fence, and gates into every road. The scent, mercifully for Daniel, was not quite what it had been; the fox had run through cattle, and also through goats (a small and odorous party, on whose behalf, indeed, some slight intervention on my part was required), and it was here, when crossing a road, that a donkey and her foal, moved by some mysterious attraction akin to love at first sight, attached themselves to me. Undeterred by the fact that the mother's foreleg was fettered to her hind, the pair sped from field to field in my wake; at the checks, which just then were frequent, they brayed enthusiastically. I thought to elude them at a steep drop into a road, but they tobogganed down it without an effort; when they overtook me the fetter-chain was broken, and clanked from the mother's hind-leg as if she were a family ghost.

There came at length a moment, outside a farm-house, when it seemed as if the fox had beaten us. Here, on the farther side of Castle Knox, I was well out of my own country, and what the fox's point might be was represented by the letter X. Nevertheless it was here that I lifted the hounds and brought off the cast of a lifetime; I am inclined to think that he had lain down under a hayrick and was warned of our approach by the voices of my attendant jackasses; my cast was probably not much more of a fluke than such inspirations usually are, but the luck was with me. Old Playboy, sole relic of my deputy mastership, lifted his white head and endorsed my suggestion with a single bass note; Rally, Philippa's prize puppy, uttered a soprano cadenza, and the pack suddenly slid away over the pasture fields with the smoothness and unanimity of the *petits chevaux* over their green cloth.

It was now becoming for Daniel and me something of an effort to keep our proud and lonely place in or about the next fields to the hounds. The fields were becoming smaller, the gaps fewer; Daniel had no intention of chucking it, but he gave me to understand that he meant to take the hills on the second speed. And, unfortunately, the hills were coming. The hounds, by this time three fences ahead, flung over a bank on the upgrade, a bank that would give pause for reflection at the beginning of a run. I tried back, scrambled into a lane, followed it up the hill, with the cry of the hounds coming fainter each minute, dragged a cart wheel and a furze bush out of a gap with my crop, found myself in a boggy patch of turnips, surrounded by towering fuchsia hedges, and realized that the pack had passed in music out of sight.

I stood still and looked at my watch. It was already an hour and twenty minutes from the word "Go!" and the hounds were not only gone but were still going. A man who has lost hounds inevitably follows the line of least resistance. I retired from the turnip field, and abandoned myself to the lane, which seemed not disinclined to follow the direction in which the hounds had been heading. Since the hayrick episode they had been running right-handed, and the lane bent right-handed over the end of the hill, and presently deposited me on a road. It was one of the moments when the greatness of the world is borne in upon the wayfarer. There was a spacious view from the hillside; three parishes, at least, offered themselves for my selection, and I surveyed them, solitary and remote as the evening star, and with no more reason than it for favouring one more than another. A harrowing, and, by this time, but too familiar cry broke on my ear, an undulating cry as of a thing that galloped as it roared. My admirers were still on my trail; I gave Daniel a touch of the spurs and trotted on to the right.

No human being was visible, but some way ahead there was a slated house at a cross-roads; there, at all events, I could get my bearings. There were porter-barrels outside it, and from some distance I heard two voices, male and female, engaged in loud and ferocious argument; I had no difficulty in diagnosing a public-house. When Daniel and I darkened the doorway the shouting ceased abruptly, and I saw a farmer, in his Sunday clothes, making an unsteady retreat through a door at the back of the shop. The other disputant, a large, middle-aged woman, remained entrenched behind the counter, and regarded me with a tranquil and commanding eye. She informed me, as from a pulpit, that I was six miles from Castle Knox, and with dignity, as though leaving a pulpit, she moved from behind the counter, and advanced to the door to indicate my road. I asked her if she had seen anything of the hounds.

"There was one of your dogs looked in the door to me a while ago," she replied, "but he got a couple of boxes from the cat that have kittens; Id'no what way he went. Indeed I was bothered at the time with that poor man that came in to thank me for the compliment I paid him in going to his sister's funeral."

I said that he certainly seemed to feel it very much. At which she looked hard at me and said that he was on his way to a wedding, and that it might be he had a drop taken to rise his heart. "He was after getting a half a crown from a gentleman—a huntsman like yourself," she added, "that was striving to get his horse out of a ditch."

"Was there a lady with him?" I asked.

"There was, faith! And the two o' them legged it away then through the country, and they galloping like the deer!"

So, in all love, we parted; before I reached the next turning renewed sounds of battle told me that the compliment was still being pressed home.

My road, bending ever to the right, strolled through an untidy nondescript country, with little bits of bog, and little lumps of hills, and little rags of fields. I had jogged a mile or so when I saw a hound, a few fields away to my right, poking along on what seemed to be a line; he flopped into a boggy ditch, and scrambled from it on to a fence. He stood there undecidedly, like any human being, reviewing the situation, and then I saw his head and stern go up. The next moment I also heard what he had heard, a faint and far-away note of the horn. It came again, a long and questing call.

The road was flat and fairly straight; far away upon it something was moving gradually into my scope of vision, something with specks of red in it. It advanced upon me, firmly, and at a smart pace; heading it, like the ram of a battleship, was Mr. Knox. With him, "of all his halls had nursed", remained only the two hounds with the hairless backs, the two who, according to Miss McRory, were always scratching. Behind him was a small and unsmiling selection from those who, like him, had lost the hunt. Lady Knox headed them; my wife and Bill brought up the rear. The hound whom I had seen in the bog had preceded me, and was now joining himself to his two comrades, putting the best face he could upon it, with a frowning brow and his hackles up. The comrades, in their official position as sole representatives of the pack, received him with orthodox sternness, and though unable, for obvious reasons, to put their hackles up, the bald places on their backs were of an intimidating pink.

My own reception followed the same lines.

"Where are the hounds?" barked Flurry, in the awful tones of a parent addressing a governess who, through gross neglect, has mislaid her charges.

Before I had time to make up my mind whether to be truculent or pacific, there was a shout away on our left. At some little distance up a by-road, a man was standing on a furze-plumed bank, beckoning to us with a driving-whip, Flurry stood in his stirrups, and held up his cap. The man yelled information that was wholly unintelligible, but the driving-whip indicated a point beyond him, and Flurry's brown mare jumped from a standstill to a gallop, and swung into the by-road.

The little band of followers swung after him. When Lady Knox was well ahead, I followed, and found myself battering between high banks behind Philippa and Bill Cunningham.

"Where's Mossoo?" my wife said breathlessly, as Daniel's head drew level with her sandwich case. "We met the man who pulled him out of the ditch—up in the hills there——"

"Yes, by Jove!" said Bill, "Flurry asked him if it was a Frenchman, and the chap said, 'French or German, he had curses as good as yourself!' I told Flurry it must have been you!"

"I don't mind Flurry, it's Lady Knox——" began Philippa.

Here we all came to a violent full-stop. Flurry's advance had been arrested by a covered-car and horse drawn across the road; the horse was eating grass, the driver, with the reins in his hand, was standing with his back to us on top of the bank from which he had hailed us, howling plaudits, as if he were watching a race. There were distant shouts, and barking dogs, and bellowing cattle, and blended with them was the unmistakable baying of hounds.

I dare say that what Flurry said to the driver did him good—did Flurry good, I mean. The car lurched to one side, and, as we squeezed past it, we saw between its black curtains a vision of a scarlet-faced bride, embedded in female relatives; two outside cars, driverless, and loaded with wedding guests, were drawn up a little farther on. Flurry, still exploding like a shell, thundered on down the lane; the high bank ended at a gateway, he turned in, and as we crushed in after him we were greeted by a long and piercing 'Who-whoop!'"

We were in a straggling field with furzy patches in it. At the farther end of it was a crowd of country people on horses and on foot, obviously more wedding-guests; back of all, on a road below, was a whitewashed chapel, and near it, still on the chestnut horse, was the priest who had headed the morning fox. Close to one of the clumps of furze the Comte de Pralines was standing, knee-deep in baying hounds, holding the body of the fox high above his head, and uttering scream upon scream of the most orthodox quality. He flung the fox to the hounds, the onlookers cheered, Miss McRory, seated on the car-horse, waved the brush above her head, and squealed at the top of her voice something that sounded like "Yoicks!" Her hair was floating freely down her back; a young countryman, in such sacrificial attire as suggested the bridegroom, was running across the field with her hat in his hand.

Flurry pulled up in silence; so did we. We were all quite outside the picture, and we knew it.

"Oh, the finest hunt ever you see!" cried the bridegroom as he passed us; "it was Father Dwyer seen him shnaking into the furze, the villyan!"

"Worry, worry, worry! Tear him and eat him, old fellows!" shouted the Comte de Pralines. "Give the hounds room, can't you, you chaps! I suppose you never saw them break up a fox before!" This to the wedding guests, who had crowded in, horse and foot, on top of the scuffling, growling pack.

Flurry turned an iron face upon me. His eye was no bigger than a pin's head.

"I suppose it's from Larkie McRory he got the English?" he said; "he learnt it quick."

"The McRorys don't speak English!" said Lady Knox, in a voice like a north-east wind.

"Seulement très petit!" Philippa murmured brazenly.

Whether Lady Knox heard her or not, I am unable to say. Her face was averted from me, and remained as inflexible as a profile on a coin—a Roman coin, for choice.

The faculty of not knowing when you are beaten is one that has, I think, been lauded beyond its deserving. Napoleon the Great has condemned manœuvring before a fixed position, and Lady Knox was clearly in a fixed position. Accepting these tenets, I began an unostentatious retirement, in which I was joined by Philippa. We were nearing safety and the gate of the field when a yearning, choking wail came to us from the lane.

"The bride?" queried my wife hysterically.

It was repeated; in the same instant my admirers, the jackasses, *mère et fils*, advanced upon the scene at a delirious gallop, and, sobbing with the ecstasy of reunion, resumed their attendance upon Daniel.

For a moment the attention of the field, including even that of the Roman coin, was diverted from the Comte de Pralines, and was concentrated upon our retreat.

THE SHOOTING OF SHINROE

Mr. Joseph Frances M'Cabe rose stiffly from his basket chair, picked up the cushion on which he had been seated, looked at it with animosity, hit it hard with his fist, and, flinging it into the chair, replaced himself upon it, with the single word:

"Flog!"

I was aware that he referred to the flock with which the cushions in the lounge of Reardon's Hotel were stuffed.

"They have this hotel destroyed altogether with their improvements," went on Mr. M'Cabe between puffs, as he lit his pipe. "God be with the time this was the old smoking-room, before they knocked it and the hall into one and spoilt the two of them! There were fine solid chairs in it that time, that you'd sleep in as good as your bed, but as for these wicker affairs, I declare the wind 'd whistle through them the same as a crow's nest." He paused, and brought his heel down heavily on top of the fire. "And look at that for a grate! A well-grate they call it—*I'd* say, 'Leave well alone!' Thirty years I'm coming to Sessions here, and putting up in this house, and in place of old Tim telling me me own room was ready for me, there's a whipper-snapper of a snapdragon in a glass box in the hall, asking me me name in broken English" (it may be mentioned that this happened before the war) and 'Had I a Cook's ticket?' and down-facing me that I must leave my key in what he called the 'Bew-ro'."

I said I knew of a lady who always took a Cook's ticket when she went abroad, because when she got to Paris there would be an Englishman on the platform to meet her, or at all events a broken Englishman.

Mr. M'Cabe softened to a temporary smile, but held on to his grievance with the tenacity of his profession.

(I don't think I have mentioned that he is a solicitor, of a type now, unfortunately, becoming obsolete.) He had a long grey face, and a short grey moustache; he dyed his hair, and his age was known to no man.

"There was one of Cook's tourists sat next me at breakfast," he resumed, "and he asked me was I ever in Ireland before, and how long was I in it. 'Wan day,' says I!"

"Did he believe you?" I asked.

"He did," replied Mr. M'Cabe, with something that approached compassion.

I have always found old M'Cabe a mitigating circumstance of Sessions at Owenford, both in Court and out of it. He was a sportsman of the ingrained variety that grows wild in Ireland, and in any of the horse-coping cases that occasionally refresh the innermost soul of Munster, it would be safe to assume that Mr. M'Cabe's special gifts had ensured his being retained, generally on the shady side. He fished when occasion served, he shot whether it did or not. He did not exactly keep horses, but he always knew someone who was prepared to "pass on" a thoroughly useful animal, with some infirmity so insignificant that until you tried to dispose of him you did not realize that he was yours, until his passing-on to the next world. He had certain shooting privileges in the mountains behind the town of Owenford (bestowed, so he said, by a grateful client) and it had often been suggested by him that he and I should anticipate some November Sessions by a day, and spend it "on the hill". We were now in the act of carrying out the project.

"Ah, these English," M'Cabe began again, mixing himself a glass of whisky and water, "they'd believe anything so long as it wasn't the truth. Talking politics these lads were, and by the time they had their ham and eggs swallowed they had the whole country arranged. 'And look,' says they—they were anglers, God help us!—'look at all the money that's going to waste for want of preserving the rivers!' I beg your pardon, says I, there's water-bailiffs on the most of the rivers. I was defending a man not long since, that was cot by the water-bailiff poaching salmon on the Owen. And what proof have

575

you? says I to the water-bailiff. How do you know it was a salmon at all? 'Is it how would I know?' says the bailiff, 'didn't I gaff the fish for him meself!' "

"What did your anglers says to that?" I inquired.

"Well, they didn't quite go so far as to tell me I was a liar," said Mr. M'Cabe tranquilly. "Ah, telling such as them the truth is wasting what isn't plenty! Then they'll meet some fellow that lies like a tooth-drawer, and they'll write to the English *Times* on the head of him!" He stretched forth a long and bony hand for the tumbler of whisky and water. "And talking of tooth-drawers," he went on, "there's a dentist comes here once a fortnight, Jeffers his name is, and a great sportsman too. I was with him to-day"—he passed his hand consciously over his mouth, and the difference that I had dimly felt in his appearance suddenly, and in all senses of the word, flashed upon me—"and he was telling me how one time, in the summer that's past, he'd been out all night, fishing in the Owen. He was going home before the dawn, and he jumped down off a bank on to what he took to be a white stone—and he aimed for the stone, mind you, because he thought the ground was wet— and what was it but a man's face!" M'Cabe paused to receive my comment. "What did he do, is it? Ran off for his life, roaring out, 'There's a first-rate dentist in Owenford!' The fellow was lying asleep there, and he having bundles of spurge with him to poison the river! He had drink taken, I suppose."

"Was he a water-bailiff too?" said I. "I hope the conservators of the river stood him a set of teeth."

"If they did," said M'Cabe, with an unexpected burst of feeling, "I pity him!" He rose to his feet, and put his tumbler down in the chimney-piece. "Well, we should get away early in the morning, and it's no harm for me to go to bed."

He yawned, a large yawn that ended abruptly with a metallic click. His eyes met mine, full of unspoken things; we parted in a silence that seemed to have been artificially imposed upon Mr. M'Cabe.

The wind boomed intermittently in my chimney during the night, and a far and heavy growling told of the dis-

576

satisfaction of the sea. Yet the morning was not unfavourable. There was a broken mist, with shimmers of sun in it, and the carman said it would be a thing of nothing, and would go out with the tide. The boots, a relic of the old regime, was pessimistic, and mentioned that there were two stars squez up agin the moon last night, and he would have no dependence on the day. M'Cabe offered no opinion, being occupied in bestowing in a species of dog-box beneath the well of the car a young red setter, kindly lent by his friend the dentist. The setter, who had formed at sight an unfavourable opinion of the dog-box, had resolved himself into an invertebrate mass of jelly and lead, and was with difficulty straightened out and rammed home into it.

"Have we all now?" said M'Cabe, slamming the door in the dog's face. "Take care we're not like me uncle old Tom Duffy, that was going shooting, and was the whole morning slapping his pockets and saying, 'Me powder! me shot! me caps! me wads!' and when he got to the bog, 'O tare an' 'oun's' says he, 'I forgot the gun!'"

There are still moments when I can find some special and not-otherwise-to-be-attained flavour in driving on an outside car; a sense of personal achievement in sitting, by some method of instinctive suction, the lurches and swoops peculiar to these vehicles. Reardon's had given us its roomiest car and its best horse, a yellow mare, with a long back and a slinging trot, and a mouth of iron.

"Where did Mr. Reardon get the mare, Jerry?" asked M'Cabe, as we zigzagged in successive hairbreadths through the streets of Owenford.

"D-Dublin, sir," replied the driver, who, with both fists extended in front of him and both heels planted against his narrow footboard, seemed to find utterance difficult.

"She's a goer!" said M'Cabe.

"She is—she killed two men," said Jerry, in two jerks.

"That's a great credit to her. What way did she do it?"

"P-pulled the lungs out o' them!" ejaculated Jerry, turning the last corner and giving the mare a shade more of her head, as a tribute, perhaps, to her prowess.

She swung us for some six miles along the ruts of the coast road at the same unflinching pace, after which, turning inland and uphill, we began the climb of four miles into the mountains. It was about eleven o'clock when we pulled up beside a long and reedy pool, high up in the heather; the road went on, illimitably it seemed, and was lost, with its attendant telegraph posts, in cloud.

"Away with ye now, Jerry," said M'Cabe; "we'll shoot our way home."

He opened the back of the dog-box, and summoned its occupant. The summons was disregarded. Far back in the box two sparks of light and a dead silence indicated the presence of the dog.

"How snug you are in there!" said McCabe; "here, Jerry, pull him out for us. What the deuce is this his name is? Jeffers told me yesterday, and it's gone from me."

"I d'no would he bite me?" said Jerry, taking a cautious observation and giving voice to the feelings of the party. "Here, poor fellow! Here, good lad!"

The good lad remained immovable. The lure of a sandwich produced no better result.

"We can't be losing our day with the brute this way," said M'Cabe. "Tip up the car. He'll come out then, and no thanks to him."

As the shafts rose heavenwards, the law of gravitation proved too much for the setter, and he slowly slid to earth.

"If I only knew your dam' name we'd be all right now," said M'Cabe.

The carman dropped the shafts on to the mare, and drove on up the pass, with one side of the car turned up and himself on the other. The yellow mare had, it seemed only begun her day's work. A prophetic instinct, of the reliable kind that is strictly founded on facts, warned me that we might live to regret her departure.

The dentist's setter had, at sight of the guns, realized that things were better than he had expected, and now preceded us along the edge of the lake with every appearance of enthusiasm. He quartered the ground with professional zeal, he splashed through the sedge, and rattled through thickets of dry reeds, and set successively a heron, a water-hen, and something, unseen, that I believe to have been a water-rat. After each of these efforts he rushed in upon his quarry, and we called him by all the gun-dog names we had ever heard of, from Don to Grouse, from Carlo to Shot, coupled with objurgations on a rising scale. With none of them did we so much as vibrate a chord in his bosom. He was a large dog, with a blunt stupid face, and a faculty for excitement about nothing that impelled him to bound back to us as often as possible, to gaze in our eyes in brilliant inquiry, and to pant and prance before us with all the fatuity of youth. Had he been able to speak, he would have asked idiotic questions, of that special breed that exact from their victim a reply of equal imbecility.

The lake and its environs, for the first time in M'Cabe's experience, yielded nothing; we struck up on to the mountain side, following the course of an angry stream that came racing down from the heights. We worked up through ling and furze, and skirted flocks of pale stones that lay in the heather like petrified sheep, and the dog, ranging deliriously, set water-wagtails and anything else that could fly; I believe he would have set a blue bottle, and I said so to M'Cabe.

"Ah, give him time; he'll settle down," said M'Cabe, who had a thankfulness for small mercies born of a vast experience of makeshifts; "he might fill the bag for us yet."

We laboured along the flank of the mountain, climbing in and out of small ravines, jumping or wading streams, sloshing through yellow sedgy bog; always with the brown heather running up to the misty skyline, and always with the same atrocious luck. Once a small pack of grouse got up, very wild, and leagues out of range, thanks to the far-reaching activities of the dog, and once a hermit woodcock exploded out of a clump of furze, and sailed away down the slope, followed by four charges of shot and the red setter, in equally innocuous pursuit. And this, up to luncheon time, was the sum of the morning's sport.

We ate our sandwiches on a high ridge, under the lee

of a tumbled pile of boulders, that looked as if they had been about to hurl themselves into the valley, and had thought better of it at the last moment. Between the looming, elephant-grey mountains the mist yielded glimpses of the far greenness of the sea, the only green thing in sight in this world of grey and brown. The dog sat opposite to me, and willed me to share my food with him. His steady eyes were charged with the implication that I was a glutton; personally I abhorred him, yet I found it impossible to give him less than twenty-five per cent of my sandwiches.

"I wonder did Jeffers take him for a bad debt," said M'Cabe, reflectively, as he lit his pipe.

I said I should rather take my chance with the bad debt.

"He might have treated me better," M'Cabe grumbled on, "seeing that I paid him seven pound ten the day before yesterday, let alone that it was me that was the first to put him up to this—this bit of Shinroe Mountain that never was what you might call strictly preserved. When he came here first he didn't as much as know what cartridges he'd want for it. 'Six and eight,' says I, 'that's a lawyer's fee, so if you think of me you'll not forget it!' And now, if ye please," went on Mr. Jeffers' preceptor in sport, "he's shooting the whole country and selling all he gets! And he wouldn't as much as ask me to go with him; and the excuse he gives, he wouldn't like to have an old hand like me conny-shooring his shots! How modest he is!"

I taunted M'Cabe with having been weak enough thus to cede his rights, and M'Cabe, who was not at all amused, said that after all it wasn't so much Jeffers that did the harm but an infernal English syndicate that had taken the Shinroe shooting this season, and paid old Purcell that owned it ten times what it was worth.

"It might be as good for us to get off their ground now," continued M'Cabe, rising slowly to his feet, "and try the Lackagreina Valley. The stream below is their bounds."

This, I hasten to say, was the first I had heard of the syndicate, and I thought it tactless of M'Cabe to have mentioned it, even though the wrong that we had done them was purely technical. I said to him that I thought the sooner we got off their ground the better, and we descended the hill and crossed the stream, and M'Cabe said that he could always shoot this next stretch of country when he liked. With this assurance, we turned our backs on the sea and struck inland, tramping for an hour or more through country whose entire barrenness could only be explained on the hypothesis that it had been turned inside out to dry. So far it had failed to achieve even this result.

The weather got thicker, and the sport, if possible, thinner; I had long since lost what bearings I possessed, but M'Cabe said he knew of a nice patch of scrub in the next valley that always held a cock. The next valley came at last, not without considerable effort, but no patch of scrub was apparent. Some small black and grey cattle stood and looked at us, and a young bull showed an inclination to stalk the dog; it seemed the only sport the valley was likely to afford. M'Cabe looked round him, and looked at his watch, and looked at the sky, which did not seem to be more than a yard above our heads, and said without emotion:

"Did ye think of telling the lad in the glass box in the hall that we might want some dinner kept hot for us? I d'no from Adam where we've got to!"

There was a cattle track along the side of the valley which might, though not necessarily, lead somewhere. We pursued it, and found that it led, in the first instance, to some black-faced mountain sheep. A cheerful interlude followed, in which the red setter hunted the sheep, and we hunted the setter, and what M'Cabe said about the dentist in the intervals of the chase was more appropriate to the occasion than to these pages.

When justice had been satiated, and the last echo of the last yell of the dog had trembled into silence among the hills, we resumed the cattle-track, which had become a shade more reliable, and, as we proceeded, began to give an impression that it might lead somewhere. The day was dying in threatening stillness. Lethargic layers of mist bulged low, like the roof of a marquee, and cloaked every outline that could yield us information. The dog, unchastened by recent events, and full of an idiot optimism, continued to range the hillside.

"I suppose I'll never get the chance to tell Jeffers my opinion of that tom-fool," said M'Cabe, following with an eye of steel the perambulations of the dog; "the best barrister that ever wore a wig couldn't argue with a dentist! He has his fist half-way down your throat before you can open your mouth; and in any case he'll tell me we couldn't expect any dog would work for us when we forgot his name. What's the brute at now?"

The brute was high above us on the hillside, setting a solitary furze bush with convincing determination, and casting backward looks to see if he were being supported.

"It might be a hare," said M'Cabe, cocking his gun, with a revival of hope that was almost pathetic, and ascending towards the furze bush.

I neither quickened my pace nor deviated from the cattle track, but I may admit that I did so far yield to the theory of the hare as to slip a cartridge into my gun.

M'Cabe put his gun to his shoulder, lowered it abruptly, and walked up to the furze bush. He stooped and picked up something.

"He's not such a fool after all!" he called out; "ye said he'd set a blue-bottle, and b'Jove ye weren't far out!"

He held up a black object that was neither bird nor beast.

I took the cartridge out of my gun as unobtrusively as possible, and M'Cabe and the dog rejoined me with the product of the day's sport. It was a flat-sided bottle, high-shouldered, with a short neck; M'Cabe extracted the cork and took a sniff.

"Mountain dew no less!" (Mr. M'Cabe adhered faithfully to the stock phrases of his youth.) "This never paid the King a shilling! Give me the cup off your flask, Major, till we see what sort it is."

It was pretty rank, and even that seasoned vessel, old M'Cabe, admitted that it might be drinkable in another couple of years, but hardly in less; yet as it ran, a rivulet of fire, through my system, it seemed to me that even the water in my boots became less chill.

"In the public interest we're bound to remove it," said M'Cabe, putting the bottle into his game bag; "any man that drank enough of that'd rob a church! Well, anyway, we're not the only people travelling this path," he continued, "whoever put his afternoon tea to hide there will choose a less fashionable promenade next time. But indeed the poor man couldn't be blamed for not knowing such a universal genius of a dog was coming this way! Did'nt I tell you he'd fill the bag for us!"

He extracted from his pockets a pair of knitted gloves, and put them on; it was equivalent to putting up the shutters.

It was shortly after this that we regained touch with civilization. Above the profile of a hill a telegraph post suddenly showed itself against the grey of the misty twilight. We made as bee-like a line for it as the nature of the ground permitted, and found ourselves on a narrow road, at a point where it was in the act of making a hairpin turn before plunging into a valley.

"The Beacon Bay road, begad!" said M'Cabe; "I didn't think we were so far out of our way. Let me see now, which way is this we'd best go."

He stood still and looked round him, taking his bearings; in the solitude the telegraph posts hummed to each other, full of information and entirely reticent.

The position was worse than I thought. By descending into the valley we should, a couple or three miles farther on, strike the coast road about six miles from home; by ascending the hill and walking four miles, we should arrive at the station of Coppeen Road, and, with luck, there intercept the evening train for Owenford.

"And that's the best of our play, but we'll have to step out," concluded M'Cabe, shortening the strap of his game-bag, and settling it on his back.

"If I were you," I said, "I'd chuck that stuff away. Apart from anything else, it's about half a ton extra to carry."

"There's many a thing, Major, that you might do that

583

I might not do," returned M'Cabe with solemnity, "and in the contrairy sense the statement is equally valid."

He faced the hill with humped shoulders, and fell with no more words into his poacher's stride, and I followed him with the best imitation of it that I could put up after at least six hours of heavy going. M'Cabe is fifteen years older than I am, and I hope that when I am his age I shall have more consideration than he for those who are younger than myself.

It was now nearly half-past five o'clock, and by the time we had covered a mile of puddles and broken stones it was too dark to see which was which. I felt considerable dubiety about catching the train at Coppeen Road, all the more that it was a flag station, demanding an extra five minutes in hand. Probably the engine-driver had long since abandoned any expectation of passengers at Coppeen Road, and if he even noticed the signal, would treat it as a practical joke. It was after another quarter of an hour's trudge that a distant sound entered into the silence that had fallen upon M'Cabe and me, an intermittent grating of wheels upon patches of broken stone, a steady hammer of hoofs.

M'Cabe halted.

"That car's bound to be going to Owenford," he said; "I wonder could they give us a lift."

A single light (the economical habit of the south of Ireland) began to split the foggy darkness.

"Begad, that's like the go of Reardon's mare!" said M'Cabe, as the light swung down upon us.

We held the road like highwaymen, we called upon the unseen driver to stop, and he answered to the name of Jerry. This is not a proof of identity in a province where every third man is dignified by the name of Jeremiah, but as the car pulled up it was Reardon's yellow mare on which the lamplight fell, and we knew that the fates had relented.

We should certainly not catch the train at Coppeen Road, Jerry assured us; "she had," he said, "a fashion of running early on Monday nights, and in any case if you'd want to catch that train, you should make like an amber-bush for her."

584

We agreed that it was too late for the preparation of an ambush.

"If the sergeant had no objections," continued Jerry, progressing smoothly towards the tip that would finally be his, "it would be no trouble at all to oblige the gentlemen. Sure it's the big car I have, and it's often I took six, yes, and seven on it, going to the races."

I was now aware of two helmeted presences on the car, and a decorous voice said that the gentlemen were welcome to a side of the car if they liked.

"Is that Sergeant Leonard?" asked M'Cabe, who knew every policeman in the country. "Well, sergeant, you've a knack of being on the spot when you're wanted!"

"And sometimes when he's not," said I.

There was a third and unhelmeted presence on the car, and something of stillness and aloofness in it had led me to diagnose a prisoner.

The suggested dispositions were accomplished. The two policemen and the prisoner wedged themselves on one side of the car, M'Cabe and I mounted the other, and put the dog on the cushion of the well behind us (his late quarters in the dog-box being occupied by half a mountain sheep, destined for the hotel larder). The yellow mare went gallantly up to her collar, regardless of her augmented load; M'Cabe and the sergeant leaned to each other across the back of the car, and fell into profound and low-toned converse; I smoked, and the dog, propping his wet back against mine, made friends with the prisoner. It may be the Irish blood in me that is responsible for the illicit sympathy with a prisoner that sometimes incommodes me; I certainly bestowed some of it upon the captive, sandwiched between two stalwarts of the R.I.C., and learning that the strong arm of the Law was a trifle compared with the rest of its person.

"What sport had you, Major?" inquired Jerry, as we slackened speed at a hill.

I was sitting at the top of the car, under his elbow, and he probably thought that I was feeling neglected during the heart-to-heart confidences of M'Cabe and the sergeant.

"Not a feather," I replied.

"Sure the birds couldn't be in it this weather," said Jerry considerately; he had in his time condoled with many sportsmen. "I'm after talking to a man in Coppeen Road station that was carrying the game bag for them gentlemen that has Mr. Purcell's shooting on Shinroe Mountain, and what had the four o' them after the day—only one jacksnipe!"

"They went one better than we did," I said, but, as was intended, I felt cheered—"what day were they there?"

"To-day sure!" answered Jerry, with faint surprise, "and they hadn't their luncheon hardly ate when they met one on the mountain that told them he seen two fellas walking it, with guns and a dog, no more than an hour before them. 'That'll do!' says they, and they turned about and back with them to Coppeen Road to tell the police."

"Did they see the fellows?" I asked lightly, after a panic-stricken pause.

"They did not. Sure they said if they'd seen them, they'd shoot them like rooks," replied Jerry, "and they would too. It's what the man was saying if they cot them lads to-day they'd have left them in the way they'd be given up by both doctor and priest! Oh, they're fierce altogether!"

I received this information in a silence that was filled to bursting with the desire to strangle M'Cabe.

Jerry leaned over my shoulder, and lowered his voice.

"They were saying in Coppeen Road that there was a gentleman that came on a mothor-bike this morning early, and he had Shinroe shot out by ten o'clock, and on with him then up the country; and it isn't the first time he was in it. It's a pity those gentlemen couldn't ketch *him*! *They'd* mothor-bike him!"

It was apparent that the poaching of the motor-bicycle upon the legitimate preserves of carmen was responsible for this remarkable sympathy with the law; I, at all events, had it to my credit that I had not gone poaching on a motor-bicycle.

Just here M'Cabe emerged from the heart-to-heart,

and nudged me in the ribs with a confederate elbow. I did not respond, being in no mood for confederacy, certainly not with M'Cabe.

"The sergeant is after telling me this prisoner he has here is prosecuted at the instance of that syndicate I was telling you about," he whispered hoarsely in my ear, "for hunting Shinroe with greyhounds. He was cited to appear last week, and he didn't turn up; he'll be before you to-morrow. I hope the Bench will have a fellow-feeling for a fellow-creature!"

The whisper ended in the wheezy cough that was Mr. M'Cabe's equivalent for a laugh. It was very close to my ear, and it had somewhere in it the metallic click that I had noticed before.

I grunted forbiddingly, and turned my back upon M'Cabe, as far as it is possible to do so on an outside car, and we hammered on through the darkness. Once the solitary lamp illumined the prolonged countenance of a donkey, and once or twice we came upon a party of sheep lying on the road; they melted into the night at the minatory whistle that is dedicated to sheep, and on each of these occasions the dentist's dog was shaken by strong shudders, and made a convulsive attempt to spring from the car in pursuit. We were making good travelling on a long down-grade, a smell of sea-weed was in the mist, and a salt taste was on my lips. It was very cold; I had no overcoat, my boots had plumbed the depths of many bogholes, and I found myself shivering like the dog.

It was at this point that I felt M'Cabe fumbling at his game-bag, that lay between us on the seat. By dint of a sympathy that I would have died rather than betray, I divined that he was going to tap that fount of contraband fire that he owed to the dentist's dog. It was, apparently, a matter of some difficulty; I felt him groping and tugging at the straps.

I said to myself, waveringly: "Old blackguard! I won't touch it if he offers it to me."

M'Cabe went on fumbling:

"Damn these woolly gloves! I can't do a hand's turn with them."

587

In the dark I could not see what followed, but I felt him raise his arm. There was a jerk, followed by a howl.

"Hold on!" roared M'Cabe, with a new and strange utterance. "Thtop the horth! I've dropped me teeth!"

The driver did his best, but with the push of the hill behind her the mare took some stopping.

"Oh, murder! oh, murder!" wailed M'Cabe, lisping thickly, "I pulled them out o' me head with the glove, trying to get it off!" He scrambled off the car. "Give me the lamp! Me lovely new teeth——"

I detached the lamp from its socket with all speed, and handed it to M'Cabe, who hurried back on our tracks. From motives of delicacy I remained on the car, as did also the rest of the party. A minute or two passed in awed silence, while the patch of light went to and fro on the dark road. It seemed an intrusion to offer assistance and an uncertainty as to whether to allude to those loss as "them" or "it", made inquiries a difficulty.

"For goodneth 'ake have none o' ye any matcheth, that ye couldn't come and help me?" demanded the voice of M'Cabe, in indignation blurred pathetically by his gosling-like lisp.

I went to his assistance, and refrained with an effort from suggesting the employment of that all-accomplished setter, the dentist's dog, in the search; it was not the moment for pleasantry. Not yet.

We crept along, bent double, like gorillas; the long strips of broken stones yielded nothing, the long puddles between them were examined in vain.

"What the dooth will I do to-morrow?" raged M'Cabe, pawing in the heather at the road's edge. "How can I plead when I haven't a blathted tooth in me head?"

"I'll give you half a crown this minute, M'Cabe," said I brutally, "if you'll say 'Sessions'!"

Here the sergeant joined us, striking matches as he came. He worked his way into the sphere of the car-lamp, he was most painstaking and sympathetic, and his oblique allusions to the object of the search were a miracle of tact.

"I see something white beyond you, Mr. M'Cabe," he said respectfully, "might that be them?"

M'Cabe swung the lamp as indicated.

"No, it might not. It's a pebble," he replied, with pardonable irascibility.

Silence followed, and we worked our way up the hill.

"What's that, sir?" ventured the sergeant, with some excitement, stopping again and pointing. "I think I see the gleam of the gold!"

"Ah, nonthenth, man! They've vulcanite!" snapped M'Cabe, more irascibly than ever.

The word nonsense was a disastrous effort, and I withdrew into the darkness to enjoy it.

"What colour might vulcanite be, sir?" murmured a voice beside me.

Jerry had joined the search-party; he lighted, as he spoke, an inch of candle. On hearing my explanation he remarked that it was a bad chance, and at the same instant the inch of candle slipped from his fingers and fell into a puddle.

"Divil mend ye for a candle! Have ye a match, sir? I haven't a one left!"

As it happened, I had no matches, my only means of making a light being a patent tinder-box.

"Have you a match there?" I called out to the invisible occupants of the car, which was about fifteen or twenty yards away, advancing towards it as I spoke. The constable politely jumped off and came to meet me.

As he was in the act of handing me his matchbox, the car drove away down the hill.

I state the fact with the bald simplicity that is appropriate to great disaster. To be exact, the yellow mare sprang from inaction into a gallop, as if she had been stung by a wasp, and had a start of at least fifty yards before either the carman or the constable could get under weigh. The carman, uttering shrill and menacing whistles, led the chase, the constable, though badly hampered by his greatcoat, was a good second, and the sergeant, making the best of a bad start, followed them into the night.

The yellow mare's head was for home, and her load

589

was on its own legs on the road behind her; hysterical yelps from the dentist's dog indicated that he also was on his own legs, and was, in all human probability, jumping at the mare's nose. As the rapturous beat of her hoofs died away on the down-grade, I recalled the assertion that she had pulled the lungs out of two men, and it seemed to me that the prisoner had caught the psychological moment on the hop.

"They'll not ketch him," said M'Cabe, with the flat calm of a broken man, "not to-night anyway. Nor for a week maybe. He'll take to the mountains."

The silence of the hills closed in upon us, and we were left in our original positions, plus the lamp of the car, and minus our guns, the dentist's dog, and M'Cabe's teeth.

Far, far away, from the direction of Coppeen Road, that sinister outpost, where evil rumours were launched, and the night trains were waylaid by the amber-bushes, a steady tapping sound advanced towards us. Over the crest of the hill, a quarter of a mile away, a blazing and many-pointed star sprang into being, and bore down upon us. "A motorbike!" ejaculated M'Cabe. "Take the light and thtop him—he wouldn't know what I wath thaying—if he ran over them they're done for! For the love o' merthy tell him to keep the left thide of the road!"

I took the lamp, and ran towards the bicyclist, waving it as I ran. The star, now a moon of acetylene ferocity, slackened speed, and a voice behind it said:

"What's up?"

I stated the case with telegraphic brevity, and the motor-bicycle slid slowly past me. Its rider had a gun slung across his back, my lamp revealed a crammed game-bag on the carrier behind him.

"Sorry I can't assist you," he called back to me, keeping carefully at the left-hand side of the road, "but I have an appointment." Then, as an afterthought, "There's a first-rate dentist in Owenford!"

The red eye of the tail light glowed a farewell and passed on, like all the rest, into the night.

I rejoined M'Cabe.

He clutched my arm, and shook it.

"That wath Jefferth! *Jefferth*, I tell ye! The dirty poacher! And hith bag full of our birdth!"

It was not till the lamp went out, which it did some ten minutes afterwards, that I drew M'Cabe from the scene of his loss, gently, as one deals with the bereaved, and faced with him the six-mile walk to Owenford.

A SELECTION OF BESTSELLERS FROM SPHERE

FICTION

FOOTFALL	Niven & Pournelle	£3.95	☐
PRIVATE AFFAIRS	Judith Michael	£4.95	☐
STREET SONG	Emma Blair	£3.50	☐
GOLDEN TRIPLE TIME	Zoe Garrison	£2.95	☐
BEACHES	Iris Rainer Dart	£2.95	☐

FILM & TV TIE-IN

MONA LISA	John Luther Novak	£2.50	☐
BLOCKBUSTERS GOLD RUN		£1.95	☐
9½ WEEKS	Elizabeth McNeil	£1.95	☐
BOON	Anthony Masters	£2.50	☐
AUF WIEDERSEHEN PET 2	Fred Taylor	£2.75	☐

NON-FICTION

MY MOTHER'S KEEPER	B. D. Hyman	£3.50	☐
BURTON: THE MAN BEHIND THE MYTH	Penny Junor	£2.95	☐
THE DISAPPEARED	John Simpson & Jana Bennett	£4.95	☐
THE LAST NAZI: THE LIFE AND TIMES OF JOSEPH MENGELE	Gerald Astor	£3.50	☐
THE FALL OF SAIGON	David Butler	£3.95	☐

All Sphere books are available at your local bookshop or newsagent, or can be ordered direct from the publisher. Just tick the titles you want and fill in the form below.

Name _____

Address _____

_____

Write to Sphere Books, Cash Sales Department, P.O. Box 11, Falmouth, Cornwall TR10 9EN.

Please enclose a cheque or postal order to the value of the cover price plus:

UK: 55p for the first book, 22p for the second book and 14p for each additional book ordered to a maximum charge of £1.75.

OVERSEAS: £1.00 for the first book plus 25p per copy for each additional book.

BFPO & EIRE: 55p for the first book, 22p for the second book plus 14p per copy for the next 7 books, thereafter 8p per book.

Sphere Books reserve the right to show new retail prices on covers which may differ from those previously advertised in the text or elsewhere, and to increase postal rates in accordance with the PO.